Musical Improvisation in the Baroque Era

Specvlvm Mvsicae

Edendum Curavit
Roberto Illiano

Volume XXXIII

Publications of the Centro Studi Opera Omnia Luigi Boccherini
Pubblicazioni del Centro Studi Opera Omnia Luigi Boccherini
Publications du Centro Studi Opera Omnia Luigi Boccherini
Veröffentlichungen des Centro Studi Opera Omnia Luigi Boccherini
Publicaciones del Centro Studi Opera Omnia Luigi Boccherini
Lucca

Musical Improvisation in the Baroque Era

EDITED BY
FULVIA MORABITO

BREPOLS
TURNHOUT
MMXIX

© BREPOLS 2019

All rights reserved. No part of this publication may be reproduced,
stored in a retrieval system, or transmitted, in any form or by any means,
electronic, mechanical, photocopying, recording, or otherwise, without
the prior permission of the publisher.

D/2019/0095/18

ISBN 978-2-503-58369-3

Printed in Italy

To Mila,
in memoriam

Contents

FULVIA MORABITO
    Introduction   xi

Improvisation into Composition

DAVID CHUNG
    French Harpsichord *doubles* and the Creative Art
    of the 17th-Century *Clavecinistes*   3

MASSIMILIANO GUIDO
    Sounding Theory and Theoretical Notes
    Bernardo Pasquini's Pedagogy at the Keyboard:
    A Case of Composition in Performance?   31

JAVIER LUPIAÑEZ – FABRIZIO AMMETTO
    Las anotaciones de Pisendel en el Concierto
    para dos violines RV 507 de Vivaldi: una ventana abierta
    a la improvisación en la obra del 'Cura rojo'   43

JOSUÉ MELÉNDEZ PELÁEZ
    Cadenze per finali: Exuberant and Extended
    Cadences in the 16th and 17th Centuries   63

MARINA TOFFETTI
    Written Outlines of Improvisation Procedures in Music
    Publications of the Early 17th Century: The Second (1611-1623)
    and Third (1615-1623) Book of *Concerti* By G. Ghizzolo
    and the Motet *Iesu Rex Admirabilis* (1625-1627) by G. Frescobaldi   81

Issues of Performance Practice

Giovanna Barbati
 «Il n'exécute jamais la Basse telle qu'elle est écrite»:
 The Use of Improvisation in Teaching Low Strings   117

Anthony Pryer
 On the Borderlines of Improvisation:
 Caccini, Monteverdi and the Freedoms of the Performer   151

Laura Toffetti
 «Sostener si può la battuta, etiandio in aria». Testi e contesti
 per comprendere l'invenzione e la disposizione del discorso musicale
 nel repertorio strumentale italiano fra Seicento e Settecento   175

Rudolf Rasch
 Improvised Cadenzas in the Cello Sonatas Op. 5 by Francesco Geminiani   195

Contemporary Treatises, Pedagogical Works, and Aesthetics

Valentina Anzani
 Il mito della competizione tra virtuosi:
 quando Farinelli sfidò Bernacchi (Bologna 1727)   223

John Lutterman
 Re-Creating Historical Improvisatory Solo Practices on the Cello:
 C. Simpson, F. Niedt, and J. S. Bach on the Pedagogy
 of *Contrapunctis Extemporalis*   241

Francesca Mignogna
 Accompagnamento e basso continuo alla chitarra spagnola.
 Una cartografia della diffusione dei sistemi di notazione stenografici
 in Italia, Spagna e Francia tra XVI e XVII secolo e loro implicazioni teoriche   261

Guido Olivieri
 Naturalezza o artificio: riflessioni su improvvisazione
 e virtuosismo italiani in Francia nel Settecento   287

NEAL ZASLAW
    «Adagio de Mr. Tartini. Varié de plusieurs façons différentes,
    très utiles aux personnes qui veulent apprendre à faire
    des traits sous chaque notte de l'Harmonie…» 301

THE ART OF PARTIMENTO

SIMONE CIOLFI
    Cantata da camera e arte del partimento in Alessandro Scarlatti.
    «An Historical Link between Baroque Recitatives and
    Development Section of the Sonata-Form Movements?» 323

MARCO POLLACI
    Two New Sources for the Study of Early
    Eighteenth-Century Composition and Improvisation 343

GIORGIO SANGUINETTI
    On the Origin of Partimento: A Recently Discovered
    Manuscript of Toccate (1695) by Francesco Mancini 353

PETER VAN TOUR
    «Taking a Walk at the Molo»: Partimento and the Improvised Fugue 371

ABSTRACTS 383

BIOGRAPHIES 391

INDEX OF NAMES 395

Introduction

Body and Soul

Everyone has had the experience of listening to a railway station or airport announcement. The speaker, non-human, is an aural scanner, that is, software that translates written information into sound. The total lack of expression and of cadence is striking, even though making sense. One has the same impression listening to a piece of music reproduced in one of the many music word processing programs — particularly the less sophisticated ones. The notes, all having identical 'specific gravity', are a dry sequence of sounds lacking that breath of life capable of transmitting any emotional content. Clearly the aural reception of music, whose end is the aesthetic enjoyment of a piece, is arrived at by stages that go beyond the mere sonic translation of the notes.

By way of analogy with the human body, musical notes constitute the skeleton of the composition, the responsibility of the composer. Body and soul are vouchsafed by interpretation and by improvisation, both the responsibility of the executant. Musical interpretation is a cluster of manifestations that somehow fall into the realm of predictability. A composer can expect that every executant will render the sounds of the score as he conceived it in a personal manner, including tempo nuances, dynamics, articulations, etc. Improvisation, on the other hand, implies an unpredictable, 'unrehearsed' gestural expressiveness, even if admissible by contemporary aesthetic canons. Into this realm falls a series of 'adulterations' of the score consisting of the addition of ornaments, cadenzas, and vocal and instrumental parts, as well as the alteration of the instrumental complement, etc.[1]

Composition, interpretation and improvisation render a unique and unrepeatable sounding version of every piece of music, even when it is the same piece, just as every human being is unique and unrepeatable.

Moreover, this concept must be placed in historic perspective. Musical notation, in its oldest form dating to Hellenic culture and before that to Mesopotamian culture, flourished in a context in which music was transmitted chiefly by oral tradition, having the primary function of an *aide-mémoire*. Only in the late Middle Ages did notation begin to become increasingly sophisticated, until the present day — sophistication understood

---

[1]. See Rasch, Rudolf. 'Preface', in: Rasch 2011.

Introduction

as the means of fixing on paper as many parameters of musical execution as possible, the will of the composer asserting itself with more and more forcefulness and with less and less concession to the inspiration of the executant. In this interactive process, Baroque music is based on an advanced notational system that nevertheless allows an ample margin for interpretation and improvisation. In other words, the notation can indicate the sounds autonomously but requires the help of an oral tradition in order to be fully intelligible.

This is even truer if we consider that the Baroque signaled the passage from *musica mensurabilis* to accompanied monody, or rather from a musical concept focused on the mathematical relationships of sounds, to a concept based on the *affects*. Music is no longer an 'abstract game' of arithmetic relationships, but aims at interpreting the human passions, in instrumental music, and even more in vocal music. The Monteverdian aesthetic takes root, according to which the *prima prattica* gives way to the *seconda prattica*, when the texts, no longer subordinate to musical exigencies, assert their ascendancy over the music, subjecting it to their dramatic effect. Thus, the musical notation of the time is distinctly inadequate to express all the dynamic shades between loud and soft, between fast and slow, and fails to distinguish «sudden or prepared interruptions, pronunciation, declamation, syllabification or murmuring, accentuation, breathing, tranquility or excitement»[2]. Just as the alphabet, by itself, indicates the words on paper but does not suggest their expressive relationships, so the Baroque score, though indicating the pitch and the relative duration of the notes, is incapable of suggesting the nuances of tempo, the intricate linkages that give meaning to the music, infusing it with the 'breath of life' referred to above. To lend significance to a verbal or musical discourse the phenomes and sounds must be subjected to the laws of τέχνη ῥητορική of classic memory. The penalty for infraction: a kind of aphasia in which, though the words are pronounced correctly, the phrase structure and the melodic coherence of the language are altered, to the detriment of expression, and ultimately of communication.

The Form of the Ephemeral

But, musically speaking, especially in the Baroque period, of what did this *quid* consist, that signaled the divide between inexpressivity and expressivity? Many techniques were called into play. One could execute simple variations, regarding embellishments — adding or omitting them —, diminutions, harmony, rhythm, texture — to be attenuated or enriched —, tessitura — transposing up or down —, chordal figuration of the bass —

---

[2]. Quoted from the article of Laura Toffetti in this volume, p. 179: «[...] l'interruzione brusca o preparata, il pronunciare, declamare, sillabare o sussurrare, il porre accenti, il respirare, l'attendere o il concitare [...]».

INTRODUCTION

broken or arpeggiated. Or one could expand a pre-existing idea by repeating notes or melodic-rhythmic patterns, and new musical material could be added, such as dissonant notes, chromaticisms, imitation, *petite reprise*, transition passages, more or less extended cadenzas, *prima volta* and *seconda volta*, refashioning of the bass etc.

It goes without saying that in such a context it is the executant that makes the difference. And the theoreticians, following with little delay the practice of performers, were also aware of this. Already in the Fifties of the sixteenth century, Vincenzo Galilei, Gioseffo Zarlino and Nicola Vicentino noted the fact that a musician who follows slavishly the written score without adding anything will be considered a sort of surveyor, a clumsy and ignorant dabbler[3]. The disparity with the past is great: music, previously esteemed among the liberal arts of the *quadrivium*, because able to embody the numerical ratios that underly all acoustical phenomena, from the most elementary to the harmony of the spheres, now descends to the 'servile' level of vocal and instrumental performance.

The phenomenon of virtuosity overflowed. Now, for the first time in the history of music, we have the exaltation of the outstanding performer, capable of ornamenting, extending and expanding a musical text, improvising *en souplesse*, that is, without stumbling when confronting *ex-tempore* what was not rehearsed. The virtuoso is a 'brand': the emotional mediator between the written text and its aural reception creates a unique and unrepeatable product, since it is the expression of the player's personal inspiration, technical ability and artistic background. From here on we have the incessant exploration for compositional/executive solutions (let us not forget that at the time there did not exist the distinction between composer and interpreter to which we have become accustomed by the history of modern and contemporary music), perpetually hovering between homage for the glorious past and succumbing to the seductiveness of the new, between restraint and excess, 'good taste' and mere athleticism, in a dialectic consummated at the personal level as well: the irregular stylistic development of Tartini is the proof[4]. Now we also have the ambivalent attitude of several virtuosos towards self-promotion: the allure of public exposure, with all that it entails, is counterpoised by the fear of revealing one's 'secret', or indeed one's own stylistic identity, which during the act of improvising exteriorizes its most tangible and genuine characteristics.

This concern manifested itself above all in the area of teaching. The attitudes of virtuosi varied from case to case, at times sharply diverging: Locatelli taught exclusively amateurs, Tartini founded the School of Nations. But it bears emphasizing that the art of improvisation, paradoxically, is learned. The elaborations of the written text are free but not anarchic, in that they benefit from pre-existing models, transmitted, in the most fortunate

---

[3]. See the article of Laura Toffetti inside this volume, pp. 182-183.
[4]. See the contribution of Neal Zaslaw in this volume.

cases, by the virtuosos themselves. In this sense one may speak of free composition and codified improvisation.

An essential element in the training of musicians in the Baroque and pre-Romantic era was the memorization of melodic and harmonic patterns that facilitated improvisation. Volumes of solfeggi, partimenti, *regole*, *principi*, *lezioni*, *zibaldoni* proliferated, that is, collections of melodies and basses, figured and unfigured, drawn from the repertory or not, to learn, to store up and dust off both in the act of composing and during performance, in order to develop expertise in the art of counterpoint, diminution, improvisation and accompaniment[5]. This didactic regime must also be followed by present-day musicians who undertake to execute correctly the repertory of the seventeenth and eighteenth centuries.

The actual practice of Baroque improvisation, an ephemeral art that dies at the moment of creation, is, for obvious reasons, not documented. Our understanding and reconstruction of the phenomenon comes from treatises and manuals, and from documentary testimonies. There are cases, however, in which improvisation has fortunately been preserved on paper. Albeit most of the music of the period has come down to us by way of 'approximate' notation of what can be done in the performance, certain cases, sporadic, but not exceptional, attest to a 'prescriptive' notation indicating what should be done in a performance, if not indeed 'descriptive' of what was done by a specific performer on a specific occasion. These sources are usually in manuscript, since published music is intended for a heterogenous public, and tends to be as generic as possible. Yet there are cases in which this type of music vividly evokes improvisatory practice: improvisation has become composition, as in *doubles*, cadenzas, caprices, toccatas, etc.

From what has been said thus far it is obvious that the aural realization of a Baroque piece of music cannot proceed without preliminary study of the historical context, of the theoretical and documentary evidence and of philological exegesis of the sources. Baroque music is a meeting ground between the competence of the musicologist and that of the musician, called upon by necessity to collaborate on the 'restoration' of the musical monument for which there exists no primary source (= sonic recording), but only secondary sources (= codified and written indications, mostly concise, of the aural realization).

As a musicologist, I would emphasize that the philological reconstruction of texts should be fashioned according to the peculiarity of the repertory in question. If it is true that the goal of philology is to restore a text shorn of the contaminations of tradition and as near as possible to the last wishes of the composer, it is also true that in a context in which

---

[5]. VAN TOUR 2015, p. 19.

Introduction

the same piece is never played twice in the same manner, there can arise several versions of equal authority. The philologist should consider all the information potentially useful to the performer without constricting the latter's improvised inspiration. As for authorial variants, one should evaluate the nature of each, distinguishing between substitutions and alternatives, and document these last without suppressing them, thereby imposing a choice. In the case of traditional variants, a heavily interpolated text can also be of great documentary value, worth at any rate placing in an appendix.

The sonic restoration of the Baroque repertory thus necessitates musicians who are 'historically informed' and 'practically trained' in improvisation.

Inside the Volume

The contributions to the present volume, which elaborate in turn upon the themes treated in this introduction, are drawn from the talks given at an International conference entitled *Musical Improvisation in the Baroque Era*, held in Lucca from 19 to 21 May 2017, organized by the Centro Studi Opera Omnia Luigi Boccherini in collaboration with *Ad Parnassum. A Journal of Eighteenth- and Nineteenth-Century Instrumental Music*. The scholarly committee consisted of Simone Ciolfi, Roberto Illiano, Fulvia Morabito, Massimiliano Sala, Rohan H. Stewart-Macdonald (†), and the keynote speakers were Guido Olivieri, Giorgio Sanguinetti and Neal Zaslaw.

The articles have been organized into the following four thematic areas: 1) 'Improvisation into composition'; 2) 'Issues of Performance Practice'; 3) 'Contemporary Treatises, Pedagogical Works, and Aesthetics'; 4) 'The Art of *Partimento*'. This grouping should not be understood as airtight compartments as the contributions, though belonging to a distinct category, often reveal a stimulating ambivalence.

This volume is not the first on musical improvisation, nor will it be the last, as it follows a path much-trodden in the past few years. The reason without doubt lies in the fact that our present way of understanding musical notation, vitiated by the Romantic and post-Romantic eras, has accustomed us to regard the score as a form of exhaustive communication — at least in so far as the fundamental parameters are concerned — to transform on the sonic level the 'sacred' intentions of the composer, no longer a craftsman, but an artist. The approach to music in the Baroque era, as we have seen, was completely different, and it is the responsibility chiefly of musicology to throw light on the subject, often extrapolating from the repertory that kind of 'soft theory' that is confirmed and completed in the 'hard theory' of traditional treatises.

✱✱✱

Introduction

I would like to to thank the editorial staff of the Centro Studi Opera Omnia Luigi Boccherini, in particular, Roberto Illiano and Massimiliano Sala, for their work. As well, a warm thank goes to Warwick Lister for having translated my Introduction, and to Jennifer Walker for her careful assistance with the revision of some English texts.

This book is dedicated to Mila, who has always exhorted me to live life intensely, also for her, when without her.

Lucca, Winter 2019

Fulvia Morabito
Translation by Warwick Lister

Bibliography

Rasch 2011
Beyond Notes. Improvisation in Western Music of the Eighteenth and Nineteenth Centuries, Turnhout, Brepols, 2011 (Speculum musicae, 16)

Van Tour 2015
Van Tour, Peter. *Counterpoint and Partimento: Methods of Teaching Composition in Late Eighteenth-Century Naples*, Uppsala, Acta Universitatis Upsaliensis, 2015 (Studia musicological Upsaliansia. Nova Series, 25).

Zarlino 1558.
Zarlino, Gioseffo. *Le Istitutioni harmoniche*, Venice, Pietro da Fino, 1558.

Improvisation into Composition

French Harpsichord *Doubles* and the Creative Art of the 17ᵀᴴ-Century *Clavecinistes*

David Chung
(Hong Kong Baptist University)

Introduction[1]

THE SEVENTEENTH-CENTURY French harpsichord repertory developed from a largely improvised art in which the notation served as an *aide-mémoire* to a form with highly sophisticated notation in which the details carefully marked by the composer were expected to be observed meticulously by the performer[2]. The lack of a single, definite source for much of this repertory continues to perplex many scholars and performers[3]. Understanding the repertory's creative evolution would undoubtedly be beneficial to all those interested in 17ᵗʰ-century French harpsichord music.

Through an in-depth study of pieces with *doubles*, this article delves into performance practice issues pertinent to this repertory and explores the creative processes of playing and teaching by 17ᵗʰ-century musicians in the quasi-improvisatory tradition. Three issues will be considered in detail: (1) the art of embellishment and variation; (2) the ways in which 17ᵗʰ-century musicians cultivated their individual artistic voices; and (3) what concordant versions tell us about the performance of this repertory.

Definitions and Functions

Doubles, a type of variation, seem to have originated in the 17ᵗʰ-century *airs de cour*, with notable examples composed by Bénigne de Bacilly (1621-1690) and Michel Lambert

---

[1]. The author acknowledges the support of a General Research Fund (HKBU 12401714) awarded by the Research Grants Council (RGC) of Hong Kong, without which the timely completion of this article would not have been possible.

[2]. See GUSTAFSON 1995, pp. 118-119: «French harpsichord music of the seventeenth century was to a significant extent an improvisatory art».

[3]. A major exception is music by Jean Henry D'Anglebert, which survives in both an autograph source (F-Pn Rés. 89ter) and a printed source meticulously prepared by the composer himself (Paris, 1689). See HARRIS 2009, vol. II, pp. 79-102 for a discussion of the latter sources and other manuscripts containing D'Anglebert's works for the keyboard.

(1610-1696) in the decades between the 1640s and the 1660s[4]. In the *airs de cour* repertory, *doubles* are the second strophes (or couplets), in which the melody of the first verse is embroidered with diminutions and passages. Those published by Bacilly typically comprise ornamented melodies alone, without the bass[5]. The word «variation» is commonly found in English manuscripts during this period, such as in the recently rediscovered Selosse manuscript (see LEECH 2008, no. 14b)[6].

In French harpsichord music, however, a *double* is usually a separate, embellished version that follows the original piece[7]. Some composers provide *doubles* of their own, but it is common practice to make a *double* from an existing piece by another composer, sometimes in homage. A piece by Marais, for example, is entitled *Rondeau redouble* in a manuscript compiled by Charles Babel[8]. In the recently rediscovered «Borel» manuscript, 10 pieces are followed by their «*redoubles*»[9].

The repertory of harpsichord *doubles* includes many courantes and menuets, as well as several bourrées, gavottes, sarabandes and other dances. Hardel's Gavotte and the C major Gavotte by Lebègue appear to have been very popular, as they were circulated in many manuscript sources.

AUTHORSHIP OF *DOUBLES*

APPENDIX 1 provides a list of *doubles* made by the composers themselves (i.e., with both the principal piece and its *double* by the same composer). With the notable exception of those by Louis Couperin, many pieces in this category were published in collections of Chambonnières, Lebègue, D'Anglebert and Jacquet de la Guerre. APPENDIXES 2 and 3 list *doubles* based on works by other composers — by D'Anglebert and Louis Couperin, respectively[10]. An instrumental version of D'Anglebert's Lully Courante, for example,

---

[4]. See GORDON-SEIFERT 2011, pp. 1-9 for an in-depth discussion of the *airs de cour* repertory.

[5]. The expressive function of embellishment was emphasized by both Marin Mersenne and Bacilly. See *ibidem*, p. 115.

[6]. See LEECH 2008, pp. v-viii and GUSTAFSON 2018, p. 22 for a discussion of the Selosse manuscript, which is privately owned by Peter Leech.

[7]. In D'ANGLEBERT 1689, the composer provided *doubles* for three courantes (G major, G minor and D minor). The shorter D minor courante and its *double* (pp. 73-74) were spread over two facing pages. For the longer G major and G minor courantes (pp. 5-8 and 41-44), the principal piece and its *double*, each engraved on two facing pages, were separated by a page turn. Similarly, the *doubles* copied by Marc Roger Normand Couperin (e.g., «Gavotte de Mr Hardel» and «Double de la Gavotte» in ff. 56ᵛ-58ʳ) are clearly separated versions of the original pieces.

[8]. Gb-Lbl Ms Add 39569, no. 163. See GUSTAFSON 1990 for a discussion of Babel's role in pieces he compiled.

[9]. See MORONEY 2005, pp. 23-26 for an inventory of the «Borel» manuscript.

[10]. See WILSON 2013, pp. 6-25 for the argument that some of the pieces attributed to Louis Couperin in the so-called Bauyn (F-Pn Rés. Vm7 674-675) and Parville (US-BEm MS778) manuscripts could instead

survives in the 1695 'Philidor' manuscript (F-Pn Rés. F. 533). D'Anglebert's own setting, published 6 years before the date ascribed to the Philidor manuscript in his *Pieces de clavecin* (1689), is adorned with the composer's characteristic ornaments, and is probably D'Anglebert's own reworking of Lully's lost original. Apart from the Lully Courante, all of the pieces in this category survive in manuscript sources. APPENDIX 4 lists remaining pieces with *doubles* that survive in various printed and manuscript sources. In the majority of these pieces, it is impossible to assume that the *doubles* were made by the composers of the principal pieces. APPENDIX 5 lists a number of *doubles* related to keyboard arrangements of Lully's music[11].

Techniques of Making *doubles*

Seventeenth-century harpsichordists from Chambonnières to Jacquet de La Guerre tapped into a wide range of techniques beyond melodic diminution. Many of these techniques, such as replacing block chords with broken-chord figurations (commonly known as *brisures*), were ubiquitous in the music of the *clavecinistes*[12]. Yet by blending these conventional procedures with distinctive ideas and musical propensities, each composer created an original musical footprint.

Chambonnières

Chambonnières' *double* to the A minor Courante (1670) demonstrates conventional techniques of making keyboard *doubles*, such as diminution (treble, bass or mixed voices), changes in tessitura, alternate ornamentation and figuration, points of imitation (bars 5, 8-9) and increased rhythmic activity (see Ex. 1). Chambonnières' avoidance of mechanical, predictable patterns (e.g., in the right hand in bar 2) imparts a sense of spontaneity[13]. These techniques were skillfully combined to give shape, variety and sometimes even drama. In bar 2 of the principal piece, for example, the bass branches out into two voices, yielding an additional tenor voice above. In the *double*, the bass also separates into two voices, but this time yields a lower bass voice and a richer sonority in bars 2-3. Significantly, the figurations and diminutions in bars 9-15 are shared equally between the voices.

---

have been composed by his brother Charles (1632-1675); however, the evidence cited is inconclusive.

[11]. See CHUNG 2015, Introduction, pp. iv, vii for a discussion of *doubles* in the repertory of keyboard arrangements of Lully's music.

[12]. For a discussion of the *style brisé* technique frequently linked to the style of the *clavecinistes*, see LEDBETTER 1987, pp. 45-48.

[13]. See MARTIN 2009, pp. 145-149, for a rhetorical analysis of Jacquet de La Guerre's Allemande in A minor (1687), a good example of «the balance between measure and *mouvement*» characteristic of the 17th-century French harpsichord style.

David Chung

Ex. 1: Jacques Champion de Chambonnières, Courante in A minor and *Double* de la Courante (*Les Pieces de clavessin, Livre Premier*, 1670, pp. 3-4), bars 1-16.

French Harpsichord *doubles* and the Creative Art of the 17th-Century *Clavecinistes*

Chambonnières' *double* above brings to mind Le Gallois' observations on his playing[14].

> [...] & toutes les fois qu'il joüoit une piece il y mêloit de nouvelles beautés par des ports de voix, des passages, & des agrémens differens, avec des doubles cadences. Enfin il les diversifioit tellement par toutes ces beautez differentes qu'il y faisoit toûjours trouver de nouvelles graces.

D'Anglebert

D'Anglebert's *doubles* reveal the composer's resourcefulness in combining and varying common procedures to create new shapes and effects. The opening of the G major Courante is a case in point (see Ex. 2). In the principal piece, the rhythmic characteristics of the dance are prominent from the start. The music begins with an upbeat shortened by a *détaché*, followed by a downbeat enhanced by a *tremblement appuyé*. In the *double*, D'Anglebert initiates movement with an upbeat of three quavers. Interestingly, the downbeat is stripped of the *tremblement*, possibly to yield more flow, and the *tremblement* on the third quaver propels the music forward. D'Anglebert uses diminution to create additional shapes. In the opening, a falling and rising shape is complemented by a subsequent rising and falling shape; next, a longer winding passage leads to a cadence in G in bars 3-4. In the *double*, improvisatory gestures and fluid movements take precedence over the rhythmic character of the dance, which is largely delegated to the left hand.

Ex. 2: opening of Jean Henry D'Anglebert's Courante in G major and *Double de la Courante* (*Pieces de clavecin*, 1689, pp. 5, 7).

A similar approach is evident in the D minor Courante (see Ex. 3). In the principal piece, the rhythmic quality of the dance is strongly highlighted. In the *double*, improvisatory gestures and melodic diminutions glue phrases into longer units. The composer makes

---

14. See Le Gallois 1680, p. 70.

ingenious use of tensions and resolutions to maintain flow. In the opening bar, for example, he adjusts the note value of the bass and tenor notes to create the expressive dissonance of a major second.

Ex. 3: opening of Jean Henry D'Anglebert's Courante in D minor and *Double* de la Courante (*Pieces de clavecin*, 1689, pp. 73-74).

D'Anglebert's propensity to recompose existing music is demonstrated in his *double* to the C major Gaillarde (Ex. 4). In the principal piece, the rhythmic character of the dance is firmly established from the outset. In the *double*, D'Anglebert creates a new gesture comprising an anacrusis (a three-note upbeat figure), a dotted rhythm, a chord and a bass note. This gesture or its elements are used to bind the piece tightly together throughout the *double*.

Ex. 4: Jean Henry D'Anglebert's Gaillarde in C major and Double (F-Pn Rés. 89ter, ff. 10ᵛ-11ᵛ), bars 1-8.

In the improvisatory tradition, alternate endings in repeats were often entrusted to the performer. In his *doubles*, however, such as the Gaillarde in C major and the Sarabande in A minor, D'Anglebert wrote out in full alternate and additional endings of increasing complexity. In his *petite reprise* of the Gaillarde in C major, the melody leaps up a fifth to a''', creating a dissonance with the bass that imparts a sense of freshness and a stronger drive towards the eventual cadence (see Ex. 5). In the Sarabande in A minor, the bass is critically retouched in the penultimate bar to produce a strong cadential gesture comprising a striking subdominant seventh chord giving way to an enriched dominant sonority in which the bass leaps down dramatically by a minor ninth (see Ex. 6). Certainly, D'Anglebert's models offer very useful lessons for the modern performer seeking to construct individualized endings.

Ex. 5: endings of Jean Henry D'Anglebert's Gaillarde in C major and *Double* (F-Pn Rés. 89ter, ff. 10ᵛ-12ʳ).

Ex. 6: endings of Jean Henry D'Anglebert's Sarabande in A minor and *Double* (US-Cn Case MS VM2.3 E58r, ff. 38ᵛ-39ᵛ).

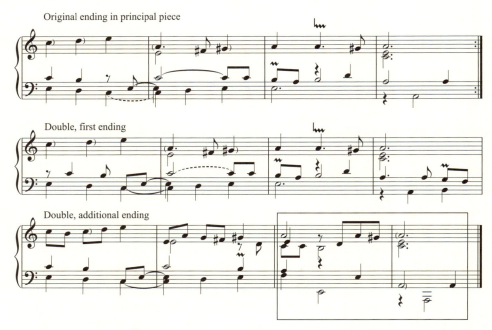

D'Anglebert's sensitivity to nuances (melodic, harmonic, rhythmic, textural) and resourcefulness in recasting existing pieces with expressive shapes and gestures is evident throughout his music. Although space does not allow a comprehensive scrutiny of his music, a few examples will suffice to indicate the palette of effects he painstakingly marked in the notation. In his *double* to Pinel's Sarabande in C major, D'Anglebert's adeptness in recasting lute-inspired textures to give effects idiomatic to the keyboard is in full display; the syncopated repeated notes in the top voice are richly supported by a sonorous accompaniment in the tenor-bass register, possibly referring to the lute's *campanella* effect (see Ex. 7)[15]. In both the principal piece and the *double*, the syncopated rhythms in bars 2-4 of the bass remove the strong accents on the first beats of bars 3-5. In bars 13-16, a quaver movement is woven throughout the texture with *brisures* and diminutions. In his *doubles* to Louis Couperin's Allemande in G and Chambonnières' Courante in G, D'Anglebert offers his signature cadential gesture of two repeated notes followed by a chord (see Ex. 8). In his *double* to Louis Couperin's Allemande, D'Anglebert's use of rhythmically enhanced texture, newly composed motivic gestures, syncopated voices and spicy dissonances add flow, fluidity and spontaneity (see Ex. 9).

---

[15]. In lute music, the *campanella* technique involves playing adjacent or repeated notes on different courses. The effect of *campanella* is known as «baigné». See LEDBETTER 1987, p. xi for an explanation of these two terms and pp. 79-81 for a nuanced discussion of the assimilation of these lute-originating effects into D'Anglebert's harpsichord music.

French Harpsichord *doubles* and the Creative Art of the 17th-Century *Clavecinistes*

Ex. 7: Jean Henry D'Anglebert's Sarabande [de] Pinel in C major and *Double* (F-Pn Rés. 89ter, ff. 6ᵛ-8ʳ), bars 1-15.

Ex. 8: cadential gesture in Henry D'Anglebert's *double* to Louis Couperin's Allemande in G major (F-Pn Rés. 89ter, ff. 69ʳ-70ᵛ).

Ex. 9: Jean Henry D'Anglebert's *double* to Louis Couperin's Allemande in G major (F-Pn Rés. 89ter, ff. 68ʳ-69ᵛ), bars 1-3.

Louis Couperin

Doubles by Louis Couperin have a strong rhythmic drive and are infused with youthfulness. Outbursts of energy and unreserved virtuosity are distinctive traits of his *doubles*, such as the *double* to Chambonnières' 'Le Moutier', whose running semiquaver passages and chains of sequences reflect a strong Italian influence (see Ex. 10). In Couperin's famous *double* to Hardel's Gavotte in A minor, the semiquaver runs extend the compass by an octave at the end of bar 1, giving clear prominence to the top voice; meanwhile, both texture and ornamentation are simplified (see Ex. 15 below). A similarly extroverted approach can be observed in the *double* to Rigaudon in C. Couperin's tendency to surprise listeners with bold gestures (bar 16) and pungent harmonic effects (bars 4-5) is clearly demonstrated in the *double* to the Menuet de Poitou (see Ex. 11)[16].

Ex. 10: Louis Couperin's *double* to Chambonnières' «Le Moutier» (F-Pn Rés.Vm7 674-675, I, ff. 1ʳ-1ᵛ), bars 1-6.

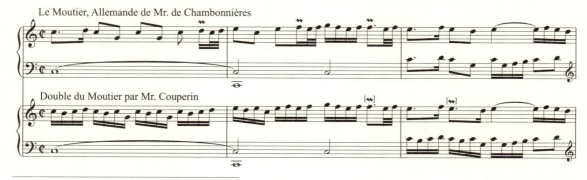

---

[16]. The piece is simply entitled «de Mr Couperin» in Bauyn II (F-Pn Rés. Vm7 674-675, II, f. 68ᵛ). The title «Menuet de Poitou» comes from Parville (US-BEm MS778, p. 100). See MORONEY 1985, p. 218 for a discussion of the differences between the two versions.

French Harpsichord doubles and the Creative Art of the 17th-Century Clavecinistes

Ex. 11: Louis Couperin, [Menuet de Poitou] de Mr Couperin and *Double* (F-Pn Rés. Vm7 674-675, II, f. 68ᵛ), bars 1-6, 13-18.

David Chung

Other composers

Many *doubles* made by other 17th-century composers incorporate the techniques discussed above, although almost every piece offers something unique and special. *Doubles* by Lebègue contain some of the finest examples of melodic diminutions, in which the avoidance of recurrent patterns results in an improvisatory effect. In the Courante de Mr Richard, the rhythmic displacement of melody and bass notes not only gives the music more fluidity and movement, but also somewhat weakens the beat and imparts a harmonic vagueness strongly alluding to lute techniques (see Ex. 12). In bar 6, the repositioning of the melodic note *e″* creates the mild dissonance of a perfect fourth (note *f″*) over the bass, which is quickly resolved. Paradoxically, the note *e″* then creates dissonance in the subsequent dominant chord, enhancing the momentum into the cadence in C. The *double* to the G minor Menuet (1687) by Jacquet de la Guerre deserves special mention (see Ex. 13). De la Guerre varies the repeat in both strains by transferring the diminutions from the melody to the bass (first, using the same bass as the principal piece; and in the repeat, reducing the right-hand melody to either chords or single notes). The *doubles* in the 1707 book demonstrate greater sophistication: existing materials are elaborated through a complex keyboard technique to give a rich contrapuntal texture.

Ex. 12: Courante de Mr Richard and *Double* (F-Psg Ms 2356, ff. 8ʳ-8ᵛ), bars 1-6.

Ex. 13: Jacquet de La Guerre, G minor Menuet and *Double* (1687, pp. 38-39), bars 1-8.

Summary of Techniques of Making doubles

Table 1 summarizes the common techniques of making *doubles* discussed above. The table reveals that 17th-century harpsichordists tapped into a wide range of techniques beyond merely the diminution of melodies. These techniques can be reduced to three main types, depending on the degree of revision of existing material: (1) variation of an idea; (2) extension and expansion of an idea; and (3) addition of new materials. These techniques can be used either in isolation or in combination to give shape and expression with endless variety, such as by forming irregular phrases and sub-phrases in the melodic line, reinforcing the tenor or bass line, injecting new expressive gestures, enhancing movement and flow by adding various degrees of dissonance and varying (usually increasing) the rhythmic energy for expressive purposes. It is in the last two types (extension/expansion of an existing idea and addition of new materials) that each composer's character and individuality are most strongly revealed; for example, in Couperin's extroverted gestures and harmonic boldness and D'Anglebert's luxuriant ornamentation and expansive textures. Significantly, *doubles* by individual composers contain a wealth of information on the composers' stylistic fingerprints and musical personalities.

Table 1: Summary of Techniques of Making *doubles*

Technique	Description
Variation of an existing idea	diminutions chords to melody block chords to *brisé* chords respaced rhythmic redistribution repositioning of melodic notes change of texture (thickening or thinning) change of tessitura (higher or lower) bass (retouched) different ornaments (including removing existing ones)
Extension/expansion of an existing idea	extending tessitura repetition of notes or musical patterns
Adding new materials	dissonant notes chromatic notes bass recomposed points of imitation new rhythms (e.g. dotted) *petite reprise* different first and second repeats linking passages new ornamentS

Concordances

Concordant versions of pieces with *doubles* contain many differences in notes, accidentals, articulation symbols and other details. Such differences, as scholars have noted, are to be expected in the manuscript tradition[17]. The late arrival of music engraving in the French harpsichord music tradition is often blamed for an imputed lack of precision in notating complex textures and sophisticated ornaments. The variant readings in concordant versions remind modern musicians of the fluidity of 17th-century notation[18].

Hardel's famous gavotte is a case in point (see Ex. 14). This gavotte has survived in more than a dozen manuscript versions, of which five stemming from sources central to the Parisian repertory have been selected for close inspection here[19]. First, the similarities

---

[17]. See GUSTAFSON 1995, pp. 123-126 for a study of three versions of Chambonnières' Courante in G.

[18]. More recent editions, such as those published by the Broude Brothers, reproduce the different versions, as reproducing different versions of a piece best demonstrates «the range of ways in which a piece was understood in its own day». See GUSTAFSON – HERLIN 2017, p. xv. See also BROUDE 2017, pp. 284-285 for a detailed discussion of the significance of reproducing multiple texts, a procedure known as «versioning», for the 17th-century French harpsichord repertory.

[19]. The five sources are as follows: Bauyn (F-Pn Rés. Vm7 674-675), Parville (US-BEm MS778), Babell (Gb-Lbl Ms Add 39569), F-Pn Rés. F. 933 and Humeau (France, private collection of Philippe Humeau).

French Harpsichord *doubles* and the Creative Art of the 17th-Century *Clavecinistes*

Ex. 14: opening of Jacques Hardel, Gavotte in A minor in Bauyn, Parville, Babell, and Humeau (see note 19).

See Gustafson 1979 for inventories of Bauyn, Parville, Babell and Rés. F. 933 and Gustafson 2018, pp. 31-33 for an inventory of the recently rediscovered Humeau manuscript.

in textural details suggest that all versions except the Humeau version derive from a single tradition, although a stemma cannot be established for these sources. In the opening, the melody thickens into two voices before thinning back into one, and the left-hand texture is virtually identical in the first strain in all non-Humeau versions. Given its simplified texture, the Humeau version may have been prepared for (or by) an amateur player. The differences are even more telling, and convey three types of performance practice information: (1) different notations of the same effect; (2) explicit performance information; and (3) alternate figurations or effects.

(1) Different notations of the same effect

The dotted rhythms in Bauyn, Parville and Humeau are obviously written-out *notes inégales*. The scribes of Babell and Rés. F. 933 considered the explicit notation of the dotted effect unnecessary. In bars 7–8, the so-called *tierce coulé*, effectively a grace note linking the interval of a third, is expressed in five ways, including a small note (with and without a slur), a symbol and a real note value (with and without a slur). And in bar 1, both the Bauyn and Parville versions have a 'drier' notation in the left hand than the Babell and Rés. F. 933 versions. This short piece shows us how the same (aural) effect is presented in different notations (visually) in three dimensions critical to interpretation, namely, rhythm (dotted and undotted notation), ornamentation and articulation.

French Harpsichord *doubles* and the Creative Art of the 17th-Century *Clavecinistes*

(2) Explicit performance information

Of the five scribes, the Bauyn scribe uses the fewest ornament symbols. The Babell and Rés. F. 933 scribes are more generous in supplying ornaments (bars 3-4, 10-12), sometimes even writing out effects in full note values (see Ex. 14, bar 13) and links at endings and repeats.

(3) Alternate figurations/effects

Some differences appear to be connected with the character of individual musicians. In bar 3 of the *double*, for example, all versions except Babell and Humeau terminate the running passage with a trill on the note *d''* over the subdominant bass (note *F*). The continuation of the run seems to reflect the distinct creative personalities of the Babell and Humeau scribes (see Ex. 15). Both the Rés. F. 933 and Humeau scribes provide explicit links to the opening in the repeat. Whilst the idea of using continuous semiquaver movement is identical, each scribe finds a different way to accomplish this task.

Ex. 15: alternate figurations in *doubles* to Jacques Hardel's Gavotte in A minor, bars 1-4.

Evidence on the page suggests that the Rés. F. 933 scribe was particularly keen on using the *port de voix* (see Ex. 14, bars 6, 9, 13). In bars 8-9, the Babell scribe makes distinctive use of the left hand — in a manner that recalls D'Anglebert — to hold on to notes to achieve greater resonance and to create textured crescendo and diminuendo effects.

Similar observations can be made on the various versions of Chambonnières' Courante in C major, including two versions of D'Anglebert's *double* (see Ex. 16). In the opening bar of the two Roper versions, the right-hand third is staggered, and in D'Anglebert's *double* (in F-Pn Rés. 89ter), the space within the third is further filled up by a gesture that recurs later in the piece (bars 8 and 9). Performance information of particular interest includes different beaming patterns (in Rés. 89ter, quavers are uniquely beamed in pairs, not groups of four), written-out ornaments (e.g., bars 6 and 10), D'Anglebert's characteristic method of substituting a long note with a note followed by an embellished chord (bars 4 and 14), an upbeat transformed into a run (bar 7), alternative ornamentation (bar 3), different notations of the same ornament (bar 13) and the so-called 'wet' and 'dry' notation (bars 2 and 9)[20].

Ex. 16: Jacques Champion de Chambonnières, Courante in C major and *doubles* by D'Anglebert, bars 1-4.

[20]. See LEDBETTER 1987, p. 68 for a discussion of the «wet» and «dry» notation.

These different notations of the same effect remind us that during the 17th century, music existed largely as sound, as notation grew out of the need to represent sound on paper. As John Butt so aptly points out (2002), notation in the manuscript tradition was sometimes an example of what could be done, sometimes a description of what had been done and sometimes a solution required by a particular musician or event[21]. Therefore, it is not surprising that different scribes took different approaches to representing music on paper[22]. These multiple versions contain various kinds of performance information (such as written-out embellishments and alternative effects), many of which are beyond the general remit of treatises and tutors. Such information provides the modern performer with an enhanced awareness of the kaleidoscopic range with which an embellished version could deviate from an existing model and more opportunities to translate the inherent richness of original notation into vivid sonic experiences.

Significance of *doubles*

Studying how a composer created an embellished version from an existing piece sheds light on the creative process. As the art of making *doubles* is closely linked to the art of embellishment, the repertory of *doubles* as a whole provides a unique window onto the hidden skills of 17th-century musicians. Without *doubles*, we would be deprived of many embellished pieces, such as the superlatively virtuosic and colouristic versions composed by Louis Couperin.

Doubles based on existing works by other composers bring to light the close relationship between imitation and creativity in 17th-century arts. In 1680, Jean le Gallois strongly promoted the idea that imitating a good model provides a solid foundation for creative development[23].

> L'on peut dire encore qu'il y en a plusieurs autres, qui ont dans leurs manieres de joüer quelque chose de particulier & de beau […] Il suffit de dire que ces autres manieres de joüer differentes participant plus ou moins des deux premieres [celles de Chambonnières et Louis Couperin], qui sont comme les deux sources d'où les autres derivent.

For Le Gallois, Chambonnierès was unquestionably the best model for other harpsichordists[24].

---

[21]. Butt 2002, pp. 96-122.
[22]. In his edition of Hardel's harpsichord pieces, Denis Herlin (in Herlin 1991, p. 20) explains that it is not possible to work towards a single and definitive text of the composer's Gavotte in A minor.
[23]. Le Gallois 1680, pp. 74-75.
[24]. *Ibidem*, pp. 70-72.

> Et c'est ce qui a fait que chacun se l'est proposé à imiter comme un parfait modele [...] apres la mort de Chambonniere Hardelle passoit avec raison pour le plus parfait imitateur de ce grand homme [...].

Interestingly, these *doubles* most clearly reveal the composers' distinctive characteristics, such as Louis Couperin's fieriness and D'Anglebert's reflectiveness and sensitivity. Similarly, many musicians stamped their musical imprints on *doubles* with characteristic gestures and ornaments.

Conclusion

The repertory of *doubles* examined here provides insights into the creative processes of performance and teaching during the 17th century and the relationship between imitation and creativity at the core of the 17th-century musical mind. Studying the techniques of making *doubles* allows us to explore in depth the elusive art of embellishment and the resourcefulness with which 17th-century musicians cultivated their individual artistic voices. A closer examination of concordant versions reveals fascinating details of performance. By distinguishing decorative elements from those integral to the musical fabric, the modern performer can cultivate spontaneity while remaining faithful to the original spirit of the music through an increased awareness of the opportunities to fuse knowledge with creativity.

French Harpsichord *doubles* and the Creative Art of the 17th-Century *Clavecinistes*

Appendixes

Abbreviations and sigla

RISM sigla for libraries are used. Manuscript sources are identified by the locations and call numbers. Codes for printed sources are derived from the year of publication and volume number, if there is more than one publication from the same year. For example, 1670-1 (first item in Appendix 1) refers to Chambonnières, Jacques Champion de, *Les Pieces de clavessin [...] Livre Premier*, Paris, Jollain, 1670. For concordances, only information of *doubles* is included. For a comprehensive list of sources and modern editions, see Gustafson 1979, Gustafson – Fuller 1990, Gustafson – Wolf 1999, and Gustafson 2017.

Other abbreviations

G.: Gustafson, Bruce. *Chambonnières: A Thematic Catalogue*, JSCM Instrumenta 1, <http://www.sscm-jscm.org/instrumenta_01>, accessed 8 October 2018.

LWV: Schneider, Herbert. *Chronologisch-Thematisches Verzeichnis sämtlicher Werke von Jean-Baptiste Lully*, Tutzing, Hans Schneider, 1981.

Appendix 1
Doubles by Original Composers

Composer	Piece (key)	Double(s)	Source(s)	Concordance(s)
Chambonnières	Courante (a), G.2	Double de la Courante,	1670-1, pp. 3–6	GB Oldham, ff. 31^r–31^v F-Pn Rés. Vm7 674–675, 1, f. 60^r
Louis Couperin (?)	Menuet de Poitou (a)	Double	F-Pn Rés. Vm7 674–675, II, f. 68^v, US-BEm Ms 778, p. 100	
D'Anglebert	Courante (G)	Double	1689, pp. 5–8	
D'Anglebert	Courante (d)	Double de la Courante	1689, pp. 73–74	
D'Anglebert	Gaillarde (C)	Double	F-Pn Rés. 89ter, ff. 10^v–12^r	
D'Anglebert	Sarabande (a)	Double	US-Cn Case MS VM2.3 E58r, ff. 38^v–39^v	
Gigault	Allemande par fugue (d)	[Double] La mesme allemande avec les ports de voix	1682, pp. 18–19	
Jacquet de La Guerre	Menuet (g)	Double	1687, pp. 38–39	
Jacquet de La Guerre	La Flamande [Allemande] (d)	Double	1707, pp. 1–4	
Jacquet de La Guerre	Courante (d)	Double	1707, pp. 5–7	
Jacquet de La Guerre	Gigue (d)	Double	1707, pp. 9–12	
Le Roux	Menuet (a)	Double du Menuet	1705, pp. 23–24	
Le Roux	Menuet (F)	Double du menuet Double de la Basse	1705, pp. 46–48	
Le Roux	Courante (f#)	Double de la Courante	1705, pp. 54–55	
Lebègue	Courante (d)	Double	1677, pp. 7–10	US-BEm MS 770, p. 333 D-B Mus. Mu. 40044. f. 87^r
Lebègue	Bourée (G)	Double	1677, pp. 43–44	US-Cn Case MS VM2.3, E58r, f. 27^r GB-Ob MS Tenbury 1508, f. 33^r Gb-Lbl Ms Add 39569, p. 63
Lebègue	2me Courante (C)	Double	1677, pp. 69–70	

Composer	Piece	Type	Source	Concordances
Lebègue	Bourée (C)	Double	1677, pp. 73-74	
Lebègue	Gavotte (C)	Double	1677, pp. 77-78	GB-Ob MS Tenbury 1508, f. 5r; Gb-Lbl Ms Add 39569, p. 42; F-Psg MS 2374, ff. 8r-8v; D-SWl Musik Hs. 619, ff. 84v-85r; F-Pn Rés. Vm7 674-675, III, f. 40r; US-BEm Ms 778, p. 143; US-BEm Ms 778, pp. 276-277; F Humeau (private collection), p. 19; US-BEm Ms 1371, ff. 75v-76r
Lebègue	Bourée (A)	Double	1687, pp. 49-51	
Lebègue	Gavotte (G)	Double	1687, pp. 91-93	
Perrine	Courante du J.G. (a)	Double	1680, pp. 53-54, 56	
Richard	Courante (a)	Double [by Richard?]	F-Psg MS 2356, ff. 8r-8v	

APPENDIX 2

DOUBLES BY D'ANGLEBERT OF OTHER COMPOSERS' PIECES

Composer	Piece (Key)	Source	Concordances
Chambonnières	Courante 'Iris' (C), G.8	F-Pn Rés. 89ter, ff. 2r-4r	US-Cn Case MS VM2.3 E58r, ff. 8Av-9Ar; Girard, pp. 9-10; GB Oldham, ff. 17v-18r; F-Pn Rés. Vmd. ms. 18, ff. 12v-13r; F-Pn Rés. Vmd. ms. 18, ff. 45r-46r; F-Pn Rés. Vmd. ms. 18, ff. 18Av-19Ar
Chambonnières	Courante 'l'Immortelle' (C), G.9	F-Pn Rés. 89ter, ff. 5r-6r	US-Cn Case MS VM2.3 E58r, ff. 10Av-11Ar
Chambonnières	Gigue. La Verdinguette. (C), G.35	F-Pn Rés. 89ter, ff. 9v-10r	GB-Cu MS. Add. 9565, p. 44 (incomplete)
Chambonnières	Courante (G), G.56	F-Pn Rés. 89ter, ff. 71v-72r	
Chambonnières	Courante (G), G.58	F-Pn Rés. 89ter, ff. 73v-74r	
Chambonnières	Sarabande 'Jeunes Zéphyrs' (G), G.59	F-Pn Rés. 89ter, ff. 75v-76r	
Chambonnières	Sarabande 'O beau jardin' (F), G.116	F-Pn Rés. 89ter, f. 52r	
Louis Couperin	Allemande (G)	F-Pn Rés. 89ter, ff. 68v-70r	
Lully	Courante, Mr. de Lully (g), LWV 75/24	1689, pp. 78-80	F-Pn Rés. 89ter, ff. 87r-89r; US-BEm Ms 778, pp. 72-73; D-Rtt Inc. IIIc/4, ff. 28v-29r
Pinel	Sarabande (C)	F-Pn Rés. 89ter, ff. 6v-8r	
Richard	Sarabande (G)	F-Pn Rés. 89ter, ff. 80v-82r	

French Harpsichord *doubles* and the Creative Art of the 17th-Century *Clavecinistes*

APPENDIX 3

Doubles by Louis Couperin of Other Composers' Pieces

Composer	Piece (key)	Source(s)	Comments
Chambonnières	Le Moutier, Allemande (C), G.67	F-Pn Rés. Vm7 674-675 I, f. 1ʳ US-BEm Ms 778, p. 118-119 Babell, pp. 148-149 US-BEm Ms 1371, ff. 70ᵛ-71ᵛ	
Hardel	Gavotte (a)	F-Pn Rés. Vm7 674-675 III, ff. 38ʳ-38ᵛ US-BEm Ms 778, p. 98-99 US-BEm MS 1372, f. 40ʳ F Humeau, p. 28 GB-Ob MS Tenbury 1508, f. 8ᵛ E-Mn MS 1360, f. 227ʳ GB-Ob: Ms. Mus. Sch. E. 426, f. 14ᵛ Jeans (private collection) F-Pn Rés. F. 933, f. 10ʳ F-Pn Vm7 137321, p. 26 US-BEm Ms 1371, ff. 57ᵛ-58ᵛ D-Rtt Inc. IIIc/4, ff. 10ᵛ-11ʳ D-Rtt Inc. IIIc/4, ff. 61ᵛ-62ʳ F Roanne, ff. 46ʳ-45ᵛ	See HERLIN 1991, p. 20 for a list of many contemporary transcriptions for lute, flute and voice, and other instruments.
Lebègue	Gavotte (C)	F-Pn Rés. Vm7 674-675, III, f. 40ʳ US-BEm Ms 778, p. 276	Both versions appear to have been corrupt; see MORONEY 1985, p. 221.
Lully	Rigaudon, from *Acis et Galatée* (1686) (D), LWV 73/6	US-BEm Ms 778, pp. 138-141	«Double du Rigaudon fait par Mr. Couprain»; see GUSTAFSON – FULLER 1990, p. 383 for comments on the authorship of the harpsichord version.

APPENDIX 4

Doubles in Other Manuscript Sources

Source(s)	Composer	Title (key)	Double	Comments
B-Bc Ms 27220, pp. 85-86		Allemande (F)	Double	
B-Bc Ms 27220, pp. 90-91		Les plaisirs derobez (d)	Double	
B-Bc Ms 50775, pp. 113-114		Gavotte (d)	Double	
D-B Lynar A-1, pp. 292-293		Courante (D)	[with interpolated variation]	GUSTAFSON – WOLF 1999, no. 20
D-B Lynar A-1, pp. 294-295		Courante (d)	[with variations]	GUSTAFSON – WOLF 1999, no. 21
D-B Lynar A-1, pp. 296-298		Courante (d)	Variatio	GUSTAFSON – WOLF 1999, no. 22
D-B Lynar A-1, pp. 298-299 I-Rvat Chigi Q IV 24, ff. 47ʳ-47ᵛ		Courante de La Barre (d)	Variatio	GUSTAFSON – WOLF 1999, no. 6c

Source	Composer	Title	Type	Notes
D-Rtt Inc. IIIc/4, ff. 17ᵛ–19ᵛ	Chambonnières	La Loureusse (D), (G.11b)	double de La Loureusse	Cfr. Gb-Lbl Ms Add 39569, pp. 136–137
D-Rtt Inc. IIIc/4, ff. 2ʳ–2ᵛ		Menuet (C)	double	Cfr. F-Pn Rés Vmd. Ms. 18, ff. 22r, 20Ar
D-Rtt Inc. IIIc/4, ff. 67ᵛ–69ʳ	Louis Couperin	Courante du vieux Couprin (d)		double by Louis Couperin?
F Humeau, p. 3	Chambonnières or Monnard	Sarabande (C), G.150	Double	Cfr. Gb-Lbl Ms Add 52363, p. 154
F Roanne, ff. 44ʳ–43ᵛ		Menuet (d)	[Double]	
F-Pn Rés. 1184, 1185, p. 174		Courante (d)	[with interpolated variation]	GUSTAFSON – WOLF 1999, no. 6
F-Pn Rés. 1184, 1185, p. 337		Courante (C)	[with interpolated variation]	GUSTAFSON – WOLF 1999, no. 3b
F-Pn Rés. Vm7 674-67, 1, f. 19ʳ	Chambonnières	Courante (d), G.92	Double du meme Auteur	
F-Pn Rés. Vm7 674-67, 1, f. 68ʳ	Chambonnières	Gaillarde (B-flat), G. 68	Double de la [...] par led' Auteur	Cfr. F Oldham, ff. 25ᵛ–26ʳ
F-Pn Rés. Vmd. ms. 18, f. 22ʳ		Menuet (C)	double du Menüet (C)	
F-Pn Rés. Vmd. ms. 18, f. 47ʳ		menüet (C)	Double	F-Pn Rés. Vmd. ms. 18, f. 47ʳ
F-Pn Rés. Vmd. ms. 18, f. 20ʳ		Menüet (C)	Double	F-Pn Rés. Vmd. ms. 18, f. 20ʳ
F-Pn Vm7 6307(2), pp. 4–5		La fustanbert (g)	Double	
GB-Cu Add 9565, p. 44	Chambonnières	Guigue (C), G.35	Double	double by D'Anglebert, incomplete
GB-Cu Add. 9565, pp. 13–15		Gavotte (G)	Double	
Gb-Lbl Ms Add 39569, p. 76	Dieupart?	Gavotte (a)		
Gb-Lbl Ms Add 39569, p. 115	Hardel	Gavotte (a)		
Gb-Lbl Ms Add 39569, p. 130	Anon.	Sarabande (g)	Double [by Louis Couperin?]	
Gb-Lbl Ms Add 39569, p. 162	Marais	Rondeau redouble (D)		
Gb-Lbl Ms Add 39569, p. 42	Lebègue	Gavotte (C)		Copy of Lebègue
Gb-Lbl Ms Add 39569, p.63	Lebègue	Bourée (G)		Copy of Lebègue
Gb-Lbl Ms Add 39569, pp. 136–137	Chambonnières	Allemande la loureuse (d), G.11	Le Double Double de La Loureusse	
D-Rtt Inc. IIIc/4, ff. 18ᵛ–19ʳ		Sarabande (e)	[with variations]	GUSTAFSON – WOLF 1999, no. 19
GB-Och Mus. Ms. 1177, f. 2ʳ		Corant (d)	[with variation]	GUSTAFSON – WOLF 1999, no. 6a
GB-Och Mus. Ms. 1236, p. 10		Courante (d)	[with variation]	GUSTAFSON – WOLF 1999, no. 14
GB-Och Mus. Ms. 1236, pp. 11–12				
US-NYp Ms. Drexel 5611, p. 103				
GB-Och Mus. Ms. 378, ff. 3ʳ–4ᵛ		Courante (G)	[with interpolated variation]	GUSTAFSON – WOLF 1999, no. 15a
I-Rsc MS A/400, f. 48ʳ	Chambonnières or Monnard	Sarabande (C), G.150	Redoublé	
I-Rvat Chigi Q IV 24, ff. 48ᵛ–49ʳ		Courante (d)	[with variation]	GUSTAFSON – WOLF 1999, no. 27
US-BEm Ms 1365, 22ʳ	Brochard	Courante de Mr. brochard (a)	Suite	
US-BEm Ms 1365, f. 11ʳ	La Barre	Pauane D'angleterre de Mr. De La Barre (d)	Redouble	
US-BEm Ms 1365, f. 20ᵛ	Chambonnières	autre. Chambonniers (d), G.152	Suite	attrib. to La Barre in D-B Lynar A-1, pp. 296–298
US-BEm Ms 1365, f. 22ᵛ		Tricotte (d)	redouble	

French Harpsichord *doubles* and the Creative Art of the 17th-Century *Clavecinistes*

Source	Composer	Title	Double	Comments
US-BEm Ms 1365, f. 23ᵛ	De La Barre	Courante de Monsieur de la barre organiste du Roy (F)	Redouble	
US-BEm Ms 1365, f. 24ʳ		Royale, courante (g)	Diminu[ti]on	top line only
US-BEm Ms 1365, f. 27ᵛ		Sarabande avec le redouble de la main droite et de la gauche (a)	redouble	
US-BEm Ms 1365, f. 28ᵛ		Sarabande (g)	redouble	top line only
US-BEm Ms 1365, f. 30ʳ		Tricottez (F)	[redouble]	
US-BEm Ms 1365, f. 9ʳ		Allemande (C)	suitte	
US-BEm Ms 1365, ff. 15ᵛ–16ʳ	La Barre	Pauane D'angleterre de Monsr. de La Barre (d)	Suitte, ou redouble	*redouble* by La Barre? Cfr. F-Pn Rés. Vm7 674-675, III, f. 29ᵛ
US-BEm Ms 1365, ff. 21ʳ–21ᵛ		Courante Chanbon (d), G.153	Suite	attrib. to La Barre in D-B Lynar A-1, p. 298-299
US-BEm Ms 1371, f. 3ʳ	Chambonnières	Sarabande	Double	
US-BEm MS 770, p. 339		Menuet (C)	Double	Cfr. US-Cn: Case MS VM2.3 E58r, f. 34ʳ
US-Cn Case MS VM2.3 E58r, f. 34ʳ		Menuet (C)	double	Cfr. US-BEm Ms 770, p. 339
US-Cn Case MS VM2.3 E58r, ff. 11ᵛ–12ʳ	Lebègue	[Double to Lebègue, Gigue (C)]	Double de le gige en C sol-ut	Cfr. 1677, pp. 75–76
US-NYp Ms. Drexel 5611, p. 78		Coranto (d) [Gibbons/Tresure?]	[variation]	Gustafson – Wolf 1999, no. 6b
GB-Och Mus. Ms. 1236, p. 3				
US-NYp Ms. Drexel 5611, pp. 104–105		Courante (G)	[with variation]	Gustafson – Wolf 1999, no. 15

Appendix 5
Doubles related to works of Lully

LWV	Work of Lully	Title (key)	Double	Source	Comments
32/7	*Ballet des Muses* (1666)	La Gauotte du ballet (G)	Double de la Gauotte du ballet	B-Bc Ms 27220, p. 42	key of Lully: B-flat
35/4	*Trios pour le coucher du Roy*	Menuet 'Dans nos bois'	2.me couplet de dans nos bois	F-Pn Rés. F. 1091, p. 17	
53/58	*Atys* (1676)	dessente de Cibelle de l'opera d'Atis | Basse Continue (a)	dessente de Cibelle de l'opera d'Atis | Basse roulante (a)	US-BEm Ms 1371, ff. 59ᵛ–61ᵛ	
54/12	*Isis* (1677)	Air de Trompette (C)	Double de Trompette	US-BEm Ms 1371, ff. 76ᵛ–77ᵛ	
54/45	*Isis* (1677)	Troisiéme Air (menuet)	Double	F-Pn Rés 476, f. 83ᵛ	
57/7	*Bellérophon* (1679)	Menuet (d)	Double	B-Bc Ms 27220, pp. 150-151	incomplete
61/27	*Phaeton* (1683)	Gauotte (C)	Double	US-BEm Ms 777, ff. 2ᵛ–3ʳ	
61/28	*Phaeton* (1683)	Gauotte (C)	[double]	US-BEm Ms 777, f. 3ᵛ	Vocal item, *double* (bars 13–24) for harpsichord only
73/6	*Acis et Galatée* (1686)	Rigaudon	Double du Rigaudon fait par Mr. Couprain	US-BEm Ms 778, pp. 138-141	See comments in Appendix 3 above
75/24		Courante, Mr. de Lully (g)	Double	1689, pp. 78-80 F-Pn Rés. 89ter, ff. 87ᵛ–89ʳ US-Bem Ms 778, pp. 72–73 D-Rtt Inc. IIIC/4, ff. 28ᵛ–29ʳ	D'Anglebert/Lully (1689)

David Chung

Bibliography

Broude 2017
Broude, Ronald. 'Paris *chez l'autheur*: Self-Publication and Authoritative Texts in the France of Louis xiv', in: *Early Music*, xlv/2 (2017), pp. 283-296.

Butt 2002
Butt, John. *Playing with History: The Historical Approach to Musical Performance*, Cambridge, Cambridge University Press, 2002 (Musical Performance and Reception).

Chung 2015
Keyboard Arrangements of Music by Jean-Baptiste Lully, edited by David Chung, 2 vols., Web Library of Seventeenth-Century Music, Monuments of Seventeenth-Century Music, vol. 1 (2015), <http://www.sscm-wlscm.org/monuments-of-seventeenth-century-music/volume-i>, accessed October 2018.

D'Anglebert 1689
D'Anglebert, Jean Henry. *Pieces de clavecin*, Paris, l'Auteur, 1689.

Gordon-Seifert 2011
Gordon-Seifert, Catherine. *Music and the Language of Love: Seventeenth-Century French Airs*, Bloomington-Indianapolis (IN), Indiana University Press, 2011.

Gustafson 1979
Gustafson, Bruce. *French Harpsichord Music of the 17th Century: A Thematic Catalog of the Sources with Commentary*, 3 vols., Ann Arbor (MI), UMI Research Press, 1979 (Studies in Musicology, 11).

Gustafson 1990
Gustafson, Bruce. 'The Legacy in Instrumental Music of Charles Babel, Prolific Transcriber of Lully's Music', in: *Jean-Baptiste Lully. Actes du colloque (Saint-Germain-en-Laye = Kongressbericht Heidelberg 1987)*, edited by Jérôme de La Gorce and Herbert Schneider, Laaber, Laaber-Verlag, 1990 (Neue Hidelberger Studien zur Musikwissenschaft, 18), pp. 495-516.

Gustafson 1995
Id. 'France', in: *Keyboard Music before 1700*, edited by Alexander Silbiger, New York, Schirmer Books, 1995 (Studies in Musical Genres and Repertoires), pp. 90-146.

Gustafson 2007
Id. *Chambonnières: A Thematic Catalogue: The Complete Works of Jacques Champion de Chambonnières (1601/02-1672)*, in: *Journal of Seventeenth-Century Music, JSCM Instrumenta*, vol. 1 (2007), <https://sscm-jscm.org/instrumenta/instrumenta-volumes/instrumenta-volume-1/>, accessed October 2018.

Gustafson 2018
Id. 'Four Decades after French Harpsichord Music of the Seventeenth Century: Newly Discovered Sources,' in: *Perspectives on Early Keyboard Music and Revival in the Twentieth Century*, edited by Rachelle Taylor and Hank Knox, London-New York, Routledge, 2018, pp. 7-45.

Gustafson – Fuller 1990
Id. – Fuller, David. *A Catalogue of French Harpsichord Music 1699-1780*, Oxford, Clarendon Press, 1990.

French Harpsichord *doubles* and the Creative Art of the 17th-Century *Clavecinistes*

Gustafson – Herlin 2017
Chambonnières, Jacques Champion de. *The Collected Works*, edited by Bruce Gustafson and Denis Herlin, 2 vols., New York, The Broude Trust, 2017 (Art of the Keyboard, 12).

Gustafson – Wolf 1999
Harpsichord Music Associated with the Name LA BARRE, edited by Bruce Gustafson and Peter Wolf, New York, The Broude Trust, 1999 (Art of the Keyboard, 4).

Harris 2009
D'Anglebert, Jean Henry. *The Collected Works*, edited by C. David Harris, 2 vols., New York, The Broude Trust, 2009 (Art of the Keyboard, 7/1-2).

Herlin 1991
Hardel, Jacques. *Pièces de clavecin*, edited by Denis Herlin, Monaco, Éditions de l'Oiseau-Lyre, 1991 (Grand Clavier, 5).

Le Gallois 1680
Le Gallois de Grimarest, Jean-Léonor. *Lettre de Mr Le Gallois à Mademoiselle Regnault de Solier touchant la musique*, Paris, Estienne Michallet, 1680.

Leech 2008
The Selosse Manuscript: Seventeenth-Century Jesuit Keyboard Music, edited by Peter Leech, Launton, Edition HH, 2008.

Ledbetter 1987
Ledbetter, David. *Harpsichord and Lute Music in 17th-Century France*, London, Palgrave Macmillan, 1987.

Martin 2009
Martin, Margot. 'The Rhetoric of *mouvement* and Passionate Expression in Seventeenth-Century French Harpsichord Music', in: *Seventeenth-Century French Studies*, xxxi/2 (2009), pp. 137-149.

Moroney 1985
Couperin, Louis. *Pièces de clavecin*, edited by Paul Brunold, new revision by Davitt Moroney, Monaco, Éditions de l'Oiseau-Lyre, 1985.

Moroney 2005
Moroney, Davitt. 'The Borel Manuscript: A New Source of Seventeenth-Century French Harpsichord Music at Berkeley', in: *Notes: Quarterly Journal of the Music Library Association*, lxii/1 (2005), pp. 18-47.

Wilson 2013
Wilson, Glen. 'The Other Mr. Couperin', in: *Early Keyboard Journal*, xxx/30 (2013), pp. 6-25.

Sounding Theory and Theoretical Notes
Bernardo Pasquini's Pedagogy at the Keyboard: A Case of Composition in Performance?

Massimiliano Guido
(Università di Pavia)

Chi avrà ottenuta la sorte di praticare o studiare sotto la scuola del famosissimo Signor Bernardo Pasquini in Roma, o chi almeno l'avrà potuto inteso o veduto sonare, avrà potuto conoscere la più vera, bella e nobile maniera di sonare e di accompagnare; e con questo modo cosí pieno avrà sentita dal suo cimbalo una perfezione di armonia meravigliosa[1].

Francesco Gasparini fully acknowledges his teacher, praising his virtue at the keyboard. Muffat, Berardi, and Pitoni echoed Gasparini's enthusiastic words, reporting about the international students sent to Pasquini by princes from around Europe to learn the true manner of playing. Muffat's parallel between Corelli as Orpheus and Pasquini as Apollo provides a vivid picture of this outstanding couple, actually making music together on many occasions[2].

Why was Pasquini so famous as a pedagogue? What was so unique about his teaching method? To cut to the case, he connected the keyboard technique with the art of composing in a coherent unity, providing the student with all the elements to extemporize music both in the old and modern style directly at the harpsichord. Two of the most excellent teachers and practitioners of historical improvisation, Edoardo Bellotti and William Porter, conclude

---

[1]. «Who has had the fortune of practicing or studying at the school of the very famous Signor Bernardo Pasquini in Rome, or has had at least the chance of hearing or seeing him playing, that one is exposed to the truest, fanciest, and noblest manner of playing and accompanying. Moreover, through this way [of playing] so full, he has heard from [Pasquini's] harpsichord an astonishing perfection of harmony». Gasparini 2001, p. 62.

[2]. Berardi's passage from *Il perché musicale* is quoted in Morelli 2016, pp. 93 and 332. Muffat studied in Rome with Pasquini during 1681-1682, when he received a paid leave from Salzburg: *ibidem*, p. 98. The comparison is taken from his preface to *Außerlesene mit Ernst- und lust-gemengter Instrumnetal-Music*, Passau, Höllerin, 1701. See Morelli 2016, p. 333.

their essay on the pedagogical perspectives of Pasquini claiming that «his example can be of great value because it stands as a synthesis between theory and praxis, composition and performance, conceived as connected and complementary moments in music making»[3].

In the closing discussion of the 2013 conference on counterpoint and improvisation that I had the privilege to organize, again Porter raised the argument if improvisation were the best word for describing what the old masters were teaching and playing in the Baroque[4]. Actually, his point was more on composition, knowing from direct experience how feeble the demarcation between the two words could be. Also, I guess — we are still debating this issue today. The more we deepen our theoretical and practical understanding, the more written-out and extemporized music-making seem to be an organic, leaving entity. On the one hand, written pieces, far from being fixed once and forever, can be interpreted as traces of an ongoing process of creation. On the other hand, innocent-looking bass lines, cadences, and mechanic patterns drafted on a page and subsequently memorized might develop into a fully-fledged piece[5]. Several scholars are convincingly demonstrating that, in many and complementary ways, these two forms are condensed vehicles for knowledge transferal. Furthermore, they are also the essence of *la più vera, bella e nobile maniera di suonare* (the truest, fanciest, and noblest manner of playing), because they constituted the fundamental skills of a mature professional[6].

Bellotti and Porter draw our attention to the possibility of looking at Pasquini's music (including both didactic works and fully-composed pieces) as a coherent repository of the art of playing. They noticed how the same basic formulas presented in *basso continuo* versets, sonate, and partimenti are inserted in many toccatas, variations, and dances. They also connected a self-evident line between the cadence and progression collections and similar formulas in Pasquini. Their assumptions are also restated and discussed in the very recent work by Arnaldo Morelli, who systematizes Pasquini's biography and the thorough discussion on the sources of his music with new historical evidence. In the chapter about keyboard music, Morelli quotes the 1716 correspondence between Forzoni Accolti and his friend Giovanni Giacomo Zamboni about the music of Domenico Anglesi, suggesting that what is discussed there can be fully applicable to Pasquini: «egli non componeva

---

[3]. BELLOTTI – PORTER 2012, p. 209. When not otherwise indicated, translations are by the author of this essay.

[4]. A condensed version is incorporated in the introduction to GUIDO 2017, pp. 1-4.

[5]. GUIDO – SCHUBERT 2014 demonstrates how a cadential pattern can generate a sophisticated piece of contrapuntal music such as a ricercare. Furthermore, it links the harmonic idea of a cadence to its linear implications, suggesting how the basso continuo practice in Italy was intimately connected to voice leading.

[6]. Improvisation has never been a *per se* event; it comes out of necessity (practical use within the liturgy or during a performance) and naturally stems from the keyboard during transferal of knowledge. A historically informed approach has to deal with this characteristic adapting it to a different context. Therefore, a particular emphasis is given in the specific literature to the learning process and the benefits of using improvisation in the present-day curriculum. See SCHUBERT – GUIDO 2016, pp. 133-134.

per far mostra del suo sapere, ma solo per la lezzione che di mano in mano conosceva opportuna all'abilità dello scolare» (he did not compose for showing off his knowledge, but for teaching that gradually knew was useful for the skill of the learner)[7]. One can immediately find an echo of Gasparini's words quoted at the opening of this chapter: the absorption of knowledge happens by looking at and listening to the master; writing out pieces or sketches is only a medium for knowledge transferal.

In Pasquini's music, there are some tiny miniatures, dedicated to noblemen, students or simple admirers. They are somewhat rudimentary and look more like drafts to be continued then the shining product of the spark of genius. Morelli stresses the importance of variation settings: Pasquini provides examples and, in some cases, literally exhorts the player to continue as long as he wants or can[8]. Morelli insists on the pieces *sopra il basso*, relating them to the growing tradition of partimento, while dismisses the *Saggi di contrappunto* as a homage to the respected but old school of strict composition. Developing Bellotti's and Porter's approach, I prefer to consider the counterpoint rules as an essential part within Pasquini's pedagogical approach. The figures disseminated within the *Saggi* as a sort of commentary to the counterpoint lines are an obvious link. Furthermore, I will point out some subtler connections.

Pasquini's commitment as a teacher can be evaluated by looking at his works, especially the *Saggi di Contrappunto* (1695), the *Sonate per uno o due cembali* (1703-1704), and the *Versetti con il solo basso cifrato* (1708)[9]. They constitute a homogenous collection in which the learner is exposed to the complexity of composing at the keyboard, from the *stile osservato* to the *stile modernissimo*, as Giuseppe Ottavio Pitoni writes in his *Guida Armonica*[10]. Pasquini deals with counterpoint practically. He does not write a counterpoint treatise, but a collection of examples, *saggi*. These are exercise sketched for the student, his nephew Felice Ricordati, during private lessons, while the master sits with him at the keyboard. As different research projects have recently demonstrated, such an approach is of extreme benefit in our educational system. After more than six decades of Early Music Movement, during which we rediscovered how to deal with historical instruments as to performance practice, technique, and organology, we are finally completing our knowledge with a more historically informed way of teaching and learning counterpoint and composition. Still, the majority of classically trained musicians see composition detached from the keyboard. As a consequence, the primary function of a written out teaching collection as the *Saggi* is obliterated and its value questioned and diminished.

---

[7]. MORELLI 2016, p. 333.
[8]. *Ibidem*, pp. 334-335.
[9]. *Saggi di Contrappunto and Regole*, in: PASQUINI 2009. *Sonate a due bassi e Versetti*, in: PASQUINI 2006A and PASQUINI 2006B. My thanks to Armando Carideo, who shared with me his musical transcriptions for setting out the examples in this chapter.
[10]. GUIDO 2009, pp. 156-157.

In Pasquini's teaching, music speaks without words[11]. In all the collection there are only a couple of annotations, explaining the avoidance of particular intervals in invertible counterpoint because they would turn into a dissonance. We do find another descriptive text, made of continuo figures, by which Pasquini indicates both the kind of chord and the voice leading. Armando Carideo, in his critical edition, suggests that these figures are Pasquini's guidelines for his nephew[12]. The learner had to follow them and realize a three, four, or five part counterpoint that had to be checked and discussed with the master at the keyboard. Rules were eventually presented aurally, and there was no need for fixing them on paper: the music was clear enough to internalize them. The act of notating voices in a score and not as keyboard tablature is also an exercise of contrapuntal clarity. On the other side, Morelli does not believe that the *Saggi* can be the basis of composing at the keyboard, because he says that they are structured according Fux's species, and he would rather focus on the recurrent harmonic tonal schemes found in the *basso continuo* pieces[13]. More than Fux, Pasquini follows Diruta's *Breve et facile regola*, sketching the usual path from note against note to florid counterpoint. It is also true that we find advanced duos in the style of *bicinia*, modally ordered. However, the quality of the given cantus firmus is evolving throughout the collection[14].

Pasquini gives only two examples of note-against-note counterpoint. The first CF is the most awkward possible, a single note plus a cadence given by a descending fourth (Ex. 1a). This is clearly just about consonances: the student has the chance of learning and memorizing all the possibilities. The only other note-against-note example comes after a few pages, dealing with perfect and imperfect consonances, chains of thirds and sixths, and contrary motion[15]. So far, nothing exciting or particularly exotic. It is like learning to write by following the marks carved on a wax tablet: your hand learns the movement and gains confidence. By now I have memorized the CF: it is so simple that I can venture in transposition without even knowing what transposition is. The only thing I need is a new starting note. I am then so confident that I can immediately play two consonances on each note of the CF and introduce passing notes: dissonances (Ex. 1b).

So now here comes the little magic. I can play a third voice, repeating what I have just played, as long as I pair the two voices using thirds: I need to check if there is a 'hole' in my hand: 1-3 or 2-4. To make it more interesting, I can use faster note values and cross the voices (Ex. 1c). If I realize that I am coming to a unison — the distance between the parts

---

[11]. See Bellotti's remarks on 'Counterpoint, the *Seconda Prattica* and the Practice of Basso continuo', in: PASQUINI 2006A, p. vi.

[12]. PASQUINI 2009, pp. v-vi.

[13]. MORELLI 2016, p. 340.

[14]. On Diruta and his integrated approach to fingering, composition, and improvisation see GUIDO 2012A.

[15]. Counterpoint XI (PASQUINI 2009, p. 6).

Ex. 1a-b: counterpoints I-III.

is narrowing (3-2-1) — I can jump an octave higher and go on. In this way, the student, at the fourth exercise in his notebook, is playing a three-voice florid counterpoint with some canonic entries: this was done more intuitively than we are used to and constitutes one of the reasons for saying that Pasquini was a good teacher.

The second CF is treated precisely in the same way: in the two voice settings, Pasquini introduces some new contrapuntal devices, such as suspension or fourth species. In so doing, he provides the student with different patterns, which can be easily memorized by repetition at the keyboard. Though patterns are explicitly used in the exercises, they are never repeated mechanically[16]. The player is, therefore, guided to develop his musical

---

[16]. See for instance Counterpoint XIII and XIV (*ibidem*, p. 6).

invention achieving *variety*. The two *bicinia* on the ascending and descending scales, with a florid realization at the bass, are an excellent example: each bar could be repeated and work under all the CF notes[17]. Ex. 2 shows the second version, Counterpoint XVIII: Pasquini mixes up the modules in coherent musical structures, usually in groups of two or three bars. Even at the early stage of a strict counterpoint exercise, we find the other fundamental principle in Pasquini's didactical approach: the variation idea. The very same concept praised by Morelli in the written out pieces.

Ex. 2: counterpoint XVIII.

[17]. This learning process is a mechanical and mental rumination of patterns through finger motions. The basic idea is the step motion of the CF that is easily fillable with diminutions underneath. Once the learner possesses this skill, the sequent exercise has leaps in the CF that imply a more accurate selection of the notes in the second voice, to avoid jumping from a dissonance.

Sounding Theory and Theoretical Notes

Pasquini comments upon some of the basses, providing figures. The exciting aspect is that the written out realization is always a polyphonic rendition, with great care about voice leading. Only one *Saggio* in the whole book, Counterpoint LII, has the annotation *io Bernardo*, suggesting that the master realizes the entire setting. It comes just after a three-voice version with fewer figures. Comparing the two exercises, it is evident that the first exercise has almost the identical implied figures (Ex. 3a-b). Pasquini shows how to add a fourth voice developing the same contrapuntal material used by his nephew at the alto part in *Saggio* LI. He also retains the melodic contour of the soprano — almost identical to bar 5 onwards — without changing the melodic range (highest note *g*). The tenor is the new part, to which some of the figures (*aka* contrapuntal movements) are transferred from the preexisting soprano line: the 4-3♯ used by his nephew at the second measure of the soprano in LI is used as the opening movement of the tenor and will be repeated in bar 4 in the soprano, creating an interesting polyphonic texture.

Ex. 3a-b: counterpoints LI-LII.

Io Bernardo

Figures are used in these exercises as shortcuts for memorizing several linear possibilities above the same basic idea given by the CF movement, following the Italian tradition from Diruta to Banchieri. The contrapuntal quality of the figures is even more evident in more extended exercises where the long-note CF is abandoned for a modern bass line. Once these conducts have been absorbed in this simplified (and regulated) environment, the basic movements can be extended to their real musical appearance, becoming bass lines shaped according to the modern style. The same CF is transformed and its figures almost identically repeated in the 5 voice setting of *Saggio* CVIII.

Ex. 4: counterpoints CVIII.

Before going on with the *Saggi*, I would like to present some other examples of the use of *basso continuo* as a pedagogical tool. In the other main autograph British Library Ms. Add. 31501, there are several collections of *versetti in basso continuo*[18]. They are the first examples of the famous school of Partimento, which would have developed in the Neapolitan conservatories about one generation after Pasquini[19]. This school combines the art of counterpoint with the ability to play diminutions and variations on a given music

---

[18]. PASQUINI 2006A and 2006B.
[19]. On Pasquini and partimento see GJERDINGEN 2012, SANGUINETTI 2012, pp. 58-50, and MORELLI 2016, pp. 335-38.

material, grounded on a set of implicit harmonic-melodic conventions, or schemata. The simplest verses are nothing but an embellished cadence, ornamented in different ways. This connects the collection on the one hand to similar works from Fattorini up to Spiridion, on the other to the same cadential patterns found in the *Saggi di contrappunto* and the written-out pieces. In their study about Pasquini's pedagogy, Bellotti and Porter identify five different categories of versetti:

    a) versetto-cadenza with or without passages in the bass;
    b) versetto with imitazioni;
    c) versetto-sequence;
    d) versetto-fugato;
    e) versetto-adagio[20].

Especially the cadential and sequential types are built on repeated patterns that had to be memorized by the student. Ex. 5 shows the first 6 versets in D, all derived from the basic cadential idea of number 1.

Ex. 5: versets in D *for answering to the choir* (1-6).

If we take Pasquini's opening rubric seriously, these versetti are not only a didactic collection *per se*, but they serve a liturgical function: respond to the choir. Since 1605, the bass as a *true and specific way* for improvising verses had been introduced in Banchieri's

---

[20]. Bellotti – Porter 2012.

Organo suonarino[21]. It insisted on the contrapuntal tradition found in both counterpoint tutors such as Diruta's *Il Transilvano* and entirely composed collections like the *Musica Nova* of 1540. Responding to the choir is a set or two of entries in imitation plus a cadence on the right ecclesiastic tone. It is no surprises that a careful examination of the figures, especially in the imitative verses, suggests a contrapuntal realization. If it is so, Pasquini uses figures in a quite similar way then he does in the *Saggi*, especially the more advanced, as shown in Ex. 6.

Ex. 6: versets in G *for answering to the choir* (5-6).

Another promising comparison is between the verses and some fully written-out pieces, especially toccatas and variations settings. Again, Pasquini seems to apply the same principles of polyphonic schemes and cadences, adding the roundness of ornamental figurations to enrich the basic idea[22]. As it is written in the Noto's partimento collection: *apre gli occhi*[23]!

I would like to come back to the 'sounding theory' in the title of this article. Thomas Christensen, in his lecture 'Fragile Texts, Hidden Theory,' given at the 2012 meeting of the Society for Music Theory, talked about a discursive theory, bound to notions of authorial agency and textual representation. He then developed the idea in his chapter

---

[21]. GUIDO 2013.
[22]. GUIDO 2012B examines the variety of compositional schemes used in Pasquini's toccatas.
[23]. I-NT, *Fondo Altieri* 28, c. 89ᵛ, quoted in MORELLI 2016, p. 330.

'The Improvisatory Moment' in *Studies on Historical Improvisation*[24]. He claims that, in the history of music theory, there are many examples in which theoretical knowledge is disseminated through 'fragile texts', from which the discursive part is almost eliminated. He concludes that it is possible to have music theory even without texts, a sort of 'hidden theory', transmitted within a pedagogical system centered on the direct making of music. Pasquini provides an outstanding example of this hidden praxis if we stop to question if we are dealing with improvisation within composition: theory is sounding, and notes are assuming a theoretical value.

Credo che la Fama abbia spezzate le trombe,
non avendo più voce per pubblicare i suoi applausi,
et io sospenderò la penna,
per non aver concetti adeguati per tesserae le sue lodi.
Ottavio Pitoni, *Guida Armonica*[25]

Bibliography

Bellotti – Porter 2012
Bellotti, Edoardo – Porter, William. 'Pasquini e l'improvvisazione: un approccio pedagogico', in: *Pasquini Symposium. Convegno Internazionale (Smarano, 27-30 Maggio 2010). Atti*, edited by Armando Carideo, Trento, Giunta della Provincia autonoma di Trento-Assessorato alla cultura, rapporti europei e cooperazione, 2012 (Quaderni Trentino Cultura – Cultura per il territorio, 17), pp. 195-210.

Christensen 2017
Christensen, Thomas. 'The Improvisatory Moment', in: *Studies in Historical Improvisation: From 'Cantare super Librum' to Partimenti*, edited by Massimiliano Guido, Abington-New York, Routledge, 2017, pp. 9-24.

Gasparini 2001
Gasparini, Francesco. *L'Armonico pratico al cimbalo*, (1708), Bologna, Arnaldo Forni Editore, 2001 (Bibliotheca Musica Bononiensis, IV/90).

Gjerdingen 2012
Gjerdingen, Robert. 'A Source of Pasqini Partimenti in Naples', in: *Pasquini Symposium* [...], *op. cit.*, pp. 177-194.

Guido 2009
Guido, Massimiliano. 'Lo stile come manifestazione degli affetti', in: *Storia dei concetti musicali. 3: Melodia, stile, suono*, edited by Gianmario Borio and Mario Gentili, Rome, Carocci Editore, 2009, pp. 145-159.

---

[24]. Christensen 2017, pp. 9-25.
[25]. «I believe that as Fame broke her trumpets, not having any more voice to praise his virtues, I shall, in the same way, drop the pen, not having adequate concepts for his eulogy».

Guido 2012a
Id. 'Counterpoint in the Fingers. A Practical Approach to Girolamo Diruta's *Breve & Facile Regola di Contrappunto*', in: *PhilomusicaOnline*, xi/1 (2012), pp. 63-76.

Guido 2012b
Id. '*Affetti cantabili* from Frescobaldi to Pasquini', in: *Pasquini Symposium* […], *op. cit.*, pp. 154-176.

Guido 2013
Id. '«Con questa sicura strada»: Girolamo Diruta's and Andriano Banchieri's Instructions on How to Improvise Versets', in: *The Organ Yearbook*, no. 42 (2013), pp. 40-52.

Guido – Schubert 2014
Guido, Massimiliano – Schubert, Peter. 'Unpacking the Box in Frescobaldi's Ricercari of 1615', in: *Music Theory Online: A Journal of the Society for Music Theory*, xx/2 (2014), <http://www.mtosmt.org/issues/mto.14.20.2/mto.14.20.2.guido_schubert.pdf>, accessed November 2018.

Morelli 2016
Morelli, Arnaldo. *La virtù in corte. Bernardo Pasquini (1637-1710)*, Lucca, LIM, 2016 (ConNotazioni, 12).

Pasquini 2006a
Pasquini, Bernardo. *Opere per tastiera. 6: London, Bl Ms. Add. 31501. I*, edited by Edoardo Bellotti, Latina, Il Levante Libreria Editrice, 2006 (Tastata. Opere d'intavolatura d'organo e cimbalo, 18).

Pasquini 2006b
Id. *Opere per tastiera. 7: London, Bl Ms. Add. 31501, II-III*, edited by Armando Carideo, Latina, Il Levante Libreria Editrice, 2006 (Tastata. Opere d'intavolatura d'organo e cimbalo, TA 19).

Pasquini 2009
Id. *Opere per tastiera. 8: Saggi di contrappunto (S.B.P.K. Landsberg 214); Regole… per ben accompagnare con il cembalo (Bc, MS. D 138/2)*, edited by Armando Carideo, Latina, Il Levante Libreria Editrice, 2009 (Tastata. Opere d'Intavolatura d'organo e cimbalo, 24).

Sanguinetti 2012
Sanguinetti, Giorgio. *The Art of Partimento: History, Theory, and Practice*, Oxford-New York, Oxford University Press, 2012.

Schubert – Guido 2016
Schubert, Peter – Guido, Massimiliano. 'Back into the Classroom. Learning Music Through Historical Improvisation', in: *Improvisation and Music Education: Beyond the Classroom*, edited by Ajay Heble and Mark Laver, Abington-New York, Routledge, 2016, pp. 130-139.

Las anotaciones de Pisendel en el Concierto para dos violines RV 507 de Vivaldi: una ventana abierta a la improvisación en la obra del 'Cura rojo'

Javier Lupiáñez – Fabrizio Ammetto
(Universidad de Guanajuato, México)

La famosa colección 'Schrank II' de la Biblioteca de la Universidad de Dresde (Sächsische Landesbibliothek – Staats- und Universitätsbibliothek Dresden) contiene unos dos mil manuscritos de música instrumental[1]. El extenso material, en el que encontramos tanto partes como partituras completas, estaba destinado a ser interpretado en la Hopfkapelle de Dresde durante la primera mitad del siglo XVIII y fue reunido en su mayor parte por el violinista y compositor Johann Georg Pisendel (1687-1755).

Pisendel entró a formar parte de la orquesta de la corte de Dresde en 1712[2], y tomó el papel de concertino en 1728, aunque no fue oficialmente reconocido como tal hasta 1730[3]. Pisendel permaneció en Dresde hasta su muerte. Los manuscritos del 'Schrank II' contienen el trabajo de recopilación y copia de Pisendel, incluyendo algunos de su colección personal compilados incluso antes de 1712 y que trajo consigo cuando ocupó su puesto en la corte[4].

La estrecha relación de Pisendel con estas partituras se hace más patente al descubrir una gran cantidad de anotaciones realizadas por él mismo sobre las mismas. Entre las anotaciones referentes a las dinámicas, o las guías de lo que hacen otros instrumentos para facilitar la labor de concertino, encontramos un tipo peculiar de anotación destinada a cambiar el discurso musical: son anotaciones destinadas a servir como ornamentación o como guía para la improvisación. Las encontramos en ciento sesenta y dos piezas. Algunas

---

[1]. Ver <https://hofmusik.slub-dresden.de/themen/schrank-zwei/>, visitado en Octubre 2018.
[2]. Köpp 2005, p. 79.
[3]. *Ibidem*, p. 236.
[4]. Entre estos manuscritos anteriores a 1712 cabe destacar la copia de la Trio Sonata RV 820 de Vivaldi (D-Dl, Mus. 2-Q-6), copiada por Pisendel durante su estancia en Ansbach, entre 1697 y 1709.

de estas anotaciones han sido comentadas y analizadas en otros estudios[5] (a partir del principio del siglo XX, con el de Arnold Schering en 1909[6]).

Este tipo de anotaciones se presentan de diversas formas, ocupando diferentes posiciones en la partitura y sirviendo para diversos propósitos. Desde simples guías para la improvisación a elaborados pasajes o, como en el caso del Concierto para violín RV 340 de Vivaldi, modificaciones sustanciales del texto musical[7]. Además es posible encontrarse en piezas de diferente naturaleza: conciertos para violín y orquesta, sonatas para violín y continuo o trio sonatas.

Podemos encontrar estas anotaciones en los más variados contextos: movimientos rápidos, lentos, como parte de cadencias en fermatas, como es el caso del siguiente ejemplo tomado del segundo movimiento de la Sinfonía para cuerdas RV 192.

Il. 1. A. Vivaldi, Sinfonía para cuerdas RV 192, II mov., Mus.2389-N-7a.

Contextualización.
Los ornamentos de Pisendel, Vivaldi y el Concierto RV 507

Parece claro que la obra de Vivaldi ocupa un papel especial y predominante en la colección de Pisendel en Dresde[8]. De entre este corpus de manuscritos que incluyen algún tipo de anotación se posiciona en un lugar especial la obra de Antonio Vivaldi. En primer lugar por la gran cantidad de manuscritos autógrafos o en copia que incluyen anotaciones, un total de treinta y seis (más que ningún otro compositor[9]).

---

[5]. Algunas de las anotaciones de Pisendel sobre el Concierto para violín RV 340 fueron enumeradas en Landmann 1981, p. 137. Algunas otras se discuten en Heller 1976, pp. 82-83. Otro trabajo donde se analizan algunas de estas anotaciones es Fechner 1980. Algunas de las disminuciones son transcritas y atribuidas a Pisendel en Landshoff 1935, 'Preface'. El trabajo más reciente lo encontramos en Lockey 2010.

[6]. Schering 1905-1906. Schering realiza además una interesante transcripción de las disminuciones.

[7]. Lockey 2010, p. 132.

[8]. Heller 2010, p. 145.

[9]. El número de manuscritos con anotaciones es el siguiente: 36 (Vivaldi); 24 (Graun); 19 (Pisendel); 16 (Fasch); 5 (Telemann); 3 (Haendel, Quantz y Geminiani); 2 (Benda, Schreyfogel y Tartini); 1 (Tartini,

Las anotaciones de Pisendel en el Concierto para dos violines RV 507 de Vivaldi

Otra de las razones que añaden interés a estas anotaciones sobre la obra de Vivaldi es que algunas de ellas fueron realizadas directamente sobre autógrafos vivaldianos, como es el caso de los conciertos para violín RV 172[10], RV 205[11], RV 237[12] y RV 340[13], o el interesante caso de la Sonata para violín y continuo RV 25[14] donde aparece un movimiento completo escrito por Pisendel insertado en una sonata autógrafa de Vivaldi.

Encontramos anotaciones de Pisendel en los siguientes manuscritos vivaldianos de Dresde (D-Dl):

- Mus. 2-O-1,1, Concierto para violín en Sol mayor, RV 326;
- Mus. 2364-O-7, Concierto para violín en Mi menor, RV 366;
- Mus. 2389-N-7a, Sinfonía en Do mayor, RV 192;
- Mus. 2389-O-42, Concierto para violín en Do mayor, RV 172;
- Mus. 2389-O-43, Concierto para violín en La mayor, RV 340;
- Mus. 2389-O-46, Concierto para violín en Re menor, RV 237;
- Mus. 2389-O-47, Concierto para violín, dos oboes, dos cornos y fagot en Fa mayor, RV 568;
- Mus. 2389-O-47a, Concierto para violín en Fa mayor compilado por Pisendel, tomando los movimientos extremos del RV 568 y el movimiento lento central del RV 202;
- Mus. 2389-O-48a, Concierto para violín en Fa Mayor, RV 571;
- Mus. 2389-O-49, Concierto para dos violines en Do mayor, RV 508;
- Mus. 2389-O-54, Concierto para dos violines en La mayor, RV 521;
- Mus. 2389-O-58, Concierto para violín en Re mayor RV 228;
- Mus. 2389-O-58b, Concierto para violín en Re mayor, RV 228;
- Mus. 2389-O-61, Concierto para violín en Re mayor, RV 213;
- Mus. 2389-O-61a, Concierto para violín en Re mayor, RV 213;
- Mus. 2389-O-67, Concierto para violín y dos orquestas en Re mayor, RV 582;
- Mus. 2389-O-74, Conciertos para violín en Re mayor, RV 205 y RV 212;
- Mus. 2389-O-92, Concierto para violín en Sol mayor, RV 298;
- Mus. 2389-O-93, Concierto para violín en Fa mayor, RV 569;
- Mus. 2389-O-93a, Concierto para violín en Fa mayor, RV 569;
- Mus. 2389-O-95, Concierto para violín en Sol mayor, RV 302;
- Mus. 2389-O-98, Concierto para dos violines en Do mayor, RV 507;
- Mus. 2389-O-105, Concierto para violín en Sol menor, RV 329;
- Mus. 2389-O-111, Concierto para violín en Mi bemol mayor, RV 259;
- Mus. 2389-O-112, Concierto para violín en La mayor, RV 343;
- Mus. 2389-O-122, Concierto para violín en Do menor, RV 202;
- Mus. 2389-O-123, Concierto para violín en Re mayor, RV 205;
- Mus. 2389-O-154, Concierto para violín en Si bemol mayor, RV 373;
- Mus. 2389-O-157, Concierto para violín en Fa mayor, RV 574;

Cattaneo, Albicastro, Somis, Torelli, entre otros).

[10]. D-Dl, Mus. 2389-O-42.
[11]. D-Dl, Mus. 2389-O-123 y D-Dl, Mus. 2389-O-74.
[12]. D-Dl, Mus. 2389-O-46.
[13]. D-Dl, Mus. 2389-O-43.
[14]. D-Dl, Mus. 2389-R-10,3.

- Mus. 2389-R-6,1, Sonata para violín en Sol menor, RV 28;
- Mus. 2456-R-21, Sonata para violín en Sol mayor, RV Anh. 98 (RV 776)[15];
- Mus. 2822-O-5, Concierto para violín en Sol mayor, RV 299/2[16];
- Mus. 4155-O-1, Concierto para violín en Re mayor, RV 213.

La estrecha relación establecida desde 1717[17] entre Pisendel y Vivaldi toma forma en estos manuscritos. Como alumno directo de Vivaldi, sus anotaciones y ornamentaciones sobre la obra vivaldiana conforman una importante referencia como fuente para la ornamentación sobre el repertorio vivaldiano.

Como ya señaló Kolneder[18] la cercanía de Pisendel con Vivaldi hace muy posible que las diminuciones de Pisendel estén muy cerca de la práctica del propio Vivaldi. Kolneder presenta incluso la posibilidad de que algunas de estas disminuciones fuesen escritas o elaboradas por el propio Vivaldi para el uso de sus estudiantes[19].

Sobre las fuentes de ornamentación de la época

Es posible analizar fuentes de las primeras décadas del siglo XVIII que muestran cómo se improvisaba en este período y que nos servirán como comparación para las anotaciones de Pisendel.

Podemos catalogar estas fuentes en dos grupos diferentes: (a) fuentes impresas y (b) fuentes de uso particular (las anotaciones de Pisendel pertenecen a este segundo grupo).

Esta catalogación nos permite comparar las anotaciones de Pisendel con otras anotaciones similares de la época y contraponerlas con las fuentes impresas, destinadas al uso pedagógico y enfocadas a un público más general. Notamos así importantes divergencias entre las fuentes destinadas a un uso privado y las de dominio público. Estas diferencias, presentes en las disminuciones de Pisendel sobre la obra de Vivaldi son de extrema importancia para entender las diferencias entre la praxis interpretativa real de alto nivel y la interpretación llevada a cabo por el público general que consumía los métodos y ediciones del momento.

---

[15]. El manuscrito contiene una sonata *pasticcio* en la que el primer movimiento se corresponde con el tercer movimiento de la sonata RV 22.

[16]. El manuscrito contiene el segundo movimiento del concierto RV 299 de Vivaldi insertado entre dos movimientos de Visconti.

[17]. Heller 1997, p. 230.

[18]. Kolneder 1979, p. 41.

[19]. «[…] the Adagio of a violin concerto (Hs Dresden Cx 1091) [Concierto para violín y orquesta en Do menor, RV 202, Mus.2389-O-122] with diminutions by Pisendel is very close to the master's usage, if not indeed elaborated by himself for a pupil's usage». Kolneder 1979, p. 41.

Las anotaciones de Pisendel en el Concierto para dos violines RV 507 de Vivaldi

Algo que llama la atención es la mayor variedad en función y tipología de las ornamentaciones en manuscritos destinados a un uso personal frente a las fuentes impresas. Al igual que ocurre con los manuscritos de Pisendel en Dresde, las ornamentaciones destinadas a uso personal afectan tanto a movimientos rápidos como lentos e incluyen no sólo ornamentos sino que incluso añaden variaciones y cadencias. Sin embargo, el rango de uso de la ornamentación en los ejemplos impresos es mucho más restringido y se ciñe exclusivamente a la ornamentación de movimientos lentos y ninguno incluye variaciones o pasajes con dobles cuerdas.

Acotaremos las fuentes que a continuación se enumeran a un período temporal cercano a la elaboración de las anotaciones de Pisendel en el concierto que nos ocupa.

(a) Fuentes impresas para la ornamentación:
- Johann Christoph Pez / anónimo, ornamentos sobre el Op. 5 de Corelli[20] (1707);
- Arcangelo Corelli (?), ornamentos sobre el Op. 5[21] (1710);
- William Babell, set de sonatas[22] con ornamentos en los movimientos lentos (ca. 1725);
- Georg Philipp Telemann, *Sonate metodiche* (Hamburgo, 1728);
- G.Ph. Telemann, *Trietti methodici e Scherzi*[23] (Hamburgo, 1731);
- G.Ph. Telemann, *Sonate metodiche* (II) (Hamburgo, 1732).

Il. 2. W. Babell, Sonata I, *incipit*.

---

[20]. *A Second collection of SONATAS for two FLUTES and a BASS, by Signr Christopher Pez* […]; RISM P1689.

[21]. *SONATE a Violino e Violone o Cimbalo DI ARCANGELO CORELLI Da Fusignano OPERA QUINTA. Troisieme Edition ou l'on a joint les agree-mens [sic] des Adagio de cet ouvrage, composez [sic] par Mr. A. Corelli comme il les joue* […]; RISM C3812.

[22]. *XII Solos for a Violin or Hautboy with a Bass, figur'd for the Harpsicord. With proper Graces adapted to each Adagio* […]; RISM A/I: B 7

[23]. Esta obra es de especial interés por dos razones: es una de las pocas fuentes que incluyen ornamentos en dos partes al mismo tiempo y porque existe una copia manuscrita en Dresde (Mus. 2392-Q-4).

Encontramos otras fuentes muy útiles en textos de la época que nos hablan sobre la ornamentación: Scheibe[24], Tosi[25], Couperin[26], Monteclair[27], Geminiani[28], o en textos algo más tardíos como Quantz[29], L. Mozart[30] o C. Ph. E. Bach[31].

(b) Manuscritos destinados a un uso personal:
- 'Colección de Pisendel'. El archivo personal de Pisendel es quizá una de las fuentes más importantes de manuscritos con disminuciones escritas. Los ornamentos se encuentran tanto en movimientos rápidos como lentos, con uso de dobles cuerdas y con una gran variedad funcional (ornamentos, cadencias, variaciones, etc.)[32];
- 'Anónimo-Walsh'. Ornamentos sobre el Op. 5 de Corelli[33]. Ornamentos sobre movimientos lentos y rápidos (ca. 1711);
- 'BL 17,853'. Disminuciones sobre el Op. 5 de Corelli[34] (ca. 1720);
- 'Dubourg'. Disminuciones sobre el Op. 5 de Corelli[35]. Ornamentos en movimientos rápidos y lentos, incluye además variaciones y dobles cuerdas (ca. 1721);
- 'Anónimo para órgano'[36]. Ornamentos sobre la Sonata Op. 5 n. 6 de Corelli[37] (ca. 1725);
- 'Vivaldi (?)'. Ornamentos sobre el *Adagio* del Concierto para violín, RV 581[38] (ca. 1726);
- 'Festing'. Disminuciones sobre el Op. 5 de Corelli[39]. Ornamentos en movimientos rápidos y lentos, incluye además variaciones y dobles cuerdas (ca. 1736);

---

[24]. Carta anónima en 'Der Critische Musicus' (1737-1740) con interesantes comentarios sobre la ornamentación e improvisación llevada a cabo en orquestas (citado en SPITZER – ZASLAW 1986).

[25]. *Opinioni de' cantori antichi e moderni* (1723).

[26]. *L'Art de toucher le Clavecin* (1716).

[27]. *Principes de musique* (1736).

[28]. *Rules for Playing in a True Taste* (1748).

[29]. *Versuch einer Anweisung die Flöte traversiere zu spielen* (1752).

[30]. *Versuch einer gründlichen Violinschule* (1756).

[31]. *Versuch über die wahre Art das Clavier zu spielen* (1753, 1762).

[32]. El estudio de estos manuscritos está siendo desarrollado en estos momentos como tema de la tesis doctoral de Javier Lupiáñez (*Las anotaciones de Johann Georg Pisendel (1687-1755) en los manuscritos vivaldianos de Dresde*, Doctorado en Artes, División de Arquitectura, Arte y Diseño, Campus Guanajuato, Universidad de Guanajuato), bajo la dirección de Fabrizio Ammetto.

[33]. Manuscrito anónimo insertado en una re-edición de Walsh & Hare (ca. 1711); RISM C3816. Anteriormente propiedad de David Boyden, actualmente en la Biblioteca Musical de la Universidad de California, Berkeley (sin signatura).

[34]. GB-Lbl, Add. Ms. 17,853.

[35]. *Dubourg Corelli's Solos Grac'd by Doburg* [sic].

[36]. Identificado por Javier Lupiáñez en junio de 2015.

[37]. Gerard Cook Coll. 2/D/MISCELLANY, pp. 35-46.

[38]. I-Vc, Busta 55.1 (*Anna Maria Partbook*).

[39]. GB-Lbl, Add. Ms. 71,244, f. 30.

Las anotaciones de Pisendel en el Concierto para dos violines RV 507 de Vivaldi

- 'Roman'. Ornamentos sobre el Op. 5 de Corelli[40] (ca. 1715). Ornamentos en movimientos rápidos y lentos, incluye además variaciones y dobles cuerdas;
- 'Geminiani'. Una fuente algo más tardía con ornamentos sobre el Op. 5 de Corelli[41], interesante porque incluye ornamentos en movimientos rápidos, variaciones y múltiples dobles cuerdas.

Il. 3: Michael Festing, disminuciones sobre la Sonata Op. 5 n. 5 de Corelli.

El Concierto para dos violines y orquesta en Do Mayor, RV 507

De entre todos los manuscritos que contienen anotaciones es el Concierto para dos violines en Do mayor el único que incluye anotaciones tanto para el primer solista como para el segundo solista.

Del RV 507 se conservan tres fuentes manuscritas, un autógrafo[42] y dos copias en Dresde: (a) el manuscrito D-Dl, Mus. 2389-O-98, copiado enteramente por Pisendel, en formato de partitura general y que contiene anotaciones y (b) el manuscrito D-Dl, Mus. 2389-O-98a, formado por un juego de partes mayormente copiado por Giovanni Battista Vivaldi, con partes copiadas además por Grundig y Pisendel (que añade dos oboes a la orquestación original)[43].

El concierto fue compuesto alrededor de 1716[44], coincidiendo con el viaje de Pisendel a Italia y su encuentro con Vivaldi en 1716-1717. Es justo esta fecha (1717) la datación de

---

[40]. S-Sk, Roman Collection, Mss. 61, 97.
[41]. El manuscrito de la Sonata Op. 5 n. 9 de Corelli elaborado por un alumno de Geminiani está perdido, pero fue posteriormente publicado en HAWKINS 1776.
[42]. I-Tn, Giordano 35, ff. 269-278.
[43]. Para una descripción detallada de las fuentes, ver AMMETTO 2013, pp. 67-87: 68-69 y 79.
[44]. Ibidem, p. 226.

la copia contenida en el D-Dl, Mus. 2389-O-98a[45], así como una muy posible fecha para la copia que nos ocupa y que contiene las anotaciones, el manuscrito D-Dl, Mus. 2389-O-98, es entre 1716 y 1725[46].

Análisis general de las anotaciones del RV 507

Algo que llama la atención desde el principio es que el Concierto para dos violines en Do mayor, RV 507 incluye anotaciones tanto para el primer violín como para el segundo violín solista[47]. Es posible observar dos tipos de tinta diferentes para cada una de las anotaciones, siendo la utilizada para el violín segundo de un característico color más rojizo[48]:

c. 50, Violín I   c. 74, Violín II

Las anotaciones se encuentran generalmente escritas en pentagramas adyacentes o en los lugares de la misma página donde se tuviese espacio libre, usando en muchas ocasiones los pentagramas que quedaban libres entre los sistemas o al final de la página.

Encontramos que, tanto para el violín primero como para el violín segundo, se dan en varias ocasiones diversas versiones de un mismo pasaje. En algunas ocasiones queda por determinar si se tratan de diferentes ideas con la misma validez, o una evolución, o un cambio de ideas sobre la ornamentación.

---

[45]. RISM ID no.: 212000209.

[46]. RISM ID no.: 212000208.

[47]. El hecho de encontrar anotaciones en ambas partes es bastante infrecuente, de hecho existen en el 'Schrank II' otros ejemplos de música escrita para dos solistas y que contienen ornamentaciones y anotaciones, aunque en esos casos las anotaciones se restringen al primer violín. Así encontramos en el 'Schrank II' ejemplos de importantes ornamentaciones en las siguientes obras para dos violines: Johann Friedrich Fasch, Trio Sonata para dos violines en Sol mayor, FaWV N:G4 (Mus. 2423-Q-2); Johann Gottlieb Graun, Trio Sonata para dos violines en Re mayor, GraunWV A:XV:6 (Mus. 2474-Q-9); Georg Friedrich Händel, Trio sonata para dos violines y continuo en Si bemol mayor, HWV 339 (Mus. 2410-N-5a); G.F. Händel, Trio sonata para dos violines y continuo en Fa mayor, HWV 361 (Mus. 2410-Q-20); Georg Philipp Telemann, Trio sonata para dos violines y continuo en La mayor, TWV 42:A 8 (Mus. 2392-Q-11) y Georg Philipp Telemann, Trio sonata para dos violines y continuo en Re mayor, TWV 42:D 1 (Mus. 2392-Q-6).

[48]. Sin embargo este hecho no nos permite afirmar que las anotaciones del segundo violín fueran hechas por una mano distinta a la de Pisendel, aunque sería una posibilidad bastante plausibile.

Las anotaciones de Pisendel en el Concierto para dos violines RV 507 de Vivaldi

Ornamentos en los movimientos rápidos (I y III)

Es interesante destacar la gran cantidad de ornamentos localizados en ambos movimientos rápidos del concierto. Si bien los métodos de ornamentación de la época se centran más en la ornamentación de los movimientos lentos, encontramos algunas referencias a la ornamentación de movimientos rápidos. Quantz, aunque se trate de una fuente más tardía, nos explica por qué: «Von willkürlichen Veränderungen leidet das Allegro nicht viel; weil es mehrenteils mit einem solchen Gesange und solchen Passagien gesetzet wird, worinne nicht viel zu verbessern ist»[49].

Podemos encontrar los ornamentos en los movimientos rápidos en las siguientes situaciones: (a) secuencias, (b) enlaces o (c) como forma de crear contraste con el otro solista.

(a) Secuencias

En secuencias formadas por patrones regulares Pisendel usa la ornamentación de dos formas distintas:

– creando un patrón diferente aunque regular (en este caso se trata de variantes para el patrón dado en la secuencia original). Pisendel escribe normalmente un solo compás con el nuevo que debería seguir como modelo para los compases siguientes[50];

Ej. 1: A. Vivaldi, Concierto RV 507, I mov., cc. 80-83.

– rompiendo una secuencia que usaba un patrón regular. En otros casos, para añadir más variedad a un pasaje articulado de forma regular, Pisendel transforma el pasaje

---

[49]. *Versuch einer Anweisung die Flöte traversiere zu spielen*, Capítulo XII, § 27.
[50]. El mismo procedimiento es descrito por Lockey en el las anotaciones de Pisendel sobre el concierto RV 340 (ver Lockey 2010, p. 132).

articulando la secuencia de forma desigual. En el siguiente pasaje Pisendel comienza con un movimiento melódico que desemboca en un nuevo patrón a mitad de la secuencia.

EJ. 2: A. Vivaldi, Concierto RV 507, I mov., cc. 49-51.

(b) Enlaces

Encontramos dos enlaces ornamentados muy idiomáticos en el primer movimiento del concierto, una interesante tirata de 14 notas del violín segundo en el compás 74 precede a la entrada del solo del primer violín.

EJ. 3: A. Vivaldi, Concierto RV 507, I mov., cc. 73-75.

El otro ejemplo son las varias versiones, también en el violín segundo, de una ornamentación en la cadencia que introduce el *tutti* del compás 104 en el primer movimiento.

EJ. 4: A. Vivaldi, Concierto RV 507, I mov., cc. 102-104.

(c) Como forma de crear contraste con el otro solista

Finalmente las encontramos con la intención de crear alguna diferencia con el otro violín solista cuando ambos repiten un mismo patrón. El primer ejemplo lo encontramos

Las anotaciones de Pisendel en el Concierto para dos violines RV 507 de Vivaldi

al final de la primera intervención de los solistas, donde ambos violines repiten el mismo patrón melódico de arpegios y escalas ascendentes, el segundo violín introduce una escala descendente justo al final (c. 20).

Ej. 5: A. Vivaldi, Concierto RV 507, I mov., cc. 19-22.

Otro ejemplo significativo de este recurso lo encontramos en el tercer movimiento, entre los compases 107 y 113 donde el primer y el segundo violín se responden con el mismo material melódico, en este caso el primer violín opta por una fuerte variación del motivo mientras que el segundo lo interpreta casi como está.

Ej. 6: A. Vivaldi, Concierto RV 507, III mov., cc. 107-113.

La última ornamentación que encontramos toma la idea de un pasaje que ya apareció en el primer movimiento y lo traslada al tercer movimiento.

Ej. 7: A. Vivaldi, Concierto RV 507, I mov., cc. 63-64 y III mov., cc. 121-122.

En la tabla que sigue se resumen los ornamentos presentes en el primer y último movimiento del Concierto RV 507.

Mov.	Compás	Solista	N. de versiones	Tipología
I	20	violín II	1	diferencia con el violín I
I	40	violín I	4	secuencia ornamentada (patrón regular)
I	50	violín I	1	secuencia ornamentada (ruptura de patrón)
I	74	violín II	1	enlace - diferencia con el violín I
I	77-80	violín I	3	secuencia ornamentada (ruptura de patrón / patrón regular)
I	81-82?	violín I	4	secuencia ornamentada (¿patrón regular?)
I	94-96	violín I	1	secuencia ornamentada (ruptura de patrón)
I	97-98	violín II	1	enlace
I	102	violín II	3	enlace (cadencia)
I	113	violín II	1	diferencia con el violín I
III	106-107	violín I	3	diferencia con el violín II
III	111	violín II	1	diferencia con el violín I
III	115-120	violín I	3	secuencia ornamentada (ruptura de patrón)
III	121-122	violín II	1	secuencia ornamentada (patrón regular)

Ornamentos en el «Largo»

Como en el caso de las anotaciones de los otros movimientos, encontramos aquí también varias versiones para el mismo pasaje, si bien aquí hay una cantidad mayor de enmiendas, tachones y otras marcas que dificultan la valorización de los ornamentos, haciendo difícil poder decir qué fragmento se conecta con qué, o qué anotaciones fueron desechadas. Véase, por ejemplo, la sección de los compases 5 y 6, donde encontramos no sólo varias versiones del mismo pasaje si no también enmiendas y líneas que parecen conectar unas ideas con otras.

Esta profusión de ornamentos y su tipología concuerda bastante bien con otras fuentes cercanas al RV 507. Encontramos, de hecho, un movimiento bastante parecido, en forma de siciliana, en el Concierto RV 340[51], también ornamentado por Pisendel, así

---

[51]. Mus. 2389-O-43.

Las anotaciones de Pisendel en el Concierto para dos violines RV 507 de Vivaldi

como los profusos ornamentos que Pisendel añadió al Concierto RV 202[52] (transcritos ya en 1906 por Schering[53]).

EJ. 8: A. Vivaldi, Concierto RV 340 (Mus. 2389-O-43), II mov., cc. 8-11.

EJ. 9: A. Vivaldi, Concierto RV 202 (Mus. 2389-O-122), II mov., cc. 14-15, (fragmento de la transcripción de Schering de las disminuciones).

---

[52]. Mus. 2389-O-122.
[53]. SCHERING 1905-1906, pp. 377-385.

Merecen también especial mención las disminuciones del Concierto para violín RV 581 contenidas en el conocido como 'Libro de Anna Maria'[54]. Estas disminuciones han sido ya objeto de estudio[55], siendo una de las fuentes más cercanas a la forma de ornamentar del propio Vivaldi.

Podemos establecer algunas concordancias entre las fuentes mencionadas (los ornamentos de Pisendel en los Conciertos RV 340, 507 y 202 y los del 'Libro de Anna Maria' sobre el 581) y que se alejan de la norma corelliana, que además coinciden con los rasgos más significativos que encontramos en algunos movimientos lentos de conciertos de Vivaldi y que hacen gala de su estilo más improvisativo. Podemos citar (en una lista no exhaustiva): el *Grave* del RV 212a[56], las versiones del *Largo* del RV 279[57], el *Grave Recitativo* del RV 208, el *Adagio* del RV 195[58], el *Adagio* del 285[59], el *Largo* del RV 318[60], el *Grave* del RV 562[61]. Además, son dignos de mención los movimientos centrales de los Conciertos RV 775 y RV 771, contenidos en el 'Libro de Anna Maria'[62] que cuentan con las repeticiones ornamentadas[63].

Veamos ahora más en detalle los ornamentos del *Largo* del RV 507 y sus peculiaridades y semejanzas con otras fuentes. Encontramos ornamentaciones ya en el *tutti* de apertura, aprovechando los silencios.

Ej. 10: A. Vivaldi, Concierto RV 507, II mov., cc. 1-4.

---

54. I-Vc, Busta 55.1.
55. TALBOT 2007.
56. Mus. 2389-O-74.
57. El Mus. 2389-O-155 contiene dos versiones del *Largo* del Concierto, ambas presentan una escritura en un estilo improvisatorio, aunque la segunda se aleja más de la norma corelliana presentando interesantes esquemas melódicos.
58. Mus. 2389-O-117.
59. Mus. 2389-O-103.
60. Mus. 2389-O-120.
61. Mus. 2389-O-94.
62. I-Vc, Busta 55.1. El RV 775 en el f. 13 y RV 771 en los ff. 16-17.
63. Hay que decir que las disminuciones del RV 775 y del RV 771 si bien se alejan de los estándares corellianos por el uso de saltos y arpegios, pueden considerarse mucho más conservadoras si se las compara con los conciertos citados o con las ornamentaciones del Concierto RV 581 del mismo libro o las disminuciones de Pisendel sobre los conciertos de Vivaldi.

Las anotaciones de Pisendel en el Concierto para dos violines RV 507 de Vivaldi

Un pasaje muy parecido se encuentra justo al final del movimiento.

Ej. 11: A. Vivaldi, Concierto RV 507, ii mov., cc. 21-23.

La ornamentación de estos silencios orquestales no es algo excesivamente peculiar, encontramos un ejemplo muy parecido en los *Trietti* de Telemann para dos violines[64].

Il. 4: G. Ph. Telemann, *Trietto Secondo, Andante* (violín primero).

Sin embargo, existen algunas peculiaridades en nuestro concierto: Telemann mantiene un claro esquema rítmico como anacrusa hacia las notas fundamentales, usando también un patrón armónico claro: el arpegio correspondiente y el arpegio con apoyaturas cromáticas (bastante similar a las ornamentaciones de Pisendel al principio), pero Pisendel es mucho más variado rítmicamente, cambiando el patrón en sólo dos compases.

Ej. 12: A. Vivaldi, Concierto RV 507, ii mov., cc. 2-3.

En el pasaje final Pisendel usa dos recursos originales y que se alejan en cierta manera de la norma: intervalos aumentados y dobles cuerdas (ver Ej. 11).

---

[64]. Telemann, *3 Trietti methodichi e 3 Scherzi* (Mus. 2392-Q-4). Trietto Secondo, *Andante* (final), Violino Primo.

Vemos también el uso de intervalos aumentados o disminuidos, algo bastante común al lenguaje vivaldiano[65]. Este tipo de 'difícil' interválica — que podríamos definir como un especial gusto por el uso de pasos y saltos 'duriusculus', y que se aleja de la práctica más académica — se hace bastante visible en el lenguaje pisendeliano y vivaldiano; además de los ejemplos expuestos esto incluye un característico uso del cromatismo[66].

EJ. 13: A. Vivaldi, Concierto RV 507, II mov., cc. 6-7.

EJ. 14: A. Vivaldi, Concierto RV 581, II mov., cc. 48-49/1[67].

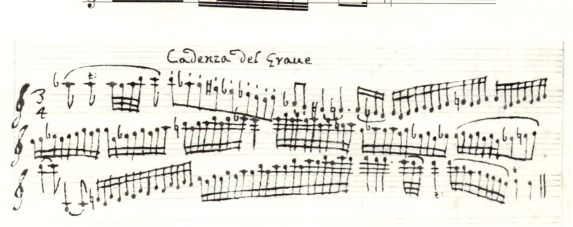

IL. 5: Cadenza para el *Grave* del Concierto RV 286, 'Libro de Anna Maria'[68].

A esto podemos unir otra característica del lenguaje pisendeliano, que también se aleja de los pulcros contornos corellianos: el uso de saltos y arpegios. Juntos, los pasajes por grados conjuntos y los saltos se mezclan para crear una heterogeneidad melódica muy característica: un ejemplo lo encontramos en el uso de arpegios invertidos (comenzando por el registro agudo).

---

[65]. TALBOT 1978, p. 75.
[66]. *Ibidem*.
[67]. I-Vc, Busta 55.1., f. 75ʳ.
[68]. I-Vc, Busta 55.1., f. 78ᵛ.

Ej. 15: A. Vivaldi, Concierto RV 507, II mov., cc. 6-7.

Ej. 16: A. Vivaldi, Concierto RV 581, II mov., c. 4[69].

Se crean, de esta forma, originales pasajes con saltos y arpegios, repletos de saltos disonantes, raros en la literatura más escolástica.

Ej. 17: A. Vivaldi, Concierto RV 507, II mov., cc. 6-7.

Ej. 18: A. Vivaldi, Concierto RV 581, II mov., c. 33[70].

Todas estas disminuciones parecen alejarse del estándar corelliano predominante en los tratados y en otros ejemplos de disminuciones publicados en la época. Enrico Gatti define el estilo de Corelli de forma sucinta: «Il principio basilare è quello di collegare le note portanti della frase tramite gradi congiunti e numerose note di passaggio. I salti sono poco numerosi e ben calibrati, in modo da poter descrivere delle forme arrotondate ad arco e non squadrate come tendevano ad essere le antiche diminuzioni a cavallo fra Cinquecento e Seicento»[71].

Tanto los ornamentos de Pisendel, como los del 'Libro de Anna Maria' parecen adecuarse más a la definición que el propio Gatti otorga a la forma de ornamentar en Venecia

---

[69]. I-Vc, Busta 55.1., f. 75^v.
[70]. I-Vc, Busta 55.1., f. 75^r.
[71]. GATTI 2014, p. 129.

en la época de Vivaldi: «A Venezia durante l'epoca di Vivaldi lo stile dell'improvvisazione era già molto diverso, più ardito e spregiudicato, molto idiomatico e colorito rispetto all'austero ed equilibrato stile della generazione di Corelli. Purtroppo non ci sono molti documenti al riguardo, essendo questa un'arte effimera riservata ai virtuosi che improvvisavano e quindi di norma non fissata in regole precedenti»[72].

Algunas conclusiones

La estrecha relación de Pisendel con Vivaldi, la importancia y la cantidad de anotaciones de Pisendel sobre obras de Vivaldi, además del estilo de las anotaciones analizadas en este artículo hacen plausible la propuesta de Kolneder: «[…] the Adagio of a violin concerto (Hs Dresden Cx 1091) [Concierto para violín y orquesta en Do menor, RV 202, Mus. 2389-O-122] with diminutions by Pisendel is very close to the master's usage, if not indeed elaborated by himself for a pupil's usage»[73].

Las anotaciones encontradas en el RV 507 (así como, de forma general las otras anotaciones de Pisendel sobre los manuscritos vivaldianos) parecen responder a la necesidad práctica de anotar ciertas ideas surgidas en el momento de una improvisación real. Hecho por el cual se hace muy difícil comparar este tipo de anotaciones con las de otras fuentes existentes. Por lo tanto, todas estas anotaciones estarían enmarcadas dentro de un contexto interpretativo donde el intérprete improvisa y modifica el texto musical *ex tempore*: de ahí su dificultad, notada por Lockey en cuanto a la Siciliana del RV 340[74], para ser transcritas y organizadas en forma de edición moderna.

El análisis de estas anotaciones nos muestra un estilo que se aleja de los tratados contemporáneos dedicados a la ornamentación y las fuentes — académicas o no — destinadas a un público más general. En este sentido es interesante hacer notar que las mayores similitudes con otras fuentes de la época las encontramos en las ornamentaciones más 'personales' contenidas en manuscritos realizados por los propios intérpretes y que no tuvieron difusión más allá del uso personal o de un reducido círculo, como las disminuciones sobre Corelli de 'Festing' o 'Roman'.

Esto concuerda con la idea ya enunciada en 1958 por Pincherle[75] y argumentada con diversas fuentes de la época de cómo los grandes músicos evitaban en lo posible hacer público «los secretos de su estilo»: «They [composers] manifest, in a certain measure, a preoccupation with business, but at the same time, they give evidence of a desire legitimate, after all to preserve the secret of their style as much as was feasible. Indeed, ornamentation

---

[72]. *Ibidem*, p. 133.
[73]. Kolneder 1979, p. 41.
[74]. Lockey 2010, p. 135.
[75]. Pincherle – Cazeau 1958.

expressed, better than any other element of the art of the interpreter, his own style, his taste, his personality. He did not always like to put it within the reach of anybody at all»[76].

Referencias bibliográficas

Ammetto 2013
Ammetto, Fabrizio. *I concerti per due violini di Vivaldi*, Florencia, Olschki, 2013 (Quaderni vivaldiani, 18).

Fechner 1980
Fechner, Manfred. 'Improvisationsskizzen und ausnotierte Diminutionen von Johann Georg Pisendel, dargestellt an in Dresden handschriftlich überlieferten Konzerten von Johann Friedrich Fasch und Johann Gottlieb Graun', en: *Zu Fragen der Verzierungskunst in der Instrumentalmusik der ersten Hälfte des 18. Jahrhunderts: Konferenzbericht der 7. Wissenschaftlichen Arbeitstagung (Blankenburg/Harz, 29. Juni bis 1. Juli 1979)*, editado por Günter Fleischhauer, Blankenburg/Harz, Kultur-und Forschungsstäate Michaelstein, 1980 (Studien zur Aufführungspraxis und Interpretation der Intrumentalmusik des 18. Jahrhunderts, 11), pp. 35-55.

Gatti 2014
Gatti, Enrico. '«Però ci vole pacientia»: un excursus sull'arte della diminuzione nei secoli XVI, XVII e XVIII «per uso di chi avrà volontà di studiare»', en: *Quaderni del Conservatorio 'Giuseppe Verdi' di Milano*, n.s. 2 (2014), pp. 71-188.

Hawkins 1776
Hawkins, John. *A General History of the Science and Practice of Music*, 5 vol., Londres, Payne, 1776.

Heller 1976
Heller, Karl. 'Zu einigen Aspekten der solistischen Improvisation im Instrumentalkonzert des frühen 18. Jahrhunderts', en: *Zu Fragen des Instrumentariums, der Besetzung und der Improvisation in der ersten Hälfte des 18. Jahrhunderts. Konferenzbericht der 3. Wissenschaftlichen Arbeitstagung (Blankenburg/Harz, 28.-29. Juni 1975)*, vol. II, editado por Eitelfriedrich Thom and Renate Borman, Magdeburg, Rat des Bezirks, 1976 (Studien zur Aufführungspraxis und Interpretation von Instrumentalmusik des 18. Jahrhunderts, 2.2), pp. 80-87.

Heller 1997
Id. *Antonio Vivaldi: The Red Priest of Venice*, Portland (OR), Amadeus Press, 1997.

Heller 2010
Id. 'Pisendels Sammlung Vivaldishcher Violinkonzerte', en: *Johann Georg Pisendel – Studien zu Leben und Werk. Bericht über das Internationale Symposium vom 23. bis 25. Mai 2005 in Dresden*, editado por Ortrun Landmann y Hans-Günter Ottenberg, Hildesheim, Olms, 2010 (Dresdner Beiträge zur Musikforschung 3), pp. 145-169.

Kolneder 1979
Kolneder, Walter. *Performance Practices in Vivaldi*, Winterthur, Amadeus-Verlag, 1979.

---

[76]. *Ibidem*, p. 158.

Köpp 2005
Köpp, Kai. *Johann Georg Pisendel (1687-1755) und die Anfange der neuzeitlichen Orchesterleitung*, Tutzing, Hans Schneider, 2005.

Landmann 1981
Landmann, Ortrun. 'Katalog der Dresdner Vivaldi-Handschriften und -Frühdrucke', en: *Vivaldi-Studien. Referate des 3. Dresdner Vivaldi-Kolloquiums: mit einem Katalog der Dresdner Vivaldi-Handschriften und -Fruhdrucke*, Dresde, Sachsische Landesbibliothek, 1981, pp. 101-167.

Landshoff 1935
Landshoff, Ludwig. *Antonio Vivaldi, Violinkonzert A dur*, Berlín, Peters, 1935.

Lockey 2010
Lockey, Nicholas Scott. 'Second Thoughts, Embellishments and an Orphaned Fragment: Vivaldi's and Pisendel's Contributions to the Dresden Score of RV 340', en: *Studi vivaldiani*, x (2010), pp. 125-142.

Pincherle – Cazeau 1958
Pincherle, Marc – Cazeau, Isabelle. 'On the Rights of the Interpreter in the Performance of 17th- and 18th-Century Music', en: *The Musical Quarterly*, xliv/2 (1958), pp. 145-166.

Schering 1905-1906
Schering, Arnold. 'Zur instrumentalen Verzierungskunst im 18. Jahrhundert', en: *Sammelbande der Internationalen Musikgesellschaft*, vii (1905-1906), pp. 365-385.

Spitzer – Zaslaw 1986
Spitzer, John – Zaslaw, Neal. 'Ornamentation in Eighteenth-Century Orchestras', en: *Journal of the American Musicological Society*, xxxix/3 (1986), pp. 524-577.

Talbot 1978
Talbot, Michael. *Vivaldi*, Londres, J. M. Dent, 1978 (Master Musicians Series).

Talbot 2007
Id. "Full of Graces': Anna Maria receives Ornaments from the Hands of Antonio Vivaldi', en: *Arcangelo Corelli fra mito e realtà storica: nuove prospettive d'indagine musicologica e interdisciplinare nel 350° anniversario della nascita. Atti del Congresso internazionale di studi (Fusignano, 11-14 settembre 2003)*, a cura di Gregory Barnett, Antonella D'Ovidio y Stefano La Via, Florencia, Olschki, 2007 (Historiae Musicae Cultores, 111), pp. 253-268.

Cadenze per finali:
Exuberant and Extended Cadences in the 16th and 17th Centuries*

Josué Meléndez Peláez
(University of Music, Trossingen)

WE ALL HAVE HEARD about improvised *cadenze* in classical and early romantic music, where a soloist displays her/his abilities and expressiveness towards the end of a musical piece. But do we know if this practice has antecedents in music before the classical period, and if yes, was it part of a common practice?

Extended virtuoso cadences that prolong the penultimate note of a musical piece are well documented in the second half of the sixteenth century and throughout the seventeenth. These cadences are mostly called *finale* (sometimes also *accadenza*) and their most remarkable characteristic is that they alter the length of the penultimate measure, prolonging it to provide space to add a richly ornamented cadence. Indeed, written examples of ornamented cadences[1] that are not called *finale* stay strictly to the number of beats given in their original unornamented figures, but the examples of *cadenze per finali*, the *finali diversi per diversi parti* and the *fini diversi* found in Francesco Rognoni's *Selva di varii passaggi*[2], as well as the *finali* in Johannes Andreas Herbst's *Musica moderna prattica*[3], the *cadenze finali* in the Estense manuscript (for the theorbo)[4] and the *concludendii* and *finalia* cadences in Spiridionis a Monte Carmelo's *Nuova Instructio*[5], all add extra beats to the penultimate note.

Could we imagine a classical *cadenza*-type ending in renaissance motets and madrigals or in early baroque monody?

---

*.   A special thank to Helen Roberts and Catherine Motuz for correcting of the English language in this article.
[1]. For general information about cadences see SCHWANNBERGER, Sven. 'Kadenzfiguration in verschiedenen Stillen', in: SCHWENKREIS 2018, pp. 134-139.
[2]. ROGNONI 1620.
[3]. HERBST 1653.
[4]. ANONYMOUS 1995 (Estense Codex G 239).
[5]. SPIRIDIONIS 1670, Pars 1-2, 1670-1671.

In this article I will explain how these *cadenze per finali* were performed, written out, or just left *a suo genio* (to the performer's own genius), providing information from sources of the time that prove that this practice was common. I suggest a term to call these cadences for analytical purposes, and propose a method for inserting them in modern performances.

Already on the front page of Francesco Rognoni's *Selva di vari passaggi secondo l'uso moderno*, we read: «[here] is shown […] the way how to *passegiar* [ornament] stepwise, with jumps of third, fourth, fifth, sixth, octave, and final cadences for all the voices, with various other examples, […]». On the front page of the second part of his *Selva*, he addresses «Difficult *passaggi* for the instruments, […] *cadentie finali*; examples, diminished songs […]»[6]. In the index of both books he seems to distinguish between *cadenze* and *finali* whereby the examples called *finali* are the only ones that add extra beats or measures to the original figure. Systematically, the examples that are called simply *cadenze*, keep strictly the values of the original figures but all those that say *finale* or *fini* or *finali*, add extra beats, more or less randomly, to the penultimate note. Let us take some examples from Rognoni's page for 'Cadenze & finali sopra il basso' (Cadences & final cadences over the bass). Here we see that the first three diminutions for each cadence stays strictly within the original values of the unornamented version, but the fourth diminution of each cadence, which has an indication «per doi battuti o finali» (*per due battute o finali*, that is, for two measures or for final cadences), extends the original values by one measure. The title of the page and its contents seem to be very clear and leave us with only one possible thought: *cadenze* = cadences and *finali* = prolonged cadences for the end of a piece (see Ex. 1).

Ex. 1: Rognoni 1620, examples from 'Cadenze & finali sopra il basso'.

---

[6]. See Rognoni 1620.

Cadenze per finali: Exuberant and Extended Cadences in the 16th and 17th Centuries

In the several pages that Rognoni dedicates to cadences we find, again in a very systematic way, that only the cadences called *finali* alter the original figure, prolonging those that consist of one semibreve by adding two more semibreves, and those ones that are originally one breve by adding one extra semibreve (in most of the cases).

J. A. Herbst's *Musica Moderna e Prattica overo la maniera del buon canto* shows the exact same procedure, as do the *cadenze finali* from the Estense Manuscript for theorbo, although here the cadences have no original unornamented figure to refer to[7].

On the other hand, all treatises mentioning *tactus* or *battuta* in relation to *passaggi* agree that it is most important to keep the length of the original values intact. Ricardo Rognoni even recommends measuring the beat by tapping your foot «because the mind is occupied with other tasks [i.e., improvising diminutions] and without that guide, one will often find oneself lost at the end»[8]. Ludovico Zacconi dedicates almost a whole page to the importance of not converting eighths into quarters, arguing against those *suministratori del tatto* (those in charge of the tactus) that do so when a *gran copia di chrome* is to be found in the score[9]. Nevertheless, Zacconi himself, as well as Giovanni Battista Bovicelli, accepts the insertion of extra measures at the final cadence, or more precisely, at the penultimate note, in order to add more ornamentation. Criticising those musicians who, in order to accommodate *passaggi* to their own wish, hold a note that is equal to a measure for two, or even three measures, Bovicelli allows an exception by saying: «I know well that it is more praiseworthy while playing *passaggi* to stay bound to the *tempo giusto* that is to be found in the written chant, except for the end, that is, the penultimate note»[10]. Zacconi's *Prattica di Musica* dedicates a whole chapter to different ways of ending a cantilena[11]. In total he describes six final cadences; the two of them that he considers principal are — or can be — prolonged: *commune* and *soggetto*.

> After having spoken about the beginning, and the middle of a piece, it is convenient that I speak about the end; which is as important as the other two: so while beginning it is necessary [to maintain] the good way and the art; and in the middle [it is important to maintain] manners, and graces: at the end one

---

[7]. Most of the cadances in the Estense Manuscript are three semibreves long, i.e., exactly the same length as all of the sources calling for *cadenze finali*.

[8]. ROGNONI 1592.

[9]. ZACCONI 1592, fol. 76ᵛ.

[10]. BOVICELLI 1594. p. 14: «Sogliono alcuni che per accomodarsi i Passaggi a modo loro, se una nota vale una battuta, tenerla due, ò tre, con che ragione, io no 'l so, so bene che è più laudabile nel Passeggiare star obligato al tempo giusto, che si trova nel Canto, fuori, che nel fine cioè nella penultima nota». Translation by Josué Mélendez.

[11]. Zacconi had defined cantilena as music on paper. Libro 1, chapter 3, fol. 4ᵛ: «[…] quando io vorò per Musica intendere le carte ove sono affisse et poste le figure Musicalli, ò che io le dirò cantilene, over libri da catare […]» («when I want to understand under the term music of paper, on which musical notes are placed, [that] I call them either cantilenae or singing book»; translated in GERHARD 1968, p. 125).

needs manners and graces with art and the proper way: and if the end seems to be an easy thing, nevertheless you will find difficulties, not known to everyone.

But by demonstrating some endings here, I say that singers should be aware while singing the end of a piece, not to do like some not-very-aware singers do, that at the end cause dissatisfaction to the ears of the listeners because they don't pay attention to the final figure[12], which can be of two principal types, that is, *commune* and *soggetto*: *Commune* is the name of that ending when all parts agree on the value of such figures [presumably, how long the figure will be], as shown here […]

Then you have to stay on the penultimate figure as long as all other parts want and are happy with; and then jump to the last figure: [the end] place where all voices agree[13].

Zacconi continues with a confusing explanation distinguishing between the *figura finale* (final figure) and the *ultima figura* (last figure), being the final figure the penultimate note of a piece. Staying (*fermare*) on the penultimate figure (note), as long as all parts want, upon an agreement on the value of that final figures seems to describe a kind of *fermata* on the penultimate note (in this case the fifth degree of a perfect cadence) to which the time values previously agreed are added. In a different chapter Zacconi tells us about soprano leading-note cadences (not necessarily cadences at the end of a piece) that can be held long: «Similarly, in cadences, that replication of sol-fa-sol; la-sol-la; fa-mi-fa; and the others can be held as long as all the time lasts that is required»[14].

Zacconi proceeds again in a very confusing way trying to explain mistakes that can be produced if a cadence is extended. Sion M. Honea has clarified that «What he [Zacconi]

---

[12]. By final figure Zacconi refers here to the penultimate note.

[13]. ZACCONI 1592, libro I, chapter 70, fol. 79: «Havendo io dunque parlato del principio, e del mezzo delle cantilene, è cosa conveniente che io parli anche del fine; il quale è si d'importanza quanto che sia l'uno e l'altro: poi che se nel dar principio ci bisogna il modo, e l'arte; e nel mezzo le maniere, e le vaghezze: nel fine ci voranno le vaghezze, e le maniere, con l'arte, e il debbito modo: E se bene il fine par che sia una cosa facile: non di meno molte difficoltà vi si trovano non cosi da tutti conosciute. / Però volendone dimostrar alcune dico, che i cantori nel finir di cantare una cantilena si guardino di far quello che fanno alcuni poco accorti, che nel finir fanno mala sodisfattione alle orecchie de gli ascoltanti per non avertire alla figura finale, la quale può esser di due sorte principalmente, cioè commune, e soggetto: Commune si chiama quel fine quando le parte tutte convengano nel valore delle istesse figure, come a dire quando le parte finiscano, come qui si vede [musical example]. Allhora su la penultima figura tanto si hà da fermare quanto che tutte l'altre parte vogliano, e si contentano; e poi salire all'ultima figura; termine e l'uoco ove convengano tutte le voci sonore: […]». I wish to thank David Yacus for revising my translation of this quote.

[14]. HONEA, translation of Zacconi's libro I, part I, chapter 66, p. 16.

CADENZE PER FINALI: EXUBERANT AND EXTENDED CADENCES IN THE 16TH AND 17TH CENTURIES

is describing is that some careless singers in wishing to ornament the very end of the cadence introduce pitches that can cause dissonance with the lower voices if the ornament is prolonged too far»[15].

Back to the chapter on how to finish a *cantilena*, Zacconi describes the cadence he calls *soggetto* as:

> [...] a figure on which all the other voices make, with a distinctive final voice, *quasi* like a windmill, or like turning around in an artful, lovely and pleasant way; joking [playing] around the mentioned end». [...]: «but we must know that not every time that we finish singing a cantilena, the singer should stop on the penultimate figure [note]: because on some occasions, by staying in [*fermandosi*] there could be discordance [*dissonanze*] with all the other parts, [...][16].

The singer cannot necessarily stay (*fermarsi*) on the penultimate note at the end of every *cantilena*. In the example that Zacconi provides, if the tenor were to stay on the penultimate note, a horrible, cacophonous collision would occur. Therefore, Zacconi's recommendation for this particular cadence is obviously correct. What intrigues me is that these and other observations of Zacconi confirm that it seems to have been common for singers to stop at the penultimate note of a cadence, and not necessarily only at the end of a piece, to add florid ornamentation. Other sources such as F. Rognoni and J. A. Herbst, both intended for performers to teach themselves by 'picking up' ornaments (*pigliare* or *servirsene*) and placing them into their performances, confirm that extending a cadence for a pair of beats or a pair of measures, was a common practice and that the usual term to define these cadences was *finale*[17]. Other composers, such as Giulio Caccini, associate

---

[15]. *Ibidem*, fn. 62.

[16]. ZACCONI 1592, libro I, chapter 70, p. 79: «La figura del fine poi che è soggetto è una figura sopra la quale tutte l'altre parte con sumministratione di voce finale fanno quasi come un poco di girandola, o' torneamento: non meno artificioso che vago, e dilettevole; scherzando intorno al detto finale: [...] però è da sapere che non ogni volta che si finisce di cantare una cantilena, il cantore su la penultima figura si ha da fermare: perche fermandosi in alcune occasione faria dissonanza con tutte l'altre parte [...]».

[17]. Remarkably interesting, in that it shows the continuity of these ornamentation traditions into the nineteenth century, is Manuel Garcia's quotation of Herbst when proposing alternative musical endings to

finali with long *passaggi*[18] although he, as well as others including Francesco Severi and some examples in the Estense manuscript, often prolongs the antepenultimate note rather than the penultimate. Severi's *Salmi passaggiati* is a collection of vespers psalms (and some Misereres) in the *falso bordone* manner of improvisation. His examples provide great evidence of prolonged passages and cadences that were otherwise mostly improvised[19].

Do we have any other surviving pieces that demonstrate this practice? Surviving pieces with long final cadences that prolong their penultimate note in order to add diminutions can be found in works by Girolamo Dalla Casa, Giovanni Bassano, Ricardo Rogniono, Francesco Rognoni, Bartolomeo de Selma, Oratio (Bassani), Ascanio Mayone and Antonio Terzi, as well as in later composers including Dario Castello, Biagio Marini, Bartolomeo Barbarino, Francesco Severi, Tarquinio Merula, Giovanni Batista Fontana, Antonio Pandolfi Mealli, Vincenzo Bonizzi, Girolamo Frescobaldi, Michael Praetorius and many others. In the case of the written-out diminutions on original motets or madrigals, it is obvious that sometimes the final cadence has been prolonged (see Ex. 3, p. 69). In compositions such as the early seventeenth-century sonata or monody, we need to understand the concept of extending or prolonging a cadence to be able to call it a *finale*. However, a quick look at different bass lines gives us a very good idea of the concept. In Ex. 2 there is a simple cadence next to a *finale* cadence. Surprisingly, we could eventually prolong the first cadence, making it look like the second one, and add a florid *finale* cadence according to our own wishes; that same procedure could be done with any motet, madrigal, chanson or monody.

Ex. 2: Fontana bass lines (FONTANA 1641).

the word Amen — presumably to be used at the end of a piece or a section of it (Manuel Garcia, *L'Art du chant*, 1847, p. 77). Garcia begins by copying Herbst's two first examples and continues, obviously inspired by Herbst, with his own solutions, in much the same way that Herbst himself does with the works of F. Rognoni, Bovicelli and Donati, who likewise praised the works of the older Girolamo da Udine (Dalla Casa) and Bassano (Giovanni).

18. See GATTI 2014, pp. 102-103.
19. SEVERI 1615.

Cadenze per finali: Exuberant and Extended Cadences in the 16th and 17th Centuries

Ex. 3: final cadence of the madrigal *Vestiva i colli* by G. P. da Palestrina. Erig 1979. The two prolonged diminutions are by F. Rognoni. The one with the indication *a cadenza* is by De Selma 1638.

*) Basso continuo

John Butt has discussed the increased tendency in the late seventeenth century for composers to include written-out embellishments in their works[20]. By comparing *cadenze finali* and other common passages included in diminution treatises to written-out music, it is possible to prove that this happens already in the early seventeenth century. Indeed, the surviving diminution pieces provide a trace of this trend also during the sixteenth century. Many compositions show a similar style to those *finali* by Francesco Rognoni, for example Castello's Sonata prima or seconda[21], the examples in the Carlo G. manuscript, or Fontana's sonata prima or seconda[22], among many others. Francesco Lomazzo writes at the end of Francesco Rognoni's second book that «the author does not deny that someone could serve himself to any kind of *passaggio* contained in the book, or of any other author, to make a cadenza, or finale, or [to place it] in any imitative passage of whatever *cantilena*, [it] being a praiseworthy thing to know how to combine them [the passages]»[23]. Musicians have always been copying works from each other to learn from them or to use or recycle specific materials in their own works. It is not surprising therefore, but nevertheless curious, that Lomazzo tells us about two or three pages of *Cadenze, ò finali* that were once stolen from his teacher (F. Rognoni).

What is surprising, though, is the artistic outpouring achieved by some sixteenth-century musicians when performing ornaments. According to Zacconi: «there are some [singers] who, at the end of a *cantilena*, desire to ornament for an hour long, and make all [their] colleagues wait for them, and even if the colleagues have waited for quite a bit, they [this singers] finish anyway after them»[24]. Likewise, more than a century later, Pier Francesco Tosi complains also about singers ornamenting too long at the final cadence. His complaint gives us a clue as to a difference in performance practice: by arguing that at the final cadence, no listener that knows about music would appreciate a cadence without a bassline, Tosi gives us a clear indication that all those not ornamenting at the end of a piece would come to a complete stop[25].

The practice of extending or prolonging a cadence might have started with the tendency of musicians to structure their works after the rhetoric discourse of the ancient Greeks. Ann Smith says that «[...] in the course of the humanist movement in the 15th century, the antique sources on rhetoric were rediscovered and soon became part of the gentle person's basic education»[26]. In this manner, «Gallus Dressler, in 1563 in his *Praecepta*

---

[20]. BUTT 1991.
[21]. CASTELLO 1629.
[22]. FONTANA 1641.
[23]. ROGNONI 1620, p. 76.
[24]. ZACCONI 1592, libro I, chapter 70, p. 79ᵛ: «[...] sono alcuni che nel fine delle cantilene, vogliano con le glorie tenerle un hora lunghe; e fanno che tutti gli altri compagni lo stiano ad aspettare, oltre che molte volte se bene l'hanno un pezzo aspettato, le finiscono dopo loro».
[25]. TOSI 1723, p. 89. TOSI 1967, pp. 44-45.
[26]. SMITH 2011, chapter 'The Rhetoric of Counterpoint', pp. 102ff.

Cadenze per finali: Exuberant and Extended Cadences in the 16th and 17th Centuries

Musicae Poeticae, began talking about the structure of a musical piece being similar to that of an oration»[27].

Conclusio, also called *finis*, is the part (or period) of a speech that defines the end. In his *Musical poetica* of 1606, in a chapter dedicated to musical analysis and arrangement, Joachim Burmeister divides a piece into three parts, writing that: «The ending is the principal cadence where either all the musical movement [*modulatio*] ceases or where one or two voices stop while the others continue with a brief passage called *supplementum*»[28]. Later on, analyzing Lasso's motet *In me transierunt irae tuae,* (according to Joshua Rifkin the first known analysis of a musical piece)[29] Burmeister subdivides a piece into nine rhetorical periods. «The Final, namely, the ninth, period is like the Epilog of the speech. This harmony displays a principal ending, otherwise called a *supplementum* of the final cadence, [...]»[30]. Indeed, the final cadence of this motet adds a kind of two bars supplement; the tenor concludes its final cadence and stays still holding its last note while the other four voices play around with the first and fourth degree of the mode. This is the cadence that Zacconi calls *soggetto*. Final cadences that have one or more voices holding the final note while the others continue for a couple of bars can be found in works of many renaissance and early baroque composers[31]. An extreme example of this type of cadence can be seen in the Sonata x by Gioanpietro del Buono[32] (see Ex. 4) where the tenor voice arrives at the final note at measure eleven while the other voices continue for another twenty measures.

A kind of sister of this *supplemento* or *soggetto* cadence seems to be the so called *accadenza* or *a cadenza*, an extra cadence that moves around the fourth and first degrees, which appears sometimes at the end of a piece as an *ad libitum* extra cadence. In the diminutions by Bortholomeo de Selma on Lasso's *Susane un jour*, an impressive amount of diminutions are placed in the last nine measures. These are to be repeated as many times as the soloist wants, with the request to warn the organist about the number of times this last section will be repeated. This section is followed, as if after ten repetitions it would not be enough to conclude the piece, by another four measures that play around the fourth and first degrees in the *soggetto-supplemento* manner with the indication *accadenza*[33].

---

[27]. *Ibidem.*

[28]. BURMEISTER 1993, p. 205.

[29]. See SMITH 2011, chapter 'The Rhetoric of Counterpoint', pp. 102ff.

[30]. BURMEISTER 1993, p. 207.

[31]. For example: the chanson *Douce Memoire* by Pier Sandrin, the already mentioned *In me transierunt* by Lasso, the madrigal *Così le chiome* (the second part of Palestrina's mottet *Vestiva i colli*), Thomas Crecquillon's *Une gay bergier* and *Oncques amour*, Adrian Willaert's *Iouissance vous donneray* and *À la Fontaine du pré*, G. B. Fontana's *Sonata prima*, etc.

[32]. DEL BUONO 1641.

[33]. See ERIG 1979, pp. 171 and 376. This same base pattern is to be found in many both vocal and instrumental 17th-century works.

Ex. 4: Gioanpietro del Buono, Sonata x sopra *Ave Maris Stella* (transcription by Lorenzo Girodo).

CADENZE PER FINALI: EXUBERANT AND EXTENDED CADENCES IN THE 16TH AND 17TH CENTURIES

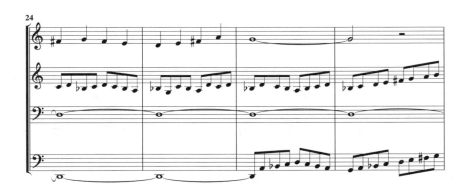

The recently discovered Carlo G. manuscript contains a great number of sketched diminutions added to passages and cadences that require the original figure in the score to be prolonged in order to fit. Additional ornaments for final cadences, intermediate cadences and other passages that alter the original score to add ornamentation are to be found throughout the whole manuscript. Thus, this manuscript provides enough information to understand how these cadences were performed and to confirm that this practice existed.

> An interesting feature of the Carlo G MS is the addition of optional variants for certain vocal passages. In many pieces, there are one or more *ossias*; these appear typically, but not always, on the final cadence, suggesting different variants for certain diminutions. These optional variants are not consistent in their nature; sometime they offer an easier and shorter passage, but sometime a longer and more virtuosic one. They are mostly not labeled with text, but when they are, it is along the line of: *passaggio altro* (another passage), or *per chi vuol variare* (for those who would like to vary)[34].

Ex. 6: Carlo G. ms., *Confiteor Deo*, bars 28-34.

---

[34]. Rotem forthcoming. Selected pieces have been edited online in <https://imslp.org/wiki/Di_Carlo_G._(Anonymous)>, accessed November 2018, by Elam Rotem. *The Carlo G Manuscript: Virtuoso Liturgical Music from the Early 17th Century*, CD, Profeti della Quinta, Glossa, 2017, GCD 922516.

Cadenze per finali: Exuberant and Extended Cadences in the 16th and 17th Centuries

Ex. 7: Carlo G. ms., *Ego Flos Campi*, bars 23ff.

One of the first questions appearing when trying to add a *finale* cadence in modern performances is how they were to be accompanied, that is, what kind of counterpoint or harmonic patterns should be used with a prolonged cadence. The Carlo G. manuscript offers us several answers for this question. In all plagal cadences, the penultimate chord is simply held during the added embellishments. In perfect cadences sometime the chord is held long, but sometimes we find a 5/3 6/4 5/4 5/3 basso continuo pattern over the penultimate note. The *cadenze finale* from the Estense manuscript for the theorbo have mostly this kind of counterpoint pattern and, in general, the *finale* examples from Herbst and Rognoni, particularly the longest ones, seem to need that cadential pattern. I have experimented by pasting cadences requiring this pattern from both F. Rognoni's and Estense's *finali* into real pieces, with a satisfactory result[35].

Another interesting source is Spiridionis a Monte Carmelo's *Nuova instructio*[36], a series of four books intended for keyboard players to learn the practice of improvisation through memorisation and transposition of a sort of «encyclopedic collection of 1251 musical segments»[37] called *cadentiae*. Spiridione explains in the introductory letter to the reader that combining and transposing different cadences is the secret for this practice, pointing out the importance of learning how to close a musical phrase quickly (*hurtig schliessen*) with a small cadence and how to play all kinds of *finalia*[38]. In the Latin version of this text Spiridione uses the terms *concludendi* and *finalia* to denote small and large cadences. In the first pages of the first book we find 72 cadences from which a prolongation of a minim is to be found from example number 32 onwards, as well as a prolongation of a semibreve after example 42 and of two semibreves after example 57. All of these cadences present a systematic use of the 5/3 6/4 5/4 5/3 basso continuo pattern already mentioned.

Could we give a term to differentiate this cadences? It is important that, for analytical purposes, we are able to distinguish between a normal cadence and one that has been prolonged in order to add florid ornamentation, regardless of whether it is intermediate or final. It seems logical to assume that for Spiridione, a cadence that closes quickly is a *concludendi* and a prolonged cadence is a *finalia*. Considering that F. Rognoni's and Herbst's '*finalia*' add at least one semibreve, and that some intermediate prolonged cadences can be found that add only one minim, I would suggest the generic terms *finalia* and *concludendi* to denote prolonged cadences both at the end and in the middle of a musical piece.

---

[35]. Some examples can be heard at <www.ifedeli.org/audio>, accessed November 2018.
[36]. SPIRIDIONIS 1670.
[37]. BELLOTTI 2003, 'Preface'.
[38]. SPIRIDIONIS 1670, 'Ad Lectorem. Dem Leser', p. 3: «[…] und lernt Mann dadurch hurtig schliessen und allerhand Finalia machen».

CADENZE PER FINALI: EXUBERANT AND EXTENDED CADENCES IN THE 16TH AND 17TH CENTURIES

Could prolonged cadences be related to any other type of contrapuntal *fioriture* such as *canti fermi* or pedal-like movements?

Are there any similarities between this extended Renaissance *finalia* and the classical *cadenza*, the long or double cadence, or the prolonged *cadenza finta* of the Neapolitan partimento?

Harmonic pattern relationships can be traced in between the partimento cadences, the *finalia* in Estense manuscript and Spiridioni's *Nuova Instructio*[39]. Furthermore, it is unlikely that the realisation of Durante's *Perfidia* partimento[40], which offers extremely elaborated passages and leaves the final cadence empty, with the remark *a suo genio*, would be concluded with an empty and short cadence. Instead, a majestic and well extended cadence, even for 'an hour long', could be expected.

Finally, the most clear difference between the renaissance *finalia* and the classical *cadenza* is that in the latter, the soloist is left completely alone to demonstrate their virtuosity. In the former, all other performers hold the harmony steady, for a previously agreed value, in order for the 'soloist' to add more ornamentation. The terms *a suo genio*, *col canto*, *colla parte* or *point d'orgue*, are indications that continue the renaissance *finalia* into the following centuries.

The exuberant ornamentations found in several diminution treatises of the renaissance and early baroque musical era include examples of prolonged cadences that can be added to any motet, madrigal, sonata or monody, regardless of the number of voices involved. Howard Mayer Brown, referring to sixteenth-century ornamentation, has pointed out that: «Any comprehensive view of musical life in the Renaissance would be incomplete that did not take into account these spontaneous sounds»[41]. Thus all these sources together provide a glimpse of an entirely lost practice that we are trying to recover today, and if authenticity is required in historically informed performance practice, copying ornaments form old treatises might be a good start. However, the final cadence might not be the first ornament we should add to our performance, as Zacconi warns: «In addition, the singer should take care at the end of any song not to do what many little wise and little practiced in this profession do, who make such a great mass of embellishments (*vaghezze*), because they want to show off everything at the end and have all the middle left empty and barren»[42].

---

[39]. For other similarities between partimento cadences and renaissance cadences see MENKE, Johannes. 'Potentiale der *Cadenza doppia*', in: SCHWENKREIS 2018, pp. 59-66.

[40]. See SANGUINETTI 2012, pp. 227-228.

[41]. BROWN 1976.

[42]. HONEA, translation of Zacconi's libro I, part I, chapter 66, p. 9. In ZACCONI 1592, libro I, p. 59: «In oltre si guardi il cantore nella fine di qual si voglia cantilena di non far ciò che fanno molti poco accorti, et molto poco prattici in questa professione: che fanno tanta gran copia di vaghezze, che ogni cosa vogliono mostrar nel fine, et hanno tutto il mezzo lasciato voto et secco».

Josué Meléndez Peláez

Bibliography

Anonymous 1995
Anonymous. *Cadenze e passaggi diversi intavolati per tiorba dal manoscritto Estense G 239 (sec. XVII)*, edited by Tiziano Bagnati, Bologna, Ut Orpheus Edizioni, 1995 (Società italiana del liuto, 1).

Bellotti 2003
Spiridionis a Monte Carmelo. *Nova instructio pro pulsandis organis, spinettis, monuchordiis, pars prima, (Bamberg, 1670); pars seconda (Bamberg, 1671)*, edited by Edoardo Bellotti, Colledara (TE), Andromeda Editrice, 2003 (Tastature: musiche intavolate per strumenti da tasto, 11).

Bovicelli 1594
Bovicelli, Giovanni Battista. *Regole, passaggi di musica, madrigali, e motteti passeggiati [...]*, Venice, G. Vincenti, 1594.

Brown 1976
Brown, Howard Mayer. *Embellishing 16th-Century Music*, London, Oxford University Press, 1976 (Early Music Series, 1).

Burmeister 1993
Burmeister, Joachim. *Musical Poetics*, (1606), translation, with introduction and notes by Benito V. Rivera, New Haven-London, Yale University Press, 1993 (Music Theory Translation Series).

Butt 1991
Butt, John. 'Improvised Vocal Ornamentation and German Baroque Compositional Theory: An Approach to "Historical" Performance Practice', in: *Journal of the Royal Musical Association*, CXVI/1 (1991), pp. 41-62.

Castello 1629
Castello, Dario. *Sonate concertate in stil moderno [...] a 1. 2. 3. Et 4. voci, Libro secondo*, Venice, Gardano appresso Bartolomeo Magni, 1629.

De Selma 1638
Selma y Salaverde, Bartolomé de. *Canzoni fantasie e correnti da suonar ad una 2. 3. 4. Con basso continuo, Libro primo e secondo*, Venice, Magni, 1638.

Del Buono 1641
Del Buono, Gioanpietro. *Canoni obblighi et sonate in varie maniere sopra l'Ave Maris Stella*, Palermo, Ant. Martarello et Santo d'Angelo, 1641.

Erig 1979
Italian Diminutions: The Pieces with more than One Diminution from 1553 to 1638, edited by Richard Erig and Veronika Gutmann, Zurich, Amadeus, 1979 (Prattica Musicale, 1).

Fontana 1641
Fontana, Giovanni Battista. *Sonate a 1. 2. 3. per il violino, o cornetto, fagotto, chitarrone, violoncino, o simile altro istromento*, Venice, Bartolomeo Magni, 1641.

GATTI 2014
GATTI, Enrico. '«Però ci vole pacientia»: un excursus sull'arte della diminuzione nei secoli XVI, XVII e XVIII «per uso di chi avrà volontà di studiare»', in: ACCIAI, Giovanni – GATTI, Enrico – TAVELLA, Konrad. *Regole per ben suonare e cantare: diminuzioni e mensuralismo fra XVI e XIX secolo*, Pisa, ETS, 2014 (Quaderni del Conservatorio 'Giuseppe Verdi' di Milano, n.s. 2/2014), pp. 71-188.

GERHARD 1968
GERHARD, Singer. *Ludovico Zacconi's Treatment of the "Suitability and Classification of All Musical Instruments" in the «Prattica di Musica» of 1592*, Ph.D. Diss., Los Angeles (CA), University of Southern California, 1968.

HERBST 1653
HERBST, Johann-Andream. *Musica moderna prattica, overo Maniera del buon canto. Das ist: Eine kurtze Anleitung wie die Knaben und andere so sonderbahre Lust und Liebe zum Singen tragen auff jetzige italienische Manier [...] können informirt und unterrichtet werden*, Frankfurt, A. Hummen, 1653.

HONEA
Lodovico Zacconi. Prattica di Musica (1596), Part 1, Book 1, Chapter 66, 'Che stile si tenghi nel far di gorgia, & dell'uso de i moderni passaggi', translated by Sion M. Honea, at <https://www.uco.edu/cfad/files/music/zacconi-prattica.pdf>, accessed November 2018.

ROGNONI 1592
ROGNONI, [ROGNONO, ROGNIONO], Riccardo. *Passaggi per potersi essercitare nel diminuire*, Venice, Vincenti, 1592.

ROGNONI 1620
ROGNONI, Francesco. *Selva de varii passaggi [...]*, (1620), edited by Alessandro Bares, Albese con Cassano (Como), Musedita, 2014.

ROTEM forthcoming
ROTEM, Elam. 'The Carlo G Manuscript. New Light on Early 17th-Century Accompaniment and Diminution Practices', in: *Basler Jahrbuch für historische Musikpraxis XXXIX-2015*, forthcoming.

SANGUINETTI 2012
SANGUINETTI, Giorgio. *The Art of Partimento: History, Theory, and Practice*, Oxford-New York, Oxford University Press, 2012.

SCHWENKREIS 2018
Compendium Improvisation: Fantasieren nach historischen quellen des 17. und 18. Jahrhunderts, edited by Markus Schwenkreis, Basel, Schwabe Verlag, 2018 (Scripta, 5).

SEVERI 1615
SEVERI, Francesco. *Salmi passaggiati per tutte le voci [...]. Libro primo*, Rome, N. Borboni, 1615.

SMITH 2011
SMITH, Anne. *The Performance of 16th-Century Music: Learning from the Theorists*, Oxford-New York, Oxford University Press, 2011.

Spiridionis 1670
Spiridionis a Monte Carmelo. *Nova instructio pro pulsandis organis, spinettis, monuchordiis, pars prima*, Bamberg, Immel, 1670.

Tosi 1723
Tosi, Pier Francesco. *Opinione de' cantori antichi e moderni*, Bologna, Lelio dalla Volpe, 1723.

Tosi 1967
Id. *Observations on the Florid Song*, translated into English by John Ernest Galliard, London, William Reeves, 1967.

Zacconi 1592
Zacconi, Lodovico. *Prattica di musica* […], Venice, G. Polo, 1592.

Written Outlines of Improvisation Procedures in Music Publications of the Early 17th Century
The Second (1611-1623) and Third (1615-1623) Book of Concerti By G. Ghizzolo and the Motet Iesu Rex Admirabilis (1625-1627) by G. Frescobaldi

Marina Toffetti
(Università di Padova)

> *And now the miracle is that this life,*
> *presenting itself immediately, streaming forth and acting spontaneously,*
> *expresses itself in a content given and shaped elsewhere.*
> Georg Simmel, *Toward the Philosophy of the Actor*[1]

Just as the script of the 'commedia dell'arte' (not by chance also called 'commedia all'improvviso', or 'commedia improvvisa', to underline its intrinsically improvisational nature) limits itself to sketching the main sequence of events and indicating the entrances and exits of the various characters, without fixing the individual lines in writing (which will be integrated extemporaneously by the actors), in the same way the musical text simply provides some of the coordinates necessary for its performance, which need to be integrated by the creative input of the performer.

While, however, all musical repertoires offer interpreters a relative freedom in terms of agogics, dynamics and expression, there are phases and repertoires in which the performer is required to provide a more significant contribution, which goes beyond the choice of how to interpret the indications provided by the composer — which are usually relatively prescriptive as far as the pitch and duration of the notes are concerned, and more indicative with regards the agogic-dynamic aspect of the performance — involving a sort of 'completion' of the compositional plan of the composer by means of extemporary integrations to the melodic texture (with an embellishing or diminutive function) and/or the harmony (with a supporting function) of the composition.

One such phase is the Baroque period, not by chance defined as the «age of the basso continuo': it comes as no surprise, then, that it is precisely the basso continuo that represents one of the elements of 17th- and 18th-century compositions which most places the performer in the dual role of performer and composer-improviser[2].

---

[1]. Simmel 1920-1921, p. 13.
[2]. See Gatti 2014.

Marina Toffetti

The basso continuo consists in an uninterrupted melodic line (hence the adjective 'continuo'), generally set in the low register (thus the noun 'basso'), destined to be played by one or more 'fundamental' instruments and realized harmonically in an improvised manner, through the introduction of chords or variously articulated simultaneous configurations, by one or more 'ornamental' instruments (in the case of multi-voice instruments, like the organ or the harpsichord, one single instrument can carry out both functions)[3].

However, the improvisational (or more precisely elaborative) role of the performer (in this case, of the continuo player) was not limited to the mere realization of the harmonies explicitly indicated in (or simply implied by) the continuo part, but also concerned its own line, which could be played as indicated in the scores, but which was frequently re-elaborated in a variously 'articulated' manner, leaving us to suppose that, over and above what was prescribed by the composer, the continuo player tended, in fact, to perform it in a different way each time.

What most interests us here is the fact that certain traces of this usage can be found within some editions of the period, and in particular by comparing different editions of the same collection (or of the same composition). When faced with such variants, one must ask oneself whether they are the will of the composer (that is, whether the composer had changed his intentions and had deliberately made some more or less substantial changes to the continuo line in the new edition), or whether they are presumably ascribable to someone other than the composer (for example the music publisher, who may also have made the changes for extra-musical reasons). In these cases, depending on the circumstances, the most appropriate editorial strategy needs to be chosen. Moreover, one must also determine whether the variants found in the basso continuo lines might supply information useful for the modern performer and thus *if*, and if deemed appropriate, *how* they should be restituted in a modern edition.

---

[3]. On the problems posed by the realization of the basso continuo see the 18th-century treatises by Agostino Agazzari (AGAZZARI 1607) and Francesco Bianciardi (BIANCIARDI 1607). Some suggestions of a practical nature, accompanied by short musical examples, can be found in the short manual by the 'Professore della musica' Pietro Paolo Sabbatini published in Rome in the mid-17th century (see SABBATINI 1650, pp. 16-18, 'Modo per sonare il basso continuo per li principianti') and in *Li primi albori musicali* by Lorenzo Penna (PENNA 1672-1679-1684). See RISM B/VI, p. 743d. The treatises of the 18th century are more copious and include those by Michael de Saint Lambert (SAINT LAMBERT 1707), *L'Armonico pratico al cimbalo* by Francesco Gasparini (GASPARINI 1708), the *Principes de l'accompagnement du clavecin* by Jean-François Dandrieu (DANDRIEU 1718), the *Versuch einer Anweisung die Flote traversiere zu spielen* by Johann Joachim Quantz (QUANTZ 1752), *Le maitre de clavecin pour l'accompagnement* by Michel Corrette (CORRETTE 1753), the *Versuch uber die wahre Art das Clavier zu spielen* by Carl Philipp Emanuel Bach (BACH 1753-1762), *Li primi albori musicali* by Lorenzo Penna (PENNA 1672-1679-1684), the *Pratica d'accompagnamento sopra bassi numerati e contrappunti a più voci sulla scala maggiore e minore* by Stanislao Mattei (MATTEI 1788), the treatise *Thorough-bass Made Easy: Or Practical Rules for Finding and Applying Its Various Chords With Little Trouble* by Nicolò Pasquali (PASQUALI 1757), while at the beginning of the 19th century it must be remembered *The Singer's Preceptor: A Treatise on Vocal Music Calculated to Teach the Art of Singing* by Domenico Corri (CORRI 1810).

Written Outlines of Improvisation Procedures in Music Publications

This article offers a reflection on the consequences that this peculiar relation between the fixed text and its extemporary realization in performance might have in editing a musical edition of compositions from the first half of the 17th century. It is an issue that has already been dealt with, first and foremost by taking into consideration the great deal of information on performance practice deducible from indirect coeval sources (manuals on realizing the basso continuo, theoretical treatises, descriptions of musical performances, iconographic sources of various kinds). The intention here is firstly to examine the information available from direct musical sources — namely the actual musical editions — focusing in particular on the information that be gleaned from a comparison of the first editions and the later reprints or re-editions. This will highlight how a new edition of a given musical collection could be transformed (and in fact this was often the case) into an opportunity to introduce corrections or to make changes to previously published works, *and in particular to the line of the basso continuo*. Setting aside the question of who was responsible for such changes, one needs to ask if, and to what extent, they might reflect aspects of coeval performance practice.

Although this peculiar relation between the written text and performance practice that was created in the 17th- and 18th-century repertoire does not bring about any radical transformation in the role of the music philologist (whose task will remain that of publishing scientifically grounded critical editions, attempting to reconstruct a text that is as close as possible to the last will of the composer) or in that of the performer (who will continue to have the task of proposing the repertoire in the context of live concerts or recordings), we nevertheless believe that it highlights the need for a closer collaboration between the editor of the edition and the 'historically informed' performer, both of whom should be intent on comprehending not only what is explicitly prescribed in the text, but also what it implies in terms of extemporary realization. We also think that this repertoire requires a greater awareness on the part of the philologist with respect to all those elements of the ancient edition which, if adequately incorporated in the modern edition, could prove useful in understanding and studying the various aspects of the performance practice of the time, as well as a greater consciousness of what should be fixed (or, on the contrary, *not* fixed) in the modern edition, making sure not to overlook any information that might be potentially useful to the performer, but at the same time not limiting his/her creative-improvisational input. In order to achieve an acceptable balance between these two requirements it could prove useful, at least in some cases, to adopt particular solutions in the presentation of the musical text that may in part be different from those commonly adopted in the restitution of other types of repertoire.

In this context any variants that come to light during the comparison of different editions of the same composition have a dual value, and will thus be examined from a dual perspective: on the one hand, we will consider what the implications might be for the way the musical text is presented in the critical edition (and therefore which elements are worth presenting to the modern user and how to present them); on the other, what impact they might have on performance practice (and therefore how to use this wide but often contradictory store of information deducible from ancient sources for the purpose of interpretation).

It will also be necessary to reflect on the nature of such variants from a strictly philological point of view. Although each case should obviously be examined in its own specific context, it can nevertheless be observed how, broadly speaking, the variants made to the vocal lines tend to be mostly a matter of substitutive variants, while those made to the basso continuo line, where the line is simply 'redesigned' in some of its rhythmic details, can be seen mostly as alternative variants and only rarely substitutive. Which suggests at least two consequences: the first is that the editor should not choose, but should limit him/herself (with appropriate strategies in presenting the text) to reporting all the solutions found in the different editions, so that the modern performer can consider and assess them one by one, drawing his/her own conclusions at an operative level. The second is that, for the purposes of performance, the presence of several alternative solutions does not imply a choice limited exclusively to *those* solutions, but should encourage the modern performer to behave like a performer of the time, that is to say like a performer-composer, able not only to choose between the solutions offered by the editions, but also to elaborate (also spontaneously) further stylistically plausible solutions.

It should be kept in mind that the composers of the early 17th century (including those we are dealing with here) were, in most cases, at the same time composers and performers-improvisers. We can thus imagine that an organist like Frescobaldi, when seated at the organ to realize the basso continuo of a motet (his or someone else's), would behave like any other continuo player of the time, and would therefore realize the part (and elaborate its line) in a different way each time, maybe growing fond of a particular solution that did not necessarily match the one fixed in the edition he was using during the performance. So it should come as no surprise if, in preparing a new edition of a motet, he had preferred to introduce the 'new' continuo line, which he had in the meantime been elaborating (and progressively fixing) under his very own fingers in the course of successive performances. In such cases the border between alternative and substitutive variants can be very flimsy; for this reason the written outlines of this process of elaboration should be reported in the edition and taken into consideration in order to study the performance practice and the creative process (which does not, in fact, mean studying just the genesis of the composition, but also its refinement)[4].

---

[4]. The interest of musicology in sketch-studies and authorial philology, stimulated by the debate on the usefulness of studying preparatory material for the purposes of musical analysis and/or of the critical edition, which emerged on the occasion of the anniversaries of the birth (1970) and death (1977) of Beethoven (see KERMAN 1982) and initially focused on the 19th-century repertoire, later gave way to a deeper reflection on the various aspects of the creative process, covering increasingly wider periods of time and also involving studies on ancient music. Worthy of particular mention on this matter is the pioneering book by Robert

Written Outlines of Improvisation Procedures in Music Publications

The compositions examined in this article are homogeneous both in genre (they are in any case motets, or *concerti*, for few voices and basso continuo), and in chronological range (the musical editions considered were printed in a period spanning from 1611 to 1627). Instead, the questions taken into consideration regard three aspects commonly associated with the sphere of practice: the elaboration of the basso continuo line (and, in some cases, the actual way of playing within, or accompanying a polyvocal work on the instrument), the introduction of diminutions in any vocal part, and the possible modal transposition of the compositions, mostly motivated by necessities of a practical order linked to the circumstances of the performance.

Revision Procedures in the Motets of Giovanni Ghizzolo's Second Book (1611/1623): *Full Score*, *Short Score* and *Basso per l'organo*

The first case examined is Giovanni Ghizzolo's *Concerti all'uso moderno*, first published in Milan by the heirs of Simon Tini and Filippo Lomazzo in 1611[5] and then reprinted in Venice by Alessandro Vincenti in 1623[6]. As I have already mentioned elsewhere, the reprinting of the collection allowed Ghizzolo to substantially revise the compositions previously published, introducing structural variants (such as to modify the form and length of the original compositions) in six motets (from a total of twenty-two)[7]. Of particular interest here are the variants found in the parts for the organist in the successive editions. In the *editio princeps* the part for the continuo player, named *Partitura*, appears as a full-score (notated on four staves) in the first eighteen compositions and as a short-score (notated on two staves) in the last four, whereas in the Venetian reprint the part for the continuo player, named *Basso per l'organo*, is notated on just one stave. Both the *Partitura* of the *princeps*, and the *Basso per l'organo* of the second edition are divided into mostly isochronic bars each with a duration of a *brevis*.

Marshall on the compositional process in the vocal music of Bach, as well as the successive work by Jessie Ann Owens on the creative process in the period from 1450 to 1600 and the recent book by Friedemann Sallis on the function of sketches and preparatory material from 1600 to today. See MARSHALL 1972; OWENS 1997; SALLIS 2015.

[5]. See the *Concerti all'uso moderno a quattro voci* by Giovanni Ghizzolo (GHIZZOLO 1611). The collection, published in separate parts (SATB) and score, has survived in two complete copies (kept respectively in I-Bc and I-VCd) and one copy that consists only of the score (A-Wn). See RISM A/I G 1783. Modern edition: GIOVANNI GHIZZOLO 2010.

[6]. See GHIZZOLO 1623A. The four surviving copies are all incomplete: I-Bc (S missing); I-CEc (S and organ part missing); I-Nc (T) and I-Rsc (S and organ part missing). The part-book of the soprano has not survived in any source. See RISM A/I G 1784.

[7]. On Giovanni Ghizzolo's compositional process and the successive revisions of his motets see TOFFETTI 2018.

Marina Toffetti

The comparison between the part-books of the single voices and the score of the first edition revealed a certain number of variants which could offer some indications about the various ways in which the organist could accompany the voices. See, for example, the summary of the variants between the part-book of the cantus and the cantus part of the score[8]:

TABLE 1: VARIANTS BETWEEN THE PART-BOOK OF THE CANTUS
AND THE CANTUS PART OF THE SCORE (1611)[9]

N.	INCIPIT	BARS/NOTES	SCORE	SEPARATE PART
1	*Pulchrae sunt genae tuae*	15, 4	A♯	A
2	*Domine exaudi*	16, 3	G	G♯
		38	**SB C B**	**CR C B QU C B C D**
5	*Exsurgat Deus*	28, 2-(3)	**CR A**	**QU A B**
6	*O Domine quis habitabit*	59	2 B♯ (♭ in the clef)	B natural
8	*Quemadmodum desiderat*	22	2 CR G♯ tied	Dotted CR G; QU G
		26,	G	G♯
		30, 1-(2)	F	F♯
15	*Laudate nomen Domini*	2, 4	CR G	CR rest, CR G

Although the variants are mostly of a minor entity (especially in the cases where they are simply erroneous omissions, in the score or in the separate parts, of accidentals referring to a single note), in some cases (written in bold in the TABLE) certain rhythmic figurations of the voice have been simplified or slightly modified in the organ score[10]. Moreover, some diminutions have been omitted in the score which are instead written out in full in the part-book of the cantus, meaning that at those points the organist should not double the voice but play a prolonged single note to sustain the more lively figuration of the voice in question. Such seemingly slight discrepancies nevertheless provide elements that can prove valuable in terms of performance practice. If, due to necessity of space or other reasons, it is decided *not* to publish the organ score in full, it would be opportune to indicate in the critical notes *all* the variants present, so as to allow a complete assessment.

Instead, on comparing the line of the bass voice of the *editio princeps* with the lowest part of the score of the same edition, one can observe how the latter mostly traces the vocal line of the bass and generally also respects the rests (when the bass voice is silent): at these points the organist, having the complete score at his disposition, could well have

---

[8]. The TABLE refers to the first eighteen motets of Ghizzolo's collection, with a full-score in the organ part.

[9]. Here, and in the following TABLES, B = breve; SB = semibreve; M = minim; CR = crotchet; QU = quaver; SQ = semiquaver.

[10]. On this topic see also FRESCOBALDI 2002.

played the line that was respectively the lowest. At other points the lowest voice of the score introduces slight rhythmic modifications to the line of the bass, mostly simplifying its profile, or more simply playing a single long note where the bass voice has shorter consecutive notes of the same pitch.

In the line of the *Basso per l'organo* of the second edition things obviously change. Since the organist no longer has a score to follow, he would risk losing his place when the bass voice is silent and find it difficult to realize the continuo. Therefore, at such points the bass line of the organ part behaves prevalently as a basso seguente (tracing the profile of the lowest voice used at that moment in the polyphony, sometimes with rhythmic variants), or else as a true basso continuo (introducing elements different from those of the voice lines with a function of harmonic support), thus guaranteeing the support of the organ even in the sections where the lowest voices are silent. Furthermore, in tracing the voice that is lowest at any given moment, the organ bass line in the reprint simplifies its physiognomy more frequently than in the lowest voice of the score of the first edition, resulting in numerous differences between the two versions.

As for the possible choices for an edition, on encountering variants one would, from a purely theoretic viewpoint, be inclined to respect the version given in the second edition, since it is presumably closer to the last will of the composer (who, it should be remembered, was still alive when the second edition was published). Moreover, in the case of Ghizzolo's second book of motets a particular problem regarding the state of the sources should be kept in mind: the first edition has come down to us in three copies, two of which are complete, while the second edition has survived in four incomplete copies, all lacking the soprano part[11].

Moreover, as mentioned above, in the second edition six motets have been substantially modified on account of variants in the structure, which alter its form and modify its overall length. In these circumstances it seems inevitable that both versions should appear in the edition, given separately in their entirety: the first version taken from the *editio princeps*, the second from the reprint. The soprano part, lacking in the reprint, could simply be omitted in the modern edition; alternatively, in the portions coinciding with the version of the *princeps*, the soprano part could be borrowed from the latter, making sure not only to detail in the introduction to the critical edition the criteria for reconstruction adopted, but also to differentiate this part from the others by means of a sufficiently clear graphic expedient (for example notating it in smaller type compared to the other voices, indicating the text in italics and clearly specifying the provenance of this part at the start of the stave). In the portions where the version of the second edition differs compared to that of the first, one could consider the possibility of reconstructing the missing part by conjecture, differentiating it not only from the other parts, but also from

---

[11]. The four surviving copies, all incomplete, are kept in the following libraries: I-Bc (S missing); I-CEc (S and organ part missing); I-Nc (T) and I-Rsc (S and organ part missing). See RISM A/1 G 1784.

the remaining portions of the same part, which, as we have said, can be taken from the first edition (for example, placing the portions reconstructed by conjecture in square brackets, and giving an adequate account of the criterion).

In the case of the motets that did *not* undergo any structural modifications, it will be possible to recreate the text based on the only single complete edition (in this case the *princeps*), mentioning in the critical notes the sporadic variants that occur in the vocal lines of the contralto, tenor and bass in the second edition. As we have seen, though, the majority of the variants concern the bass line for the organ. In this case they are mostly alternative variants, which involve octave shifts or slight changes in the rhythmic pattern of the bass line. Variants of this type provide the organist with suggestions about how to proceed, they offer plausible alternatives in the shaping of the bass and are therefore worth including in the critical edition so that they can be adequately considered and assessed by the players. The best way to present such instances will be to reproduce both of the bass lines, one above the other, making the edition more 'transparent' by indicating their relative provenance[12].

Revision Procedures in the Motets of Giovanni Ghizzolo's Third Book (1615/1623): The Problem of Transposition

The history of the transmission of another collection of motets by the same Ghizzolo presents several analogies with that of the previous collection: the *Terzo libro delli concerti* was published first in Milan by Filippo Lomazzo in 1615[13] and was reprinted in Venice by Alessandro Vincenti in 1623[14].

Unlike in the second book, only one concerto from the third book presents a structural variant in its second edition (the motet *Omnes de Saba venient*, of which the concluding section has been modified by Ghizzolo in the 1623 version). This is the only case, then, that will require the edition of the two distinct versions (or, at least, the publication *in extenso* of both versions of the final part, to allow a comparison).

In this collection the greatest point of interest is the comparison between the organ part of the *princeps* and that of the second edition. In this case the part destined for the organist is named *Partitura* both in the *editio princeps* and in the reprint; in the first case, though, it is presented as a short-score (on two staves), while in the second it assumes the form of a basso continuo (on just one stave). Moreover, the score of the *princeps*, in which

---

[12]. An optimal solution could be to transcribe the four voices in a score, including both the organ *Partitura* of the first edition (transcribed onto a double stave), and the single line of the *Basso per l'organo* as it appears in the second edition (remembering to indicate the provenance of this line at the start of the stave).

[13]. Ghizzolo 1615. RISM A/I G 1787.

[14]. Ghizzolo 1623b, RISM A/I G 1788.

the bass part for the continuo player also supports the sections where the vocal bass is silent, has no numbering above the lowest line, whereas the reprint provides some numberings and indicates accidentals useful for the realization of the bass. In addition, the bass part of the reprint contains various melodic variants with respect to that of the *princeps*, similar to those found in the second edition of the motets of the second book: including the transformation of several short notes into a single longer note, the division of a long note into shorter notes, and the inversion of the trend of rising or falling intervals (see Ex. 1; in the following example lines 2 and 3 have been re-transposed *in tono*).

Ex. 1: Giovanni Ghizzolo, *Super flumina Babylonis* (from the *Terzo libro dei concerti*, 1615/1623), bars 21-32.

The most significant aspect, though, is the fact that in the organ part of the first edition all the compositions are notated *in tono* (like the vocal parts), whereas in the reprint the seven motets (out of twenty-three) notated in *chiavette* are transposed down a fourth and/or a fifth (while the vocal parts are in any case notated *in tono*).

In his article on vocal ranges, cleffing and transposition in the sacred music of Giulio Belli, Jeffrey Kurtzman investigated the «relationship between notation and sounding pitch, with regard to transposition of notated pitch levels» considering the question in terms of many interrelated aspects, such as the modes and psalm tones, the use of *mollis* signature, the vocal ranges of contemporary voices, the pitch standards of accompanying organs and other instruments, the notational conventions, and the divergent practices of individual composers[15]. «The particular significance of Giulio Belli for this study», explains Kurtzman, «resides in the fact that a number of his sacred music collections have organ part-books with specific rubrics for transposition for some of the pieces»[16].

In dealing with the «relationship between notation and sounding pitch», Kurtzman focuses not only on the usual conventions of notation, but also on the variation in their usage from one composer to another, in the awareness that «trying to make coherent sense of how composers and performers understood the notation and the issues of transposition and performance is an ongoing process, and the present study is only one further stage in that process»[17].

Considering that Giovanni Ghizzolo's *Terzo libro di concerti* includes precise indications regarding the transposition of certain compositions, it appears useful to compare them with those found in the sacred collections of Giulio Belli and examined by Kurtzman[18].

In assessing the differences between Belli's approach and that of Ghizzolo, it should be remembered that, in most cases, compositions notated in standard clefs (C_1 C_3 C_4 F_4) were usually performed *in tono* or a full step (1 tone) or a minor third downward, while compositions notated in high clefs, or *chiavi alte*, or *chiavette* (G_2 C_2 C_3 C_4 or F_3) were usually performed a fourth or a fifth lower than notated, depending on the pitch standard (according to Adriano Banchieri only a fifth below).

It is interesting to observe that in compositions notated in high clefs, while some composers of the time preferred the transposition to a fourth below, Belli shows a preference for the transposition to a fifth below, specifying on each occasion his precise choice. In the

---

[15]. KURTZMAN 2014, p. 141.
[16]. *Ibidem*.
[17]. *Ibidem*.
[18]. It should also be remembered that both Ghizzolo and Belli belonged to the Order of Friars Minor, and that both had worked at the Veneranda Arca di Sant'Antonio in Padua: Giulio Belli between 1606 and 1608, Giovanni Ghizzolo between 1622 and 1623, leading one to suppose that Ghizzolo may have encountered Giulio Belli's sacred works during his brief period in Padua, from which the reprint of his first book dates.

second edition of Ghizzolo's third book of *concerti*, in such cases both solutions are given, thus leaving open both possibilities.

It should also be pointed out that in the organ parts of Belli's compositions we find both the version *in tono* and the transposed version, while in the organ part of the second edition of Ghizzolo's third book there are one or more transposed versions, but *not* the version *in tono*. More precisely: in the organ part the motets notated in the *cantus mollis* signature we find *only* the version transposed to a fourth below:

Ad te Domine	F *cantus mollis*	4th →	C *cantus durus*
Gaudens gaudebo	G *cantus mollis*	4th →	D *cantus durus*

while the motets notated in the *cantus durus* signature are given in versions transposed a fourth *and* a fifth below, or just a fifth below:

Super flumina	CTB	G *cantus durus* [7th]	4th → D in *cantus durus*
			5th → C in *cantus mollis*
Congratulamini	CAB	G *cantus durus* [7th]	4th → D in *cantus durus*
			5th → C in *cantus mollis*
Confitebor tibi	CATB	A *cantus durus* [10th]	4th → E in *cantus durus* [D♯]
			5th → D in *cantus mollis*
Confitemini gentes	CATB	D *cantus durus* [1st]	4th → A in *cantus durus*
			5th → G in *cantus mollis*
O Domine	CATB	C *cantus durus* [11th]	5th → F in *cantus mollis*

TABLE 2 summarizes the clefs used for each motet, with the relative *finalis* and realization of the bass part in the booklet of the *partitura* of the 1623 edition[19].

---

[19]. The clef is indicated with the letter and the number of the stave (e.g.: C clef in the first stave: C_1). A ♭ indicates the presence of a flat in the clef. The TABLE is taken from TASCHETTI 2016.

Table 2: Giovanni Ghizzolo, *Terzo Libro di Concerti* (Repr. 1623): Transpositions

Incipit	Voices	Clefs	Finalis	Score
For Two Voices				
Indica mihi	Two Cantus, or Tenors	C$_1$♭, C$_1$♭	F	*in tono*
Gaudete et exultate	Two Cantus, or Tenors	C$_1$♭, C$_1$♭	F	*in tono*
O dies infelices	Cantus and Tenor	C$_1$♭, C$_4$♭	G	*in tono*
Vias tuas demonstra mihi	Cantus, and Tenor, Dialogue	C$_1$♭, C$_4$♭	F	*in tono*
Exaudi Deus	Cantus and Bass	C$_1$♭, F$_4$♭	G	*in tono*
Decantabat populus Israel	Cantus and Bass	C$_1$, F$_4$	A	*in tono*
For Three Voices				
Super flumina	Cantus, Tenor and Bass	G$_2$, C$_3$, F$_3$	G	4th ↓, 5th ↓
O quam metuendus	Cantus, Tenor and Bass	C$_1$, C$_4$, F$_4$	G	*in tono*
Paratum cor meum	Cantus, Tenor and Bass	C$_1$♭, C$_4$♭, F$_4$♭	F	*in tono*
Cantabo Domino	Two Cantus or Tenors and Basso	C$_1$♭, C$_1$♭, F$_4$♭	F	*in tono*
Florete flores	Two Cantus or Tenors and Bass	C$_1$, C$_1$, F$_4$	G	*in tono*
Gaudete in Domino	Cantus, Alto and Bass	C$_1$, C$_3$, F$_4$	D	*in tono*
Congratulamini	Cantus, Alto and Bass	G$_2$, C$_2$, F$_3$	G	4th ↓, 5th ↓
For Four Voices				
Confitebor tibi Domine Rex	C, A, T, B	G$_2$, C$_2$, C$_3$, F$_3$	A	4th ↓, 5th ↓
Ad te Domine clamabo	"	G$_2$♭, C$_2$♭, C$_3$♭, F$_3$♭		4th ↓
Exultate iusti in Domino	"	C$_1$♭, C$_3$♭, C$_4$♭, F$_4$♭	F	*in tono*
Iubilate deo omnis terra	"	C$_1$♭, C$_3$♭, C$_4$♭, F$_4$♭	G	*in tono*
Eripe me	"	C$_1$, C$_3$, C$_4$, F$_4$	D	*in tono*
Omnes de Saba venient	"	C$_1$♭, C$_3$♭, C$_4$♭, F$_4$♭	F	*in tono*
Gaudens gaudebo in Domino	"	G$_2$♭, C$_2$♭, C$_3$♭, F$_3$♭	G	4th ↓
Mulier quid ploras	"	C$_1$, C$_3$, C$_4$, F$_4$	F	*in tono*
O Domine semper laudabo te	"	G$_2$, C$_2$, C$_3$, F$_3$	C	5th ↓
Confitemini gentes	"	G$_2$, C$_2$, C$_3$, F$_3$	D	4th ↓, 5th ↓
Letanie B. M. Virginis	C, A, Q, T, B	C$_1$, C$_3$, C$_4$, C$_4$, F$_4$	D	*in tono*

Therefore, contrary to what occurs in the collections of most of his contemporaries, in this collection Ghizzolo not only specifies all the transpositions he considers acceptable, but provides the organist with the part *already transposed*, saving him the trouble of having to transpose it extemporaneously: this would certainly make the task easier, but at the same time would limit the possibilities of choice. On the other hand, the organ part of the 1623 edition is not given *in tono*[20]. Without going into who was responsible for such a choice — it could have been either composer or the publisher — what interests us here is how to present these compositions within the modern edition. If, in fact, we consider that the transposition of the compositions was carried out in an extemporaneous fashion, any written outlines of this procedure should be rendered in the modern edition so as not to lose any information that could be drawn from them, without however 'fixing' a single solution, given that at the time more than one would, in some cases, have been possible.

Basically, it is a question of deciding whether to present the composition *in tono*, as in the notation of the vocal parts, or in the transposed version (or else, in the case of the compositions where the organ part appears in a double version, in one of the two transposed versions, or in both). In line with the notational usages of the time, the first solution seems decidedly preferable, leaving any transpositions made necessary for contingent reasons to the practical realm (such as the comfort pitch of the choir, the instruments used for any doubling or substitutions, or even the diapason of the organ used to accompany the voices). By opting for the solution of transcription *in tono*, it will then be necessary to re-transpose the organ part and place it beneath the vocal parts in the score. Nevertheless, it would be opportune to also publish, possibly in an appendix, the transposed version (or the two different transposed versions) of the organ part.

A further issue remains to be resolved: the comparison between the organ bass line of the *editio princeps* and that of the second edition revealed a fair number of variants, mostly of an alternative nature, as if the new edition had become an opportunity to introduce different versions reflecting alternative ways of performing the same line. Moreover, in the cases where the organ part of the 1623 edition presents *two different transpositions*, these differ in numerous details not only from the version of the organ part appearing in the first edition, but also from each other. In other words, while in the case of nineteen motets we have *two different bass lines for the organ*, for the four motets where the organ part in the second edition has two possible transpositions, to the fourth and the fifth below (*Super flumina*, *Congratulamini*, *Confitebor tibi* and *Confitemini gentes*), we have as many as *three organ bass lines* that are certainly very similar, but nevertheless slightly different from one another. So which of the two (or three) versions should we choose to present in the score beneath the vocal parts? Since there appear to be no reasons to prefer one version to the other, any choice would be purely arbitrary (and still more arbitrary would be any contamination between the different versions). Given this situation, it seems reasonable to present *all* the versions of the bass in the score: the one notated *in tono* in the first edition, and the one (or ones) notated at a fourth and/or fifth below in the second edition (after re-transposition *in tono*). This solution, although quite costly in terms of space, presents the

---

[20]. The choice to present the organ part in this way could perhaps be ascribed to the publisher, who wished to make his edition as appealing as possible, also in virtue of these strategies aimed at simplifying the task of the organist.

no small advantage of allowing a synthetic view of all the versions available, thus making their comparison much simpler.

In such a case the potentials of an electronic edition (which the performer could also access with a tablet) could be of great help in the presentation of the musical text, making it possible to visualize *all* the solutions (*in tono*, or transposed to the fourth and/or the fifth below) in the study phase, and then being able to obscure them during the performance, without effecting the transparency criteria of the critical edition.

Revision Procedures in the Two Editions of Girolamo Frescobaldi's Motet *Iesu Rex Admirabilis* (1625-1627)

Revisions in the Basso Continuo Line

In the context of the issues dealt with here, a particularly interesting case is that of Girolamo Frescobaldi's motet *Iesu Rex admirabilis*, which first appeared within the *Sacri affetti*, a miscellaneous collection compiled by Francesco Sammaruco, published in Rome by Luca Antonio Soldi on the occasion of the 1625 jubilee and which survives complete[21]. The same motet reappeared two years later, with numerous modifications, in the only individual collection of motets by Frescobaldi that has survived, the *Liber secundus diversarum modulationum*, published in Rome by Andrea Fei and come down to us without the *cantus secundus*[22].

The interesting aspect of this motet is that it is the only vocal work by Frescobaldi which has reached us in two different editions, and thus the only one allowing us a glimpse into Frescobaldi's approach to writing vocal music especially in the phase of revision, which is in itself no less relevant or significant than the gestational phase of the creative process. In addition, the examination of the double version of this motet allows us to deepen

---

[21]. See *Sacri affetti* 1625; RISM B/I 1625¹. The anthology has survived in two copies, the first of which (kept in the Museo internazionale e biblioteca della musica in Bologna) is complete, while the second (kept in the Biblioteca comunale Luciano Benincasa in Ancona) contains only the Bass part.

[22]. See *Liber secundus diversarum modulationum* 1627; RISM A/I F 1853. Partial modern edition edited by Christopher Stembridge: Frescobaldi 1987. The motet *Iesu Rex admirabilis* and another three motets by Frescobaldi included in three different Roman anthologies (*Peccavi super numerum*, *Angelus ad pastores* and *Ego sum panis vivus*) have been published in another modern edition edited by Lorenzo Ghielmi and Mario Valsecchi (Frescobaldi 1983). This collection, which survived without the *cantus secundus*, was recently published in a critical edition edited by Marco Della Sciucca and Marina Toffetti, with a complete reconstruction of the missing part, in the context of the *opera omnia* of the composer (Frescobaldi 2014). To avoid any undue *contaminatio* between the two versions, which present several variants, the incomplete version of 1627 was included with the other motets of the *Liber secundus*, while the complete version of 1625 was reported in its entirety in an appendix. The criteria adopted for the reconstruction of the missing part are described in Toffetti 2013.

our knowledge on certain aspects of Frescobaldi's technique and style as a composer of sacred vocal music, an area that remains one of the least studied within the otherwise vast literature on Girolamo Frescobaldi's output[23].

As well as *Iesu Rex admirabilis*, another three motets by Frescobaldi had appeared in Roman anthologies of the time: *Peccavi super numerum*, included in Fabio Constantino's *Selectæ cantiones* published by Bartolomeo Zannetti in 1616[24]; *Angelus ad pastores*, in *Scelta di motetti* again compiled by Constantino and published by Zannetti in 1618[25]; and *Ego sum panis vivus*, in the collection *Lilia campi* compiled and published by Giovanni Battista Robletti in 1621[26]. Why, then, does only the motet *Iesu Rex admirabilis* appear in the *Liber secundus*? We might suppose that Frescobaldi was particularly fond of this motet — the composition produces, in fact, a great impact on the listener on account of its extraordinary effectiveness in rendering the affects[27]. On the other hand, it cannot be ruled out that the other three motets, or at least some of them, had already been reprinted in the now lost 'Liber primus', which is hypothesized to have been published before 1627, when the surviving *Liber secundus* was published.

As has already been documented, the edition of the *Sacri affetti*, in which the motet *Iesu Rex admirabilis* appears for the first time, contains numerous misprints and inaccuracies in all the fascicles[28]. One reason that prompted Frescobaldi to have this particular motet reprinted may have been the simple wish to see it published in a more correct form. Whatever the case, the inclusion of this motet in his individual collection clearly became an opportunity to revise the whole composition, introducing numerous modifications of various kinds. As a result, the comparison between the two versions not only allows a deeper insight into Frescobaldi's creative process, but also raises other questions regarding the relation between the written composition and its improvised realization.

---

[23]. See ROCHE 1986; LUISI 1986; STEMBRIDGE 1986.

[24]. See *SELECTÆ CANTIONES* 1616; RISM B/I 1616¹. Frescobaldi's composition is for two sopranos, tenor and basso continuo.

[25]. See *SCELTA DI MOTETTI* 1618; RISM B/I 1618³. Frescobaldi's motet is for two voices, cantus, tenor and basso continuo.

[26]. See *LILIA CAMPI* 1621; RISM B/I 1621³. Frescobaldi's composition is for two sopranos, tenor and basso continuo.

[27]. As far as the form is concerned, the motet *Iesu Rex admirabilis* has a very fragmented structure, characterized by the use of frequent cadenzas. In the opening section there is a cadenza after each word: the first after «Iesu», the second after «Rex», the third after «admirabilis». As happens in many coeval works, here too there is an alternation between different constructive techniques and ensemble combinations: the *incipit*, for example, opens with an imitative episode on the word «Iesu», and is followed by a homorhythmic passage on the words «Rex admirabilis», an imitative episode on the words «et triumphator nobilis», a passage for two cantos on the word «dulcedo», and an imitative episode based on a more sprightly motive on the words «ineffabilis». In addition, as in several motets and in many multi-instrumental canzonas by Frescobaldi, here too there are two sections in ternary mensura, using a harmonic-vertical compositional technique.

[28]. See FRANCHI 2006, pp. 504-506: 505.

The comparison between the surviving parts highlighted numerous variants in the basso continuo part as well as in those of the cantus and tenor. Generally speaking, the composition published in 1627 does not simply represent (as one might have expected) a 'more correct' redaction of the previous one, but introduces many slight modifications that fix certain improvisation procedures — especially in the basso continuo part — which would otherwise have remained confined to the realm of performance practice, and in so doing offers an alternative version to the one published two years before. In its double guise, this motet therefore allows us to integrate what has already been learned about Frescobaldi's *modus operandi* from the study of the multiple versions of his instrumental canzonas[29].

To the line of the studies devoted to creative process mentioned previously[30] we can add the two studies by Niels Martin Jensen and John Harper on the revision of Frescobaldi's first book of instrumental canzonas, published first in Rome in 1628 in two separate editions — that of Masotti in a score[31] and that of Robletti in separate parts[32] — and later reprinted in Venice in 1635 (1634 *more veneto*)[33]. The two essays investigate the recomposition procedure, almost certainly attributable to the same composer, which was applied to numerous canzonas[34], leading in various cases to a significant expansion of the form[35]; they also reveal how, irrespective of the type of variants introduced, the canzonas that present the greatest number of interventions are those for one or two basses and basso continuo[36], which allows us to understand that in the 1620s Frescobaldi was dedicating particular attention to the study of the relation between the lowest respective voice and the instrumental bass support, experimenting with various different solutions.

The types of revision highlighted in these studies range from structural modification (involving the addition, removal, re-working or shifting of entire sections) to the rewriting

---

[29]. See JENSEN 1986; HARPER 1987. See also HARPER 1975.

[30]. See note 4.

[31]. See FRESCOBALDI 1628A; RISM A/I F 1869. The edition includes 37 canzonas.

[32]. See FRESCOBALDI 1628B; RISM A/I F 1868. The edition includes 35 canzonas, 34 of which also appear in the score printed in the same year by Masotti, while one is not present. For the contents of the three editions of the *Primo libro* see HARPER 1987, p. 271, Table 1.

[33]. See FRESCOBALDI 1634; RISM A/I F 1870. The edition includes 40 canzonas, 10 of which do not appear in the score printed in 1628 by Masotti, and does not include 8 canzonas present in Masotti's score. See HARPER 1987, p. 271. Critical edition by Étienne Darbellay: FRESCOBALDI 2002. Among the practical editions the following volumes are worthy of mention: FRESCOBALDI 1933; FRESCOBALDI 1959; FRESCOBALDI 1966A and FRESCOBALDI 1966B; FRESCOBALDI 1969-1970; FRESCOBALDI 1966A; FRESCOBALDI 1974-1977.

[34]. Among the canzonas that appear both in the score and in the 1635 edition, thirteen present only minor modifications, while seventeen have been substantially and extensively reworked. See HARPER 1987, pp. 270-271.

[35]. See JENSEN 1986, p. 323.

[36]. See HARPER 1987, p. 277.

of one or more voices[37], the basso continuo being the part most commonly affected. Some changes show a new conception of style, no longer anchored on polyphonic writing, but oriented towards a more modern approach, with frequent echo effects and chromaticisms and a greater number of textural combinations[38]. As in the instrumental canzonas, also in the motets of the *Liber secundus diversarum modulationum* we find vestiges of late-Renaissance usages alongside a clear assimilation of more up-to-date styles[39]: this happens especially in the motets for three or four voices and basso continuo, in which the availability of a richer palette of timbres allowed the composer to try out novel textural combinations creating contrasting effects of colour.

Jensen focuses mainly on the canzonas for one voice and basso continuo and compares them with the coeval solo sonatas by the principal exponents of violin literature in the early 17th century, with particular attention to the changes made to the basso continuo line. In the 1635 edition the basso continuo is often simplified and modified on the basis of harmonic criteria, it is less linked to the other parts and, in some passages, is transposed an octave down — perhaps in view of its realization at the organ. Moreover, in the second version, the continuo often no longer acts as a basso seguente, but assumes the function of providing a harmonic support to the composition[40].

The comparison between the different versions of the canzonas highlighted elements that proved useful in understanding the nature of the interventions introduced, in the same period or in the immediately preceding years, in the second version of the motet *Iesu Rex admirabilis*. Conceived in the same period, the *Liber secundus diversarum modulationum* and *Il primo libro delle canzoni* present a similar structure, underpinned by the criterion of a progressive thickening of the texture, from one to four voices and basso continuo[41]. Despite being, still today, among the least studied and performed works of Frescobaldi[42], these two collections, both produced in a phase of experimentation and stylistic transition, are of particular historic and aesthetic interest, as testified by the musical quality of many of the compositions contained within them, including the motet *Iesu Rex admirabilis*.

---

[37]. See *ibidem*, p. 272.

[38]. See *ibidem*, p. 276.

[39]. See the concluding remarks of the introduction to the critical edition of the *Liber secundus* published in the series of Frescobaldi's *opera omnia*: «Frescobaldi's motets reveal the hand of a gifted composer, well versed in the art of imitation, and at the same time are characterized by a style that is not only modern but also decidedly original, arising from the fusion between a strictly observed counterpoint and a monodic style featuring an extensive use of diminutions and particular care for the rendering of the *affetti* evoked by the text». See FRESCOBALDI 2014, p. lxxxiii.

[40]. See JENSEN 1986, p. 322.

[41]. See STEMBRIDGE 1986, pp. 195-213.

[42]. This situation, which Niels Martin Jensen already noted thirty years ago, is still true today. See JENSEN 1986, p. 315.

Unlike in the different versions of the instrumental canzonas, in the motet *Iesu Rex admirabilis* Frescobaldi did not make any changes to the structure; on the contrary, the variants, often introduced in a single voice, involve passages lasting a maximum four semibreves[43]. The examination of these changes allow us to focalize on the concluding phases of the creative process, showing us a Frescobaldi intent on refining a composition that had already been published and defining it more precisely in some small details. As in the instrumental canzonas, in this motet too the part most affected by the revision what that of the basso continuo.

Out of a total of twenty-six variants found between the two versions, sixteen involve the basso continuo part, seven the cantus part and three that of the tenor; apart from these, is reasonable to imagine that Frescobaldi made some changes (which in philological terms would be defined 'compensatory variants', introduced to balance the other interventions) also to the cantus part that, in the second edition, has been lost. It should, in fact, be underlined that the lack of one part-book prevents us from assessing the overall impact of the variants made to the surviving parts, since it is impossible to establish whether they were accompanied — and possibly balanced — by further modifications in the part that has been lost.

Among the variants found, some simply involve the addition (or elimination) of figuring in the basso continuo or of accidentals (mostly in cadenzas), aimed at specifying the use of one chord instead of another; while others transform a passage in *cantus durus* to one in *cantus mollis*, and are thus interventions of a modal nature. The most significant variants are those involving the melody and/or rhythm, aimed at a greater elaboration (or, on the contrary, a simplification) of a rhythmic-melodic line.

As already observed in the motets of Giovanni Ghizzolo, also in this motet by Frescobaldi most of the variants found in the basso continuo part derive from the need to change the rhythmic profile of the supporting line.

TABLE 3: FRESCOBALDI, *IESU REX ADMIRABILIS*: VARIANTS IN THE BASSO CONTINUO

Bars	1625	1627	Notes
5, I-III [IV]	SB G; dotted M C; SM C	dotted SM G; QU G; M G; SB C	rhythmic variant (greater rhythmic articulation)
7, IV-[V-VI]	QU M	SM E; QU F G	rhythmic-melodic variant; change in the state of the chord (indicated with the number 6); passing notes added
8, II-III [IV-V]	M A¹; M A²; dotted CR E; QU F	SB A; M E	rhythmic variant (simplification: octave shift removed); rhythmic-melodic modification (passing note removed)

---

[43]. As we have seen, it is not possible to establish whether in the version published in 1627 Frescobaldi also introduced variants in the *cantus secundus* part, which is now lost.

9, I [II]	M G²; M G¹ M	SB G	rhythmic variant (simplification: octave shift removed); figuring removed
13, III [IV]	M C³ M; M C²	SB C³	rhythmic variant (simplification: octave shift removed)
14, I-II	SB F¹; F²	SB F² ; D	change of octave; melodic variant
18, I [II]	B G	dotted SB G; M G	rhythmic variant (greater rhythmic articulation)
22, I [II]	dotted B G	B G; SB G	rhythmic variant (greater rhythmic articulation)
24, III	SB A² SB	SB A¹ SB	octave changed (and relative numbering removed)
25, I-IV	SB A¹; [M D]; CR A² [D]	SB A² SB; [M D]; CR A¹ [D]	octave change
26, I	G²	G¹	octave change (relative numbering added or removed)
31, I [II]	C C	B C	rhythmic variant: simplification (repeated note removed)
34, I [II]	F F	B F	rhythmic variant: simplification (repeated note removed)
36, I [II]	B E SB E	dotted B E	rhythmic variant: simplification (repeated note removed)
37, I-IV	SB A; CR A F	M A; dotted M A; CR F♯	rhythmic variant (repeated note added); melodic variant (accidental added); numbering removed
39, IV [V-VI]	M G²	CR G² SM; QU F E	melodic variant (two passing notes added that double the tenor line)

In some cases the changes made to the bass line introduce a greater rhythmic articulation, as happens in bar 5, where the basso becomes more animated and proceeds homorhythmically with the other voices (see Ex. 2). In the same passage, however, Frescobaldi has removed the repetition on the second *brevis*, evidently satisfied with the effect created by the polyrhythmic overlapping of the upper voices.

Ex. 2: *Iesu Rex admirabilis*, bar 5.

2a (1625)

2b (1627)

In other cases the changes make the bass line more elegant, as in the following example where the bass, thanks to what we might nowadays call a different inversion of the triad, proceeds parallel to the highest voice at a distance of a tenth (see Ex. 3).

Ex. 3: *Iesu Rex admirabilis*, bar 7.

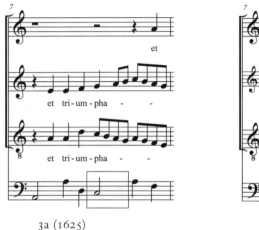

3a (1625)   3b (1627)

Considering that, throughout the composition, the bass line acts at times as a basso continuo and at others as a basso seguente, it could effectively be ruled out that this variant may have been introduced to avoid the parallel octaves (D-D C-C) between the tenor part and that of the basso continuo, even more so given that, in the second version, consecutive unisons (G-G, A-A) are created between same parts[44].

Just as in the coeval instrumental canzonas, also in the motets for 1-4 voices the bass could act both as a basso continuo and a basso seguente. In the first case it was autonomous with respect to the lowest voice and complementary to the upper voices; in the second case it doubled the lowest voice of the polyphonic texture. The passage from one approach to the other could occur not only within the same composition, but also in the same bar, and even in the space of just a few notes.

A similar situation can be observed in other motets from the *Liber secundus diversarum modulationum*. This collection includes six motets for three voices and basso continuo, one of which is divided into a *prima* and *secunda pars*[45]. On examining the relation between

---

[44]. Also in bars 39-40 the 1625 version has a succession of octaves (G-G / F-F), even though separated by two notes each lasting a quaver, while in that of 1627 there is a succession of direct octaves (E-E / F-F).

[45]. See the motets *O sacrum convivium* for two cantus and tenor; *Vox dilecti mei pulsantis* for two cantus and tenor, with the *secunda pars Quam pulchra es, et speciosa Virgo*; *Sic amantem diligite* for alto and two tenors; *Ego flos campi* for two cantus and bass; *Iesu Rex admirabilis* for two cantus and tenor; and *Exaudi nos Deus* for alto, tenor and basso.

the bass and the lowest line in the six motets several passages can be found where, in the space of just a few bars, the organ bass changes its function various times, behaving in a different manner also with respect to the tenor part. This happens, for example, in the opening episode of the motet *Quam pulchra es*, which makes up the *secunda pars* of the motet *Vox dilecti mei*. In the first two bars the bass assumes a complementary role with respect to the upper voices, providing a harmonic support typical of the basso continuo; in the two following bars it doubles the tenor part in unison and thus acts as a basso seguente; it then continues its role as a basso seguente, but moves parallel to the tenor at a distance of an octave; finally, at the words «et speciosa Virgo», it continues to double the tenor at the lower octave, but plays a single long note instead of the series of repeated shorter notes (see Ex. 4).

Ex. 4: *Quam pulchra es*, bars 1-7.

Coming back to the motet *Iesu Rex admirabilis*, the modification made in the following bars (see Ex. 5) involves the simplification of the bass line at a point where the voices have a quite lively profile and is aimed at producing a greater rhythmic contrast between the basso continuo line and those of the three vocal parts.

Ex. 5: *Iesu Rex admirabilis*, bars 8-9.

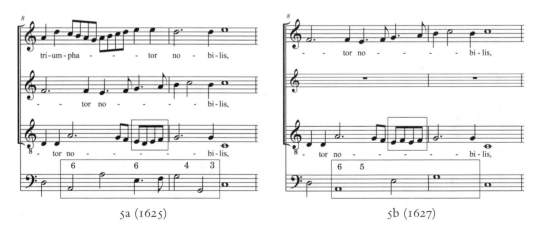

5a (1625) 5b (1627)

While it is true that, generally speaking, the variants introduced in the 1627 version, the outcome of a final careful polishing, offer mostly 'better' solutions[46], it is also true that some of them — particularly those concerning the bass line — could be considered more as alternative than substitutive variants. Examples of such *ad libitum* versions can also be identified in the passages where the revision simply consists of changes in register, frequently involving changes from one octave to the octave higher or lower (see Ex. 6). In the improvised realization of the basso continuo such octave shifts were common practice.

Ex. 6: *Iesu Rex admirabilis*, bars 24-26.

6a (1625) 6b (1627)

Also of interest are the rhythmic modifications made to the bass line in the two episodes in ternary *mensura*, where Frescobaldi appears inclined to adopt different approaches apparently for the sake of variety: in some cases, in fact, a long note in the 1625 version is split into two or more short repeated notes in the 1627 version, while elsewhere precisely the opposite occurs.

Such an approach to composition is by no means an isolated case: on the contrary, it can be considered paradigmatic of Frescobaldi's *modus operandi*. In the section of the motet *Sic amantem diligite* in ternary *mensura*, for example, a similarly erratic behavior can be observed (see Ex. 7).

Ex. 7: *Sic amantem diligite*, bars 26-31.

---

[46]. See, for example, the variants introduced in bars 31, 34 and 36, where the basso continuo is differentiated rhythmically from the vocal parts.

Written Outlines of Improvisation Procedures in Music Publications

As we have said, the *Liber secundus diversarum modulationum* has come down to us incomplete, without the part of the *cantus secundus*. For the complete critical edition of this collection, in the context of the publication of Frescobaldi's *opera omnia*, a reconstruction was made of all the parts missing from the motets that have survived incomplete. The task raised many questions about extremely specific compositional aspects, including the function of the bass, the relation between the bass and the lowest voice at any given moment, as well as the identification of typical harmonic-melodic behaviours, especially in cadenzas. When reconstructing missing parts one tends, understandably, to look in the complete compositions — or in the surviving parts of the composer's incomplete compositions — for corresponding passages (or ones that are as similar as possible) to those to be reconstructed, so as to be able to imitate, as far as possible, the style of the composer. In the case of Frescobaldi, however, this approach did not always prove productive, since his way of working was not, at least apparently, always coherent, but on the contrary tended to approach similar passages in slightly different ways not only in different compositions but also within the same composition. In other words, the fact that at a given point he approached a passage in a certain way does not necessarily mean that he would have adopted the same solution a few bars later or in another composition. For this reason it is not only difficult to deduce 'rules' for the analysis of his works, but even when it was possible to identify them, it did not seem opportune to respect them consistently. In some ways, then, Frescobaldi's writing, being open to alternative solutions, is like the transcription of an extemporaneous improvisation, where the same passage can be played each time in a slightly different way.

In the ternary section of the motet *Sic amantem*, for example, when the voice repeats the same note, the bass tends to unite the two neighbouring notes (see Ex. 8 above). This results in a trochaic rhythm (strong-weak, or long-short), which however is not used right from the beginning: in the first bar the basso continuo doubles the voice (three breves, the first two repeating the same note). Had we found ourselves in the condition of having to reconstruct the basso continuo part, for the sake of homogeneity we would probably have introduced the long-short rhythm right from the start of the ternary episode; but in doing so we would have 'normalized' — and thus in some way betrayed — the composer's improvisatory and extempory style.

On the other hand it should be kept in mind that whoever realizes a basso continuo always has a relatively free hand in interpreting what is written. Phenomena like the splitting of a long note into two short repeated notes, or, on the contrary, incorporating two or more short notes into a longer one, or else changing the octave, are approaches that concern performance practice and are often enacted irrespectively of what is actually fixed on the page. Every continuo player is used to making slight modifications to the rhythm of the bass line, considering what is written as an outline that can be integrated or modified according to one's tastes and taking into consideration the behavior (also spontaneous) of the voices and the specific acoustic conditions of the relative environment[47]. The analysis of Frescobaldi's works that accompanied the task of reconstructing the missing part in the incomplete motets of the *Liber secundus diversarum modulationum* certainly helped us to understand how Frescobaldi, who was used to adopting a relatively free approach when acting as an organist, maintained some of these habits also when he composed, and tended to tackle similar passages in different ways, allowing imagination to prevail over coherence and variety over uniformity.

Changes Made to the Vocal Lines

While the variants introduced in the basso continuo line are mostly alternative ones, and appear to be the result of a fixing in writing of improvisation procedures, the greatest part of the variants introduced in the vocal parts seem instead to be the result of an act of final polishing: most of the variants are improvements, offering us a photograph of the last phase of the creative process.

Let us look, then, in more detail at the discrepancies encountered between the first and second edition in the cantus and tenor parts. A comparison of the two corresponding cantus parts reveals, in the first place, that the part named *cantus secundus* in the 1625 version has become *cantus primus* in that of 1627 (and obviously *vice versa*). There seem to be no reasons for such an exchange, given that the voices are both notated in the soprano clef and have a substantially similar profile[48]. In any case, there are seven variants between the two corresponding cantus parts, of which four simply involve the addition or deletion of accidentals, two modify the rhythm and one helps to define the articulation of the phrase.

TABLE 4: VARIANTS IN THE PART OF THE *CANTUS SECUNDUS* (1625) / *CANTUS PRIMUS* (1627)

Bars	1625	1627	Type of intervention
	Cantus secundus	*Cantus primus*	names of the two upper voices exchanged
6, II-III	QU G F♯	QU G♯ F	accidental moved (accidental added; accidental removed)
12, IV	CR F♯	CR F	accidental removed

---

[47]. On this matter see WESTRUP 1962; BORGIR 1987; CARCHIOLO 2007. Interesting considerations can also be found in ROMAGNOLI 2012. Manuals and teaching tools on the realization of the continuo can, in turn, offer useful points for reflection: CHRISTENSEN 1992; DEL SORDO 2004; ARNOLD 1965. For further bibliographic references see also the site <www.bassus-generalis.org>, accessed November 2018.

[48]. The first *cantus* part in the 1625 version ranges from $C\sharp_3$ to F_4, while the second spans from D_3 to E_4.

Written Outlines of Improvisation Procedures in Music Publications

13, VIII-IX	QU E C	QU E dotted SQ C	rhythmic variant: dotted rhythm introduced
14, VI	QU F♯	QU F	accidental removed
26, III	M F♯	M F	accidental removed
41, I-IV	QU A G A B♭	QU A-G A-B♭, slurred in pairs	two slurs introduced specifying the articulation of the phrase
42, III-IV	QU G F	QU G dotted SQ F	rhythmic variant: dotted rhythm introduced

Some of the variants do not involve any substantial changes: see, for example, the addition of an accidental and the removal, apparently inopportune, of another accidental in an intermediate cadenza[49]. The change made in bar 12 seems instead to respond to a modal expedient: by removing the F♯ on the word «ineffabilis», the passage links more fluidly with the immediately following entry of the tenor. In the next bar there is a rhythmic variant that gives the cantus line greater impetus thanks to the introduction of the dotted figuration (a dotted quaver followed by a semiquaver in place of the two quavers of the previous version)[50].

Ex. 8: *Iesu Rex admirabilis*, bars 12-13.

8a (1625)   8b (1627)

In a later passage Frescobaldi has added some slurs to make the articulation of a motive more precise. In this case it is not so much a modification as an integration that specifies a particular way of playing. A similar occurrence can be found in the tenor part

---

[49]. In the second version of the motet (1627) at bar 6, the first of the two Gs is given a sharp, while the sharp before the following F is not given.
[50]. Similar variants are found in the same part in bar 42 and in the tenor part in bar 16 (see below).

in the immediately following bar; and it is likely that slurs of the same kind were added in bar 40 of the *cantus secundus*, which is now lost (see Ex. 9).

Ex. 9: *Iesu Rex admirabilis*, bars 40-41.

9a (1625)　　　　　　　　　　　　　　9b (1627)

The tenor line, which is the part that undergoes the least reworking, reveals only three variants.

Table 5: Variants in the Tenor Part

Bars	1625	1627	Type of intervention
16, VIII-XI	QU dotted G; SQ A; dotted QU G; SQ A	QU G A G A	rhythmic variant: removal of a dotted rhythm
36, IV-V	M G♯ G	M G G♯	accidental moved
40, I-IV	QU F E F D	QU F-E F-D slurred in pairs	two slurs added to specify the articulation of the phrase

One modification made to the tenor part involves the moving of an accidental in a cadenza. As in a similar variant found in the cantus part[51], here too the intervention does not seem totally appropriate, since in the 1627 version a necessary accidental is missing, which is correctly marked in the previous redaction. In another passage, a rhythmic figure originally based on the dotted figuration is simplified in the new redaction and transformed into a simple group of four quavers (see Ex. 10). While the solution in the 1627 version

---

[51]. See note 49 above.

is in reality more homogeneous with respect to the rhythmic patterns used for the other voices, it should nevertheless be noted that the dotted rhythm present in the 1625 redaction avoided the clash of a second between the A and G in the tenor and *cantus secundus* parts[52].

Ex. 10. *Iesu Rex admirabilis*, bar 16.

10a (1625)

10b (1627)

Finally, as far as the choices to be made in a critical edition are concerned, considering that the motet *Iesu Rex admirabilis* was published twice, and that the surviving second edition is incomplete and contains variants with respect to the first edition, the most appropriate solution, and the one adopted in the *opera omnia* of Frescobaldi, seems to be that of publishing the two distinct versions separately. The presence of numerous variants (which, as we have seen, are not always simple corrections) would make every choice between the two redactions somewhat arbitrary. Given that Frescobaldi was still alive at the time of the second version, included in an individual collection of his works and thus certainly revised by the composer himself, one is inclined to opt for the publication only of the second redaction: but this is the one that has come down to us incomplete. The hypothesis of 'completing' the second version by inserting the *cantus secundus* of the previous version would give rise to a *monstrum*, a composition that never existed (and that was never performed), the outcome of the contamination between two versions that are very similar, but contain a large number of modifications of various kinds. The choice to publish only the first redaction (the only one that has survived complete) would instead deny the reader the chance to assess the nature, extent and significance of the modifications later made by the composer.

---

[52]. Moreover, the tenor part is also involved in the addition of two slurs that specify the articulation of a motive, in analogy with those introduced in the cantus part in the following bar (see Ex. 9 above).

Marina Toffetti

Conclusions

The cases examined — the *concerti* from Giovanni Ghizzolo's second (1611-1623) and third book (1615-1623) and Girolamo Frescobaldi's motet *Iesu Rex admirabilis* (1625-1627) — have highlighted how the publication of a new edition could present an opportunity to review one or more compositions already printed and in particular to re-manage the basso continuo line.

The comparison between successive editions revealed some interesting elements regarding various aspects of performance practice, including the articulation of the basso continuo line and the way of accompanying the voices with the organ (and in particular the strategies to adopt at the points where the voices have diminutions or lively passages), as well as useful information about how to tackle the question of modal transposition in vocal compositions accompanied by the organ.

Taking for granted that the strategies to adopt in an edition should necessarily consider the specific history of transmission of each work (or collection of works) and the greater or lesser significance of the variants emerging from the comparison of sources, certain indispensable criteria should nevertheless be taken into account when preparing a critical edition. In particular, with regards the *restitutio textus* editors should *avoid contaminating two or more distinct versions of the same composition*, mixing parts or portions of one redaction with those of a later one. Two distinct versions of the same work should therefore be published separately, as in the case of the 'structurally' different versions of the motets of the second book — and in one case also of the third — by Giovanni Ghizzolo. Also with Frescobaldi's motet, of which we have two redactions, one complete and another incomplete, it would be opportune to produce two separate editions; though not structurally different, these two versions contain several variants in all the voices, making it impossible to combine them in order to 'recomplete' the second version, which moreover lacks the *cantus secundus*.

In the same way, editors should *avoid fixing elements that were not fixed in the 17th century edition*. Where clear indications about the transposition are specified by captions, clefs or accidentals in the key signature, or else the organ part has been rewritten a fourth and/or a fifth below, in the modern edition the composition should be written *in tono*, as in the notation of the vocal parts in the ancient edition. Moreover, all the indications contained in the ancient edition should be reported in the modern edition (possibly showing the transposed versions of the organ bass in an appendix, either in a reproduction or in a modern transcription), so as to allow the player to draw all possible information not only about the different transpositions suggested by the composer, but also about the different form assumed by the organ bass in the transposed versions. It would, in fact, be a great loss if all this information were to end up in the philologist's bin[53].

---

[53]. See Toffetti 2004.

Written Outlines of Improvisation Procedures in Music Publications

Bibliography

AGAZZARI 1607
AGAZZARI, Agostino. *Del sonare sopra 'l basso con tutti li stromenti e dell'uso loro nel conserto*, Siena, Falcini, 1607.

ARNOLD 1965
ARNOLD, Franck Thomas. *The Art of Accompaniment from a Thorough-Bass as Practised in the XVIIth & XVIIIth centuries*, 2 voll., New York, Dover, 1965 (Dover Books on Music).

BACH 1753-1762
BACH, Carl Philipp Emanuel. *Versuch uber die wahre Art das Clavier zu spielen. Zweiter Teil, in welchen die Lehre von dem Accompagnement und der freyen Fantasie abgehandelt wird*, 2 vols., Berlin, Henning-Winter, 1753, 1762.

BIANCIARDI 1607
BIANCIARDI, Francesco. *Breve Regola per imparar' a sonare sopra il Basso con ogni sorte d'Instrumento*, Siena, s.n., 1607.

BORGIR 1987
BORGIR, Tharald. *The Performance of Basso Continuo in Italian Baroque Music*, Ph.D. Diss., Ann Arbor (MI), UMI Research Press, 1987 (Studies in Musicology, 90).

CARCHIOLO 2007
CARCHIOLO, Salvatore. *Una perfezione d'armonia meravigliosa: prassi cembalo-organistica del basso continuo italiano dalle origini all'inizio del XVIII secolo*, revised edition, Lucca, LIM, 2007.

CHRISTENSEN 1992
CHRISTENSEN, Jesper Bøje. *Die Grundlagen des Generalbaßspiels im 18. Jahrhundert. Ein Lehrbuch nach zeitgenössischen Quellen*, Kassel, Bärenreiter, 1992.

CORRETTE 1753
CORRETTE, Michel. *Le maitre de clavecin pour l'accompagnement, methode theorique et pratique*, Paris, L'Auteur-Bayard-Le Clerc-Castagnère, 1753.

CORRI 1810
CORRI, Domenico. *The Singer's Preceptor: A Treatise on Vocal Music Calculated to Teach the Art of Singing*, London, Chappel, 1810 ca.

DANDRIEU 1718
DANDRIEU, Jean-François. *Principes de l'accompagnement du clavecin*, Paris, Bayard, 1718.

DEL SORDO 2004
DEL SORDO, Federico. *Il basso continuo. Una guida pratica e teorica per l'avviamento alla prassi dell'accompagnamento nei secoli XVII e XVIII*, Padua, Armelin, 2004 (Intelligere & concertare, 1).

FRANCHI 2006
FRANCHI, Saverio. *Annali della stampa musicale romana dei secoli XVI-XVII. Volume I/1: Edizioni di musica pratica del 1601 al 1650*, in collaboration with Orietta Sartori, Rome, IBIMUS, 2006 (ASMUR-Annali della stampa musicale romana / Istituto di Bibliografia Musicale a cura di Saverio Franchi, 1/1).

Marina Toffetti

FRESCOBALDI 1628A
FRESCOBALDI, Girolamo. *In partitura il primo libro delle canzoni a una, due, tre, e ouattro [sic] voci. Per sonare con ogni sorte di Stromenti. Con dui Toccate in fine, una per sonare con Spinettina sola, overo Liuto, l'altra Spinettina è Violino, ouero Liuto, è Violino del Sig. Girolamo Frescobaldi organista in S. Pietro di Roma. Date in luce da Bartolomeo Grassi organista in S. Maria in Acquirio di Roma. Con privilegio*, Rome, Paolo Masotti, 1628.

FRESCOBALDI 1628B
ID. *Il primo libro delle canzoni ad una, due, trè, e quattro voci. Accomodate, per sonare ogni sorte de stromenti*, Rome, Giovanni Battista Robletti, 1628.

FRESCOBALDI 1634
ID. *Canzoni da sonare a una due tre, et quattro voci con il basso continuo*, Venice, Alessandro Vincenti, 1634.

FRESCOBALDI 1933
ID. *Canzoni a due canti col basso continuo: per sonare con ogni sorte di stromenti, für zwei beliebige hohe Instrumente mit Generalbass*, edited by Hans T. David, Mainz, Schott, 1933.

FRESCOBALDI 1959
ID. *6 canzoni*, edited by Gustav Leonhardt, Vienna, Universal, 1959 (Classical Scores Library, 1).

FRESCOBALDI 1966A
ID. *Canzoni per canto solo* e *Canzoni per basso solo: Baßstimme und Generalbaß*, edited by Friedrich Cerha, Vienna-Munich, Doblinger, 1966 (Diletto musicale, Doblinger Reihe Alter Musik, 87).

FRESCOBALDI 1966B
ID. *Canzoni per basso solo: Baßstimme und Generalbaß*, edited by Friedrich Cerha, 2 vols., Vienna-Munich, Doblinger, 1966 (Diletto musicale, Doblinger Reihe Alter Musik, 88-89).

FRESCOBALDI 1969-1970
ID. *Canzonas*, London, Musica Rara, 1969-1970.

FRESCOBALDI 1974-1977
ID. *The Ensemble Canzonas of Frescobaldi*, edited by Bernard Thomas, 4 vols., London, Pro Musica, 1974-1977.

FRESCOBALDI 1983
ID. *Mottetti: a 2 e 3 voci e basso continuo*, edited by Lorenzo Ghielmi and Mario Valsecchi, Bergamo, Carrara, 1983.

FRESCOBALDI 1987
ID. *Mottetti a 1, 2 e 3 voci con continuo*, edited by Christopher Stembridge, Padua, Zanibon, 1987 (Capolavori musicali dei secoli XVII e XVIII).

FRESCOBALDI 2002
ID. *Opere complete. 8: Il primo libro delle canzoni a una, due, tre e quattro voci per sonare et cantare nelle edizioni di Roma 1628 e Venezia 1635 con l'aggiunta di tre canzoni pubblicate nella raccolta Raverij 1608*, edited by Étienne Darbellay, Milan, Suvini Zerboni, 2002 (Monumenti Musicali Italiani, 22).

Written Outlines of Improvisation Procedures in Music Publications

Frescobaldi 2014
Id. *Opere Complete. 11: Liber secundus diversarum modulationum singulis, binis, ternis, quaternisque vocibus* (1627), critical edition and reconstruction of the missing part by Marco Della Sciucca and Marina Toffetti, Milan, Suvini Zerboni, 2014 (Monumenti Musicali Italiani, 26).

Gasparini 1708
Gasparini, Francesco. *L'Armonico pratico al cimbalo*, Venice, Bortoli, 1708.

Gatti 2014
Gatti, Enrico. '«Però ci vole pacientia»: un excursus sull'arte della diminuzione nei secoli xvi, xvii e xviii «per uso di chi avrà volontà di studiare»', in: Acciai, Giovanni – Gatti, Enrico – Tavella, Konrad. *Regole per ben suonare e cantare: diminuzioni e mensuralismo fra xvi e xix secolo*, Pisa, ETS, 2014 (Quaderni del Conservatorio 'Giuseppe Verdi' di Milano, n.s. 2), pp. 71-188.

Ghizzolo 1611
Ghizzolo, Giovanni. *Concerti all'uso moderno a quattro voci. Con la partitura accomodata per suonare. Di Giovanni Ghizzolo nuovamente dati in luce. Libro secondo, et opera settima*, Milan, erede di Simon Tini e Filippo Lomazzo, 1611.

Ghizzolo 1615
Id. *Il terzo libro delli concerti a due, 3 e quattro voci, con le Letanie della B. Vergine a cinque, et la parte per l'organo. Di Giovanni Ghizzolo Maestro di Cappella dell'eccell.mo Sig. Prencipe di Correggio. Opera xii. Nuovamente data in luce*, Milan, Filippo Lomazzo, 1615.

Ghizzolo 1623a
Id. *Il secondo libro de concerti a quattro voci di Giovanni Ghizzolo Maestro di Capella della Veneranda Arca di Santo Antonio di Padova. Nuovamente ristampati, & dall'istesso Auttore corretti, et accomodati in varij lochi. Opera settima*, Venice, Alessandro Vincenti, 1623.

Ghizzolo 1623b
Id. *Il terzo libro delli concerti a due tre e quattro voci, Con le litanie della Beata Vergine a 5 voci, et la parte per l'organo. Di Giovanni Ghizzolo Maestro di Cappella di Santo Antonio di Padova. Opera duodecima nuovamente ristampata et corretta dall'istesso auttore*, Venice, Alessandro Vincenti, 1623.

Giovanni Ghizzolo 2010
Concerti all'uso moderno a quattro voci 1611/1623. Giovanni Ghizzolo OFMConv. (1580c.-1624c.), introduction and transcription by Daniele Gambino, Padua, Centro Studi Antoniani, 2010 (Corpus Musicum Franciscanum, 18/6).

Harper 1975
Harper, John Martin. *The Instrumental Canzonas of Girolamo Frescobaldi: A Comparative Edition and Introductory Study*, Ph.D. Diss., Birmingham, University of Birmingham, 1975.

Harper 1987
Id. 'Frescobaldi's Reworked Ensemble Canzonas', in: *Frescobaldi Studies*, edited by Alexander Silbiger, Durham, Duke University Press, 1987 (Sources of Music and Their Interpretation, 1), pp. 269-283.

JENSEN 1986
JENSEN, Niels Martin. 'La revisione delle canzoni ed il suo significato per la comprensione del linguaggio frescobaldiano', in: *Girolamo Frescobaldi nel IV centenario della nascita. Atti del convegno internazionale di studi (Ferrara, 9-14 settembre 1983)*, edited by Sergio Durante and Dinko Fabris, Florence, Olschki, 1986 (Quaderni della rivista italiana di musicologia, 10), pp. 315-327.

KERMAN 1982
KERMAN, Joseph. 'Sketch Studies', in: *19th-Century Music*, VI/2 (Autumn 1982), pp. 174-180.

KURTZMAN 2014
KURTZMAN, Jeffrey. 'Vocal Ranges, Cleffing and Transposition in the Sacred Music of Giulio Belli', in: *Barocco padano e musici francescani: l'apporto dei maestri conventuali. Atti del XVI Convegno internazionale sul barocco padano (secoli XVII-XVIII) (Padova, 1-3 luglio 2013)*, edited by Alberto Colzani, Andrea Luppi and Maurizio Padoan, Padua, Centro Studi Antoniani, 2014 (Centro studi antoniani, 55. Contributi musicologici del Centro ricerche dell'A.M.I.S., 20), pp. 141-164.

LIBER SECUNDUS DIVERSARUM MODULATIONUM 1627
FRESCOBALDI, Girolamo. *Liber secundus diversarum modulationum singulis, binis, ternis, quaternisque vocibus*, Rome, apud Andream Phæum, 1627.

LILIA CAMPI 1621
Lilia campi binis, ternis, quaternisque vocibus concinnata cum basso ad organum. A Jo. Baptista Robletto excerta atque luce donata, Rome, apud Jo. Baptistam Roblettum, 1621.

LUISI 1986
LUISI, Francesco. 'Il *Liber secundus diversarum modulationum* (1627): proposte di realizzazione della parte mancante', in: *Girolamo Frescobaldi nel IV centenario della nascita* […], op. cit., pp. 163-195.

MARSHALL 1972
MARSHALL, Robert Lewis. *The Compositional Process of J. S. Bach. A Study of the Autograph Scores of the Vocal Works*, 2 vols., Princeton (NJ), Princeton University Press, 1972 (Princeton Studies in Music, 4).

MATTEI 1788
MATTEI, Stanislao. *Pratica d'accompagnamento sopra bassi numerati e contrappunti a più voci sulla scala maggiore e minore*, Bologna, s.n., 1788.

OWENS 1997
OWENS, Jessie Ann. *Composers at Work: The Craft of Musical Composition 1450-1600*, Oxford-New York, Oxford University Press, 1997.

PASQUALI 1757
PASQUALI, Nicolò. *Thorough-bass Made Easy: Or Practical Rules for Finding and Applying Its Various Chords With Little Trouble*, Edinburgh, Nicolò Pasquali-Bremner, 1757.

PENNA 1672-1679-1684
PENNA, Lorenzo. *Li primi albori musicali, libro primo, libro secondo, libro terzo*, Bologna, Monti, 1672, 1679, 1684.

Written Outlines of Improvisation Procedures in Music Publications

Quantz 1752
Quantz, Johann Joachim. *Versuch einer Anweisung die Flöte traversiere zu spielen*, Berlin, Voss, 1752.

RISM A/I
Répertoire International des Sources Musicales, Einzeldrücke vor 1800, 15 vols., Kassel [...], Bärenreiter, 1971-2003.

RISM B/I
Répertoire International des Sources Musicales, Recueils Imprimés XVI-XVII siècles, edited by François Lesure, Munich-Duisburg, Henle, 1960.

Roche 1986
Roche, Jerome. 'I mottetti di Frescobaldi e la scelta dei testi nel primo Seicento', in: *Girolamo Frescobaldi nel IV centenario della nascita* [...], *op. cit.*, pp. 153-161.

Romagnoli 2012
Romagnoli, Angela. '«Con varietà di bei contraponti render vaga la melodia»: The Practice of Basso Continuo with the Brain and the Hands', a panel discussion with Edoardo Bellotti, Nicola Cumer, Thérèse de Goede, Mara Galassi, and Pietro Prosser, in: *Philomusica on-line*, XII (2012), pp. 99-109.

Sabbatini 1650
Sabbatini, Pietro Paolo. *Toni ecclesiastici colle sue intonazioni, all'uso romano. Modo per sonare il basso continuo, chiavi corrispondenti all'altre chiavi generali, et ordinarie, per beneficio de' principianti, date in luce da Pietro Paolo Sabbatini professore della musica. Libro primo, opera decima ottava*, Rome, Lodovico Grignani, 1650.

Sacri affetti 1625
Sacri affetti contesti da di veersi [sic] *eeclentissimi* [sic] *autori, raccolti da Francesco Sammaruco*, Rome, Luca Antonio Soldi, 1625.

Saint Lambert 1707
Saint Lambert, Michael de. *Nouveau traité de l'accompagnement du clavecin, de l'orgue, et des autres instruments*, Paris, Christophe Ballard, 1707.

Sallis 2015
Sallis, Friedemann. *Music Sketches*, Cambridge, Cambridge University Press, 2015 (Cambridge Introductions to Music).

Scelta di motetti 1618
Scelta di motetti di diversi eccellentissimi autori, à 2, à 3, à 4 e à 5. Posti in luce da Fabio Constantini romano, Rome, Bartolomeo Zannetti, 1618.

Selectæ cantiones 1616
Selectæ cantiones excellentissimorum auctorum binis, tenir, quaternisq. vocibus concinendæ, a Fabio Constantino romano insignis Basilicæ S. Mariæ Trans Tyberim musices moderatore, simul collecta, Rome, Bartolomeo Zannetti, 1616.

Simmel 1920-1921
Simmel, Georg. 'Zur Philosophie des Schauspielers', in: *Logos: Internationale Zeitung für die Philosophie der Kultur*, IX (1920-1921), pp. 339-362. English translation by Philip Lawton, *Towards the Philosophy of the Actor*, at <https://papers.ssrn.com/sol3/papers.cfm?abstract_id=2897044>, accessed November 2018.

STEMBRIDGE 1986
STEMBRIDGE, Christopher. 'Questioni di stile nei mottetti di Frescobaldi', in: *Girolamo Frescobaldi nel IV centenario della nascita […], op. cit.*, pp. 195-213.

TASCHETTI 2016
TASCHETTI, Gabriele. *Procedimenti di revisione nelle due edizioni de* Il terzo libro delli concerti *(Milano, 1615 - Venezia, 1623) di Giovanni Ghizzolo*, diss., Padua, University of Padua, 2016.

TOFFETTI 2004
TOFFETTI, Marina. 'Il cestino del filologo. Diasistema, dialisi e detriti del non autentico', in: *Hortus musicus*, V/20 (October-December 2004), pp. 216-217.

TOFFETTI 2013
EAD. 'Restoring a Masterpiece. Some Remarks on the Reconstruction of the Missing Part in Girolamo Frescobaldi's *Liber secundus diversarum modulationum* (Rome, 1627)', in: *Musica Iagellonica*, VII (2013), pp. 5-24.

TOFFETTI 2018
EAD. 'Note sul processo creativo nel primo Seicento: le due edizioni dei Concerti all'uso moderno di Giovanni Ghizzolo (Milano, 1611 - Venezia, 1623)', in: *Barocco padano e musici francescani, II. L'apporto dei maestri conventuali. Atti del XVII Convegno internazionale sul Barocco padano (secoli XVII-XVIII) (Padova 1-3 luglio 2016)*, edited by Alberto Colzani, Andrea Luppi and Maurizio Padoan, Padua, Centro Studi Antoniani, 2018 (Barocco Padano, 9), pp. 287-322.

WESTRUP 1962
WESTRUP, Jack. *The Cadence in Baroque Recitative*, in: *Natalicia musicologica: Knud Jeppesen septuagenario collegis oblata*, edited by Bjørn Hjelmborg and Søren Sørensen, Hafniae, Hansen, 1962, pp. 243-252.

Issues of Performance Practice

«Il n'exécute jamais la Basse telle qu'elle est écrite»: The Use of Improvisation in Teaching Low Strings

Giovanna Barbati
(Città Sant'Angelo, Pescara)

Historical Improvisation, Low Strings Didactic, Partimenti and Solfeggi

Every [...] study that confines itself exclusively to the practical and theoretical sources that have come down to us in writing or print, without taking into account the improvisational element in living musical practice, must of necessity present an incomplete, indeed a distorted picture [...] For there is scarcely a single field in music that has remained unaffected by improvisation, scarcely a musical technique or form of composition that did not originate in improvisatory performance or was not essentially influenced by it[1].

The opportunity to imagine a systematic path for teaching cello or viola da gamba based on improvisation is offered to us from the rediscovery of the didactical and pedagogical practice of partimento[2]. This method was based on learning directly at the keyboard and on the progressive memorization of patterns; it rapidly developed the skill of composing, therefore of improvising, on a given bass. Since low strings have a double function, providing the continuo and *cantus*, it is very likely that also for these instruments a method similar to the partimenti was used; the traces found in the sources may confirm this hypothesis. «*Partimenti*, or instructional basses, were central to the training of European court musicians from the late 1600s until the early 1800s. [...] From seeing only one feature of a particular schema — any one of its parts — the student learned to complete the entire pattern [committing] every aspect of the schema to memory»[3]. In the baroque period besides partimenti were used *solfeggi*, or studies on melody, formed of melodic lines

---

[1]. Ferand 1961, p. 5. See also Todea 2014, p. 30. Moore 1992, p. 61: «Written documentation supports Ferand's position on the importance of improvisation in every musical era of the Western classical tradition excepting the present. Even well into the 19th century it is clear that improvisation remained an indispensable ability for most professional musicians».
[2]. Sanguinetti 2012; Gjerdingen 2007a; Cafiero 1993.
[3]. Gjerdingen 2017a.

on basses and different from those that we use nowadays. «Collections of solfeggi were thus like a lexicon of stylistically favored melodic utterances. For the future improvisor [...] solfeggi provided a storehouse of memorized material»[4]. Teaching improvisation on a given line had been already at the core of musical education: the practice of the *cantare super librum*, that is, the improvisation of other voices on the *tenor*, can be found in many sources from 1475 to 1783 and it is today well documented[5].

The central aim of this article is to look for a historical pedagogical method, a process that probably we can still use today, in the study and in the practice of baroque music, to learn creating *ex tempore* musically relevant expressions in the baroque style. To facilitate the acquisition of this skill, which we regard as fundamental and which we will discuss further in this essay, the suggestion is to supplement the didactical method, so that the interest towards improvisation is cultivated from the beginning, rather than being required at the end of a long training. Probably it is better to set from the beginning an active method based on schemes to elaborate, in which there is room also for the student's creativity within the didactical path. Moreover, we have to consider that music is a language and there are many considerations that advice to learn languages inside meaningful contexts[6]. In order to apply this approach to the pedagogy of a musical instrument, we need to contextualize the 'technical' formulas in musical structures.

During the baroque the term *exercise* had a different meaning, compared to how it is commonly understood today. Sanguinetti describes the concepts of 'exercise' and 'artistic work':

> [In] a nineteenth-century, romantic perspective, [...] every school exercise is only a preparatory work, a sort of gymnastic exercise for fingers and brain, and in no way to be confused with Art, which is inspired by the Spirit. This distinction had no real meaning for the eighteenth century music. In the pre-idealistic world there was a continuous interchange between school and art, and the boundaries between the two realms were indistinct. As W. Dean Sutcliffe writes [...] «The assumption that there is a necessary gulf between the two areas, that one either composes proper music or satisfies pedagogical demands, is creatively and historically unrealistic». [...] A great part of the music we cherish today as masterpieces — Scarlatti's *Essercizi*, Bach's *Well tempered Clavier*, *Klavierübungen*, l'*Orgelbüchlein* [...] originated as school works[7].

---

[4]. GJERDINGEN 2017B.

[5]. HAYMOZ 2017; SCHUBERT 2014; CANGUILHEM 2013. The complete list of the methods on *cantare super librum* has been published within the FABRICA project at the following link: <http://blogs.univ-tlse2.fr/fabrica/files/2014/01/Sources-th%C3%A9oriques-du-chant-sur-le-livre.pdf>, accessed October 2018.

[6]. «Figured bass could provide the vocabulary of chords — the lexicon — for filling the open-choice slots, but a master would be required to teach the large repertory of unitized phrases — the *phrasicon* — needed for fluency. Without the *phrasicon*, the result would sound like the utterances of a nonnative speaker»: GJERDINGEN 2007B, p. 123. See also STROBBE – VAN REGENMORTEL 2012; STROBBE 2014.

[7]. SANGUINETTI 2012, p. 16.

«Il n'exécute jamais la Basse telle qu'elle est écrite»

In the baroque era, exercises were therefore intended as small pieces of different degrees of difficulty. We will follow then the traces of a didactical method in which single learning elements are always integrated in a larger musical context, for instance, a trill in a cadence or an arpeggio in a harmonic progression. First we will consider the improvisational demands of the repertoire; then we will consider some historical evidence and the traces found in documents; we will finally describe our pedagogical proposal. Before examining the sources, however, it is necessary to provide a short enquiry of the terms *composition* and *improvisation*.

The Terms *Composition* and *Improvisation*

> [According to] misguided conceptions of genius and creativity [...] today these are to be understood in terms of striking originality. [...] According to an earlier conception of musical creativity, creative composers learn from the works of their predecessors, [...] Borrowing has been a staple of musical composition since composition began[8].

The difficulty of learning how to operate on the text in accordance with the early performance practice, complying with the rules and the spirit of the baroque musical language, is increased today also by the confusion derived from the change of meaning of the terms *composition* and *improvisation* over time. As concerns composition, in Gjerdingen's opinion «the popular view of the composer — a Romantic view [...] — does not fit eighteenth-century reality [...] the galant composer lived the life of a musical craftsman, [...] who produced a large quantity of music for immediate consumption [...]»[9]; the schematization of courtly musical utterances was so pervasive as to constitute a dominant mode of thought [...] musicians learned, wrote, and taught this way»[10]. Such a concept of composition, as 'elaboration, variation, extension and expansion'[11] of pre-existing elements and patterns within a shared language, not only allows the development of personal formulas within the historical language, but implies a didactic that include these too. The first step in this direction lies in the learning and storage of musical patterns, collected from the repertoire and organised so that they could be later reused, following shared rules[12].

---

[8]. Young 2014, p. 23.
[9]. Gjerdingen 2007a, p. 6.
[10]. *Ibidem*, p. 448.
[11]. Byros 2015, p. 1.
[12]. For 'musical pattern' we mean a *figure*, such as for example a repeated note or a scale fragment, in relation to a chord or to a multiple chords path; combinations are endless, but each style has its own characteristic figures.

To learn to improvise Callahan suggests «a flexible and hierarchical model that draws an explicit distinction between long-range improvisational goals (*dispositio*), generic voice-leading progressions that accomplish these goals (*elaboratio*), and diminution techniques that apply motives to these progressions to yield a unique musical surface (*decoratio*)»[13]. For 'voice-leading' Callahan means a polyphonic writing, to be realized on a keyboard. However, this is not possible on a monodic instrument, except for very short sections: its typical writing is with broken or alternated voices[14], or through the accompaniment of a second instrument. The pair composition/improvisation has been investigated by scholars such as Dalhaus[15] and Canguilhem, which suggested more levels of division into parts between the two poles, as well as for the pair orality/writing[16].

Historical Improvisation Practice: Evidences and Hypotheses

> Then doubts arise, which can be summed up by this objection: how could such a simultaneous improvisation of many people happen without arousing confusion? […] But what is remarkable is that scholars of musical matters look as if they avoid dwelling on that question […] which is very inconvenient […] and perhaps it being doubtful and inconvenient is the reason why they talk about it as much as scholars avoid it[17].

We do not know how baroque cello and viola da gamba players improvised, but it is recognised that it was a widespread practice, 'a solo' and in group. Pietro Della Valle provides a detailed report of the improvisation practice in the baroque orchestra[18]:

> […] those singing and playing well in group have to give time each other, and instead of using too complicated contrapuntal artifices, they have to jest with light imitations. They will show their skill doing again and readily what others

---

[13]. Callahan 2010, p. vii.

[14]. *Cfr.*, *infra*, note 68.

[15]. «Analysed soberly, improvisation almost always relies to a large extent on formulas, tricks of the trade and models […] The improviser must be able to fall back […] on a store of prefabricated parts, which he may indeed modify or combine differently […] The idea that he can commit himself entirely to the vagaries of chance is […] an aesthetically legitimate fiction»: Dahlhaus 1987, p. 268. See also Dahlhaus 2010.

[16]. «While [musicology] has the tendency to define the whole musical production through the screen of the binary opposition improvisation/composition, […] there was a great variety of solutions that the singers found to arrange writing and orality performing these music. […] the musicologist Jean-Yves Hamelin proposed a very useful categorization [among] spontaneous, customary, and compositional practices, while these three categories aren't mutually exclusive»: Canguilhem 2010, pp. 274-275.

[17]. Torchi 1894, p. 8. When not otherwise indicated, translations are by the author of this essay.

[18]. Rose 1965. The orchestral improvisational practice is treated also in Torchi 1894.

did before; then allowing another redoing what they did, and a proper chance,
and so [...] they will show their skill among the others[19].

From the earliest sources of ornamentation practice, we find so many pleas not to diminish[20] and to observe the right rules, that we can imagine this was a habit practised not only by the most skilled musicians, but also by beginners. We will divide the subject depending on the different contexts in which the low string instrument acts: (1) 'a solo' without accompaniment; (2) as principal voice — or *cantus* — to be accompanied; as accompaniment of a *cantus* in two different ways, either (3) within a continuo group which can consist of two or more instruments[21], or (4) alone without additional instruments at the continuo (therefore without harmonic support, a documented setting, but today very seldom used in performances).

1. 'A solo' improvisation, without accompaniment, is one of the basic skills that the baroque musician had, and on which was judged[22]. If keyboard players improvised preludes, canzonas, ricercari, fantasias etc., this also happened with monodic instruments[23], including viola da gamba and cello. We find an example of what they played solo in the testimony of André Maugars, 1639:

> [...] in this worthy house [Leonora Baroni's house] I was induced for the first time to exhibit in Rome. [...] I played *studied things* very well, on the second occasion I gave them so many kinds of *preludes and fantasias* that they really granted me more appreciation than the first time. [But] the experts doubted if I were capable of *extemporising a theme and playing variations on it*. [...] The next day I was given fifteen to twenty notes, in order to make myself heard [...] with the accompaniment of a small organ. *This subject I treated with such infinite variety* that great satisfaction was shown[24].

---

[19]. DELLA VALLE 1763, p. 254.
[20]. ESSES 1992, p. 4; COLLINS 2001, pp. 142-146.
[21]. Usually with the cello or the viola da gamba we find an harpsichord and/or a theorbo, or we can add in a wider context more bass instruments like the double bass, the bassoon, or harmonic ones like harp etc.
[22]. «It's above all preluding that the great Musicians [...] let shine those cultivated modulations that ravish the Listeners. It's there that it's not enough to be a good Composer, nor to well dominate the Harpsichord [...] but that it is still necessary to abound in this fire of genius & this inventive spirit»: ROUSSEAU 1768, *sub voce* 'Preluder'. «[It] is the perfection of the viol [if] a man may show the excellency both of his hands and his invention»: SIMPSON 1665, p. 27. Cfr., *infra*, note 24.
[23]. «[...] the Prélude has to be produced on the spot without any preparation, and [...] it includes a countless variety»: HOTTETERRE 1719, p. 3.
[24]. The text continues: «[in Rome] it is thought here that we are not capable of *improvising on a given theme*. In fact, whoever plays an instrument deserves no *extraordinary consideration*, unless he shows himself equal to such a demand»: WASIELEWSKI 1894, pp. 13-15 (italics added). Cfr. MAUGARS 1672, pp. 173-175.

Still at the end of the eighteenth century, Carl Friedrich Abel, cellist and one of the last great viola da gamba players, is so described by Gerber: «With his dexterity on the gamba he also possessed the talent, like many other older virtuosi, of exciting the astonishment and admiration of his hearers by free fantasias and learned modulations [...] his cadences especially were excellent»[25].

The most common forms used to improvise in solo performance were the prelude, the toccata and the ricercare. This topic is very wide and would need a specific space.

2. As a *cantus* the low string instrument follows the same rules of the other melodic instruments and of the voices. A clarifying source is that of Bartolomeo Barbarino, who published a collection of sacred monodies with a diminished version next to an undiminished one, writing: «they will be useful to 1) singers without disposition, who can be satisfied to sing the plain version, 2) singers with disposition, but without a counterpoint knowledge, who can sing the diminutions as written and 3) singers who have both disposition and counterpoint knowledge, who can sing from the plain version, improvising their own versions»[26].

Therefore, as musicians had different dispositions towards improvisation, several possibilities of performance were considered, all valid. The performance of the plain text was considered for beginners and it was considered natural that the most skilled could develop it. For the most talented performers, besides the usual diminution and variation of the melodic line in the refrain, there were some 'musical spaces' predisposed just for improvisation. In instrumental music, besides grounds (bassi ostinati), dance forms could have a varied repetition, called *double*[27]. In various collections we also find very simple minuets and gavottes, that make you think at ready material to improvise variations; several were indeed composed that could be used as samples[28]. In vocal music,

---

[25]. Gerber's quote is in WASIELEWSKI 1894, p. 33.

[26]. BARBARINO 1614, quoted in COLLINS 2001, p. 141. Another clarifying passage is this by Luigi Zenobi, quoted in BLACKBURN – LOWINSKY 1993, pp. 83-85: «The soprano is obliged, and has the freedom to diminish, to joke and in sum embellish a musical body [...] He must have excellent counterpoint, because without it he sings randomly, and makes thousands bad mistakes [...] Now, all or most of the mentioned conditions must be followed by a player on the Cornett, or Viola da Gamba, [...] or similar of only one voice».

[27]. Marin Marais composed many *doubles*, for exemple: *1 Livre, Suite I*: 2 *Allemande*, 1 *Courante* and 2 *Gigue*; *Suite II*: 1 *Allemande* and 1 *Courante*; *Suite IV*: 1 *Allemande*; see MARAIS 1686. «There is this difference between the *Double* and the diminutions [that the musician] can make or leave when he wants, to catch the plain text up. But the *Double* can't be stopped»: ROUSSEAU 1768, p. 175. «Variations. We mean with this term every way of embellishing and make *doubles* of an air [...] Players make often improvised or so assumed variations; but more often they write them [...] we find them also often in French songs & in short Italian airs for violin or cello»: FRAMERY 1791, vol. II, pp. 550-551.

[28]. See LANZETTI 1750, *Gavotta*, Sonata no. 6; see also MARAIS 1689, p. 90, *Sujet Diversitez* (20 variazions on a bass).

instead, the space dedicated to the *ex tempore* contribution of an instrument were the refrains between the vocal verses. In some compositions they are written, in others we guess that performers are free to propose as they wish. A gorgeous model can be find in Monteverdi's aria *Et è pur dunque vero*[29] (see Ex. 1, p. 124). If in verses, for example, you have at the continuo a viola da gamba, in refrains it can take on the role of *cantus*.

The literature on melodic embellishment and variations on the *cantus* is immense; we will focus our attention instead on the less clear features of the performing practice of the low string instrument: the opportunities offered by the presence of more instruments at the continuo and the continuo function at the solo low string instrument.

3. In the continuo group instruments are classified in «two groups: as foundation and as ornament»; the low string instrument belongs to both categories, provided at least one bass line is played as foundation, as Agazzari explains[30]. Bismantova describes the difference between the *basso cantante*, a bass line rich of movement[31], and the *basso continuo*, a simpler bass with a foundation task, warning to always work out a simpler line for the continuo[32]. Therefore we can infer that if the writing of the bass line is too developed the continuo player has to simplify, when instead it is too simple, the *basso cantante* can enrich it. We find clear examples of reduction, in which simpler bass lines for the continuo are extracted from more articulated ones, in Supriani's *Sonate*, which will be treated later[33]. Improvisation on the bass was so widespread that it was often exaggerated: «We generally listen in the Music only to a thorough bass always doubled, that frequently is a kind of *battérie*, of chords, & an arpeggio […] of those accompanying or at the harpsichord, or at the viol; it should be then that of the two instruments, there is one that plays the plain bass, & the other the *double*»[34].

We notice in this passage that bass players enriched the continuo with *battéries* and chords; these were troubling if performed by more players together, instead if one played the plain bass line and the other the *double*, they were enjoyable to listen to. The practice of adding chords at the viola da gamba is documented in HOFFMANN 2010.

4. In absence of a polyphonic instrument the matter is more complicated, as it is very much debated if and how to realize the harmony, in instrumental and vocal chamber

---

[29]. The refrain is written in treble clef, it has been thought for a high compass, we freely infer that it is suitable for the viola da gamba. MONTEVERDI 1632.
[30]. AGAZZARI 1607, p. 3.
[31]. The movement comes from adding to the basso cantante passing notes, which connect the main harmonic notes that mostly form the basso continuo, and diminutions.
[32]. BISMANTOVA 1677, p. 59.
[33]. See paragraph 'Solfeggi per violoncello'.
[34]. BONNET 1715, pp. 434-435. See BOL 1973, p. 50.

Ex. 1: Claudio Monteverdi, *Et è pur dunque vero*, SV 250 (Monteverdi 1632).

music or in the recitatives. A practice somewhat documented is that of the recitatives at the cello[35]. As concerns the *recitativi secchi*, the practice of enriching the bass is attested since the earliest cello virtuosi, who realized the thorough bass together with the harpsichord or other instruments. For example «Giuseppe Jacchini was particularly famous for the way he accompanied singers in their recitatives: he seems to have made broad use of chords and melodic ornamentation in his continuo parts»[36].

In the period between the end of the eighteenth century and the first half of the nineteenth, when harpsichords disappeared from theatres, the *recitativi secchi* were instead performed mostly by the cello together with the double bass, which played the fundamental line. The use of the double bass allowed the cello to realize a good motion of the voices with some freedom in choosing the notes of the chord to use. Then it presumably consisted not of a series of chords originating by the production of simultaneous sounds 'a solo', but rather of double stop chords[37], helped by a second instrument that guaranteed the thorough bass line[38], alternated with full chords, more or less arpeggiated.

The practice of the recitatives at the cello lasted until about the middle of the nineteenth century[39]; in 1882 Amintore Galli wrote:

> [...] the cellist and the double bassist at the harpsichord were educated in the study of the figured bass, that allowed them to adorn the modulations, recurring at the end of each phrase of the recitative, with elegant embellishments [...] If singers able to perform the *recitativo secco* are rare like white flies, equally we have to say of the *violoncellisti partimentisti*. With today's instrumental polyphony, players are reduced to a merely mechanical duty, and none of them finds anymore necessary to study harmony and partimento[40].

5. We can assume what the *violoncellisti partimentisti* did when looking at some cantatas by Gaffi and Gasparini, both pupils of Pasquini, who is considered one of the founders of the didactical method based on partimenti[41]. We have for example two Cantatas by Gaffi,

---

[35]. For example see BACCIAGALUPPI 2006; ROMANOU 2009; LYMENSTULL 2014.

[36]. VANSCHEEUWIJCK 1996, p. 89. About Jacchini see also MARTINI 1776, p. 15.

[37]. At the string instruments the number of the notes of chords played with simultaneous sounds corresponds to the number of the strings necessary to execute it.

[38]. «It is also important to note that since the Violoncellist will often omit the root due to the difficulty of the hand position, the Contra Bass is absolutely necessary; but in the absence of a Contra Bass, the Violoncellist is obliged never to omit the root»: STIASTNY 1834, p. 21. *Cfr.* LYMENSTULL 2014, p. 18.

[39]. Most likely the tradition of realizing the recitatives at the cello had different features and histories depending on the places. Wasielewski says that he listened to it in Italy in 1873, and that in Germany since at least ten years it was no more practiced. WASIELEWSKI 1894, p. 42.

[40]. GALLI 1882, pp. 131-132 (italics added). *Cfr.* BACCIAGALUPPI 2006, p. 105.

[41]. «Yet the idea that the use of partimento as a teaching method had one of his earliest advocates in Pasquini is not without foundation», SANGUINETTI 2012, p. 59.

Allor che'l vostro lume and *Dalle oziose piume*[42] (Exs. 1a and 1b) in which now and then a voice is inserted: this could be the entry of an *obbligato* cello.

Ex. 2a: excerpt from Tommaso Gaffi, *Allor che'l vostro lume* (Gaffi a).

As we see in Ex. 2a and 2b, in some passages the bass line doubles: the upper voice once follows the melody in thirds, another time creates an imitative counterpoint on the bass. These written examples, in which the bass gets 'concertante' only in a few moments, let us speculate that in vocal music a good *partimentista* could freely take the opportunity to insert a parallel voice or a countermelody.

I agree with Gjerdingen when, speaking of Cimarosa's realization of partimenti, says that the young composer «would surely have noticed an incongruity when a busy, interesting opening passage leads into a boring passage»[43], and would have got around that by filling the spaces deliberately left empty, but I would add that most likely a good musician would have always done like this. We have so many vocal compositions in which spaces are deliberately left empty, with the bass line sometimes thematic, sometimes as a simple continuo. If, for example, the continuo is realized besides the harpsichord by a cello, the latter has room to improvise.

---

[42]. Gaffi a, Gaffi b. I am grateful to Pierluigi Morelli, who kindly suggested me these cantatas.

[43]. «In the process of learning Durante's A-minor *partimento*, a talented boy like Cimarosa would surely have noticed an incongruity when a busy, interesting opening passage leads into a boring passage», Gjerdingen 2010, p. 46.

Ex. 2b: excerpt from Tommaso Gaffi, *dalle oziose piume* (GAFFI B).

In the prefaces of the Cantatas published in Rome by Mascardi, Gasparini and Gaffi explain that, when we find more lines at the bass, there is freedom to play everything at the harpsichord or to arrange if there is available a cello, or an archlute or a violin as well. Gasparini says: «You will find in some Arias two Basses one for convenience, or easy to accompany; as it was necessary to adapt to the Print, so that I could not fully show my intention. But where you find above the Bass some Voice or Violin keys, you will play it with the right hand like a tablature. Here still the Archlute and the Cello will be able to be satisfied»[44].

Bernardo Gaffi gives more details:

> You will find some Arias with two Basses, and that one above with key changes like Violin or Tenor, there the Violin or the Violone could be satisfied, & without these will supply the virtue of a good Harpsichord player making both Basses, i.e. the Violin key with the right hand, and the others with the left, as the Author has not the intention to present Cantatas with instruments, but only to make the Harpsichord play like as a Tablature[45].

We notice the equivalence between playing at the harpsichord and arranging with strings. Certainly cello writing until about the half of the eighteenth century largely

---

[44]. GASPARINI 1695, 'A gl'amatori della Musica'. See GIALDRONI 2013, p. 133.
[45]. GAFFI 1700, 'L'Autore a gl'Amatori della Musica'. See GIALDRONI 2013, p. 133.

coincides with the one of the left hand at the harpsichord (melodic elements, arpeggios and *battéries*[46]), we hypothesize then that not only music for upper voice and bass was played at the harpsichord solo and that for harpsichord was arranged for violin and cello[47], but in general we believe quite possible that the low string instrument used techniques of the continuo line elaboration similar to those that today are common in the performance practice of polyphonic instruments.

The considerable use of the *obbligato* or *concertante* cello in Rome can be explained by the presence of a very important cello school, described by La Via in his works[48]. This arranging practice was probably widespread and also improvised in different ways, sometimes with bad taste if Benedetto Marcello says: «the cello virtuoso […] in the arias will divide the bass whimsically, varying each evening, even if variations are not at all related with the musician's or the violins's part»[49].

6. For the realization of the continuo 'a solo' in chamber instrumental music were used the same skills of the *violoncellisti partimentisti*. We have evidence of the various tours that some duos violin-cello did: Tartini accompanied by Vandini, pupil of Jacchini; Veracini accompanied by Lanzetti; Manfredi by Boccherini[50]. What the cellist did accompanying 'a solo' it's a debated topic. Many sustain the thesis of a chordal accompaniment[51], instead the thesis suggested here, given the monodic nature of the cello and given the evidence that a good two-voices counterpoint is enough to create masterpieces, is that the cello solo accompaniment was similar to what the left hand does in a classical Sonata: sometimes it performs an Alberti bass or broken chords patterns, sometimes it accompanies the

---

[46]. «As concerns *battéries* […] if the harpsichord doesn't swell its sounds, if the double beats on the same note don't work extremely well on it, it has other advantages»: COUPERIN 1716. From this quote in my opinion we can infer how the bass line writing was thought for different instruments, with the presence in the Sonata of passages clearly written for the low string instrument; moreover we read how features of the string sound were highly esteemed. From here we could guess that also a plain long notes accompaniment could be appreciated.

[47]. An example that could confirm this practice is the *Avvertissement* in the *Pièces de théorbe et de luth mises en partition*, where De Visée states: «The goal of this print is the Harpsichord, the Viol and the Violin, on which instruments they always have been arranged». We infer that it was common practice to arrange on strings score composed for polyphonic instruments. DE VISÉE 1716.

[48]. During his roman stay G. F. Handel composed his Cantatas *Tra le fiamme*, with concertante viola da gamba, 1707 and *Non s'afferra d'amor il porto*, with concertante cello, 1708. Cfr. HOFFMANN 2016; LA VIA 1983-1984; LA VIA 1987.

[49]. MARCELLO 1720, p. 53. Cfr. NUTI 2007, p. 110. Also Halton (HALTON 2008, p. 317) draws similar conclusions: «It is possible that this division [in Scarlatti's music] of the bass part into two specialised functions […] has its origins in improvisation practices of the new generation of violoncello virtuosi».

[50]. WHITTAKER 2012, pp. 46-47.

[51]. Cfr. LYMENSTULL 2014, p. 5; WHITTAKER 2012. We believe that the chordal realization (with simultaneous sounds) is one of the choices, but not the most idiomatic one. In our opinion a good bass realization can use various alternatives, like a theorbo does.

melody with a parallel line in thirds or sixths, sometimes it creates a countermelody, sometimes, for harmonic clarity, adds a few notes forming double stop chords or full chords. In fact, this is the kind of writing that we find in the compositions by Cervetto[52] or by other composers of the time for violin and cello. We know besides that also the violin in various contexts could add important notes to the harmony, for example with double stop chords[53].

The Historical Pedagogy

> Up to a few years ago, in almost all schools in Italy, harmony was taught more or less in the following way. Just after having learned the intervals, one studied the Rule of the Octave [...] Afterwards one went on to the study of partimento, with little or no care in the first stages [...] for knowing chords. These [...] step after step became clear[54].

The thesis suggested here is that in baroque times the teaching method was organised so that pupils could improvise, that is to say was based on patterns which could be reused in different contexts, namely based on different kind of figures. Considering the importance of arpeggios and *battéries*, it seems that these were from the beginning typical *figures* of the cello, as also François Couperin states: «as concerns *battéries*, or *arpègements* [...], whose origin comes from the Sonatas, my opinion would be that we need to limit their amount when we play them on the harpsichord. This instrument has its own features, such as the violin has its own»[55]. Towards the end of the eighteenth century, together with the decline of the harpsichord, we witness the development of figures belonging exclusively to the cello, like the special arpeggio-figures, often present in the methods.

In many sources concerning the training of a cellist or viola da gamba player, immediately after the basic instructions, we find exercises to master intervals and play arpeggios and *battéries*. For instance, in De La Borde's *Essai*, after the explanation of the left hand positions one goes directly to the *battéries*[56], and after one finds a scale harmonised in accordance with the rule of the octave, as was usual in the partimenti school. The voice

---

[52]. James Cervetto, pupil of his father Giacobbe, from Venice, was well known for the performance of recitatives and taught to Nochez and Robert Lindley, one of the most famous cellists at the operatic continuo.

[53]. Stein 2014, pp. 11-34.

[54]. Cav. Maestro Ettore De Champs, Sanguinetti 2012, p. 96.

[55]. Couperin 1716, p. 35. This could be a reference to the improvised accompaniment made of arpeggios and two-notes broken chords at the cello.

[56]. We infer that for *battéries* they meant many kinds of broken chords, from alternated thirds to arpeggios on three strings, all performed *détaché*, whereas *harpegés* was used only for *legato* figures. Cfr. De La Borde 1780, p. 314.

Ex. 3: Examples of *battéries* from De La Borde's *Essai* and the first part of a *Rondeau* by Nochez.

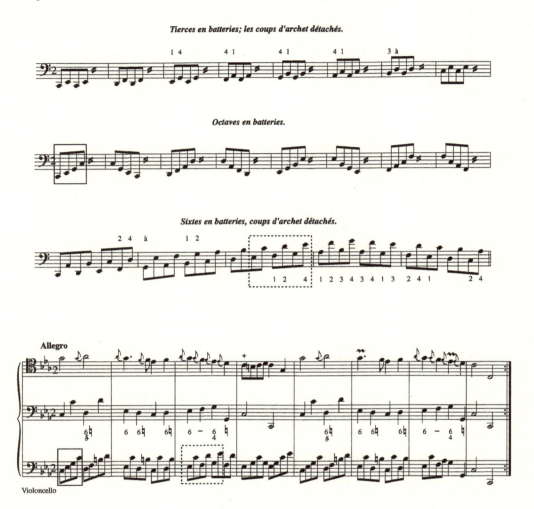

violoncelle in the *Essai* was written by Nochez, cellist at the Opera in Paris, who had studied with Cervetto and Dell'Abaco[57].

By Nochez we have also a precious bass realisation of a *Rondeau*, kindly provided by Christophe Coin (Ex. 3). The melody is written in the first stave, in the second there is a simple bass line, in the third we find an elaborated version of the latter. Analyzing the elaborated version, we notice the precise application of the figures shown by Nochez in De La Borde's *Essai*: exclusive use of arpeggios and alternated consonances of thirds and sixths (there are also occasional broken octaves) within a quavers perpetual motion, interrupted only at the cadences.

---

57. WASIELEWSKI 1894, p. 93.

In various cello methods we find simple arias with the accompaniment bass line in several versions, usually in a first variant at the bass we find crotchets, then quavers, then semiquavers in different kinds of arpeggio figures. We hypothesize that these realisations work as true bass harmonisations, having already said that the cello realises chords trough its specific figures. For instance, there are many alternatives in the methods by Gunn[58] and Breval; in the latter we read: «The following Arias can be performed not only with the written bowings, but with every other we will choose among the previous examples»[59]. This let us assume that the goal was to master some chosen figures, to learn applying them later in the accompaniment of other melodies. It was therefore a matter of learning patterns that the student would later reuse in complete autonomy.

Also the interesting anonymous German viola da gamba method, probably written around 1730, edited by Bettina Hoffmann in 2014, shows the same didactic approach: a few explanations, many ready diminution patterns, arpeggios and *battérie*, with the final statement: «When a scholar has understood and put into practice these instructions, he needs no further information, and can assist himself»[60]. We interpret this expression as an exhortation to learn by heart and apply, with the implicit certainty that through experience one learns what he needs... In Ex. 4 (p. 132) we see some chords followed by a few figures, which can be used to realise those chords at the viol: slurred and separated arpeggios, simple two-notes chords, two-notes chords with repeated notes, broken thirds with an applied dotted rhythm. In other pages there are also diminutions that refer to the division — or *passaggi* — tradition. So we lie in-between the early art of ornamentation on interval basis and the art of harmonic realisation. Going back a few decades, we notice that Simpson had clearly distinguished among different kinds of *divisions*: «[We have] two kinds of divisions: a breaking of the ground and a descanting upon it: out of which two, is generated a third sort […] to wit a mixture of those, one with the other. […] Descant division differs from the former [because] that breaks the notes of the ground, this descant upon them […] in any of the concords»[61]. According

---

[58]. GUNN 1789, p. 22, 63. John Gunn published also a very interesting treatise on the study and the performance of harmony at the cello: GUNN 1802. Here at pp. 35-36 there is the realisation of a scale with the rule of the octave at the cello, first with chords, then with arpeggios; at p. 39 there are examples of accompaniments of arias at the cello with arpeggios.

[59]. BREVAL 1804, pp. 121-132. Also in DUPORT 1840 pp. 80-87 are dedicated to arpeggio variants, with the note: «Those who practice them can vary them according to their own fantasy». It is taken for granted the practice of introducing variants to the musical text proposed.

[60]. ANONYMOUS 2014, p. 30.

[61]. The phrase continues: «But in the main business of division, they are much the same: for all Division, whether Descant or Breaking the Bass, is but a Transition from Note to Note, or from one Concord to another, either by Degrees or by Leaps, with an Intermixture of such Discords as are allowed in Composition». SIMPSON 1665, p. 28. We assume that the freedom to use any of the consonances is given from the not completely tonal context.

to Simpson we have two options: to follow faithfully the bass outline, to enrich with divisions, or to create a new line above it (*descant*). To create this new line we can lean on any of the consonances (*concords*) in relation to the bass, anyway the two kind of *division* are very similar.

Ex. 4: Excerpt from Anonymous, *Instruction oder eine Anweisung auff der Violadigamba*, around 1730.

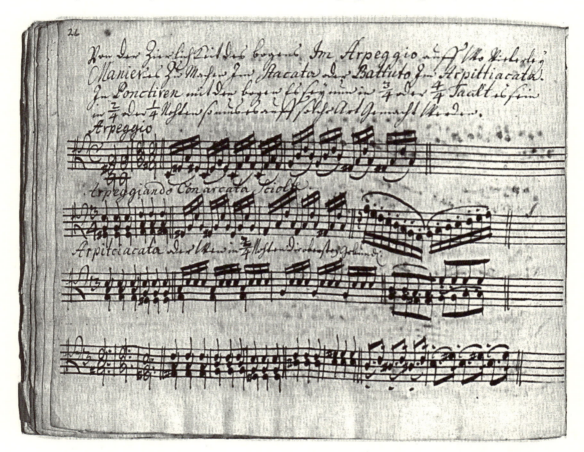

Another interesting didactical source are Sanguinazzo's sonatas for cello. In the collection we find both a whole sonata with an empty bass staff[62], probably to realise extemporaneously, and several variations on the bass[63]. This may prove the practice of the bass variation training, even at a not advanced grade of technical preparation, given the amateur level of these sonatas.

---

[62]. In the fourth sonata, SANGUINAZZO A, pp. 15-17, the bass staff is empty, in contrast to the others sonatas, all complete.

[63]. All the variations on different basses are 230 in: SANGUINAZZO B and SANGUINAZZO C.

«Il n'exécute jamais la Basse telle qu'elle est écrite»

Very important sources, which can give new light to this research, turned out to be some works for cello by Lanzetti, Supriani and Caldara, already known to few specialists, but so far lacking comprehensive studies[64].

Solfeggi for Cello

*Longum iter est per praecepta,
breve et efficax per exempla*
Seneca

Scholars have already written on improvisation at the bass and on the continuo realisation at the cello without accompaniment of a polyphonic instrument, in recitatives and in chamber music[65], but still there is not a thorough study on the teaching methods that brought to these skills. Following the rediscovery of the didactical and pedagogical practice of partimento, we investigated the possibility of the existence of a similar historical method suited to the cello and viola da gamba characteristics. The first step is to define the specific features of the low string instruments, regarding the continuo realization: the cello and the viola da gamba are not polyphonic instruments; the cello is similar to the viola da gamba, with which shares texture and role; the two-strings chords on the cello have always a good effect, whereas three- or four-strings chords are marked by great performing troubles and by a strong character, that makes them suitable for cadences, but not to accompany long progressions or melodic phrasing; as for easiness, the three- or four-strings chords on the viol are equivalent to the two-strings chords on the cello; anyway at the cello the two-strings chords were considered already difficult to perform, as clearly indicated by Jean-Louis Duport[66]. Baumgartner suggests to harmonize at the cello often using two-strings chords instead of three «as you will be extremely embarrassed & exposed to play out of tune»[67]; when the most virtuoso players wrote music for viola da gamba and for cello often they inserted passages with double strings, limiting instead the use of three- and four-strings chords on the cello and more than three for the viol only to cadences[68].

---

[64]. Except the works of Olivieri. See Olivieri 2009.
[65]. Watkins 1996; for the realization of the recitatives see above note 35.
[66]. «Nothing more agreeable to the ears than the diatonic sequences of thirds, but unfortunately these sequences are very difficult to play on the cello, especially on the neck [...] one needs absolutely to make the hand jump every third that comes next, which makes the slurring and the sound continuity extremely difficult»: Duport 1840, p. 55.
[67]. Baumgartner 1774, p. 20.
[68]. A very important model for the cello chordal writing is the collection of J. S. Bach's *Suites*. Here three/four-strings chords are very much used only in the sarabandes, the slowest movements of the suites;

Therefore, searching for didactical works of bass realization at the string instruments and having as a reference point the partimenti, we did not look for polyphonic or chordal realizations, instead for two-voices realizations, of which one is the given bass and the other is derived from the first according to various techniques. This second voice realizes a *concertato* line, which can be a principal or a secondary voice, useful for musical ideas in 'empty' spaces of the score. The teaching goal would then exactly correspond to that of the partimento, with a specific application of the improvisation skills in the 'musical spaces' suited to the low string instrument. «A partimento is a solo piece, whose goal is teaching composition via improvisation, whereas the aim of a basso continuo playing is accompaniment»[69]. For cello the three sources which could be somehow included in the category of 'realized partimenti or solfeggi for cello' are Supriani's *Sonate*, Lanzetti's *Principes* and Caldara's *Lezioni*[70]. We could postulate that, despite the different names, the three works document three aspects of a single didactical method to the training of improvisation skills for cellists. Supriani's *Sonate*, already examined by Guido Olivieri[71], are composed on the toccatas published from the same author together with *Principij*[72], a short cello treatise. Each toccata is the foundation of a *Sonata*[73]: this last one appears in a triple staff, in the first one top line a toccata is reproduced; the staff in the middle has a version of it enriched according to various techniques; finally, in the lower staff there is a 'reduced' version of the toccata, in which a thorough bass is extracted through a reduction process[74]. Both processes, of enrichment and of reduction, are very interesting. The Fondo Noseda of the Conservatory in Milan preserves Lanzetti's *Principes ou l'application du Violoncelle par tous les tons*[75]. A meaning of *application* is 'put into practice, put into use, opposed to the

---

in the other movements they appear only at the beginning or at the conclusion of sections. Polyphony and harmony at the cello and at the viol alone are then obtained not with the keyboards' techniques, but rather with those described to adapt the polyphonic repertoire to the lute (VACCARO 1981, p. 131), further arranged to the string instrument. The viola da gamba has definitely a greater predisposition to the chordal writing and some viol players composed pieces in chordal style; anyway, in general, chords with more than three strings have a specific punctuation (phrase opening or closing) or accentuation role in the musical discourse.

[69]. SANGUINETTI 2012, p. 98.

[70]. SUPRIANI 2010, LANZETTI 1770, CALDARA 17--.

[71]. «[…] it's possible that these pieces represent written-out examples of the type of elaborations that cello players improvised when accompanying aria or recitatives, or in solo performances». OLIVIERI 2009, p. 124.

[72]. SUPRIANI 2008.

[73]. It comes naturally a comparison for example with the *Toccate* (14 for harpsichord) by Leonardo Leo, some of which have been realized by the composer himself. See SANGUINETTI 2012, p. 222.

[74]. A clarifying help is given by distinguishing between the bass line meant as a voice (*basso cantante*, see above note 31) and the line of the *basso continuo*. If the first has the priority of the melodic motion (prevalence of steps), the second has instead the task of making explicit the harmonic functions (presence of leaps mostly between fundamentals and thirds of the chords). In the repertoire usually the different functions are found together. Clear examples are in GUNN 1802, pp. 34-37.

[75]. LANZETTI 1770.

theory'. So we may interpret the title this way: 'Principles, that is the practice at the cello in all the tonalities', i.e. what the cello can do in all the tonalities. Let's see an example: the *Andante* in Ex. 5 (p. 136). The bass realization takes place through arpeggios, that keep almost always the same shape, often enriched by the addition of appoggiaturas that make the harmony more interesting[76].

Next exercise is a G major scale, first simple, then elaborated with virtuosities and figures, reusable for example in a cadence. Also in these exercises by Lanzetti, like in Supriani, we have easier realizations, with patterns repeated identical in the harmonic sequences, and further realizations more elaborated, with thematic ideas and virtuoso elements added. We presume that we are dealing with exercises to be transposed and which figures are to be learned as patterns to reuse in different contexts, as variations of arias, refrains, introductions, cadences etc. A different approach have the *Lezioni per il violoncello con il suo basso*[77] by Caldara[78] (Ex. 6, p. 137).

These are 44 lessons, each one seems to deepen one specific type of composition on the bass, that could be a model for autonomous creations by the student. One common feature among the three cellists' works is that there are not technical differences among the exercises, namely it is not a matter of single exercises dedicated for example to the study of one position, of hard bowings or strings leaps[79], even if in Supriani and Lanzetti there is a clear path towards virtuosity. Another common feature is that in all the three kind of works, figures (mostly melodic-rhythmical figures in Caldara and patterns with arpeggios, scale fragments and diminutions in Supriani and Lanzetti) are repeated through transposition and arranged to different harmonic sequences; that is we are talking about application of figures and patterns. This is exactly the didactical path for the improvisation skills that we hypothesize: the student should learn some patterns — as those we saw in the methods — and later reuse them, choosing and arranging according to the context. The three works represent three different approaches: in Supriani many elaborations can be defined divisions and the text on which they are applied are toccatas; in Lanzetti the majority of the exercises is comparable to the elaboration of figures based on scales and

---

[76]. Adding one note to an arpeggio has one more important result: we obtain an even number of notes, for instance, four instead of three, which allows for instance a quavers perpetual motion.

[77]. They are preserved in a manuscript belonged to Elisabeth Cowling; the original is in the Österreische Nationalbibliothek, Vienna. I'm grateful to the Library of the North Caroline University, that kindly provided a copy of the microfilm, in particular to Mrs. Stacey Krim.

[78]. «Caldara was often in Rome and besides got in touch with the Roman cello school, which featured virtuoso cellists and gave the cello a main role in the musical production within various genres [...]. Going round with Ottoboni and Ruspoli (probably also cardinal Benedetto Pamphilj and the queen of Poland) was in close contact with Corelli, Alessandro and Domenico Scarlatti, Haendel, Cesarini and Pasquini»: KIRKENDALE – KIRKENDALE 1973.

[79]. I thank Francesco Maschio for the precious help in analysing the texts and Alessandro De Marchi for his precious comments on the belongings of these works to the area of the Solfeggi.

Ex. 5: Salvatore Lanzetti, *Andante*, in: *Principes ou l'application du Violoncelle par tous les tons*, p. 1ᵛ.

arpeggios, applied to the scale degrees; in Caldara the text on which the student learn to improvise thematic fragments is made of thorough bass phrases typical of arias or sonatas. The common method is nevertheless presumably that of learning directly at the instrument the improvising techniques. These lie between two poles, the division and the *discantus*, with the use of early figures, such as diminution patterns, and modern figures, connected to

«Il n'exécute jamais la Basse telle qu'elle est écrite»

Ex. 6: Antonio Caldara, *Lezione no. 1* (Caldara 17--).

scales and arpeggios in various versions. The main difficulty, for the *violoncellista partimentista*, is not related to the instrumental technique[80], but instead concerns the *extempore* practical

---

[80]. Today the instrumental technique is usually undertaken in a way completely unrelated to the musical language, also because of the multiplicity of languages that the contemporary musician has to master.

application to the instrument of the harmonic and contrapuntal rules, using the figures. If in the modal system the logic of the consonances is enough to create a *discantus*, instead in the tonal system a precise harmonic reference is essential, hence the necessity of figured bass. Therefore the *violoncellista partimentista* along with the study of counterpoint, with which he learned to compose *extempore* a two-voices counterpoint on a given bass or melody, had to study harmony extensively and, above all, practice at the cello exercises like those we see in Supriani, Lanzetti and Caldara.

Updates and Research Developments

This research on solfeggi for cello has been further developed in the paper 'Un'ipotesi di ricostruzione'[81]. The main remarks[82] of this work are: in Supriani the most used enrichment techniques consist of: single notes ornaments; scale fragments or diminution patterns inserted to fill the space between notes originally approached by leaps; divisions of the rhythmic values into *battéries* (broken two-notes chords or full chords); two-notes chords or full chords additions in cadence; additions of a second alternating voice, formed by a pedal or a parallel line in consonances of thirds and sixths. The continuo line is a rare witness of the reduction practice applied to toccatas. As concerns Lanzetti, analysing all the pieces of the *Principes*, it appears that they are always composed on a scale proceeding by repeated steps, strictly following the Octave rule. A different approach, mostly based on cadence patterns, proves instead to be Caldara's *Lezioni*. Cadences, scale fragments and progressions are proposed in a large number of variants, in particular there are always progressions of fifths, from the second lesson, with numerous different figures.

Antonio Guida's «Sonate per il violoncello»

Further confirmation that the study method based on the scale and the rule of the octave was common in the Neapolitan cello didactic[83], is provided to us by Antonio

---

[81]. The final writing of this article follows the paper focused on the works by Supriani, Lanzetti e Caldara: BARBATI – MASCHIO 2017.

[82]. In this paper there are also the biographical data of the three authors examined here, that witness their long collaboration in different contexts: Supriani and Lanzetti served together at the Neapolitan court musical chapel; Supriani and Caldara collaborated most probably in Barcelona, 1708, to perform Caldara's *Il più bel nome* during Charles III's wedding.

[83]. «The counterpoint and partimento teaching methods […] were largely based on the scale, […] the student spent many years training improvisation on partimento, which foundation […] was the scale placed at the bass and accompanied according to the rule of the octave»: SANGUINETTI 2009, p. 66.

Guida's manuscript[84], kindly provided to me by Guido Olivieri, who has recently confirmed the attribution. This is a collection of pieces entitled *Sonate per il violoncello*[85], which appears to be a complete course, from the first to the thumb position, formed by exercises, with no explanatory texts. After reaching an advanced skill on the four neck positions and on various bowings, we find fifteen exercises similar to those by Lanzetti, in which figures patterns are proposed according to the rule of the octave on all the scale degrees (Ex. 7). The very first exercises are simple diminution and broken chord patterns applied to the scale degrees, supporting the modular setting from the beginning of the studies.

Ex. 7: exercises from Antonio Guida, *Sonate per il violoncello* (GUIDA 17--).

---

[84]. Antonio Guida was string teacher at the Conservatorio di Sant'Onofrio a Capuana from 1785 to 1797; see DI GIACOMO 1924, p. 138. According to COLUMBRO – MAIONE 2008 he was cellist at the Tesoro di S. Gennaro in 1777-1780 and 1790-1800.

[85]. GUIDA 17--. The title *Sonate* has been probably added because there are short minuets and gavottes, but we assume that it is a complete method, which includes all the didactic path steps.

Giovanna Barbati

Suggestions for Using Improvisation in the Early Music Didactic

We suggest that today too it is possible to choose, in the early music training, a method based on musical elements and processes, that the students can learn and later modify. Using as a reference the tripartite plan described by Callahan[86], we can choose some figures patterns, for example diminutions or arpeggios, and arrange them in relation to the bass, according to the voice leading rules. Applying the classical terminology, it is a matter of putting the *Decoratio* on the *Elaboratio* schemes. Going a step further, even the whole structure, the *Dispositio*, would be planned by the student, who will compose short pieces like for example preludes, ricercari or minuets. Then, if on the theoretical side the order is: general structure — voice leading scheme — application of embellishment patterns, on the pedagogical side we have to start from the last level, the simplest one, to go back towards those levels that require more advanced skills in harmony, counterpoint and composition. The student will then start applying the various patterns, taken from the treatises or directly extracted from the repertoire, to harmonic sequences. At the beginning it would be highly advisable the variations on ground basses, which have been experimented also in improvisation workshops at the Frosinone Conservatory in 2015 and at the Conservatorio Regional de Ponta Delgada in 2017[87]. One can start with diminutions from the sixteenth- and seventeenth-century treatises[88], which enable to form a rich vocabulary of ready-to-use musical patterns, but it is very useful to extract patterns also directly from the general repertoire, not necessarily from that specifically for low strings. The exercises on ground basses can be carried out in groups and enable a quick and funny learning[89]. Given at the beginning the diagram of the parts[90], the rules are:

> 1) once chosen the pattern, it must be strictly used until the end of the sequence. If the student modifies the pattern, usually after two-three times he will have exhausted his inventiveness and will repeat himself;
> 2) the pattern can be melodic of rhythmic, it can be composed on arpeggios, or it can be a combination of these elements. The basic rule is the variety of solutions;
> 3) usually the ground bass includes two large phrases; it is possible to add or modify something to the pattern in the second half of the bass;

---

[86]. Callahan 2010.

[87]. Students attending to the workshops were either already trained in early music practice (Frosinone), or beginners and advanced students in a traditional academic path (Ponta Delgada).

[88]. A rich list of the sources around the sixteenth and seventeenth centuries can be found, with an annotated anthology, in Dongois 2014.

[89]. «It's more funny: then it's more useful»: Rodari 1973, p. 37. For the individual study we experimented the use of the loop station, which enables to improvise on one's own bases.

[90]. As we see for example in Ortiz 1553, before each *Recercada* there is the corresponding voices scheme.

4) the simplest variation is composed on one of the four voices that constitute the harmonic scheme; additional virtuoso variations can be made *alla bastarda*, that is, passing through the different voices;

5) while a colleague is improvising the task is to accompany without interfering, or add some complementary patterns.

For the whole didactic path the suggestion is to take as a model the method that Couperin explains in *L'Art de toucher le clavecin*:

> Separately from the examined embellishments, such as trills, mordents, appoggiaturas, etc., I always made my pupils make some little fingers' motions, either diminutions, or different battéries starting with the easiest, and in the most comfortable tonalities; and imperceptibly I brought them until the most nimble, and the most transposed, [...] the knowledge of intervals, of modes and their cadences, either perfect or imperfect, of chords and their *supposition*. That gives them a kind of local memory that makes them more confident, and which is useful to reset, with knowledge, when they failed[91].

We can do it also today: the student has to repeat with variations the given exercises; these consist of patterns which later will be useful as material to improvise; the first exercises are on basic embellishments (on single notes, the easiest), then one goes to study diminutions and *battéries*[92]; the study is based on transposition, starts from the nearest tones to go to the farthest and it starts from easier patterns to go to the most complex; at the same time of the technique (which consists of the clarified exercises) it is necessary to instruct pupils about intervals, modes, cadences, then about chords (starting then at two-voices to proceed with three-voices and more). This instruction has to come gradually, either from the theoretical side or from the technical one, so as to allow the student an active approach from the beginning.

We think these basic principles can be valid for all instruments. In conclusion, the exam of the sources concerning pedagogy and in particular the Solfeggi for cello brings us to the following remarks: in a path towards historical improvisation it is recommended to start with single embellishments and easy diminutions to practice with transpositions and on various schemes. If we consider the scale and the arpeggio as basic schemes, these, with a conceptual shift to an 'active technique', can be treated also as building elements, to elaborate (for example juxtaposition of scale fragments in the two directions to form endless figures, arpeggios broken and/or enriched with non-chord tones[93]). Together with

---

[91]. COUPERIN 1716, pp. 8-9, 34.

[92]. We can notice that this collection of embellishments, diminutions and battéries already forms a sort of vocabulary for the student's improvisations.

[93]. In Fig. 5 by Lanzetti, we can notice that the scale is used first as foundation for the exercise within the rule of the octave, and after as a compositional element, in exploring its virtuosistic potential.

the study of the first notions of harmony and counterpoint one can practice the first divisions (for example alternated consonances of parallel thirds and sixths) and *battéries* in the easiest harmonic sequences.

If enriching the bass is easier to achieve, composing a *discantus* on a bass is a true composition exercise, it is then more suitable to advanced students. Together with studying partimento directly at the keyboard, practicing directly at the instrument the works of Supriani, Lanzetti, Caldara and Guida, intended as exercises to transpose and to vary further, probably helps to develop from the beginning the skills necessary to an excellent improvisation in style.

From this point of view we interpret Ancelet's polemic statement referred to Forqueray the young («He never performs the Bass as it is written»[94]), as the observation of a common practice, but performed by a Master, who shows his ability in the continuos variation of the bass[95].

Bibliography
Primary Sources

Agazzari 1607
Agazzari, Agostino. *Del sonare sopra 'l basso con tutti li stromenti*, Siena, Falcini, 1607.

Ancelet 1757
Ancelet. *Observations sur la musique, les musiciens, et les instruments*, Amsterdam, Aux dépens de la Compagnie, 1757.

Anonymous 2014
Anonymous. *Instruction oder eine Anweisung auff der Violadigamba*, facsimile edition edited by Bettina Hoffmann, Heidelberg, Güntersberg, 2014.

Barbarino 1614
Barbarino, Bartolomeo. *Secondo Libro delli Mottetti*, Venice, Magni, 1614.

Baumgartner 1774
Baumgartner, Johann Baptist. *Instructions de musique, théoriques et pratiques, à l'usage du violoncelle*, The Hague, D. Monnier, 1774.

Bismantova 1677
Bismantova, Bartolomeo. *Compendio musicale*, Ferrara, s.n., 1677.

---

[94]. «He never executes the bass just as it is written; he claims to greatly improve it with the great number of brilliant traits he throws at it; he fights, so to say, with the person playing the solo; and often the Composer is just as unhappy as the violinist who is playing», Ancelet 1757, *cfr*. Bol 1973, p. 50.

[95]. I am very grateful to Guido Olivieri, who helped me to use English more correctly, to Ilaria Zamuner, for her advices on editorial criteria and to Bettina Hoffmann, for her kind suggestions.

«Il n'exécute jamais la Basse telle qu'elle est écrite»

Bonnet 1715
Bonnet, Jacques. *Histoire de la Musique, et de ses effets, depuis son origine jusqu'à présent*, Paris, J. Cochart, 1715.

Breval 1804
Breval, Jean-Baptiste-Sébastien. *Traité du violoncelle*, Op. 42, Paris, Janet & Cotelle, 1804.

Caldara 17--
Caldara, Antonio. *Lezioni per il Violoncello con il suo Basso*, Vienna, Österreichische Nationalbibliothek, EM.69 Mus; Cowling box 3-2, Martha Blakeney Hodges Special Collections and University Archives, The University of North Carolina at Greensboro.

Couperin 1716
Couperin, François. *L'Art de toucher le clavecin*, Paris, Foucaut, 1716.

De La Borde 1780
De La Borde, Jean-Benjamin. 'Violoncelle', in: *Essai sur la musique ancienne et moderne. Tome Premier*, Paris, Ph.-D- Pierre, 1780, pp. 309-323.

De Visée 1716
De Visée, Robert. *Pièces de théorbe et de luth: mises en partition, dessus e basse*, Paris, Roussel, 1716.

Della Valle 1763
Della Valle, Pietro. 'Della musica dell'età nostra', in: Doni, Giovan Battista. *De' trattati di musica […] tomo secondo […]*, Florence, Stamperia Imperiale, 1763.

Duport 1840
Duport, Jean-Louis. *Essai sur le doigté du violoncelle, et sur la conduite de l'archet*, Paris, Cotelle, 1840.

Framery 1791
Framery, Nicolas E. *Enciclopédie metodique. Musique*, 2 vols., Paris, Panckoucke, 1791-1818.

Gaffi 1700
Gaffi, Tommaso. *Cantate da cammera a voce sola […]*, Rome, Mascardi, 1700.

Gaffi a
Id. *Allor che il vostro lume*, manuscript, Modena, Biblioteca Estense, MO008918060, in: <www.internetculturale.it>, accessed November 2018.

Gaffi b
Id. *Dalle oziose piume*, manuscript, Modena, Biblioteca Estense, MO008918064, in: <www.internetculturale.it>, accessed November 2018.

Gasparini 1695
Gasparini, Francesco. *Cantate da camera a voce sola*, Op. 1, Rome, Mascardi, 1695.

Guida 17--
Guida, Antonio. *Sonate per il violoncello*, Berkeley (CA), University of California, Jean Gray Hargrove Music Library, MS 1016.

GUNN 1789
GUNN, John. *The Theory and Practice of Fingering the Violoncello*, London, The Author, 1789.

GUNN 1802
ID. *An Essay theoretical and practical […] on the Application of the Principles of Harmony, Thorough Bass and Modulation to the Violoncello*, London, Preston, 1802.

HOTTETERRE 1719
HOTTETERRE, Jacques. *L'Art de préluder*, Paris, Foucault, 1719.

LANZETTI 1750
LANZETTI, Salvatore. XII *Sonate à Violoncello Solo e Basso Continuo Op. 1*, Paris, Le Clerc-Boivin, [1750].

LANZETTI 1770
ID. *Principes ou l'application du Violoncelle par tous les tons*, Amsterdam, J. J. Hummel, [1770].

MARAIS 1686
MARAIS, Marin. *Pièces de viole Livre I*, Paris, L'auteur-J. Hurel, 1686.

MARAIS 1689
ID. *Basse-Continuës des Piéces à une et à deux violes*, Paris, L'auteu-J. Hurel, 1689.

MARCELLO 1720
MARCELLO, Benedetto. *Il teatro alla moda*, (1720), Milan, Ricordi, 1883.

MARTINI 1776
MARTINI Giovanni Battista. *Serie Cronologica de' Principi dell'Accademia de' Filarmonici di Bologna*, Bologna, L. della Volpe, 1776.

MAUGARS 1672
MAUGARS, André. 'Discours sur la musique d'Italie et des opera' (1639), in: *Divers traitez d'histoire, de morale et d'éloquence. 1: La Vie de Malherbe*, Paris, C. Thiboust et E. Esclassan, 1672, pp. 154-179.

MONTEVERDI 1632
MONTEVERDI, Claudio. *Scherzi musicali*, Venice, Magni, 1632.

ORTIZ 1553
ORTIZ, Diego. *Tratado de Glosas*, Rome, Valerio e Luigi Dorico, 1553.

ROUSSEAU 1768
ROUSSEAU, Jean-Jacques. *Dictionnaire de musique*, Paris, Vve Duchesne, 1768.

SANGUINAZZO A
SANGUINAZZO, Nicolò. *Suonate à violoncello e basso*, Vienna, Österreichische Nationalbibliothek, E. M. 41, 1700-1720.

SANGUINAZZO B
ID. *Suonata violoncello solo*, Vienna, Österreichische Nationalbibliothek, E. M. 42a, 1700-1720.

«Il n'exécute jamais la Basse telle qu'elle est écrite»

Sanguinazzo c
Id. *3 Sonatas*, Vienna, Österreichische Nationalbibliothek, E. M. 43a, 1700-1720.

Simpson 1665
Simpson, Christopher. *The Division Viol*, London, W. Godbid, 1665.

Stiasny 1834
Stiastny, Bernhard. *Méthode pour le Violoncelle*, Mainz, Schott, 1834.

Supriani 2008
Supriano, (Supriani, Scipriani) Francesco P. *12 Toccate per violoncello solo; Principij da imparare à suonare il violoncello*, edited by Marco Ceccato, Albese con Cassano, Musedita, 2008 (Minghèn dal viulunzèl).

Supriani 2010
Id. *Sonate a due violoncelli*, edited by Alessandro Bares, Albese con Cassano, Musedita, 2010 (Minghèn dal viulunzèl).

Secondary Literature

Bacciagalupi 2006
Bacciagaluppi, Claudio. 'Primo violoncello al cembalo: l'accompagnamento del recitativo semplice nell'Ottocento', in: *Rivista italiana di musicologia*, xli/1 (2006), pp. 101-134.

Barbati – Maschio 2017
Barbati, Giovanna – Maschio, Francesco. 'Un'ipotesi di ricostruzione, un percorso formativo per il violoncellista improvvisatore al basso continuo', paper presented at the *xxiv Convegno annuale Sidm (Lucca 20-22 October 2017)*, unpublished.

Blackburn – Lowinsky 1993
Blackburn, Bonnie J. – Lowinsky, Edward E. 'Luigi Zenobi and His Letter on the Perfect Musician', in: *Studi musicali*, xxii/1 (1993), pp. 61-114.

Bol 1973
Bol, Hans. *La basse de viole du temps de Marin Marais et d'Antoine Forqueray*, Bilthoven, A. B. Creyghton, 1973 (Utrechtse bijdragen de muziekwetenschap, 7).

Byros 2015
Byros, Vasili. 'Prelude on a Partimento: Invention in the Compositional Pedagogy of the German States in the Time of J. S. Bach', in: *Music Theory Online*, xxi/3 (September 2015), <http://www.mtosmt.org/issues/mto.15.21.3/mto.15.21.3.byros.html>, accessed November 2018.

Cafiero 1993
Cafiero, Rosa. 'La didattica del partimento a Napoli fra Settecento e Ottocento: note sulla fortuna delle 'Regole' di Carlo Cotumacci', in: *Gli affetti convenienti all'idee, studi sulla musica vocale italiana*, edited by Maria Caraci Vela, Rosa Cafiero and Angela Romagnoli, Naples, Edizioni Scientifiche Italiane, 1993 (Archivio del teatro e dello spettacolo, 3), pp. 549-579.

Callahan 2010
Callahan, Michael. *Techniques of Keyboard Improvisation in the German Baroque and Their Implications for Today's Pedagogy*, Ph.D. Diss., Rochester (NY), University of Rochester, 2010.

Canguilhem 2010
Canguilhem, Philippe. 'Le projet FABRICA: oralité et écriture dans les pratiques polyphoniques du chant ecclésiastique (xvi-xx siècle)', in: *Journal of the Alamire Foundation*, II/2 (2010), pp. 272-281.

Canguilhem 2013
Id. *Chanter sur le livre a la Renaissance: une édition et traduction des traités de contrepoint de Vicente Lusitano*, Turnhout, Brepols, 2013 (Epitome musical).

Collins 2001
Collins, Timothy A. 'Reactions Against the Virtuoso. Instrumental Ornamentation Practice and the Stile Moderno', in: *International Review of the Aesthetics and Sociology of Music*, XXXII/2 (2001), pp. 137-152.

Columbro – Maione 2008
Columbro, Marta – Maione, Paologiovanni. *La Cappella musicale del Tesoro di San Gennaro di Napoli tra Sei e Settecento*, Naples, Turchini, 2008 (I Turchini saggi).

Dahlhaus 1987
Dahlhaus, Carl. 'Composition and Improvisation', in: Id. *Schoenberg and the New Music: Essays by Carl Dahlhaus*, translated by Derrick Puffett and Alfred Clayton, Cambridge-New York, Cambridge University Press, 1987, pp. 265-273.

Dahlhaus 2010
Id. 'Qu'est-ce que l'improvisation musicale?', translated by Marion Siéfert and Lucille Lisack, in: *Tracés: Revue de Sciences humaines*, no. 18 (2010), pp. 181-196.

Di Giacomo 1924
Di Giacomo, Salvatore. *Il Conservatorio di Sant'Onofrio a Capuana e quello di S. M. della Pietà dei Turchini*, Palermo, R. Sandron, 1924 (Collezione settecentesca, 26).

Dongois 2014
Semplice ou passeggiato: diminution et ornementation dans l'exécution de la musique de Palestrina et du stile antico, directed by William Dongois, Droz, Geneva, 2014 (Musique & recherche).

Esses 1992
Esses, Maurice. *Dance and Instrumental Diferencias in Spain During the 17th and Early 18th Centuries. 1: History and Background, Music and Dance*, Stuyvesant (NY), Pendragon Press, 1992.

Ferand 1961
Ferand, Ernst T. *Improvisation in Nine Centuries of Western Music, an Anthology with an Historical Introduction*, Cologne, Arno Volk Verlag, 1961 (Musikwerk, 12).

Galli 1882
Galli, Amintore. 'Forme liriche. Saggio storico e tecnologico. Recitativo semplice', in: *Il teatro illustrato*, II (1882), pp. 131-132.

«Il n'exécute jamais la Basse telle qu'elle est écrite»

Gialdroni 2013
Gialdroni, Teresa. 'La cantata a Roma negli anni del soggiorno italiano di Händel', in: *Georg Friedrich Händel Aufbruch nach Italien*, edited by Helen Geyer and Birgit Johanna Wertenson, Rome, Viella, 2013 (Venetiana / Centro tedesco di studi veneziani, 11), pp. 113-136.

Gjerdingen 2007a
Gjerdingen, Robert O. *Music in the Galant Style*, Oxford, Oxford University Press, 2007.

Gjerdingen 2007b
Id. 'Partimento, que me veux-tu?', in: *Journal of Music Theory*, LI/1 (2007), pp. 85-135.

Gjerdingen 2010
Id. 'Partimenti Written to Impart a Knowledge of Counterpoint and Composition', in: Christensen, Thomas – Gjerdingen, Robert – Sanguinetti, Giorgio – Lutz, Rudolf. *Partimento and Continuo Playing in Theory and in Practice*, Leuven, Leuven University Press, 2010 (Collected Writings of the Orpheus Institute, 9), pp. 43-70.

Gjerdingen 2017a
Id. *Monuments of Partimenti*, 2017, at <http://faculty-web.at.northwestern.edu/music/gjerdingen/partimenti/aboutParti/histOverview.htm>, accessed November 2018.

Gjerdingen 2017b
Id. *Monuments of Solfeggi*, 2017 <http://faculty-web.at.northwestern.edu/music/gjerdingen/solfeggi/index.htm>, accessed November 2018.

Halton 2008
Halton, Rosalind. 'Nicola Porpora and the Cantabile Cello', paper presented at the *Convegno Sidm. Nicola Porpora musicista europeo. Le corti, i teatri, i cantanti, i librettisti (Reggio Calabria, 2-3 October 2008)*, unpublished, online at <http://www.academia.edu/5016315/Nicol%C3%B2_Porpora_and_the_cantabile_Cello>, accessed November 2018.

Haymoz 2017
Haymoz, Jean Yves. 'Discovering the Practice of Improvised Counterpoint', in: *Studies in Historical Improvisation: from Cantare super librum to Partimenti*, edited by Massimiliano Guido, Abington-New York, Routledge, 2017, pp. 90-111.

Hoffmann 2016
Hoffmann, Bettina. ''Einige praetendiren gar einen General-Bass darauff zu wege zu bringen' – Die Gambe als akkordisches Generalbassinstrument', in: *Repertoire, Instrumente und Bauweise der Viola da gamba: XXXVIII. Wissenschaftliche Arbeitstagung und 31. Musikinstrumentenbau-Symposium, Michaelstein, 19. bis 21. November 2010*, edited by Christian Philipsen, Monika Lustig and Ute Omosky, Augsburg, Wissner-Verlag; Blankenburg, Stiftung Kloster Michaelstein, 2016 (Michaelsteiner Konferenzberichte, 80), pp. 251-279.

Kirkendale – Kirkendale 1973
Kirkendale, Ursula – Kirkendale, Warren. 'Antonio Caldara', in: *Dizionario Biografico degli Italiani*, vol. XVI (1973), on line at <http://www.treccani.it/enciclopedia/antonio-caldara_%28Dizionario-Biografico%29/>, accessed November 2018.

LA VIA 1983-1984
LA VIA, Stefano. *Il violoncello a Roma al tempo del Cardinale Ottoboni*, Ph.D. Diss., Rome, Università di Roma 'La Sapienza', 1983-1984.

LA VIA 1987
ID. 'Un'aria di Händel con violoncello obbligato e la tradizione romana', in: *Händel e gli Scarlatti a Roma: Atti del Convegno internazionale di studi (Roma, 12-14 giugno 1985)*, edited by Nino Pirrotta and Agostino Ziino, Florence, Olschki, 1987, pp. 49-71.

LYMENSTULL 2014
LYMENSTULL, Eva. *Chordal Continuo Realization on the Violoncello*, M.Mus. Diss., The Hague, Royal Conservatory of The Hague, 2014.

MOORE 1992
MOORE, Robin. 'The Decline of Improvisation in Western Art Music: An Interpretation of Change', in: *International Review of the Aesthetics and Sociology of Music*, XXIII/1 (1992), pp. 61-84.

NUTI 2007
NUTI, Giulia. *The Performance of Italian Basso Continuo: Style in Keyboard Accompaniment in the Seventeenth and Eighteenth Centuries*, Aldershot, Ashgate, 2007.

OLIVIERI 2009
OLIVIERI, Guido. 'Cello Teaching and Playing in Naples in the Early Eighteenth Century: Francesco Paolo Supriani's Principij da imparare a suonare il violoncello', in: *Performance Practice: Issues and approaches*, edited by Timothy D. Watkins, Ann Arbor (MI), Steglein, 2009, pp. 109-136.

RODARI 1973
RODARI, Gianni. *Grammatica della fantasia: introduzione all'arte di inventare storie*, Turin, Einaudi, 1973 (Piccola biblioteca Einaudi, 221).

ROMANOU 2009
ROMANOU, Katy. *A Cembalo for Nabucco? - Basso Continuo Improvisation in 19th-Century Opera Performances in Italy and Corfú*, paper presented at the Biennial Euro-Mediterranean Music Conference, University of Nicosia, 18-20 September 2009, unpublished, online at <https://www.academia.edu/3256291/A_cembalo_for_Nabuco_-_Basso_continuo_improvisation_in_19th_century_opera_performances_in_Italy_and_Corf%C3%B9>, accessed November 2018.

ROSE 1965
ROSE, Gloria. 'Agazzari and the Improvising Orchestra', in: *Journal of the American Musicological Society*, XVIII/3 (1965), pp. 382-393.

SANGUINETTI 2009
SANGUINETTI, Giorgio. 'La scala come modello per la composizione', in: *Rivista di analisi e teoria musicale*, XV/1 (2009), pp. 69-94.

SANGUINETTI 2012
ID. *The Art of Partimento: History, Theory, and Practice*, Oxford, Oxford University Press, 2012.

SCHUBERT 2014
SCHUBERT, Peter. 'From Improvisation to Composition: Three 16th Century Case Studies', in: *Improvising Early Music: The History of Musical Improvisation from the Late Middle Ages to the Early Baroque*, edited by Dirk Moelants, Leuven, Leuven University Press, 2014 (Collected Writings of the Orpheus Institute, 11), pp. 93-130.

STEIN 2014
STEIN, Daniel. *Figure It Out: An Approach on Playing Basso Continuo on the Violin*, Ph.D. Diss., Bloomington (IN), Indiana University, 2014.

STROBBE 2014
STROBBE, Lieven. *Tonal Tools: For Keyboard Players*, Antwerpen, Garant, 2014.

STROBBE – VAN REGENMORTEL 2012
STROBBE, Lieven – VAN REGENMORTEL, Hans. 'Music Theory and Musical Practice: Dichotomy or Entwining?', in: *Dutch Journal of Music Theory*, XVII/1 (2012), pp. 19-30.

TODEA 2014
TODEA, Flavia C. *Eighteenth Century Techniques of Classical Improvisation on the Violin: Pedagogy, Practice and Decline*, Ph.D. Diss., Perth, Western Australian Academy of Performing Arts, Edith Cowan University 2014.

TORCHI 1894
TORCHI, Luigi. 'L'accompagnamento degl'istrumenti nei melodrammi italiani della prima metà del Seicento', in: *Rivista musicale italiana*, I/1 (1894), pp. 7-38.

VACCARO 1981
VACCARO, Jean-Michel. *La Musique de luth en France au XVI siècle*, Paris, CNRS, 1981.

VANSCHEEUWIJCK 1996
VANSCHEEUWIJCK, Marc. 'The Baroque Cello and Its Performance', in: *Performance Practice Review*, IX/1 (1996), pp. 78-96.

WASIELEWSKI 1894
WASIELEWSKI, Wilhelm J. von. *The Violoncello and Its History*, translated by Isabella S. E. Stigand, Novello, London, Novello, 1894.

WATKINS 1996
WATKINS, David. 'Corelli's Op. 5 Sonatas: "Violino e violone o cimbalo?"', in: *Early Music*, XXIV/4 (1996), pp. 645-663.

WHITTAKER 2012
WHITTAKER, Nathan H. *Chordal Cello Accompaniment: The Proof and Practice of Figured Bass Realization on the Violoncello from 1660-1850*, D.M.A. Diss., Seattle (WA), University of Washington, 2012.

YOUNG 2014
YOUNG, James O. 'Congetture sulle composizioni non originali', in: *Estetica. Studi e ricerche* [*Ladri di Musica, filosofia, musica e plagio*, edited by Alessandro Bertinetto, Ezio Gambia and Davide Sisto], IV/1 (2014), pp. 23-34.

On the Borderlines of Improvisation: Caccini, Monteverdi and the Freedoms of the Performer

Anthony Pryer
(Goldsmiths' College, University of London)

The Baroque in Context: Rethinking the Oral/Written Divide

Improvisation during the Baroque period stands more or less at the midpoint in the documented history of the practice. Moreover, what that history reveals is that the activities we subsume under the single term 'improvisation' comprise a complex and varied field of musical behaviour, not all elements of which are quite as spontaneous or 'in the moment' as they might appear. Improvisation is usually a 'cross-border' product arising from the interaction of both oral and written cultures, or rehearsed and spontaneous musical activity, or the routine application of performance conventions to written cues within the notation. In the middle of this activity it is sometimes difficult to distinguish between embellished compositions and *impromptu* explorations, and moments of genuine freedom often coexist alongside routine habits of decoration associated with certain genres. Moreover, there is always a framework of 'common practice' musical styles which both guide and constrain the limits of supposed 'spontaneous' creativity. To paraphrase the philosopher (and musician) Schopenhauer, musicians may do as they will, but they cannot will as they will[1] — that is, they cannot freely control or be conscious of all the forces that help to bring their apparently 'spontaneous' musical ideas, situated within a particular style, into being.

If the list above covers how, and under what circumstances, people employ improvisatory practices, then we are still left with the issue of why they pursue them at all — that is, why 'improvisation' is deemed in any society to be desirable and valuable. In fact it fulfills many functions. It can operate as a valued manifestation of technical skill and virtuosity, or as a means of producing melodic beauty, expression, and rhetorical

---

[1]. Schopenhauer 1960, p. 18.

enhancement. It may also serve to confirm a performer's understanding of style and performance conventions, and on some occasions be a symptom of a person's inspiration, spiritual possession or ecstasy. Nor is it entirely unknown for improvisation to be taken as a convenient medium of self-advertisement and individualism, or as an indicator of that artistic inspiration and creativity proper to musical geniuses. Not surprisingly, these complex factors make it difficult to know on any particular occasion what kind of 'improvisation' we are witnessing, and whether we should take the event as an unquestionable confirmation of the creativity and imagination of the performers involved. Clearly any clarification of the meaning of Baroque improvisational practices must involve some understanding of the traditions in that field and what they bequeathed to the seventeenth century. It must also re-assess the concepts under which define and judge improvisation.

The most obvious place to start is the issue of the supposed separation of oral and written cultures, a 'separation', as we shall see, that is hopelessly compromised in the Baroque period. Of course, there have been times in western history when musical cultures seem to have been almost entirely oral in nature. For example, Isidore of Seville, writing in the early seventh century of the Christian era, tells us that «unless sounds are held by the memory of man they perish because they cannot be written down»[2]. What we should notice, however, is that Isidore accepts that even in his society there is at least one possible substitute for written notation — memory, which in itself can act as a kind of 'virtual notation'. Indeed many cultures in the world still employ systems of rote learning under a 'master' (they are usually men) to train novices in the replication of traditional repertories[3]. Moreover, the identities of 'works' and their performances can sometimes be more stable under an oral system than under a written one — a phenomenon which is exemplified in modern times in the West by the tendency of some performers surreptitiously to replicate CD performance interpretations by admired artists in baroque and other repertories. The danger is that such a practice copies the musical achievement without fully understanding the knowledge and musical judgments that make that achievement possible and its procedures adaptable to new circumstances. Quantz, writing in 1752, highlights exactly this dilemma when he reports on what he clearly considers to be deceptive practices in Italy: «as it is the mode with most singers, you must keep a master constantly at hand from whom you can learn variations [...] and if you do this you will remain a student all your life and will never become a master yourself»[4].

From the point of view of defining improvisation the principle we should draw from this is that the most telling divide when it comes to 'creativity' in performance is not that between oral and written practices, but between the rehearsed and un-rehearsed elements. FIG. 1 represents this important distinction in visual form. It allows for the location of

---

[2]. ISIDORE OF SEVILLE 2006, , Book III, Section XIV, p. 95.
[3]. For a comparison of western and non-western practices see NETTL 1974.
[4]. QUANTZ 1966, Chapter XIV, Section 3, p. 163.

the 'creative' demands of different types of music by plotting them on a grid — the oral/written divide is shown by the left hand axis and the prepared/unprepared axis runs along the top. For example, 'oral' popular music tends to have almost no written transmission of the music (though there may be of its texts), and even its apparently 'spontaneous' performance effects, are frequently learnt by rote in rehearsal, with relatively few diversions in the live event. By contrast, Baroque vocal music is deeply embedded in a notated culture but is typically open to a large number of unprepared features in performance.

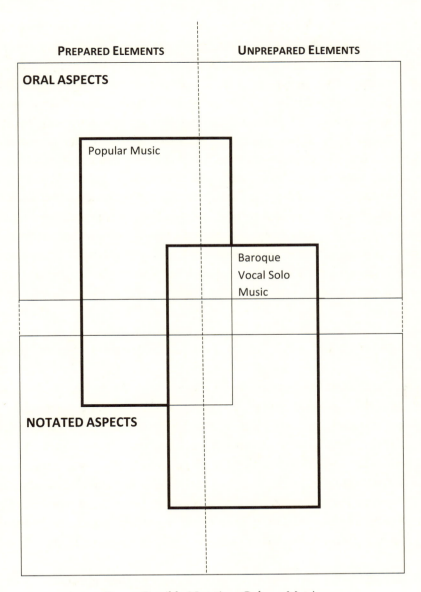

Fig. 1: Possible Notation-Culture Matrix

What Fig. 1 also suggests is that musical performances rarely derive 'purely' from one tradition or the other — the oral or the written — and history reveals some of the reasons why this might be so. For example, we know that the Ancient Greeks had musical notation (many musical fragments, including settings of the choruses of plays by Euripides, survive)[5], but some performances were certainly learnt by rote, and within those notation-free performances strong stylistic limits were placed on acceptable experimentation and embellishment. Indeed, one instance is described by Aristophanes in an episode from his play *Clouds* (lines 961-972). Village boys are rehearsing a song by ear, and the master tells us «if any of them fooled around with the tune or twisted» the mode like the composer Phrynis «he was soundly beaten for obliterating the true Muses»[6]. Clearly it was not enough that a melody might be well known, or even that a version of it might exist in a written copy; the correct approach still had to be conveyed by a person who understood the conventions of performance and the limits of style. Nineteen hundred years later in Italy a very similar approach was also in operation. A letter survives from the composer Cesare Marotta in Rome to Enzo Bentivoglio in Ferrara (3 March 1614) concerning a certain singer called Francesca. He explains that he normally «teaches Francesca by rote, and not because she cannot read music, but because the notation is insufficient to communicate the [...] monodic style»[7]. Notational systems may seem to provide independent records of music but they still require some oral transmission of the appropriate 'reading cultures' that will enable the performer to transform the signs into culturally understood music. When it comes to the performing arts, the menu is never the meal — a fact that Caccini and others struggled to compensate for when their semi-improvised music hit the cultures of print in the early seventeenth century, as we shall see shortly.

Improvisation and the Constraints of 'Common-Practice' Styles

An understanding of the boundaries of style is central for the art of improvisation. It is no accident that the Baroque, which in some ways was obsessed with the definition of styles (*stile antico, stile moderno, stile concitato, stile rappresentativo, style brisé, style galant*, etc.; the division of music into church, chamber or stage types; the increasing separation of instrumental styles from vocal styles; the French *clavecin* style; the Italian violin style; the distinct national styles of operatic singing; and so on), was also a period where improvisation flourished. The more secure and clear those stylistic boundaries were, the more easily could performers exercise freedoms within those boundaries and, in the moment, draw on a fully understood and accepted musical language. Moreover, the dramatic shift in

---

[5]. Sixty-one surviving examples are documented and transcribed in POHLMANN – WEST 2001.
[6]. Translation from BARKER 1984, pp. 101-102.
[7]. HILL 1997, vol. I, pp. 128-129.

common practice around 1600 from polyphony to melodies with harmonic accompaniment (exemplified in the pervasive use of figured bass), freed up the opportunities for performance ornamentation without endangering too much the harmonic structures of works or their textural clarity.

In those periods where common practice breaks down, as in the twentieth century for example, there tends to be a reduction in the general employment of improvisation, even if it is preserved in certain subcultures (such as Jazz, aleatoric avant-garde music, or improvised piano accompaniments to early silent films), each of which develops its own 'local' common practices with its own self-imposed limits. After all, no one would have expected Miles Davis or La Monte Young to burst into pastiche Bartók, let alone embrace Mozartian musical procedures. What this 'common-practice principle' does indicate is that 'improvised' performances are rarely completely invented or whimsically free, and this has important implications for the quality of 'spontaneity' often said to be associated with improvisations. Within a common-practice context 'spontaneity' in performance frequently turns out to be, not a compositional 'cause' (that is, not the process by which the music is 'invented'), but rather a somewhat arch 'style of presentation' — a fact evidenced, to take but one example from the Baroque period, by the care with which Giulio Caccini attempted to convey in his *Le nuove musiche* (1602) the importance in performance presentations of «a certain noble negligence of song» (una certa nobile sprezzatura di canto)[8]. Indeed, in a certain sense we may take this to mean that performers who cannot fake spontaneity cannot be successful performers at all, a precept with which many performers today would agree — it is part of the 'stylishness' of performing, even if it does on occasion offend against the claims of creativity on the part of performers. Moreover, the equivalent in compositional terms can be found in the way in which many genres — capriccios, fantasias, impromptus, rhapsodies, *etc.* — attempt to mimic the attributes of spontaneously created music despite being carefully crafted and notated.

Of course, common practice styles are frequently made manifest through, and preserved by, the notated examples of music from their culture. Hence it should not surprise us that apparently un-written 'spontaneous' improvisations have often been developed in relation to notated ideas. For example in the final chapter — on improvisation — of C. P. E. Bach's *Essay on the True Art of Playing Keyboard Instruments* he offers many notated examples of bass-lines that he will «leave to the private study of my reader» before attempts are made to elaborate them into improvised preludes and fantasias[9]. There were, long before the eighteenth century, already well-established traditions of improvised

---

[8]. HITCHCOCK 1970B, p. 44; CACCINI 1602, 'Ai Lettori' (To the Readers), unnumbered p. 1. The term *sprezzatura* famously occurs in Baldassarre Castiglione's *Il Cortegiano* completed in 1521. See SACCONE 1983. According to PIRROTTA 1984, p. 227, its musical use added a new application to a term already used to denote «the agile suppleness of the ideal dancer».

[9]. BACH 1974, p. 436.

music constructed on various schematic chord sequences — such as ostinato-based pieces, variations, figurational preludes and many other types. Indeed, the pre-determined chordal basis of the figurational-prelude type is obvious in several works from Book 1 of J. S. Bach's *Well-Tempered Clavier*. For example, Preludes numbers 2 in C minor, 6 in D minor, 8 in E-flat minor, and 15 in G major all begin with embellishments of the same figured bass sequence: 5/3; 6/4; 7/4/2; and 5/3[10].

The tension between improvisatory opportunities and written or rehearsed preparation reached a kind of crisis in the seventeenth and eighteenth centuries, a crisis most easily observed in relation to what many take to be that most obvious manifestation of momentary invention — the *ad libitum* cadenza. The dilemma is best illustrated by the practices of Beethoven at the end of our period. Descriptions exist of Beethoven apparently improvising dazzling cadenzas for several of his works around 1800 — as in his First Piano Concerto, for example, or the Piano Quintet Op. 16 (a work in any case closely modeled on Mozart's Quintet, K 452) — but he none-the-less seems to have written down sketches of cadenza material for those works before their performances happened[11]. This was probably because he was trying to reconcile the traditions of *ad libitum* performance with his desire for greater compositional control, the desire to produce a perfectly formed work on the spur of the moment. He is reported as saying that no artist deserved the title of 'virtuoso' unless his improvisations could pass for written compositions[12]. His solution seems to have been partly to plan his 'improvisations' in writing before he developed them in performance, because 'pure' improvisations almost inevitably have different characteristics from written compositions. A summary of these differing tendencies can be found in TABLE 1, and they suggest that it is not helpful to think of improvisations as simple equivalents to compositions in un-notated form.

Free improvisations tend to be pretexts for certain kinds of event[13], rather than the primary, if virtual, texts of musical works[14], and in that sense Beethoven was not so much drawing together improvisations and compositions, as intervening in the former to such a great extent that they in fact became the latter. This impulse should be distinguished from the use of written templates to guide performers who have to insert improvisations during fluid situations to fill the time. Girolamo Frescobaldi, for example, speaking of church services in the 'Preface' to his *Fiori musicali* (1635), tells us that the pieces «may be used as one pleases», but it is «a matter of great importance» for players to refer to the scores he has provided «because this practice, like a touchstone, distinguishes and makes known the true gold of the *virtuosi* from the actions of the ignorant. Nothing else need be said except

---

[10]. Further on improvising preludes and fantasias in the Baroque see MOERSCH 2009, pp. 160-164.
[11]. See KINDERMAN 2008.
[12]. WHITMORE 1991, p. 202.
[13]. See COOK 2017.
[14]. See also the discussion in DAHLHAUS 1987.

that practice is the master of all»[15]. Clearly the implication here is that imaginative and worthwhile improvisations need to be built upon the study and understanding of relevant models, and are very unlikely to emerge from an unsullied field of ignorance.

TABLE 1: DIVERGENT TENDENCIES BETWEEN COMPOSITIONS AND IMPROVISATIONS

COMPOSITION	IMPROVISATION
1. The material is integrated before the performance. The whole, or 'idea', may be conceived in an inspired moment, but the details are then 'composed out' prior to the performance.	1. The material is integrated experientially in virtue of the performance. There is a tendency to arbitrary voice leading, isolated splashes of sound, unbalanced forms, etc. Some details may be conceived beforehand, but the 'whole' 'emerges' or has to be constructed.
2. All elements of the musical material tend to play an equal role in the composition.	2. There is a tendency to privilege only one or two parameters (melody, or rhythm, or methods of sound attack or manipulation, or harmony, etc.).
3. Style arises from the techniques employed.	3. Style tends to control the techniques employed.
4. Performers are primarily concerned with the reproduction of the music as a 'text'.	4. Performers tend to use the prepared elements as 'pretexts' for the display of individualism, virtuosity, spontaneous decision-making (characterized as 'risk'), and the presentation of unpredictable events (characterized as 'discoveries').
5. Performances are primarily characterized as presentations of a work.	5. Performances are primarily seen as a celebration of a performer or an event.

There have been several junctures in the history of Western music where oral and written cultures have clashed. Major examples include the struggle to transfer the plainsong repertory into notated form in the ninth and tenth centuries[16], the collision between improvisational practices and the cultures of print in the late sixteenth century (of which more soon), and the transformation currently taking place in the field of composition between traditional methods employing score notation and the new technologies of computer generated music and sound art. In such cases important questions arise as to how a 'composition' might emerge from the mix of oral and written cultures, and how effective a notation (or other retrieval system) might be in preserving and transmitting the necessary ingredients of the 'work' (a problematic concept in itself, especially when improvisation might be involved). Moreover, what freedoms are given to, and expected of, the performer to add to the preserved information and reconstitute it as sounding music. These issues interact in complex ways in a famous source from the early Baroque that gives us a great deal of information about the works it contains — Caccini's *Le nuove musiche* published in Florence in 1602.

---

[15]. Translation from MCCLINTOCK 1979, pp. 135-136.

[16]. For a fascinating cultural and musicological examination of the emergence of chant compositions and their ultimate preservation in distorting notational systems, see JEFFERY 1992.

Anthony Pryer

Writing the Unwritable: The Case of Caccini's *Le Nuove Musiche*

The plural reference to 'new musics' in Caccini's title (the singular form would have been '*La nuova musica*') implies not only that the volume represents a decisive break with practices from the past, but also that the innovations are of more than one kind. Just exactly which types of multiple developments the collection might contain is not immediately clear. After all, Caccini himself did not invent monody nor, for that matter, its application to opera; clear traces of disputes over precedence with other protagonists in that venture survive not only in the prefaces by Jacopo Peri and himself in their respective settings of the opera *L'Euridice*, but also in a number of other sources[17]. Moreover, *Le nuove musiche* was quite probably not even the first volume of monodies published — that distinction seems to belong to Domenico Melli's *Musiche composte sopra alcuni madrigali* of 1602[18]. Again, we should recognise that it is not even Caccini's famous codification of ornaments that is especially innovative. Rather it is his holistic approach to their application[19], his insistence on linking their use to expressive intentions and detailed sensitivity to the words, and his careful calibration of the interplay between patterned, written ornaments and improvised 'characterisation' elements applied in the moment of performance by the singer with grace and nobility.

These attributes may be striking in Caccini's 'Preface', but in fact not even these were wholly his invention. His comments about demeanour, grace, nobility, ideal accompaniments, and tasteful ornamentation largely parallel those advocated in great detail some twenty years before in a document sent to him by Giovanni Bardi (a founder of the Florentine Camerata) — the *Discourse Addressed to Giulio Caccini Called the Roman, on Ancient Music and Good Singing*[20].

---

[17]. For texts and translations of the relevant documents by Jacopo Peri, Giulio Caccini, Emilio de' Cavalieri, Marco da Gagliano and Ottavio Rinuccini, see CARTER – SZWEYKOWSKI 1994. Also see STRUNK 1998, pp. 523-525, for a letter of 1634 from Pietro de' Bardi to Giovanni Doni which retrospectively recounts the origins of the new style. On Emilio de' Cavalieri's difficulties with Caccini and Antonio Nardi (purported inventor of the *Chitarrone*), see PALISCA 1994, p. 405. The attacks on Nardi provoked a fierce defence from Caccini in the final paragraph of the Preface to his 1602 print, but when the volume was reprinted in 1608 and 1615 that paragraph was omitted (see HITCHCOCK 1970B, p. 56.)

[18]. As reported in FORTUNE 1953, p. 176, n. 16.

[19]. HITCHCOCK 1970B, p. 48; CACCINI 1602, 'Ai Lettori', [unnumbered] p. 3: «non servono solo le cose particolari, ma tutte insieme la fanno migliore».

[20]. *Discorso mandato a Giulio Caccini detto romano sopra la musica antica, e 'l cantar bene*. The original Italian with parallel translation appears complete in PALISCA 1989, pp. 90-131. The shared topics and their respective page numbers in the Bardi essay (*ibidem*) and the Caccini preface (HITCHCOCK 1970B) include: Plato's view on music and speech (93; 43); the preference for the archlute as an accompanying instrument (117 and 125; 45 and 56); the irrelevance of counterpoint (111; 46), the singer must be guided by the words (115; 46); long syllables should not be placed on short notes (121; 46); the use of long and misplaced *passaggi* is

As for the distinction between performance elements provided by the composer and those supplied by the singer, Bardi provides an interesting metaphor. He tells us that the singer must adjust his voice «like a good cook who adds to the food that he has seasoned well a little sauce or condiment to make it pleasing to his Lord»[21]. Here Bardi seems to be suggesting that, although before the performance the work might exist together with some written in ornaments (that have 'seasoned' it well), the singer's task is to add yet further elements (the 'sauce') that make the overall presentation of the work more fitting and appetizing for its discerning recipients. This leaves us with the thought that even those works printed with ornamental runs or local embellishments in *Le nuove musiche* are open to yet further decoration and expressive enhancement. Moreover, this point is made clear in Caccini's 'Preface' addressed to the readers (*Ai Lettori*) where, after giving fully marked up examples of decoration and sung articulations in relation to 'Deh dove son fuggiti' and other compositions, he tells us «thus they may serve as models from which may be recognized similar places in the following pieces»[22] — that is, the various techniques should be adapted and added to the printed versions of works published in the body of the collection.

This requirement to transfer various types of performance articulation onto the particular poetic and musical situations of the individual works in the volume (which already contain some notated embellishments) is rarely carried through by modern singers. Indeed the relative uniformity of the many performances of one of Caccini's better-known works, 'Amarilli mia bella' demonstrates this very clearly. The performances tend to fall into one of two broad groups. The first comprises those derived from the edition in Parisotti's 1888 anthology, *Arie antiche*[23]. They can be recognised by the characteristic type of accompaniment provided, the substitution in the fifth line of the words 'Dubitar non ti vale' for the original 'Prendi questo mio strale', and the use (notated in the 1888 score) of brief anticipations of the pitches of certain notes at the end of the notes immediately preceding them (following nineteenth century vocal practice). Beniamino Gigli's 1939 recording[24] provides a clear example of a literal performance of Parisotti's edition, complete with vocal 'swoops' from note to note. There are also numerous modern singers who do not specialise in the early music but simply add the piece to their concerts for the sake of repertorial variety, and follow the Parisotti model closely. They rarely employ ornaments of any kind; instead they attempt to give the bare music import by overlaying it with a kind

---

distasteful (127; 46); nobility and grace are important in the demeanour of the singer (111; 43 and 47); and the enthusiasms of plebs (121, «indotta plebe»; 44, «plebi esaltati») should be ignored.

[21]. PALISCA 1989, pp. 114-115.

[22]. HITCHCOCK 1970B, p. 55; CACCINI 1602, 'Ai Lettori', [unnumbered] p. 8: «et accio[c]ché servano per esempio, in riconoscere, in esso musiche i medesimi luoghi».

[23]. PARISOTTI 1888, vol. II, pp. 15-17.

[24]. Recorded on 12 May 1939 and first issued on HMV DB 3895. Now available on Naxos Historical, *The Gigli Edition*, vol. X, Naxos 8.110271, track 5.

of sub-operatic intensity, usually delivered relatively slowly and with a 'beat-counting' uniformity of pulse.

By contrast those dependent on Hitchcock's 1970b edition or a facsimile of the original print (see Ex. 1) tend to add occasional trills (which Caccini calls *gruppi*) and tremolos (which he rather confusingly calls *trilli*), but by and large they follow Caccini's score closely. However, even in this group (which includes singers such as Emma Kirkby[25] and Roberta Invernizzi[26]) it is rare for the performers to improvise those many other expressive and dramatic vocal effects related to the rhetoric of the text that Caccini recommends such as the *esclamazione* (a light, quick attack but with low intensity), the *crescere e scemare della voce* (*crescendo* followed by a *diminuendo* on long notes), the *cascata* (a cascade of notes, applied in various forms) and so on[27].

This hesitancy to go beyond the printed text, even for those with knowledge of appropriate style, may well partly be Caccini's fault. Although in the 'Preface' to *Le nuove musiche* he discuss a range of effects that might be introduced by the performer, his detailed printed examples almost inevitably give the impression that the essentials of the style can still be captured in notation. Moreover, this impression is reinforced in his 1614 publication *Nuove musiche e nuova maniera di scriverle* (New Musics and a New Manner of Writing Them)[28], which asserts on the title page that «all the delicacies of this art can be learned without having to hear the composer sing», and in the 'Preface' to 'discriminating readers' (A Discreti Lettori) where Caccini refers to his style of singing «which I *write out exactly as it is sung*» (my italics: «la quale io scrivo giustamente, come si canta»).

Given the range of vocal effects described in his publications, it is clear that Caccini's assertion cannot be completely true because: a) some effects cannot be put into exact notation; b) certain improvisatory elements are part of the performance style; and c) notation itself can have different functions. In terms of notation functions we make take the example of figured bass. Firstly it acts as an *archive* in that it records exactly what the bass line and harmonies are. However, at the same time it is also a *strategy* for allowing the performer to decide upon certain kinds of textural and voice-leading effects, as well as decorations and responses to the melodic features of the vocal part. We can see therefore that notated instructions can also imply or encapsulate improvisatory practices, not only in relation to figured bass but also elements such as cadenzas, melodic figuration (think of the mathematically suspect decorative embellishments in some of Chopin's melodies)[29], or even

---

[25]. Emma Kirkby, *Arie Antiche*, Columns Musica Oscura 070988 (1993), track 2.

[26]. Roberta Invernizzi and Accademia Strumentali Italiana, *Dolcissimo Sospiro*, Divox CDX 70202-6 (2005), track 9.

[27]. For a full exploration of the complete range of Caccini's suggested vocal effects (and their multiple manifestations) see HITCHCOCK 1970A.

[28]. CACCINI 1614; HITCHCOCK 1978.

[29]. For mathematically incorrect examples from Francesco Rasi's 1608 collection *Vaghezze di musica* see CARTER 2000, p. 15. Minor instances also occur in *Le nuove musiche*, for example in 'Vedrò 'l mio sol' (no. 7), and 'Io parto' (no. 14).

Ex. 1: facsimile of 'Amarilli mia bella' from Caccini's 1602 print.

the notated example of a *trillo* which Caccini gives in his 1602 'Preface'[30]. Although the *trillo* is given in a mathematically correct form (that is, its notes add up to the correct number of beats in the measure) he makes it clear that this is an exercise which he employed while teaching his wife and daughter how to execute and control a particular vocal technique. Therefore the exact notation is merely indicative and the ornament should be delivered more freely in performance[31]. Clearly we cannot discern by simply staring at an example of notated music what the subtle interplay between its strategic and archival functions might be. Moreover, those functions typically exist simultaneously in the same symbol and their implications for the improvising performer rest upon a complex field of understanding.

A more common categorisation of notation employed is that which distinguishes between its prescriptive and descriptive functions, a separation first suggested by the ethnomusicologist Charles Seeger in 1958[32]. Seeger's terms attempt to capture two distinct motivations for writing down music. In prescriptive notation the intention is to tell the performer exactly what to do in a forthcoming performance, whereas with descriptive notation the intention is to record what *was done* in a past performance.

Often early Baroque notated sources contain a complex mix not only of strategic and archival functions, but also of descriptive and prescriptive motivations. Caccini's *Le nuove musiche*, for example, presents some interesting examples among the items included from his stage work *Il rapimento di Cefalo* performed in the Uffizi palace in Florence in 1600 (items 13 a, b, and c in HITCHCOCK 1970B). At the head of the aria 'Muove si dolce' (item 13b) Caccini tells us «This air was sung with the passaggi as given by Melchior Palantrotti, excellent musician of Our Lord's Chapel». Thus this is a clear example of descriptive notation — it tells us what Palantrotti did — even though the figured bass and certain vocal indications (*trillo, esclamazione*) are of a strategic kind. A more complex case is the aria 'Qual trascorrendo' (item 13d) for which Caccini tells us: «This air was sung, with *some* of the *passaggi* as given and *some* according to his own taste, by the famous Francesco Rasi, nobleman of Arezzo, most obliging servant of His Highness, the Duke of Mantua». So the music here is descriptive in so far as it contains sections of *passaggi* performed by Rasi according to his own taste, and yet its general motivation is prescriptive since it largely offers a version of how Caccini would like it to be sung.

In terms of improvisatory freedoms on the part of the performer a complex picture is now beginning to emerge, and it seems clear that those freedoms can operate in relation to three rather different arenas. First we have the particular demeanour, characterisation and stylized attitude chosen and projected by the performer — grace, elegance, *sprezzatura*, real or simulated spontaneity, the particular display of the role of a protagonist in the narrative, and so on. Next we have a range of 'execution techniques' selected by the performer from

---

[30]. HITCHCOCK 1970B, p. 50.
[31]. See the discussion in HITCHCOCK 1970A, pp. 389-390.
[32]. SEEGER 1958.

their repertory of skills and employed for articulating and underlining particular emotive or rhetorical elements in the text and/or music (in Caccini's case, *esclamazione, intonazione della voce, passaggi*, etc.). And thirdly, although less frequently mentioned by theorists, we have the use of improvised embellishment to enhance or even create the structural goals and organization of a work.

This structural use of embellishment is frequently written into the music itself (as in variations for example), or very conventionally applied (as in many performances of *da capo* arias). Its improvised application in early Baroque vocal music is less common, even when the music clearly offers the opportunity. In the case of 'Amarilli mia bella' for example, we can see from TABLE 2 that the text divides into two sections 'A' and 'B' (with the last line repeated at the end as a brief coda). In his print Caccini repeats the text and the music of the long 'B' section exactly. Only in the Coda, which appears after that repetition, and in which he repeats the last line of the text, does he then add new decoration. The long repetition of the 'B' music is almost never subjected to any kind of improvised embellishment in performance (though an interesting exception is provided by Roberta Invernizzi in the recording mentioned above).

TABLE 2: MUSICAL STRUCTURE, TEXT AND TRANSLATION OF CACCINI'S 'AMARILI MIA BELLA'

MUSIC	TEXT	TRANSLATION
A	1. *Amarilli mia bella*	1. Amarilli my love
	2. *Non credi, o del mio cor dolce desio*	2. Do you not believe, o sweet desire of my heart
	3. *D'esser tu l'amor mio?*	3. That you are my love?
B	4. *Credilo pur, e se timor t'assale*	4. Believe it indeed, and if fear torments you
	5. *Prendi questo mio strale*	5. Take this arrow of mine
	6. *Aprim'il petto, e vedrai scritto il core*	6. Open my breast, and you will see written on my heart
	7. *'Amarilli è 'l mio amore'*	7. 'Amarilli is my love'
Coda	7. *'Amarilli è 'l mio amore'* [In the 1602 printed version, after the fully written out repeat of the **B** section (Hitchcock ed., bars 28-44), Line 7 is again repeated with new music (bars 44-50) and *passaggi*. This coda is not in the early manuscript versions.]	7. 'Amarilli is my love'

This nervousness about the improvised structural use of embellishment in forms where it is not absolutely conventionally applied seems to change significantly only at the end of the Baroque period. It is interesting that C. P. E. Bach in his *Essay* keeps distinct his remarks on embellishment (which are in Part I, Chapter 2) from those on improvisation as such (in Part II, Chapter 7). He also separates embellishments into two types: the conventional (indicated by established signs); and the free (which lack signs and consist of many short notes)³³. What we do find in C. P. E. Bach is the use of increasingly elaborate and carefully graded ornamentation to complement the structural drive of the movement. For example, in the third movement of his third Sonata from his *Sech sonaten [...] mit verändarten Reprisen* (Wq. 50), the published version clearly shows this tendency (bars 74-94). Moreover, in the British Library there is a copy of the print (GB-Lbl. K.10.a23) with C. P. E. Bach's additional annotated embellishments which intensify yet further the formal unfolding of the work. It is in this sense that ornamentation in the late Baroque becomes structurally integral to the music, and is not just focused on those decorative or expressive functions that we find more generally in the period[34].

Given the many complications associated with the functions and placing of improvised embellishments in Baroque works, and also the multiple functions of the notations involved, it would be difficult to take at face value the claim that Caccini's printed scores should be seen as «frozen improvisations» that require a certain «interpretative flexibility, and above all *sprezzatura*, to bring them to life»[35]. As we have seen the notation hardly functions solely as an archive of a past act of performance by Caccini or anyone else, and the term «interpretative flexibility» covers a range of complex interventions (some restricted by pattern-book formulas, performance conventions, common-practice styles, and much else besides) concerned variously with the elaboration and characterisation of the music, the elucidation of form, and with individual acts of performer display.

However, there is another sense in which we may construe the term «frozen improvisations» in relation to the works in Caccini's print. They are not records of actual (now fixed) past improvisations, but rather are tangible traces of an ongoing process through which the identity of the works continue to emerge and gain meaning — not in a straight line from oral creation to written record but from a sometimes opaque confluence of the two. 'Amarilli mia bella' for example exists in at least two manuscript versions that seem to predate the 1602 publication — Florence, Biblioteca Nazionale, I-Fn: ms. Magl. xix. 66 (folio 18ʳ), and Brussels, Bibliotheque du Conservatoire, B-Bc: ms. 704 (p. 46)[36]. Both

---

[33]. BACH 1974, p. 80.

[34]. It is interesting to note that when Frederick Neumann published his acclaimed study on ornamentation in the Baroque (NEUMANN 1978) he divided the chapters into types of ornament, but in his later work on Mozart (NEUMANN 1986) he treated ornamentation in relation to the different movement forms in which they were employed. This tendency to see structural musical goals as being made manifest through the intensification and embellishment of basic music material is exactly what we find in the early twentieth-century analytic methods of Heinrich Schenker. His approach was to see the goal-directed foreground and middle ground textures of a work as elaborations of a basic *Ursatz* and a proto-melodic *Urline*. It can hardly be a coincidence that Schenker did his Ph.D. on C. P. E. Bach, produced performing editions of his music, and published a pioneering study of ornamentation (see SCHENKER 1903).

[35]. CARTER 1984, p. 217.

[36]. For a survey of the sources of 'Anima mia bella' see CARTER 1988, which contains (p. 254) a facsimile of the Brussels source. The Florence source is reproduced in DONINGTON 1981, Plate VI (between pp. 64-65).

of these provide much simplified forms of the printed version. As such they are unlikely to present actual performed improvisations at all, and we should not assume that all 'plain' versions necessarily represent an earlier stage of the conception of the work.

Ex. 2: edited musical extracts from 'Amarilli mia bella'.

a) CACCINI 1602, opening of Section A (= HITCHCOCK 1970B, bars. 1-5).

I-Fn ms. Magl. XIX.66, f. 18ʳ.

Passamezzo antico bass.

b) CACCINI 1602, close of Section B (= HITCHCOCK 1970B, bars. 20-27, and repeated 37-44).

I-Fn ms. Magl. XIX.66, f. 18ʳ.

c) CACCINI 1602, Coda (= HITCHCOCK 1970B, bars. 44-50).

As Ex. 2 reveals, the version in Florence is slightly 'squarer' in its rhythms (lacking the opportunity for an *esclamazione* on the first syllable of 'Amarilli' for example), and at the close of the 'B' section it lacks the small embellishments, chromaticisms and palpitating rests. Also the extensively decorated final impassioned cry of 'Amarilli è 'l mio amore' (Ex. 1c) in the Coda is entirely missing from the manuscript. It is possible that someone may have learnt the skeletal framework of the song from the Florence 'template' source but it is unlikely to preserve the details of an actual performance. It could perhaps serve for the performer as the beginning of an improvisatory process, but not the end of one; the notation comes before the improvisation not after it from this perspective. From the point of view of the composer, however, the written version might well contain the ghostly trace of genuine improvisatory exploration in relation to the creation of the song. The bass line of the 'A' music is clearly an elaboration of the passamezzo antico scheme — a scheme also adumbrated in several other items in *Le nuove musiche*, most clearly in no. 13b, 'Muove sì dolce'.

These interlocking layers of compositional exploration, notated templates and elaborations by a performer (who is sometimes also the composer) leave questions of creativity, ownership, and improvisation problematically entwined in this repertory. Another intriguing example, which I have discussed (together with music examples) in some detail elsewhere[37], is 'Possente spirto' from Monteverdi's 1607 opera *Orfeo*, an aria for which Monteverdi famously provided two versions of the vocal line sections — one 'plain' and the other decorated. The first surprise is that the 'plain' version is already decorated since this is another one of those works based on the passamezzo antico. Even more surprisingly 'Monteverdi's' elaborated version of a passamezzo antico shows a remarkable similarity to an aria contained in Caccini's 1602 *Le nuove musiche*, 'Qual trascorrendo' (no. 13d), an item originally composed for Caccini's stage work *Il rapimento di Cefalo*. We do know from the rubric in Caccini's volume that 'Qual trascorrendo' was sung by Francesco Rasi and, and, interestingly enough, it is precisely Rasi who seems to have sung the role of Orfeo in Monteverdi's opera.

There are some differences of ornamentation between Caccini's piece and those in 'Possente spirto', but we should remember that we are not looking at all the embellishments sung by Rasi in Caccini's printed version. As we have seen, Caccini tells us that Rasi sang some of the *passaggi* according to his own taste and not as written, therefore Rasi's original embellishments for Caccini's aria may have been even closer to the decorated version in Monteverdi's score than is now apparent. Also the words of 'Qual trascorrendo' are so close to the situation in Monteverdi's opera that it would be surprising if some kind of adaptation had not recommend itself to both Rasi and Monteverdi. After all, Orfeo — an offspring of the Sun God Apollo — has just embarked on an unworldly journey amongst

---

[37]. See PRYER 2007, pp. 12-14.

the shades of Hell to rescue his love. She will not in the end return to earth but will be placed to shine among the stars. And what does the text of Caccini's aria say? «As the sun brings day to the shades of night, as it proceeds on its ethereal journey, so love shines among the stars, brightening our lives and luring us with its splendour»[38]. It seems then that 'Qual trascorrendo', already composed by Caccini as a variation on the improvisatory structural model of the passamezzo antico, and enlivened and adapted in performance by Rasi's personal repertory of improvisatory *passaggi*, finally found itself embedded in Monteverdi's grand aria as it was customised for use in his opera. Clearly 'Monteverdi's' work was only the latest manifestation in a series of improvisatory adaptations that inevitably emerged from the constant interchange between the cultures of unwritten performance and written compositions during the period.

IMPROVISATION, AUTHORSHIP AND CREATIVE FREEDOMS

This interdependence of oral and written cultures may help to explain why definitions of the term 'improvisation' that we find in dictionaries and theoretical writings around 1600 turn out to be surprisingly brief and unhelpful. For example, the various editions of John Florio's dictionary of Italian and English, first published in 1598, says that *improvvisare* means «to sing or speake extempore»[39] — a description that was repeated in many dictionaries of the time and one that simply equates being 'out of time' or in free rhythm with any kind of spontaneous composition. We get a different emphasis from the famous Accademia della Crusca dictionary of 1612 which illustrates the word with reference to the suddenness and anti-rational nature of certain improvised actions[40]. What is particularly interesting is that neither Florio nor Crusca, nor any Italian source at all before the eighteenth century seems to contain the noun for an 'improviser' (*improvvisatore*), presumably because it was not considered a special skill distinct and separable from performance or composition.

Monteverdi's attitude is intriguing here since he seems to claim 'Possente spirto' as his own in a letter of 9 December 1616 when he tells us «*Arianna* led me to a just lament, and *Orfeo* to a righteous prayer»[41]. However, it may be that Monteverdi was implying, not ownership of the aria model, nor of the background traditions that went into it, but

---

[38]. See HITCHCOCK 1970B, p. 21: «Qual trascorrendo per gli eterei campi / Il sol quaggiù l'ombre notturne aggiorna / Tale amor sulle stele almo soggiorna / E cosparge fra noi fulgidi lampi / Per invogliare altrui de sol splendore».

[39]. 'Improvvisare', in: FLORIO 1611.

[40]. CRUSCA 1612 records *improvviso*, both as an adjective («il rumore [...] improvviso» [sudden, unexpected or unforseen noise]) and as an adverb («Il Conte Tegrino rispuose improvviso, e subito, cioè senza pensare, o premeditare» [Count Tegrino replied suddenly and hastily, which means without thinking or premeditation]). Both examples are taken from *Storia di Giovanni Villani* (Florence, 1587).

[41]. LAX 1994, p. 49: «L'Arianna mi porta ad un giusto lamento e l'Orfeo ad una giusta preghiera».

rather the 'invention' of his grand adaptation and its effects. 'Invention' (*invenzione*) is the term most often associated with creativity in his writings[42], but a word that he seems never to have used — and, indeed, it cannot be found in any Italian dictionaries of the period — is originality (*originalità*), that quality of being creatively first and unique. This should not surprise us since it was standard practice for composers of Monteverdi's time to imitate, emulate and pay homage to their colleagues through the medium of quotation, and then subtly re-work their musical material in a new ways. Moreover, it is precisely the techniques of re-combination, variation, invention, and adaptation that form the bedrock of an improvisatory process whether considered from the perspective of performance or composition[43]. These interlocking chains of intertextuality, bringing together both oral and written elements, were also common in 'literary' cultures as well, and seem to have bred few hesitations in relation to the perceived authorship and ownership of the works[44].

Throughout this article we have been attempting to differentiate between relevant and irrelevant factors in relation to our understanding of acts of improvisation. Much of our discussion comes down to the background notion of the role of freedom and its relation to creativity. In fact the difficulties we uncovered with the traditional oral/written divide discussed earlier rest on a confusion between two rather different types of freedom — what we might call 'escape' freedoms and 'fulfilment' freedoms[45]. To claim that *freedom from* notation in oral cultures automatically guarantees that we have the *freedom to* (or the capacity to) create something new is clearly not the case, most obviously in societies were the performance and transmission of music are dominated by rote learning, but also where there may be a lack of creativity to bring the desired fulfilment about. Furthermore, if fulfilment freedoms are to have a chance to operate, to play out creatively as it were, there needs to be some receptivity in at least sections of the community where those achievements can be agreed to be interesting and meaningful. This is where the importance of common-practice musical styles come into play, and why the Baroque was so successful as an 'improvising age'. Its stylistic frameworks were constantly being defined and better

---

[42]. See for example in LAX 1994, p. 28 (letter of 10 September 1609) where he praises a 'certain novel invention' («qualche invenzione nova») in the canzonas of Galeazzo Sirena; or p. 79 (letter of 1 February 1620) where he records that, in relation to his *Lamento di Apollo*, certain gentlemen were 'pleased in the manner of its invention' («piaciuto in maniera nella invenzione»).

[43]. On the cognitive and creative skills needed for these processes see BERKOWITZ 2010.

[44]. To take but one example, the story of Troilus and Cressida was developed out of events in Homer's tale of the Trojan war; it was elaborated in a French source, the *Roman de Trois*, by the twelfth-century poet Benoit de Sainte-Maure, which then influenced the version in Boccaccio's *Il Filostrato*. This in turn formed the basis of Chaucer's poem, which then lent inspiration to Shakespeare's play of the same name. None of this prevented Chaucer from claiming ownership of the work and fixing its identity in a written copy. Thus towards the end of the poem (Book v, line 1795) we find him pleading: «So pray I God that none mis-write thee». For the oral dimensions of Chaucer's poem see MANGUEL 1996, pp. 252-255.

[45]. See the discussion in, for example, BERLIN 2009. Philosophers often refer to the two types as 'freedom from' and 'freedom to'.

understood, and therefore its musical 'liberties' entered into a more nuanced transaction than that of mere *permission*, and its improvisatory practices gained import in ways that mere *licence* or *anarchy* could not. In other words, the art world began to establish a kind of aesthetic equivalent to Rousseau's social contract (*avant la lettre*), so that communal discourses could find ways of negotiating between uniquely interesting products and merely bizarre ones, between imaginative insights with wider import, and the banal fancies of lone individuals.

These restrictions should not be seen as a dreary moral plea for compromise, or some kind of officious insistence that artistic creativity should be curtailed. Clearly composers such as Caccini and Monteverdi managed to produce interesting and enduring works, and ones that played a part in gradually enabling the musical language to evolve ('revolution' is usually too extreme and simplistic a term for cultural change). This they did by moving freely between oral and written influences, and employing a range of improvisatory mechanisms and borrowing techniques in the performance and making of musical works. As the French writer Chateaubriand said: «An original writer is not one who imitates nobody, but one whom nobody can imitate»[46].

Bibliography

Bach 1974
Bach, Carl Philipp Emanuel. *Essay on the True Art of Playing Keyboard Instruments*, (1753), translated and edited by William Mitchell, London, Eulenberg Books, 1974.

Barker 1984
Greek Musical Writings. Volume 1: The Musician and His Art, edited by Andrew Barker, Cambridge-New York, Cambridge University Press, 1984 (Cambridge Readings in the Literature of Music).

Berkowitz 2010
Berkowitz, Aaron. *The Improvising Mind: Cognition and Creativity in the Musical Moment*, Oxford-New York, Oxford University Press, 2010.

Berlin 2009
Berlin, Isaiah. 'Two Concepts of Liberty', in: *Isaiah Berlin: Liberty*, edited by Henry Hardy, Oxford-New York, Oxford University Press, 2009, pp. 166-217.

Caccini 1602
Caccini, Giulio. *Le nuove musiche*, Florence, Marescotti, 1602 [more veneto, 1601].

Caccini 1614
Id. *Nuove musiche e nuova maniera di scriverle*, Florence, Zanobi Pignoni, 1614.

---

[46]. Chateaubriand 1802, vol. II, Chapter 3, p. 153: «L'écrivain original n'est pas celui qui n'imite personne, mais celui que personne ne peut imiter».

CARTER 1984
CARTER, Tim. 'On the Composition and Performance of Caccini's *Le nuove musiche* (1602)', in: *Early Music*, XII/2 (May 1984), pp. 208-217.

CARTER 1988
ID. 'Caccini's 'Amarilli, mia bella': Some Questions (and a Few Answers)', in: *Journal of the Royal Musical Association*, CXIII/2 (1988), pp. 250-273.

CARTER 2000
ID. 'Printing the "New Music"', in: *Music and the Cultures of Print*, edited by Kate van Orden, New York, Garland, 2000 (Garland Reference Library of the Humanities, 2027 / Critical and Cultural Musicology, 1), pp. 3-37.

CARTER – SZWEYKOWSKI 1994
Composing Opera: from Dafne to Ulisse Errante, translated and edited by Tim Carter and Zygmunt Szweykowski, Kraków, Musica Jagellonica, 1994 (Practica Musica, 2).

CHATEAUBRIAND 1802
CHATEAUBRIAND, François-Auguste René vicomte de. *Génie du christianisme*, 5 vols., Paris, Chez Migneret, 1802.

COOK 2017
COOK, Nicholas. 'Scripting Social Interaction: Improvisation, Performance and Western "Art" Music,' in: *Improvisation and Social Aesthetics*, edited by Georgina Born, Eric Lewis and Will Straw, Durham (NC), Duke University Press, 2017, pp. 59-77.

CRUSCA 1612
Vocabolario degli accademici della Crusca, Venice, Giovanni Alberti, 1612.

DAHLHAUS 1987
DAHLHAUS, Carl. 'Composition and Improvisation' in: *Schoenberg and the New Music: Essays by Carl Dahlhaus*, edited and translated by Derrick Puffett and Alfred Clayton, Cambridge-New York, Cambridge University Press, 1987, pp. 265-273.

DONINGTON 1981
DONINGTON, Robert. *The Rise of Opera*, London, Faber and Faber, 1981.

FLORIO 1611
FLORIO, John. Revised as *Queen Anna's New World of Words, or Dictionarie of the Italian and English tongues*, London, Edward Blount and William Barret, 1611.

FORTUNE 1953
FORTUNE, Nigel. 'Italian Secular Monody from 1600 to 1635: An Introductory Survey', in: *The Musical Quarterly*, XXXIX/2 (April 1953), pp. 171-195.

FORTUNE 1954
ID. 'Italian 17th-century Singing', in: *Music & Letters*, XXXV/3 (July 1954), pp. 206-219.

HILL 1997
HILL, John Walter. *Roman Monody, Cantata, and Opera from the Circles around Cardinal Montalto*, 2 vols., Oxford, Clarendon Press, 1997 (Oxford Monographs on Music).

HITCHCOCK 1970A
HITCHCOCK, H. Wiley. 'Vocal Ornamentation in Caccini's *Nuove Musiche*', in: *The Musical Quarterly*, LVI/3 (July 1970), pp. 389-404.

HITCHCOCK 1970B
CACCINI, Giulio. *Le nuove musiche*, edited by H. Wiley Hitchcock, Madison, A-R Editions, 1970 (Recent Researches in the Music of the Baroque Era, 9).

HITCHCOCK 1978
ID. *Nuove musiche e nuova maniera di scriverle (1614)*, edited by H. Wiley Hitchcock, Madison, A-R Editions, 1978 (Recent Researches in the Music of the Baroque Era, 28).

ISIDORE OF SEVILLE 2006
ISIDORE OF SEVILLE. *The Etymologies*, translated by Stephen Barney, W. Lewis, Jennifer Beach and Oliver Berghof, Cambridge, Cambridge University Press, 2006 (Etymologiæ).

JEFFERY 1992
JEFFERY, Peter. *Re-envisioning Past Musical Cultures: Ethnomusicology in the Study of Gregorian Chant*, Chicago, Chicago University Press, 1992 (Chicago Studies in Ethnomusicology).

KINDERMAN 2008
KINDERMAN, William. 'A Tale of Two Quintets: Mozart's K. 452 and Beethoven's Op. 16', in: *Variations on the Canon: Essays from Bach to Boulez in Honor of Charles Rosen's Eightieth Birthday*, edited by Robert Curry, David Gable and Robert L. Marshall, Rochester (NY), Rochester University Press, 2008, pp. 55-77.

LAX 1994
Claudio Monteverdi: Lettere, edited by Éva Lax, Florence, Leo Olschki, 1994 (Studi e testi per la storia della musica, 10).

MANGUEL 1996
MANGUEL, Alberto. *A History of Reading*, London, Harper Collins, 1996.

MCCLINTOCK 1979
Readings in the History of Music in Performance, selected, edited and translated by Carol McClintock, Bloomington (IN), Indiana University Press, 1979.

MOERSCH 2009
MOERSCH, Charlotte Mattax. 'Keyboard Improvisation in the Baroque Period', in: *Musical Improvisation: Art, Education and Society*, edited by Gabriel Solis and Bruno Nettl, Urbana (IL), University of Illinois Press, 2009, pp. 150-170.

NETTL 1974
NETTL, Bruno. 'Thoughts on Improvisation: A Comparative Approach', in: *The Musical Quarterly*, LX/1 (January 1974), pp. 1-19.

NEUMANN 1978
NEUMANN, Frederick. *Ornamentation in Baroque and Post-Baroque Music*, Princeton, Princeton University Press, 1978.

NEUMANN 1986
ID. *Ornamentation and Improvisation in Mozart*, Princeton, Princeton University Press, 1986.

PALISCA 1989
PALISCA, Claude. *The Florentine Camerata: Documentary Studies and Translations*, New Haven, Yale University Press, 1989 (Music Theory Translation Series).

PALISCA 1994
ID. *Studies in the History of Italian Music and Music Theory*, Oxford, Clarendon Press, 1994.

PARISOTTI 1888
Arie antiche ad una voce per canto e pianoforte, edited by Alessandro Parisotti, 3 vols., Milan, Ricordi, 1888.

PIRROTTA 1984
PIRROTTA, Nino. *Music and Culture in Italy from the Middle Ages to the Baroque: A Collection of Essays*, Cambridge (MA), Harvard University Press, 1984 (Studies in the History of Music, 1).

POHLMANN – WEST 2001
Documents of Ancient Greek Music: The Extant Melodies and Fragments, edited and transcribed with commentary by Egert Pohlmann and Martin L. West, Oxford-New York, Oxford University Press, 2001.

PRYER 2007
PRYER, Anthony. 'Approaching Monteverdi: His Cultures and Ours', in: *The Cambridge Companion to Monteverdi*, edited by John Whenham and Richard Wistreich, Cambridge, Cambridge University Press, 2007 (Cambridge Companions to Music), pp. 1-19.

QUANTZ 1966
QUANTZ, Johann Joachim. *On Playing the Flute*, (1752), translated by Edward R. Riley, London, Faber and Faber, 1966.

SACCONE 1983
SACCONE, Eduardo. '*Grazia, Sprezzatura, Affettazione* in the *Courtier*', in: *Castiglione: The Ideal and the Real in Renaissance Culture*, edited by Robert Hanning and David Rosand, New Haven, Yale University Press, 1983, pp. 45-67.

SCHENKER 1903
SCHENKER, Heinrich. *Ein Beitrag zur Ornamentik: als Einführung zu Ph. Em. Bachs Klavierwerken*, Vienna, Universal Edition, 1903.

Schopenhauer 1960
Schopenhauer, Arthur. *Essay on the Freedom of the Will*, translated by Konstantin Kolenda, New York, Bobbs-Merrill, 1960.

Seeger 1958
Seeger, Charles. 'Prescriptive and Descriptive Music Writing', in: *The Musical Quarterly*, XLIV/2 (April 1958), pp. 184-195.

Strunk 1998
Strunk, Oliver. *Source Readings in Music History*, revised edition by Leo Treitler, New York, W. W. Norton, 1998 (Books that Live in Music).

Whitmore 1991
Whitmore, Philip. *Unpremeditated Art: The Cadenza in the Classical Keyboard Concerto*, Oxford, Clarendon Press, 1991 (Oxford Monographs on Music).

«Sostener si può la battuta, etiandio in aria»
Testi e contesti per comprendere l'invenzione e la disposizione del discorso musicale nel repertorio strumentale italiano fra Seicento e Settecento

Laura Toffetti
(Conservatoire de Musique H. Dutilleux, Belfort /
Conservatoire de Musique H. Dreyfus, Mulhouse)

Premessa

Il dibattito sulla relazione tra musica, *ratio* logico-matematica, natura umana e soggettività ha caratterizzato la storia della musica da che se ne ha memoria e alimenta ancora oggi interessanti riflessioni in contesti scientifici diversi.

Nell'ambito di questa vasta discussione, la partitura barocca, intesa come insieme di segni appartenenti a un codice preciso, rappresenta un significativo terreno di scambio, soprattutto qualora si accetti di considerarla come un'emanazione del pensiero cristiano medievale, per cui ogni forma altro non è se non il rivestimento di un'idea che assegna all'arte in generale, come alla dottrina stessa, un carattere universale e la funzione di rappresentare il mondo nella sua globalità.

Vincenzo Galilei, figura di grande rilievo durante il periodo di affermazione della rivoluzione scientifica operatasi in Italia tra la fine del '500 e l'inizio del '600, fornisce, ad esempio, un'interessante analisi della pagina musicale barocca e, per estensione, della genesi della composizione musicale stessa. Ricalcando le orme di Leonardo da Vinci, il quale afferma che la pittura pre-esistendo al quadro nella mente del suo speculatore assurge a rango di vera scienza, nelle sue teorizzazioni Galieli afferma il sussistere, prima di tutto, dell'immagine musicale nella mente del compositore:

> Quando vorrete intavolare qual si voglia cantilena, esaminate prima molto bene qual sia stata l'intenzione del Compositore di essa, et poi cercate con il vostro sano giudizio d'intender non solo quello che dice, ma ben spesso quello che ha voluto dire[1].

Gli scritti di Leonardo chiariscono, inoltre, che la pittura non solo rappresenta l'universo, ma che essa è in grado di farlo in modo da permettere al pubblico di identificare in

---

[1]. Galilei 1568, p. 28.

maniera inequivocabile i soggetti rappresentati, assumendo, quindi, il ruolo di strumento di trasmissione delle idee: «l'occhio, che si dice finestra dell'anima, è la principal via donde il comune senso pò più copiosamente e magnificamente considerare le infinite opere de natura»[2].

Nel caso della musica, definita dallo stesso da Vinci quale «sorella minore della pittura» perché «si va consumando mentre ch'ella nasce» e che «s'eterna [solo] collo scriverla»[3], la comunicazione dei significati passa attraverso l'operare del 'musico prattico', incaricato della decodificazione dei segni e della conseguente comunicazione dei significati.

Le indicazioni che Vincenzo Galilei fornisce nel trattato *Fronimo, Dialogo di Vincentio Galilei fiorentino nel quale si contengono le vere et necessarie regole del intavolare la musica nel liuto*, permettono di meglio comprendere la centralità, l'importanza del ruolo e la responsabilità nella mediazione affidata alla figura che oggi chiamiamo interprete:

> [...] non vi venisse in animo volervi difendere con la sciocca scusa di alcuni, i quali dicono non essere tenuti a far più di quello che trovano stampato o scritto, perché quando ei volessero ciò osservare, non havrebbono a fare il semitono in quelle cadentie, dove rare volte per non dir mai, si trova segnato [...][4].

È importante ricordare che, nell'organizzazione medievale del sapere, solo la teoria musicale, la quale non considerava l'aspetto fisico dei fenomeni sonori, apparteneva alle arti liberali del *quadrivium*, mentre l'*ars cantus* e la *musica instrumentalis*, attività esclusivamente artigianali, erano considerate alla stregua di *artes serviles*. Vincenzo Galilei, sostenitore della nuova visione del mondo basata sull'osservazione diretta della natura come unica via capace di formulare le leggi che ordinano i fenomeni, 'sporca' l'opera teorica con le mani del 'musico prattico', legittimando, all'interno della relazione tra arte e scienza, la presenza e l'individualità dell'interprete dei segni che compongono il codice musicale.

Dal momento in cui le consonanze non sono più considerate pitagoriche manifestazioni dell'armonia del mondo ma risultato dell'interazione tra vibrazioni della corda o dell'aria con il sistema percettivo, si realizza l'importante spostamento della musica dal cielo alla terra, dalla magia dei numeri alla materialità del suono percepito dall'individuo.

Oggi un numero sempre più elevato di partiture di quest'epoca appare in pubblicazioni moderne, consegnando agli esecutori un patrimonio che, sebbene indubbiamente sempre più conosciuto, si presta ancora a esecuzioni inappropriate o monche.

L'edizione moderna, infatti, porta con sé una carica simbolica legata ad altre epoche e ad altri stili, più recenti e strettamente legati a modelli di interpretazione basati sulla fedele

---

[2]. Da Vinci 1890, parte I, 1/15.
[3]. *Ibidem*, parte I, 1/27.
[4]. Galilei 1568, p. 28.

riproduzione dei segni scritti, considerati, oggi, se non del tutto esaustivi del fatto sonoro, per lo meno in grado di suggerirne tutte le caratteristiche necessarie.

La scrittura musicale barocca, invece, si rivela, all'attenta lettura delle fonti, carente di indicazioni interpretative: sono rare le indicazioni dinamiche o agogiche, spesso totalmente assenti quelle relative alle articolazioni o al fraseggio. Questo aspetto, che solo a un'analisi superficiale appare effetto di un sapere primitivo o incompleto, cela, in verità, una vasta scelta di possibilità interpretative. L'apparente ambivalenza, in parte dovuta alla tecnica ancora rudimentale della stampa musicale, è conseguenza di due ragioni diverse e complementari. La prima, come già si è intuito dalle parole di Vincenzo Galilei, è legata alla prassi esecutiva barocca, che lasciava all'esecutore ampio spazio per l'arricchimento del testo scritto. La seconda, indubbiamente più importante ai fini di questa ricerca poiché direttamente connessa al processo della codificazione del pensiero musicale, è implicita alla genesi della composizione stessa, che si struttura grazie alle regole e alle consuetudini della retorica classica più che a quelle delle diverse teorie musicali.

Appare, quindi, evidente la necessità di arricchire queste musiche, la cui forma scritta è chiaramente 'non finita', con quelle informazioni che permettono la corretta comprensione del suo contenuto originario, elaborando un'ipotesi di 'ricostruzione' basata sull'analisi dettagliata non solo dei testimoni e delle teorie musicali dell'epoca, ma anche delle convenzioni editoriali ed esecutive. Situare la ricerca su questi repertori all'interno del loro contesto intellettuale e individuare le interazioni tra le diverse discipline coesistenti in quella cultura umanistica che, ancora nel primo Seicento, coniugava erudizione e oralità rappresenta quindi, a mio avviso, la chiave di volta per la comprensione della partitura di quest'epoca, al fine di poter capire e valutare i segni e restituirne i significati.

La pagina musicale diventa, così, il prezioso, anche se virtuale, luogo di incontro tra il musicologo e il musicista: dove le ricerche dell'uno assumono un assetto definitivo, inizia il percorso dell'altro e ciò non tanto per affrontare le necessità tecnico-esecutive, quanto per risolvere i quesiti posti proprio dal dover scegliere i processi adatti alla decodificazione del testo scritto.

Il procedimento di ricostruzione può considerarsi, allora, l'omologo musicale del restauro in materia d'arte o d'architettura. Purtroppo, però, se in questi ambiti la natura e l'utilità di qualsiasi intervento sono oggi facilmente comprensibili, al contrario la riflessione sulla qualità della restituzione dei monumenti musicali non è ancora altrettanto matura, concentrandosi spesso su metodologie esclusivamente pertinenti alla loro forma scritta. Inoltre, e forse proprio per questa ragione, solo un numero ristretto di addetti ai lavori è cosciente che questa forma di 'restauro musicale' è indispensabile ai fini di una corretta divulgazione della composizione del passato.

Si considerano quindi, per questa ricerca che si limita al repertorio strumentale e più precisamente violinistico delle scuole italiane tra Sei e Settecento, i risultati dei lavori di quelle discipline che, contrariamente alla musica, la quale non possiede alcuna fonte primaria (avendo per ovvie ragioni ereditato solo trascrizioni e nessuna fonte sonora), hanno la fortuna di disporre dell'oggetto della loro indagine, quali musicologia, storia dell'arte, architettura, retorica o linguistica.

La partitura barocca: chiavi di lettura

Se «l'occhio è la finestra dell'anima», come dice Leonardo, quali sono le immagini e le idee che influenzano il compositore? Qual è il contesto nel quale egli sviluppa la partitura scritta e quali sono i significati protetti da questo codice? Qual è di conseguenza il raggio d'azione del 'musico prattico', quanto può e deve, cioè, arricchire la lettura della musica, ossia quali e quanti tipi di improvvisazione devono essere considerati dall'esecutore odierno?

Si è già chiarito come la partitura barocca, primo strumento di 'registrazione' dei suoni, assolva principalmente la funzione di trasmettere la composizione allo scopo di conservarla e renderla eterna.

Questo processo si esplicita attraverso due percorsi complementari: il primo ha origine nel pensiero musicale e individua, all'interno della propria matrice culturale, i segni adatti alla trascrizione sulla pagina di altezze e durate dei suoni percepiti (percorso musica-immagine); il secondo attinge più alla sfera delle arti visive, poiché teso a sviluppare un modello di organizzazione spaziale delle figure musicali che favorisca l'evocazione del discorso attraverso un itinerario opposto al primo, ossia dalla figura all'idea musicale (percorso immagine-musica). Individuare gli archetipi di questo processo permette al musicista odierno di decodificare lo spartito in modo più pertinente e, di conseguenza, di comprenderne più in profondità il pensiero.

Confrontando la partitura con un monumento istoriato, ad esempio, è facile evincere che anche le figure musicali, come le immagini che compongono il bassorilievo, ossia i segni appartenenti al codice, possano, in contesti diversi, avere valore esclusivamente decorativo, ma anche simbolico e semantico. Sappiamo che durante tutto il Medioevo, la rappresentazione di storie, principalmente bibliche, assolve un'importante funzione non solo di ornamentazione, ma anche sociale, pedagogica e divulgativa. Questa forma d'arte rappresenta, infatti, in una società ancora profondamente influenzata da modelli di trasmissione orale, la dimensione visiva del racconto, tanto quanto la partitura ne declina la variante musicale.

Diversamente dallo spazio architettonico, però, nel caso della pagina musicale la narrazione della 'storia' necessita di un interprete in grado di decodificare le figure e veicolarne i significati. Egli, nell'assumere il ruolo di traduttore, non solo si atterrà al contenuto della composizione nel suo duplice aspetto tecnico e semantico, ma dovrà considerare tutte le variabili che riguardano il tempo necessario alla sua condivisione.

Il discorso musicale così concepito, oltre a giustificare per ogni figura la relazione con un 'momento assoluto' esprimibile in termini matematici di durata, è sostanzialmente intonazione di figure sonore, le quali acquistano valore e interesse principalmente grazie alla loro disposizione nel tempo: l'anticipare o il ritardare gli elementi di una sequenza, il dire piano, forte, veloce, lento, l'interruzione brusca o preparata, il pronunciare, declamare, sillabare o sussurrare, il porre accenti, il respirare, l'attendere o il concitare dipendono, allora, più che dalla padronanza di teorie musicali, dall'uso di tecniche declamatorie che si riferiscono a eventi semantici e a fattori psicologici.

La *Response faite à un curieux sur le sentiment de la musique en Italie*[5] di André Maugars, nella quale il famoso virtuoso di viola da gamba descrive i sentimenti suscitatigli dall'ascolto della musica eseguita durante le celebrazioni per la solennità di S. Domenico, il 6 agosto 1639 nella Chiesa della Minerva a Roma, fornisce una testimonianza di questa prassi:

> C'est sans doute dans ces sorties agréables, où consiste tout le secret de l'Art; la Musique ayant ses figures aussi bien que la Rhétorique, qui ne tendent toutes qu'à charmer et tromper insensiblement l'Auditeur[6].

Un esempio di questo doppio ruolo della scrittura musicale (computo di valori e organizzazione di distanze), più tardi ma eloquente e emblematico di questa cultura musicale, è rappresentato dall'inizio della Sonata Op. 5 n. 1 di Arcangelo Corelli.

Ex. 1: versione originale e ornata delle prime battute della Sonata Op. 5 n. 1 nell'appendice della stampa di Estienne Roger (Amsterdam 1710).

Qui minime e seminime assumono un valore più simbolico che quantitativo (suono di apertura di un ciclo di sonate, *finalis* del *Protus*, contenitore di vaste figure ornamentali sottintese) e si prestano a esecuzioni che nulla hanno a che vedere con la durata misurabile dal moderno metronomo, soprattutto considerando l'importante dato

---

[5]. MAUGARS 1639.
[6]. *Ibidem*, p. 3 («come la retorica, la musica ha le sue figure che tendono tutte ad incantare e ingannare l'auditore, ingannandolo inavvertitamente»). Anche in MAUGARS 1985.

che uno strumento capace di calcolare il tempo in musica sarebbe stato realizzato solo alla fine del XVII secolo, non in Italia, ed esclusivamente allo scopo di permettere l'esecuzione, in assenza del compositore, di un brano musicale alla velocità da lui immaginata:

> Éléments ou principes de musique, […] Avec l'estampe, la description & l'usage du chronometre ou Instrument de nouvelle invention par le moyen duquel, les compositeurs de musique pourront désormais marquer le veritable mouvement de leurs compositions & leurs ouvrages marquez par rapport à cet instrument, se pourront executer en leur absence comme s'ils en battoient eux-mesmes la mesure[7].

Da queste considerazioni si evince che l'interprete deve saper restituire il messaggio codificato secondo i criteri che erano all'origine della sua creazione. Questi criteri, per quanto riguarda il ritmo, non corrispondono alle regole del moderno solfeggio (alle quali la partitura odierna fa naturalmente riferimento), ma a quelle dell'organizzazione del discorso, ossia della retorica classica.

Teoria delle proporzioni *versus* estetica della diminuzione

Oltre alla preoccupazione di descrivere e condividere i fenomeni, il pensiero rinascimentale è pervaso dalla ricerca di un'estetica capace di conciliare aspetti ed elementi diversi di una stessa realtà. La teoria delle proporzioni, che presenta lo spazio come la dimensione della relazione tra le cose ed è fondamento del concetto umanistico di bellezza come «accordo e armonia delle parti in relazione al tutto»[8], rappresenta un ulteriore principio intorno al quale si articola il dialogo tra il mondo della musica e quello degli spazi architettonici che lo ospitano. Se nell'ambito delle arti figurative e dell'architettura questo canone estetico definisce la relazione tra le parti e il tutto come armonia delle forme[9], in musica esso stabilisce anche le basi del sistema notazionale, affermando la necessità di rispettare determinati principi aritmetici.

Così, Giovanni Maria Bononcini, ne *Il Musico prattico* ribadisce, ancora nel 1673, questo concetto: «La proporzione (lasciando altre cose, che non fanno al nostro proposito) altro non è, (secondo il Crivellati nelli suoi Discorsi Musicali Capitolo secondo) che una comparazione di numero a numero[…]»[10].

---

[7]. Loulié 1696, p. 1.
[8]. Alberti 1847, p. 239.
[9]. A proposito della Basilica di Santa Maria Novella a Firenze: «L'intero edificio sta rispetto alle sue parti principali nel rapporto di uno a due, vale a dire nella relazione musicale dell'ottava, e questa proporzione si ripete nel rapporto tra la larghezza del piano superiore e quella dell'inferiore […]». Wittkower 1964, p. 48.
[10]. Bononcini 1673, p. 3. Crivellati 1624.

Secondo questa teoria, il 'bello' si configura come simmetria degli elementi che compongono un insieme: nella bellezza armonica, la molteplicità di questi elementi viene ricondotta a unità; un'idea, però, mai disgiunta da quella di misura fra i diversi elementi di un'opera.

Se questa teoria è universalmente accettata in ambiti quali la pittura o l'architettura, basti pensare all'attenzione portata dagli artisti allo studio della sezione aurea e al conseguente condizionamento esercitato sulla vita di tutti i giorni dal gran numero di immagini costruite secondo questo principio, meno evidente appare l'influenza esercitata sul mondo musicale. Ciò nonostante, oltre ai numerosi esempi forniti dall'analisi formale delle opere di quest'epoca e a osservazioni di tipo organologico, quali ad esempio il rilevare che Stradivari costruì il suo violino racchiudendone la forma in quattro poligoni regolari, negli scritti del teorico Gioseffo Zarlino sulla notazione l'origine filosofico-scientifica appare chiara:

> Dico adunque ch'essendo la breve madre e generatrice di qualunque altra figura cantabile, è di bisogno primieramente ragionar de tutti quelli accidenti che possono accascare intorno a lei, percioché gli antichi le attribuirono il tempo. Laonde dico che in questo luogo io non chiamo tempo quello che significa lo stato buono o la buona fortuna d'alcuno, come quando si dice: «Francesco è uomo di buon tempo», cioè mena tranquilla e lieta vita; né meno quella buona temperatura d'aria, come si suol dire: «Oggi è buon tempo», cioè oggi è giorno sereno, chiaro e lieto; neanco nomino tempo quello che 'l filosofo definisce esser numero o misura di movimento o d'alcun'altra cosa successiva; ma dico tempo, secondo la definizione degli antichi musici, essere una certa e determinata quantità de figure minori, contenute o considerate in una breve. E questo tempo è di due maniere, perfetto e imperfetto[11].

L'avvento della *musica mensurabilis* aveva, quindi, risolto già da tempo il problema della struttura ritmica, proponendo un sistema di proporzioni che permettono di stabilire, grazie a un elevato numero di segni e di combinazioni di segni, a regole, misure e alla considerazione di numerose eccezioni, il tempo dell'esecuzione e il valore proporzionale dei suoni, senza però fornire sufficienti informazioni circa la loro distanza reciproca.

Un'ulteriore considerazione per la decodificazione di questa notazione da parte del musicista odierno consiste nel riflettere sulla pratica di assumere come unità di misura per l'esecuzione il valore più piccolo, mentre risulta chiaro, alla lettura delle parole di Zarlino, che il riferimento era quello alla figura 'di contenimento', da lui identificata con la breve.

A sostegno di questa affermazione, è sufficiente osservare la struttura dei numerosi trattati di diminuzione apparsi dall'inizio del '500 e fino ai primi decenni del '600, dai quali si evince, oltre ad alcune indicazioni tecnico-stilistiche fondamentali per chiunque

---

11. ZARLINO 1558, 'Del Tempo, del Modo, & della Prolazione', parte III, cap. 67.

si interessi alla prassi esecutiva, l'informazione che la composizione musicale era tributaria di un'operazione di 'ricostruzione attiva' da parte dell'esecutore attraverso la pratica estemporanea dei passaggi, ossia quelle formule create per riempire, appunto, le figure estese del canto.

Senza soffermarmi, per ovvie ragioni di tempo e spazio, sull'analisi di queste opere già ampiamente discusse[12], è interessante osservare, nell'analisi delle relazioni tra la musica e il suo contesto culturale, che l'assetto editoriale e dell'impaginazione di queste opere rivelano lo sviluppo del pensiero estetico-scientifico tardo-rinascimentale dalla summa medievale, cioè quella forma chiusa e compiuta che propone una visione del mondo rassicurante davanti all'infinito, verso, la lista, ossia l'enumerazione, un concetto lineare ed estraneo, cioè, a ogni rapporto di gerarchia, che proietta il sapere, nella dimensione dell'infinito e dell'*et-cætera*[13].

Teoria degli affetti e notazione

Alle soglie della seconda pratica e dell'emergere delle esigenze di grande espressività teorizzate nell'ambito della nuova estetica sviluppatasi dopo i lavori della Camerata de' Bardi e gli scritti dei fratelli Monteverdi[14], questa notazione musicale, inizia ad andare 'stretta':

> […] il modo di comporre in tal maniera (mensurata) non solamente non è utile ma anco dannoso, per la perdita del tempo ch'è più prezioso d'ogni altra cosa, e che i punti, le linee, i circoli, i semicircoli e altre cose simili, che si dipingono in carte, sono sottoposte al sentimento del vedere e non a quello dell'udito; e sono cose considerate dal geometra; ma i suoni e le voci (come quelli che veramente sono il proprio oggetto dell'udito, dai quali nasce ogni buona consonanza e ogni armonia) sono principalmente dal musico considerate, ancora che consideri per accidente eziandio molt'altre cose[15].

e ancora

> […] si deve il cantore di stare attento a considerare mille chimere che cadono sotto il Modo, il Tempo, la Prolazione, le note nere, i vari tipi di punto; essendo che se facesse altrimenti, sarebbe reputato un Goffo ed un Ignorante[16].

---

[12]. A titolo di esempio si veda Gatti 2014, pp. 71-188.
[13]. Eco 2009, p. 18.
[14]. Monteverdi 1605.
[15]. Zarlino 1558, 'Dell'utile che apportano i mostrati accidenti nelle buone armonie', parte III, cap. 71.
[16]. *Ibidem*.

Dalle parole di Gioseffo Zarlino, e nonostante le accese polemiche di cui l'Artusi si fa interprete, si evince che il dato quantitativo della notazione cinquecentesca, quella nozione di misura di cui si è parlato in precedenza, non fornisce più elementi sufficienti all'esecuzione di un repertorio nel quale si va affermando l'ideale monteverdiano di una musica che esce dal gioco astratto dei rapporti aritmetici, proponendosi invece di riprodurre e dipingere le passioni umane.

Anche Nicola Vicentino, noto compositore, ma soprattutto famoso teorico della musica, lamenta in modo ancora più esplicito l'inadeguatezza del sistema di notazione misurata, incapace di esprimere le importanti indicazioni esecutive relative alla dinamica, al carattere, ma soprattutto all'agogica:

> […] qualche volta si usa un certo ordine di procedere nella composizione che non si può scrivere, come sono il dir piano e forte, il dir presto e tardo e, secondo le parole, muover la misura per dimostrare gli affetti delle passioni, delle parole e delle armonie […][17].

Ex. 2: Biagio Marini, 'Sonata quarta per il violino per suonar con due corde', in: *Sonate e Symphonie a 1, 2, 3, 4, 5 e 6 voci*, Op. 8, Venezia, appresso Bartolomeo Magni, 1624.

Un riscontro pratico di questa importante affermazione si trova in due sonate di Biagio Marini, l'Op. 8 e l'Op. 22, stampate a Venezia rispettivamente nel 1629 e 1655, nelle quali i termini «presto» e «tardo» vengono aggiunti sotto le note, oltre alle più frequenti indicazioni quali «affetti» «groppo» «piano» o «forte» o «dolcemente»[18].

Sempre in ambito romano, Giovanni Battista Doni, studioso di musica, uomo di eccezionale cultura e segretario del Collegio dei Cardinali presso Francesco Barberini, afferma in modo chiaro che il violinista che suona in teatro deve far prova di un'interpretazione ritmica delle note che trascenda le ordinarie conoscenze musicali, come oggi le intendiamo:

---

[17]. VICENTINO 1555, p. 89.
[18]. MARINI 1626: nella *Sonata prima a due violini* appare il termine «affetti» (nella parte staccata del vl I); nella *Sonata quarta per suonar con due corde* appaiono i termini «presto», «tardo» e «affetti» (nella parte staccata del violino e del BC). MARINI 1655: nella *Sonata per due violini* appare il termine «dolcemente» (nelle parti staccate del vl I, vl II e BC); nella *Sonata per violino e basso* appare il termine «affetti» (nella parte staccata del vl I).

> Sopra questa base poi dovrà il violino fabricare le sue diminuzioni, come più gl'aggradirà, […] per far spiccare massimamente le consonanze in quelle sillabe accentuate, con qualche nota un poco più lunghetta; perché anco nel parlare ordinario tali sillabe si sogliono talvolta allungare più dell'altre […][19].

Doni descrive qui un metodo di lettura della partitura secondo una logica ritmica mutuata all'arte del discorso; un modo di procedere, cioè, in parte intuitivo, basato sull'organizzazione delle figure musicali come fossero parole e che fa riferimento al pensiero musicale quale fonte primaria, di cui la pagina scritta è l'incompleta rappresentazione.

La musica dipinge le passioni

> Il dire dunque che la battuta per se stessa formi diversità di ritmi, è fuor d'ogni ragione; come sarebbe chi dicesse che i diftongi consistino nella scrittura, e non nella pronuntia[20].

Per Doni il ritmo della recitazione, e come abbiamo visto dell'esecuzione strumentale, è un parametro molto importante al quale egli dedica, nella sua produzione, tempo e attenzione nei confronti di ogni dettaglio.

Anche Vincenzo Giustiniani, mecenate e collezionista d'arte, noto soprattutto per aver contribuito alla fama del Caravaggio, nel *Discorso sopra la musica dei suoi tempi* accorda notevole importanza alla trattazione delle tematiche relative alle esecuzioni musicali e all'interpretazione, conciliando, però, il principio della proporzione aritmetica con la descrizione del sentimento, contenuto, questo, destinato ad acquisire uno spazio sempre maggiore, nonostante l'impossibilità di misurarne i limiti. Autentico compositore è, dunque, secondo l'erudito romano, «colui che possiede tanto la conoscenza delle regole e le giuste proporzioni dei numeri», quanto «la pratica degli effetti che da queste derivano negli animi degli uomini»[21].

Ecco chiarita la nuova concezione del musicista che, come l'artista, determina d'ora in poi, in modo sempre più autonomo e soggettivo, l'orientamento culturale del proprio lavoro. In altri termini, anche la musica, come ogni attività scientifica, diventa un processo di conoscenza il cui fine ultimo è la conoscenza stessa.

Utilizzando ancora una volta il procedimento dell'analogia, proprio l'osservazione della produzione pittorica di uno degli artisti più amati da Giustiniani, Michelangelo Merisi da Caravaggio, mette in luce il passaggio, avvenuto contemporaneamente in musica e pittura, verso un'estetica che si carica di significati psicologici e drammatici.

---

[19]. Doni 1640a, p. 372.
[20]. *Ibidem*.
[21]. Giustiniani 1981, p. 19.

Ill. 1: Michelangelo Merisi da Caravaggio (1571-1610), *Giuditta e Oloferne* (1597), Galleria nazionale di arte antica, Palazzo Barberini, Roma.

Ill. 2: Fede Galizia (1578-1630), *Giuditta con la testa di Oloferne* (1596), John and Mable Ringling Museum of Art Sarasota, Florida USA.

L'estremo realismo e la teatralizzazione nell'uso della luce hanno un influsso evidente sul ritmo dei dipinti caravaggeschi, rendendo i contorni più malleabili, come in una frase musicale nella quale si suona «con qualche nota un po' più lunghetta»[22].

Caravaggio, a Roma, frequentava gli stessi ambienti in cui i musicisti erano soliti prodursi e nei dipinti che eseguì per i suoi committenti appare sulla tavolozza un nuovo soggetto: la musica. Egli, trascrivendo in termini pittorici le stesse tematiche che animavano i salotti e le accademie musicali, testimonia di quell'intenso dibattito interdisciplinare tra artisti e intellettuali che aveva portato ai profondi mutamenti stilistici, e quindi esecutivi, annunciati, per quanto riguarda la nuova moda musicale, dai fratelli Monteverdi[23].

---

[22]. *Ibidem*.

[23]. A questo proposito è interessante il volume DE PASCALE – MACIOCE 2012, che promuove un proficuo confronto tra gli studi di storia dell'arte e quelli di musicologia, in relazione alle diverse metodologie d'indagine.

Comparando la *Giuditta e Oloferne* di Caravaggio (Ill. 1) e la *Giuditta con la testa di Oloferne* di Fede Galizia (Ill. 2), due dipinti anche cronologicamente vicini, è facile cogliere la volontà caravaggesca di liberare il soggetto da ogni ornamento per fissare il fuoco sulla natura dell'uomo. Questa stessa esigenza viene espressa da Giulio Caccini nella prefazione alle *Nuove Musiche*: «I passaggi sono stati ritrovati per gli orecchi di quelli che meno intendono che cosa sia cantare con affetto […]»[24].

La produzione musicale evolve, così, dalla prassi dell'ornare e dell'abbellire con gusto a quella del descrivere, dell'esprimere con introspezione. Questa trasformazione, percepibile in modo intuitivo all'osservazione dell'opera pittorica, è registrata in modo chiaro dallo stesso Giustiniani, il quale descrive musici di entrambe la categorie, ossia gli antichi, che

> […] facevano a gare […] nell'ornamento di esquisiti passaggi tirati in opportuna congiuntura e non soverchi […] e di più col moderare e crescere la voce forte o piano, assottigliandola o ingrossandola […] ora tirando passaggi lunghi, seguiti bene, spiccati, ora gruppi, ora a salti, ora con trilli lunghi, ora con brevi […] e principalmente con azione del viso, e de' sguardi e de' gesti che accompagnavano appropriatamente la musica e li concetti […][25].

e i moderni

> […] perché avendo lasciato lo stile passato, che era assai rozzo, et anche li soverchi passaggi con li quali si ornava, attendono ora per lo più ad uno stile recitativo ornato di grazia et ornamenti appropriate al concetto […] e sopra tutto con far bene intendere le parole, applicando ad ogni sillaba una nota or piano or forte, or adagio, or presto[26].

La melodia 'eloquente'

Anche il naturalismo caravaggesco è quindi impregnato dalla progressiva tendenza a scrutare la natura, spesso quella umana, nei minimi dettagli: questo nuovo modo di concepire l'arte implica, nel caso della composizione musicale, il graduale abbandono di quella forma di improvvisazione sul testo rappresentata dall'aggiunta dei passaggi, così simili all'ordinato apparato ornamentale e simbolico di Fede Galizia, in favore di una lettura della partitura che si espleta nella libertà agogica come eco di una natura umana il cui intelletto è in continuo movimento. L'interpretazione di questa partitura non è, però, arbitraria, ma un'applicazione specifica degli insegnamenti tratti dall'*ars oratoria*.

---

[24]. Caccini 1602, 'Ai lettori'.
[25]. Giustiniani 1981, p. 22.
[26]. *Ibidem*, p. 31.

La nozione fondamentale che permette di studiare le caratteristiche della retorica, è contenuta nella definizione di *numerus*. Questo termine polisemantico ricorrente nei trattati dell'antichità e presso gli umanisti traduce il greco ρυθμός (ritmo, ordine) e designa qualità proprie alle arti visive, quali la proporzione e la simmetria di una statua e di una facciata, o il movimento armonioso del gesto teatrale e pittorico, ma si riferisce anche alla poesia, regolando allora il concatenarsi dei piedi o delle sillabe lunghe e brevi nel *metrum*.

È necessario, però, specificare che il rapporto tra musica e retorica è di natura duplice. Le referenze fondamentali in questo campo per il mondo latino sono senza dubbio contenute negli scritti di Cicerone e Quintiliano. Quest'ultimo ci informa che le diverse concatenazioni metriche della poesia si sono sviluppate grazie alla misura percepita dall'orecchio sensibile dei poeti. È la musica quindi, che dà origine alla poesia, e in questo atto generatore trasmette al verso le sue qualità ritmiche[27].

Il rapporto con la prosa è, invece, più complesso. Contrariamente alla poesia, infatti, in una normale sequenza di parole, prosa o discorso, il susseguirsi di sillabe lunghe e brevi è inevitabilmente irregolare; ciononostante anche in questo caso viene percepita una forma di ritmicità dovuta non agli accenti o alle durate misurate in quantità di sillabe o seminimine, ma grazie alle relazioni di spazialità che vengono messe in gioco.

Dagli scritti di Cicerone si evince che l'eloquenza degli antichi poteva perdere il suo carattere austero e acquistare piacevolezza: «solo grazie all'introduzione di pause determinate non dalla stanchezza dell'oratore, né dai segni di punteggiatura, ma dalla misura ritmica delle parole e dei pensieri»[28].

E ancora:

> […] se unire la prosa in versi è un errore, tuttavia l'oratore deve congiungere le parole in modo armonioso affinché combacino tra loro e abbiano la necessaria completezza ritmica, poiché nessuna cosa distingue maggiormente un oratore dall'uomo inabile a parlare, quanto il fatto che l'uomo inesperto butta fuori senza alcun ordine tutto ciò che gli viene in mente e misura ciò che dice sulla base del fiato e non dell'arte, mentre il vero oratore lega il pensiero con le parole in modo da stringerlo in un ritmo che è ad un tempo libero e obbligato. Infatti, dopo averlo vincolato in una determinata maniera e ritmo, allenta il freno e lo libera, mutando l'ordine delle parole, in modo che le parole non siano né legate ad una determinata legge ritmica, né libere così da poter andare dove vogliono[…][29].

A partire dagli ultimi decenni del '500 il rapporto di dipendenza del discorso dalla musica rappresenta il fulcro di interesse nelle opere di molti eruditi, i quali, come testimonia Giustiniani, erano formati anche all'arte della musica. Questa complessa relazione è da

---

[27]. SUEUR 2013.
[28]. CICERONE 2005, Libro III, p. 173.
[29]. *Ibidem*, Libro III, pp. 175-176.

considerarsi, però, reciproca. Proprio l'influenza dell'*ars oratoria* sulla musica è, infatti, riconosciuta in svariate fonti, e ciò con riferimento tanto all'opera del compositore quanto al ruolo dell'esecutore. A questo proposito, fin dai primi anni del Seicento si sviluppa, per opera di alcuni teorici fra cui Athanasius Kircher o Joachim Burmeister, un'oratoria specificamente musicale. Quest'ultimo, appoggiandosi alla teoria di Quintiliano, scrive che «ciò che conta non è tanto la qualità della composizione, ma il modo in cui la comunichiamo, poiché è ascoltando che l'uomo si commuove»[30].

La notazione musicale, fallendo come abbiamo già osservato proprio laddove si deve portare la dimensione della comunicatività all'interno della forma, libera il campo all'interprete, che assume il ruolo di medio proporzionale tra l'aspetto visivo e quello contenutistico dell'opera del compositore. In Italia questa prassi dell'improvvisare raggiunge, secondo le testimonianze di cronisti e teorici, altissimi livelli di virtuosismo. Oltralpe, invece, mentre i viaggiatori francesi rimanevano stupiti dalla grande libertà dei musici italiani, la trattatistica tedesca assegnava il ruolo di mediazione alla forma scritta, compilando cataloghi di figure retoriche specificatamente musicali. È interessante ricordare che questo termine traduce il greco *schema* o *ordine*, o anche *euritmia*, cioè *bella apparenza*, ossia l'aspetto sontuoso, coerente, eloquente che si produce quando il rapporto tra le parti e il tutto è retto dalle leggi della simmetria.

Ex. 3: Giuseppe Colombi, *Sonata da camera*, Libro settimo, Mus. F277, Modena, Biblioteca Estense Universitaria[31].

A questo stadio della riflessione, solo l'ascolto comparato di brani eseguiti in modo 'eloquente' potrebbe elucidare i concetti esposti. In mancanza di questo supporto, si propone la trascrizione di una sonata di Giuseppe Colombi tratta dal *Libro VII*, nella quale si

---

[30]. BURMEISTER 1601, p. 5. *Cfr.* QUINTILIANO 2001.
[31]. L'esempio è tratto da SUESS 1999, p. 152.

è palesata, attraverso la spazializzazione grafica, la qualità prosodica delle figure ornamentali, ossia il ritmo della recitazione, quella forma di improvvisazione musicale basata, cioè, sulla ripartizione 'eloquente' del materiale sonoro.

Ex. 4: Giuseppe Colombi, *Sonata da camera*, Libro settimo. L'esempio trascrive la disposizione delle figure scritte e ornamentali (a cura dell'autore) delle misure 1-3[32].

In questo tipo di processo creativo a quattro mani, il compositore, secondo i dettami dell'*ars oratoria* di Quintiliano, s'incarica dell'*inventio*, ossia dell'inventare o scegliere il tema musicale, mentre il compito dell'*elocutio*, ossia dell'individuare un repertorio di moduli espressivi, è affidato all'improvvisazione dell'interprete con la precisa finalità di muovere gli affetti.

A questo proposito Giulio Caccini, nella prefazione alle *Nuove musiche* precisa:

> [...] questi intendentissimi gentiluomini m'hanno sempre confortato [...] ad attenermi a quella maniera cotanto lodata da Platone et altri filosofi, che affermarono la musica altro non essere che la favella e il ritmo et il suono per ultimo [...] a volere che ella possa penetrare nell'altrui intelletto e fare quei mirabili effetti[33].

Nell'analisi della partitura composta secondo questi criteri non basta quindi esaminare la relazione tra le note e le parole, anche se sottintese, o calcolare le durate dei suoni rispetto a quelle delle sillabe, occorre piuttosto ricercare i criteri d'organizzazione e di ripartizione del discorso musicale.

La Sonata Op. 4 n. 6 di Antonio Pandolfi Mealli, *La Vinciolina*, è esemplificativa di come la composizione musicale barocca sia fondata su nuclei linguistico-semantici diversi per natura e funzione dalle figure ritmiche alle quali siamo oggi abituati, poiché basati sull'imitazione di gesti verbali e non sull'assemblaggio matematico di valori ritmici. Quando il testo non c'è, infatti, ci si comporta come se fosse 'implicito', come chi, abituato a questa estetica vocale, ne abbia assimilato la prosodia applicandola spontaneamente al 'testo strumentale'.

La forma della Sonata Sesta, dedicata «Alla mia illustre Signora Teodora Vincioli mia signora singolarissima» si presta, inoltre, a un'esecuzione preceduta, nella tradizione retorica di questo repertorio, da un'intonazione libera e improvvisata, un'introduzione preludiata,

---

[32]. La sonata è contenuta nel CD *Duo in Rondeau, Dance Music at the Court of Francesco d'Este*, Ensemble *Antichi Strumenti*, Stradivarius, 2006, STR 33764.

[33]. CACCINI 1602.

cioè, nello stile dell'*exordium* di Quintiliano. L'uso del preludio come anticipazione è infatti, non a caso, strettamente legato alla logica del tempo inteso come spazio di esperienze (sonore) e di riflessione, di memoria e di apprendimento, in grado anche di costruire nuovi inizi.

Oltre a curarsi dell'*elocutio*, l'interprete assume, in questo caso, anche il compito della *dispositio*, cioè del predisporre il piano di svolgimento dell'opera, partecipando quindi attivamente al processo di creazione dell'opera stessa.

Pandolfi Mealli, come spesso accadeva agli strumentisti di quest'epoca, era vicino alla sfera dei cantori: lo stile vocale e recitativo delle sue sonate ne sono, infatti, una testimonianza, e la Sonata IV è un buon esempio di quanto Giovanni Battista Doni esprime nel suo *Discorso sopra il Violino Diarmonico*[34]:

> Tra tutti gli strumenti musicali, meravigliosa è veramente la voce del violino […] e che meglio esprime la voce humana non solo nel canto, ma nella favella istessa […] tanto più che noi udiamo talvolta esprimere col Violino alcuni accenti e parole che par proprio ch'eschino dalla bocca humana […].

Gli elementi compositivi di questa sonata — come la figura melodica ascendente o discendente, lenta o rapida, breve o estesa e la disposizione degli intervalli — devono quindi essere considerati come strutture semantiche minime che, giustapposte nel tempo e distanziate tra loro in base al potenziale drammatico, costruiscono il discorso musicale secondo le regole della retorica.

Girolamo Frescobaldi, organista e compositore citato da Maugars nella sua cronaca per le «mille sorte d'invenzioni sopra il suo clavicembalo, sopra delle note tenute ferme dall'organo»[35], appone all'edizione delle *Toccate Libro Primo* (FRESCOBALDI 1616/1637) numerose indicazioni di grande aiuto per l'interprete, dalle quali si evince l'importanza da lui attribuita proprio alla prosodia nell'esecuzione anche strumentale:

> Nelle Partite quando si troveranno passaggi et affetti sarà bene di pigliare il tempo largo; il che osservarassi anche nelle toccate. L'altre non passeggiate si potranno sonar alquanto allegre di battuta, rimettendosi al buon gusto e fino giuditio del sonatore il guidar il tempo; nel qual consiste lo spirito e la perfettione di questa maniera e stile di sonare[36] […].
>
> Primieramente che non dee questo modo di sonare stare soggetto a battuta […] perché la perfettione di sonare principalmente consiste nell'intendere i tempi[37].

---

34. DONI 1640B, p. 337.
35. MAUGARS 1639, p. 6, traduzione dell'autore del presente saggio.
36. FRESCOBALDI 1637, 'Avvertimenti'.
37. *Ibidem*.

Conclusione

Come in tutte le forme d'espressione, è la comunicazione a svolgere, in ultima istanza, il ruolo decisivo. Roman Jakobson, in uno studio sui disturbi del linguaggio, afferma che l'atto comunicativo implica la selezione di alcune entità semantiche e la loro combinazione in unità più complesse[38]. Durante lo scambio di informazioni, prosegue, il mittente e il suo ascoltatore sono legati dall'impiego di un codice comune, costituito, appunto, da tali sequenze, il cui significato non può essere dedotto dalla semplice somma di ogni componente lessicale: il tutto non è, quindi, uguale alla somma delle parti.

Nel caso della restituzione musicale, questo codice si costruisce grazie alla relazione di contiguità dei suoni trattati come eventi semantici, alla ripartizione, cioè, della frase musicale in periodi comprensibili e non attraverso la riproduzione di valori musicali ritmati in modo matematico.

L'esecuzione che si adegua a queste regole[39] mostra come l'operazione di adattamento continuo delle durate e delle distanze del materiale sonoro sia particolarmente funzionale alla sintassi del discorso musicale.

La distanza tra le figure, paragonabili alle parole che insieme formano le frasi e i pensieri musicali, assume un'importanza predominante rispetto al valore della nota stessa. Come la sintassi lega i pensieri e permette di comprendere il messaggio, così il ritmo 'eloquente', ossia il concatenamento delle formule musicali, risulta essere il procedimento adeguato all'interpretazione della composizione barocca.

Quando, viceversa, l'approccio al repertorio si focalizza sulla scrittura in senso stretto, cioè sulla lettura dei segni piuttosto che della relazione tra di essi, si genera un fenomeno di incomprensione. I linguisti definiscono questa alterazione della facoltà di combinare unità linguistiche più semplici (le note e le figure) in unità più complesse (le frasi) con il termine di 'agrammatismo', «la malattia che si manifesta con una degenerazione della frase in semplice mucchio di parole»[40].

Bibliografia

Testi antichi

ALBERTI 1847
 ALBERTI, Leon Battista. *Arte edificatoria*, in: *Opere volgari*, vol. IV, Firenze, Tipografia Galileiana, 1847.

---

[38]. JAKOBSON 1976.
[39]. Si faccia riferimento, ad esempio alla *Sonata IV a Violino e Viola* di Pietro Sorosina, contenuta nel CD *Duo in Rondeau, Dance Music at the Court of Francesco d'Este*, citato.
[40]. JAKOBSON 1976, p. 36.

Cicerone 2005
Cicerone, Marco Tullio. *De Oratore*, a cura di Pietro Li Causi, Rosanna Marino e Marco Formisano, Alessandria, Dell'Orso, 2005 (Culture antiche, 28).

Da Vinci 1890
Da Vinci, Leonardo. *Trattato della pittura condotto sul Cod. Vaticano Urbinate 1270*, a cura di Gaetano Milanesi, Roma, Unione cooperativa editrice, 1890.

Quintiliano 2001
Quintiliano. *Institutio Oratoria*, a cura di Adriano Pennacini, Torino, Einaudi, 2001 (Biblioteca della Pleiade, 38), Libro ix.

Trattati

Bononcini 1673
Bononcini, Giovanni Maria. *Il musico prattico*, Bologna, Giacomo Monti, 1673.

Burmeister 2007
Burmeister, Joachim. 'Musica Autoschédiastikè (1601)', in: Id. *Musica Poetica (1606): augmentée des plus excellentes remarques tirées de Hypomnematum musicae poeticae (1599) et de Musica autoschédiastikè (1601)*, a cura di Agathe Sueur e Pascal Dubreuil, Wavre, Mardaga, 2007 (Ars musices iuxta variorum scriptorium. 1. Reinassance et période préclassique. Domaine germanique, 1).

Caccini 1602
Caccini, Giulio. *Le Nuove Musiche*, Firenze, Marescotti, 1602.

Crivellati 1624
Crivellati, Cesare. *Discorsi musicali, nelli quali si contengono non solo cose pertinenti alla teorica, ma etiandio alla pratica*, Viterbo, Agostino Discepoli, 1624.

Doni 1640a
Doni, Giovanni Battista. 'Discorso sesto sopra il Recitare in Scena con l'accompagnamento di strumenti musicali', in: Id. *Annotazioni sopra il compendio de' generi, e de' modi della musica* [...], Roma, Andrea Fei, 1640, pp. 359-379.

Doni 1640b
Id. 'Discorso sopra il Violino Diarmonico', in: Id. *Annotazioni sopra il compendio de' generi, e de' modi della musica* [...], *op. cit.*, pp. 337-358.

Galilei 1568
Galilei, Vincenzo. *Il Fronimo: dialogo di Vincentio Galilei fiorentino nel quale si contengono le vere et necessarie regole del intavolare la musica nel liuto*, Girolamo Scotto, Venezia, 1568.

Giustiniani 1981
Giustiniani, Vincenzo. 'Discorso sopra la musica dei suoi tempi', (Lucca 1628), in: *Discorsi sulle arti e sui mestieri*, a cura di Anna Banti, Firenze, Sansoni, 1981 (Raccolta di opere inedite e rare), pp. 15-36.

«Sostener si può la battuta, etiandio in aria»

LOULIÉ 1696
LOULIÉ, Étienne. *Éléments ou principes de musique*, Parigi, Christoph Ballard, 1696.

MAUGARS 1639
MAUGARS, André. *Response faite à un curieux sur le sentiment de la musique en Italie*, Rome, 1er octobre 1639, Parigi, BnF, RES-V-2469 e 2471.

MAUGARS 1985
ID. 'Risposta data a un curioso sul sentimento della musica d'Italia', a cura di Jean Lionnet, in: *Nuova rivista musicale italiana*, XIX/4 (1985), pp. 681-707.

VICENTINO 1555
VICENTINO, Nicola. *L'antica musica ridotta alla moderna prattica*, Roma, Antonio Barre, 1555.

ZARLINO 1558
ZARLINO, Gioseffo. *Le Istitutioni harmoniche*, Venezia, Pietro da Fino, 1558.

Musiche

FRESCOBALDI 1616/1637
FRESCOBALDI, Girolamo. *Toccate, e partite d'intavolatura di cimbalo* [...] *libro primo*, Roma, Nicolò Borbone, 1616.

FRESCOBALDI 1637
ID. *Il secondo libro di toccate canzone versi d'hinni Magnificat gagliarde correnti et altre partite d'intavolatura di cimbalo et organo*, Roma, Nicolò Borbone, 1637

MARINI 1626
MARINI, Biagio. *Sonate, symphonie, canzoni, passemezzi, baletti, corenti, gagliarde e retornelli: per ogni sorte d'instrumenti: opera ottava*, Venezia, Bartolomeo Magni, 1626.

MARINI 1655
ID. *Diverse sonate da chiesa e da camera a due, tre e quattro*, Op 22, Libro III, Venezia, Francesco Magni, 1655.

MONTEVERDI 1605
MONTEVERDI, Claudio. *Il V libro dei madrigali*, Venezia, Ricciardo Amadino, 1605.

ROGNONI 1620
ROGNONI, Francesco. *Selva di vari passaggi*, Milano, Filippo Lomazzo, 1620.

Testi moderni

DE PASCALE – MACIOCE 2012
La musica al tempo del Caravaggio, a cura di Enrico De Pascale e Stefania Macioce, Roma, Gangemi, 2012.

Eco 2009
Eco, Umberto. *Vertigine della lista*, Milano, Bompiani, 2009.

Gatti 2014
Gatti, Enrico. 'Però ci vuole pacientia', in: *Regole per ben suonare e cantare: diminuzioni e mensuralismo tra 16. e 19. secolo*, Pisa, ETS, 2014 (Quaderni del Conservatorio 'Giuseppe Verdi' di Milano, n.s. 2/2014), pp. 71-188.

Jakobson 1976
Jakobson, Roman. 'Due aspetti del linguaggio e due tipi di afasia', in: *Saggi di linguistica generale*, a cura di Luigi Heilmann, Milano, Feltrinelli, ³1976 (Sc/10, 37), pp. 22-45.

Suess 1999
Suess, John G. 'Giuseppe Colombi's Dance Music for the Estense Court of Duke Francesco II di Modena', in: *Marco Uccellini. Atti del Convegno Marco Uccellini da Forlimpopoli e la sua musica (Forlimpopoli, 26-7 ottobre 1996)*, a cura di Maria Caraci Vela e Marina Toffetti, Lucca, LIM, 1999 (Strumenti della ricerca musicale), pp. 141-162.

Sueur 2013
Sueur, Agathe. *Le Frein et l'Aiguillon: éloquence musicale et nombre oratoire (16ᵉ-18ᵉ siècle)*, Parigi, Classique Garnier, 2013 (Renaissance latine, 2).

Wittkower 1964
Wittkower, Rudolf. *Principi architettonici nell'età dell'umanesimo*, traduzione italiana a cura di Renato Pedio, Torino, Einaudi, 1964.

Improvised Cadenzas in the Cello Sonatas Op. 5 by Francesco Geminiani

Rudolf Rasch
(Utrecht University)

Improvisation always has been a standard element of the performance of early music. This must have been the case in historical times, while it applies equally to today's performance practice. No score was or is ever performed exactly as it is written down, if only because of the many elements left undefined such as tempo and much of articulation, dynamics and ornamentation. Performers must fill in what the composer or the publisher (or the copyist) has left open. These 'unforeseen' elements could be called 'improvisation', but it is more in conformity with terminological practice to reserve this term for extra notes, not provided in the score.

These extra notes can be applied in two ways. First, they can be used to adorn or embellish the melody as written down, in the way of diminutions or figuration or written-out ornamentation, either in the form of notes with exact time values or as notes with undefined values. The second way to add notes to a composition is to play short separate passages that are inserted in to places that seem appropriate for such an elaboration. Additions of the second kind are called 'cadenzas', because they most often occur as a part of the final cadence of a movement. Cadenzas play an important role in the performance of solo concertos from the Classical and Romantic periods, but they have a history that goes much further back than the second half of the eighteenth century.

Johann Joachim Quantz

There is little attention to the cadenza in early eighteenth-century music theory. By far the most comprehensive account is found in Johann Joachim Quantz's *Versuch einer Anweisung, die Flöte traversière zu spielen* (Berlin, 1752). Quantz spends an entire chapter on the subject: 'Das XV. Hauptstück: Von den Cadenzen' (pp. 151-164); it is divided into 33 numbered short sections. These sections allow us to summarize his argument point by point:

1. A cadenza consists of «embellishments produced, in concerting parts, at the end of a piece, over the penultimate note, namely, the fifth over the tonic, according to the will and pleasure of the performer».

2. Introduced by the Italians fifty years ago (that is, around 1700). First, there were a few small passages and trills in the cadence, then, from «about between 1710 and 1716», the ordinary cadenza with a prolonged bass note under it came into use.

3. Cadenzas are probably invented by performers, not by composers.

4. Unfortunately, cadenzas are often added to movements where they do not belong.

5. The aim of a cadenza is to surprise the listener just before the end of the movement.

6. Many cadenzas are bad or inappropriate.

7. There are no strict rules for cadenzas.

8. Cadenzas must match the character of the movement.

9. Describes a one-voice cadenza: «They must be short and new, and surprise the listener, as a *bon mot*. Therefore they must sound like they were conceived of at the moment they are played. Do not be wasteful with them, but treat them as a good host; in particular when you have the same listener more often before you».

10. Because cadenzas are short, they must not have too many figures.

11. The repetition of figures more than once, such as in the following example, where two figures are repeated three times, is better avoided (Tabula XX, Fig. 1):

It is better to repeat figures only once and to insert other figures between the repeated ones (Fig. 2):

This one is also better because the metre is irregular. It is meant for an *Allegro*. For an *Adagio* one must extract the main notes (Fig. 3):

12. One must avoid repeats of figures on the same pitch.

13. Dissonances (that is, alterations) must be treated properly, that is, followed by their proper resolutions (Fig. 4):

14. Cadenzas can go to neighbouring keys, but one must be cautious. An example is given in a major key (F major), where by the application of alterations modulations to the fourth (B-flat major, at [a]) and fifth (C minor, at [b]) and the return to the main key (F major, at [c]) are inserted (Fig. 5):

A similar example is given for a minor key (G minor; Fig. 6):

15. A cheerful cadence has jumps, triplets and trills (Fig. 7)…

…a sad cadence has steps and dissonances (Fig. 8):

16. Cadenzas need not obey a regular time or metre.

17. Then comes Quantz's famous advice for the length of a cadenza: when for the voice or a wind instrument it must be possible to perform the cadenza on one breath; when for a stringed instrument there is no limit, but shortness is advised.

18. He does not provide written-out examples of perfect and fully-fledged cadences.

19-31. About cadenzas for two instruments (Figs. 9-14, Tab. XXI, Figs. 1-6).

32-33. About cadenzas when the movement ends on an imperfect cadence with a seventh-sixth suspension (Figs. 7-8):

34. Cadenzas for two instruments on an imperfect cadence (Fig. 9).
35. Cadenzas on words like "vado", "parto", and so on, as a kind of tone painting (Figs. 10-11).
36. The final trill in a cadenza, with a reference to Tabula XV, Fig. 21.

Quantz's cadenzas given for a perfect authentic cadence (Tabula XX, Figs. 2-8) could serve well as practical examples for today's performers, as also the one given for an imperfect cadence (Tabula XI, Fig. 8).

Arcangelo Corelli

Although Quantz states that in Corelli's sonatas there are no cadenzas (only written-out embellishments, as in the 1710 Amsterdam edition), yet the Sonatas Op. 5 provide two written-out examples of cadenzas on the penultimate note of a movement, just as in Quantz's definition. The second movement of Sonata 1 ends with an arpeggio passage concluded by a little flourish which together can be considered as a cadenza:

Note that the first sonority of the arpeggio passage is a 6/4 chord on the dominant.

The diminished-seventh chord on G-sharp that precedes is can be considered as a chord that prepares the cadenza.

The second movement of Sonata 3 concludes with a much longer but still quasi-improvisatory passage on the penultimate note, first with broken intervals, then with broken chords, everything above the penultimate note of the bass part:

Improvised Cadenzas in the Cello Sonatas Op. 5 by Francesco Geminiani

After Corelli, many composers followed suit, and soon wrote cadenzas also without an underlying bass note, thereby creating a much wider tonal space. Well-known examples of large cadenzas are the harpsichord cadenza in the first movement of the Fifth Brandenburg Concerto of Johann Sebastian Bach, just before the last repeat of the ritornello, and the Capricci that Pietro Antonio Locatelli wrote for his violin Concertos Op. 3 published as *L'arte del violino* (Amsterdam, 1733). Less known is the extensive written-out cadenza that Willem de Fesch inserted in the first movement of his Violin Concerto in A minor Op. 3 no. 6 (published in Amsterdam in 1719), just before the final ritornello.

Francesco Geminiani

The *Sonate a violino, violone e cimbalo* by Francesco Geminiani, published in London in 1716, contain two written-out cadenzas, one in Sonata 2, the other one in Sonata 3. The cadenza that is found just before the end of the second movement of Sonata 2 is of a different type than those in Corelli's sonatas. It is different in two respects. First, it is an elaboration of the diminished-seventh chord on the raised fourth degree of the key, which functions as a secondary dominant, a chord that prepares the dominant, instead of a series of sonorities that start with a 6/4 chord on the dominant. And secondly the bass note stops after the cadenza is 'launched':

The cadenza in the first movement in Sonata 3, in E minor, a movement in 'prelude style' consisting of sections in various metres and tempos, conforms to the model of the cadenza on a penultimate note that is the fundamental note of the dominant. It differs from the cadenza in Corelli's Sonata 3 mainly in the melodic figures used: instead of broken intervals and broken chords there are nearly continuously little diatonic figures:

In the reworked version of the Sonatas of 1716 that Geminiani published in 1739 under the title *Le prime sonate a violino e basso* the cadenza in Sonata 2 has disappeared, that in Sonata 3 is found there in a slightly rewritten version.

At some point between 1700 and 1739 the habit must have been established not to write out cadenzas such as the ones presented above, but to write a corona or fermata sign on the place where such a cadenza could be played. Geminiani's *Sonate a violino e basso, Opera quarta*, published in London in 1739, provide two such examples. One is towards the end of the first movement of Sonata 1:

The arrangement of this movement in the *Pièces de clavecin* (Paris and London, 1743) has an extensive written out cadenza for this passage:

Improvised Cadenzas in the Cello Sonatas Op. 5 by Francesco Geminiani

This is certainly not a representation of a cadenza as played in the violin sonata.

The second cadenza example in Geminiani's Violin Sonatas Op. 4, towards the end of the first movement of Sonata 6, is somewhat problematic because the fermata is placed only in the bass part and is placed over a pause sign in the figuring, between the 6/4 suspension and the 5/3 resolution:

In a way this notation suggests that the cadenza has to be played by the continuo player, although the sketchy melodic contour of the violin part rather is also indicative of a cadenza in that part. The pause sign in the bass could simply mean that no chords are played by the continuo player for a while, until the cadenza in the violin part comes to an end.

The little flourish in *Stichnoten* in the last bar of the first movement of Sonata Op. 4 No. 3 can be considered as a very short written-out cadenza:

Interesting for this discussion is the copy of Geminiani's Op. 4 Sonatas in Ann Arbor, Michigan, USA[1]. Extra notes in pencil were written by an early possessor, either in the late eighteenth or the early nineteenth century, on various places in the main text, and several music notations can also be found in the margins. The notations in the margins appear to be cadenzas that can be played when performing the sonatas. Two examples may be given here. The third movement of Sonata 7, *Moderato*, ends in this way in the main text:

---

[1]. US-AA, M219 .G32 S71 1739.

The early owner has placed an 'X' mark above the violin part where the harmony is a 6/4 suspension of the dominant. In the upper margin a cadenza is pencilled in that can be played at the place marked by an 'X':

The fourth movement of Sonata 11, *Allegro*, is in rondeau form. In the upper margin a little cadenza is written down that can be added just before the final cadence of the refrain when it is played to conclude the movement, «zum Schluß», as the anonymous, but certainly German author of these additions, wrote next to it. The final bars of the refrain are:

The X marks the place where a cadenza can be inserted:

Note that these cadenzas are not suggested in the score; they are elaborations by an early interpreter.

Geminiani's Cello Sonatas Op. 5

Geminiani's *Sonates pour le violoncelle et basse continue, Ouvrage cinquième*, first published in The Hague, by the composer himself, early 1747, despite the year 1746 on the title page, contain more fermata signs that can be interpreted as referring to cadenzas then any of his earlier (or later) works. There are six sonatas in the set and at eight places fermata signs are found that can be interpreted as cadenzas. They occur in the following places:

	Place	Position	Suspension	Cadence	Cadence	Key	Comments
1	I/i/15	halfway	6/4 5/3	E major	PAC	A major	
2	I/i/35	final	6/4 5/3	E major	imperfect	A major	
3	II/i/21	final	7 6	A major	imperfect	D minor	
4	IV/ii/36	halfway	6/4 5/3	D minor	PAC	B♭ major	«Fantasia ad libitum»
5	V/i/4	final	7 6	A major	imperfect	F major	
6	V/iii/9	halfway	6/4 6/5	A minor	PAC	D minor	«Cadenza al solito»
7	V/iii/24	pre-final	4 ♯3	D minor	PAC	D minor	
8	VI/i/6	final	7 6 ♯6	E major	imperfect	A minor	

This overview shows a few interesting relations. Half of the cadenzas (nos. 2, 3, 5, 8) occur on the penultimate note of an imperfect cadence that ends a slow movement. They follow the suspension note on this penultimate note and they end with the resolution of the suspension, always a note with a trill. The suspension is usually of the 7-6 type, in one case (no. 2) of the 6/4-5/3 type.

The other half of the cadenzas (nos. 1, 4, 6, 7) occur on other positions within the movement, either 'halfway' or 'pre-final'. ('Pre-final' here means 'just before the final cadence'.) These cadenzas occur as part of perfect authentic cadences (PAC). Also these cadenzas follow a suspension note and end with the resolution with a trill. Suspensions are here most often of the 6/4-5/3 type, once only 4-3. Most often they occur in slow movements, only once (no. 4) in a fast movement: it is placed just before the return to a *da capo* section. This cadenza is also exceptional because of the extra comment «Fantasia ad libitum». This may be read as an invitation to insert a cadenza that is longer than the usual one, perhaps some kind of Capriccio. The remark «Cadenza al solito» in the next Sonata (V/iii/9) may then be a reminder that this cadenza should *not* be a Fantasia, but just a regular cadence.

Most cadences with a cadenza have a trill on the note that precedes the tonic. The note before it is the note with the fermata, where there is a 6/4 or a 7 suspension in the bass, but this more often is *not* the dissonant note of which the note with the trill is the resolution. Geminiani's cadences with cadenzas often have a non-regular structure, in several cases with a rather large interval (fifth or seventh) between the note with the fermata and the note with the trill (cadenzas nos. 1, 3, 7). The cadenza can be used to bridge this interval. Sometimes it is a note which is a fourth above the bass that has the fermata, while the note with the trill that follows is a fifth above the bass (cadenzas nos. 4, 6).

Realisations of the Cadenzas

How the cadenzas of Geminiani's Cello Sonatas Op. 5 were realized in the eighteenth century we do not know. On the other hand, how they were realized during the last half century is amply documented by the LP and CD recordings that have been made of the works. Actually, Geminiani's Cello Sonatas Op. 5 are his most often recorded works, with nine complete recordings since 1976 and numerous recordings of single sonatas. The first recording was an LP, performed by Anthony Pleeth on cello, with Christopher Hogwood (harpsichord) and Richard Webb (cello) as continuo players, brought out by L'Oiseau-Lyre in 1976 and later (1991) reissued by the same label on CD. Directly on CD the sonatas were recorded by the cellists David Simpson (1984), Hidemi Suzuki (1990), Gaetano Nasillo (2001), Alison McGillivray (2005), Jaap ter Linden (2007), Bruno Cocset (2008), Enrico Bronzi (2010) and Loretta O'Sullivan (2015). More details on the recordings are given in the Appendix.

How do these nine cellists play the cadenzas in Geminiani's Cello Sonatas? Transcriptions of the cadenzas are included in the Appendix and from these transcriptions several conclusions can be drawn[2].

First of all it is clear that not all the fermata signs were interpreted in the same way. The fermata on the imperfect cadence of the first movement of Sonata 5 was never used as a starting point for a cadenza. Probably the little flourish that Geminiani inserted there himself has discouraged the performers from adding a cadenza of their own. The fermata sign near the end of the first movement of Sonata 6 has given rise to a cadenza only once (O'Sullivan) and this is a very rudimentary one at best. Here, the fermata is placed over the resolution of the suspension, which is a bit awkward, and this was probably enough reason for the performers not to play any further cadenza.

Also the final cadence of the first movement of Sonata 1 did not equally inspire the performers to insert a cadenza there. Five performers did play a cadenza there; four did not. That means that the final cadence of the first movement of Sonata 2 was the only instance of final (imperfect) cadence of a slow movement where all performers felt the need to insert a cadenza.

---

[2]. As a matter of fact, the transcriptions are approximate; they have done by ear. No attempts have been made to measure exactly the durations of the notes. Also there is no absolute certainty about the pitch of very short notes and notes of double stops in a low register. The transcriptions have not been checked by the players themselves.

Improvised Cadenzas in the Cello Sonatas Op. 5 by Francesco Geminiani

The four fermatas on the suspension of a perfect authentic cadence, either in slow or in fast tempo, on the other hand, were always interpreted as meaning that a cadenza should be played there. The second of these is halfway through the second movement of Sonata 4, with the remark «Fantasia ad libitum». In three cases the performers indeed play a true Fantasia or Capriccio (Simpson, Nasillo, O'Sullivan); the other six play a cadenza that is either not different or hardly different from the other cadenzas and can rather be described as «al solito» than as a Fantasia.

The normal length of the cadenzas «al solito» falls somewhere between ten and twenty notes. Some are very short (three or four notes), other are long or very long (up to 37 notes) but are certainly not a Fantasia or Capriccio. The number of notes is, of course, a very crude measure of the length of a cadenza, but given the unmeasured and free structure of them, there is no better way available. The following table lists the lengths of the cadenzas expressed in the number of notes:

	Pleeth	Simpson	Suzuki	Nasillo	McGillivray	Linden	Cocset	Bronzi	O'Sullivan
1	4	10	3	7	13	4	7	4	12
2	7	18	—	—	—	—	14	13	7
3	7	21	14	5	10	8	13	9	12
4	37	145	20	96	17	12	20	17	127
5	—	—	—	—	—	—	—	—	—
6	17	43	12	17	13	10	7	13	5
7	20	17	19	15	8	11	52	9	34
8	—	—	—	—		—	—	—	3

The style of the cadenzas varies — of course — from player to player. They are all characterized by the lack of a clear metrical structure. They employ various note durations, which were transcribed as crotchets, quavers, semiquavers and demisemiquavers and their dotted variants. Triplets are very common. There is a variety of figures, among them triadic figures and scale runs, the latter both ascending and descending. Double and triple stopping is employed only occasionally (Simpson, nos. 4 and 6; O'Sullivan, no. 4). Most cadenzas can be conveniently written down with a tenor clef, the clef always used by Geminiani when writing the passage with the cadenza. Some cadences use the high register of the cello, that is, between $a1$ and $e2$ (Simpson, nos. 4 and 6; Cocset, no. 4); some — sometimes the same — the low register, that is, between C and c (Simpson, nos. 4 and 6; Cocset nos. 2, 4 and 7; O'Sullivan nos. 4 and 7). But in most cases the tenor register, between, say, d and $a1$, is preferred.

There is hardly any resemblance among the cadenzas. This probably means that all performers 'composed' their own cadenzas entirely independent of the others. Only Bruno Cocset seems to quote Anthony Pleeth with the first notes of his cadenza at the end of the first movement of Sonata 2, which must perhaps be seen as a homage rather than an imitation.

Quantz Again

To what extent do the cadenzas played by these nine performers adhere to the rules given by Johann Joachim Quantz? Not all of Quantz's points are relevant here, but some provide interesting opportunities for comparison. First of all, the cadenzas connected with perfect authentic cadences certainly conform to Quantz's basic definition that cadenzas are «embellishments produced, in concerting parts, at the end of a piece, over the penultimate note, namely, the fifth over the tonic, according to the will and pleasure of the performers» (point 1). The cadenzas connected with imperfect cadences can be connected with Quantz's points 32-33. Quantz does not acknowledge the application of cadenzas halfway through a movement. In this respect, Geminiani's cadences nos. 1, 4 and 6 fall outside the scope of Quantz's discussion.

Quantz's description of the cadenza as something «short and new, to surprise the listener, as a *bon mot*» and something «that must sound like it was conceived at the moment it was played» (point 9) can certainly be applied to the cadenzas as performed in the recordings of Geminiani's sonatas. They have little internal structure and will indeed sound as if invented on the spot, not pre-composed. Regarding the repetition of figures (Quantz's point 11), the cadenzas in principle follow Quantz's advice as well: there are few repeated figures. The application and treatment of alterations agrees with Quantz's point 13. Modulations (Quantz's point 14) are found only in the worked-out Fantasias. The main cadence there is to D minor. The Fantasias inserted there show modulations to F major and G minor, for example. In the other cases the continuing bass note on the dominant may have been a reason not to introduce any modulation to a different key.

Apart from the Fantasias for the second movement of Sonata 4, the cadenzas added to Geminiani's cello sonatas obey Quantz's rule for the length of a cadenza (point 17). The examples that Quantz gives himself vary in length mostly from sixteen to 27 notes, but two are definitely longer: his Figs. 2 (46 notes) and 7 (61 notes), and these seem to defy his own rule.

So in general 'Quantz's rules' were obeyed by the performers of Geminiani's cello sonatas. Whether that means that they have studied Quantz's text before designing their cadenzas, is impossible to tell. They may also just follow general habits that are current in the performance of early music during the last half century.

Improvised Cadenzas in the Cello Sonatas Op. 5 by Francesco Geminiani

In one respect the cadenzas for Geminiani's cello sonatas do differ from the examples given by Quantz in his *Versuch*: the 'Geminiani cadenzas' are much more irregular in their figures, both regarding pitch and duration, than Quantz's examples. The latter ones always have a more compact structure and nearly always have a melodic contour that first rises to an octave above the starting note and then falls towards the note with the trill.

Conclusion

There are many more examples to study regarding the cadenzas in Geminiani's cello sonatas. The many single sonatas recorded by a variety of musicians will undoubtedly provide further examples of cadenzas. Written-out cadenzas are also provided in the editions of Sonatas 2 and 6 edited by Frank Merrick as *Sonata in D minor (A minor) for Violoncello and Piano (Harpsichord) Op. 5 No. 2 (No. 6)* (London, Schott, 1959), with cadenzas probably by Ivor James (who took care of the bowing and phrasing of the violoncello part), and of all six edited by Walter Kolneder as *Sechs Sonaten für Violoncello und Basso continuo Opus V* (Frankfurt, Peters, 1964), with cadenzas probably by Walter Schultz (who edited the cello part). In general the written-out cadenzas found in these editions are longer, more complex and technically more demanding than the cadenzas found in recordings.

Geminiani also published his cello sonatas in a version adapted to the violin, under the title *Sonates pour le violon avec un violoncelle ou clavecin* (The Hague, 1747). Recordings of these sonatas add further examples of cadenzas. Kolneder's edition of these works as *Sechs Sonaten für Violine und Basso continuo* (Frankfurt, Peters, 1965) simply transposes the cadenzas from his edition of the cello sonatas.

In short, it would not be difficult to assemble further examples of cadenzas to Geminiani's Op. 5 Sonatas for the study of improvisation as practised today as part of the performance of early music. It is, however, not to be expected that this will add any new elements to the above discussion. Whether the practice described there reflects early practice is impossible to say. Perhaps this is a question that should not be asked. Not only do we not know how representative the preserved contemporary examples of performed cadenzas 'frozen' into notation — either in practical editions or in theoretical discussions — are, there will also always have been and always will be as many ways of performing cadenzas as there are performers.

Appendix

Cadenza Marks in Francesco Geminiani, Sonates pour le violoncelle et basse continue, Ouvrage cinquième (The Hague, Author, 1747; London, Author, 1747)

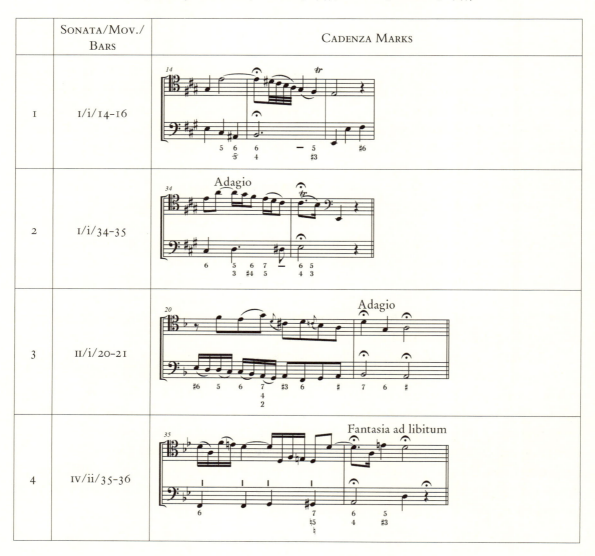

	Sonata/Mov./Bars	Cadenza Marks
1	I/i/14–16	
2	I/i/34–35	
3	II/i/20–21	
4	IV/ii/35–36	

Improvised Cadenzas in the Cello Sonatas Op. 5 by Francesco Geminiani

	Sonata/Mov./Bars	Cadenza Marks
5	v/i/4	
6	v/iii/8-9	
7	v/iii/23-25	
8	v/i/5-6	

Rudolf Rasch

Complete Recordings of Geminiani's Cello Sonatas Op. 5.

1. Anthony Pleeth (1976)

Geminiani, 6 Cello Sonatas, Op. 5, LP Decca L'Oiseau-Lyre DSLO 513, 1976. CD L'Oiseau-Lyre 433 192-2, 1992. Anthony Pleeth (cello), Christopher Hogwood (harpsichord), Richard Webb (cello continuo).

2. David Simpson (1984)

Francesco Geminiani, Les six sonates Op. 5 pour violoncello et continuo, Solstice SOCD 34, [1984]. David Simpson (cello), Noëlle Spieth (harpsichord), Claire Giardelli (cello continuo).

3. Hidemi Suzuki (1991)

Francesco Geminiani, VI Sonate di Violoncello, Ricercar RIC 095077, 1991. Hidemi Suzuki (cello), Guy Penson (harpsichord), Rainer Zipperling (cello continuo).

4. Gaetano Nasillo (2001)

Geminiani, Cello Sonatas, Pan Classics PC 10232, 2001, 2011. Gaetano Nasillo (cello), Jesper Christensen (harpsichord), Tobias Bonz (cello continuo).

5. Alison McGillivray (2005)

Francesco Geminiani, Sonatas for Violoncello & Basso Continuo, Op. 5, Linn BKD 251, 2005, 2015. Alison McGillivray (cello), David McGuinness (harpsichord), Eligio Quinteiro (also Baroque guitar), Joseph Crouch (cello continuo).

6. Jaap ter Linden (2007)

Geminiani, Cello Sonatas Op. 5, Brilliant Classics 93636, 2007. Jaap ter Linden (cello), Lars Ulrik Mortensen (harpsichord), Judith-Maria Becker (cello continuo).

7. Bruno Cocset (2008)

Francesco Geminiani, Sonates pour violoncelle avec la basse continue, Alpha 123, 2008. Bruno Cocset (cello), Luca Pianca (theorbo), Bertrand Cuiller (harpsichord), Mathurin Matharel (cello continuo), Richard Myron (double bass).

8. Enrico Bronzi (2010)

Francesco Geminiani, 6 Sonate Op. 5, Concerto CD 2061, 2010. Enrico Bronzi (cello), Michele Barchi (harpsichord).

9. Loretta O'Sullivan (2015)

Francesco Geminiani, Sonatas for Cello Continuo Op. 5a – George Fredric Handel, Suite V for Harpsichord in E Major, Orchid ORC 100049, 2015. Four Nations Ensemble: Loretta O'Sullivan (cello), Andrew Appel (harpsichord), Beilang Zhu (continuo cello), Scott Pauley (theorbo and guitar).

Improvised Cadenzas in the Cello Sonatas Op. 5 by Francesco Geminiani

Cadenzas in Recordings of Geminiani's Cello Sonatas Op. 5

Anthony Pleeth (1976)

Geminiani, Cello Sonatas, Op. 5, Decca, L'Oiseau-Lyre, 1976, CD L'Oiseau-Lyre 433 192-2, 1992.

Sonata/Mov./Bar	Cadenza
I/i/15	
I/i/35	
II/i/21	
IV/ii/36	Fantasia ad libitum
V/i/4	none
V/iii/9	Cadenza al solito
V/iii/24	
VI/i/6	none

Rudolf Rasch

David Simpson (1984)

Francesco Geminiani, Les six sonates op. 5 pour violoncelle et continuo, Solstice SOCD 34, 1984.

Sonata/Mov./Bar	Cadenza
I/i/15	
I/i/35	
II/i/21	
IV/ii/36	
V/i/4	none
V/iii/9	
V/iii/24	
VI/i/6	none

Improvised Cadenzas in the Cello Sonatas Op. 5 by Francesco Geminiani

Hidemi Suzuki (1990)

Francesco Geminiani, Sonatas for Cello and Continuo. Ricercar RIC 095077, 1990.

Sonata/Mov./Bar	Cadenza
I/i/15	*(musical notation)*
I/i/35	*(musical notation)*
II/i/21	*(musical notation)*
IV/ii/36	Fantasia ad libitum *(musical notation)*
V/i/4	none
V/iii/9	Cadenza al solito *(musical notation)*
V/iii/24	*(musical notation)*
VI/i/6	none

Rudolf Rasch

Gaetano Nasillo (2001)

Geminiani, Cello Sonatas, Pan Classics PC 10232. 2001, 2011.

Improvised Cadenzas in the Cello Sonatas Op. 5 by Francesco Geminiani

Alison McGillivray (2005)

Francesco Geminiani, Sonatas for Violoncello & Basso Continuo Op. 5, Linn BTK . 2005, 2015.

Sonata/Mov./Bar	Cadenza
I/i/15	*(musical notation)*
I/i/35	none
II/i/21	*(musical notation)*
IV/ii/36	*(musical notation, Fantasia ad libitum)*
V/i/4	none
V/iii/9	*(musical notation, Cadenza al solito)*
V/iii/24	*(musical notation)*
VI/i/6	none

Rudolf Rasch

Jaap ter Linden (2007)

Geminiani, Cello Sonatas Op. 5, Brilliant Classics 93636. 2007.

Sonata/Mov./Bar	Cadenza
I/i/15	[music notation, bar 15]
I/i/35	none
II/i/21	[music notation, bar 21]
IV/ii/36	[music notation, bar 36, "Fantasia ad libitum"]
V/i/4	none
V/iii/9	[music notation, bar 9, "Cadenza al solito"]
V/iii/24	[music notation, bar 24]
VI/i/6	none

Improvised Cadenzas in the Cello Sonatas Op. 5 by Francesco Geminiani

Bruno Cocset (2008)

Francesco Geminiani, Sonates pour violoncelle avec la basse continue, Alpha 123. 2008.

Sonata/Mov./Bar	Cadenza
i/i/15	
i/i/35	
ii/i/21	
iv/ii/36	
v/i/4	none
v/iii/9	
v/iii/24	(35 sec)
vi/i/6	none

Rudolf Rasch

Enrico Bronzi (2010)

Francesco Geminiani, 6 Sonate Op. 5, Concerto CD 2061. 2010.

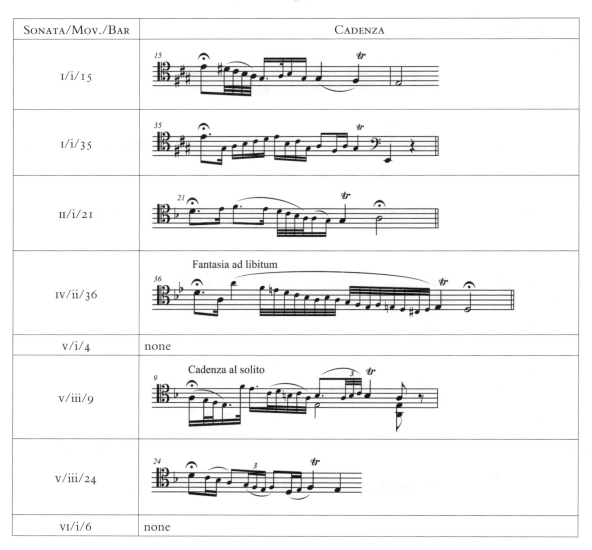

Improvised Cadenzas in the Cello Sonatas Op. 5 by Francesco Geminiani

Loretta O'Sullivan (2015)

Francesco Geminiani, Sonatas for Cello and Continuo, Orchid ORC 100049. 2015.

Sonata/Mov./Bar	Cadenza
I/i/15	
I/i/35	
II/i/21	
IV/ii/36	*Fantasia ad libitum*
V/i/4	none
V/iii/9	*Cadenza al solito*
V/iii/24	
VI/i/6	

Contemporary Treatises, Pedagogical Works, and Aesthetics

Il mito della competizione tra virtuosi: quando Farinelli sfidò Bernacchi (Bologna 1727)

Valentina Anzani
(Università di Bologna)

Una sfida sui palchi bolognesi

Nell'estate del 1727 i castrati Antonio Bernacchi, all'epoca quarantaduenne, e Farinelli (Carlo Broschi), ventiduenne, si trovarono per la prima volta ingaggiati per una stessa opera: *Antigona, ovvero la fedeltà coronata* di Giuseppe Maria Orlandini, dramma di Benedetto Pasqualigo, dato al Teatro Malvezzi di Bologna.

Nel giugno 1727 il Teatro Malvezzi, dopo cinque anni d'inattività veniva riaperto con grande sfarzo artistico: per *Antigona* erano infatti stati scritturati alcuni tra i cantanti di maggior grido del tempo, ovvero Bernacchi, Nicola Grimaldi, Antonia Merighi e Carlo Broschi Farinelli, quest'ultimo caldamente raccomandato dal conte Sicinio Pepoli. Il nobile aveva un ruolo di primo piano nel nuovo comitato impresariale del teatro; pochi mesi prima gli era stato introdotto il giovane musico dai suoi parenti romani, il cognato don Fabrizio Colonna e il cardinale Carlo Colonna, zio della moglie: fu questa scrittura che consacrerà alla scena internazionale il giovane cantante ventiduenne, che già raccoglieva successi in patria[1].

La riapertura del teatro e lo speciale dramma per musica erano dovuti al soggiorno in città di Giacomo III Stuart (1688-1766), l'esule pretendente giacobita al trono inglese e scozzese, accolto in Italia con tutti gli onori per il suo tentativo di ripristinare il culto cattolico in Inghilterra. Di madre italiana, figlio di Giacomo II Stuart e di Maria Beatrice d'Este, considerava la musica fra i suoi passatempi più graditi. A Roma si distingueva come uno dei maggiori mecenati dei teatri d'opera: nel suo preferito, l'Alibert, gli erano assegnati eccezionalmente tre palchi e ogni allestimento era dedicato a lui o alla consorte Maria Clementina[2]. Particolari onori gli erano riservati anche quando si recava altrove,

---

[1]. *Cfr.* Vitali 1992, p. 2.
[2]. *Cfr.* Corp 2011, pp. 82-84.

come avvenne a Bologna, seconda città dello Stato Pontificio, dove si trattenne per diversi mesi, omaggiato lussuosamente: il 31 dicembre 1726, per il genetliaco del figlio primogenito Carlo Edoardo (1720-1788), fu dato un fastosissimo ricevimento a Palazzo Marescotti, in via Barberia 391 (oggi 4):

> In esso giorno [martedì sera], per il compleanno del principino di Galles figlio primogenito di questo re britannico, fu gran galla in sua corte, e nella sera questa nobiltà vuolle dimostrare quanto sia la stima faccino della maestà sua: sol fare per tal effetto da dodici di questi primari cavaglieri una festa di ballo nel palazzo del signore senatore Marescotti, avendo perciò nel giorno antecedente fatto dispensare polizze a bello studio stampate, colle quale invitavano tutta questa nobiltà ad intervenire a detta festa nella più sontuosa galla; come in fatti vi comparvero con superbissimi abiti, ed era illuminato detto palazzo dentro e fuori con gran quantità di lumi di cera, avendola poscia decorata la comparsa fatta di sua maestà e 'l prencipino di Galles, quali si compia[c]quero di danzare in minuetti, e contradanze, e di più la maestà sua vuole fare danzare questa nobiltà in balli all'inglese, delli quali non sapendogli fare, sua maestà ne era il maestro con gran suo contento, e vi si trattenne sino all'ore sei e mezza; e riuscì tanto più decorosa detta festa, quanto che fu fram[m]ischiata da superfluità delli più rari rinfreschi, e per certo è stata una festa delle più singolari siansi fatte mai in questa città, e tanta satisfazione ne ha riportata la maestà sua, che non si puole esprimere, conoscendo quanta parzialità, e stima abbi questa nobiltà per la reale gran casa Stuarda[3].

Come molti altri allestimenti dedicati all'esule re inglese, anche il dramma che si allestì a Bologna l'estate 1727 si prestava a interpretazioni 'giacobite': i temi trattati nella trama di *Antigona, ovvero La fedeltà coronata* erano il trionfo del bene sul male, il premio dato alla pazienza e la restaurazione di una monarchia legittima[4]. Gli *Avvisi* della città testimoniano che:

> La sera di detto giorno [2 giugno] si diede principio alle recite della grandiosa opera musicale intitolata *La fedeltà coronata* nel Teatro Malvezzi, ornata di s[c]enario di nuove invenzioni de' più celebri pennelli in simile sfera, con nobilissimo vestiario, essendo la musica del virtuoso Orlandini recitata da' primi cantanti d'Europa, fra' quali li due famosi musici Bernachi e Farinello, fatti venire di Baviera e Napoli a forza di contanti, riuscendo a meraviglia[5].

---

[3]. I-Bu, ms. 770 vol. XCI: GHISELLI. *Memorie antiche manoscritte di Bologna, Avvisi secreti di Bologna*, 4 gennaio 1727.

[4]. *Cfr.* CORP 2011, pp. 89, 92.

[5]. I-Bu, ms. 225/IV: BARILLI, Antonio. *Zibaldone, ossia Giornale di Antonio Barilli Bolognese di quanto è seguito in Bologna dal principio dell'anno 1726 per tutto l'anno 1728. Tomo quarto.* c. 139ᵛ.

Il mito della competizione tra virtuosi: quando Farinelli sfidò Bernacchi

Narrazioni distorte, narrazioni ricche

Una tradizione diffusa vorrebbe che durante l'allestimento dell'opera Farinelli e Bernacchi avessero ingaggiato una gara: il primo incontro tra i due cantanti è narrato in numerose fonti secondarie come un momento di tensione e rivalità, in cui un borioso Farinelli avrebbe voluto dimostrare la propria superiorità all'anziano collega. Scatenata una disputa canora, entrambi si sarebbero lanciati in esecuzioni di difficilissimi passaggi, improvvisazioni estemporanee e di reciproche imitazioni, al cui termine Bernacchi non solo ebbe la meglio, ma indusse addirittura Farinelli ad accantonare la propria vanità per chiedere lezioni di canto al collega.

Il racconto iniziò a prendere questa forma nelle parole di Giovenale Sacchi, primo biografo di Farinelli (1784), che fu informato dei dettagli della sua vita da Padre Martini. Sacchi per primo affermò che quando si ritrovarono a cantare insieme, Farinelli decise di ostentare la propria abilità, che Bernacchi gli dimostrò invece di essergli superiore, e che una volta sconfitto, i due si sarebbero accordati per studiare insieme a Roma:

> Il giovine Broschi, cantando la prima volta insieme con lui privatamente, giudicò che il valore del Bernacchi non fosse uguale alla fama di cui godeva; onde con certa *animosità giovanile* cominciò a fare ostentazione della propria abilità, ciò che il più vecchio non faceva. Si accorse il Bernacchi di essere provocato, ed accesosi alquanto, fecegli sentire che egli non era ancora a tempo di uguagliarlo, non che di superarlo. Questo accidente, che avrebbe disgiunto due altri che fossero amici, congiunse questi due in amicizia che fu poi indissolubile; perché erano ambedue *di ottimo animo*, e oltre a ciò fu questa un'occasione a Farinello di farsi migliore che non era perché, compresa la superiorità del Bernacchi nell'arte del canto, lo pregò che volesse riceverlo alla sua scuola. Subito poi trasferitisi amendue a cantare a Roma, quivi ogni mattina il Broschi frequentava la casa del Bernacchi, ed apprendeva da lui quelle grazie sopraffine delle quali non era ancora abbastanza fornito[6].

Il Fétis (1860) nel suo compendio enciclopedico dedicato ai musicisti aggiunse un dettaglio sulla tipologia di duello canoro in cui i due si sarebbero confrontati: un duetto, il quale divenne sede di una vera e propria gara in cui ogni variazione proposta da Farinelli era immediatamente ripresa identica da Bernacchi, ma eseguita molto meglio. Farinelli gli aveva chiesto consiglio, e Bernacchi era stato felice di portare a compimento la formazione del cantante più talentuoso del Settecento:

> Nel 1727 [Farinelli] andò a Bologna dove doveva cantare con Bernacchi. Orgoglioso di tanto successo, fiducioso nell'incomparabile bellezza della sua voce e nella facilità prodigiosa d'esecuzione che non lo aveva mai tradito,

---

[6]. Sacchi 1784, pp. 13-14; corsivi aggiunti.

> temeva poco la prova cui stava per sottoporsi. L'abilità di Bernacchi era tale, tuttavia, che gli aveva fatto guadagnare l'appellativo di *Re dei cantori*; ma la sua voce non era bella, ed era solo per i mezzi dell'artificio che Bernacchi aveva trionfato sui suoi difetti. Non dubitando di una vittoria simile a quella ottenuta a Roma cinque anni prima [sul trombettiere tedesco], l'allievo di Porpora esibì tutti i tesori della sua bellissima voce, tutte le coloriture che avevano fatto la sua fama, nel duetto che cantò con Bernacchi. Il pubblico, nel delirio, rispose con applausi furiosi a ciò che aveva ascoltato. Bernacchi, per nulla turbato dalla meraviglia e dall'effetto che aveva prodotto, iniziò a sua volta la frase che doveva ripetere, e, riproducendo tutte le variazioni del giovane cantante, senza dimenticarne alcuna, mise in ogni dettaglio una perfezione così meravigliosa che Farinelli fu obbligato a riconoscere il suo maestro nel suo rivale. Dopo di che, invece di reagire con orgoglio ferito come un artista ordinario avrebbe fatto, ammise la sconfitta e chiese consiglio Bernacchi, che fu lieto di dare l'ultima rifinitura al talento del cantante più straordinario [*chanteur le plus extraordinaire*] del XVIII secolo[7].

Come sottolinea Ortkemper, il racconto suona però pericolosamente simile a un passo del trattato di Piefrancesco Tosi, tanto da far supporre che il duetto citato da Fétis non sia altro che un'aggiunta di sua mano:

> Mi sovviene, o mi sognai d'aver sentito un famoso duetto messo in pezzi minuti da due professori di grido, impegnati dalla emulazione a proporre, e vicendevolmente a rispondersi, che infine terminò in una gara a chi faceva più spropositi[8].

In un articolo pubblicato sulla *Revue des deux Mondes* del 1861, Paul Scudo riprese quasi per intero il passo di Fétis, aggiungendovi un dettaglio suggestivo: in breve, l'ultima frase ripresa da Bernacchi avrebbe conquistato il pubblico non solo perché era eseguita

---

[7]. «En 1727 il [Farinelli] se rendit à Bologne: il y devait chanter avec Bernacchi. Fier de tant de succès, confiant dans l'incomparable beauté de sa voix et dans la prodigieuse facilité d'execution qui ne l'avait jamais trahi, il redoutait peu l'épreuve qu'il allait subir. L'habilité de Bernacchi était telle, à-la-vérité, qu'elle l'avait fait appeler *Le rois des chanteurs*; mais sa voix n'était pas belle, et ce n'était qu'a force d'art que Bernacchi avait triomphé de ses défauts. Ne doubtant pas d'une victoire semblable à celle qu'il avait obtenue à Rome cinq ans auparavant [du trompette allemande], l'élève de Porpora prodigua dans le duo qu'il chantait avec Bernacchi tous les trésors de son bel organe, tous les traits qui avaient fait sa gloire. L'auditoire, dans le délire, prodigua des applaudissements frénétiques à ce qu'il venait d'entendre. Bernacchi, sans être ému du prodige e de l'effet qu'il avait produit, commença à son tour la phrase qu'il devait répéter, et redisant tous les traits du jeune chanteur, sans en oublier un seul, mit dans tous les détails une perfection si merveilleuse, que Farinelli fut obligé de reconnaître son maître dans son rival. Alors, au lieu de se renfermer dans un orgueil blessé, comme n'aurait pas manqué de faire un *artiste ordinaire*, il avoua sa défaite et demanda des conseils à Bernacchi, qui se plut à donner la dernière perfection au talent du *chanteur le plus extraordinaire* du dix-huitième siècle». FÉTIS 1860, p. 83; corsivi aggiunti.

[8]. TOSI 1723, p. 96.

Il mito della competizione tra virtuosi: quando Farinelli sfidò Bernacchi

tanto bene quanto quella di Farinelli, ma anche perché la sua esecuzione era naturale, l'emissione semplice e l'interpretazione piena di sentimento:

> Farinelli debuttò a Bologna in un'opera in cui aveva un duetto da cantare con Bernacchi, la cui voce era sorda e mediocre [=*la voix était sourde et mediocre*]. Il brillante allievo di Porpora, che doveva solo mostrare la sua figura snella e una figura affascinante per voltare il pubblico a suo favore, cominciò sfoggiando nella frase melodica che gli fu affidata tutti i gioielli delle sue fioriture vocali, tutta l'inventiva della sua immaginazione, che gli erano così ben riusciti a Roma. Dopo lo straordinario tumulto che la prestigiosa bravura di Farinelli aveva suscitato nella sala, Bernacchi riprese con modestia il motivo già sentito, lo espose con gusto, senza il minimo artificio, e lo espresse con un tale carattere di semplicità e sentimento [=*reprit modestement le motif déjà entendu, l'exposa avec goût, sans le moindre artifice, et lui imprima un tel cachet de simplicité et de sentiment*] che anche il suo giovane rivale ne rimase commosso. Il pubblico si pronunciò a favore di Bernacchi, e Farinelli, lungi dal sentirsi umiliato da questa vittoria, si dichiarò sconfitto: chiese a Bernacchi consigli durante tutto il tempo che trascorse a Bologna[9].

Scudo fu il primo a trasformare Bernacchi in un fautore del canto patetico, e fu riproposto quasi pedissequamente nell'articolo inglese anonimo di due anni dopo 'Singing to Some Purpose'[10]. Anche Enrico Panzacchi a fine secolo narrò la propria versione dello stesso episodio in un saggio intitolato 'La musica' (1897), che appare una sua libera traduzione dei testi citati, che dunque doveva conoscere (s'inventò però l'autore dell'opera e omise ogni riferimento alla richiesta di lezioni da parte di Farinelli).

Nelle parole di Panzacchi l'esecuzione di Bernacchi fu tanto più sorprendente e inaspettata perché quest'ultimo, invece di aggiungere nuovi trilli alla frase melodica, ebbe l'ingegnosa trovata di ripresentarla al pubblico nella purezza del tema originale:

---

[9]. «Farinelli se rendit à Bologne en 1727. Il y rencontra le sopraniste Bernachi, qui devait avoir sur sa carrière d'artiste la plus salutaire influence. Bernacchi était un virtuose dèjà célèbre, que ses contamporains avaient surnommé le *roi des chantaurs*. Élève de Pistochi, qui avait fondé à Bologne une ècole de chant très estimée, Bernachi à continué avec succès l'enseignement de son maitre en formant ò son tour un grand nombre de virtuoses distingués. Farinelli débuta à Bologne dans un opéra où il avait un duo à chanter avec Bernachi, dont la voix était sourde et mediocre. Le brillant élève de Porpora, qui n'avait qu'à montrer sa taille svelte et une charmante figure pour prévenir le public en sa faveur, commença par dérouler sur la phrase mélodique qui lui était confiée tout l'écrin de ses fioritures vocales, toutes les ingéniositès de sa fantaisie, qui lui avaientsi bien réussi à Rome. Après un tumulte extraordinaire qu'avait soulevé dans la salle la bravoure prestigieuse de Farinelli, Bernachi reprit modestement le motif déjà entendu, l'exposa avec goût, sans le moindre artifice, et lui imprima un tel cachet de simplicité et de sentiment que son jeune rival en fut ému lui-même. Le public se prononça en faveur de Bernachi, et Farinelli, loin de se trouver humilié de cette victoire, s'avoua vaincu: il demanda des conseils à Bernachi pendant tout le temps qu'il passa à Bologne». Scudo 1861, p. 759.

[10]. Singing to Some Purpose 1863.

> Il Bernacchi e il Farinello divennero col tempo *rivali*, e una volta s'incontrarono a Bologna verso la metà del secolo. Il pubblico li attendeva in un duetto del maestro Hasse, detto il Sassone, dove ognuno dei due doveva dare prova del proprio talento. Raccontano che in mezzo ad una trepida aspettazione, ad un silenzio profondo i due campioni prima espressero il puro tema melodico su cui cadeva la *gara*. Il Farinello, più giovane, stupì il pubblico con variazioni audacissime, e il Bernacchi di rimando sulle prime *tenne validamente testa all'avversario*; ma poi, crescendo sempre le difficoltà inaspettate e le ardue bizzarrie del canto farinelliano, il Bernacchi ebbe l'astuzia da *vecchio lottatore*. Ad un tratto abbandonò il sistema delle variazioni e dei trilli, e ripresentò al pubblico il bel tema melodico in tutta la sua primitiva purezza e semplicità. L'entusiasmo del pubblico, a quell'effetto inatteso, non ebbe più confini. Fu domandato il bis e il Bernacchi lo concesse; ma quando fu per riprendere la sua frase, sentì nell'orchestra una certa inquietudine, una certa titubanza. Si volse a guardare, e si avvide che anche i suonatori, anche il direttore d'orchestra piangevano[11].

Panzacchi postdatò l'accaduto di un quarto di secolo («verso la metà del secolo»), forse equivocando con il *Siroe* di Hasse del 1733, con Farinelli e Caffarelli, e aggiunse dettagli romanzeschi che tradiscono la sua attitudine alla narrativa di fantasia[12]. Nella tradizione successiva questo passo venne spesso acriticamente considerato come un indizio inequivocabile del riconoscimento di Bernacchi come ultimo esponente di quello stile patetico tipico di coloro che Tosi chiama «gli antichi», contrapponendolo allo stile moderno (di cattivo gusto) di Farinelli, illustre esponente della 'scuola' napoletana.

Realtà storica

Ad uno sguardo complessivo risulta però chiaro che l'episodio tramandato dal biografo più vicino ai fatti (Sacchi 1784), subì la corruzione apologetica tipica dei biografi del XIX secolo e che una volta rielaborato da Fétis (1861), Scudo (1861) e Panzacchi (1897) la verosimiglianza storica diventa improbabile. Ognuno dei racconti riporta imprecisioni. La modalità di somministrazione delle lezioni proposta da Fétis è incongruente con la realtà dei fatti, poiché il confronto tra le carriere dei due conferma che non furono mai a Roma insieme: dopo le recite di Bologna si ritroveranno per due estati successive a Parma, dove entrambi saranno impegnati nell'allestimento del *Medo* di Frugoni/Vinci nel 1728 e nel *Lucio Papirio dittatore* di Frugoni/Giacomelli nel 1729.

---

[11]. La presente citazione proviene da Panzacchi 1897, pp. 522-524 (corsivi aggiunti).

[12]. Questa attitudine di Panzacchi è testimoniata anche dalla pubblicazione dei suoi *Racconti* (Panzacchi 1889), tra cui ve ne è anche uno, *Cantores*, dedicato ai cantanti castrati che poté udire nella Cappella Sistina.

Il mito della competizione tra virtuosi: quando Farinelli sfidò Bernacchi

Molto di più fu il tempo che condivideranno a Bologna: nella primavera del 1728, prima di dirigersi a Parma per le recite di *Medo*, saranno entrambi nella città felsinea, e si esibiranno in separate sedi durante le celebrazioni pasquali[13]. I due saranno di nuovo insieme a Bologna per il *Farnace* di Lucchini/Porta del 1731, estate in cui canteranno anche «in casa del Principe senator Riario, dove vi fu una nobile accademia di suono e canto»[14]; e ancora nei mesi estivi del 1732: Bernacchi arrivò in giugno[15] e Farinelli passò verosimilmente l'estate in città[16].

Sempre Fétis afferma che i due si confrontarono in un duetto; tuttavia nell'opera in scena al Teatro Malvezzi nel 1727 non ne era previsto alcuno tra loro due. Si potrebbe forse ipotizzare un'aggiunta estemporanea o non registrata da libretto o partitura, il che andrebbe a favore dell'attribuzione che Panzacchi fa del brano, dicendolo di Hasse e non dell'autore dell'opera in cartellone, che era invece Orlandini; ma all'altezza del 1727 non c'è alcun dramma per musica che contenga un duetto tra due 'primi uomini'. Si potrebbe anche immaginare che l'esibizione sia avvenuta in ambito privato («cantando la prima volta insieme con lui privatamente», come vorrebbe Sacchi), non in teatro, forse a latere dell'informale prova generale organizzata in casa Pepoli di cui parlano gli *Avvisi*, oppure in tutt'altro contesto, durante un'esecuzione di musica sacra[17].

Preso atto di tutte le inverosimiglianze presenti in questi racconti, sembra probabile che in realtà la contesa non avvenne mai, ma fu piuttosto deliberatamente inventata dai

---

[13]. Bernacchi cantò il 16 marzo durante un'Accademia degli alunni del Collegio dei Nobili (I-Bu, ms. 225/IV: Barilli, Antonio. *Zibaldone* [...], c. 237^v); pochi giorni dopo, il 26 marzo «fu fatta grandiosa cappella a S. Petronio per la commemorazione della Risurrezione del Redentore con la presenza de' Regi Stuardi e de' signori Superiori, dove vi cantò il famoso Farinelli con gran lode, come pure il Minelli et altri accreditati musici, e la loro armonia fu accompagnata dallo sfarzo del cannone e moschettaria svizzera su questa pubblica piazza» (*ibidem*, c. 238^r).

[14]. I-Bu, ms. 225/V: Barilli, Antonio. *Zibaldone* [...]. *Tomo quinto*, c. 256^{r-v}.

[15]. I-Bu, ms. 92, busta IV, n. 8: *Lettere 233 di Francesco Zambeccari al fratello Alessandro dal 1709 al 1745*, 2 luglio 1732.

[16]. Il diarista Barilli è prodigo di notizie a riguardo: «A dì 2 settembre: avere gl'impresari dell'opera musicale a recitarsi in Piacenza accordato a questa cantatrice signora Vittoria Tesi duecento luigi di suo onorario, oltre il regalo per la recita della medesima, la quale si dispone alla partenza, come fa il famoso musico Farinelli» (I-Bu, ms. 225/VI: Barilli, Antonio. *Zibaldone* [...]. *Tomo sesto*, 2 settembre 1732). Già in quel periodo Farinelli pensava di stabilirsi a Bologna: «A dì 22 settembre: Sèntesi che il famoso musico Farinelli sia risoluto di stabilire qui il suo soggiorno, sento in trattato di fare acquisto di decoroso stabile»; «A dì 23 ottobre: Dall'eccelso Senato è poi stato decretato della cittadinanza con il beneficio del Terminale, il famoso musico Farinelli, che fa ora un acquisto di stabili per 2800 lire di pronti contanti» (*ibidem*, 22 settembre 1732; 23 ottobre 1732).

[17]. «Da Monaco di Baviera in quattro giorni giunse in questa città il famoso musico signore Bernacchi, per la qual cosa nelli susseguenti giorni furono fatte alcune prove della nota grand'opera nel palazzo dell'eccellenza il signor conte Sicinio Pepoli. È riuscita a meraviglia, e questa sera si dovrà fare nel teatro la prova generale per dare incominciamento alle recite lunedì venturo». I-Bu, ms. 770 vol. XCI: Ghiselli. *Memorie antiche manoscritte di Bologna*, *Avvisi secreti di Bologna*, 31 maggio 1727.

biografi: è infatti altamente improbabile che proprio quegli stessi *Avvisi* (o *Zibaldoni*) che informano così diffusamente sull'arrivo dei cantanti in città, sulle loro cene e pranzi, sulle prove private e sull'andamento delle repliche non abbiano speso una riga su una disfida canora fra i due divi. Un tanto eclatante duello e l'altrettanto eclatante esito sarebbero di certo stati riportati in un tale genere di fonti che, paragonabili a moderne riviste di gossip, registravano tutte le attività degne di nota avvenute in città.

Il sonetto

L'unico documento in nostro possesso che rivela un clima di ostilità è un sonetto che circolò in città durante quell'estate[18].

In favore del musico Bernacchi e contro il Farinello

Avre ch'am dsissi cosa è mai st' gran fiach cha fà person cun st' vostr Farinel[!] Per Crispel, av dig ch'avi pers al cervel, e s' v' sò dir ch'al canta mei Bernach[!]	*Vorrei che mi diceste cos'è mai questo gran rumore che la gente fa con questo vostro Farinelli! Per Cristo, vi dico che avete perso il cervello, e vi dico che canta meglio Bernacchi!*
Quest n'è spar d' raz, ne di tich tach e s' n' fà da lusgnol, nè da franguel. L'è un capon, ch'è castrà qusi ben ugual ch'int la sò vos an spò truvar intach.	*Questo non spara né razzi né mortaretti e non imita né l'usignolo né il fringuello! È un cappone che è castrato così ben ugualmente che nella sua voce non si può trovare intaccatura.*
Donca, chi ha la passion la lassa andar. Es spò dir a sti tal ch'ijn in error che quand s' dis Bernach, più in là n' s' po' andar.	*Pertanto, chi ne è dispiaciuto si vada a nascondere. E dico a questi tali che sono in errore, che quando si è detto "Bernacchi", più in là non si può andare.*
Diga, chi vol Bulogna[:] n' n'a scador, qui as fà di mustaz ch'an al cular l'in tutt l' scienzi i portin via l'unor.	*Dicano ciò che vogliono: a Bologna non danno fastidio e ciò alla faccia dei cani che disonorano tutte le scienze.*

L'anonimo autore bolognese del sonetto si schiera apertamente in favore del proprio concittadino e sostiene di non condividere l'entusiasmo di coloro che parteggiano per Farinelli; inoltre mette i due a paragone enumerando con disapprovazione le caratteristiche interpretative di Farinelli, senza però pronunciarsi su quelle di Bernacchi. Farinelli è descritto come un cantante che «spara razzi» e «mortaretti» e che «imita l'usignolo» e «il fringuello»; Bernacchi al contrario non fa nulla di tutto questo, eppure canta meglio: l'autore non

---

[18]. I-Bu, ms. 239, fasc. v, c. 7: *Sonetto in favore del musico Bernacchi e contro il Farinello*; trad. it. di Gabriele Musenga <http://www.haendel.it/interpreti/old/bernacchi_aneddoti.htm>, visitato nell'Ottobre 2018; *cfr.* Verdi 2008, p. 129.

aggiunge a sostegno di tale affermazione null'altro che l'assunto — non privo di humor — che egli è «castrato così bene che la sua voce non ha intaccature». Sembrerebbe insomma che il canto di Farinelli non fosse apprezzato perché implicava un'esecuzione inadeguatamente o eccessivamente ornata, una critica, questa, conforme a quanto si legge ampiamente nella letteratura coeva e successiva, a partire di nuovo da Tosi: nella contrapposizione che egli fa tra *antichi* e *moderni*, condanna i moderni di «rompere [le arie], e [...] sminuzzarle in guisa che non è possibile di poter più sentire né parole, né pensieri, né modulazioni, né discernere un'aria dall'altra a cagione di tal somiglianza, ché una che se ne senta serve per mille»; condanna inoltre l'indugiare nel «torrente de' passaggi alla moda», nelle «capricciose cadenze», nell'«artificio prodigioso di cantar come i grilli [...] dieci o dodici crome in fila», arrivando a «tritolar[l]e a una a una con un certo tremor di voce che passa da poco tempo in qua sotto nome di mordente fresco»; stigmatizza infine «l'invenzione di rider cantando, o di cantar come le galline quando han fatto l'uovo», nella «velocità continua d'una voce errante senza guida e senza fondamento»[19].

Come Tosi, molti successivi detrattori del canto ornato procedettero sulla medesima linea: Vincenzo Martinelli condanna «tutti quei voli bizzarri e poco significanti»[20] e Stefano Arteaga, contrario a quei «mille impertinentissimi gruppi di note», vorrebbe proscrivere «tutte le cadenze eseguite nello stile di *bravura*, cioè quelle cadenze arbitrarie inventate all'unico fine di far brillare una voce accumulando senza disegno una serie prodigiosa di tuoni e raggirandosi con mille *ghirigori insignificanti*»[21].

Il canto di Farinelli dunque, con i suoi «razzi e mortaretti», aveva quelle caratteristiche ritenute proprie dei *moderni*, e per questo condannate come nocive al buon gusto. Per negazione ci si aspetterebbe in Bernacchi un modo di cantare del tutto opposto (come Scudo e Panzacchi centocinquant'anni dopo vollero insinuare: «e Bernacchi *ripresentò al pubblico il bel tema melodico in tutta la sua primitiva purezza e semplicità*»). Se sul modo di cantare di quest'ultimo l'autore del sonetto non si pronuncia, è possibile però rifarsi a testimonianze relative agli stessi anni, tra cui la più esplicativa e sintetica è forse la caricatura di Antonio Zanetti risalente al 1729 in cui il cantante è impegnato in una cadenza tanto lunga da innalzarsi fin sopra il campanile di Piazza S. Marco a Venezia, ridiscendere ondeggiando sopra la libreria Sansoviniana (l'odierna biblioteca marciana) e terminare in un trillo[22].

È solo la più immediata di una serie di testimonianze che descrivono il cantante come uno degli interpreti che più indugiavano in abbellimenti, passi, cadenze e fioriture e che gli causarono le aspre critiche di alcuni detrattori del canto ornato.

---

[19]. Tosi 1723, pp. 67, 81-82, 105-106.
[20]. Martinelli 1758, p. 358.
[21]. Arteaga 1783, pp. 130, 122.
[22]. La caricatura di Antonio Bernacchi è di mano di Anton Maria Zanetti e proviene da I-Vcini, *Album di caricature di Anton Maria Zanetti e altri, appartenuto a Francesco Albergati Capacelli*, ed è pubblicata in Lucchese 2015, p. 107.

A metà Settecento Vincenzo Martinelli disapprovava Bernacchi perché era solito «voler trascorrere tutti i possibili [artifici] della musica nel breve compasso d'un'aria»[23], mentre Algarotti racconta che il maestro Pistocchi avrebbe addirittura redarguito l'allievo: «"Tristo a me, io t'ho insegnato a cantare e tu vuoi suonare", rimproverava Pistocco a Bernacchi, che si può tenere come il caposcuola, il Marini della moderna licenza» e annovera Bernacchi tra quei moderni virtuosi che «pensano in contrario, che tutta la scienza stia nello isquartar la voce, in un saltellar continuo di nota in nota, non in iscegliere quello che vi ha di migliore, ma in eseguire ciò che vi ha di più straordinario e difficile»[24].

Voler associare Bernacchi, come fecero Scudo e Panzacchi, a un tipo di canto non ornato è un'evidente forzatura, poiché era anch'egli cantante che fioriva ampiamente le sue arie. Verosimilmente l'unica competizione della stagione operistica bolognese del 1727 fu quella documentata dal sonetto citato, sviluppatasi interamente tra le fazioni del pubblico, parte del quale si era schierato campanilisticamente e acriticamente a favore del concittadino: una competizione del tutto priva delle considerazioni stilistiche fatte dai biografi successivi.

A testimoniare la diffusione di situazioni di antagonismo in ambito operistico, proprio allo stesso anno risale forse il più chiacchierato litigio tra primedonne del secolo, avvenuto sui palchi londinesi durante le rappresentazioni dell'*Astianatte* di Bononcini: l'ostilità tra Faustina Bordoni (1697-1781) e Francesca Cuzzoni (1696-1778) diede luogo a racconti secondo cui le due cantanti si avventarono l'una contro l'altra in un litigio tanto violento che i commentatori lo definirono un uragano («hurricane»[25]). La risonanza di questo evento fu abbastanza ampia, seppur anche in quel caso, come sembra essere accaduto a Bologna, le narrazioni coeve (due pamphlet senza alcuna pretesa di verosimiglianza e con finalità puramente satirica[26]) abbiano di molto esagerato la realtà dei fatti, che si limitò a un astio profondo tra le due, alimentato da opposte fazioni del pubblico[27].

Bernacchi insegnante di canto

Bernacchi fu uno dei più celebrati maestri di canto del Settecento. Poter dire di aver studiato con lui era sinonimo di legittimità degli studi compiuti e un ottimo biglietto da visita per futuri ingaggi. Tra coloro che restarono sotto il suo magistero per diversi anni vi furono Ventura Rocchetti, Giovanni Tedeschi Amadori, Anton Raaff, Carlo Carlani e Tommaso Guarducci. Di Ventura Rocchetti, soprano, non si conoscono le date di nascita e morte; tuttavia quando iniziò a vivere con Bernacchi, nel 1735-1736, era attivo

---

[23]. Martinelli 1758, p. 358.
[24]. Algarotti 1763, p. 46.
[25]. *The Devil* 1727, p. 4.
[26]. Si vedano *The Devil* 1727 e *The Contre-Temps* 1727.
[27]. La questione è affrontata ampiamente in Aspden 2013.

nei teatri italiani da un lustro e aveva già cantato a Dresda e a Londra. Giovanni Tedeschi Amadori (1715-1787), contralto, aveva almeno 24 anni quando nel 1739 si trasferì a Bologna, e dal 1732 aveva già cantato in una decina di opere in teatri romani. Anton Raaff (1714-1797), tenore, arrivò nel 1740, essendosi esibito nei tre anni precedenti a Monaco, Firenze e Venezia.

Tutti i sopracitati avevano dunque iniziato a prendere lezioni da Bernacchi già adulti e a carriera avviata, avendo prima studiato con altri maestri, perlopiù compositori: Raaff era stato allievo di Giovanni Battista Ferrandini (ca. 1710-791), Giovanni Tedeschi di Giuseppe Amadori (1670-1730); lo stesso fecero anche altri cantanti che studiarono con Bernacchi per un più breve periodo: tra questi un certo «signor Tomasini» virtuoso della reale maestà di Portogallo, giunto da Lisbona a Bologna nel maggio del 1751 appositamente per avere lezioni da Bernacchi[28]. Nel '51 risiedevano nella sua casa anche il ventiseienne Lorenzo Memel e Antonio Ratti, trentaseienne; erano probabilmente allievi, ma non riuscirono ad avviare una carriera teatrale[29]. «In Bologna si trattenne alcuni mesi assistito dal maestro Bernacchi» anche Pietro Paolo Carnoli (1752-1802), poi al servizio dell'elettore palatino[30], e forse pure Vincenzo Caselli (1710-1799), poi alla corte di Dresda.

Altri suoi allievi furono Giuseppe Appiani detto l'Appianino (1712-1742), e Gioacchino Conti detto Gizziello (1714-1761), entrambi provenienti da scuole napoletane: il primo era stato, come Farinelli, allievo del compositore Nicola Porpora (1686-1766); il secondo del soprano Domenico Gizzi (1680-1758), da cui il soprannome artistico (talvolta storpiato in 'Egiziello'). Appiani giungeva a Bologna con una solida carriera alle spalle, nei teatri del Nord d'Italia; dal canto suo, Conti aveva già conquistato il pubblico di Londra, dove nel 1736-1737 aveva anche assistito alle esibizioni di Farinelli. Non sappiamo se, rientrando in Italia, la scelta di rivolgersi a Bernacchi sia stata suggerita da quest'ultimo; di fatto, la fiducia riposta — già famosi — nella didattica di Bernacchi venne letta da Mancini come un encomiabile segno di umiltà artistica:

> Il giovanetto Gizziello, quantunque lontano dal suo maestro [Gizzi], non lasciò di mettere in pratica tutti gli avvertimenti acquistati, e di seguire lo studio sulle regole del suo Maestro. Passò in Inghilterra per alcuni anni, dove perfezionò lo stile e si fé raro. Non ostante però l'alto nome che ivi avea alzato,

---

[28]. «Scrivo intanto questa per domani consegnarla in caso che partisse la detta [nave] avanti martedì, e in questa nave parte un musico di Sua Maestà per portarsi a studiare sotto la direzione del nostro famosissimo signor Antonio Bernacchi, il quale me lo potrà divertire con tutta la stima e che li sono e fui sempre suo buon amico e servitore». I-Bc, I.4.29: *Lettera di Gaetano Maria Schiassi a Giovanni Battista Martini*, Lisbona, 6 maggio 1751.

[29]. I-Bgd, Parrocchie Soppresse, Ss. Giacomo e Filippo de' Piatesi, *Stati delle anime*, anno 1751.

[30]. «Mi ricordai che avevo nella corte Palatina un mio amico chiamato Pietro Paolo Carnoli, che serve quella corte in qualità di tenore. [...] Questo giovine l'ha dovuto conoscere in Bologna, dove si trattenne alcuni mesi assistito dal maestro Bernacchi. Comunque sia, se non è morto deve rispondere». I-Bc, L.117.76: *Lettera di Giovanni Battista Mancini a Giovanni Battista Martini*, Vienna, 4 gennaio 1769.

ritornando in Italia, quasi non contento di sé stesso, volle fermarsi in Bologna sotto la direzione del gran Bernacchi. Fatto, che potria essere di regola e di rossore a molti, che presumono di sé stessi. Lo stesso praticò l'amabile Giuseppe Appiani detto Appianino, trattenendosi anch'esso in Bologna per studiare presso lo stesso Bernacchi. Questo studio fatto da questi due Professori fu da loro eseguito in quel medesimo tempo che ambidue erano riconosciuti ed acclamati fra il numero de' primari cantanti[31].

Vittoria Tesi era stata allieva del compositore Giovanni Redi (1685-1769) a Firenze; trasferitasi a Bologna, studiava quotidianamente con Francesco Campeggi (16??-1742), pur «non tralasciando nel medesimo tempo di frequentare la scuola di Bernacchi»[32]; aveva studiato con Bernacchi lo stesso Giovanni Battista Mancini (1714-1800): allievo di Leonardo Leo per due anni a Napoli, nel 1728 si era spostato a Bologna per perfezionarsi con quello che nei *Pensieri e riflessioni pratiche sopra il canto figurato* (1774) innalzerà poi a principe della didattica vocale.

La scuola di Bernacchi come tappa di perfezionamento

Al tempo della comparsa sulla scena bolognese, la carriera di Farinelli era in piena ascesa, tuttavia l'anno precedente questi aveva rifiutato un'importante scrittura per Londra e, secondo l'impresario inglese in esilio Owen McSwiny, non lo si sarebbe potuto convincere ad andare in Inghilterra per i successivi due o tre anni, «poiché egli ha in mente di studiare la *maniera lombarda*, che lo farà migliorare al cento per cento»[33]. Il passo testimonia in Farinelli un atteggiamento che Tosi descrive nel suo trattato come il più apprezzabile in un cantante, nonché necessario per raggiungere i più alti livelli di carriera: l'apertura continua verso nuovi studi e i consigli di nuovi mentori:

> Chi nutre però sentimenti migliori cercherà una più nobile e più ristretta compagnia. Conoscerà il bisogno che ha d'altri lumi, d'altri documenti, e d'altro

---

[31]. Mancini 1774, pp. 184-185.

[32]. *Ibidem*, p. 19.

[33]. «I am just returned from Parma where I heard ye Divine Farinelli (another blazing star) but I am sorry to tell you that I m'e affraid he'l not be p[e]rsuaded to goe for England these two or three years yet, for he has a mind to study ye Lombard Manner, which will improve him Cent per Cent: I think I told your Grace in my last letter that he was engaged to sing in one of the theatres of Rome the next winter». GB-West Sussex Record Office, Chichester, Goodwood MS 105/401, 3: *Letter by Owen McSwiny dated Venice 31 May 1726 to the Duke of Richmond*, trascritta in Llewellyn 2009, p. 228. Nel suo contributo del 2014, Anne Desler ha evidenziato l'inverosimiglianza dei testi di Sacchi e Fétis, escludendo la possibilità che i due cantanti abbiano intrapreso una gara canora, ma supportando la reale possibilità che Farinelli sia stato istruito, pur non formalmente, da Bernacchi, supportando la sua ampia argomentazione anche con questa testimonianza. *Cfr.* Desler 2014, pp. 107 e 110.

Il mito della competizione tra virtuosi: quando Farinelli sfidò Bernacchi

> maestro ancora. Da questo vorrà apprendere coll'arte di ben cantare quella di saper vivere, che tutta consiste nelle belle convenienze della vita civile. Unita che questa sia al merito che si farà nel canto, allora ei potrà sperare la grazia de' monarchi e la stima universale[34].

Farinelli era di certo un cantante con la piena padronanza delle proprie capacità tecniche, acquisite presso Nicola Porpora a Napoli: se avesse avuto gravi lacune non gli sarebbe stata possibile una carriera così ottimamente avviata; tuttavia, almeno già dall'anno precedente al suo incontro con Bernacchi, tutt'altro che compiaciuto di sé, desiderava migliorare il proprio stile esecutivo e rinunciava a un'importante occasione lavorativa perché aveva intenzione di imparare a cantare alla «maniera lombarda». Mancini (1774) conferma che in effetti portò a compimento il proposito:

> Nacque il Cavaliere Don Carlo Broschi nella Provincia di Bari nel Regno di Napoli. […] I suoi *primi studi* furono diretti dal celebre Niccolò Porpora. […] i Teatri delle primarie città d'Italia fecero a gara per averlo, e in ogni parte ov'egli cantò, ne riportò un ben meritato applauso, a tal segno che ognuno pretese di rifermarlo. Molte corti d'Europa non tardarono di farlo chiamare, e da per tutto fu ammirato, contraddistinto e ben premiato. Questo florido suo corso fu ne' primi anni della sua gioventù. Non per questo il nostro valent'uomo *cessò mai di studiare a un tanto segno che gli riuscì di cambiare in gran parte il suo primo fare, scegliendone un altro migliore; e tutto ciò fu da esso intrapreso in quel medesimo tempo che si avea già fatto il gran nome*[35].

Se Mancini non si pronuncia su cosa fece Farinelli per migliorarsi, la risposta è negli appunti manoscritti di Padre Martini, amico stretto di entrambi i soggetti coinvolti:

> 1727: [Farinelli] recitò in Bologna assieme col famoso Antonio Bernacchi, del quale è viva ancora la memoria fra' tanti scolari nel signor Giovanni Amadori, Raaff, signor Tommaso Guarducci, i quali passano fra i più eccellenti cantori de' nostri tempi. Terminato il dramma in Bologna, essendo chiamati ambedue a recitare nel teatro di Parma *ed avendo ammirata il Broschi la grand'arte del Bernacchi nel cantare, fu pregato a darle alcune istruzioni che conosceva mancargli*; e infatti ogni mattina, levato dal letto lui e il Bernacchi passavano assieme al cembalo ed attendeva quelle sottigliezze che conosceva mancargli. Da tutto ciò non è da meravigliarsi se riuscì così eccellente il cavaliere Broschi e fu ricercato dalle principali teste coronate d'Europa[36].

Dunque il giovane cantante in ascesa Farinelli, una volta avuta la fortuna di lavorare al fianco di Bernacchi, lo riconobbe come «a quel tempo il primo cantante d'Italia per

---

[34]. Tosi 1723, p. 90.
[35]. Mancini 1774, pp. 105-107; corsivi aggiunti.
[36]. I-Bc, ms. H.60: Martini, Giovanni Battista. *Zibaldone Martiniano. Contiene notizie di musicisti, ed altre cose relative alla storia della musica*, p. 132; corsivi aggiunti. Il documento è già citato in Verdi 2008, p. 129.

gusto e sapienza»[37], ritrovò in lui un esponente di quella «maniera lombarda» diversa dalla sua 'napoletana' di cantare, e decise quindi di rivolgersi allo stimato collega per qualche consiglio, che il didatta fu pronto a dare: molto probabilmente, dopo quel primo incontro, trovarono del tempo per studiare insieme quando ebbero l'occasione di lavorare nelle stesse città e durante i frequenti soggiorni di Farinelli a Bologna.

Versioni di un mito

Avendo stabilito che in realtà non ci fu alcuna competizione, è chiaro che alcuni biografi hanno messo in atto una reinvenzione estrema, tanto estrema da suggerire che l'importanza di queste fonti 'alterate' non risieda nella loro riconduzione ad una realtà storicamente attendibile, ma nell'immagine che ci offrono della recezione postuma del personaggio Bernacchi e del rapido processo di mitizzazione cui fu sottoposto. In quest'ottica, queste diverse e successive versioni, piuttosto che essere ritenute distorte, possono essere ritenute legittime per comprendere il pensiero coevo all'autore. La chiave di lettura è dunque quella di narrazioni che possano essere esemplificative di una più ampia visione: quella del mito. Come un mito, rappresentano un episodio che possa avere caratteri universali, e per raggiungere quel grado di importanza usano come 'attori' delle figure iconiche, come erano appunto Farinelli e Bernacchi. Entrambi «di ottimo animo», il primo è l'incarnazione del virtuoso di talento (Fétis: «chanteur le plus extraordinaire») nel pieno del proprio successo e ancor giovane (Sacchi: «animosità giovanile»), l'altro è l'incarnazione del maestro di canto paterno, comprensivo, intelligente, la validità dei cui metodi d'insegnamento è confermata dal fatto che egli è a sua volta un cantante di rilievo sul piano internazionale. Il narratore attinge al repertorio di altre storie di cui dispone ed estremizza le caratteristiche di entrambi i cantanti, alterandole quanto serve perché aderiscano ai cliché che gli serve vengano impersonati: solo così il racconto mitico acquisisce adeguata forza comunicativa.

In questi racconti l'identità degli 'antagonisti' non è nemmeno troppo fondamentale per la delineazione del messaggio retorico, come dimostra una versione modificata del racconto sopracitato di Algarotti pubblicata su un giornale milanese del 1827, secondo cui Bernacchi sarebbe diventato il primo cantante d'Europa solo dopo aver rinnegato il canto ornato:

> Pistochi capo-scuola di canto del secolo passato, avendo udito dalle scene
> di un Teatro di Londra il suo allievo Bernachi, «Ah sciagurato!», esclamò fra il

---

[37]. «From Rome he [Farinelli] went to Bologna where he had the advantage of hearing Bernacchi, a scholar of the famous Pistocchi, of that city, who was then the first singer in Italy, for taste and knowledge; and his scholars afterwards rendered the Bologna school famous». BURNEY 1773, pp. 214-215.

Il mito della competizione tra virtuosi: quando Farinelli sfidò Bernacchi

profondo silenzio del pubblico, «Io ti ho insegnato a cantare e tu vuoi suonare!».
Gli inglesi applaudirono l'ardire di Pistocchi, ed il Bernacchi fu d'allora in poi
il primo cantante in Europa[38].

Si vede bene un *pattern* che si ripete, invariabilmente applicabile anche su colui che in altre testimonianze è il mitico maestro salvatore e risanatore di un allievo troppo dedito alle fioriture: gli attori che impersonano l'allievo troppo audace e il maestro molto raffinato sono intercambiabili, a riprova del trattamento di mitizzazione che ricevono; ciò che viene preservata è la contrapposizione tra due generazioni in contrasto fra loro, in cui «la scuola antica si rivoltava contro le innovazioni della nuova»[39].

Nei diversi racconti le figure di Farinelli e Bernacchi assurgono dunque *ad exempla* e, come nella tradizione agiografica delle *Vite dei santi*, incarnano più di quello che furono, ovvero gli stereotipi (vuoi positivi o negativi) delle rispettive categorie. In questo modo il cantante di successo diventa vanesio, il maestro furbo ma pacato, il loro primo incontro una competizione in campo aperto e la risoluzione commovente schiude le porte per un insegnamento morale: un cantante non deve smettere di studiare e migliorarsi; un cantante più bravo di un altro non deve ostentare la propria superiorità, ma consentire all'altro di attingere in modo costruttivo dalla sua esperienza al fine di mantenere viva l'arte del canto e permetterne la trasmissione; un cantante deve essere umile e non credersi migliore di quello che è, non deve mettersi in competizione e deve comportarsi in modo rispettoso. I biografi successivi delineeranno dunque un nuovo *topos*: quello dei colleghi che si imitano in un rapporto virtuoso.

Oscurata dall'abbondanza di fonti primarie e letteratura secondaria che indugiano in forse più succulenti, pruriginosi, divertenti episodi concentrati sulla competizione, la collaborazione tra virtuosi è un aspetto della realtà di quel periodo (e di tutti gli altri) troppo spesso trascurato, sebbene non manchino altri esempi coevi che testimoniano che fosse pratica comune, come ad esempio il rapporto tra Felice Salimbeni (1712-1755) e Giuseppe Appiani (1712-1742):

> L'eccellente contraltista Giuseppe Appiani, detto Appianino, [...] aveva un timbro particolarmente bello e sapeva cantare in modo brillante e pulito. Questo suscitò in Salimbeni una lodevole ammirazione per lui che lo stimolò a imitarlo. I due erano grandi amici e studiarono insieme, con la suddetta intenzione di migliorarsi e con pari diligenza, soprattutto i duetti di Steffani[40].

---

[38]. *I TEATRI* 1827, p. 10.

[39]. LEMAIRE – LAVOIX 1881, p. 388.

[40]. «[...] vortrefliche Contraltist, Giuseppe Appiani, insgemein Appianino genannt, bey seiner besonders schönen Stimme, auch viel Geschicklichkeit in der ausgehaltenen, gezogenen, doch aber auch dabei netten und brillanten Singart besaß: so erregte dies bey Salinbeni die löbliche Eifersucht, ihm es darinne gleich zu thun. Sie waren gute Freunde, und studirten, hauptsächlich in der erwähnten Absicht, die Steffanischen Duette, mit großem Fleiße, nochmals miteinander durch». HILLER 1784, p. 232.

Valentina Anzani

Se improvvisazione nell'opera del Settecento significava saper applicare in un contesto quasi estemporaneo formule appropriate precedentemente apprese, la modalità di apprendimento era tanto importante quanto le potenzialità vocali dell'interprete. Senza bravi maestri, bravi esempi, stimoli al continuo miglioramento, una voce *per se* non aveva nulla di straordinario. Fondamentale dunque l'apertura del cantante/allievo ai nuovi insegnamenti, e fondamentale l'atteggiamento di accoglienza, paterno, del maestro di canto, pronto a trasmettere dalla propria voce a quella dell'allievo, come le formule melodiche e testuali delle tradizioni orali, le tecniche (o i segreti) dell'improvvisare.

BIBLIOGRAFIA

ALGAROTTI 1763
ALGAROTTI, Francesco. *Saggio sopra l'opera in musica*, Livorno, Coltellini, 1763.

ARTEAGA 1783
ARTEAGA, Stefano. *Le rivoluzioni del teatro musicale italiano dalla sua origine fino al presente*, 3 voll., Bologna, Trenti, 1783-1788, vol. I.

ASPDEN 2013
ASPDEN, Suzanne. *The Rival Sirens: Performance and Identity on Handel's Operatic Stage*, Cambridge, Cambridge University Press, 2013 (Cambridge Studies in Opera).

BURNEY 1773
BURNEY, Charles. *The Present State of Music in Germany, the Netherlands and United Provinces*, 2 voll., Londra, Beckett and Strand, 1773, vol. I.

CORP 2011
CORP, Edward. *The Stuarts in Italy, 1719-1766: A Royal Court in Permanent Exile*, Cambridge, Cambridge University Press, 2011.

DESLER 2014
DESLER, Anne. *"Il novello Orfeo". Farinelli: Vocal Profile, Aesthetics, Rhetoric*, Ph.D. Diss., Glasgow, University of Glasgow, 2014.

FÉTIS 1860
FÉTIS, François-Joseph. *Biographie universelle des musiciens et bibliographie générale de la musique. 2*, Parigi, Firmin Didot, ²1860.

HILLER 1784
HILLER, Johann Adam. *Lebensbeschreibungen berühmter Musikgelehrten und Tonkünstler neuerer Zeit*, Lipsia, Dyk, 1784.

I TEATRI 1827
I teatri: giornale drammatico, musicale e coreografico, 1 (1827).

Il mito della competizione tra virtuosi: quando Farinelli sfidò Bernacchi

Lemaire – Lavoix 1881
Lemaire, Théophile – Lavoix, Henri, fils. *Le chant, ses principes et son histoire*, Parigi, Heugel, 1881.

Llewellyn 2009
Llewellyn, Timothy D. *Owen McSwiny's Letters, 1720-1744*, Verona, Scripta, 2009 (Lettere artistiche del Settecento veneziano, 4; Fonti e documenti per la storia dell'arte veneta, 14).

Lucchese 2015
Lucchese, Enrico. *L'album di caricature di Anton Maria Zanetti alla Fondazione Giorgio Cini*, Venezia, Lineadacqua-Fondazione Giorgio Cini, 2015.

Mancini 1774
Mancini, Giovanni Battista. *Pensieri, e riflessioni pratiche sopra il canto figurato*, Vienna, Ghelen, 1774.

Martinelli 1758
Martinelli, Vincenzo. 'Al signor conte di Buckinghamshire: sulla origine delle Opere in Musica', in: *Lettere Familiari e Critiche*, Londra, Giovanni Nourse, 1758, pp. 353-363.

McGeary 2005
McGeary, Thomas. 'Farinelli's Progress to Albion: The Recruitment and Reception of Opera's "Blazing Star"', in: *British Journal for Eighteenth-Century Studies*, XXVIII/5 (2005).

Panzacchi 1889
Panzacchi, Enrico. *I miei racconti*, Milano, Treves 1889.

Panzacchi 1897
Id. 'La Musica', in: *La vita italiana durante la Rivoluzione francese e l'Impero. 3*, Milano, Treves, 1897, pp. 509-540.

Sacchi 1784
Sacchi, Giovenale. *Vita del Cavaliere Don Carlo Broschi*, Venezia, Coleti, 1784.

Scudo 1861
Scudo, Paul. 'Les sopranistes - Farinelli', in: *Revue des deux mondes*, XXXV/3 (1861), pp. 759-769.

Singing to Some Purpose 1863
'Singing to Some Purpose', in: *All the Year Round: A Weekley Journal Conducted by Charles Dickens*, 15 marzo 1863, pp. 21-24.

The Contre-Temps 1727
The Contre-Temps; or Rival Queens: a Small Farce, Londra, Moore, 1727.

The Devil 1727
Anonimo. *The Devil to Pay at St. James, or a Full Account of a Most Horrible and Blody Battle between Madam Faustina and Madam Cuzzoni*, Londra, s.n., 1727.

Tosi 1723
Tosi, Pier Francesco. *Opinioni de' cantori antichi e moderni o sieno Osservazioni sopra* il *canto figurato*, Bologna, Lelio dalla Volpe, 1723.

Verdi 2008
Verdi, Luigi. 'Del musico Antonio Maria Bernacchi nel 250° della morte', in: *Un anno per tre filarmonici di rango: Perti, Martini e Mozart: un principe, un definitore e un fuoriclasse da celebrare nel 2006. Atti del convegno (Bologna, Accademia Filarmonica, 3-4 novembre 2006)*, a cura di Piero Mioli, Bologna, Pàtron, 2008, pp. 125-146.

Vitali 1992
Vitali, Carlo. 'Da «schiavottiello» a «fedele amico». Lettere (1731-1749) di Carlo Broschi Farinelli al conte Sicinio Pepoli', in: *Nuova rivista musicale italiana*, n. 1 (1992), pp. 1-36.

Re-Creating Historical Improvisatory Solo Practices on the Cello
C. Simpson, F. Niedt, and J. S. Bach on the Pedagogy of *Contrapunctis Extemporalis*

John Lutterman
(University of Alaska Anchorage)

While those of us interested in historically-informed performing practices recognize that anachronistic nineteenth-century traditions have continued to influence the treatment of early music in today's conservatory and concert life, it is easy to forget that modern practices of presenting public concerts and studying at conservatories are themselves nineteenth-century inventions. We see that even *urtext* editions are often colored by nineteenth-century traditions, but often lose sight of the fact that the very idea of publishing critical editions of early music is itself a nineteenth-century invention. In light of this, it is perhaps less surprising that we rarely stop to consider the still more insidious ways in which another nineteenth-century idea about the nature of musical practices has come to govern the ways that we understand the meaning of musical notation: the idea that written compositions should be understood as fixed musical works.

The work of Roman Ingarden, Carl Dahlhaus, and Lydia Goehr[1] has prompted much of the recent scholarly writing that has questioned the ontological status of compositions before Beethoven. However, in addressing the practical concerns of performing musicians, I have found Arthur Mendel's 1957 formulation of the problem refreshingly succinct:

> Western musicians of today have such strong habits of associating a piece of music with its graphic notation that they need constant reminding, by every possible means, of the limitations of notation as applied to either old or exotic music. The hunt for the authentic version of a piece by even so recent a composer as J. S. Bach [...] is a vain one. Neither Bach nor any other good musician up to at least Bach's time probably ever played a piece exactly the same way twice. And by 'the same way' we mean nothing so narrow as the musician of today may understand. We mean that he probably never played exactly the same notes twice, or played them in exactly the same rhythm[2].

---

[1]. Ingarden 1986, Ingarden 1989, Dahlhaus 1989, Dahlhaus 1994, Goehr 1992.
[2]. Mendel 1957, pp. 10-11.

John Lutterman

As David Schulenberg has suggested, in the course of his analysis of the three-part ricercar from *The Musical Offering* as a kind of record of Bach's improvisation on the royal theme:

> In its printed form the three-part *ricercar* might be seen in the same light as those engravings of Baroque opera scenes in which heroes rise to heaven or armies attack one another without any visible inconvenience from gravity or balky stage machinery[3].

While Bach's written music may represent an idealized portrait of practices that he was illustrating for his students and patrons, we should be able to make some educated guesses about the nature of «the inconvenient effects of gravity» and the kinds of «balky stage machinery» that may have shaped these improvisatory practices. Viewed through an analytic lens, free from the blinders of a modern work concept, the written compositions of Bach and his contemporaries may be understood as more-or-less systematically organized inventories of formal models, and as idiomatic vocabularies of motivic, harmonic and contrapuntal ideas or 'inventions', all of which are ripe for improvisatory appropriation and elaboration. Indeed, as I have argued elsewhere, I would suggest that it is these somewhat abstract, enduring 'ideas' which are best understood as Bach's contribution to the canon of musical 'works', rather than any particular instantiation of such ideas[4].

Accounts of J. S. Bach's solo performances invariably focus on his improvisatory prowess. Indeed, the only reference to his use of written music in an unaccompanied performance is found in an account by his Leipzig contemporary, Theodor Pitschel, in which Bach is said to have used organ compositions by lesser composers as a springboard for his improvisations.

> You know, the famous man who has the greatest praise in our town in music, and the greatest admiration of connoisseurs, does not get into condition, as the expression goes, to delight others with the mingling of his tones until he has played something from the printed or written page, and has [thus] set his powers of imagination in motion [...] The able man whom I have mentioned usually has to play something from the page that is inferior to his own ideas. And yet his superior ideas are the consequence of those inferior ones[5].

Recent scholarship has brought a broadening recognition of the important roles that improvisatory practices continued to play in concert life well into the nineteenth century, and this recognition poses one of the most significant challenges to the adequacy of representing historical performing practices by means of programs that consist solely of written compositions[6]. In an attempt to solve this dilemma, I often include performances of

---

[3]. SCHULENBERG 1995, p. 5.
[4]. LUTTERMAN 2006.
[5]. PITSCHEL 1741.
[6]. RASCH 2011

unaccompanied, semi-improvised suites of pieces in my concert programs, drawing upon the written compositions by a number of eighteenth-century composers as frameworks, and employing eighteenth-century techniques and styles of improvisatory elaboration. In these programs, I have sought to re-create eighteenth-century musical practices of unaccompanied solo cello playing, rather than simply performing a fixed set of musical 'works'.

Clues to the technical means of re-creating relevant historical improvisatory practices appropriate to unaccompanied cello performance can be found in a number of sources, including Christopher Simpson's *The Divison Viol*[7], Friedrich Niedt's *Musicalische Handleitung*[8], and the earliest cello methods, which invariably included instruction in the art of chordal thoroughbass realization[9]. The rich trove of Italian partimento exercises also offer invaluable insights into historical techniques of improvisatory elaboration and development.

The particular improvisatory techniques that I have employed, and which I would like to discuss include: 1) the use of sequences of double-stops and arpeggiated patterns to create a prelude, 2) practices of thoroughbass realization on the cello and the incorporation of a basso continuo line into an unaccompanied performance of an existing work, and 3) the use of «points of division» or «inventions» over a bass framework to generate complete movements in particular genres.

Clues to the employment of sequences of double-stops and arpeggios for preluding can be found in several of the early cello methods, starting with Baumgartner[10], whose treatise was the first to provide explicit instruction in chordal thoroughbass realization, but the most systematic treatment is Duport[11]. Fingerings of double-stops in the early cello treatises is invariably arranged in patterns designed to facilitate the performance of common contrapuntal sequences, which may be easily memorized and employed as a kind of vocabulary when preluding. In my experiments, I frequently adapt this vocabulary to harmonic patterns derived from Bach's preludes as a framework to provide a large-scale formal structure for my improvisations.

Duport (see Ex. 1, p. 244) begins with sequences of 2-3 suspensions, and then expands this treatment by adding a 6th as preparation for each suspension. This is followed by circle-of-5^{ths} sequences, using alternating 6^{ths} and 3^{rds}, sequences of diminished 5^{ths} and 3^{rds}, and then examples of sequences of augmented 4^{ths} resolving to 6^{ths} which conclude with various 4-3 and 7-6 cadential formulas. After this, we get sequences of 5-6 progressions. At the end come sequences with 7^{ths}: 7-6 suspensions, a rising-4th sequence of alternating 7ths and 3^{rds}, and finally, diminished 7^{ths} alternating with 5^{ths}.

---

[7]. SIMPSON 1659.
[8]. NIEDT 2003.
[9]. LUTTERMAN 2011.
[10]. BAUMGARTNER 1774.
[11]. DUPORT 1806.

Re-Creating Historical Improvisatory Solo Practices on the Cello

While Baumgartner's treatise was the first to offer explicit instruction in chordal thoroughbass realization on the cello, it is clear from his text that he is documenting an established practice. His written examples included idiomatic realizations of common cadential patterns in which octave placement and inversions are treated quite freely. Written examples of figured bass realizations in the other cello treatises also frequently treat inversions (including 2nd inversion) interchangeably. The most thorough treatment of figured bass realization on the cello is found somewhat later in a treatise by John Gunn[12], who illustrates several idiomatic 'rule of the octave' progressions, with a number of alternative cadences (see Ex. 2, p. 246). Gunn also illustrates the application of thoroughbass treatment to unaccompanied playing with examples of arpeggiated realizations of two well-known eighteenth-century «standards»: the folk-song *Ah! Vous dirai-je maman* and *La Folia* (or, as Gunn puts it: «a Spanish melody from Corelli's Opera 5ta»).

At this point, before continuing my discussion of thoroughbass realization, I would like to briefly consider a set of six pieces by Boismortier, entitled *Suite de pieces qu'on peut jouer seul*, found as an *addendum* to his Op. 40 Sonatas, which are often held up as early examples of unaccompanied works[13] (see Ex. 3, p. 247).

These pieces, which are somewhat more idiomatic for bassoon than cello, do in fact work reasonably well in an unaccompanied performance, but the textures are not substantially different from the accompanied continuo sonatas which make up the bulk of the Op. 40 collection (see Ex. 3, A). Indeed, unaccompanied performance is much more effective for several movements from Boismortier's Op. 50[14], in which he incorporates the basso line as well as its chordal realization into the solo part to a degree that frequently makes a basso accompaniment superfluous (see Ex. 3, B).

This observation supports my hypothesis that thoroughbass training would have played an essential role in unaccompanied solo practices of the eighteenth century. In my experiments with chordal realization of figured bass on the cello, I have discovered that I often find myself incorporating the solo part into my own part when preparing a thoroughbass realization of an aria or solo sonata. By the same token, when practicing a solo concerto or sonata, I have frequently found myself incorporating a realization of the basso into the solo part. And this is what I often attempt to do when generating unaccompanied versions of several of the 'framework' compositions in my little fantasy suites. Here, you can see two small samples from my experiments: the first, a *Largo* in ritornello form from Boismortier's Op. 50 Sonatas (see Ex. 3, C1 and C2); the second an *Adagio* in the form of a *da capo* aria, from Vivaldi's G minor Cello Concerto, RV 416 (see Ex. 3, D1 and D2).

---

[12]. Gunn 1802.
[13]. Boismortier 1732.
[14]. Boismortier 1734.

Ex. 2: John Gunn, examples of thoroughbass realization on the cello.

"Rule of the octave" progressions

Arpeggiated realization of *Ah! vous dirai-je maman*

Arpeggiated realization of "Corelli's" *La folia*

Re-Creating Historical Improvisatory Solo Practices on the Cello

Ex. 3: Excerpts from works by Boismortier and Vivaldi that may be realized and performed by an unaccompanied cello.

The next step would be to improvise an entirely new solo part above such a realization, much as Kirnberger suggests in his charming tract entitled, *Methode Sonaten aus'm Ermel zu Schüdeln*[15] (How to shake a sonata out of one's sleeve), in a process which I view as 'dialogic' in a Bakhtinian sense. This dialogic sense has also informed my experiments in improvising complete movements by employing motivic ideas ('inventions') drawn from historical sources to elaborate contrapuntal frameworks that I have extracted from Bach's unaccompanied works. As for the working out of 'inventions' or 'points of division', I would like to consider Christopher Simpson's and Friedrich Niedt's pedagogical methods, and offer two (written-out) samples of my experiments in a partimento-style of improvisation, in which I have employed a number of strategies outlined by Simpson and Niedt.

Christopher Simpson's *The Division Viol* is one of the most comprehensive treatises on improvisation ever written, offering valuable clues to the nature of a number of historical improvisatory practices, particularly his method of teaching the art of extemporaneous implied polyphony, which Simpsons terms a 'mixt' style of divisions. While the importance of Simpson's treatise for understanding the practices of seventeenth-century British musicians is well known, *The Division Viol* had a greater influence on the continent than has generally been recognized. The popularity of the *Division-Viol* led to the printing of a second edition with a parallel Latin translation in 1667, in order «that it might be understood in Foreign Parts», and this edition found its way into a number of continental collections[16]. Demand for copies of *The Division-Viol* was strong enough to warrant additional printings of the second edition, and a third edition was published in 1712[17]. Mattheson discusses Simpson's work in his *Critica Musica* of 1722-1725[18] and *The Division Viol* remained influential enough to be mentioned in Walther's *Musicalisches Lexicon* as late as 1732[19].

Simpson's approach to counterpoint is more harmonically conceived than has generally been recognized (he anticipates Rameau in demonstrating the inversional equivalence of triads), and the organization of his treatise shows interesting parallels to Niedt's *Musikalische Handleitung*, which itself appears to reflect Italian partimento practices. While I would not posit a causal link of influence between these three important approaches to the pedagogy of improvisation in the seventeenth century, I do suggest that a better understanding of the similarities between them can offer valuable insights into the mechanics and the underlying grammatical and syntactical structures of the elusive improvisatory practices that they were meant to teach. My discussion here will focus primarily on Simpson's contributions, in large part because his work has received less scholarly attention than Niedt's treatise or the partimento tradition has in recent years.

---

[15]. KIRNBERGER 1783.
[16]. SIMPSON 1667.
[17]. SIMPSON 1712.
[18]. MATTHESON 1722-1725.
[19]. WALTHER 1732.

Re-Creating Historical Improvisatory Solo Practices on the Cello

The *Division-Viol* is divided into three parts, preceded by a glossary of terms that gives translations in Latin, French and Italian. The set of translations for the English term 'Descant' that Simpson presents in his glossary is of particular interest, suggesting several shades of meaning to the improvisatory process of contrapuntally elaborating an idea: Latin – *Contrapunctus ex-temporalis*; French – *Contrepoint a première veüe*; and Italian – *Contrapunto a mente*.

Part III of the treatise contains perhaps the most valuable insights into Simpson's approach to teaching improvised counterpoint, in particular chapters three, four and five, which introduce three broad approaches to elaborating a bass line: 'Breaking the Ground', 'Descant Division', and 'Mixt Division'. These chapters elaborate three fundamental categories of skills that a student was expected to develop: 1) ornamenting a bass line, 2) improvising a new contrapuntal line, and 3) using real or implied polyphony to project several lines at once. These skills are interdependent, and each would have been an essential component of earlier improvisatory practices, but Simpson's decision to treat them systematically is surely one of his most important contributions to the pedagogy of improvisation.

Friedrich Niedt employs a similar organization of topics in the *Musicalische Handleitung*. Methods of varying the bass (the left hand) are presented first, followed by instructions for creating a new part above the bass (varying the right hand realization in various ways). As for the 'mixt' style, while Niedt doesn't explicitly label this as an individual category of variation, several of his later examples clearly demonstrate the realization of an underlying contrapuntal texture as a compound melody.

Simpson's chapter three, 'Breaking the Ground', gives detailed and systematically ordered instructions for varying a bass line. He outlines five progressive steps for learning this style of divisions: 1) simple rhythmic division of each note of the ground, 2) examples of simple turns and short linear ornamental passages that begin and end on each note of the ground before moving on, 3) examples in which the end of each point of division makes a smooth stepwise transition to the following pitch without returning to the pitch being divided, 4) examples which, as in the second, begin and end on each note of the bass, but make use of intermediate skips to consonant pitches, and 5) examples in which the arpeggiations introduced in part four are filled in with scalar passages to create smoother transitions.

After systematically describing these five procedures, Simpson offers three general guidelines for improvising an effective «broken ground»:

> First, That it be harmonious to the holding Note. Secondly, That it come off so, as to meet the next Note of the *Ground* in a smooth and natural passage. Thirdly, Or if it pass into Discords, that they be such as are aptly used in Composition[20].

---

[20]. SIMPSON 1667, p. 30.

Simpson then gives several examples in which the connection is rather mechanically made smooth «by making the last three, or more of the Minute Notes (at least two of them) ascend or descend by degrees, unto the next succeeding Note»[21]. This last point is followed by an admonishment that «this requires not only a Notion but a Habit also, which must be got by practice»[22].

As further illustration of the above points, and in order to provide more material for practice, Simpson then gives an example of divisions over a longer ground bass line. The student's attention is called to several new points here: the appropriate use of accidentals, the inversional equivalence of 2nds and 7ths, 3ds and 6ths, etc., and the need to sharpen the leading tone in minor ('flat') keys and at internal 'closes'. Simpson also uses this opportunity to introduce several examples in which a point of division begins on a pitch other than the one given in the ground. This pitch must be consonant with the ground, of course, which provides a nice segue to his discussion of descant division in chapter four.

Descant division is defined as «that which makes a Different-concording-part unto the *Ground*». This is distinguished from breaking the ground by the fact that the latter «takes the liberty to wander sometimes beneath the *Ground*», while descant «(as in its proper sphere) moves still above it»[23]. In breaking the ground one «meets every succeeding Note [...] in the *Unison* or *Octave*», while in descant one may proceed to any of the concords. Simpson's discussion of descant is surprisingly concise. As justification, he argues that the skills involved in improvising descant division are much the same as breaking the ground:

> For all *Division*, whether *Descant* or *Breaking the Bass*, is but a Transition from Note to Note, or from one Concord to another, either by Degrees or Leaps, with an intermixture of such Discords as are allowed in Composition[24].

Simpson's chapter on 'mixt' division, which is of great importance to understanding the heritage of Bach's solo music, is still more concise. His description touches on both the desired effect, and the means to achieve this end:

> *Mixt Division* which mixeth *Descant* and *Breaking the Ground*, one with the other [...] presents to our Ears the Sounds of *Two* or more Parts moving together: And, this is expressed either in single Notes, by hitting first upon One String and then upon an Other; or in double Notes, by touching two or more Strings at once with the Bow. This is more excellent than the single ways [...] so it is more intricate, and requires more of judgement and skill in Composition; by reason of the Bindings and intermixtures of Discords, which are as frequent in This as in any other *Figurate Musick*[25].

---

[21]. *Ibidem*, p. 31.
[22]. *Ibidem*.
[23]. *Ibidem*.
[24]. *Ibidem*.
[25]. *Ibidem*, p. 36.

Re-Creating Historical Improvisatory Solo Practices on the Cello

As in his introduction to descant, Simpson's examples are left to the later chapters, which also serve to broach other considerations of effective improvisation. While the explanation of descant and 'mixt' division is confined to simple general rules, the remainder of the treatise provides an inventory of concrete, systematically organized practical examples of their application.

In fact, chapters six through eleven each present numerous short, easily memorized examples of breaking the ground, descant and 'mixt' division over various common short bass patterns. These patterns include 4-3 and 7-6 contrapuntal cadences, rising and falling scales, and scales in broken thirds. In the process of introducing these patterns, he also discusses the treatment of accidentals, and of thirds, sixths, fifths and octaves in descant division. Each type of ground that he illustrates begins with the ground bass, followed by examples of breaking the ground, examples of descant and then examples of his two types of 'mixt' division: 1) broken-chord jumping between voices of an implied polyphony and 2) multiple-stop chordal progressions.

Since he is always careful to identify these short passages of divisions as examples, it is clear that Simpson means for them to be memorized as a kind of vocabulary to be drawn on in extemporaneous performance. This is made explicit in chapter eleven:

> It now only remains that I give you some little assistance, by taking you (as it were) by the Hand, and leading you into the easiest way of Playing *Ex tempore* to a *Ground*.
>
> First, you are to make choice of some *Ground* consisting of *Semibreves* or *Minims*, or a mixture of these two [...]
>
> Next, you ought to be provided of ten, twelve, or more points of Division (the more the better) each consisting of a *Semibreve* or *Minim* [...]
>
> Being thus prepared, take one of the said Points, and apply it first to One Note, and then to another, and so through the whole *Ground*. When you can do this, take another Point, and do the like with it, and so after another so many as you please[26].

At this point he lists 24 'points of division', which are short motivic ideas, closely related to seventeenth-century German theorists' treatment of 'inventions' or *Manieren*, each with a distinctive melodic/rhythmic profile. Next, he proceeds to systematically apply each 'point of division' to a ground bass. Apart from the fact that the metric and rhythmic profile of Simpson's ground remains more-or-less constant, the procedures which he employs are strikingly similar to those employed in Niedt's examples showing how to generate a suite of dances from a common figured bass line. Simpson's treatment of 'points of division' is similar to Niedt's suggestion that once a figure has been chosen «the whole bass can then be worked out in the same way» and is also closely related to Forkel's definition of an invention:

---

[26]. *Ibidem*, p. 53.

> A musical subject which was so contrived that, by imitation and transposition of the parts, the whole of a composition might be unfolded from it was called an invention. The rest was only elaboration, and if one but knew properly the means of development, did not need to be invented[27].

Here is an example in which I have employed one of Niedt's simple motivic ideas to create a prelude, using a bass line which I have extracted from the corresponding movement of Bach's Suite for Solo Cello in G Major, BWV 1007 (Ex. 4):

Ex. 4: Method for improvising a prelude by applying one of Friedrich Niedt's 'inventions' to a framework abstracted from the prelude of BWV 1007.

---

[27]. FORKEL 1998, p. 467.

While many of Simpson's examples seem rather mechanical and tedious, it should be kept in mind that they are presented as steps in a didactic method — they are clearly not meant to be considered finished musical works. On the other hand, while he is keenly aware of the pedagogical value of varied repetition, Simpson does not rigidly maintain a single point of division for each variation, and the change from one idea to another does not always coincide with repetitions of the ground. He does point to the unifying aesthetic value of carrying an idea through, but this notion of a single unifying affect should not be unduly stressed. In the complete sets of divisions with which Simpson concludes his treatise, as in so much seventeenth-century instrumental music, there is often a strong contrast in character between individual variations, but a degree of freedom is allowed in extemporaneously carrying a point of division through each repetition of the ground. Indeed, a given point of division will often require modification to allow for smooth connection and appropriate voice leading.

> This driving or carrying on of a *Point*, doth much ease the Invention, which hath no further trouble, so long as the *Point* is continued, but to place and apply it to the several Notes of the *Ground*: Besides, it renders the *Division* more uniform and more delightful also; provided you do not cloy the Ear with too much repetition of the same thing; which is easily avoided with a little variation, as you can see I have done in carrying on some of the foregoing *Points*. Also you have liberty to change your *Point* in the middle or in any other part of the *Ground*: or you may mingle one *Point* with another, as best shall please your fancy[28].

Chapters twelve through fourteen give advice on various ways of structuring a set of divisions. Chapter twelve is primarily concerned with divisions as variations over a basso ostinato. The performer is advised to begin with a performance of the ground itself, followed by a slow point of division. The speed of divisions should gradually increase, but slow divisions should be interspersed, and variety should be sought through the use of suspensions, alternation between leaping and scalar motion, and dynamic and rhythmic

---

[28]. SIMPSON 1667, p. 56.

variation. «You must so place and dispose your *Division*, that the change of it from one kind to another may still beget a new attention»[29].

Most of Simpson's divisions make use of relatively short bass patterns, but his suggestion to use a longer «continued ground», such as «the Through-Bass of some Motet or Madrigal», as a framework for improvising divisions foreshadows the exercises found in Niedt's treatise and the Italian partimento sources. While Simpson does not give written-out examples of longer pieces, following his advice to use a bass from a pre-existent composition as a formal schema would result in a structured approach to improvisation similar to that which German and Italian partimento practices were designed to cultivate. Here is an example of an allemande which I have created by using one of Simpson's 'points of division' over a bass line that I have extracted from the corresponding movement of Bach's Suite for Solo Cello in G Major, BWV 1007 (Ex. 5).

Ex. 5: Method for improvising an allemande by applying one of Christopher Simpson's 'points of division' to a framework abstracted from the allemande of BWV 1007.

[29]. Ibidem.

Chapters fourteen through sixteen are concerned with arranging divisions for various combinations of viols and continuo. Simpson's discussion of divisions for a single viol is quite short, but does make an important point about contemporary attitudes toward the compositions of other musicians, which were regarded as examples, as inventories of musical ideas or inventions to be learned and deployed when improvising. Simpson directs his students to «peruse the *Divisions* which other men have made upon *Grounds* [...] observing and noting in their *Divisions*, what you find best worthy to be imitated»[30]. This point is reinforced in the concluding paragraph of the treatise, which also points to financial constraints that limited Simpson's ability to provide further illustrations of his improvisatory practices.

> Myself, amongst others more eminent, have made divers Compositions, which perhaps might be useful to young Musicians, either for their Imitation or Practice; but the Charge of Printing *Divisions* (as I have experienced in the *Cuts* of the *Examples* in this present Book) doth make that kind of Musick less communicable[31].

Chapter fifteen concerns the performance of extemporaneous divisions by two viols, and is of particular interest because of the historical evidence it offers of sophisticated improvisatory skills similar to the jazz practices of 'trading fours' and 'cutting contests'. Simpson suggests arranging divisions for two viols into four large sections. At the beginning, the performers are to take turns playing the ground and improvising divisions, each player continuing in their role until a new repetition of the ground begins. He also gives advice on effective ordering of these solos.

---

[30]. *Ibidem.*
[31]. *Ibidem*, p. 61.

> The *Ground* thus Play'd over, *C.* may begin again, and Play a Strain of quicker *Division*; which ended, let *B.* answer the same with something like it, but of a little more lofty Ayre: for the better performance whereof, if there be any difference in the Hands or Inventions, I would have the better Invention *lead*, but the more able Hand still *follow*, that the Musick may not seem to flaccess or lessen, but rather increase in the performance[32].

After trading choruses in this manner for as long as they like, perhaps with the continuo player taking a turn, comes a passage in which the two soloists improvise simultaneously. This is managed by having one violist break the ground in such manner that his divisions begin and end on each note of the bass before moving on to the next. The other violist is then free to improvise descant above the ground. In the third section, the two viols alternate roles as in the opening section, but this time each plays a shorter passage, the pace of dialogue quickens and the performance becomes a contest:

> *C.* may begin some Point of *Division*, of the length of a *Breve* or *Semibreve*, naming the said work, that *B.* may know his intentions; which ended, let *B.* answer the same upon the succeeding Note or Notes to the like quantity of Time […].
>
> This contest in *Breves*, *Semibreves*, or *Minims* being ended, they may give the Signe to *A.* [the continuo player] if (as I said) he have ability of Hand, that he may begin his Point as they had done one to another; which point may be answered by the *Viols*, either singly or jointly[33].

In the final section, the viols are to:

> […] joyn together in a Thundering Strain of *Quick* Division; with which they may conclude; or else with a Strain of slow and sweet Notes, according as may best sute the circumstance of time and place[34].

This kind of extemporaneous performance requires highly developed skills, and Simpson speaks of having «some experimental knowledge» of it. It is perhaps not likely that many musicians of his day were capable of successfully performing this kind of group improvisation, but clearly some were. Simpson recalled:

> I have known this kind of *Extemporary* Musick, sometimes (when it was performed by Hands accustomed to Play together) pass off with greater applause, than those Divisions which had been most studiously composed[35].

---

[32]. *Ibidem*, p. 58.
[33]. *Ibidem*, p. 59.
[34]. *Ibidem*.
[35]. *Ibidem*.

Re-Creating Historical Improvisatory Solo Practices on the Cello

The examples of fully formed («studiously composed») solo preludes and divisions over repeated bass patterns with which Simpson's treatise concludes are meant to be studied and imitated. They contain new points of division, which we can extract and use in our own improvisations. They also illustrate his advice for pacing and structuring a set of divisions effectively, and can serve as models for framing large-scale structures. Finally, for performers who are capable of facing the considerable technical challenges which they present, but lack the necessary skills of invention, written examples such as Simpson's may be performed «as if» extemporized, «though less to be admired, as being more studied».

> He that hath it *not* in so high a measure as to play *ex tempore* to a *Ground*, may, notwithstanding give both himself and hearers sufficient satisfaction in playing such Divisions as himself or others have made for that purpose; in the performance whereof he may deserve the Name of an excellent Artist; for here the excellency of the Hand may be shewed as well as in the Other, and the Musick perhaps better, though less to be admired, as being more studied[36].

Bibliography

BAUMGARTNER 1774
BAUMGARTNER, Johann Baptist. *Instructions de musique theorique et pratique: a l'usage du violoncello*, The Hague, Monnier, 1774.

BOISMORTIER 1732
BOISMORTIER, Joseph Bodin de. *6 Sonates suives d'un nombre de pieces qu'on peut jouer seule, Op. 40*, Paris, l'Auteur, 1732.

BOISMORTIER 1734
ID. *6 Sonates don't la dernier est en trio, Op. 50*, Paris, l'Auteur, 1734.

DAHLHAUS 1989
DAHLHAUS, Carl. *Geschichte der Musiktheorie. 11. Die Musiktheorie im 18. und 19. Jahrhundert. 2: Deutschland*, edited by Ruth E. Müller, Darmstadt, Wissenschaftliche Buchgesellschaft, 1989.

DAHLHAUS 1994
ID. 'Das Musikalische Kunstwerk als Gegenstand der Soziologie', in: *The International Review of the Aesthetics and Sociology of Music*, XXV/1-2 (1994), pp. 115-130.

DAVID – MENDEL 1998
DAVID, Hans T. – MENDEL, Arthur. *The New Bach Reader: A Life of Johann Sebastian Bach in Letters and Documents*, revised edition by Christoph Wolf, New York, W. W. Norton, 1998.

---

[36]. *Ibidem.*

DUPORT 1806
DUPORT, Jean-Louis. *Essai sur le doigté du violoncelle, et sur la conduite de l'archet*, Paris, Imbault, 1806.

FORKEL 1998
FORKEL, Johann Nikolaus. *Ueber Johann Sebastian Bachs Leben, Kunst und Kunstwerke* (Leipzig, Hoffmeister und Künet, 1802), English translation by Hans T. David in: DAVID – MENDEL 1998.

GOEHR 1992
GOEHR, Lydia. *The Imaginary Museum of Musical Works: An Essay in the Philosophy of Music*, Oxford-New York, Clarendon Press, 1992.

GUNN 1802
GUNN, John. *An Essay Theoretical and Practical, with Copious and Easy Examples on the Application of the Principles of Harmony, Through Bass, and Modulation to the Violoncello*, London, Preston, 1802.

INGARDEN 1986
INGARDEN, Roman. *The Work of Music and the Problem of its Identity*, English translation by Adam Czerniawski, edited by Jean G. Harrell, Berkeley (CA), University of California Press, 1986.

INGARDEN 1989
ID. *Ontology of the Work of Art: The Musical Work, the Picture, the Architectural Work, the Film*, Athens (OH), Ohio University Press, 1989 (Series in Continental Thought, 12).

KIRNBERGER 1783
KIRNBERGER, Johann Philipp. *Methode Sonaten aus'm Ermel zu schüdeln*, Berlin, F. W. Birnstiel, 1783.

LUTTERMAN 2006
LUTTERMAN, John Kenneth. *Works in Progress: J. S. Bach's Suites for Solo Cello as Artifacts of Improvisatory Practices*, Ph.D. Diss., Ann Arbor (MI), UMI Research Press, 2006.

LUTTERMAN 2011
ID. '«Cet art est la perfection du talent». Chordal Thoroughbass Realization and Improvised Solo Performance on the Viol and Cello in the Eighteenth Century', in: RASCH 2011, pp. 111-128.

MATTHESON 1722-1725
MATTHESON, Johann. *Critica Musica*, 2 vols., Hamburg, the Author, 1722-1725.

MENDEL 1957
MENDEL, Arthur. 'The Services of Musicology to the Practical Musician', in: *Some Aspects of Musicology*, edited by Arthur Mendel, Curt Sachs and Carroll C. Pratt, New York, Liberal Arts Press, 1957.

NIEDT 2003
NIEDT, Friedrich Erhard. *Musikalische Handleitung. Teil I-III in Einem Band (1710, 1721, 1717)*, facsimile reprint, Hildesheim, Olms, 2003.

PITSCHEL 1741
PITSCHEL, Theodor Leberecht. 'Letter' (1741), in: SCHULZE 1969, p. 397; English translation by Hans T. David, in: DAVID – MENDEL 1998, pp. 333-334.

Rasch 2011
Beyond Notes: Improvisation in Western Music of the Eighteenth and Nineteenth Centuries, edited by Rudolf Rasch, Turnhout, Brepols, 2011 (Speculum Musicae, 16).

Schulenberg 1995
Schulenberg, David. 'Composition and Improvisation in the School of J. S. Bach', in: *Bach Perspectives. 1*, edited by Russell Stinson, Lincoln-London, University of Nebraska Press, 1995, pp. 1-42.

Schulze 1969
Bach-Dokumente. Supplement zu Johann Sebastian Bach neue Ausgabe Samtlicher Werke. 2: Fremdschriftliche und Gedruckte Dokumente zur Lebensgeschichte Johann Sebastian Bachs, 1685-1750, edited by Werner Neumann and Hans-Joachim Schulze, Leipzig, Bärenreiter, 1969.

Simpson 1659
Simpson, Christopher. *The Division-Violinist: or, The Art of Playing Ex-Tempore Upon a Ground*, London, W. Godbid, 1659.

Simpson 1667
Id. *Chelys, Minuritionum Artificio Exornata, Sive, Minuritiones ad Basin, Etiam Ex Tempore Modulandi Ratio in Tres Partes Distributa / The Division-Viol, or, The art of Playing Ex Tempore Upon a Ground, Divided into Three Parts, Early English Books, 1641-1700*, London, W. Godbid for Henry Brome, ²1667.

Simpson 1712
Id. *Chelys, Minuritionum Artificio Exornata […] The Division-Viol […]: Prioribus Longe Auctior*, London, William Pearson for Richard Mears, ³1712.

Walther 1732
Walther, Johann Gottfried. *Musikalisches Lexikon; oder Musicalische Bibliothec*, Leipzig, W. Deer, 1732.

Accompagnamento e basso continuo alla chitarra spagnola

Una cartografia della diffusione dei sistemi di notazione stenografici in Italia, Spagna e Francia tra XVI e XVII secolo e loro implicazioni teoriche

Francesca Mignogna
(Université de Paris-Sorbonne/IReMus)

La questione riguardante il rapporto tra orizzontalità e verticalità — quello che oggi definiamo armonia funzionale — prima della teorizzazione del sistema tonale coinvolge numerosi aspetti della pratica e della teoria della musica. Come sottolineato da Massimo Preitano in un articolo apparso nel 1994 sulla *Rivista Italiana di Musicologia*[1] e che ancora oggi resta uno dei rari studi in lingua italiana consacrati al ruolo della chitarra barocca spagnola nell'evoluzione del linguaggio tonale, le significative evoluzioni della pratica musicale avvenute nel periodo di tempo che va dalle *Istituzioni Harmoniche* di Zarlino[2] al *Traité* di Rameau[3] non trovano reale corrispondenza nelle opere di speculazione teorica coeve, ma sono piuttosto da ricercare nella manualistica[4]. La (apparente) netta distinzione tra musica pratica e musica teorica risulta ancora radicata nel pensiero del musico negli anni della teorizzazione del basso continuo; ciò nonostante, le vere origini di quest'ultimo non sono rintracciabili in un trattato propriamente teorico e la sua formulazione risulta essere una sistematizzazione a posteriori di una pratica preesistente. Come sottolineato da John Walter Hill, a proposito delle origini dello stile recitativo:

---

[1]. Preitano 1994.
[2]. Zarlino 1558.
[3]. Rameau 1722.
[4]. «Se è lecito considerare le date di pubblicazione di questi due trattati [*Istituzioni Harmoniche* di Zarlino e *Traité* di Rameau, n.d.a.] come due ideali capisaldi di altrettante distinte concezioni musicali in una fase di acquisita consapevolezza dei rispettivi orizzonti stilistici, risulta un lasso di tempo piuttosto ampio all'interno del quale il passaggio dall'una all'altra è, in pratica, avvenuto, ma mai direttamente testimoniato da una formulazione teorica compiuta: nell'ambito strettamente speculativo, difatti, la trattatistica secentesca non si discosta in maniera significativa dalla tradizione zarliniana, evidenziando però un progressivo scollamento dalla prassi musicale, intorno alla quale le informazioni più attendibili sono desumibili, piuttosto, dalla letteratura specifica di tipo 'manualistico'». Preitano 1994, pp. 27-28.

> Si tratta, almeno in parte, del seguente problema più generale: se nel mutamento dello stile musicale siano da considerarsi più importanti le cause interne (musicali) o esterne (intellettuali) e, di questo problema più specifico, se l'ultima fase della storia della musica protomoderna — spesso indicata come l'età barocca — si originasse dalla fissazione in forma di notazione musicale di precedenti tradizioni non scritte, o solo parzialmente scritte. Finché non si giunge alla comprensione dello stile recitativo, non si potrà comprendere pienamente come è potuta cominciare l'età barocca[5].

L'interesse musicologico relativo alla realizzazione del basso continuo è stato per lungo tempo rivolto quasi esclusivamente agli strumenti a tastiera; un numero di studi comunque rilevante ha portato l'attenzione sul ruolo degli strumenti a corde pizzicate in questa pratica. Tali studi, tra i quali l'eccellente articolo di Thomas Christensen che pone il continuo barocco come una delle applicazioni più importanti della tecnica chitarristica spagnola del *rasgueado*[6], hanno mostrato il sorgere, tra XVI e XVII secolo, di sistemi stenografici di notazione per tale strumento, le cui caratteristiche permettono di considerarli non solo un primo esempio di notazione 'aleatoria' dal punto di vista armonico ma anche un primitivo tentativo di cifrare il basso. Tali sistemi sono basati sulla corrispondenza di un numero o una lettera con ciascun agglomerato armonico verticale che, sovrapposti al testo o al basso, servono da soli a realizzare l'accompagnamento senza rispondere alle regole di condotta delle parti. Benché questi sistemi sopravvivano — in progressivo declino — fino al 1800, verrà qui proposta una cartografia corrispondente al periodo compreso tra i due trattati sopracitati, dunque tra il 1558 e il 1722, considerando queste date come punti di apertura e di chiusura della lunga elaborazione del concetto teorico di accordo. Ci si riferirà esclusivamente alle opere spagnole, italiane e francesi, a stampa o manoscritte, nelle quali vengono fornite 'istruzioni' riguardo ai sistemi stenografici; tra di queste, solo alcune sono definibili trattati (o manuali), mentre nella maggior parte dei casi l'apporto teorico è costituito solamente da tavole esplicative anteposte alle raccolte di musica. Le raccolte di musica nelle quali sono utilizzati tali sistemi di notazione ma che sono prive di qualunque istruzione sono invece numerosissime: basti pensare che solo in Italia, tra il 1610 e il 1665, ne vengono pubblicate circa 100[7]. In questo articolo, che vede come punto di partenza le riflessioni proposte da Christensen e Preitano nei due articoli sopracitati, non sarà proposta una descrizione dettagliata di tutti i manuali, né tantomeno un confronto sistematico tra di essi; verranno estrapolate le caratteristiche chiave di questo tipo di notazione per metterle in relazione all'evoluzione della notazione e della teoria tonale. Soltanto i dettagli del primo sistema in esame, quello di Amat, saranno proposti, a titolo rappresentativo.

---

[5]. Hill 2003, pp. 35-36.
[6]. Christensen 1992, p. 20.
[7]. *Cfr.* Gavito 2006.

Accompagnamento e basso continuo alla chitarra spagnola

Per comprendere il contesto nel quale questi sistemi si collocano e la loro importanza dal punto di vista teorico, risulta necessaria qualche riflessione sulla notazione, in particolare sulla notazione per strumenti a corde pizzicate. L'evoluzione della musica 'a suoni simultanei'[8] si accompagna in maniera indissolubile all'evoluzione della notazione musicale; i differenti stadi evolutivi di quest'ultima sono al tempo stesso rivelatori della concezione musicale di un determinato periodo storico e catalizzatori nel processo di ideazione di nuove forme musicali, in particolare di nuove forme polifoniche: l'introduzione dei modi ritmici (scuola di Notre Dame) e la conseguente precisione nella notazione ha reso possibile l'evoluzione di una scrittura polifonica più articolata[9]. La più precisa sovrapposizione di suoni che questo sistema ha generato non può non aver avuto influenza sull'evoluzione di una scienza esatta della verticalità in musica. In questo senso, il passo fondamentale arriverà circa quattro secoli più tardi, con la riapparizione della notazione in forma di partitura[10]. La questione è stata oggetto di ampia discussione: l'avanzamento degli studi e la scoperta di nuove fonti sembra anticipare progressivamente l'avvento di questa pratica. Se per William Apel la disposizione in parti separate è da considerarsi l'unica utilizzata fino al XVII secolo (eccezion fatta per alcune composizioni in stile di conductus del XIV e XV secolo[11] e il motteto *Laus Domino*[12]) gli studi di Kinkeldey, Schwartz, Haas, Smijers e Lowinsky[13] hanno provato l'esistenza di musica notata in partitura già nel XVI secolo. Il concetto di partitura, al suo primo stadio[14], non concerne in modo diretto il processo compositivo. Tra le partiture del XVI secolo identificate da Lowinsky, sono identificabili tre tipologie che differiscono in base alla loro funzione: si potrebbero identificare con i nomi di 'false partiture' (sovrapposizioni casuali di parti, dovute a questioni editoriali), 'partiture di esecuzione' (trascrizioni in partitura preparate dagli strumentisti per agevolare l'esecuzione)[15] e 'partiture di elaborazione' (la partitura è utilizzata nell'atto compositivo)[16]. La pratica di trascrivere in partitura le composizioni polifoniche in vista di un'esecuzione

---

[8]. Il termine, utilizzato per indicare le musiche armoniche e polifoniche in un'ottica storicizzante, è preso da Coussemaker 1852, p. 1.

[9]. *Cfr.* Apel 1998, p. 196.

[10]. Fatto interessante rispetto a l'ipotesi, da me sostenuta, di una progressiva orizzontalizzazione della polifonia nel corso del medioevo, una disposizione definibile 'in partitura' caratterizzava le prime composizioni polifoniche (*Musica enchiriadis* — notazione dasiana —, il *Micrologo* di Guido d'Arezzo, i manoscritti di San Marziale, di Compostela e di Notre Dame; *cfr. ibidem*, p. 14).

[11]. *Ibidem*, p. 241.

[12]. *Ibidem*, p 14.

[13]. *Cfr.* Lowinsky 1948, p. 17.

[14]. Ci si riferisce solamente al percorso evolutivo della partitura in era moderna, non considerando in questa affermazione le forme di 'notazione sovrapposta' utilizzate per la notazione teorica durante il medioevo.

[15]. La stessa espressione è usata da Jean-Michel Vaccaro in relazione alla tablatura (*cfr.* Vaccaro 1981, p. 121).

[16]. Le espressioni non sono di Lowinsky. *Cfr.* Lowinsky 1960.

alla tastiera o al liuto, corrispondente alla seconda tipologia di partiture individuata da Lowinsky, rivela il fatto che la concezione orizzontale delle voci come entità autonome è perdurata, in quanto «apparent maintenance of the old order»[17], meno presso i compositori che presso i teorici, e ancor meno presso gli strumentisti. Come sottolineato da Apel, uno dei criteri fondamentali di classificazione della notazione per la musica a suoni simultanei concerne il numero di esecutori coinvolti: una distinzione di base è istituita tra musica per *ensemble* e musica per un solo strumentista (strumenti a tastiera o a corde pizzicate)[18]. La pratica di trascrivere la musica polifonica vocale per uno strumento a corde pizzicate rappresenta, in qualche maniera, una conciliazione tra le due categorie identificate da Apel, ed è origine di un riallineamento verticale che vede la pratica musicale — e non la riflessione teorica — come principale propulsore dell'evoluzione di una coscienza armonica verticale. Il XVI secolo vede il fiorire della musica strumentale amatoriale, sotto la spinta dei precetti dell'umanesimo italiano del Quattrocento: l'ideale platonico dell'uomo in equilibrio, che pratica la ginnastica e la musica, trova la sua manifestazione più ricca nelle corti italiane, prima fra tutte la corte di Isabella d'Este a Mantova. In questo contesto dall'*allure* popolare, ispirato all'arte dei menestrelli, la pratica di uno strumento musicale diventa elemento imprescindibile per il buon cortigiano. In *Il libro del Cortegiano*, Baldesar Castiglione si riferisce al liuto (alla viola, più precisamente) mostrando le ragioni per le quali questo strumento è da preferire agli altri:

> Bella musica [...] parmi il cantar bene a libro sicuramente e con bella maniera; ma ancor molto più il cantare alla viola perché tutta la dolcezza consiste quasi in un solo e con molto maggior attenzion si nota ed intende il bel modo e l'aria non essendo occupate le orecchie in più che in una sol voce, e meglio ancor vi si discerne ogni piccolo errore; il che non accade cantando in compagnia perché l'uno aiuta l'altro. Ma sopra tutto parmi gratissimo il cantare alla viola per recitare; il che tanto di venustà ed efficacia aggiunge alle parole, che è gran maraviglia[19].

In questa breve affermazione sono messi in evidenza due concetti importanti. In primo luogo, Castiglione osserva che il liuto permette a un solo individuo di riprodurre tutta la ricchezza armonica della polifonia, sottolineando così la capacità del liuto di 'sintetizzare'

---

[17]. «When harmonic phenomena [...] are explained as contrapunctually conceived, it is little wonder that the author of this explanation finds it necessary to consider the bass progressions that are fundamental to cadential structures in tonal music as nonstructural and nonessential in the cadence formulas of fifteenth- and sixteenth-century. [...] [This position] ignores a fundamental and delicate historic process: the transition from an old mode of artistic conception to a new one within the apparent maintenance of the old order. This is what we are in fact witnessing in the phenomena of harmony and incipient tonal orientation emerging within the contrapuntal and modal matrix of fifteenth-century music». LOWINSKY 1989, pp. 889-890.

[18]. *Cfr.* APEL 1998, p. 14.

[19]. CASTIGLIONE 1528, libro II, cap. XIII.

le voci che, nella polifonia propriamente detta, costituiscono degli elementi distinti; tale osservazione sembra preconizzare il concetto di accordo in quanto entità integra. In secondo luogo, Castiglione sottolinea che suonare il liuto permette di eseguire al canto una sola voce, estrapolata dal complesso polifonico; il testo di questa voce sarà quindi più intelligibile che nel contesto polifonico. Il nuovo interesse a donare priorità al testo che è tipico del pensiero rinascimentale marca l'inizio di un processo che avrà grande influenza sul sistema musicale: dare priorità al testo comporterà la prevalenza di forme dotate di uno schema armonico fisso, in contrapposizione alla *varietas* musicale che governava le leggi del contrappunto. La diffusione del liuto si accompagna alla nascita di un sistema di notazione appositamente ideato, la tablatura, che resterà per secoli l'unico sistema utilizzato per notare la musica per strumenti a corde pizzicate. L'ideazione della tablatura è senza dubbio da ricondurre in primo luogo alla necessità di semplificare la lettura della musica polifonica[20]. La semplificazione non riguarda solamente l'essere accessibile a un pubblico che non conosce le regole della notazione mensurale — in altre parole, l'amatore — ma coinvolge anche un altro fattore importante, ben sintetizzato nella seguente definizione di tablatura: «A score in which the voice-parts are 'tabulated' or written so that the eye can encompass them»[21]. Questa problematica — ossia che tutte le voci possano essere comprese in un solo sguardo — troverà risoluzione generale nella realizzazione in partitura della musica polifonica; ma, nel caso specifico degli strumenti a corde pizzicate, si aggiunge una seconda problematica, di carattere tecnico: le voci della composizione polifonica devono poter essere comprese non solamente in un solo sguardo, ma anche in una stessa posizione della mano (sinistra) dello strumentista. Si potrebbe così riformulare la frase citata: la tablatura per strumenti a corde pizzicate è una partitura nella quale le differenti voci sono intavolate in maniera da poter essere comprese in un solo sguardo e da poter essere suonate, verticalmente, con un'unica posizione della mano. Questa necessità genera inevitabilmente un *découpage* della linearità temporale del contrappunto in blocchi verticali dalla durata variabile, durata che corrisponde al tempo in cui una stessa posizione della mano è mantenuta. Alcuni elementi riscontrabili nelle intavolature per liuto del XVI secolo testimoniano questo fenomeno. Come sintetizzato da Howard Mayer Brown:

---

[20]. «Bermudo [*Declaracion des instrumentos musicales*, 1555, fol. 83, n.d.a.] offers three reasons for the use of tablature: (1) convenience in preparing an "improvised" rendering of a motet; (2) economy in paper, since a score takes four times as much space as a tablature; (3) simplicity, since even a beginner can use with ease a tablature in which every key on the harpsichord is designated by a number. He censures those who, "ignorant of counterpoint, are yet desirous to compose through mere calculation of consonances: they bar the music paper so as not to get lost in their calculation. Although this method is crude, I give an example for those who need and wish to use it" [*ibidem*, fol. 134, n.d.a.]. The example is a score — this time the meter is alla breve and hence the unit a breve per bar — and the music is so primitive an example of three-part harmony, almost completely homophonic, as to be without either melodic or rhythmic interest». LOWINSKY 1960, pp. 146-148, nota.

[21]. DART – MOREN – RASTALL 2001.

> The evident attempt of the lutenists to reproduce literally the vocal polyphony succeeds in spite of small variants of a sort we can expect from all lute music: ties are broken; some long notes are divided into notes of smaller value, or more rarely the reverse; a few rhythms are dotted or undotted; and the polyphony is occasionally rearranged slightly in order to make it fit better under the instrumentalist's hand[22].

Vaccaro analizza tali modificazioni del modello nel passaggio da notazione mensurale a tablatura in termini di «réduction de l'espace vocal à l'espace du luth»[23] e identifica otto parametri interessati da questa riduzione: altezza, durata, timbro, intensità, articolazione (di suoni e frasi), struttura polifonica, rapporto intensità-durata, rapporto struttura polifonica-timbro. Tre di queste categorie risultano di particolare interesse nell'evoluzione del sistema contrappuntistico e in direzione di una coscienza dell'accordo e della tonalità. Prima fra tutte, la categoria delle altezze: la riorganizzazione del materiale dallo spazio vocale a quello strumentale comporta talvolta la trasposizione e condiziona la tonalità — fittizia — dell'intavolatura sulla base di questioni pratiche (a questo proposito, bisogna ricordare che esistevano strumenti di differenti dimensioni e dal tipo di accordatura differente); inoltre, tale riorganizzazione corrisponde anche, inconsapevolmente, a una trasposizione da un sistema non temperato a un sistema temperato[24]. Al livello della struttura polifonica, sono le relazioni di comunicazione interna tra le voci a essere stravolte: se nella polifonia vocale si sviluppano in modo orizzontale, nella tablatura diventano verticali (la relazione tra una nota di una voce e la nota successiva della stessa voce è meno forte che la relazione tra una nota di una voce e quella emessa simultaneamente da un'altra voce); questo comporta un indebolimento dell'identità di ogni voce e la polarizzazione delle parti esterne, oltre che un aumento di variabilità dello spazio polifonico (il raddoppio o l'aggiunta di suoni non alterano lo svolgimento logico della struttura musicale)[25]. L'identità di ogni voce è

---

[22]. Brown 1973-1974, p. 55.

[23]. Vaccaro 1981, pp. 131-138.

[24]. «[…] l'accordatura et la tasteggiatura de l'instrument établirent nécessairement ce tempérament égal (gamme tempérée) que le génie du grand Bach appliqua plus tard au clavier pour mettre en œuvre toutes les tonalités, en détruisant définitivement toutes traces de l'ancien système des modes ecclésiastiques. Il est curieux de voir qu'au XVIe siècle on discutait avec passion [cfr. Galilei, Vincentio. *Della musica antica e della moderna*, 1581] sur la manière de plier la gamme naturelle aux exigences de l'évolution que subissait l'art musical, tandis que dans la pratique le seul moyen propre était déjà en usage sur le luth, sans qu'on s'en fût aperçu». Chilesotti 1912, p. 637. Si veda anche Lindley 1984.

[25]. «[…] l'espace vocal [de la polyphonie, n.d.a.] peut être qualifié de "pluri-linéaire". Il est engendré par la superposition de plusieurs "lignes" indépendantes ayant leurs déroulements spécifiques: les voix. Ces lignes sont, si l'on peut dire, parallèles […]. Il n'existe entre elles aucune communication possible. À cause de cette individualité irréductible, elles engendrent un espace de caractère discontinu. À cette discontinuité en quelque sorte "verticale" (dans la simultanéité) s'oppose, organiquement, une continuité "horizontale" (dans la succession). L'espace sonore du luth, comme d'ailleurs celui de tout instrument polyphonique soliste, se caractérise par l'opposition inverse. L'émission sonore est unifiée; la polyphonie s'élabore dans un

ulteriormente indebolita dal nuovo rapporto struttura polifonica-timbro: nel contesto del contrappunto del XVI secolo, che abbonda di incroci e imitazioni, la condotta di ogni voce, sul liuto, diventa ambigua a causa della mancanza del differenziale timbrico[26]. Questo tipo di trasformazioni sono peculiari delle tablature per strumenti a corde pizzicate. È quanto dimostrato da uno studio comparativo condotto da Wolfgang Boetticher sulle intavolature per organo e per liuto delle opere di Lasso comprese nel periodo tra 1566 e 1603. Tale studio ha rivelato che:

> 1) le déroulement harmonique semble fixé avec plus de précision dans les transcriptions pour luth que dans celles pour instruments à clavier de la même époque; 2) le Fingerfall de l'orgue, le suspirium, est remplacé la plupart du temps, dans les transcriptions pour luth, par des accords brisés de grande amplitude; 3) la polyphonie factice du luth tend souvent à simplifier la basse en tant que soutien harmonique et fait ainsi partiellement disparaître l'exécution en legato des parties inférieures; 4) les diminutions enveloppant les notes principales des petits intervalles qui correspondaient à un vieux principe fondamental du style des instruments à clavier cède de plus en plus le pas, dans les pièces pour instruments à cordes pincées à la main, au jeu par amples accords; 5) les fausses relations latentes du modèle vocal sont largement compensées […] par la fugacité des sons; 6) le riche travail figuratif de la basse se conforme moins aux lois du contrepoint vocal qu'au broderies et aux retards de la partie supérieure, contrairement à ce qui se passait pour les tablatures d'orgue restées plus fidèles à l'original […][27].

Inoltre, l'intavolatura della musica polifonica vocale comporta un'altra conseguenza significativa: considerato che la tablatura non è una rappresentazione astratta della musica ma la descrizione dell'azione fisica necessaria alla produzione del suono[28], la *musica*

---

geste unique et une communication peut s'établir à tout moment entre les différentes parties créant ainsi une continuité "verticale". […] Les voix n'ont plus qu'une existence virtuelle […]. Cette transformation entraîne nécessairement une discontinuité "horizontale" caractéristique. Unifié du grave à l'aigu, le champ des hauteurs se dessine en fonction des seuls contours extérieurs, les parties extrêmes. La polyphonie se polarise autour d'un axe supérius-basse; l'autonomie et la continuité des parties intermédiaires s'effacent. C'est en ce sens que le contrepoint du modèle vocal tend à se transformer en harmonie». VACCARO 1981, p. 136.

[26]. «Lorsque les parties polyphoniques ne sont opposées ni par leurs régimes de valeurs de durée ni par leurs registres comme dans le cas d'un croisement passager d'imitations ou d'un canon à l'unisson, le mouvement contrapuntique se fige en ostinato. Les voix fusionnent entre elles pour ne laisser émerger que leurs contours combinés. Le mouvement en avant des imitations se transforme en piétinement rythmique et harmonique; la mélodie, fixée dans ses superpositions successives, s'immobilise en sonorité harmonique». *Ibidem*, p. 138.

[27]. BOETTICHER 1958, pp. 147-148.

[28]. «The term 'tablature' generally signifies a notational system using letters of the alphabet or other symbols not found in ordinary staff notation, and which generally specifies the physical action required to

ficta vi è obbligatoriamente notata. Questo fenomeno ha senza dubbio contribuito alla sistematizzazione dell'uso e della funzione delle alterazioni[29].

Tutto quanto evidenziato fino a questo momento appartiene comunque al dominio della musica scritta. Benché delle modificazioni avvengano rispetto al modello polifonico, non c'è discrepanza — se non per quanto riguarda la fioritura — tra la musica scritta in tablatura e il prodotto risultante dall'esecuzione. Tutto quello che è scritto in tablatura (sebbene non risponda più, come abbiamo visto, alle regole che reggevano la costruzione contrappuntistica originale) non contempla ulteriori interventi da parte dell'esecutore per quello che riguarda la struttura armonico-polifonica; semmai, il contrario: la tablatura non è che la descrizione dell'azione fisica necessaria alla produzione del suono ed è dunque un mero sistema semiografico che non rimanda ad alcun sistema teorico. Inoltre, anche se la tablatura, in quanto sistema di notazione distinto dal sistema mensurale, sancisce in un certo senso l'indipendenza della musica strumentale[30], è nella musica originale per strumenti a corde pizzicate che le caratteristiche idiomatiche e stilistiche di questi ultimi emergono in maniera più evidente. Come sottolineava circa un secolo fa Chilesotti:

> [...] la transformation de la tonalité ancienne dans nos modes majeur et mineur a été favorisée ou, mieux encore, presque déterminée d'une manière décisive par la musique originale du luth, dont le caractère absolument mélodique fait de l'accord un élément essentiel de l'art, et non un fait accidentel dans la rencontre des diverses parties de la polyphonie. [...] Il faut encore noter que dans la musique originale du luth fonctionne évidemment ce basso continuo dont l'invention, selon les histoires de l'art, appartiendrait au père Lodovico Grossi de Viadana. Celui-ci donc, au lieu de découvrir un nouveau moyen de structure pour la composition, aurait seulement appliqué aux voix la basse instrumentale naturelle sur laquelle la musique de luth était déjà basée[31].

La notazione in tablatura è idealmente destinata all'esecuzione *punteado*: è la tecnica che è propria all'esecuzione di musiche polifoniche al liuto, e che permette,

---

produce the music from a specific instrument, rather than an abstract representation of the music itself». BENT 2001.

[29]. «De cette évolution enfin [l'identificazione del rapporto tonica-dominante, n.d.a.], au cours de laquelle on employait des altérations chromatiques, qui faisaient perdre à la tonalité antique la caractéristique de ses divers modes, nous pouvons suivre les phases dans les compositions polyphoniques transportées sur les cordes du luth. Ici, en efffet, la notation (tablature) pour l'instrument était établie [...] de façon à représenter l'exécution matérielle de la musique sur les touches; de sorte qu'il n'y a point de doute au sujet des notes altérées que les chanteurs, guidés par le sentiment artistique qui devinait l'art nouveau, employaient en faveur de la transformation de la tonalité, et que les joueurs de luth marquaient naturellement dans leurs tablatures». CHILESOTTI 1912, p. 637. Si veda anche BROWN 1973-1974.

[30]. «Y es más lógico, para destacar su independencia y emancipación frente a la música vocal, aplicar un sistema casi completamente distinto del de la notación mensural». SCHMITT 1997, p. 182.

[31]. CHIESOTTI 1912, p. 637.

grazie all'utilizzazione indipendente di ogni dito della mano destra, di eseguire melodie e di escludere determinate corde nell'esecuzione di agglomerati armonici. Tale tecnica sembrerebbe la logica derivazione della tecnica liutistica a plettro del xv secolo[32]; inoltre, è recentemente stato mostrato che già all'epoca coesistevano la tecnica del plettro (utilizzata per i passaggi accordali) e quella delle dita (utilizzata per i passaggi melodici)[33]. Ma l'evoluzione del linguaggio accordale e di un proto basso continuo alla chitarra spagnola è ascrivibile a un altro stile esecutivo, comunemente noto come *rasgueado* (ma anche come battuto — in Italia — e *golpeado* — in Spagna) e pertinente all'ambito della danza e dell'accompagnamento della canzone popolare. Tecnicamente, il *rasgueado* prevede la sollecitazione simultanea di tutte le corde della chitarra, senza la possibilità di escludere l'una o l'altra. *Nella Declaracion des intrumentos* del 1555[34], Bermudo testimonia l'esistenza dello stile *golpeado* sulla chitarra a 4 corde[35], ma è sulla chitarra a 5 corde che tale stile si sviluppa in modo più sistematico. Lex Eisenhardt sottolinea che l'aggiuta della quinta corda potrebbe essere vista non soltanto come la naturale evoluzione dello strumento, ma come un avanzamento tecnico necessario a migliorare l'esecuzione del *rasgueado*: uno strumento a quattro corde, infatti, generalmente non permetteva l'esecuzione di armonie complete; in questo senso, è fortemente influente anche il tipo di accordatura dello strumento[36]. In quest'ottica, estendendo la riflessione di Eisenhardt, si può affermare che è lo sviluppo della chitarra a cinque corde a permettere l'evoluzione di un sistema di notazione per il *rasgueado* che, come era stato per la tablatura, riposa su un sistema di relazioni tra semiografia e prodotto musicale proprio e distinto dal sistema mensurale. Un sistema di notazione completamente dedicato al *rasgueado* sancisce, in un certo senso, l'affrancamento di quest'ultimo, come aveva fatto la tablatura per la musica per liuto.

In base alle fonti a noi pervenute, il primo sistema di notazione stenografica del *rasgueado*, detto 'catalano', appare in Spagna nel manuale *Guitarra española* di Juan Carles Amat; sebbene l'esemplare più antico a noi pervenuto sia un'edizione del 1626 (Lérida, Anglada & Llorens), l'*imprimatur* data al 1596. Brown[37] riporta l'ipotesi di una prima edizione del 1586, secondo quanto indicato da Fray Leonardo de San Martin in una lettera ad Amar datata 30 aprile 1639 e riportata nell'edizione di Barcellona del 1639; considerato che nel 1586 Amat avrebbe avuto solamente quattordici anni, l'ipotesi di un errore nella lettera di Fray Leonardo sembrerebbe la più realistica[38]. Il trattato di Amat, diviso in nove

---

[32]. *Cfr.* DANNER 1972.
[33]. IVANOFF 2005.
[34]. BERMUDO 1555.
[35]. *Ibidem*, pp. xcixv e xxviiiv.
[36]. EISENHARDT 2015, pp. 13-14.
[37]. BROWN 1965, p. 343.
[38]. Riguardo a questa data, si veda: ESSES 1992, p. 117; HALL – TYLER 1976, pp. 227-229; PUJOL 1950.

capitoli, è esplicitamente consacrato al *rasgueado*[39]. Il secondo capitolo è completamente dedicato al concetto di accordo, che per l'autore è il primo argomento da dover trattare, una volta terminata la descrizione tecnica della chitarra: «Pues tienes la gúitarra ya téplada y puesta a punto de tañer, rason es agora enseñarte que cosa es punto, quátos son, y como se llaman»[40]. Nel descrivere quello che è un accordo (*punto*), Amat non fa alcun riferimento al sistema intervallare contrappuntistico; inoltre, ci lascia dedurre che l'idea di accordo in quanto entità integra era già affermata all'epoca, poiché esistevano già diversi termini per indicare l'accordo[41]. Nel terzo capitolo, in cui descrive le diteggiature degli accordi previsti nel suo sistema, non fa alcun riferimento ai nomi delle note (descrive solamente il gesto strumentale) ma identifica, di ogni accordo, quale siano la fondamentale, la terza e la quinta. È nel completamento della descrizione della diteggiatura, nel quinto capitolo, che la descrizione del gesto strumentale finisce per diventare sistema: gli accordi, con la loro diteggiatura e una cifra corrispondente, sono disposti in un cerchio (i maggiori — *naturales* — nella metà superiore, i minori — *mollados* — nella metà inferiore) in successione di quarte in senso orario.

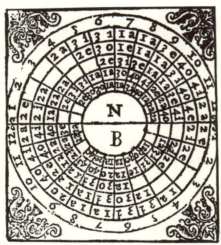

Ill. 1: Amat 1627, quinto capitolo, descrizione della diteggiatura.

---

[39]. «Considerando pues yo la falta que havia en toda esta tierra por nó haver algú auctor tartado desto (alomenos que yo fepa) le querido escrivir, con este estilo el modo de templar y tocar rasgado. esta guitarra de cinco, llamada Española por ser mas recibida en esta tierra que en las otras, y el modo de poner en ella, qualquier tono, paraque sirua de maestro, y tambien para que los dicipulo della no esten sujetos a tanta miseria como es la que nos da este humor». Amat 1627, f. [2ᵛ].

[40]. *Ibidem*, f. [6ʳ].

[41]. «Llamanse estos pútos de muchas maneras como es cruzado mayor y cruzado menor, vacas altas, y vacas baxas, puente, y de otras infinitas suertes que los muficos, unos y otros les han puestos nombres diferentes; pero yo aqui no las ılamare sino primero, segundo, tercero, y quarto, &c.y estos o naturales,o b, mollados», *Ibidem*, f. [6ᵛ].

Questa rappresentazione grafica è alla base del riconoscimento dell'enarmonia proclamato implicitamente nel capitolo successivo:

> En la susodicha tabla estan puestos todos los puntos que se pueden hazer en esta guitarra, y si alguno dize que y ay otros, como son aquellos que se hazen en el quinto, sexto, septimo, y en los otros trastes, buelvo por mi, y digo, que todos aquellos tienen la mesma consonancia, y la misma boz que tienen estos que havemos trahido: porque, el punto treze, que es el que viene despues del doze, tiene la misma consonancia y bos que tiene el primero [...]⁴².

In questo capitolo, Amat fa riferimento alla solmizzazione e spiega come il sistema — che noi definiremmo temperato — dei 12 semitoni della chitarra permetta di superare il sistema degli esacordi. Il settimo capitolo si apre con un'immagine che conferma che è l'accordo, e non il singolo intervallo, l'elemento di base della composizione in stile *rasgueado*:

> Todo lo que se ha tratado hasta aqui, es como la materia, de la qual se puede hazer muchas formas. El bueno y platico pintor tiene aparejadas todas las colores que son neccessarias para pintar, de las quales està a su alvedrio si quiere pintar, o un hombres, o un Leon, o un buey, del a mesma manera, nosotros hasta aqui havemos aparejados todos los puntos, que son como materia, y como las colores del pintor, de los quales, se pueden formar toda manera y suerte de tonos, saltando del uno al otro⁴³.

Sulle basi di tale osservazione, Amat mostra come sia semplice trasportare qualsiasi successione armonica senza dover ricorrere alla solmizzazione⁴⁴: «[...] y lo que es de maravillar (lo que a muchos parecera ímpossible) que cóestos puntos, puede qualquier ajuntar,o acomodar, por las dichas doze partes, todo lo que se tañe; y puede tañer, có qualquier instruméto de musico [...]»⁴⁵. L'utilità di poter trasporre in tutti i 12 toni sembra evidente per Amat: non soltanto si potrà accompagnare qualsiasi registro vocale, ma sarà possibile suonare con strumenti accordati in modo differente: «Desta manera se pueden tocar doze guitarras juntas cada una por sus puntos, y todas haran una misma consonancia»⁴⁶. Nell'ottavo capitolo si trova una vera e propria 'istruzione' per poter improvvisare una riduzione di qualsiasi composizione polifonica, secondo una tecnica di invenzione dell'autore (questo ci fa dedurre che tale pratica non fosse già diffusa prima di allora)⁴⁷. Il sistema che Amat propone si basa sull'identificazione del basso della

---

42. *Ibidem*, f. [13ᵛ].
43. *Ibidem*, f. [15ʳ].
44. Anche in questo caso, Amat si avvale di un grafico.
45. *Ibidem*, f. [15ʳ-15ᵛ].
46. *Ibidem*, f. [17ʳ].
47. *Ibidem*, f. [17ᵛ-18ʳ].

composizione polifonica e corrisponde a una vera e propria — seppur rudimentale — armonizzazione della scala diatonica: una volta individuato l'esacordo al quale le note del basso della composizione polifonica appartengono, si faranno corrispondere a ogni 'grado' gli accordi corrispondenti individuati da Amat e riportati, ancora una volta, in una tabella. Come sottolineato da Christensen:

> In most cases this will be a "root-position" major or minor triad determined by the numbers found intabulated in the circle printed earlier in his treatise. If, however, the chord does not seem to fit well with any of the upper parts, one can find a chord that does fit by means of the letters ciphered above mi, ut-sol, and la-mi, and match these with other chords through an algorithm that Amat describes. The net result of Amat's table is that the third, fifth and seventh scale degrees of the major and minor diatonic scales can support one of four different triads: the root-position consonant triad, first inversion (6) major and minor triads, and a second inversion (6) major triad. Evidently Amat did not find it necessary to offer inversional substitutes on the remaining scale degrees (which consequently permit only root-position triads)[48].

Amat afferma addirittura di essere riuscito a improvvisare la riduzione di opere di Palestrina grazie al suo sistema[49]. Sebbene tale affermazione sia da circostanziare alla retorica autocelebrativa dell'epoca e nonostante il sistema preveda una reale corrispondenza tra armonie scritte e armonie ridotte solo statistica e adattabile solo a procedimenti armonici elementari[50], l'idea di partire della sola lettura del basso per sviluppare le armonie ci permette di definire tale sistema come il primissimo esperimento di basso cifrato.

La chitarra spagnola, e con essa lo stile *rasgueado*, trovano rapidissima diffusione in Italia. In un articolo del 2002, John Walter Hill[51] mette in relazione il rasgueado allo stile recitativo fiorentino, presentendoci l'evidenza che l'accompagnamento ad accordi lunghi fosse noto non solo in Spagna, ma anche a Napoli, già intorno agli anni '50 del Cinquecento, e di come questi fosse in possesso di tutte le caratteristiche accordali riscontrate in una serie di accompagnamenti fiorentini in intavolatura per liuto degli anni '90 del Cinquecento. È in Italia che la notazione stenografica degli accordi per chitarra troverà la più ampia diffusione, secondo un sistema differente ma fondato sullo stesso principio di base: la rappresentazione di un accordo per mezzo di un unico simbolo. Nel caso dell'Italia, sono le lettere dell'alfabeto a essere utilizzate, ed è 'alfabeto' il nome attribuito al sistema. La paternità del sistema alfabetico italiano viene comunemente attribuita al manuale di Girolamo Montesardo del 1606[52]; in realtà, la notazione alfabetica è riscontrabile in due

---

[48]. CHRISTENSEN 1992, p. 26.
[49]. AMAT 1627, f. [18ᵛ].
[50]. A questo proposito, si veda: O'DONNELL 2011, pp. 134-136.
[51]. HILL 2003.
[52]. MONTESARDO 1606.

opere del 1599, una conservata alla biblioteca vaticana e una (spagnola) nella biblioteca privata di Szayas[53]. Il sistema montesardiano, dal quale gli altri derivano, sostituisce i numeri del sistema di Amat con le lettere ma si regge sugli stessi principi fondamentali; pur non utilizzando il sistema a cerchio, gli elementi fondanti restano gli stessi: equivalenza dei rivolti, enarmonia e assenza di condotta contrappuntistica delle parti. La Francia manterrà una posizione per lo più di importazione rispetto ai sistemi stenografici. Il primo ad apparire è il sistema alfa-numerico detto castigliano, a opera di Luis de Briçeno, nel 1626[54]; il fatto che sia edito a Parigi da Ballard è testimonianza di una diffusione non secondaria. È francese, inoltre, l'unica apparizione dei sistemi in esame in un trattato teorico: il sistema numerico spagnolo, come quello alfabetico italiano, fanno apparizione nel terzo volume dell'*Harmonie Universelle* di Marin Mersenne[55]. L'avvento dell'alfabeto italiano nella pratica francese è tardivo, e di autore italiano: Corbetta, *La guitarre royale*[56]; sarà ripreso poi da Derosier nel 1696[57]. Il sistema italiano è quello che conoscerà la diffusione più ampia. Per questo studio, una distinzione netta tra questi tre sistemi non è rilevante; si farà dunque riferimento agli 'alfabeti' per riferirci ai tre sistemi, e le riflessioni proposte saranno basate sulle caratteristiche comuni a essi. Una cartografia della diffusione di manuali o raccolte contenenti istruzioni per gli alfabeti è proposta nella Tavola 1 (p. 283).

In Italia, il sistema alfabetico diviene strumento di preferenza per l'accompagnamento della monodia sulla chitarra, principalmente a causa dell'immediatezza e facilità di lettura per l'amatore; la presenza della notazione alfabetica nelle raccolte di monodie è, come già accennato, quantitativamente significativa. Molto spesso, però, gli accordi indicati dalle lettere dell'alfabeto risultano essere addirittura incompatibili con un'armonizzazione corretta del basso. Questo ha suscitato l'ipotesi, oggi ritenuta valida, che spesso fossero gli editori ad aggiungere l'alfabeto per ragioni commerciali; a supporto di ciò, osserviamo che circa la metà delle raccolte apparse tra il 1610 e il 1660 sono edite a Venezia, e la maggior parte di esse da un solo editore, Vincenti[58]. In ogni caso, l'accompagnamento tramite alfabeto è da considerarsi come tipicamente chitarristico e, come evidenziato da Natasha Miles, come l'incontro della tradizione popolare di accompagnamento e la realizzazione del continuo[59]; a questo si può aggiungere, per le ragioni brevemente investigate qui sopra, l'eredità liutistica dalla pratica della riduzione. L'elemento di collegamento tra l'alfabeto e il basso continuo sono le cosiddette 'scale di musica', paradigmi di armonizzazione solitamente proposte nei manuali in due versioni, per B quadro e per B molle, e che

---

[53]. I-Rvat Chigi L.vi.200; E-Szayas A.iv.8, *Cancionero de Matheo Bezón* (Napoli).
[54]. Briçeno 1626.
[55]. Mersenne 1636.
[56]. Corbetta 1671.
[57]. Derosiers 1696.
[58]. O'Donnell 2011, p. 130.
[59]. Miles 2013, p. 105.

rappresentano degli antecedenti alla regola dell'ottava di Campion del 1716. Già in Amat abbiamo visto esistere una tabella contenente un sistema per armonizzare il basso nei dodici toni; in un manoscritto italiano del 1613 (I-Bc Ms. Q. 34, f. 94ᵛ) è rappresentata una scala di musica armonizzata con alfabeto, nella quale è interessante notare non solo un'armonizzazione quasi diatonica dell'intervallo fa-fa, ma anche che le note alterate sono armonizzate come un primo rivolto. Questa sarà una costante in tutte le scale di musica: non tutte le note del basso sono considerate come fondamentali. Foscarini, nella sua regola per suonare sopra la parte del 1640[60], propone addirittura una scala cromatica nella quale tutte le note alterate con un diesis sono armonizzate in 3/6. La scala che ha avuto il maggior successo è quella proposta da Milanuzzi[61] nel 1622, e verrà sistematicamente riutilizzata, anch'essa, dall'editore Vincenti di Venezia. Nell'armonizzazione di queste scale non è comunque individuabile alcun tipo di funzionalità tonale né tantomeno una vera identificazione dei modi maggiore/minore. Tale armonizzazione non si discosta molto dai precetti per suonare sopra la parte di Bianciardi e degli altri teorici del basso continuo, aderendo alla visione 'probabilistica' del basso continuo proposta da Preitano: l'aggiunta delle lettere dell'alfabeto si basava sul fatto che le probabilità che l'esecutore avrebbe suonato il giusto accordo sul basso erano molte[62]. A partire dalla metà del secolo, i limiti del sistema alfabetico nella realizzazione del basso continuo cominciano a farsi evidenti. Si comincia a quest'epoca ad aggiungere cifrature supplementari per precisare meglio le note da suonare sul basso e rendere l'esecuzione più coerente dal punto divista dei ritardi e delle dissonanze. L'alfabeto decadrà progressivamente a partire dalla metà del secolo, in favore di una notazione mista costituita da alfabeto e tablatura. Inoltre, è di particolare rilevanza il fatto che, a partire dal 1640 (Foscarini) si assiste all'uso sistematico delle cosiddette 'lettere false' e, in seguito, delle 'lettere tagliate', forme di accordi dissonanti e che cercano, in un certo senso, di reintrodurre le tensioni melodiche proprie al contrappunto, con lo scopo — presumibilmente — di ottenere una più realistica corrispondenza tra il modello polifonico e l'esecuzione accordale.

Nonostante non sia assolutamente adeguato parlare di armonia funzionale riferendosi a tali sistemi, la messa in evidenza delle loro caratteristiche fondanti fa scaturire delle riflessioni che possono legittimamente essere relazionate ai concetti di armonia e funzionalità, considerati individualmente[63]. Uno degli aspetti più interessanti dei sistemi

---

[60]. Foscarini 1640.
[61]. Milanuzzi 1622.
[62]. Preitano 1994, p. 29.
[63]. «We use the term "functional harmony" so often that we say "functionalharmony" — one word with the accent on the fourth syllable. We forget that there are two words with two different meanings; that there might be "non-functional harmony", or even "function" in the absence of "harmony". Now it seems clear that "function", since Riemann, refers to relationships between triadic chords, relationships that may be actual or implied. Armed with a more comprehensive view of history, we can proceed cautiously to speak of functions between two-note entities instead of between triads. [...] The formulas of the 15th century, then,

alfabetici è che non solo viene individuato, implicitamente, l'accordo in quanto unità integra, ma viene anche censita formalmente l'equivalenza dei rivolti: già in Amat, nonostante vengano indicate la fondamentale, terza e quinta di ogni triade, si sottolinea che la disposizione di esse non è importante. Tale affermazione appare in Amat ben in anticipo rispetto al trattato di Lippius del 1612 nel quale appariva, secondo Dahlhaus, la primissima teorizzazione del concetto di rivolto[64] (derivante, in Lippius, dalla divisione aritmetica della quinta). L'individuazione di questa equivalenza deriva da una questione strumentale: nella tecnica del *rasgueado* le corde vengono suonate tutte simultaneamente (o quasi) in un unico movimento della mano, dunque la nota che si trova 'al basso' non è determinata da nient'altro che dalla corda più grave. Questa contingenza tecnico-strumentale ci fa immaginare che la corrispondenza dei rivolti fosse una realtà di fatto esistente nella pratica chitarristica già prima della stesura del trattato di Amat. Un discorso analogo è applicabile ai raddoppi. I sistemi alfabetici prevedono un principio di sostituzione tra accordi equivalenti, tra i diversi rivolti: questo vuol dire che sono riconosciute delle caratteristiche alle quali applicare la variazione in base a caratteristiche comuni; agli accordi, che diventano entità autonome giustapponibili liberamente e che non rispondono più alla condotta delle parti (si veda il paragone fatto da Amat tra il pittore e il compositore, riportato più in alto), è riconosciuta un'identità di 'funzione', a prescindere delle disposizioni intervallari al loro interno. Quello che è interessante del sistema alfabetico, che da mero veicolo didattico finisce, attraverso il principio di sostituzione degli accordi, per essere linguaggio compositivo estemporaneo, non è tanto il fatto che sia fondato su delle sonorità triadiche ma che, seppur estraneo a un sistema di funzionalità tonale, esclude ogni legame col pensiero intervallare. Nel motetto *Sicut lilium* di Antoine Brumel (ca. 1500), ad esempio, che secondo Lowinsky costituisce un paradigma dell'armonia tonale a causa delle armonie di terza e quinta risultanti dal contrappunto, queste armonie triadiche non erano, come sottolinea Dahlhaus, il punto di partenza ma il risultato della composizione, aspetto estetico esteriore[65]; nell'alfabeto, invece, si assiste al fenomeno inverso: gli accordi costituiscono il punto di partenza del processo creativo. Il contrappunto, per definizione, riposa su due elementi fondamentali: la condotta melodica delle parti e l'opposizione tra consonanze e dissonanze[66]. Il sistema alfabetico, considerato nella sua forma iniziale puramente triadica, si distacca dall'idea che reggeva il contrappunto non soltanto perché non è gestito dalla legge della condotta delle parti, ma ancor di più perché non prevede l'alternanza consonanza/dissonanza; in questo senso, è da

---

are indeed functional: they depend upon the two-note progressions of discant. They also sound like the familiar progressions of "functionalharmony", which simply means that triadic functions and progressions develop in unbroken continuity out of discant. The difference between discant and "functionalharmony" has to do not with "function" (although the specific functions are slightly different in the two systems) but with harmony». CROCKER 1962, p. 16.

[64]. *Cfr.* DAHLHAUS 1993, p. 116.
[65]. *Ibidem*, p. 111.
[66]. *Ibidem*, p. 128.

considerarsi più simile alla diafonia parallela medievale. La sopracitata introduzione di accordi dissonanti a partire dagli anni '40 del Seicento e l'avvento della notazione mista di alfabeto e tablatura alla metà del secolo sono sintomo che il semplicismo di un sistema costituito solo di triadi maggiori e minori comincia a essere percepito come un limite. La scrittura chitarristica risponde così, nuovamente, alla chiamata del movimento melodico, restando però legata agli stilemi idiomatici (accordali) di cui la scrittura alfabetica è stata veicolo e catalizzatore.

Interessante è la questione concernente l'ordine di presentazione degli accordi nei sistemi alfabetici. Nel cerchio di Amat sono avanguardisticamente disposti in un circolo di quarte, in senso orario. Quello di Amat può essere largamente ritenuto il primo caso di circolo 'armonico'[67]. Il primissimo circolo di quinte in un trattato teorico appare solamente alla fine degli anni '70 del Seicento, nel trattato di contrappunto del russo Nikolai Diletskii *Idea Grammatiki Musikiiskoi*. Anche in questo trattato, l'idea del circolo sembra essere originata dalla volontà di semplificare il lavoro compositivo dello studente:

> The second part of the treatise covers composition. Diletskii lays out a series of rules designed to help the student compose sections of a *kontsert*. In one passage he describes two series of progressions by fifths, using first major and then minor triads, illustrated on circular staves to show how each series begins and ends on the same pitch[68].

Nell'alfabeto italiano, gli accordi non sono presentati secondo un ordine scalare ma secondo un ordine apparentemente casuale che mostra avere una relazione con le strutture armoniche tipiche delle danze spagnole (le stesse danze per le quali il *rasgueado* era lo stile di elezione)[69]: nei sistemi italiano e castigliano sono individuabili raggruppamenti corrispondenti alla successione I-IV-V, corrispondente allo schema tipico della passacaglia spagnola. Un altro aspetto fondamentale dei sistemi di armonizzazione proposti (già presente in Amat) è interessante: il mi e il si, e in seguito anche le note alterate, sono armonizzati in 3/6 per evitare il tritono, fatto che per Dahlhaus rappresenta il primo passo verso l'organizzazione del sistema di accordi in gradi principali e secondari[70]. Se a questo si aggiunge il fatto che non solo la passacaglia, ma tutte le danze tipiche del *rasgueado* sono generalmente basate su soli 3 o 4 accordi di base sostituibili in base al principio di 'equivalenza funzionale'[71], in Amat si assiste all'inizio del processo di individuazione dei gradi forti della scala diatonica, processo che culminerà in quello che per Dahlhaus è il principio fondante dell'armonia tonale, ossia la dipendenza del III e VI grado dal I[72].

---

[67]. *Cfr*. PREITANO 1994, p. 76.
[68]. JENSEN 1992, p. 307.
[69]. *Cfr*. HUDSON 1970.
[70]. *Cfr*. DAHLHAUS 1993, pp. 123-124.
[71]. *Cfr*. HUDSON 1970.
[72]. *Cfr*. DAHLHAUS 1993, p. 124.

Un'altra questione importante, che emerge già in Amat, è quella concernente la trasposizione. Già dal sistema di Amat, e in tutti i sistemi a venire, si rende possibile — grazie al riconoscimento dell'enarmonia degli accordi — la trasposizione sui 12 toni senza dover ricorrere alla solmizzazione: una certa cifra o lettera corrispondente alla posizione dell'accordo deve solamente essere spostata sul manico della chitarra di un dato numero di tasti. Questo è strettamente legato alla fisionomia della chitarra che, in quanto strumento dotato di tasti, beneficia di un sistema quasi temperato e si presta dunque a fare da propulsore al temperamento equabile. Certamente, il fatto che un proto sistema temperato esista sugli strumenti a corde non rivela, di per sé, l'esistenza di un sistema tonale:

> Lindley considère un tempérament égal acquis en ce qui concerne les années 1550-1650 [LINDLEY 1984, p. 19] soit la période qui me concerne; il signale d'ailleurs qu'une des toutes premières sources musicales faisant preuve du tempérament égal est un morceau destiné aux instruments à frettes. [*Ibidem*, p. 22. Il s'agit d'un morceau de Valderrábano 1547, pp. 48-50] En effet, ces instruments ont alors un rapport particulier avec la transposition, en raison du tempérament quasi-égal qui fait que la transposition par *n* nombre de demi-tons correspond au déplacement par *n* nombre de frettes sur le manche. [...] La présence d'un tempérament quasi-égal a permis aux musiciens et théoriciens d'établir un système chromatique sous-jacent, sans pour autant susciter derechef un nouveau système musical. Un système tonal n'advient pas nécessairement une fois le tempérament égal admis. Il est simplement dès lors plus envisageable[73].

In ogni caso, gli espedienti grafici utilizzati da Amat e Doizi de Velasco[74] ci rimandano ancora al trattato di Diletskii. In Doizi de Velasco sono proprio dei cerchi il sistema grafico utilizzato per la trasposizione[75] e in Amat, come si è visto, è il cerchio rappresentante gli accordi ad essere lo strumento di base per la trasposizione. Il circolo delle quinte di Diletskii è presentato come funzionale all'idea di 'trasposizione', intesa in un senso più ampio:

> The circles of fifths appear in the Grammatika's long final chapter, a miscellany appropriately headed 'On Things I Forgot to Write about Earlier'. The circles are part of a section called 'On Amplification', which describes ways of expanding or spinning out a musical idea and is one of several rhetorically-inspired sectional headings in the work. [...] The circles of fifths (Diletskii calls them musical circles) represent yet another way to expand a composition. Diletskii takes a brief melody and shows how it might pass through all of the musical letters and wind up back in its original position. The author explains

---

[73]. O'DONNELL 2011, pp. 77-78.
[74]. DOIZI 1640.
[75]. *Ibidem*, p. 61.

his musical circles in terms already familiar to his readers: the circles are labelled "happy" or "sad" and each statement of the melody as it moves around the circle is identified by its *kliuch*[76].

A differenza del sistema di Amat, in Diletskii il riferimento alla teoria dell'esacordo è ancora esplicitamente presente, anche se si è ipotizzato che l'autore lo abbia utilizzato solo in riferimento al canto e che nel suo pesiero teorico fosse invece già ben definito il concetto di bimodalità:

> Diletskii's division of music into happy and sad and his illustrations of these categories in the musical circles raise the important and difficult question of his understanding of the evolving system of major/minor tonality. Protopopov [DILETSKII 1979, pp. 584-586] believes that the *Grammatika* refers unambiguously to the two-mode system and that Diletskii's references to the hexachordal syllables are included only as practical aids for singers and have no part in his overall theoretical scheme[77].

Quello che emerge da questa riflessione è che la ragione per la quale il sistema di Amat ci appare più avanzato dal punto di vista della bimodalità risiede nel fatto che quest'ultimo è basato su un tipo di notazione che, come si è visto, non intrattiene alcun legame con un sitema astratto quale è quello mensurale. In Amat (nel suo sistema di base, astrazion fatta dalla sua tecnica di 'armonizzazione del basso') decade ogni vestigia dell'antico sistema di solmizazione; i due sistemi non sono relazionabili direttamente, in quanto basati su codici 'linguistici' completamente differenti[78].

Quest'ultima osservazione di carattere particolare ci conduce ad una conclusione generale. A pochi decenni di distanza dal tempo in cui Sánchez de Lima, nella sua *Arte poetica en romance castellano* (Alcala de Henares, 1580) osservava che «[e]verything that is usually sung and played nowadays is in the strummed fashion and nothing is sung or played with understanding»[79], il rapporto tra 'causa ed effetto' (e, con esso, tra teoria e pratica) nella nascita di un linguaggio armonico chitarristico si mostra ambiguo. Se è vero che, come si è dimostrato, la nascita di un sistema di notazione indipendente si rivela essere la «conseguenza di un'idea»[80], è allo stesso tempo vero che sono la particolarità e, in un certo senso, il confinamento subito dal linguaggio

---

[76]. JENSEN 1992, p. 319.

[77]. *Ibidem*, p. 320.

[78]. *Cfr*. PREITANO 1994, pp. 86-87.

[79]. Citato in EISENHARDT 2015, p. 12.

[80]. Si è presa in prestito l'espressione usata da Schmitt in riferimento alla tablatura: «[…] fenómeno histórico que vamos a considerar no tanto como evento estático […] sino más bien como algo que ocurrió en los siglos XV y XVI como consecuencia de algo, quizá como consecuencia de una idea». SCHMITT 1997, p. 177.

chitarristico ad averlo reso propulsore dell'evoluzione teorica del linguaggio musicale. Citando Thomas Christensen: «Paradoxically, one might say that it was precisely the wide gulf separating the conservative Spanish traditions of received music theory from the empirical practice of the guitarists (to say nothing of the social distinctions) that freed the latter to reconceptualize harmony so radically»[81].

BIBLIOGRAFIA

AMAT 1627
AMAT, Joan Carles. *Guitarra Española* [...] *de cinco ordenes* [...], Lérida, Viuda Anglada y Andres Lorenço, 1627.

APEL 1998
APEL, Willi. *La notation de la musique polyphonique. 900-1600*, traduzione francese di Jean-Philippe Navarre, Sprimont, Mandraga, 1998 (Musique-musicologie).

BENT 2001
BENT, Ian D. *et alii*. 'Notation', in: *Grove Music Online*, <http://www.oxfordmusiconline.com>, visitato nell'ottobre 2018.

BERMUDO 1555
BERMUDO, Fray Juan. *Declaración de instrumentos musicales*, Osuna, s.n., 1555.

BOETTICHER 1958
BOETTICHER, Wolfgang. 'Œuvres de Lassus mises en tablature de luth', in: *Le luth et sa musique: Neuilly sur Seine, 10-14 sept. 1957*, a cura di Jean Jaquot, Parigi, CNRS, 1958 (Colloques internationaux du Centre de la recherche scientifique, 12), pp. 143-153.

BRICEÑO 1626
BRICEÑO, Luis de. *Metodo mui facilissimo para aprender a tañer la guitarra a lo Español*, Parigi, Pierre Ballard, 1626 (fac-simile, Ginevra, Minkoff Reprint, 1972).

BROWN 1965
BROWN, Howard Mayer. *Instrumental Music Printed before 1600. A Bibliography*, Cambridge (MA), Harvard University Press, 1965.

BROWN 1973-1974
ID. 'Embellishment in Early Sixteenth-Century Italian Intabulations', in: *Proceedings of the Royal Musical Association*, C (1973-1974), pp. 49-83.

CASTIGLIONE 1528
CASTIGLIONE, Baldassarre. *Il libro del Cortegiano*, Firenze, per li heredi di Philippo Giunta, 1528.

---

[81]. CHRISTENSEN 1992, pp. 11-16.

CHILESOTTI 1912
CHILESOTTI, Oscar. 'Notes sur les tablatures de luth et de guitare – XVIe et XVIIe siècles', in: *Encyclopédie de la Musique et Dictionnaire du Conservatoire. 1.1: Histoire de la Musique: Antiquité, moyen age*, fondato da Albert Lavignac e diretto da Lionel de la Laurencie, Parigi, Delagrave, 1912, pp. 636-684.

CHRISTENSEN 1992
CHRISTENSEN, Thomas. 'The Spanish Baroque Guitar and Seventeenth-Century Triadic Theory', in: *Journal of Music Theory*, XXXVI/1 (1992), pp. 1-42.

CORBETTA 1671
CORBETTA, Francesco. *La guitare royalle dediée Au Roy de la Grande Bretagne*, Parigi, Bonneuil, 1671 (fac-simile Ginevra, Minkoff, 1975).

COUSSEMAKER 1852
COUSSEMAKER, Charles Edmond Henri de. *Histoire de l'harmonie au moyen âge*, Parigi, V. Didron, 1852.

CROCKER 1962
CROCKER, Richard L. 'Discant, Counterpoint, and Harmony', in: *Journal of the American Musicological Society*, XV/1 (1962), pp. 1-21.

DAHLHAUS 1996
DAHLHAUS, Carl. *La tonalité harmonique. Étude des origines*, tradotto dal tedesco da Anne-Emmanuelle Ceulemans, Liegi, Madraga, 1993.

DANNER 1972
DANNER, Peter. 'Before Petrucci: the Lute in Fifteenth Century', in: *Journal of the Lute Society of America*, n. 5 (1972), pp. 4-17.

DART – MOREN – RASTALL 2001
DART, Thurston – MOREHEN, John – RASTALL, Richard. 'Tablature', in: *Grove Music Online*, <http://www.oxfordmusiconline.com>, visitato nell'ottobre 2018.

DEROSIERS 1696
DEROSIERS, Nicolas. *Les principes de la guitarre*, Amsterdam, Antoine Pointel, ca. 1696.

DILETSKII 1979
DILETSKII, Nikolai. *Idea Grammatiki Musikiiskoi*, a cura di Vladimir Protopopov, Mosca, Muzyka, 1979 (Pamiatniki russkogo muzykal'nogo iskusstva, 7).

DOIZI 1640
DOIZI DE VELASCO, Nicolás. *Nuevo modo de cifra para tañer la guitarra con variedad, y perfección, y se muestra ser instrumento perfecto, y abuntantissimo*, Napoli, [Egidio Longo], 1640.

EISENHARDT 2015
EISENHARDT, Lex. *Italian Guitar Music of the Seventeenth Century: Battuto and Pizzicato*, Rochester, University of Rochester Press, 2015 (Eastman Studies in Music).

Esses 1992
Esses, Maurice. *Dance and Instrumental «Diferencias» in Spain during the 17th and Early 18th Centuries. Vol. 1: History and Background, Music and Dance*, Stuyvesant (NY), Pendragon, 1994 (Dance and Music Series, 2).

Foscarin 1640
Foscarini, Giovanni Paolo. *Li cinque libri della chitarra alla spagnola [...] con il modo di sonare sopra la parte*, Roma, s.n., 1640 [fac-simile Firenze, Studio per edizioni scelte, 1979 (Archivum musicum. Collana di testi rari, 20)].

Gavito 2006
Gavito, Cory Michael. *The Alfabeto Song in Print, 1610 - ca. 1665: Neapolitan Roots, Roman Codification, and «il Gusto Popolare»*, Ph.D. Diss., Austin (TX), University of Texas at Austin, 2006.

Hall – Tyler 1976
Hall, Monica – Tyler James. 'The 'Guitarra Española', in: *Early Music*, IV/2 (1976), pp. 227, 229.

Hill 2003
Hill, John Walter. 'L'accompagnamento rasgueago di chitarra: un possibile modello per il basso continuo dello stile recitativo?', in: *Rime e suoni alla spagnola. Atti della Giornata internazionale di studi sulla chitarra spagnola (Firenze, Biblioteca Riccardiana, 7 febbraio 2002)*, Firenze, Alinea, 2003 (Secoli d'oro, 33).

Hudson 1970
Hudson, Richard. 'The Concept of Mode in Italian Guitar Music during the First Half of the Seventeenth-Century', in: *Acta Musicologica*, XLII/3-4 (1970), pp. 163-183.

Ivanoff 2005
Ivanoff, Vladimir. 'An Invitaton to the Fifteenth-century Plectrum: the Pesaro Manuscript', in: *Performance on Lute, Guitar and Vihuela: Historical Practice and Modern Interpretation*, a cura di Victor Coelho, Cambridge (UK), Cambridge University Press, 2005 (Cambridge Studies in Performance Practice, 6).

Jensen 1992
Jensen, Claudia R. 'A Theoretical Work of Late Seventeenth-Century Muscovy: Nikolai Diletskii's 'Grammatika' and the Earliest Circle of Fifths', in: *Journal of the American Musicological Society*, XLV/2 (1992), pp. 305-331.

Lindley 1984
Lindley, Mark. *Lutes, Viols & Temperaments*, Cambridge, Cambridge University Press, 1984.

Lowinsky 1948
Lowinsky, Edward E. 'On the Use of Scores by Sixteenth-Century Musicians', in: *Journal of the American Musicological Society*, I/1 (1948), pp. 17-23.

Lowinsky 1960
Id. 'Early Scores in Manuscript', in: *Journal of the American Musicological Society*, XIII/1-3 (1960), pp. 126-173.

Lowinsky 1989
Id. 'Canon Technique and Simultaneous Conception in the Fifteenth-Century Music: A Comparison of North and South', in: Id. *Music in the Culture of the Renaissance & Other Essays*, a cura di Bonnie J. Blackburn, 2 voll., Chicago, University of Chicago Press, 1989, vol. II, pp. 884-910.

Mersenne 1636
Mersenne, Marin. *Harmonie universelle*, 3 voll., Parigi, S. Cramoisy, 1636 (fac-simile Parigi, CNRS, 1963).

Milanuzzi 1622
Milanuzzi, Carlo. *Primo scherzo delle ariose vaghezze* […], Venezia, Bartholomeo Magni, 1622.

Miles 2013
Miles, Natasha Frances. *Approaches to Accompaniment on the Baroque Guitar c. 1590 - c.1730*, 2 voll., Ph.D. Diss., Bimingham, University of Bimingham, 2013.

Montesardo 1606
Montesardo, Girolamo. *Nuova inventione d'Intavolatura: per sonare li Balletti sopra la chitarra spagnuola, senza numeri e note; per mezzo della quale da se stesso ogn'uno senza maestro potrà imparare*, Firenze, Christofano Marescotti, 1606.

O'Donnell 2011
O'Donnell, Aidan. *Le rôle de l'alfabeto dans le développement de la pensée harmonique en Italie, 1600-1650*, Ph.D. Diss., Parigi, Université de Paris-Sorbonne, 2011.

Preitano 1994
Preitano, Massimo. 'Gli albori della concezione tonale: aria, ritornello strumentale e chitarra spagnola nel primo Seicento', in: *Rivista Italiana di Musicologia*, XXIX/1 (1994), pp. 27-88.

Pujol 1950
Pujol, Emilio. 'Significación de Joan Carlos Amat, 1572-1644, en la historia de la guitarra', in: *Anuario musical*, V (1950), pp. 125-146

Rameau 1722
Rameau, Jean-Philippe. *Traité de l'harmonie*, Parigi, Ballard, 1722 (fac-simile [Parigi], Fondation Singer-Polignac, 1986).

Schmitt 1997
Schmitt, Thomas. 'Sobre la necesidad de las tablaturas', in: Bordas Ibañez, Cristina – Vicente, Alfonso de. *Los instrumentos musicales en el siglo XVI. Primer encuentro Tomás Luis de Victoria y la Música Española del Siglo XVI. Ávila, mayo de 1993*, Avila, Fundación Cultural Sta. Teresa, 1997, pp. 177-185.

Vaccaro 1981
Vaccaro, Jean-Michel. *La musique de luth en France au XVIe siècle*, Parigi, CNRS, 1981 (Chœur des muses. Corps des luthistes français).

Zarlino 1558
Zarlino, Gioseffo. *Le istitutioni harmoniche*, Venezia, Pietro da Fino, 1558.

Accompagnamento e basso continuo alla chitarra spagnola

Tavola 1: Trattati e raccolte contenenti istruzioni o tavole per alfabeto/cifras

	Spagna	Italia	Francia
[1596]	J. C. Amat, *Gvitarra Española*		
1599		I Rvat Chigi L.VI.200	
		E Szayas A.vi.8, *Cancionero de Matheo Bezón* (Napoli)	
1606		G. Montesardo, *Nuova inventione d'Intavolatura* (Firenze, Christofano Marescotti, 1606)	
1608		Pico, *Nuova scelta di sonate* (Napoli, Giovanni Francesco Paci, 1608)	
1609		Anon, I-Fr Ms. 3145, *Intavolatura della chitarra spagniola* (1609)	
		Palumbi, F-Pn Ms. Esp. 390, *Libro de villanelle spagnuol' et italiane* [...] (ca. 1610-1620)	
		F. Palumbi, I-Fr Ms. 2804 (ca. 1610-1620)	
		F. Palumbi, I-Fr Ms. 2849 (ca. 1610-1620)	
		Anon, I-Fr Ms. 2973/3, *Canzonette musicali spagnoli e Italiane* (ca. 1610-1620)	
		Anon, I-Fl Ashb 791 (inizi Seicento)	
		Petrus Jacobus Pedruil, I-Bc Ms. V.280, *Libro de sonate diverse alla chitarra spagnola* (1614-1625)	
1616		F. Corradi, *Le stravaganze d'amore* (Venezia, Giacomo Vincenti, 1616)	
		B. Sanseverino, *El segundo libro de los ayres, villançicos, y cancioncillas* (Milano, Filippo Lomazzo, 1616)	
		A. Falconieri, *Libro primo di villanelle* (Roma, Giovanni Battista Robletti, 1616)	
1618		F. Corradi, *Le stravaganze d'amore* (Venezia, Giacomo Vincenti, 1618)	
		R. Romano, *Prima raccolta* (Vicenza, Angelo Salvadori, 1618; rist. 1622; rist. Torino, F. Cavaleri, 1624)	
1619		G. G. Kapsberger, *Libro secondo di villanelle* (Roma, Giovanni Battista Robletti, 1619)	
		G. G. Kapsberger, *Libro terzo di villanelle* (Roma, s.n., 1619)	
	I-Fl Ashb 791 (inizio Seicento)	Anon, F-Pn Res Vmc. Ms. 59 (ca. 1620-1630)	
		Anon, I-Fr Ms. 2951 (ca. 1620-1630)	
		Anon, I-Fr Ms. 2952 (ca. 1620-1630)	
		I-Fr Ms. 2868 vol. II (ca. 1620-1640)	
		Anon, I-Fr MS 2774, *Intavolatura della chitarra spagnola* (ca. 1620)	
1620		G. A. Colonna, *Intavolatura di chitarra alla spagnuola* (Milano, eredi di G. B. Colonna, 1620)	
		G. A. Colonna, *Il secondo libro d'intavolatura di chitarra alla spagnuola*, Milano	
		B. Sanseverino, *Intavolatura facile* (Milano, Filippo Lomazzo, 1620)	
1621		G. Stefani, *Affetti amorosi* (Venezia, Alessandro Vincenti, 1621)	
1622		G. Stefani, *Scherzi amorosi* (Venezia, Alessandro Vincenti, 1622)	
		B. Marini, *Scherzi, e canzonette* (Parma, Anteo Viotti, 1622)	
		B. Sanseverino, *Il primo libro d'Intavolatura per la chitarra spagnuola* (Milano, Filippo Lomazzo, 1622)	
		C. Milanuzzi, *Primo scherzo delle ariose vaghezze* (Venezia, Bartholomeo Magni, 1622)	

			C. Milanuzzi, *Secondo scherzo delle ariose vaghezze* (Venezia, Alessandro Vincenti, 1622)
1623			R. Romano, *Prima raccolta* ([Vicenza], Angelo Salvadori, 1618, rist.)
			G. Stefani, *Concerti amorosi* (Venezia, Alessandro Vincenti, 1623)
			C. Milanuzzi, *Terzo scherzo delle ariose vaghezze* (Venezia, Alessandro Vincenti, 1623)
			G. Ghizzolo, *Frutti d'amore* (Venezia, Alessandro Vincenti, 1623)
			D. Manzolo, *Canzonette* (Venezia, Alessandro Vincenti, 1623)
			G. A. Colonna, *Il terzo libro d'intavolatura*, (Milano, erede di G. B. Colonna, 1623)
1624			C. Milanuzzi, *Quarto scherzo delle ariose vaghezze* (Venezia, Alessandro Vincenti, 1624)
			G. P. Berti, *Cantade et arie* (Venezia, Alessandro Vincenti, 1624)
1625			R. Romano, *Prima raccolta* (Pavia, G. B. de Rossi, 1625)
			C. Milanuzzi, *Secondo scherzo delle ariose vaghezze* (Venezia, Alessandro Vincenti, 1625)
1626	J. C. Amat, *Guitarra Española* (Lerida, Viuda Anglada y Andres Lorenço, 1626)	L. de Briceño, *Metodo muí facilissimo* (Parigi, Pierre Ballard, 1626)	A. Grandi, *Cantade et arie* (Venezia, Alessandro Vincenti, 1626)
1627			G. P. Berti, *Cantade et arie* (Venezia, Alessandro Vincenti, 1627)
			D. Obizzi, *Madrigali et arie a voce sola* (Venezia, Alessandro Vincenti, 1627)
			P. Millioni, *Seconda impressione del Quarto libro d'intavolatura* (Roma, Guglielmo Facciotti, 1627)
			P. Millioni, *Prima impressione del Quinto Libro d'Intavolatura* (Roma, Guglielmo Facciotti, 1627)
			G. B. Abatessa, *Corona di vaghi fiori* (Venezia, Bartholomeo Magni, 1627)
			M. Aldigatti da Cesena, *Gratie et affetti amorosi* (Venezia, s.n., 1627)
			F. Costanzo, *Fior novello* (Bologna, Nicolò Tebaldini, 1627)
			G. Miniscalchi, *Arie di Guglielmo Miniscalchi Libro Primo* (Venezia, Alessandro Vincenti, 1627)
			G. Miniscalchi, *Arie di Guglielmo Miniscalchi Libro Secondo* (Venezia, Alessandro Vincenti, 1627)
1628			C. Milanuzzi, *Sesto libro delle ariose vaghezze* (Venezia, Alessandro Vincenti, 1628)
1629			G. P. Foscarini, *Intavolatura di chitarra spagnola, libro secondo* (Macerata, Gio. Battista Bonomo, 1629)
			Anon. I-Fc Ms. B. 2556 (=CF.108), *Sonate di chitarra spagniola* (metà Seicento)
			Anon, I-Fr Ms. 3121 (metà Seicento)
1630			G. Miniscalchi, *Arie di Guglielmo Miniscalchi Libro Terzo* (Venezia, Alessandro Vincenti, 1630)
			C. Milanuzzi, *Settimo libro delle ariose vaghezze* (Venezia, Alessandro Vincenti, 1630)
			G. P. Foscarini, *Il primo, secondo e terzo libro della chitarra spagnola* (s.l., s.n., [1630])
1632			G. P. Foscarini, *I quattro libri della chitarra spagnola* (s.l., s.n., [1632])
1633			Anon, I-Fn Ms. Magl.VII.894 (1633)
1635			G. B. Abatessa, *Cespuglio di varii fiori* (Orvieto, Gio. Battista Robletti, 1635)
			C. Milanuzzi, *Ottavo Libro delle Ariose Vaghezze* (Venezia, Alessandro Vincenti, 1635)
			P. Millioni, *Quarto libro d'intavolatura di chitarra spagnola* (Roma, Paolo Masotti, 1635)

ACCOMPAGNAMENTO E BASSO CONTINUO ALLA CHITARRA SPAGNOLA

1636		P. Millioni, *Corona del primo, secondo, e terzo libro d'intavolatura* (Roma e Torino, Giovanni Manzolino & Domenico Roveda, 1635; rist. Milano, Filippo Ghidolfi, G. B. Cerri & C. Ferrardi, 1636)	M. Mersenne, *Harmonie universelle* (Parigi, Sebastien Cramoisy, 1636)
		M. Pesenti, *Arie a voce sola* (Venezia, Alessandro Vincenti, 1636)	
		L. Monte, *Vago fior di virtù* (Venezia, Angelo Salvadori, ca. 1636)	
		G. F. Sances, *Il quarto libro delle cantate* (Venezia, Alessandro Vincenti, 1636)	
1637		G. A. Colonna, *Intavolatura di chitarra spagnuola del primo, secondo, terzo, & quarto Libro* (Milano, Dionisio Gariboldi, 1637)	
		P. Millioni – L. Monte, *Vero e facil modo d'imparare a sonare* (Roma e Macerata, eredi di Salvioni & Agostino Grisei, 1637)	
		G. B. Abatessa, *Cespuglio di varii fiori* (Firenze, Zanobi Pignoni, 1637)	
1638		C. Busatti, *Arie a voce sola* (Venezia, Alessandro Vincenti, 1638)	
1639	J. C. Amat, *Guitarra Española* (Barcellona, Lorenço Déu, 1639)	F. Corbetta, *De gli scherzi armonici trouati* (Bologna, Giacomo Monti, 1639)	
		A. Trombetti, *Intavolatura di sonate [...] Libro Primo, et secondo* (Bologna, Nicolò Tebaldini, 1639)	
1640		Anon, I-Fn Ms. Magl.XIX.143 (ca. 1640)	
		A. M. Bartolotti, *Libro P.° di chitarra spagnola* (Firenze, s.n., 1640)	
		G. P. Foscarini, *Li cinque libri della chitarra alla spagnola* (Roma, s.n., 1640)	
		A. Carbonchi, *Sonate di chitarra spagnola* (Firenze, Amador Massi e Lorenzo Landi, 1640)	
		N. Doizi de Velasco, *Nuevo modo de cifra* (Napoli, Egidio Longo, 1640)	
		A. Carbonchi, *Sonate per chitarra spagnola*, I-PEc Ms H72 (metà Seicento)	
1643		A. Carbonchi, *Le dodici chitarre spostate* (Firenze, Francesco Sabatini, 1643)	
		F. Corbetta, *Varii capricii per la ghittara spagnola* (Milano, Bianchi, 1643)	
1646		F. Valdambrini, *Libro primo d'intavolatura di chitarra* (Roma, s.n., 1646)	
		G. B. Granata, *Capricci armonici sopra la chittariglia spagnola* (Bologna, Giacomo Monti, 1646)	
		C. Calvi, *Intavolatura di chitarra* (Bologna, Giacomo Monti, 1646)	
1647		P. Millioni – L. Monte, *Vero e facil modo d'imparare a sonare, et accordare da se medesimo la Chitarra Spagnola* (Roma e Macerata, Agostino Grisei, 1647)	
1648		S. Pesori, *Lo scrigno armonico* (Verona, s.n., 1648)	M. Mersenne, *Harmonicorum libri* (Parigi, Guillaume Baudry, 1648)
		S. Pesori, *Galeria Musicale* (Verona, Gio. Battista, & Fratelli Merli, 1648)	
1650	F. Corbetta, *Guitarra española y sus differencias de sonos* (Madrid, s.n., ca. 1650)	D. Pellegrini, *Armoniosi concerti sopra la chitarra* (Bologna, Giacomo Monti, 1650)	
		G. B. Abatessa, *Ghirlanda di varii fiori* (Milano, Lodovico Monza, ca. 1650)	
1655		A. M. Bartolotti, *Secondo Libro di chitarra* (Roma, s.n., ca. 1655)	
1660		T. Marchetti, *Il primo libro d'intavolatura della chitarra spagnola* (Roma, Francesco Moneta, 1660)	
		S. Pesori, *I Concerti Armonici di Chitarriglia* (Verona, Andrea Rossi, ca. 1660)	

1661		P. Millioni, *Nuova corona d'intavolatura di chitarra spagnola* (Roma, eredi di Mancini, 1661)
1666		P. Millioni – L. Monte, *Vero e facil modo d'imparare a sonare* (Venezia, Giacomo Bortoli, 1666) Anonimo, *Novissime canzonette musicali de diversi autori* (Venezia, Camillo Bortoli, 1666)
1671		F. Corbetta, *La guitarre royalle* (Parigi, H. Bonneuil, 1671)
1674	G. Sanz, *Instrucion de musica sobre la guitarra españiola* (Saragozza, eredi di Diego Dormer, 1674)	F. Corbetta, *La guitarre royalle* (Parigi, H. Bonneuil, 1674)
1675		S. Pesori, *Ricreationi armoniche* (s.l., s.n., ca. 1675)
1677	L. Ruiz de Ribayaz, *Luz y norte musical* (Madrid, Melchor Alvarez, 1677)	G. P. Ricci, *Scuola d'intavolatura* (Roma, Paolo Moneta, 1677)
1678		P. Millioni – L. Monte, *Vero e facil modo d'imparare a sonare* (Venezia, Giacomo Zini, 1678) Anonimo, *Novissime canzonette musicali* (Venezia, il Zini, 1678)
1680		A. Micheli, *La nuova chitara di regole* (Palermo, P. Coppula, 1680)
1696		[N. Derosier, *Les principes de la guitarre* (Amsterdam, Antoine Pointel, ca. 1696)]
1697	G. Sanz, *Instrucion* (Saragozza, eredi di Diego Dormer, 1697)	
1698		F. Pico, *Nuova scelta di sonate per la chitarra* (Napoli, Giovan. Francesco Paci, 1698)
1699	A. de Santa Cruz, E-Mn Ms. M.2209, *Livro donde se veran [...] escribia y asia Dn. Antonio de Santa Cruz, para D. Juan de Miranda* (ca. 1699)	Derosier, *Nouveaux principes pour la guitare* (Parigi, Christophe Ballard, 1699)
		[Anon, CZ-Pu Ms. II.Kk.77, *Pièces composee par le Conte Logis* (1700-1725)]
1717	S. de Murcia, *Resumen de acompañar la parte con la guitarra* (Madrid, s.n., 1717)	

Naturalezza o artificio: riflessioni su improvvisazione e virtuosismo italiani in Francia nel Settecento

Guido Olivieri
(University of Texas, Austin, TX)

Il termine 'improvisar' è puramente italiano[1]. Questa categorica definizione, apparsa nel 1768 nel *Dictionnaire de musique* pubblicato da Jean-Jacques Rousseau, è anche una delle prime relative all'uso di questo termine che diverrà di uso comune in Francia solo verso la fine del secolo.

È certamente sorprendente incontrare, ancora nella seconda metà del Settecento, una definizione della pratica dell'improvvisazione musicale così circoscritta e, in fondo, limitata. Sebbene alcuni studiosi abbiano di recente messo in guardia da un'estensione e un'applicazione indiscriminata del concetto di improvvisazione a qualsiasi fenomeno di produzione musicale spontanea[2], l'improvvisazione è tuttavia oggi considerata un fenomeno complesso e presente praticamente in tutte le culture musicali, seppure a diversi livelli e con diverse modalità di attuazione.

La voce del *Dictionnaire* sembra volutamente ignorare questa complessità e connette, invece, l'improvvisazione a una pratica percepita come appartenente esclusivamente alla tradizione musicale italiana contemporanea. Si tratta, dunque di una definizione molto distante da quella che siamo soliti fornire modernamente e che ha poco a che fare con lo sviluppo dell'improvvisazione considerata — ben prima del Settecento — come cifra caratterizzante del virtuosismo vocale e strumentale.

La definizione del *Dictionnaire* mostra evidentemente che in Francia il termine improvvisazione era ancora praticamente sconosciuto e che il suo uso si limitava a indicare una pratica diversa da quella francese. Ovviamente l'approccio all'improvvisazione non era sconosciuto alla musica francese che applicava da tempo la pratica dell'ornamentazione. Già alla fine del Seicento un altro Rousseau, Jean, nel suo *Traité de la viole* del 1686 affermava — in quello che è forse uno dei primi esempi della metafora del gusto riferita alla musica — che

---

[1]. Rousseau 1768, p. 255. «Le mot *improvisar* est purement Italien». Se non è ulteriormente specificato, le traduzioni italiane sono dell'autore del presente saggio.

[2]. Treitler 2015.

> […] gli ornamenti sono un sale melodico che condisce il canto e che gli dona il gusto (goût), senza i quali esso sarebbe scialbo e insipido; e come il sale dev'essere usato con prudenza, cosicché non ne serve né troppo, né troppo poco, e come esso occorre più nel condimento di alcune carni e meno in altre, così bisogna far un uso moderato degli ornamenti e saper discernere dove ne siano necessari di più e dove meno[3].

Nell'estetica francese, dunque, l'ornamentazione è governata dal gusto e controllata dalla moderazione. Ma si tratta di aggiunte, ornamenti appunto, al testo scritto che hanno la funzione di abbellire e rendere interessante la pagina musicale, senza stravolgerne la struttura e travisare le intenzioni del compositore.

Lo ribadisce Michel Pignolet de Montéclair qualche anno più tardi, a proposito delle diminuzioni, i *Passages*:

> I *Passaggi* sono arbitrari, ciascuno può farne più o meno a seconda del proprio gusto e della propria disposizione. Si praticano meno nella musica vocale che in quella strumentale, soprattutto adesso che gli strumentisti, per imitare il gusto degli italiani, sfigurano la nobiltà delle melodie semplici, con delle variazioni spesso ridicole[4].

Per comprendere meglio i motivi per i quali Rousseau indica l'improvvisazione come prassi tipicamente italiana occorre leggere fino in fondo la definizione che appare nel *Dictionaire*. Per Rousseau l'improvvisazione consiste nel «fare e cantare all'improvviso delle canzoni, arie e parole che vengono accompagnate di solito da una chitarra o altro strumento simile». Il filosofo francese sottolinea come non ci sia «nulla di più comune in Italia del vedere due maschere incontrarsi, sfidarsi, attaccarsi e replicare con coppie di versi sulla stessa Aria con una vivacità di dialogo, di canto, di accompagnamento cui bisogna aver assistito per poterlo comprendere»[5].

---

[3]. Rousseau 1687, p. 75: «[…] les Agrémens sont un Sel Melodique qui assaisonne le Chant, & qui luy donne le goût, sans lequel il seroit fade & insipide, & comme le Sel doit estre employé avec prudence, en sorte qu'il n'en faut ny trop, ny trop peu, & qu'il en faut plus dans l'assaisonnement de certaines viandes, & moins en autres: Ainsi dans l'usage des Agrémens il faut les appliquer avec moderation, & sçavoir discerner où il en faut plus, & où il en faut moins».

[4]. Monteclair 1736, p. 86: «Le Passages sont arbitraire, chacun peut en faire plus ou moins suivant son goût et sa disposition. Ils se pratiquent moins dans la Musique vocale que dans l'instrumentale, sur tout à present que les joüeurs d'instruments, pour imiter le goût des Italiens, defigurent la noblesse des chants simples, par des variations souvent ridicules».

[5]. Rousseau 1768, p. 255: «C'est faire & chanter impromtu des Chansons, Airs & paroles, qu'on accompagne communément d'une Guitarre ou autre pareil Instrument. Il n'y a rien de plus commun en Italie, que de voir deux Masques se rencontrer, se désier, s'attaquer, se riposter ainsi par des couplets fur le même Air, avec une vivacité de Dialogue, de Chant, d'Accompagnement dont il faut avoir été témoin pour la comprendre».

Naturalezza o artificio

L'improvvisazione di stampo italiano appare dunque cosa ben diversa dalla pratica di ornamentazione alla francese e si caratterizza già in queste descrizioni come creazione spontanea che nasce al di fuori delle regole e di ogni moderazione. Se nei confronti del testo musicale l'improvvisazione opera a diversi livelli — come libera creazione, ri-creazione (o completamento), oppure elaborazione (ornamentale) — si può affermare che la tradizione musicale francese coltivi prevalentemente l'ultima, mentre in Italia si preferivano le prime due.

È evidente che l'improvvisazione descritta nel *Dictionnaire* coinvolge anche altre manifestazioni artistiche e letterarie, non esclusivamente musicali. La prassi improvvisativa va ricondotta all'aspetto linguistico oltre che quello musicale e si identifica almeno in parte con un fenomeno di natura letteraria. L'improvvisazione italiana è per Rousseau invenzione spontanea e immediata condotta su testi posti in musica. Inoltre il riferimento alle maschere incluso nella definizione fa senza dubbio riferimento alla tradizione della commedia dell'arte e all'espressione musicale che di quella cultura teatrale era erede, ovvero l'intermezzo. Sarà opportuno notare che la voce del *Dictionnaire* venne pubblicata a distanza di appena una quindicina di anni dalla famosa *Querelle des Bouffons* (1752-1754), controversia in cui lo stesso Rousseau ebbe un ruolo centrale. Una *querelle*, com'è noto, centrata sulla performance della *Serva padrona* di Pergolesi e di altri intermezzi, e sulle abilità improvvisative della compagnia teatrale della commedia dell'arte di Eustachio Bambini[6].

In realtà, questa consuetudine improvvisativa ha un momento di rinascita e rivalutazione nell'Italia del XVII secolo; poeti quali Giovan Battista Zappi, Paolo Rolli, Metastasio, Vincenzo Monti furono celebri improvvisatori. È già nell'ambito dell'Accademia dell'Arcadia che si riprendono ideali presenti nei circoli letterari e intellettuali italiani che risalgono almeno a due secoli prima:

> Ai nostri tempi l'improvvisare si è avanzato di stima e di reputazione [...] ci ha di nobilissimi personaggi e di Letterati nulla meno eccellenti che sovente godono di esercitarlo [...] anzi il glorioso Principe Cardinal Pietro Ottoboni Vice Cancelliere di Santa Chiesa, il cui ingegno, e la cui prontezza è mirabile in ogni cosa, e particolarmente nelle materie letterarie, istituì gli anni passati una conversazione privata di lettere, la quale ogni Lunedì si adunava nel suo Palagio, e talora in altri luoghi di sua giurisdizione, e in essa si operava improvvisamente con eruditi discorsi e con poesie d'ogni genere, tessendosi anche, talora col suono, e talora senza, poemetti d'ottave, capitoli, catene di sonetti, di canzoni, di canzonette, e arrivandosi infine a comporvi corone perfette, e a stendersi le disfide degli improvvisatori per quattro, sei ore continue[7].

---

[6]. Sulla *Querelle des Bouffons* si veda SACALUGA 1968.

[7]. CRESCIMBENI 1731, p. 220. Nella sua *Storia dell'Accademia degli Arcadi*, Crescimbeni ribadisce la partecipazione dei più eminenti letterati alle adunanze dell'accademia, facendo anche un accenno all'uso di 'maschere': «Per maggiormente coltivare lo studio delle scienze, e risvegliare in buona parte d'Italia il buon gusto nelle lettere umane, ed in particolare nella Poesia Volgare, alquanto addormentato, fu da alcuni

In Arcadia l'improvvisazione poetica si coltiva come parte della ricerca di una nuova armonia classica fra naturalezza e artificio: «La poesia doveva ritrovare l'equilibrio tra cultura e ispirazione, tra tecnica e spontaneità, e le sfide tra gli improvvisatori ricreavano l'illusione di tornare nell'età dell'oro, quando i pastori si sfidavano in tenzoni poetiche, lasciandosi guidare dal fiume rapido e senza indugi dell'estro»[8].

È Crescimbeni, fra i fondatori dell'Arcadia e acceso sostenitore del valore dell'improvvisazione poetica, a riferirci delle gare poetico-musicali che avevano luogo in Arcadia, in particolare frutto della collaborazione fra Terpandro — Alessandro Scarlatti — e Tirsi — l'avvocato e poeta Giovan Battista Felice Zappi. In una occasione, invitato da Scarlatti a prestare i suoi versi per un'improvvisazione musicale, Zappi risponde:

> 'Deh per grazia, Terpandro, toglietene d'altrui; e lasciate star me; sapendo voi molto bene, che simili componimenti, fatti solamente in grazia della Musica, poco sono confacevoli al delicato gusto de' cospicui letterati, quali sono i Pastori di questo congresso: e massimamente ciò dee dirsi de' miei, che da me si producono senza alcuno studio all'improvviso, e per lo più al tavolino medesimo del Compositor della Musica, come più volte avete voi stesso e veduto e sperimentato; e particolarmente quando eravamo nelle Campagne della deliziosa Partenope'. 'Egli è il vero, allora Terpandro; ma ciò rende più mirabile il vostro ingegno, dappoiché all'improvviso producete voi ciò che altri con comodo studio mal sa produrre'. […] Restava intanto ognuno soprafatto in vedere, come mai gareggiassero que' due sì eccellenti Maestri, l'uno di Poesia, l'altro di Musica; ed il loro gareggiamento giunse a tal segno, che appena ebbe l'uno terminato di replicare l'ultimo verso della novella Aria, che l'altro chiuse l'ultima riga della sua Musica[9].

L'abilità improvvisativa degli italiani, non solo in musica e poesia, ma in ogni espressione artistica, provoca stupore e ammirazione, soprattutto presso i viaggiatori stranieri. La scrittrice Anne-Marie Fiquet du Boccage, in visita a Roma nel 1757 descrive un'improvvisazione di Orazio Arrighi Landini: «Il Signor Landini prese il suo mandolino e, con melodie varie, seguendo il loro uso, cantò su un soggetto propostogli dei versi spesso straordinari. Questo talento, sconosciuto presso di noi, ci stupisce»[10].

---

letterati instituita in Roma l'anno 1690 a' 5 d'Ottobre una Conversazione letteraria in forma di repubblica democratica, che abbraccia quasi tutti i Letterati d'Italia, e non pochi anche di là da i monti, e per togliere ogni riguardo di preminenza e precedenza tra i personaggi, che la dovevano formare, e anche per allettare coll'amenità e novità, si stabilì d'andar tutti mascherati sotto la finzione de' Pastori dell'antica Arcadia, dalla quale la Conversazione prese il nome; e i suggetti che la compongono Pastori Arcadi s'appellarono, e s'appellano». CRESCIMBENI 1806, p. 5.

[8]. FINOTTI 2003, p. 31.
[9]. CRESCIMBENI 1708, pp. 289-293.
[10]. 'Recueil des œuvres de madame Du Boccage', vol. III, p. 157, citato in GIULI 2009, p. 304.

Lo stupore dell'uditorio nasce, naturalmente, non solo dalla maestria, dall'essere gli improvvisatori e improvvistrici «mostri d'ingegno»[11], ma soprattutto dall'abilità di celare ogni sforzo e artificio. Il fine ultimo degli Arcadi improvvisatori è quello di unire la cultura e tecnica derivanti da una lunga tradizione letteraria a un potere creativo apparentemente spontaneo e naturale, quasi una nuova *sprezzatura*, «che nasconda l'arte e dimostri ciò che si fa e dice venir fatto senza fatica e quasi senza pensarvi»[12].

Il momento più alto di ispirazione si manifesta quindi non tanto nell'elaborazione testuale, ma anche, e forse soprattutto, nella fase della *performance*, genuina espressione della transitorietà dell'improvvisazione poetico-musicale: «Non erano solo i testi, ma la recitazione, il tono della voce, gli atteggiamenti, e persino gli sguardi dell'improvvisatore a conquistare l'uditorio»[13]. Saverio Bettinelli fornisce una dettagliata enumerazione delle fasi dell'ispirazione poetica che va dalla «immaginazione» alla «trasfusione», passando per la «visione» e la «passione»:

> Un eccellente poeta estemporaneo più volte considerai nel più forte accesso dell'estro poetico per buona mia sorte, e il vidi in prima cheto e pensoso incominciare con difficoltà, urtando or colla rima or colla frase quasi ancor si restasse nel basso e terra terra; ed eccolo a un punto raccendersi, ed elevarsi quasi a volo spiegando l'ale. Gli brillano gli occhi, serena il volto, guarda alto ed astratto dagli oggetti presenti, e il più spesso esprime questa elevazione dicendo ove sono? chi mi leva sopra di me? sdegno l'umili cose, il basso suolo, sorgiamo, o musa etc. Tali sono gli esordi più frequenti.
>
> […] Onde affrettasi e affolla concetti ed immagini, s'incalzano i versi, e trae seco il suonatore fuor di tempo; spesso tronca e finisce per tal violenza. […] Giubila ed arde affezionandosi a quelle viste ed attrattive di grandi oggetti, e belli, l'anima tutta s'affaccia, e commosso anche fuori da quel fuoco, che gli serpe entro le vene, onde gli occhi s'infiammano, arrossan le guance, sorridon le labbra, e freme la persona. […]
>
> Il qual fremito e fuoco diffondesi negli uditori, che gridan per gioia tratto tratto, e s'alzan dal luogo, e applaudono, e paiono in lui assorti, e trasformati, e trasportati con lui, ripercotendosi come palla da lui a loro, da loro a lui l'entusiasmo[14].

---

[11]. Un secolo più tardi Ugo Foscolo rimarca l'importanza dell'improvvisazione e il ruolo delle poetesse italiane: «Il dono dell'improvvisazione, che può essere definito innato in quel paese [Italia], diede celebrità a due o tre poetesse e sembra invero che la dolcezza delle voci femminili, la mobilità della loro fantasia e la scioltezza delle loro lingue le rendano più adatte degli uomini alla poesia estemporanea. Ma le donne che godono di tanta celebrità sono rare in Italia, e sono considerate non tanto con rispetto, quanto con meraviglia, come mostri d'ingegno; né vanno immuni dalle pene e dai tormenti del ridicolo». FOSCOLO 1826.

[12]. CASTIGLIONE 1528, vol. XXVI, p. 44.

[13]. FINOTTI 2003, p. 35.

[14]. BETTINELLI 1799, p. 48.

Non è difficile accostare questa animata descrizione dell'ispirazione poetica a quella dell'espressività esecutiva del musicista virtuoso, ispirato e quasi posseduto dalla potenza creatrice dell'improvvisazione: «Non ho mai incontrato nessuno soffrire delle proprie passioni nel suonare il violino da esserne quasi trasfigurato quanto il famoso Arcangelo Corelli, i cui occhi diventavano talvolta rossi come il fuoco; il suo aspetto si altera, i suoi occhi roteano come in agonia, ed egli è così preso da ciò che esegue che non sembra quasi la stessa persona»[15].

L'abilità improvvisativa, la potenza del genio creativo si connettono in ambiente italiano con l'idea del virtuosismo e ne divengono cifra caratterizzante. Nei primi anni del Settecento emerge e si afferma la figura del virtuoso moderno, una figura che diverrà centrale per lo sviluppo della musica francese e europea nel corso del secolo.

È proprio negli anni dell'incontro della cultura francese con la tradizione musicale italiana che troviamo una delle prime definizioni del virtuoso in ambito musicale; è un altro dizionario francese, il *Dictionnaire de musique* compilato da Sébastien de Brossard nel 1703, a fornircela:

> *VIRTÙ* vuol dire in italiano non soltanto quella predisposizione dell'anima che ci rende graditi a Dio e che ci fa agire secondo le regole della giusta ragione; ma anche quella *Superiorità di genio, di destrezza*, o *di abilità*, che ci fa *eccellere* sia nella *Teoria* che nella *Pratica* delle *belle arti*, al di sopra di quelli che vi si applicano tanto quanto noi. Da questo gli Italiani hanno creato l'aggettivo *VIRTUOSO* o *VIRTUDIOSO*, al femminile *Virtuosa*, da cui ottengono anche spesso dei sostantivi per appellare o per lodare coloro cui la Provvidenza ha voluto donare questa *eccellenza* o questa *superiorità*. Dunque secondo loro un eccellente *Pittore* o un *Architetto* di talento etc. è un *Virtuoso*; ma danno più comunemente e più specificamente questo bel Epiteto ai *Musicisti eccellenti* e tra questi piuttosto a quelli che si applicano alla *Teoria*, o alla *Composizione* della musica, che a quelli che eccellono nelle altre arti, tanto che nel loro linguaggio dire semplicemente che un uomo è un *Virtuoso* significa quasi sempre che è un *eccellente Musicista*. Il nostro linguaggio non ha che la parola *Illustre* che possa in qualche modo corrispondere a *Virtuoso* degli Italiani; quanto a *Vertueux*, l'uso non gli ha ancora dato lo stesso significato[16].

---

[15]. L'originale si trova nelle glosse anonime a RAGUENET 1709, pp. 20-21: «I never met with any man that suffered his passions to hurry him away so much whilst he was playing on the violin as the famous Arcangelo Corelli, whose eyes will sometimes turn as red as fire; his countenance will be distorted, his eyeballs roll as in an agony, and he gives in so much to what he is doing that he doth not look like the same man». Il testo che viene commentato, fa riferimento anch'esso all'intensa espressività della tradizione esecutiva dei virtuosi italiani: «A symphony of furies shakes the soul; it undermines and overthrows it in spite of all its care; the artist himself, whilst he is performing it, is seized with an unavoidable agony; he tortures his violin; he racks his body; he is no longer master of himself, but is agitated like one possessed with an irresistible motion».

[16]. «*VIRTU.* veut dire en Italien non seulement cette habitude de l'ame qui nous rend agréables à Dieu & nous fait agir selon les regles de la droute raison; mais aussi cette *Superiorité de genie, d'adresse* ou *d'habilité*,

Naturalezza o artificio

Se per Brossard il termine sembra applicarsi a quei musicisti che si dedicano alla teoria e alla composizione, piuttosto che alla 'pratica' della musica, occorre ricordare come l'autore scriva in un periodo in cui è ancora lontana la separazione fra esecutore e compositore e che, particolarmente nel caso dell'improvvisazione, il confine fra composizione ed esecuzione è sempre molto evanescente.

Non è un caso che questa definizione avvenga nell'ambiente culturale francese. Anche in questa circostanza è l'incontro della prassi musicale italiana con la tradizione francese a determinare la necessità di una definizione. La cultura musicale italiana gioca un ruolo fondamentale nello sviluppo dell'improvvisazione musicale e soprattutto nel legame fra questo fenomeno e quello del virtuosismo 'internazionale' sia vocale che strumentale. Appena due anni dopo la pubblicazione del *Dictionaire* di Brossard, il termine 'virtuoso' riappare, questa volta con connotazioni negative, in uno dei pamphlet che alimenta la famosa controversia sui rispettivi meriti della musica italiana e di quella francese. La *querelle* si sviluppa a partire dalla contrapposizione fra i difensori della musica italiana, il cui portavoce, l'abbate François Raguenet, pubblica nel 1702 il *Paralèle des italiens et des françois, en ce qui regarde la musique et les opéra*, e i sostenitori della tradizione francese, capeggiati da Jean Laurent Lecerf de la Viéville che risponde con la *Comparaison de la musique italienne et de la musique Françoise*, pubblicata in tre parti fra il 1704 e il 1706.

Le opposte visioni vengono efficacemente sintetizzate in un articolo (probabilmente attribuibile a Monsieur de La Tour) apparso nel *Mercure galant* nel novembre 1713: «Un [partito] ammiratore eccessivo della musica italiana, disprezza completamente la musica francese in quanto piatta e priva di gusto; l'altro, fedele al gusto della propria patria [...] tratta la Musa italiana come bizzarra e capricciosa»[17].

Il dibattito non coinvolge certo esclusivamente la dimensione estetico-musicale, ma riflette il momento di profondo cambiamento politico e sociale che investe la capitale francese all'inizio del secolo. Al tramonto dell'*ancien régime*, la musica italiana diventa il vessillo della nuova cultura proclamata e sostenuta da un'aristocrazia non più di stampo

---

qui nous fait *exceller* soit dans la *Théorie*, soit dans la *Prattique* des *beaux Arts* au dessus de ceux qui s'y apliquent aussi bien que nous. C'est de-là que les Italiens ont formé les Adjectifs *VIRTUOSO*, ou *VIRTUDIOSO*, au feminin *Virtuosa*, dont même ils sont souvent des Substantifs pour nommer, ou pour loüer ceux à qui la Providence a bien voulu donner cette *excellence* ou cette *superiorité*. Ainsi selon eux un excellent *Peintre*, un habile *Architecte*, &c. est un *Virtuoso*; mais ils donnent plus communément & plus specialement cette belle Epithete aux *excellens Musiciens*, & entre ceux là, plûtot à ceux qui s'apliquent à la *Théorie*, ou à la *Composition* de la Musique, qu'à ceux qui excellent dans les autres Arts, en sorte que dans leur langage, dire simplement qu'un homme est un *Virtuoso*, c'est presque toûjours dire que c'est un *excellent Musicien*. Nôtre langue n'a que le mot *Illustre* qui puisse en quelque maniere répondre au *Virtuoso* des Italiens, car pour celuy de *Vertueux*, l'usage ne luy a pas encore donné cette signification, du moins en parlant serieusement». 'Virtu', in: BROSSARD 1703, p. 71.

[17]. L. T. M. DE [LA TOUR?]. 'Dissertation sur le bon gout et la musique italienne et de la musique françoise, et sur ses opéras', in: *Mercure galant*, novembre 1713, pp. 3-62: 7-8.

ereditario, ma basata sul censo. I nuovi banchieri, ricchi mercanti e finanzieri che controllano le leve del potere, si distanziano gradualmente dalla politica del Re: dalle lussuose residenze di Parigi favoriscono e sponsorizzano gli artisti italiani e impongono in Francia una moderna visione estetica. Nascono in tal modo le serie di concerti pubblici, che culmineranno nel 1725 con l'istituzione dei *Concerts Spirituels* e si assiste alla creazione di un pubblico che applaude e accoglie criticamente le esecuzioni dei virtuosi internazionali.

Nei suoi scritti in difesa della tradizione francese, Le Cerf riafferma la contrapposizione fra natura e artificio, fra semplicità e «mostruosità d'ingegno»: «Da un lato il naturale e la semplicità, dall'altro l'affettazione e la brillantezza. Qui il vero, abbellito con proprietà, lì il falso, mascherato da mille raffinatezze, e carico degli eccessi di una scienza mostruosa»[18].

L'aderenza alle regole di imitazione della natura determina il buon gusto in musica e rende le composizioni musicali intelligibili e razionali:

> La musica francese è dunque saggia, uniforme e *naturale*, e non sopporta che di tanto in tanto e alla lontana i toni inusuali e gli ornamenti troppo ricercati. La musica italiana, al contrario, sempre forzata, sempre al di fuori dei confine della natura, senza unità, senza coerenza, rifiuta i nostri abbellimenti dolci e semplici. Non è sorprendente che gli italiani trovino la nostra [musica] scialba e insipida[19].

All'origine di questa contrapposizione c'è l'incontro con la tradizione virtuosistica e improvvisativa italiana. È di nuovo Le Cerf che nel 1705 dichiara apertamente la sua avversione e scagliandosi contro certi «*Virtuosi* de l'Italie» che si curano solo di «un'abilità folle e futile»[20]. Il virtuosismo esasperato è dunque percepito in Francia come una cifra caratteristica degli esecutori italiani. I commenti alle esecuzioni dei virtuosi italiani sottolineano gli elementi di sorpresa, ammirazione, ma anche sconcerto e opposizione a un tipo di esecuzione che viene sempre definita come al di fuori dei limiti stabiliti dalla natura, in altri termini 'artificiale' e innaturale. Ciò che provoca l'entusiasmo o l'aspra critica è precisamente lo stupore di fronte a musicisti che eccellono nell'esecuzione densa di passaggi virtuosistici, padroni di una tecnica di improvvisazione brillante e del tutto sconosciuta in terra francese. Per i virtuosi italiani, sia vocali che strumentali, la pagina scritta non è

---

[18]. Le Cerf 1705-1706, vol. I, p. 183. «D'un côté le naturel & la simplicité: de l'autre l'affectation & le brilliant. Là le vrai, embelli avec justesse: ici le faux, masqué par mille raffinemens, & chargé des excés d'une science monstrueuse».

[19]. *Ibidem*, vol. II, pp. 34-35. «La Musique Françoise est donc sage, unie et naturelle, et ne souffre que de tems en tems, et à loin les tons extraordinaires et les agrémens si recherchés. La Musique Italienne, au contraire, toujours forcée, toujours hors des bornes de la nature, sans liaison, sans suite, rejette nos agrémens doux et aisés. Il n'est pas étonnant que les Italiens trouvent la notre fade et insipide».

[20]. *Ibidem*, pp. 118-119.

che una traccia sempre e in modo variabile trasformata dall'aggiunta di improvvisazioni, abbellimenti e articolazioni idiomatiche. La natura estemporanea dell'esecuzione porta l'esecutore in un ruolo di primo piano rispetto al compositore — qualora le due figure siano effettivamente diverse — e, stabilendo un'equivalenza fra esecutore e virtuoso, esalta la figura del musicista professionista.

Che tra i musicisti che diffusero questa prassi in Francia vi fossero in una prima fase soprattutto strumentisti di origine e formazione napoletana non sorprende. Nei quattro antichi Conservatori napoletani già dalla metà del Seicento un approccio sistematico all'insegnamento formava musicisti professionisti, dotati di un'avanzata tecnica esecutiva e di una specifica abilità nell'elaborazione improvvisativa applicata alla composizione.

I nomi dei virtuosi che Le Cerf include nella sua critica sono quelli dei violinisti che si erano mossi in quegli anni da Napoli e che avevano incontrato fama e successo nella capitale francese. Virtuosi quali Giovanni Antonio Piani e Giovanni Antonio Guido che insieme a Michele Mascitti erano autori di collezioni che influenzano lo sviluppo della musica strumentale francese e fra i protagonisti delle *soirées* musicali organizzate dai più illustri mecenati di Parigi[21]. Se già nei suoi *Petits motets* pubblicati nel 1707 Giovanni Antonio Guido aveva inserito passaggi solistici per il violino con l'uso di doppie corde, nella sua collezione di Sonate per violino e basso continuo, pubblicata nel 1726, il violinista napoletano fa ricorso a un evidente virtuosismo, includendo successioni di accordi e arpeggi ed estesi passaggi di agilità che dimostrano, come afferma Moser, che Guido doveva essere «un violinista molto abile»[22].

Quanto a Giovanni Antonio Piani, la sua collezione di 12 Sonate stampata nella capitale francese già nel 1712 si apre con un'inusuale premessa nella quale il compositore fornisce la spiegazione di segni e colpi d'arco che vanno utilizzati per dare «brillantezza all'esecuzione». È evidente che con queste spiegazioni — scritte in francese, mentre la dedica è in italiano — l'autore intendeva illustrare tecniche espressive e virtuosistiche che facevano certamente parte del bagaglio professionale dei virtuosi italiani, ma che erano evidentemente ancora poco note e diffuse in ambito francese.

La formazione professionale dei musicisti realizzata nei conservatori napoletani favoriva evidentemente lo sviluppo di un'abilità improvvisativa, trasmessa oralmente da allievo a maestro — e dunque di per sé evanescente — e sistematicamente applicata alla prassi e alla creazione musicale. Ne resta traccia nella pratica del partimento, metodologia al confine fra improvvisazione e creazione estemporanea, basata sull'elaborazione di modelli compositivi[23]. Non diversamente dai poeti improvvisatori dell'Arcadia, questa metodologia

---

[21]. Su Antonio Guido si veda Olivieri 1996, Nestola 2004; su Mascitti e più in generale sull'influenza dei violinisti napoletani sulla scuola francese si veda Olivieri *in corso di stampa*.

[22]. «Ohne Zweifel muß Guido ein sehr tüchtiger Geiger gewesen sein». Moser 1923, p. 171.

[23]. Sui partimenti e sulla loro relazione con l'improvvisazione si veda Sanguinetti 2012 e la sezione sui partimenti in questo volume.

si muoveva fra artificio e spontaneità, forniva al virtuoso i modelli e le tecniche per un'elaborazione improvvisativa che apparisse spontanea, estemporanea e libera.

Questa pratica e lo sviluppo di una superiore abilità improvvisativa come bagaglio del virtuoso veniva tuttavia esercitato in modo particolare dagli strumentisti. In aggiunta ai partimenti, fra i mezzi didattici con cui veniva trasmessa questa tradizione vi erano i duetti e le variazioni su basso ostinato. Di questo approccio didattico rimane qualche traccia in alcuni manoscritti napoletani: da un lato un relativamente ampio repertorio di duetti, genere da sempre deputato principalmente a scopi didattici (si vedano per esempio le Sonate per due violini di Francesco ed Emanuele Barbella, che tuttavia elevano il genere a risultati di alto livello artistico)[24]; dall'altro le raccolte di variazioni per due violoncelli in cui il compositore-esecutore elabora e esperimenta le potenzialità virtuosistiche e di supporto armonico dello strumento[25]. Basti ricordare le Sonate per due violoncelli di Francesco Paolo Supriani, in cui undici Toccate originariamente parte del suo metodo per lo strumento diventano la base per un'ulteriore elaborazione virtuosistica che espande i limiti tecnici dello strumento[26].

Un esempio significativo della combinazione dei due approcci didattici sembra essere un manoscritto risalente al 1699 che include duetti per violoncelli basati su elaborazioni del basso di Passacaglia o su temi liturgici, attribuiti rispettivamente a Gaetano Francone e da Rocco Greco[27]. Anche in questo caso la scelta di due strumenti uguali, anche se non sempre impiegati allo stesso livello tecnico, suggerisce una destinazione didattica del manoscritto. La presenza e organizzazione sistematica della variazioni sulla Passacaglia e i riferimenti ai versetti liturgici rafforzano questa impressione, particolarmente evidente nelle indicazioni di improvvisazione e persino di elaborazione estemporanea presenti in alcune Sinfonie di Rocco Greco. Sono queste fonti che ci permettono di gettare uno sguardo sui metodi didattici del tempo, di chiarire alcuni aspetti della prassi esecutiva e di valutare quanto l'improvvisazione fosse parte integrante della formazione del musicista di stampo italiano.

Non c'è dubbio che in un'epoca in cui gli approcci esecutivi peculiari di una tradizione potevano circolare e diffondersi quasi esclusivamente grazie a esecutori che ne padroneggiassero le tecniche e i principi, la presenza dei musicisti italiani in Francia contribuì in modo determinante allo sviluppo di una nuova estetica e un nuovo linguaggio.

---

[24]. Una delle numerose collezioni di duetti di Emanuele Barbella è apparsa nel CD *A Due Viole*, esecutori: Stefano Marcocchi e Simone Laghi, Passacaille, 2018 (PAS 1046).

[25]. Sulla didattica del violoncello e sul repertorio di duetti si veda anche il saggio di Giovanna Barbati in questo volume.

[26]. Su questa collezione e in generale sull'attività di Supriani, si veda OLIVIERI 2009.

[27]. Ho presentato uno studio preliminare di questo manoscritto, conservato presso la biblioteca del Conservatorio di Napoli, alla *16th International Baroque Conference* tenutasi a Salisburgo nel 2014. Ho in preparazione un contributo dedicato a questo manoscritto e alla sua importanza nell'ambito della tradizione violoncellistica napoletana.

Naturalezza o artificio

Negli anni centrali del XVIII secolo si sviluppa la figura del musicista virtuoso che fa dell'arte improvvisativa uno dei cardini dell'avanzamento tecnico e del successo presso un più ampio pubblico. L'incontro di questa tradizione tutta italiana con l'ambiente culturale francese e la sua apertura a fenomeni sociali e di promozione musicale che erano invece in gran parte sconosciuti in Italia contribuiranno alla trasformazione del linguaggio musicale verso i *goûts réunis* e verso gli esiti dello stile galante, e produrranno nel secolo successivo la straordinaria fioritura della figura del solista virtuoso. È di fronte al sorgere e all'inarrestabile sviluppo di questo fenomeno e a partire dalle considerazioni sulle peculiarità dello stile strumentale italiano, che intellettuali e musicisti francesi del XVIII secolo avanzano le prime riflessioni sui caratteri costitutivi dell'improvvisazione e sul suo legame con il virtuosismo musicale.

Bibliografia

BETTINELLI 1799
BETTINELLI, Saverio. *Dell'entusiasmo delle belle arti*, 24 voll., Venezia, Adolfo Cesare, vol. I, 1799.

BROSSARD 1703
BROSSARD, Sébastien de. *Dictionaire de musique*, Parigi, Ballard, 1703.

CASTIGLIONE 1528
CASTIGLIONE, Baldassarre. *Il libro del Cortegiano*, Firenze, per li heredi di Philippo Giunta, 1528.

CRESCIMBENI 1708
CRESCIMBENI, Giovan Mario. *Arcadia*, Roma, 1708.

CRESCIMBENI 1731
ID. *Dell'istoria della volgar poesia*, vol. I, lib. III, Venezia, Basegio 1731.

CRESCIMBENI 1806
ID. *Storia dell'Accademia degli Arcadi, Istituita in Roma l'anno 1690 per la coltivazione delle scienze delle lettere umane e della poesia... pubblicata l'anno 1712 d'ordine della medesima adunanza*, Londra, Thomas Becket, 1804.

FINOTTI 2003
FINOTTI, Fabio. 'Il canto delle Muse: improvvisazione e poetica della voce', in: *Corilla Olimpica e la poesia del Settecento europeo. Atti del convegno tenuto in occasione delle celebrazioni del secondo centenario della morte di Maria Maddalena Morelli (Pistoia, Antico Palazzo dei Vescovi, 21-22 ottobre 2000)*, a cura di Moreno Fabbri. Pistoia, M&m, 2003, pp. 31-42.

FOSCOLO 1826
FOSCOLO, Ugo. 'The Women of Italy', in: *London Magazine*, VI/22 (ottobre 1826), pp. 204-219.

GIULI 2009
GIULI, Paola. 'Monsters of Talent: Fame and Reputation of Women Poets in Arcadia', in: *Italy's*

Eighteenth-Century Gender and Culture in the Age of the Gran Tour, a cura di Paula Findlen, Wendy Wassyng Roworth e Catherine M. Sama, Stanford (CA), Stanford University Press, 2009.

Le Cerf 1705-1706
Le Cerf de la Viéville, Jean-Laurent. *Comparaison de la musique italienne et de la musique françoise*, (1705-1706), ripr. facs., Ginevra, Minkoff Reprint, 1972.

Monteclair 1736
Monteclair, Michel Pignolet de. *Principes de musique*, Parigi, s.n., 1736.

Moser 1923
Moser, Andreas. *Geschichte des Violinspiels*, Berlino, Max Hesse, 1923.

Nestola 2004
Nestola, Barbara. 'Giovanni Antonio Guido e il *petit motet* all'inizio del Settecento: dal *dessus* al violino solo', in: *Florilegium Musicae*, a cura di Patrizia Radicchi e Michael Burden, 2 voll., Pisa, ETS, 2004, vol. II, pp. 737-755.

Olivieri 1996
Olivieri, Guido. '«Si suona a Napoli!» I rapporti fra Napoli e Parigi e i primordi della Sonata in Francia', in: *Studi Musicali*, XXV/1-2 (1996), pp. 409-427.

Olivieri 2009
Id. 'Cello Playing and Teaching in Eighteenth-Century Naples: F. P. Supriani's *Principij da imparare a suonare il violoncello*', in: *Performance Practice: Issues and Approaches*, a cura di Timothy D. Watkins, Ann Arbour (MI), Steglein Publishing, 2009, pp. 109-136.

Olivieri *in corso di stampa*
Id. 'Forgotten Virtuosi: The Violin Tradition in 17th- and 18th-Century Naples', in: *The Italian Violin Tradition: 1650-1850*, a cura di Simone Laghi, Bologna, Ut Orpheus Edizioni, in preparazione (Ad Parnassum Studies, 13).

Piani 1975
Piani, Giovanni Antonio. *Sonatas for Violin Solo and Violoncello with Cembalo. Opera Prima*, a cura di Barbara Garvey Jackson, Madison (WI), A-R Editions, 1975 (Recent Researches in the Music of the Baroque Era, 20).

Raguenet 1709
Raguenet, Francois. *A Comparison between the French and Italian Musick and Operas, Translated from the French with some Remarks*, (1709), edizione in facsimile, Farnborough, Gregg International Publishers, 1968.

Rousseau 1687
Rousseau, Jean. *Traité de la viole*, Parigi, Christoph Ballard, 1687.

Rousseau 1768
Rousseau, Jean-Jacques. *Dictionnaire de musique*, Parigi, Duchesne, 1768.

SACALUGA 1968
SACALUGA, Servando. 'Diderot, Rousseau, et la querelle musicale de 1752: nouvelle mise au point', in: *Diderot Studies*, X (1968), pp. 133-173.

SANGUINETTI 2012
SANGUINETTI, Giorgio. *The Art of Partimento: History, Theory and Practice*, Oxford, Oxford University Press, 2012.

TREITLER 2015
TREITLER, Leo. 'Speaking of the I-Word', in: *Archiv für Musikwissenschaft*, LXXII/1 (2015), pp. 1-18.

ADAGIO DE MR. TARTINI. VARIÉ DE PLUSIEURS FAÇONS DIFFÉRENTES, TRÈS UTILES AUX PERSONNES QUI VEULENT APPRENDRE À FAIRE DES TRAITS SOUS CHAQUE NOTTE DE L'HARMONIE...

Neal Zaslaw
(Cornell University, Ithaca, NY)

GIUSEPPE TARTINI was perhaps the most influential teacher of violinists of the mid-eighteenth century. Violinists traveled to Padua from around Europe to apprentice at his so-called Scuola degli nazioni. During five decades of training violinists, Tartini developed an arsenal of teaching materials, which (with the exception of his *L'arte del arco*[1]) neither he nor anyone else published during his lifetime. Some of the pedagogical materials circulated in manuscript, as attested to by Leopold Mozart's unacknowledged borrowings from Tartini's *Regole per arrivare a saper ben suonar il violino* in his *Versuch einer gründlichen Violinschule* (1756)[2]. After Tartini's death in 1770, a few of his former students did publish, or allow to be published, things they possessed from their time with him. Two such posthumous publications are well known: the *Lettera alla signora Maddalena Lombardini*[3], dated «Padova li 5. Marzo 1760» and published in 1770, as well as

---

[1]. PINELLI 174?; RISM T 277 (17 variations). An expanded, separate edition of *L'arte del arco* — Paris, Leclerc, [1758]; RISM T 278 (38 variations) — can be consulted at <http://imslp.org/wiki/L'arte_del_arco_%28Tartini%2C_Giuseppe%29>, accessed November 2018. An even more expanded, posthumous edition (Rome, Mareschalchi, 178?; RISM T 279) contains 50 variations. For details see SELETSKY 1989.

[2]. PETROBELLI 1968, pp. 1-17.

[3]. The *Lettera alla signora Maddalena Lombardini* attracted international interest, judging by frequent republications and translations: TARTINI 1770; *Una importante lezione per i suonatori di violino* (Bologna, Sassi, 1770); *Una importante lezione per i suonatori di VIOLINO* (Milan, Galeazzi, 1770); *Una importante lezione per i suonatori di VIOLINO* (Venice, Colombani, 1770); *A Letter from the Late Signor Tartini to Signora Lombardini* [...], translated by Charles Burney (London, Bremner, 1771); 'Lettre de Feu Tartini à Madame Madeleine Lombardini [...]', translated by Antoine-Léonard Thomas, in: *Journal de Musique*, II (1771), pp. 15ff.; *A Letter from the Late Signor Tartini to Signora Lombardini* [...], translated by Charles Burney (London, Bremner, 1779); *Brief des Joseph Tartini an Magdalena Lombardini* [...], translated by Johann Adam Hiller (Leipzig, Dykische Buchhandlung, 1784); *Brief an Magdalena Lombardini, enthaltend eine wichtige Lection für*

a French translation of the *Regole* as *Traité des agrémens de la musique*, the following year[4]. A third instructional item, which was and has remained controversial at least in part because it was believed to have been published for the first time only in 1798, provides the impetus for this essay. This is the

> ADAGIO de M[r]. TARTINI. Varié de plusieurs façons différentes, très utiles aux personnes qui veulent apprendre à faire des traits sous chaque notte de l'Harmonie. On pourra remplir les lacunes qui se trouvent dans les variations par une des lignes au dessus et au dessous et par des traits arbitraires. [( ]Prix 5[tt].)
> Celle Seconde Édition est Gravé D'après les soins de J. B. CARTIER. Chez Decombe, Editeur. Luthier, Facteur d'Instruments en tout genre, M[aît]r[e] de Musique et Professeur, Successeur de Salomon. Place de l'École près le Pont-neuf N°. 45 à Paris.
> Gravé Par Melle. Potel F[em]. Callaudaux[5].

This text, presented above as if transcribed from an ordinary title page, is in fact spread across the tops of the four pages of a folio-size, gatefold score inserted in J. B. Cartier's *L'Art du violon*[6] (see ILLS. 1a-d).

In the nearly two-and-a-half centuries since the first edition of the «Adagio varié» was published, its reception has been almost entirely negative. Paul Brainard, the formidable cataloguer of Tartini's sonatas, believed it most likely inauthentic[7] and many other violinists and scholars have agreed. Questions have been raised not only about the publication's authenticity but also about its possible utility. Here are four such questions.

---

die Violinspieler, translated by Leopold Rohrmann (Hannover, Pochwitz, 1786); *Un'importante lezione per i suonatori di violino* (Venezia, Paolo Marescalchi, 1799); 'Tartini's Brief an Madame B** [*sic*] seine Schülerin', in: *Allgemeine musikalische Zeitung*, VI/9 (30 November 1803), cols. 134-138. See BERDES 1994 and TENI 2007, p. 124.

[4]. TARTINI 1771.

[5]. Missing diacritical marks supplied by N.Z. «Adagio by Mr. Tartini. Varied in several different fashions, most useful to persons who wish to learn to make variations upon each note of the harmony. One can fill in the blank spaces found in the variations from the staves above and below, and by arbitrary variations. This second edition is engraved through the good offices of J. B. Cartier. Available at the premises of [Jacques-François] Decombe, publisher, luthier, maker of every sort of musical instrument, music-master and professor, in succession to [Jean Baptiste Dehaye] Salomon. Place de l'École near the Pont-neuf, No. 45, Paris. Engraved by Mlle. Potel, wife of Callaudaux». <http://hz.imslp.info/files/imglnks/usimg/b/bc/IMSLP333435-PMLP538968-lartduviolonoucoooocart_cartier.pdf>, last 4 images, accessed November 2018.

[6]. «L'Art du violon, ou Collection choisie dans les sonates des écoles italienne, françois et allemande, précédée d'un abrégé des principes pour cette instrument» (1st ed.: Paris, Decombe, [1798]); RISM, Series BII, p. 100).

[7]. BRAINARD 1975, p. xl and 58: «La tesi di Arnold Schering, che considerava tali variazioni come spurie, è probabilmente corretta»; cfr. *Sammelbände der Internationalen Musikgesellschaft*, VI (1905-1906), pp. 365ff.

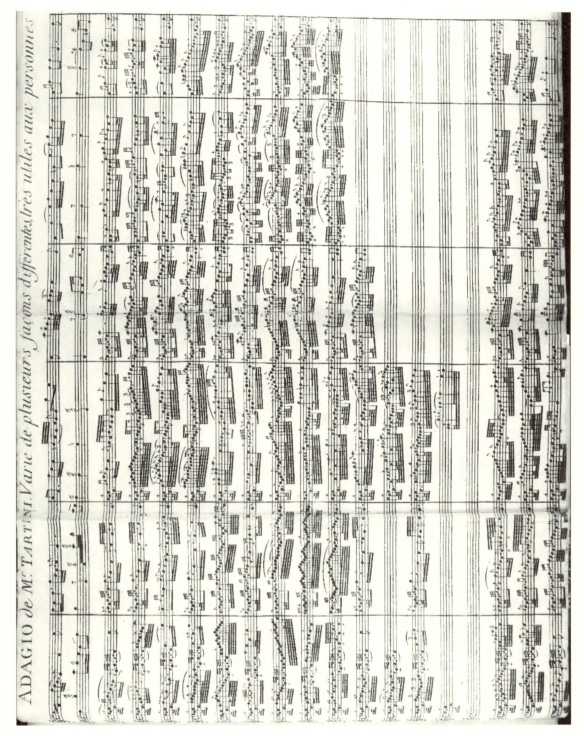

Ills. 1a–d: Tartini, *Adagio varié* from Cartier, *L'Art du violon*.

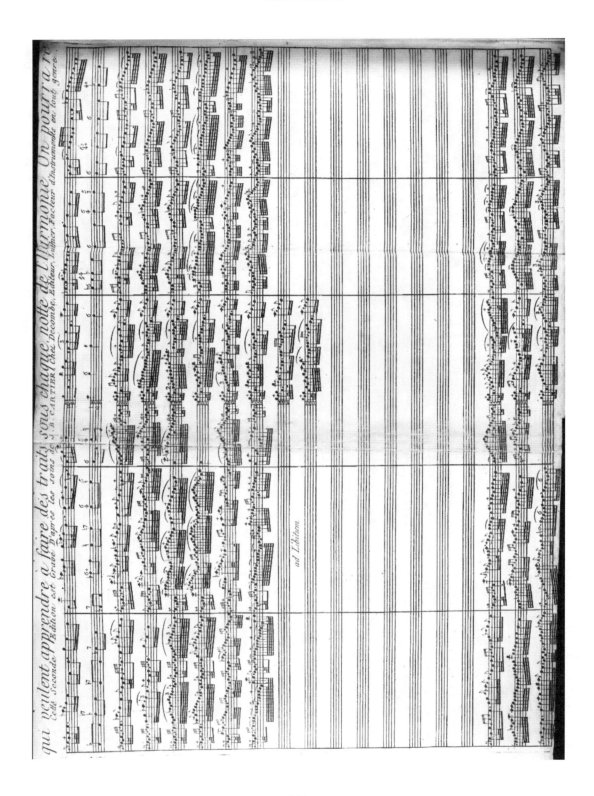

Adagio de Mr. Tartini

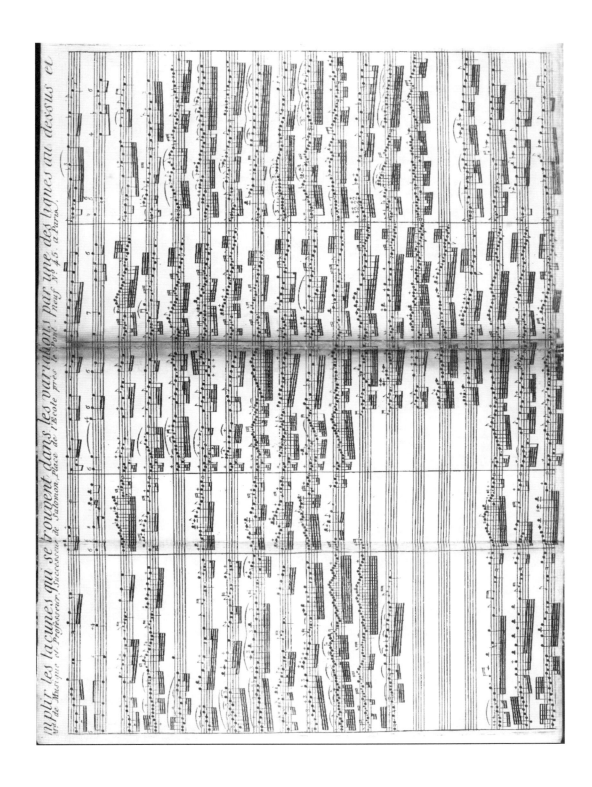

Why Should a Publication that Appeared 26 Years after Tartini's Death, and for Which There Were Apparently No Earlier Sources, Be Accepted as Genuine?

Jean-Baptiste Cartier did not reveal his source for the *Adagio varié*, remarking only that, «Ce Recueil contient surtout une pièce que j'ai le Bonheur d'avoir sauvé d'une perte presque certaine: c'est le chef-d'oeuvre appellé la feuille de Tartini»[8]. Yet the *Adagio varié* did have an earlier publication history, one that can be documented to a few years after Tartini's death — in other words, to the period when Tartini's students made available their maestro's *Lettera alla signora Maddalena Lombardini* and his *Traité des agréments*. Tracing earlier sources of the *Adagio varié* is the concern of the rest of this essay.

Given that the *Adagio varié* as inserted into Cartier's *L'Art du violon* bears the indication 'second edition', there presumably was a first edition. Robert Eitner[9] believed that he had located a reference to that item, for sale at the antiquarian dealer Leo Liepmannssohn. Eitner's imprecise reference can be traced to number 616 of a Liepmannssohn catalogue of 1872[10], which reads:

> Tartini. Adagio de M. Tartini, varié de plusieurs façons différentes, très-utiles aux personnes qui veulent apprendre à faire des traits sous chaque note de l'harmonie. Gravé par Mlle Potel, f^{em} Callaudaux. *Paris, s.d.* (vers 1750).
>
> 5 fr.
>
> Quatre feuilles in-fol. oblong, qui sont collées ensemble pour former un seul tableau de plus de deux mètres de longueur. Chaque variation (elles sont au nombre de 17), est contenue dans une seule ligne. Elles sont places les unes sous les autres, mesure par mesure, «pour qu'on puisse remplir les lacunes qui se trouvent dans les variations par une des lignes au-dessus ou au-dessous». *Fort rare.*

Liepmannssohn's «vers 1750» is mistaken: «Melle Potel, wife of Monsieur Callaudaux» was active as an engraver in Paris no earlier than the mid-1780s[11].

A copy of the *Adagio varié* reproduced in Alberto Bachmann's *Les Grands violonistes du passé*[12] on which the notation 'second edition' is absent was certainly printed from the same Cartier/Potel engraved plates, however in this exemplar the texts in the upper margin were applied in a free calligraphic hand, and Potel's name is nowhere to be seen. I suspect that Bachmann's facsimile may have been tampered with in production and is unreliable, although unfortunately I have not yet been able to investigate this. Bachmann's exemplar was probably not the putative 'first edition' implied by Cartier's 'second edition'[13].

As Cartier's publisher Decombe prepared to issue *L'Art du violon*, he solicited subscriptions in the press. Among the publication's principal attractions Decombe chose

---

[8]. CARTIER 1798, p. i. «Above all, this collection contains an item that I have had the good fortune to save from almost certain loss: the masterpiece known as 'Tartini's Sheet'».

[9]. 'Tartini', in: EITNER 1904-1916.

[10]. LIEPMANNSSOHN 1872, p. 43.

[11]. RISM, Series A/I, index of engravers, pp. 237-238: Mme Callaudaux *née* Potel died in 1811.

[12]. BACHMANN 1913, 2 unnumbered folded leaves between pp. 316 and 317.

[13]. BACHMANN indicates that the source for his facsimile of the *Adagio varié* was «B. Conserv. de Paris» (= F-Pc); according to RISM, vol. BII *Recueils*, F-Pc owns two copies of Cartier's anthology, which I have not yet been able to examine.

to single out «[...] le fameux *Adagio*, connu sous le nom de *Feuille de Tartini* [...]. Cet Ouvrage [Cartier's entire volume], qui paroîtra dans le courant du mois prochain, coûtera 20 liv., y compris le *Feuille de Tartini*. Les personnes qui souscriront jusqu'au moment où il paroîtra, ne paieront le tout que 12 liv.»[14].

A possible clue to the earlier origin of the *Adagio varié* emerges from an edition published in 1802 in Vienna by Giovanni Cappi (RISM T 289). The beginning of the violin part of Cappi's *Caprices, ou Étude du violon dediés aux Amateurs par Tartini* is labeled: «Adagio. Con Variazioni. Del Sig: Tartini»[15]. Unlike Cartier's edition, where the 17 sets of ornaments are stacked vertically below Tartini's original melody and bassline, Cappi's is organized as a traditional set of 17 variations, presented sequentially. Assuming (as I do) that Cartier's vertical arrangement reproduced Tartini's original concept, the horizontal one reproduced by Cappi can be seen as following Cartier's instructions «remplir les lacunes qui se trouvent dans les variations par une des lignes au dessus et au dessous», even if not actually by «des traits arbitraires».

Knowing that Cappi acquired the musical holdings of the Viennese publisher Artaria & Comp. in 1801[16], I thought to investigate Artaria's music catalogues, where I discovered in his firm's supplement to its 1779 music catalogue the following item[17]:

> Tartini. Adagio. Varié de plusieurs façons differentes, tres utiles aux personnes qui veulent apprendre à faire des traits sous chaque note de l'Harmonie. On pourra remplir les lacunes qui se trouvent dans les variations, par une des lignes au dessus & au dessous ou par des traits arbitraries.
> Paris   Op. — / 1 fl. / 48 kr.

This item reveals that Artaria's offering was derived from a Paris edition that, unlike Cappi's but like Cartier's, presented the 17 variations stacked up one below

---

[14]. *Journal typographique et bibliographique*, no. 4 (9 brumaire an VI [= 30 October 1797]), pp. 31-32: «[...]the famous *Adagio*, known by the name *Tartini's Leaf* [...]. This work [*L'Art du violon*], which will appear next month, will cost 20 pounds, including *Tartini's Leaf*. Those who subscribe before the volume's appearance, will pay only 12 pounds for all of it». Decombe subsequently (in the same journal [no. 18, 28 Pluviôse, an 6 = 16 February 1798, pp. 143-144]), informed his subscribers that Cartier's volume would be ready in a fortnight. Decombe subsequently (in the same journal [no. 18, 28 Pluviôse, an 6 = 16 February 1798], pp. 143-144), informed his subscribers that Cartier's volume would be ready in a fortnight.

[15]. RISM T 289 and TT 289a. <http://imslp.org/wiki/Caprices_%28Tartini%2C_Giuseppe%29>, accessed November 2018. Cappi advertised this edition in the *Wiener Zeitung*, XLI (22 May 1802), p. 1927: «Tartini, Caprices ou Etude du Viol. 1 fl. 30».

[16]. WEINMANN 1967, pp. iii-viii.

[17]. BIBA – FUCHS 2006, p. 45; RIDGEWELL 2007. I thank Rupert Ridgewell for his kind assistance in the preparation of this article.

another[18]. So far I haven't found a Paris edition of the *Adagio varié* from 1779 or earlier. Note, however, that between the late 1750s and 1768 the publisher Le Duc advertised otherwise unidentified 'Variations' by Tartini[19]. Given that Tartini's *L'arte dell'arco* was readily available from other Parisian publishers and that some years later Le Duc published his own edition of *L'arte dell'arco*, clearly identified as such (RISM T 279), these unidentified variations published between the late 1750s and 1768 may have been what Artaria offered for sale in 1779.

TABLE 1 proposes a timeline for the *Adagio varié* that, if correct, traces the work's earliest dissemination to no later than 1779 — in other words, to the decade during which Tartini's students published two other items of their maestro's pedagogical materials[20].

TABLE 1: A HYPOTHETICAL PUBLICATION HISTORY OF TARTINI'S *ADAGIO VARIÉ*[21]

late 1750s-1768	Paris: Le Duc advertises unidentified 'Variations' by Tartini (no copy known)
1779	Vienna: Artaria advertises a Paris edition of the *Adagio varié* (no copy known)
ca. 1796	Paris: Decombe's 1st printing of the *Adagio varié*, sold separately (RISM TT 262a)
1798	Paris: 2nd printing of same, a separate gatefold folio inserted in Cartier's *L'Art du violon*
1802	Vienna, Cappi, 1802 (RISM T 289)

WAS THE UNORNAMENTED VERSION OF THE *ADAGIO* REALLY BY TARTINI?

This question was raised only prior to the publication of Paul Brainard's catalogue of Tartini's sonatas[22]. Had the skeptics been more diligent, they could have satisfied themselves that the unornamented movement was to be found in Tartini's readily available Op. 2, as the first movement of a Sonata in F major, No. 5 in the Paris edition (Le Cène, [1743];

---

[18]. As an aside, I wonder if Tartini associated the number 17 with a particular symbolic or mystical meaning, given that the first edition of his *L'arte del arco* also contained 17 variations.

[19]. DEVRIÈS – LESURE 1979, plates 131-133.

[20]. Tartini pupils active in Paris in the 1770s included Pierre La Houssaye, André Noël Pagin, the no-given-name Petit, and possibly also Pietro Denis, responsible for the French translation of Tartini's treatise on ornamentation.

[21]. RISM Series A/1 T 290 bears a passe-partout title page: «Caprices ou étude du violon, Paris, Auguste Le Duc & Co.». This served in the early 19th century as the title page for sonata movements excerpted from Cartier's *L'Art du violon*, not however for the *Adagio varié*, whose engraved plates were too large to be used in that format. The passe-partout's annotation, «gravé d'après l'édition originale d'Amsterdam de J. J. Hummel», refers to Hummel's much earlier editions of Tartini's Opp. 1 and 2 violin sonatas (RISM T 242, T 252); Hummel never published the *Adagio varié* (JOHANSSON 1972). The Sidney Cox Library of Music and Dance at Cornell University, holds an exemplar of the passe-partout title identical to that cited as RISM T 290; it contains movements from Tartini's Opp. 1 and 2.

[22]. For instance, by BACHMANN 1913.

RISM T 251) and No. 4 in the London edition (Walsh, [1746] RISM T 256). While Brainard of course knew that the movement itself was genuine, he remained among those who questioned the authenticity of the 17 ornamented versions[23].

Don't the Bizarrely Dense Variations of the *Adagio varié* Seem more a Parody of Late-baroque Ornamentation than a Potential Rosetta Stone Intended to Convey and Preserve a Fading Tradition?

Cartier's *Traité du violon* was an attempt to honor his forebears by means of a grand anthology of 18th-century violin music from around Western Europe. His motivation was to provide a resource for young violinists, especially those whose teachers lacked access to a large music collection. That motivation may have been intensified by concern that the French Revolution was sweeping away some good old things along with the bad old ones, inflicting injury upon French musical culture. He was certainly announcing to the world a belief that the Paris Conservatoire was then the center of Europe's musical universe. Perhaps he regarded Tartini's ornaments as an instructive 'blast from the past'.

In any case, surviving ornamentation for many 18th-century adagios are just as dense as those for Tartini's *Adagio varié* — for instance, some of the ornamented versions of the adagios of Corelli's Op. 5 violin Sonatas[24]. The same can be said for a stand-alone instruction manual for ornamenting adagios by the Italian violinist and composer Carlo Zuccari[25]. And perhaps most tellingly, dozens of manuscripts containing a wealth of just-as-elaborately-ornamented adagios from Tartini's own sonatas and concertos survive in his hand and the hands of his students[26]. In some musical circles north of the Alps, Italian adagios were much valued, even if the training required for their idiomatic performance was not as easy to come by there as it was on the Italian peninsula. This is revealed, for instance, by the fact that most surviving notated sets of ornaments for Corelli's adagios originated in the north, as did the already-mentioned instruction manual for adagios by Italian violinist Carlo Zuccari. Consider, too, a rather defensive letter from one of Tartini's most successful students, Pietro Nardini (1722-1793), writing to his own former pupil Joseph Otter (1760-1836), whose patrons had rejected copies of Nardini's string quartets:

---

[23]. See note 7. Tartini's autograph manuscript of Op. 2 is in F-Pn, non-autograph manuscripts are in D-B, I-AN, I-Rsc, I-Vnm, and B-Bc; published editions are available in many libraries. The movement is labeled *Grave* in some 18th-century sources, *Adagio* in others.

[24]. Zaslaw 1996, pp. 95-115; Zaslaw 2015, pp. 179-192. See also Hogwood – Mark 2013.

[25]. Zuccari 1760.

[26]. For the largest collection of manuscripts containing ornaments for Tartini's violin sonatas see Duckles – Elmer 1963, especially pp. 380-384; also Brainard 1975. For ornamented concerto movements see Canale 2011.

Adagio de Mr. Tartini

> When I promised my quartets, I didn't specify how many movements they would have, because that decision is the composer's prerogative; and you know very well that my adagios aren't suitable for quartets, since they belong to another genre. Therefore, that excuse [lack of adagios] from those who promised to buy them [the quartets] doesn't seem reasonable to me. Maybe they didn't like them [the quartets], or maybe they didn't know how to perform them. [I reject their excuses] because I've sent many copies to Italy, Germany, England and other countries, and no-one raised this problem with me[27].

But Wasn't Tartini Understood to Have Rejected this Elaborate Style of Ornamentation When, after Long Exploration and Experimentation, He Believed that He Had Discovered 'Truth and Beauty' in a Simplified, Cantabile Approach to Composition and Performance?

The most frequently cited accounts of Tartini's reforms of his aesthetic date from after his death, from obituaries, reminiscences and tributes to Tartini written by people who had known him. There is, however, an account from his lifetime, which is, in effect, an extended interview of him at age 66 written down as it took place — that is, a dozen years before he died. This account was recorded in the travel diary of Achilles Ryhiner-Delon (1731-1788), a Swiss violinist who spent three weeks in Padua in the summer of 1758[28].

Table 2: Tartini's Artistic Evolution as Reported in Ryhiner-Delon's Diary
with words rendered in bold-face font by NZ

Key to numbers added by NZ
[1] = extreme technical difficulties the principal goal
[2] = impasse
[3] = rebellion against technical difficulties, and opting for radical simplicity
[4] = simplicity overloaded with ornaments
[5] = realization that full success requires aspects of **1** and **2**

---

[27]. Pietro Nardini, Letter to Joseph Otter, 27 May 1783, Paris, BNF, Richelieu VM BOB 21584. Laghi 2017, pp. 62-63: «Quando io ho promesso i miei quartetti non ho specificato di quanti tempi dovevano essere, perché ciò appartiene alla volontà del compositore, ed ella sà molto bene, che i miei adagj non sono proprj per i quartetti, essendo questi di altro genere; onde questa scusa non mi pare a proposito per quelli che Le hanno promesso di pigliarli: potrebbe darsi che non piacessero, o potrebbe anche darsi che ciò dipendesse dal non li sapere eseguire, perché avendone dati tanti fuori, sì in Italia come in Germania[,] in Inghilterra ed in altri Luoghi, nessuno mi ha fatto queste difficoltà». English translation by Simone Laghi.

[28]. Translated from Staehelin 1978, pp. 251-274.

I [Rhyner] formed [...] a personal acquaintanceship [...] with the famous violinist, Mr. Tartini. I visited him several times to discuss music. He assured me that, even though he had, during his lifetime and right up to the present, continually investigated the **[5] True Manner** of violin-playing, he nonetheless succeeded only recently; that in his youth he had believed **[1] Beauty inhered in difficulties**, but that he discovered he had been wrong; that he had fallen into a manner **[1] overloaded with ornaments**; that [he discovered] much later that that had led to **[2] Falsehood**, that thereafter he had for some time **[2] truly been stuck, not knowing what to do**. He had thought about the idea of trying the **[3] totally simple and completely unified manner**, but it hadn't seemed to him worthy or capable of sustaining his reputation.

Finally, [however,] not having a better idea of what to do, he undertook to put it to the test by trying **[3]** [the **totally simple and completely unified manner**], and he quickly perceived that not only did the **[3] Truly Beautiful** and **Good Taste** reside therein, but also that **[3] this simplicity, this unity**, was deceptive; that it was even more difficult than any other manner; that for those who played **[1] technically difficult pieces**, difficulties excused other defects; that everyone judged such a person a great violinist, but that they pleased only a very small number of people — and perhaps no-one; that on the other hand, those who, **[4] without creating extremely difficult things, had overloaded the piece with embellishments**, had taken the work's meaning and obscured it to such an extent that one no longer knew what it meant; that he had compared such people to authors who filled their writings with parentheses to such a degree that one lost the meaning of the text.

«These sorts of musicians **[4]** have yet another advantage over the first **[3]**», he continued, «They **conceal many of their weaknesses with ornaments**, and earn more applause. But neither of these two sorts of people **[3 or 4]** is capable of playing consistently [in a simple manner], which they consider unworthy of them».

«In the end I believe that the one and only **[5] true Good Taste** comprises a unified, clear tone, **instrumental** [«sonant»] **in one passage and singing** [«chantant»] **in another.** A sigh, a trill, a passing tone, a detached bow stroke, another slurred, a mordent; finally, all those different manners of varying the sounds that can be employed in the proper time and place; and even though that is necessary to impart expression to what one plays, it is [likewise] necessary to make use of it [the instrumental style] only in spots where absolutely required in order to relieve the simplicity of the unified, cantabile sounds».

«There are some movements in which **[5]** it is absolutely necessary to play in an **instrumental style**, and others in a **singing style**; the latter, more flattering to the ear than the previous, is consequently judged yet finer in **Good Taste**. This is the very reason that instruments with fixed pitches — like the harpsichord, lute, harp, zither, guitar, mandolin, and others — are considered inferior to others that are not so fixed. You cannot play **cantabile** on the former instruments, since creating cantabile is possible only during sustained sounds that you can hold as long as you please while nuancing them a bit; on the harpsichord, etc., you aren't able to sustain and are forced to repeat notes».

«Once I had discovered **[5] Good Taste**, I studied it with the utmost patience; it gave me more trouble than any other [study], and at the present moment I cannot say that I am satisfied with myself» [...]

To return to Signore Tartini: here is how I [Ryhiner] spent my time with him. He's a bit of a philosophe, but one of those likeable philosophes, gentle, obliging and very sociable. He doesn't object if you beg him to play. He plays best especially in the adagios. It is true that he's no longer in his prime, but that doesn't prevent him from being the most capable and the best suited person in the world for teaching. His method is excellent; he has a surprising amount of patience and attention. He doesn't seek to advance himself, but he strives to bring honor to his students. I don't know what about me merited a personal acquaintanceship with this man; he was pleased to instruct me. He had me play an entirely easy solo for him without accompanying me. He wanted to hear me all alone. He followed every note with his eyes. Once I had played in as unified and neat manner as I could, he had the graciousness to praise the good disposition that I had for this instrument and even, as far as he had seen, for music in general.

Dounias's foundational catalogue of Tartini's concertos argued at length for a division of Tartini's career into an apprenticeship followed by three canonical, Beethovenian biographical periods[29], and many other writers have followed suit. If one superimposes on Dounias's tripartite schema what Tartini told Achilles Ryhiner in 1758, something like TABLE 3 results. However, even though Ryhiner's account can readily be mapped onto three imagined biographical periods, real lives as lived seldom (perhaps almost never?) sort themselves into such tidy Trinitarian patterns.

TABLE 3: HYPOTHETICAL PROGRESSION OF TARTINI'S ARTISTIC DEVELOPMENT

Youth
Short 'Corelli' bow/difficulties valued
Suonabile

★★★

***Crisis 1: encounter with Francesco Maria Veracini (July 1716)
leading to a retreat to reformulate his technique***
First flowering = long 'Tartini' bow/simplicity rejected
Suonabile[30]

★★★

---

[29]. DOUNIAS 1935, pp. 33-232.
[30]. DURANTE 2017, p. 23.

Crisis 2: Self doubt
«Lacking a better idea of what to do...»
Truth and Beauty/Imitation of Nature
Cantabile

✴✴✴

Crisis 3: Injury to bow arm
Suonabile and Cantabile both essential

Tartini's own binary formulations of his ideas about musical styles and concepts are also troubling; these are matters for which mixtures, permeable boundaries and continua are what one requires (see TABLE 4). Thankfully, Sergio Durante has recently provided a finely-nuanced debunking of such historiographical tactics[31].

Some light may be shed on Tartini's self-fashioning during the period when he favored suonabile, from remarks he made in 1739 or 1740 to the French amateur musician Charles de Brosses. According to de Brosses, Tartini complained about

> [...] [an] abuse in which the composers of instrumental music want to meddle in creating vocal music and *vice versa*. «These two species», he said to me, «are so different that music proper to one can hardly be proper to the other; each person must remain within the bounds of his talent. I have», he said, «been asked to work for the theaters of Venice, and I never wanted to do it, knowing that a throat is not the neck of a violin»[32].

Do Tartini's binaries may reflect something about the culture of his time or about his idiosyncratic ways of thinking? Does the prevalence of binary thinking reveal something behind the opaque prose style of his non-performance-oriented theoretical writings? Or could these binaries be a manifestation of his well-documented fascination with Platonic reasoning? After all, the best-known likeness of Tartini portrays him in an oval hovering above his symbolic attributes: violin, bow, score by Corelli, and learned tomes by Zarlino and Plato (ILL. 2).

TABLE 4: TARTINI'S BINARIES
(ALSO KNOWN AS FALSE DICHOTOMIES)

Allegro	Adagio
Artifice	Nature
Ugliness	Beauty
Bad taste	Good taste

---

[31]. *Ibidem*, pp. 70-74.
[32]. BROSSES 1858, vol. II, pp. 360-361.

Adagio de Mr. Tartini

Suonabile	Cantabile
Difficulty	Simplicity
Early style	Late style
False	True
Inferior (harpsichord)	Superior (violin)

Ill. 2: engraving by Carlo Calcinotto (Padua, 1761) after an anonymous oil painting in the Conservatorio musicale G. B. Martini, Bologna.

In Tartini's defense, however, he did in the end conclude (at least according to Ryhiner) that «the one and only true Good Taste comprises a unified, clear tone, instrumental [*sonant*] in one passage and singing [*chantant*] in another», in that way adumbrating in a flexible manner the fading of baroque notions of unified affect and the concomitant rise of a style that is more favorable to juxtaposing contrasting elements in the same movement.

***

In a program note about Tartini's *Adagio varié*, the baroque violinist Patrick Oliva wrote something that captures, as well as anything I've read on the subject, my understanding of the Maestro's ideas about ornamentation in general and the *Adagio varié* in particular:

> Giuseppe Tartini's ornamentation [...] combines Corelli's Italian diminutions [actually «free ornamentation», not diminutions] with the application of agréments to notes pushed to the extreme [...]. «L'Adagio orné de plusieurs manières différentes» [...] is subjected to seventeen sets of ornamentation, one more exuberant than another. Mordents, trills, appoggiaturas literally invade the melodic line. Behind this overabundance one notices a certain logic in the manner of varying the different passages. Like his contemporaries, Tartini employs a rich system of ornamentation. Certain characteristic figures appear in a recurrent manner [...][33].

As one example of what might be learned about 18th-century ornamentation from close study of Tartini's teaching materials, I gloss the final sentence of this excerpt from Oliva's note. Early in my own musical apprenticeship, I understood from remarks and performances by leading performers of 18th-century music that the norm when it came to ornamenting the three iterations of a rising melodic sequence was this: leave the first «come sta», ornament the second modestly, and then ornament the third more intensely. On the contrary, judged by his notated ornamentations, Tartini more often preferred to characterize the first iteration with a notable ornamental pattern, which he re-applied *verbatim* twice more, transposed[34]. This can be confirmed in many slow movements for which Tartini and his students have left us (sometimes multiple) ornamented versions.

---

[33]. «L'ornementation de Giuseppe Tartini [...] allie l'héritage des diminutions [recte: ornementation libre] italiennes de Corelli et une agrémentation des notes poussée à l'extrême [...]. L'Adagio orné de plusieurs manières différentes [...] extrait d'une des sonates du maître soumis à dix-sept ornementations toutes plus exubérantes les unes que les autres. Les mordants, les trilles, les appoggiatures envahissent littéralement la ligne mélodique. Derrière ce foisonnement, on observe une certaine logique dans la manière de varier les différents passages. Tartini, à l'instar de ses contemporains, utilise un riche système ornemental. Certaines figures caractéristiques apparaissent de manière récurrente [...]». OLIVA 2012, p. 4.

[34]. I owe this *aperçu* to my former student, Hannah Krall.

Therefore, what I had previously understood about ornamenting melodic sequences offers an illustration of an anachronistic, *ad hoc* «rule of thumb» hardened into an inviolable and misleading commandment.

The manuscripts of ornamented movements from Tartini's 'Scuola delle nazioni' (of which the *Adagio varié* is but a singularly curious example) preserve a large reservoir of patterns to be dipped into, mixed, matched and imitated, as occasions warrant. These idiomatic patterns ('riffs') can serve as models for decorating characteristic openings, middles and endings of phrases — especially cadences, of course — of late baroque music, to be learned by ear, by musical notation, by verbal suggestions, and incorporated into performers' conscious knowledge and muscle memory, thereby providing a mass of raw materials for spontaneous ornamentation and improvisation.

BIBLIOGRAPHY

BACHMANN 1913
BACHMANN, Alberto. *Les Grands violonistes du passé*, Paris, Fischbacher, 1913.

BERDES 1994
BERDES, Jane L. 'L'ultima allieva di Tartini: Maddalena Lombardini Sirmen', in: *Tartini, il tempo e le opere*, edited by Andrea Bombi and Maria Nevilla Massaro, Bologna, Il Mulino, 1994 (Temi e discussioni), pp. 213-225.

BIBA – FUCHS 2006
BIBA, Otto – FUCHS, Ingrid. *Die Sortimentskataloge der Musikalienhandlung Artaria Comp. in Wien aus dem Jahren 1779, 1780, 1782, 1785 und 1788*, Tutzing, Hans Schneider, 2006 (Veröffentlichungen des Archivs der Gesellschaft der Musikfreunde in Wien, 5).

BRAINARD 1975
BRAINARD, Paul. *Le sonate per violino di Giuseppe Tartini: catalogo tematico*, translated by Claudio Scimone, Padua, Accademia Tartiniana, 1975.

BROSSES 1858
BROSSES, Charles de. *Le president De Brosses en Italie: lettres familiéres écrit d'Italie en 1739 et 1740*, second edition edited by Romain Colomb, 2 vols., Paris, Dider, 1858.

CANALE 2011
CANALE, Margherita. *I concerti solistici di Giuseppe Tartini: testimoni, tradizione e catalogo tematico*, 2 vols. and 1 DVD_ROM, Ph.D. Diss., Padua, Università di Padova, 2011.

CARTIER 1798
CARTIER, Jean-Baptiste. *L'Art du violon, ou Division des écoles choisies dans les sonates itallienne, françoise et allemande, précédée d'un abrégé de principes pour cet instrument*, Paris, Decombe, 1798 [RISM Series BVI[1], p. 209].

DEVRIÈS – LESURE 1979
DEVRIÈS, Anik – LESURE, François. *Dictionnaire des éditeurs de musique français: des origins à environ 1820. 1.2: des origins à environ 1820: catalogues*, Geneva, Minkoff, 1979 (Archives de l'édition musicale française, 4/1).

DOUNIAS 1935
DOUNIAS, Minos. *Die Violinkonzerte Giuseppe Tartinis als Ausdruck einer Künstlerpersönlichkeit und einer Kulturepoche*, Munich, Salesianischen Offizin, 1935.

DUCKLES – ELMER 1963
DUCKLES, Vincent – ELMER, Minnie. *Thematic Catalog of a Manuscript Collection of Eighteenth-Century Italian Instrumental Music*, Berkeley-Los Angeles, University of California Press, 1963.

DURANTE 2017
DURANTE, Sergio. *Tartini, Padova, l'Europa*, Leghorn, Sillabe, 2017.

EITNER 1904-1916
EITNER, Robert. *Biographisch-bibliographisches Quellen-Lexikon der Musiker und Musikgelehrten der christlichen Zeitrechnung bis zur Mitte des neunzehnten Jahrhunderts*, 11 vols., Leipzig, Breitkopf & Härtel, ²1904-1916.

HOGWOOD – MARK 2013
HOGWOOD, Christopher – MARK, Ryan. *Corelli: Sonaten für Violine und Basso continuo, Op. 5, mit zeitgenössischen Verzierungen sowie einer Aussetzung für Tasteninstrument von Antonio Tonelli (1686-1765)*, 2 vols. Kassel, Bärenreiter, 2013 (Bärenreiter Urtext).

JOHANSSON 1972
JOHANSSON, Cari. *J. J. & B. Hummel. Music-Publishing and Thematic Catalogues*, 3 vols., Stockholm, Almquist & Wiksell, 1972.

LAGHI 2017
LAGHI, Simone. *Italian String Quartets and Late Eighteenth-Century London: Publication and Production. With a Critical Edition of the Quartets, Opp. 2 and 7 by Venanzio Rauzzini (1746-1810)*, Ph.D. Diss., Cardiff, Cardiff University, 2017.

LIEPMANNSSOHN 1872
LIEPMANNSSOHN, Leo. *Catalogue No. 37 de la Librairie ancienne et moderne*, Paris, s.n., [1872].

OLIVA 2012
OLIVA, Patrick. 'L'imaginaire galant. Aperçu de l'ornementation pour violon en Europe au milieu du xviiiᵉ siècle', 2012, <http://www.conservatoiredeparis.fr/fileadmin/user_upload/Voir-et-Ententre/jeunes_solistes/CREC_JS_livret_PatrickOliva_1712.pdf>, accessed November 2018.

PETROBELLI 1968
PETROBELLI, Pierluigi. *Giuseppe Tartini: le fonti biografiche*, Vienna, Universal, 1968 (Studi di musica veneta, 1).

PETROBELLLI 1992
ID. *Tartini, le sue idee e il suo tempo*, Lucca, LIM, 1992 (Musicalia, 5).

PINELLI 174?
PINELLI, Petronio. *Nouvelle étude pour le violon, ou Maniere de varier et orner un pièce dans le goût du cantabile italien, augmenté d'une Gavotte de Corelli, travailez et doublez par Mr. Giuseppe Tartini*, Paris, Boivin et al., [174?].

RIDGEWELL 2007
RIDGEWELL, Rupert. Review of BIBA – FUCHS 2006, in: *The Library: The Transactions of the Bibliographical Society*, VIII/3 (September 2007), pp. 345-347.

SELETZKY 1989
SELETZKY, Robert Eric. *Improvised Variation Sets for Short Dance Movements in Violin Repertory, circa 1680-1800, Exemplified in Period Sources for Corelli's Violin Sonatas, Opus 5*, D.M.A. Diss., Ithaca (NY), Cornell University, 1989 <https://newcatalog.library.cornell.edu/catalog/1666315>, accessed November 2018.

STAEHELIN 1978
STAEHELIN, Martin. 'Giuseppe Tartini über seine künstlerische Entwicklung. Ein unbekanntes Selbstzeugnis', in: *Archiv für Musikwissenschaft*, XXXV/4 (1978), pp. 251-274.

TARTINI 1770
TARTINI, Giuseppe. 'Lettera del Defunto Sig. G. T. alla Signora Maddalena Lombardini', in: *Europa Letteraria*, IV/1 (1 June 1770), pp. 70ff.

TARTINI 1771
ID. *Traité des agrémens de la musique*, French translation by Pietro [Pierre] Denis. Paris, l'auteur, 1771 [RISM Series BVI², p. 820].

TENI 2007
TENI, Maria Rosaria. *Una donna e la sua musica: Maddalena Laura Lombardini Sirmen e la Venezia del XVIII secolo*, Novoli, Bibliotheca Minima, 2007 (Scriptorium, 36).

WEINMANN 1967
WEINMANN, Alexander. *Verlagsverzeichnis Giovanni Cappi bis A. O. Witzendorf*, Vienna, Universal, 1967 (Beiträge zur Geschichte des alt-Wiener Musikverlages, 2/11).

ZASLAW 1996
ZASLAW, Neal. 'Ornaments for Corelli's Violin Sonatas, Op. 5', in: *Early Music*, XXIV/1 (1996), pp. 95-115 [reprinted in *Baroque Music*, edited by Peter Walls, Farnham-Burlington, Ashgate, 2011 (The Library of Essays on Music Performance Practice), pp. 325-345].

ZASLAW 2015
ID. '"Graces" and "Vermin": Problems with the Ornaments for Corelli's Opus 5', in: *Basler Jahrbuch für historische Musikpraxis*, XXXIX (2015), pp. 179-192.

ZUCCARI 1760
ZUCCARI, Carlo. *The True Method of Playing an Adagio, Made Easy by twelve Examples, First, in a Plain Manner with a Bass, Then with all their Graces. Adapted for those who Study the Violin*, London, R. Bremner, [ca. 1760] [RISM Z 354].

The Art of Partimento

Cantata da camera e arte del partimento in Alessandro Scarlatti
«An Historical Link between Baroque Recitatives and Development Section of the Sonata-Form Movements?»

Simone Ciolfi
(Conservatorio 'Arcangelo Corelli' di Messina)

Il mito di Alessandro Scarlatti iniziatore o codificatore di una tradizione nonché compositore 'ricercato', ha origine all'epoca di Scarlatti stesso ed echeggia ancora oggi in varie pubblicazioni. Eccone alcuni esempi, settecenteschi e contemporanei, riguardanti la forma dell'aria e il carattere stilistico del repertorio scarlattiano. All'inizio del Capitolo IV della sua *General History of Music*, Burney cita il fatto che «it has been said that the *Da Capo* is a new invention; that [...] was first used by Alessandro Scarlatti, in his *Theodora*, 1693; and that in 1715 there was no an air without it in Gasparini's opera of *Il Tartaro alla China*». Lo stesso Burney, poco dopo, confuta questa affermazione erronea, ma essa prova la fama di Scarlatti nel Settecento come iniziatore di una tradizione[1]. Alberto Basso ritiene Scarlatti il codificatore dell'aria col da capo non l'inventore, anche se la codificazione è una forma di paternità[2].

Nell'ambito della cantata da camera, di cui Scarlatti fu prolifico autore, si riporta, in relazione con l'aria di cui il nostro compositore dovrebbe essere stato 'inventore' o 'codificatore', l'opinione di Helen T. Harris che concorda con Malcolm Boyd sul fatto che il «1697 represents a significant stylistic break in the style of Alessandro Scarlatti's cantatas [...]. After 1697 Scarlatti's cantatas illustrate the supremacy of the *da capo* aria [...]»[3]. Si deve specificare però che nelle cantate e nelle opere scarlattiane a cavallo tra Seicento e Settecento, l'aria col da capo conviveva con forme più aperte, e con diverse forme dello

---

[1]. Burney 1789, vol. IV, p. 169.
[2]. Basso 1991, p. 11. Jack Westrup scrive che la codificazione dell'aria col da capo «certainly does not have the connection with Alessandro Scarlatti that many writers, mainly out of a limited knowledge of the repertory, have suggested». Westrup 2001.
[3]. Harris 2001, p. 64.

stesso 'da capo'[4]. Per i molti lusinghieri apprezzamenti fatti sui recitativi delle cantate da camera di Scarlatti, rimando ad altre mie pubblicazioni[5]. Il loro stile è retrospettivo: le soluzioni altamente cromatiche e dissonanti di certi recitativi li apparentano a una scuola del ricercato e dell'estroso prettamente seicentesca.

Tuttavia, l'analisi del repertorio delle cantate scarlattiane rivela che soluzioni stilisticamente retrospettive potrebbero occultare strumenti compositivi nuovi. Alessandro Scarlatti si colloca infatti all'inizio di un'altra importante tradizione: quella del partimento. «It was only with Alessandro Scarlatti's surviving partimenti collections that an unmistakable pedagogical project is clearly visible», scrive Giorgio Sanguinetti in *The Art of Partimento*[6]. Se dunque Scarlatti si pone all'inizio di una tradizione, questa fu sicuramente quella del 'partimento'. Il presente scritto ha la finalità di evidenziare come le regole del partimento siano presenti nella musica delle cantate scarlattiane, e di sottolineare come, una volta mutati i gusti del pubblico da metà Settecento in poi, le cantate acquisirono valore didattico anche in virtù del loro legame con il partimento.

Clausole prearmoniche e regole del partimento nella cantata

La produzione di cantate di Alessandro Scarlatti inizia nell'alveo della libertà formale della cantata secentesca, continua con un'utilizzazione sempre più frequente dell'aria col da capo, ed è emblematica di quella standardizzazione della forma che si ebbe a cavallo tra Seicento e Settecento anche in questo genere. Tuttavia, all'interno di questa produzione,

---

[4]. Si usa qui come riferimento la matura aria col da capo, quella che segue il modello AA'BAA' con la doppia ripetizione di A, e non dei modelli precedenti nei quali è assente la doppia ripetizione di A (ABA), o ve ne è una tripla (ABABA). La tripla ripetizione di A nelle arie delle cantate di Scarlatti è riscontrata da Laura Damuth, che sottolinea come la forma ABABA possa talvolta costituirsi anche come ABACA oppure come ABCA. A seguito di un'accurata casistica sul tipo di arie presenti nelle cantate di Scarlatti, la Damuth evidenzia come la forma bipartita AB possa costituirsi anche senza la ripetizione di B e di A, e non necessariamente come $A^1B^2B^1$ o $A^1A^2B^2B^1$. Inoltre, nella forma ABCA, la C può essere ripetuta secondo il modello A(a1a2)BC(c1c2)A(a1a2). Nelle forme col da capo, la studiosa individua poi quattro possibilità: ABA semplice senza ripetizione di alcuna sezione; A(a1a2)BA(a1a2), con doppia ripetizione di A secondo il modello che diverrà predominante nell'aria col da capo del Settecento maturo; il modello AB(b1b2)A dove solo la parte B è ripetuta in una differente tonalità. Infine, è reperibile lo schema di aria col da capo dove le tre sezioni sono tutte ripetute A(a1a2)B(b1b2)A(a1a2). Damuth 1993, pp. 166-189. Nel suo volume su Scarlatti, Edward Dent sostiene che: «the irregularity of form is one of the distinguishing characteristics of Scarlatti's early cantatas [...]. To the early period also belong airs in binary form, airs on a ground bass, and all airs, in whatever form, that have two stanzas». Dent afferma di aver reperito nelle prime cantate soprattutto arie in forma bipartita del tipo $A^1B^2B^1$, $A^1A^2B^2B^1$, oppure forme come $A^1B^2B^1C^2C^1$ e, con più rarità, i tipi $A^1B^2A^1B^1$ e $A^1B^2A^2B^1$ (si riporta qui la sua grafia nella quale la lettera rappresenta il testo e i numeri la differente tonalità). Dent 1905, p. 12 per la citazione e p. 21 per il tipo di arie. *Cfr.* anche Strohm 1976, pp. 22-32, 72-87.

[5]. Ciolfi 2012, pp. 3-5.

[6]. Sanguinetti 2012, p. 15.

Cantata da camera e arte del partimento in Alessandro Scarlatti

Scarlatti non rinunciò mai alla qualità e alla sorprendente fattura dei recitativi e delle arie. Anzi, secondo Laura Damuth, nelle cantate di Scarlatti «there are more instances of tonal surprise and unusual modulations [...] from 1704-1705»[7].

Per iniziare con il caso dei recitativi, i movimenti cadenzali tipici dello stile recitativo compaiono nei trattati teorici attribuiti a Scarlatti, di cui alcuni probabilmente autografi. Egli, dunque, aveva piena coscienza dei moduli armonici di base di tali movimenti, sebbene l'indagine sui recitativi ha fatto emergere come tali formule subiscano elisioni e trasferimenti di risoluzione ispirati dal testo anche nelle cantate della maturità. I moduli cui si fa cenno si trovano nei *Principi del sig.re Cavaliere Alessandro Scarlatti* (d'ora in poi *Principi*) che contengono quelle «series of rules» sulle quali si accordano, come Sanguinetti afferma, i partimenti presenti nello stesso volume, 'rules' che vedremo fra poco. I *Principi* non sono l'unica pubblicazione di natura teorica attribuita a Scarlatti: vi sono anche manoscritti di *Regole*, sull'analisi delle quali rimando ad altre mie pubblicazioni[8].

Lo sforzo di chiarificazione didattica necessaria a Scarlatti per redigere queste trattazioni lo ha portato a evidenziare modelli compositivi di base (utili per scrivere recitativi ma non solo), soprattutto porzioni di basso continuo, che sono in sostanza regole del partimento. È necessario sottolineare subito che, all'interno di una partitura scarlattiana, la dialettica tra il modello e la sua trasgressione può essere innescata all'uopo dal compositore, quando un destinatario esigente, un testo particolare, o altro, lo richiedono. Questi fenomeni armonici arricchiscono e variano la natura musicale di un recitativo che è lungi dalla noia ed è ricco di soluzioni interessanti.

Si prenda, per esempio, l'inizio della cantata attribuito ad Alessandro Scarlatti, *Crudo amor empie stelle iniqua sorte*, contenuta nell'edizione che Etienne Roger ha stampato ad Amsterdam nel 1701[9]. Il tragico testo iniziale che dà il titolo alla cantata ispira al compositore l'uso di un tetracordo discendente collegato al primo verso. Tale formula, anche in versione cromatica, è frequente all'inizio dei recitativi per cantata di Scarlatti, ed è una strategia d'esordio ispirata al secentesco tetracordo di lamento. Col suo percorso dalla tonica al V grado, il tetracordo dissipa l'energia collocata nella fase iniziale del recitativo facendola giungere a una stasi sulla dominante, stasi adatta a mimare disperazione e abbandono. Tale soluzione è reperibile in celebri cantate di Scarlatti come *Andate o miei sospiri* (H53), *Amor Mitilde è morta* (H49), *Al fin m'ucciderete* (H21), *D'altr'uso serbate* (H12).

L'uso del tetracordo dà un tocco di tradizionalismo al recitativo di Scarlatti. Tale soluzione d'apertura è reperibile nei recitativi delle cantate di Atto Melani, scritte intorno al 1650. Il richiamo alla forma dell'aria lamento, dove il tetracordo diatonico o cromatico era utilizzato per arie di sconforto, testimonia il valore espressivo che Scarlatti conferiva al

---

[7]. Damuth 1993, p. 122.
[8]. Ciolfi 2011, pp. 84-88 e Ciolfi 2014, pp. 195-199.
[9]. *CANTATE / a I & II voci / col basso continuo / del Sig. SCARLATI / opera prima*, A Amsterdam, chez Estienne Roger, Marchand Librerie, [1701].

recitativo, in una visione di parità tra questo e l'aria. Tale esordio si ricollega alla tradizione seicentesca anche per un altro genere: quello del lamento recitativo da camera[10]. In questa forma dalle ampie potenzialità drammatiche non era di norma usato il tetracordo discendente, ma la situazione dipinta dal testo era patetica e psicologicamente cangiante, come accade nei testi delle cantate (talvolta basate anche su temi di famosi lamenti, come la cantata *Arianna*, H209, dello stesso Scarlatti).

Quando il testo poetico ha i caratteri dell'abbattimento tragico, Scarlatti predilige dunque una forma ibrida dove il vecchio lamento recitativo da camera ha assorbito i tratti ariosi del tetracordo discendente, trasformandosi con probabilità nell'esordio-lamento del repertorio in questione. Il recitativo di Scarlatti è infatti erede del recitativo affettuoso, animato da salti, contrasti di registro, ritardi, dissonanze e sorprese nell'armonia, che già nelle prime favole per musica si affiancava a quello che riprendeva il parlare ordinario, più lineare e armonicamente stabile rispetto al precedente[11].

Viene spontaneo collegare il genere del lamento e del tetracordo discendente che lo contraddistingue, alla tradizione letteraria e teatrale del Seicento[12]. Riguardo al fatto musicale, il tetracordo discendente è imparentato con la clausola prearmonica ⑧⑥⑤, ampiamente diffusa al basso come formula d'apertura nella musica madrigalistica nonché nel recitativo barocco, e mostrata come movimento armonico da molti trattatisti, per esempio da Lorenzo Penna (che la connette al recitativo), e dallo stesso Scarlatti nelle *Regole* e nei *Principi* (Ess. 1 e 2)[13]. È stato qui usato il termine clausola, frequente ormai nella moderna letteratura analitica e mutuato dalla trattatistica musicale prebarocca e barocca, perché evidenzia la tendenza di alcuni movimenti armonici a punteggiare il discorso più che a chiuderlo, un potere che spetta solo al salto V-I, l'unico per il quale si mantiene la terminologia di cadenza[14]. La clausola ⑧⑥⑤ circoscrive infatti un verso, ne punteggia la struttura, ma non esaurisce mai il potenziale espressivo di un intero periodo del testo. Tale

---

[10]. Si veda PORTER 1995, pp. 73-110, in particolare pp. 96-107, dove Porter evidenzia l'uso del tetracordo cromatico discendente negli autori di cantate d'ambiente romano. Il rapporto fra recitativo in stile cromatico e scena di lamento nel secondo Seicento è evidenziato anche in MURATA 1979, pp. 45-73: 68-73 (si veda anche MURATA 1981, pp. 161-176). Per il rapporto tra lamento polifonico e lamento monodico si veda CARACI VELA 1993, pp. 339-383.

[11]. STAFFIERI 2014, p. 41.

[12]. Su Monteverdi come modello per il genere del lamento monodico si veda TOMLINSON 1981, pp. 60-108. Sul tetracordo discendente si veda ROSAND 1979, pp. 346-59; ROSAND 1991, pp. 361-386; ROSAND 2007, pp. 224-248; BIANCONI 1991, pp. 219-235. Per approfondimenti sulla versione parodistica del lamento si veda GIALDRONI 1987, pp. 125-150: 132-134. Sul tetracordo cromatico discendente in ambito sacro si veda MARX 1971, pp. 1-23: 9-10.

[13]. PENNA 1684, pp. 180-181 (facsimile: Bologna, Forni, 1996). Per gli esempi di Scarlatti si vedano le note seguenti. Per la comprensione dei simboli sia detto che i numeri arabi racchiusi nel cerchio (①, ②, ③, ecc.) indicano i gradi della scala nel basso. I numeri romani (I, II, III...) indicano il grado armonico.

[14]. Sui termini 'clausula' e 'cadenza' si veda MEIER 2015, p. 79. Si veda poi il capitolo 'Clausulae' in GJERDINGEN 2007, pp. 139-176.

esaurimento avviene solo con una cadenza perfetta. Nel tetracordo ⑧⑦⑥⑤ utilizzato nel recitativo in questione, l'aggiunta del ⑦ deriva probabilmente da un processo di rilettura della ⑧⑥⑤ (come di molte altre clausole prearmoniche) nei processi tonali della Regola dell'ottava, la scala armonizzata ascendente e discendente che tanto successo ha avuto nella teoria del partimento già dal primo Settecento[15].

Nell'esempio n. 3 viene mostrato l'inizio del recitativo della cantata *Crudo amor empie stelle iniqua sorte*, dopo una selezione di clausole presenti nel trattato *Principi* di Scarlatti (Ess. 1 e 2)[16].

Es. 1: A. Scarlatti, *Principi*, sequenza di clausole ⑧⑥⑤.

Es. 2: A. Scarlatti, *Principi*, 'arpeggio di cembalo' in Do minore (di cui viene mostrato solo l'iniziale tetracordo ⑧⑦⑥⑤).

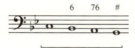

Es. 3: A. Scarlatti, tetracordo discendente dal primo recitativo (bb. 1-3) della cantata *Crudo amor empie stelle iniqua sorte*.

Nel passaggio fra Seicento e Settecento, infatti, la Regola dell'ottava si prestò a inglobare e organizzare in un pensiero coerentemente tonale una serie di formule contrappuntistiche che avevano avuto origine nella pratica precedente. La sovrapposizione tra schemi preesistenti e Regola dell'ottava, attestata in quasi tutti i trattati di fine Seicento e inizio Settecento (quelli di Scarlatti compresi), portò a una convivenza tra antiche clausole e porzioni di detta Regola. Infatti, per fare un esempio, l'antica regola di armonizzazione del semitono ascendente o discendente, chiamata '*mi-fa*' (la regola prescriveva che se due

---

[15]. Le numerose attestazioni della Regola dell'ottava in manoscritti e pubblicazioni del primo Settecento sono elencate in CHRISTENSEN 1992, pp. 91-117. Per un riassunto delle varie attestazioni reperibili nelle 'regole' manoscritte italiane del Settecento riguardanti l'uso parziale della Regola dell'ottava si consulti SANGUINETTI 2012, pp. 114-116. Alla storia del tetracordo cromatico dal tardo Cinquecento alla modernità è dedicato il testo di WILLIAMS 2006, che tocca il tema del recitativo e del lamento alle pp. 51-76.

[16]. SCARLATTI [1715-1716], f. 4ᵛ per l'Es. 1 e f. 70ʳ per l'Es. 2.

suoni salgono di semitono il primo porterà l'accordo di 6/3 e il secondo di 5/3, mentre se due suoni scendono di semitono accadrà il contrario), che nella versione ascendente costituisce la clausola ⑦①, può comparire in serie oppure acquisire elementi di definizione tonale più pronunciati grazie a una cadenza che ne conferma la triade. Ancora, alcune clausole antiche, presenti nei trattati e assai utilizzate come la ①⑦① (in cui il ⑦ porta l'accordo di 6/3, 6/5 o 7-6/3) o la ①②① (in cui il ② porta l'accordo di 6/3, 7-6/3 o 6/5), possono benissimo manifestarsi al basso come tali[17]. Seguono alcuni esempi di clausole tratte dai *Principi* scarlattiani[18].

Es. 4: A. Scarlatti, *Principi*, regola del semitono ascendente ('*mi-fa*' ascendente) ovvero clausola ⑦①.

Es. 5: A. Scarlatti, *Principi*, esempi di clausole ⑧⑥⑤, ①②① e ①⑦①.

Nel recitativo scarlattiano la formula ①⑦① ha spesso il ruolo di armonizzare il *topos* retorico dell'evocazione del nome dell'amata o dell'amato. Tale formula ha una funzione d'esordio confermata da numerosi studi nonché dalla sua facile reperibilità nel repertorio settecentesco, sia nell'ambito strumentale sia in quello vocale[19]. La novità non è il suo uso in forma d'esordio né la sua natura musicale. Ciò che si sottolinea è che, nel repertorio in questione, formule armoniche assai semplici si prestano a costituire l'ambientazione sonora per versi dal contenuto ricorrente, nell'ambito di una tradizione in cui luoghi letterari e luoghi musicali, che potremmo definire *topoi* retorici, si integrano catalizzando il senso del testo e materializzando le suggestioni antiche che la natura letteraria della cantata comportava. Suggestioni antiche che appartennero al recitativo fin dalla sua origine, essendo questo stile la ricreazione di una prosa musicale, di un'arte retorica a cavallo tra parola e canto, stile composto da versi sciolti evocanti la prosa oratoria, che per gli antichi non era poesia, non era prosa, ma una 'cosa mezzana' tra le due.

Tuttavia, l'analisi del primo recitativo di *Crudo amore empie stelle iniqua sorte* rivela anche altro (l'analisi si può seguire nell'Es. 7). In connessione al secondo endecasillabo 'che pretendete più da questo core' compare una clausola discendente di due suoni, anch'essa assai diffusa nella trattatistica di fine Seicento: al basso troviamo infatti *re-do♯* (un semitono

---

[17]. La sovrapposizione e nuova lettura delle clausule prearmoniche con porzioni della Regola dell'ottava sono approfonditamente discusse in CIOLFI 2012, pp. 45-57.
[18]. SCARLATTI [1715-1716], f. 41ᵛ per l'Es. 4 e ff. 6ʳ e 10ᵛ per l'Es. 5.
[19]. GJERDINGEN 2007, pp. 77-88.

discendente) che sono rispettivamente i gradi melodici ④③ della scala discendente di La maggiore (Es. 7, battuta 4). In questa formula il ④ porta sempre l'accordo di quarta aumentata e scende al ③ in 6/3, stabilizzando una triade in consonanza imperfetta. Sebbene non si tratti della nota cadenza frigia (che dal ⑥ abbassato scende al ⑤, unica clausola sopravvissuta come tale a secoli di tonalità), l'effetto prodotto dal semitono è quello dello stupore patetico perché corrisponde nel testo a una domanda retorica («Amore, stelle, che pretendete più da questo core?»).

Il terzo verso, un settenario, recita «di Doriste infelice», ed è inizialmente sostenuto al basso da due suoni, *si* e *do♯*, che costituiscono rispettivamente il ② e il ③ grado melodico della scala di La maggiore, triade che verrà tonicizzata dal ⑤① (v-i) successivo. Si tratta qui di altre due clausole assai note: la ②③ con la sesta aumentata sul ② che termina sul terzo grado della scala in consonanza imperfetta (6/3), e il movimento cadenzale ⑤① che diventerà il punto culminante della progressione cadenzale iv-v-i (Es. 7, battute 5 e 6).

La parola 'infelice' ben si sposa alla forza conclusiva del salto ⑤①, dove accentua la costatazione d'infelicità dell'io narrante e gli dona inesorabilità. Si tratta, però, di un movimento non preceduto da un iv grado, e dunque tale cadenza è 'inaspettata', tipica dell'apertura formale dello stile recitativo, sebbene armonicamente preparata dalle clausole ④③ e ②③ nella stessa tonalità. L'assenza del iv grado ci porta a considerare ②③ e ⑤① come due entità separate, non riconducibili a una progressione cadenzale pienamente tonale.

Prima di proseguire il discorso, nell'esempio successivo compaiono, in una versione standard in Do maggiore, le principali clausole utilizzate nella musica recitativa. Non sono altro che le clausole prearmoniche utilizzate nel sistema modale (*cantizans*, *altizans* e *tenorizans*, cioè i movimenti cadenzali tipici delle voci d'ambito polifonico) rilette, all'inizio del Settecento, alla luce del sistema tonale, per il quale poi la clausola con il salto v-i, ovvero la *basizans* ⑤① (non mostrata nell'Es. 6) è diventata la cadenza per eccellenza[20]. Nell'Es. 7 esse vengono mostrate all'interno del recitativo in questione, divise da una linea tratteggiata.

Es. 6: Principali clausule prearmoniche di due suoni e loro condotta delle voci.

---

[20]. SANGUINETTI 2007, p. 67: «Furno describes four bass motions that may induce a scale mutations, two ascending and two descending [...]. When the bass moves up a semitone, the two notes a minor second apart become ⑦ and ① of the new scale. When the bass moves up a whole tone, the two notes a major apart become ④ and ⑤ if the new scale. When the bass moves down a semitone, the two notes a minor second apart become ⑥ and ⑤ of the new scale. When the bass moves down a whole tone the two notes a major second apart become ② and ① of the new scale».

Es. 7: A. Scarlatti, cantata *Crudo amore, empie stelle, iniqua sorte*, primo recitativo (con clausole).

Le clausole ④③ con l'accordo di 6/4 con la quarta aumentata e la ②③, sono entrambe porzioni di Regola dell'Ottava sia se appartenenti a scale diverse sia se appartenenti alla stessa scala; la ①⑦①, la ⑦① ovvero la regola del *mi-fa* (utilizzabile anche in sequenza ascendente o discendente, oppure come ①⑦), la ①②①, la ②①, sono tutti movimenti cadenzali ricorrenti nella teoria del partimento, alcune delle quali potevano anche assumere il nome di «terminazioni di tono»[21]. Anche il tetracordo cromatico discendente fa parte del

---

[21]. Per le 'terminazioni di tono' si veda SANGUINETTI 2012, p. 159. Per un inquadramento storico generale delle clausole e della cadenza perfetta si veda MEIER 2015, pp. 79-93. Per un approfondimento sulle caratteristiche della cadenza autentica si veda NEUWIRTH – BERGÉ 2015, pp. 287-307.

gruppo di regole del partimento. Tutte queste regole includevano una loro condotta delle voci, specificata da Sanguinetti in *The Art of Partimento*[22].

Nel mondo del recitativo scarlattiano questi moduli armonici hanno una collocazione sequenziale. Tali moduli sono facilmente reperibili anche nei partimenti attribuiti allo stesso. Le clausole ④③ e ②③ sono tipiche formule che nel recitativo di Scarlatti seguono la fase d'esordio (dove si prediligono moduli che prolungano una tonica come la ①⑦① o la ①②①) appartengono a una fase successiva definibile come 'narrazione', fase seguita e conclusa da una figura cadenzale vera e propria, che si può chiamare 'epilogo' (dove troviamo cadenze perfette col salto ⑤①). Sebbene nelle prime 5 battute del primo recitativo di *Crudo amor, empie stelle* si trovino tutte apparentate alla stessa triade (La maggiore, si veda Es. 7), la sensazione è che questi movimenti armonici scandiscano il testo poetico come entità autonome. L'autonomia tonale delle formule l'una dall'altra è infatti la vera peculiarità dello stile recitativo.

La musica successiva lo conferma, perché una nuova clausola ④③ (*sol-fa♯*) tonicizza la triade di Re maggiore in 6/3 sul settenario 'siete troppo tiranna' (Es. 7, b. 6), e ancora la stessa formula (clausola ④③, Mi-Re) tonicizza la triade di Si minore in 6/3 sui versi 'se dopo tanti affanni ancor volete / con barbaro rigor condurla a morte', per poi cadenzare in Fa♯ minore sulla parola 'morte', la cui inesorabilità richiama la cadenza perfetta (⑤①).

Nella ripetizione finale del verso d'apertura ('crudo amor empie stelle iniqua sorte') abbiamo ancora una clausola ④③ e una cadenza ⑤① (non preceduta dal IV grado) sulla parola 'sorte', la cui inesorabilità, ricordata anche dalla sua rima con 'morte', si accompagna alla cadenza perfetta. Tale verso di cornice è musicato con due clausole (④③ e ⑤①) nella stessa tonalità di Do♯ minore (c'è dunque qui una coerenza tonale simile a quella dei primi tre versi del recitativo), che è, tuttavia, una tonalità assai lontana da quelle toccate in precedenza (Es. 7, bb. 10-12).

La relazione tra queste tonalità non può essere giustificata, infatti, dal circolo delle quinte, ma da una concezione locale dell'armonia, dove ogni clausola si lega a un verso, più raramente a due o a una parola specifica, innescando un peregrinare armonico in cui la musica, qui davvero serva dell'orazione, dona sfumature sempre diverse al susseguirsi dei versi e dei loro affetti[23].

La tripartizione del 'periodo recitativo' e le clausole nell'aria

Riepilogando, il recitativo (almeno quello del repertorio di Scarlatti) è costituito da una sequenza di moduli specifici legati a un periodo di senso compiuto (la concezione antica di periodo non è quella in due proposizioni come nel periodo moderno, ma poteva essere composto anche da una sola proposizione) nei quali la tensione delle formule si regola sia sul

---

[22]. Sanguinetti 2012, pp. 105, 112-123 (p. 114 per l'uso parziale della Regola dell'ottava, p. 117 per le clausole ①⑦① e ①②①), pp. 159-163 (§ 'Bass Motion Inducing a Scale Mutation').

[23]. Per il rapporto tra clausole e affetti si veda Ciolfi 2012, pp. 243-266.

senso del testo sia sulla sua scansione metrica, per cui le clausole musicali combaciano con le clausole metriche, cioè con il piede finale del verso. In questo tipo di periodo letterario musicato verso per verso con formule ordinate in sequenze c'è tutta la logica di questo stile. Si tratta, in estrema sintesi, di una serie di clausole e porzioni di Regola dell'ottava, armonicamente indipendenti e collocate all'esordio, al centro e all'epilogo del periodo[24].

Come si può vedere negli esempi, nel primo recitativo di *Crudo amor, empie stelle, iniqua sorte* è presente l'armatura di chiave. Talvolta ciò accade nei recitativi più antichi di Scarlatti. Si tratta di un elemento destinato a scomparire nei primi anni del Settecento, che illumina un momento ambiguo nella vita dello stile recitativo. Ci fu, talvolta, la volontà di organizzare il recitativo, principalmente sostenuto da clausole prearmoniche eredi della tradizione modale, in un quadro tonale più coerente? Potrebbe sembrare così per i primi tre versi del recitativo in questione, ma la soluzione adottata nel resto del brano vede le stesse formule vagare in tonalità lontane. Sarà questa la strada che prenderà il recitativo nel repertorio di Scarlatti e in quello della maggior parte dei compositori: assenza dell'armatura e libertà armonica in un quadro di rispetto per il testo poetico e per la correlazione dei versi con le clausole, organizzate, come detto, in una sequenza che va dal prolungamento di una tonica (esordio) alla rapida mutazione di triade (narrazione) fino alla cadenza perfetta (epilogo).

Ecco, in sintesi, le formule recitative organizzate secondo la sequenza standard, da me definito 'periodo recitativo' reperita durante l'analisi del repertorio:

PERIODO RECITATIVO[25]

1.	ESORDIO	Prolungamento di una tonica: ①⑦①, ①②①, pedale di tonica (5/3, 6/4, 7/5, 5/3), ⑧⑥⑤, ⑧⑦⑥⑤ (tetracordo cromatico e diatonico), ①②③④⑤ (Regola dell'ottava ascendente).

---

[24]. La sequenza di formule del periodo nel recitativo, poiché ha la possibilità di eliminare una o più funzioni, manifesta le stesse caratteristiche che William Caplin reperisce nei temi subordinati delle forme classiche, caratteristiche da lui definite *looser sentential functions*. Mi riferisco soprattutto alla «omission of an initiating function» («a subordinate theme can acquire formal loosening by giving the impression of starting in medias res»), che porta il tema a iniziare con una funzione di continuazione «by means of sequential harmonic progressions» o addirittura con una funzione cadenzale («a subordinate theme occasionally begins directly with a cadential progression»). Particolarmente importante per le funzioni formali nel sequenza di formule del periodo nel recitativo è l'affermazione di Caplin sulla «capacity for a passage to express the sense of beginning middle, or end indipendent of the passage's actual temporal location. Because formal functions are so conventionalized, because they are so well defined by specific characteristics, we can sometimes identify a given function without necessarily taking into account its position». CAPLIN 1998, pp. 111 e 113, e in generale, pp. 99-119.

[25]. CIOLFI 2011, pp. 90-93, CIOLFI 2012, pp. 123-151. CIOLFI 2014, pp. 203-213. Per una categorizzazione delle formule recitative dal punto di vista melodico si veda: SHERRILL – BOYLE 2015, pp. 1-61.

Cantata da camera e arte del partimento in Alessandro Scarlatti

2.	Narrazione	Rapida mutazione di triade: ②①, ⑦①, (⑤)④③, ⑦③, ②③, ⑥⑤.
3.	Epilogo	Cadenze perfette: ④⑤①, ③⑤①, ⑥⑤①.

Proseguendo nell'analisi della cantata *Crudo amor, empie stelle, iniqua sorte*, dopo il primo recitativo si incontra un'aria monostrofica su questi versi: «ma sprezza la morte / si ride del fato / un'anima forte / un core sdegnato». La rima alternata, il verso senario, sono caratteristiche che spettano all'aria, in questo caso sentenziosa. Tuttavia, quest'aria (anche per via della congiunzione iniziale 'ma') sembra sgorgare dal recitativo precedente, quasi come una conseguenza concettuale. La differenzia dal recitativo, però, il piglio energico che si deve a un'affermazione del genere, in contrapposizione con l'ambientazione languida del recitativo. Legame e separazione, dunque, il primo evidenziato dalla presenza della stessa tonalità iniziale del recitativo (La maggiore), dalla stessa armatura di chiave, dalla natura breve dell'aria che è in sostanza in forma AA con la ricomparsa di A variata e condensata (elementi che ne fanno quasi un'appendice ariosa al recitativo, pur non essendo il brano un arioso), dallo stesso andamento di quartine discendenti per grado congiunto, che ricorda la discesa del tetracordo iniziale del recitativo.

La separazione è invece evidenziata dalla dinamicità del basso continuo, dal ritornello introduttivo e finale nonché dalla dizione melismatica dei versi (molto contenuta) e dalla loro ripetizione (frequente). Da notare come l'inizio del ritornello prolunghi la tonica La tramite un movimento con nota di volta inferiore (*la – sol♮ – la*) simile alla clausola ①⑦① d'esordio che, con le sue tipiche armonie, compare all'inizio del canto e all'inizio di ogni mutazione di tono fra le due enunciazioni della strofa (entrambe nella tonalità di impianto).

Es. 8: A. Scarlatti, cantata *Crudo amore, empie stelle, iniqua sorte*, aria 'Ma sprezza la morte' (bb. 1-12).

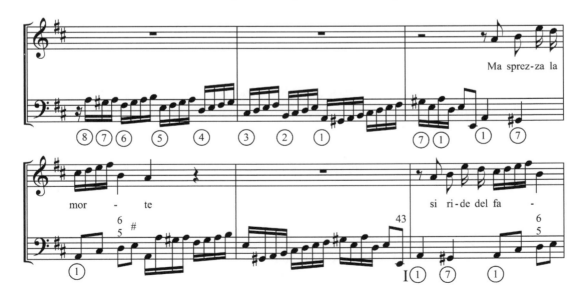

Le clausole sembrano essere dunque un elemento comune tra recitativo e aria. La loro funzione di apertura, narrazione e chiusura, in generale si potrebbe dire di 'punteggiatura', si dispiega nel recitativo in forma esclusiva e preponderante, ma è necessaria anche all'aria, sebbene qui vengano inserite in un discorso armonico strutturato. Tuttavia, contrariamente a quanto accade nel recitativo, nell'aria il circolo delle quinte diventa normativo e dunque guida i processi modulanti senza la libertà reperibile nel recitativo, il quale è libero di vagare di triade in triade.

La 'modulazione circolare' per terze

Sebbene non possa essere involontaria la similarità fra la tonalità dell'aria e quella iniziale del recitativo, il compositore ha separato la fine del recitativo dall'inizio dell'aria con uno spostamento di terza dalla triade di Do♯ minore a quella di La maggiore. Si tratta di una delle strategie più diffuse nel passaggio tra recitativo e aria, all'epoca cosciente, e di cui oggi si sono perse le tracce. È una strategia di modulazione neutra, cioè libera dalla consequenzialità tonale delle quinte; è spesso presente anche fra i periodi di un recitativo e come strategia di connessione fra aria e recitativo e fra recitativo e aria[26]. Tracce di questa tecnica si trovano in un'osservazione di Johann David Heinichen contenuta nei

---

[26]. Tali osservazioni trovano conferma nell'analisi della Damuth, che afferma come «Recitatives/aria pairs for major-key arias from later years show an increasing use of third relationships. In 1701-1705 the most common relationship is that of iii-I (with the occasional III-I)». E anche per la relazione tra aria e recitativo «some kind of third relationship is the most common choice» (DAMUTH 1993, pp. 112 e 114. Si vedano le tabelle delle pp. 115-116).

paragrafi 840 e 841 del suo *Der General-Bass in der Composition*, stampato a Dresda nel 1728. Egli racconta come, in gioventù, volendo passare da una tonalità maggiore a una tonalità minore che non fosse la relativa, i precetti del suo insegnante Kuhnau non lo avessero soddisfatto e «che nulla ancora sapevo all'epoca della modulazione circolare per terze»[27]. Si potrebbe a ragione ipotizzare che, poiché non ne aveva avuto notizia durante il suo apprendistato in Germania, Heinichen ne fosse venuto a conoscenza in Italia (Francesco Gasparini fa cenno nell'*Armonico pratico al cimbalo* alla «mutazione di tono per terza»)[28]. Inoltre, troviamo una descrizione di questo tipo di modulazione anche nel *Musicalische Handleitung* di Friderich Erhard Niedt, stampato ad Amburgo nel 1700. Nel capitolo IX, 'Wie man manierlich aus einem Thon in den andern fallen sol' ('Come passare elegantemente da una tonalità a un'altra') egli sostiene che la modulazione per terze si può realizzare discendendo alternativamente di una terza maggiore e di una minore, oppure ascendendo alternativamente di una terza maggiore e di una minore[29]. Tuttavia, Neidt, negli esempi che dà di questa pratica, non rispetta l'alternanza tra maggiore e minore, e passa, per esempio, da Si♭ maggiore a Sol minore e da Sol minore a Mi maggiore (invece che a Mi♭). Ebbene il passaggio di terza in terza era prescritto nelle regole del partimento come strategia tonale neutra[30]. Di questa tecnica di modulazione la storia della teoria musicale sembra aver perso traccia, almeno fino alla riscoperta operata in recenti studi sull'opera ottocentesca[31].

Clausole prearmoniche in alcuni partimenti scarlattiani

Passiamo ora a osservare alcuni esempi di partimenti scarlattiani. Come si può vedere nell'Es. 9, le modalità di inizio con clausola con nota di volta ①⑦① e prosecuzione con due clausole, una ④③ (preceduta da ⑤, eventualità frequente) e una cadenza frigia, sono esattamente quelle che ritroviamo nei bassi dei recitativi. Anche la loro struttura sequenziale è simile: all'inizio viene prolungata la triade di tonica ed essa è poi seguita da due clausole più brevi. La fermata sul ③ e sul ⑤ accentua l'indipendenza armonica delle clausole brevi, pur essendo qui collocate in un contesto tonalmente coerente e non all'interno di un recitativo.

---

[27]. Citato in BUELOW 1992, p. 286.
[28]. GASPARINI 1708, p. 44.
[29]. Per approfondimenti sul *Musicalische Handleitung* di Niedt si veda ARNOLD 1965, vol. I, pp. 213-236. L'argomento della modulazione per terze è toccato a p. 235.
[30]. SANGUINETTI 2012, p. 158.
[31]. Tale pratica è frequentemente reperibile fra le tecniche di modulazione dell'opera italiana di primo Ottocento. Si veda ROTHSTEIN 2008, cap. IV, § 17: «[...] the characteristically Rossinian move of a major third downward, from one major triad to another, was far from unknown in eighteenth-century music».

Es. 9: A. Scarlatti, *Principi*, partimento (bb. 1-4)[32].

Stesso discorso per il partimento che segue (Es. 10), dove l'inizio è ancora effettuato con una clausola con nota di volta, questa volta superiore, nella triade di Sol, seguita da due tetracordi discendenti alle tonalità di Re minore e di La minore, realizzate tramite due gruppi di due clausole (④③ + ②①). Pur trattandosi qui di un basso tonalmente coerente, la cifratura ci indica sequenze armoniche simili che ci permettono di considerare queste formule anche come elementi indipendenti, in modo simile alla concezione locale dell'armonia che troviamo in un recitativo (nella seconda battuta, la comparsa dell'accordo di 4/2 con la quarta alterata trasforma il ① in ④ della triade di Re).

Es. 10: A. Scarlatti, *Principi:* partimento (bb. 1-5).

«An Historical Link between Baroque Recitatives and the Development Sections of the Sonata-Form Movements»?

Constatata la neutralità di queste formule del partimento per il fatto che esse viaggiano tra generi diversi, si prenda ora in considerazione la seguente osservazione di Michael Talbot: «[…] althought there is no historical link between Baroque recitatives and the development sections of the sonata-form movements of the Classical period and later, one cannot help noticing of the advanced techniques of modulations employed. Would it be too bold to suggest that recitatives in chamber cantatas (and, of course, in dramatic genres) served as a useful laboratory, during the first half of the eighteenth century, for harmonic and tonal processes that became widely applied to closed forms only in the second?»[33].

Per tentare di rispondere a questa stimolante domanda proviamo a procedere per gradi. Abbiamo constatato che alcune regole del partimento sono comuni agli esercizi del partimento così come alla musica della cantata. Mentre nelle arie esse sono immerse nella coerenza tonale delle forme chiuse, nei recitativi sono usate in forma indipendente, peregrinando da triade e a triade al fine di sottolineare porzioni di testo. Si noti poi che in

---

[32]. Scarlatti [1715-1716], f. 41ʳ per l'Es. 12 e 46ʳ per l'Es. 13.
[33]. Talbot 2009, p. 272.

vari trattati, come per esempio i *Principi* di Scarlatti (si veda sopra), appaiono vari recitativi o bassi di recitativo presentati come esercizi. Il peregrinare armonico tipico del recitativo faceva forse parte di un training che potremmo definire come appartenente a quello del partimento. L'instabilità tonale, il viaggio di triade in triade in effetti caratterizza anche la sezione di sviluppo della forma-sonata. Osserviamo ora la riduzione sintetica delle battute 7-19 dello sviluppo nel primo movimento della Sonata per pianoforte in Do maggiore Op. 2 n. 3 di Beethoven (Es. 11).

Es. 11: Beethoven, Sonata Op. 2 n. 3, riduzione delle batt. 7-19.

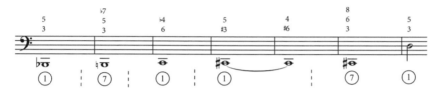

Il basso di questo esempio è in semibrevi come nella composizione originale di Beethoven (la presenza della stessa figurazione in due battute è stata ridotta a una sola battuta), gli accordi spezzati alla mano destra sono qui trasformati in cifre del basso. Nel processo armonico è possibile leggere le caratteristiche di un basso per recitativo: l'inizio prevede una tonica momentanea in *si*♭, *si*♭ che poi diventa naturale e sostiene una settima diminuita che evita di risolvere a *do* (una 'catacresi', ovvero una elisione della risoluzione). Nel successivo accordo è però implicita la risoluzione a *do*, perché l'accordo che compare è il tipico secondo *step* di quelle figure iniziali di recitativo che aprono con la triade e, tenendo il pedale di tonica, si spostano alla 6/4 per poi approdare alla settima e tornare in 5/3 (gli ultimi due passi eliminati sempre per catacresi). Ciò accade proprio nei due *do*♯ successivi, il primo sostenente la triade perfetta, il secondo l'accordo di 6/4. Anche qui manca il completamento della figura (accordo di settima e ritorno all'accordo in 5/3 sono elisi). La figura finale è un semplice '*mi-fa*'.

In sostanza un basso del genere potrebbe benissimo comparire in un recitativo, perché ne ha la classica peregrinazione armonica a tonalità lontane (Si♭ maggiore, Do♯ maggiore, Re maggiore), perché ne possiede le clausole, perché ne usa i procedimenti cromatici (come l'elisione della risoluzione), perché la concezione dell'armonia è locale, come in un recitativo. L'ipotesi di Talbot ha dunque un suo fondamento, anche se l'indagine è tutta da compiere: è molto probabile che nell'apprendistato di un compositore i processi armonici del recitativo siano serviti da modello per la conduzione di uno sviluppo nella forma-sonata (almeno nel primo classicismo viennese), ed è dunque possibile che i recitativi delle cantate, dove sono evidenti formule del partimento, abbiano costituito un banco d'esercizio per compositori poi dedicatisi ad altro. Dietro questi fenomeni l'arte del partimento giace come processo fondativo le cui potenzialità si applicano a generi diversi e talvolta apparentemente lontani tra loro.

Simone Ciolfi

Bibliografia

Arnold 1965
Arnold, Franck Thomas. *The Art of Accompaniment from a Thorough-Bass as Practised in the XVIIth & XVIIIth centuries*, 2 voll., New York, Dover, 1965 (Dover Books on Music).

Basso 1991
Basso, Alberto. *Storia della musica. 6: L'Età di Bach e di Händel*, nuova edizione riveduta e ampliata, Torino, EdT, 1991 (Biblioteca di cultura musicale).

Bianconi 1991
Bianconi, Lorenzo. *Storia della musica. 5: Il Seicento*, nuova edizione riveduta e ampliata, Torino, EdT, 1991 (Biblioteca di cultura musicale).

Buelow 1992
Buelow, George J. *Thorough-Bass Accompaniment According to Johann David Heinichen*, edizione riveduta, Lincoln, University of Nebraska Press, 1992.

Burney 1789
Burney, Charles. *A General History of Music, from the Earliest Ages to the Present Period*, 4 voll., Londra, The Author, 1776-1789, vol. IV (1789).

Caplin 1998
Caplin, William E. *Classical Form: A Theory of Formal Functions for the Instrumental Music of Haydn, Mozart and Beethoven*, Oxford, Oxford University Press, 1998.

Caraci Vela 1993
Caraci Vela, Maria. 'Lamento polifonico e lamento monodico da camera all'inizio del Seicento: affinità stilistiche e reciprocità di influssi', in: *Seicento inesplorato. Atti del III convegno internazionale sulla musica in area lombardo-padana del secolo XVII (Lenno-Como, 23-25 giugno 1989)*, a cura di Alberto Colzani, Andrea Luppi e Maurizio Padoan, Como, Antiquae Musicae Italicae Studiosi, 1993 (Contributi musicologici del Centro ricerche dell'A.M.I.S., 7), pp. 339-383.

Christensen 1992
Christensen, Thomas. 'The *Régle de l'Octave* in Thorough-Bass Theory and Practice', in: *Acta Musicologica*, LXIV/2 (1992), pp. 91-117.

Ciolfi 2011
Ciolfi, Simone. 'Formule e improvvisazione nei recitativi delle cantate di Alessandro Scarlatti', in: *Beyond Notes: Improvisation in Western Music of the Eighteenth and Nineteenth Centuries*, a cura di Rudolf Rasch, Brepols, Turnhout, 2011 (Speculum musicae, 16), pp. 83-96.

Ciolfi 2012
Id. *Il recitativo semplice nelle cantate di Alessandro Scarlatti: aspetti formali e funzionali*, tesi di dottorato, Roma, Università degli studi di Tor Vergata, 2011-2012.

CIOLFI 2014
ID. 'L'espressione degli 'affetti' nei recitativi delle cantate di Alessandro Scarlatti. Nuovi elementi per una teoria del recitativo', in: *Devozione e Passione: Alessandro Scarlatti nella Napoli e Roma Barocca*, a cura di Luca Della Libera e Paologiovanni Maione, Napoli, Turchini, 2014, pp. 191-213.

DAMUTH 1993
DAMUTH, Laura. *Alessandro Scarlatti's Cantatas for Soprano and Basso Continuo (1693-1705)*, Ph.D. Diss., New York (NY), Columbia University, 1993.

DENT 1905
DENT, Edward Joseph. *Alessandro Scarlatti: His Life and Works*, Londra, E. Arnold, 1905.

GASPARINI 1708
GASPARINI, Francesco. *L'Armonico pratico al cimbalo*, Venezia, Antonio Bortoli, 1708.

GIALDRONI 1987
GIALDRONI, Teresa Maria. 'Francesco Provenzale e la cantata a Napoli nella seconda metà del Seicento', in: *La musica a Napoli durante il Seicento. Atti del convegno internazionale di studi, Napoli (11-14 aprile 1985)*, a cura di Domenico Antonio D'Alessandro e Agostino Ziino, Roma, Torre d'Orfeo, 1987 (Miscellanea musicologica, 2), pp. 125-150.

GJERDINGEN 2007
GJERDINGEN, Robert. *Music in the Galant Style*, Oxford, Oxford University Press, 2007.

HARRIS 2001
HARRIS, Ellen T. *Handel as Orpheus: Voice and Desire in the Chamber Cantatas*, Cambridge (MA), Harvard University Press, 2001.

MARX 1971
MARX, Hans Joachim. 'Monodische Lamentationen des Seicento', in: *Archiv für Musikwissenschaft*, XXVIII/1 (1971), pp. 1-23.

MEIER 2015
MEIER, Bernard. *I modi della polifonia vocale classica descritti secondo le fonti*, edizione italiana a cura di Alberto Magnolfi, Lucca, LIM, 2015 (Teorie musicali, 1).

MURATA 1979
MURATA, Margaret. 'The Recitative Soliloquy', in: *Journal of the American Musicological Society*, XXXII/1 (1979), pp. 45-73.

MURATA 1981
EAD. *Operas for the Papal Court (1631-1668)*, Ann Arbor (MI), UMI Research Press, 1981 (Studies in Musicology, 39).

NEUWIRTH – BERGÉ 2015
'Towards a Syntax of the Classical Cadence', in: *What is a Cadence? Theoretical and Analytical Perspectives on Cadences in the Classical Repertoire*, a cura di Markus Neuwirth e Pieter Bergé, Lovanio, Leuven University Press, 2015.

PORTER 1995
PORTER, William E. 'Lamenti recitativi da camera', in: *'Con che soavità'. Studies in Italian Opera, Song, and Dance, 1580-1740*, a cura di Iain Fenlon e Tim Carter, Oxford, Clarendon Press, 1995.

PENNA 1684
PENNA, Lorenzo. *Li primi albori musicali per li principianti della musica figurata*, Bologna, Giacomo Monti, 1684.

ROSAND 1979
ROSAND, Ellen. 'The Descending Tetrachord: An Emblem of Lament', in: *The Musical Quarterly*, LXV/3 (1979), pp. 346-359.

ROSAND 1991
EAD. *Opera in Seventeenth-Century Venice: The Creation of a Genre*, Berkeley (CA), University of California Press, 1991.

ROSAND 2007
EAD. *Monteverdi's Last Operas: A Venetian Trilogy*, Berkeley (CA), University of California Press, 2007.

ROTHSTEIN 2008
ROTHSTEIN, William. 'Common-Tone Tonality in Italian Romantic Opera: An Introduction', in: *Music Theory Online*, XIV/1 (2008), <http://www.mtosmt.org/issues/mto.08.14.1/mto.08.14.1.rothstein.html>, visitato nel novembre 2018.

SANGUINETTI 2007
SANGUINETTI, Giorgio. 'The Realization of Partimenti: An Introduction', in: *Journal of Music Theory*, LI/1 (2007), pp. 51-83.

SANGUINETTI 2012
ID. *The Art of Partimento*, Oxford, Oxford University Press, 2012.

SCARLATTI [1715-1716]
SCARLATTI, Alessandro. *Principi della musica del Sig.^re Cavaliere Alessandro Scarlatti*, GB-Lbl Add. 14244.

SHARRILL-BOYLE 2015
SHARRILL, Paul – BOYLE, Matthew. 'Galant Recitative Schemas', in: *Journal of Music Theory*, LIX/1 (2015), pp. 1-61.

STAFFIERI 2014
STAFFIERI, Gloria. *L'opera italiana: dalle origini al secolo dei Lumi (1590-1790)*, Roma, Carocci, 2014 (Frecce, 171).

STROHM 1976
STROHM, Reinhard. *Italienische Opernarien des Frühen Settecento (1720-1730). 1: Studien*, Colonia, Volk Verlag H. Gerig KG, 1976 (Analecta Musicologica, 16/1).

TALBOT 2009
TALBOT, Michael. 'Patterns and Strategies of Modulation in Cantata Recitatives', in: *Aspects of the Secular Cantata in Late Baroque Italy*, a cura di Michael Talbot, Aldershot, Asghate, 2009, pp. 255-272.

TOMLINSON 1981
TOMLINSON, Gary. 'Madrigal, Monody, and Monteverdi's «Via naturale alla immitatione»', in: *Journal of the American Musicological Society*, XXXIV/1 (1981), pp. 60-108.

WESTRUP 2001
WESTRUP, Jack. 'Aria', in: *The New Grove Dictionary of Music and Musicians*, seconda edizione, a cura di Stanley Sadie, 29 voll., Londra, Macmillan, 2001, vol. I, p. 889.

WILLIAMS 2006
WILLIAMS, Peter. *The Chromatic Fourth during Four Centuries of Music*, Oxford, Clarendon Press, 2006 (Oxford Monographs on Music).

Two New Sources for the Study of Early Eighteenth-Century Composition and Improvisation

Marco Pollaci
(Nottingham University)

In recent years, the role of musical improvisation has increasingly interested both musicians and scholars, together with the revival of a keyboard repertoire from the seventeenth and the eighteenth centuries[1]. The Romantic idea of creative genius being inspired by virtue of the sheer power of creativity in the composer is being steadily eclipsed by the study of pedagogic traditions that more specifically emphasise the role of musical improvisation in composition teaching[2]. In fact, until the beginning of the nineteenth century, composition was taught almost entirely through practice and indeed improvisation at the keyboard[3].

Recent studies dedicated to improvisation in history highlight a close link between improvisation, composition pedagogy, and practical musicianship[4] to re-establish the inextricably entwined nature of theory and practice through examples from the past[5]. Significant data, derived from eighteenth century primary sources preserved in European libraries, attest to this legacy of improvisation, which undoubtedly held much significance for most composers of the period. Beyond proving that improvisation and composition were interwoven in musical training, these sources also testify to the importance of the main pedagogic tool in the compositional practice of the eighteenth century: the partimento tradition and its rules.

This work does not intend to explore the history and the rules of the partimento tradition and the Neapolitan school[6]; rather, it seeks to describe two manuscript

---

[1]. Among other works, see Christensen 2017.
[2]. Mann 2013, Lester 1994.
[3]. Guido 2017.
[4]. Erhardt 2013.
[5]. These aspects are investigated in the significant work by Bernstein – Hatch 1993.
[6]. The essential result of the *partimento* research studies has been the publication by Sanguinetti 2012. See also Gjerdingen 2007, Gjerdingen 2009, Van Tour 2015, Cafiero 1993, Cafiero 2007, Cafiero 2009. See also Van Tour 2014a— and Van Tour 2014b—.

sources preserved in the Staatsbibliothek zu Berlin Preussischer Kulturbesitz: *Regole per accompagnare nel Cimbalo ò vero Organo*[7] and *Principi di Cembalo*[8] and their reflections on this pedagogic tool.

The art of partimento has become increasingly prominent in recent musicological literature. Noteworthy studies have been dedicated to the centrality of the Neapolitan school and indeed the solfeggi traditions in the eighteenth century[9]. Although the partimento derives from the teaching and practice of the thoroughbass, it differs from the latter in certain musical aspects and compositional purposes. Collections of partimenti show exercises written on a bass line, figured or not, and intended to develop and refine one's ability to improvise and to compose at the keyboard. Settled on one voice, they can have key changes and provide thematic proposals for the extemporaneous processing and elaboration of the music itself.

Naples and its four conservatories (Santa Maria di Loreto, Santa Maria della Pietà dei Turchini, Sant'Onofrio a Capuana, and I Poveri di Gesù Cristo)[10], became the *fulcrum* of what may be seen as a response to the considerable demand of musicians and of the teaching of composition, in which partimento was a useful tool. From at least the end of the seventeenth to the beginning of the nineteenth century, through the teaching methods of musicians such as Francesco Durante (1684-1755), Leonardo Leo (1694-1744) and Nicola Porpora (1686-1768), *inter alia*, the partimento technique became an essential skill and its importance in musical improvisation an essential lesson for any student seeking to become a professional musician regardless of specialisation, assuring a gateway to widespread exposure.

Recent debates on the genesis of partimento have given rise to new hypotheses[11]. It is speculated that the technique's origins may lie in Roman ecclesiastical circles, where the production of organ music necessitated keyboard improvisation skill[12]. This milieu would have unknowingly supported the incorporation of partimento into music teaching methodologies. Such approaches would view either possession or assimilation of thoroughbass and liturgical music as essential requisites for seventeenth-century musicians involved in ecclesiastic expression. Therefore, the two contexts in which our partimento sources are examined are the aforementioned Neapolitan conservatories and the Roman institutions.

---

[7]. D-Bsb Mus.ms.theor. 1483.

[8]. D-Bsb Mus.ms.theor. 1417.

[9]. See BARAGWANATH 2014. Baragwanath is currently working on the first book-length study regarding solfeggi's theory and practice, titled *The Solfeggio Tradition: A Forgotten Art Melody in the Long Eighteenth Century* (BARAGWANATH forthcoming)

[10]. More details in SANGUINETTI 2012, pp. 29-40.

[11]. See CIPRIANI, forthcoming and Giorgio Sanguinetti's article in this volume.

[12]. This aspect has been discussed in SANGUINETTI 2012, pp. 20-23.

Two New Sources

Sources referring to this Roman circle are scarce since the teaching of music was, at that time, restricted to religious, welfare or charitable entities or private institutions, which were not driven to preserve or transmit pedagogical traditions like the Neapolitan conservatoires were. In fact, the teaching of composition in the Rome of the time generally operated from musically inclined chapels and religious institutions, and often involved private teaching from teacher to pupil rather than formalized groups like in the conservatoires of Naples with established cultures of musical instruction. This deficiency of source data is noted but does not undermine the interest of the Roman *milieu*.

This work includes an initial, but not exhaustive, investigation of the sources; it will introduce us to two manuscripts that remain unexplored in scholarship. It should be noted that it is not always possible to attribute, with certainty, the sources relating to the partimento as they are often *Principi*, *Lezioni*, *Regole* or *Zibaldoni*, aggregated collections of autographs or of material for didactic use from various copyists. The styles and ink found therein indicate content that cannot be regarded as homogeneous or attributable to a single master. As Sanguinetti argues:

> With perhaps the exception only of the chamber cantatas, no other repertoire is affected by such great uncertainty about authorship as are partimenti. This uncertainty is most clearly discernible in the several anonymous manuscripts and zibaldoni […][13].

For this reason, I attribute the manuscripts described in this article to the Roman circle without certitude, given some indicative, but still not exhaustive, detailing in the reconstruction of the collections. This study aims to inspire scholars to further investigate such unexplored sources in the hope that firmer knowledge of the Roman circle may be uncovered, by means of anonymous manuscripts like these two partimenti sources.

This work highlights the improvisational aspects of the partimento tradition and its rules. What emerges from the analysis of the collections under the spotlight here is certain stylistic characteristics that confirm the importance of improvisation and inspiration for students to improvise accordingly. Let us examine the two in succession.

The first of the two, the anonymous manuscript 1417 entitled *Principi di Cembalo*, may be dated around the seventeenth century or early eighteenth century, although this remains an estimation. The collection of rules and musical examples includes 36 partimenti without realizations. Following the modalities typical of Neapolitan school sources, which inform the transmission of musical elements without extensive prescriptive and written treatise, the manuscript begins with a brief introduction to the first elements with musical examples. What follows is a series of examples of harmonised ascending scales, following

---

[13]. Sanguinetti 2012, p. 63.

the Rule of the Octave[14]. This is one of the prototypical Neapolitan school pedagogical instruments for instructing on harmonising a scale[15]. In fact, the approach to harmonising each note of the diatonic scale reflects the common practice of accompaniment of a scale and can have several variants with different chords. The RDO was described by Sanguinetti as having a range of variants as employed by the likes of Alessandro Scarlatti (1660-1725), Giacomo Tritto (1733-1824), Giovanni Paisiello (1740-1816), and the renowned Fedele Fenaroli (1730-1818)[16].

Ex. 1 shows the RDO presented in manuscript 1417, but an interesting and new detail concerns the harmonisation of the ascending scale. The schema does not entirely correspond with other such chord successions generally. It is similar to Francesco Durante's and Fedele Feranoli's version, following Sanguinetti's synoptic view of the different versions of the RDO[17]. Yet, it does not correspond entirely to those versions either. The second degree is prescribed to use a 3/6 chord instead of 3/4/6.

Ex. 1: the Rule of the Octave according to the anonymous manuscript D.Bsb Mus.ms.theor.1417, folio 4ʳ.

Following this first part dedicated to the scales, a larger section then presents the series of 36 partimenti that do not correspond with other sources, as far as current literature is able to inform us. The partimenti are presented progressively by complexity, from the simplest patterns to the most difficult. Each of the more or less figured partimenti suggests examples to practice the study of cadences, suspensions, RDO, sequences, and schematic bass. Ex. 2 shows two examples of these partimenti at the beginning of the source from the collection 1417. The manuscript does not trace the date of composition, and therefore links with any musical institute cannot be identified. Following my investigation, I can assert that this is the only copy of these partimenti in existence.

Ex. 2: two partimenti from the manuscript Mus.ms.theory 1417, folio 10ʳ.

---

14. Hereafter abbreviated as RDO (= *Regola dell'Ottava*).
15. HOLTEMEIER 2007.
16. SANGUINETTI 2012, pp. 113-125.
17. *Ibidem*, p. 123.

Two New Sources

One more detail might be interesting about the origin of this source. The last partimento, at the end of the manuscripts, is presented as a bass written by Signor Cavalieri Alessandro Scarlatti (Ex. 3). Located across other sources for comparison and verification, this partimento is included in the collection entitled *Principi del Sig.^{re} Cavaliere Alessandro Scarlatti*, preserved in the British Library as Ms. Add. 14244.

Ex. 3: *Basso del Signor Cavaliere Allesandro Scarlatti*, from the manuscript Mus.ms.theory 1417, folio 18^r.

The presence of this particular partimento might be a detail suggesting links with the Roman circle, in which Alessandro Scarlatti was himself a protagonist. The handwriting looks consistent throughout the manuscript; there is no difference in the paper or ink between the last page and the rest of partimenti collection.

The second manuscript to be examined is preserved at the Staatsbibliothek zu Berlin Preussischer Kulturbesitz as well as in the manuscript 1483. It contains rules and partimento for keyboard accompaniment; it is entitled *Regole per accompagnare nel Cimbalo ò vero Organo*. This source is certainly one of the earliest manuscripts to exhibit a collection of partimenti and it is dated 1696[18]. It presents a brief and general introduction to the music languages, the names of the notes, keys, and cadences. Similarly, in only five pages, including musical examples themselves, the rules appear as short written explanations directing the reader to consistent musical examples. The largest part presents only partimenti, to assist the student in practising and improvising accordingly to late seventeenth-century partimenti function.

These anonymous partimenti are often presented as unfigured bass lines, and they exhibit changes in texture and clef, following the partimento rules found in Neapolitan compositional practice. It should be noted that all these partimenti present typical contrapuntal patterns, showing a tight link to pedagogic exercises that help students improvise and practice at the keyboard. Students could rehearse the ascending 5-6 technique sequences on bass motions, diminution techniques, descending 5-6 motion bass and ascending chromatic motions, segments of RDO, as shown in one example from the collection 1483 (Ex. 4).

Ex. 4: partimento from the anonymous manuscript D.Bsb Mus.ms.theor.1438m folio 8ʳ.

---

[18]. This document has been mentioned by Sanguinetti with a short description: «As the title makes clear, it is a series of rules and precepts for through bass interspersed with exercises and more demanding pieces in partimento notation, such as organ versets». *Ibidem*, p. 20.

A second section of this source is an explanation on harmonising scales, *Regole per accompagnare i Toni*. On close inspection, we can observe a link with the Roman chapel master Raimondo Lorenzini, whose *Grammatica per il Bassetto* (1787) is preserved at the Biblioteca Casanatense in Rome[19]. The second section of the manuscript 1438 appears to be a replication of Lorenzini's rules. It seems clear that this section from the manuscript is related to but not written by the same author, perhaps nor in the same period. This second part presents scales as a principal contrapuntal tool in studying elementary counterpoint. For each scale and example, a small collection of partimenti follows, of which some are completely original, however, and do not exhibit such correlations with Lorenzini's sources, nor with any others.

Once again, the presence of musical examples, rather than of written rules and theoretical guidelines, testify to the will to steer student proficiency towards improvisation though actual practice of partimento methods at the keyboard. As mentioned before, detailed instructions and long descriptions of theory were less important in the partimento art. What was crucial was practising; the conceptual frameworks simply served to briefly support and ultimately empower the internalising of such exercises, which gradually enable the art of improvising. This practical transmission, as mentioned in the introduction, resonates with oral pedagogical traditions; the fundamental idea is that of physical guidance through spoken instruction. Over time, the teacher aids the student in creating a space in their competence for fluid improvisation, a skill essential for the latter to graduate as professional musicians.

Indeed, the conceptual and instructive components that do exist can also be lent to this idea. Manuscript 1483 contains some written guidance mandating that a composer's

---

[19]. LORENZINI 1787.

core idea should be variability in the music and that this is what makes a real musician, especially when combined with a good voice leading. They steer the reader to focus on the experiential nature of what the musician plays or hears[20]. They comment that even rules themselves are inherently inclined to give rise to more specific rules, depending on the composer's thinking in the moment.

This needs to be seen in a broader context. The series of tips and exercises on how to learn music and improvise at the keyboard, derived from expanding on such models as these, inspired generations of students and professional musicians throughout the baroque period and thereafter. Yet currently, even specialist senior musicians would seldom consider these notions of improvisation when playing or singing eighteenth century music. They often consider such repertoires to be untouchable, even inviolable in a sense, as written and transmitted, thereby needing to be preserved as faithfully as possible. The paradigmatic shift away from the Romantic ideal that music should be original — that is, born from the inspiration of genius — did not undermine the importance of improvising in the eighteenth century. Furthermore, improvisation did not mean avoiding repeating oneself. On the contrary, repetitions, the art of diminution, varied sequences, and partimenti patterns such as those evident in the described sources, all these can serve to heighten the students' and audience's depth of engagement as well as the musician's own proficiency, through the layers of familiarity — even intimacy — with the patterns to produce them instinctively.

Music improvisation and the strong connection between theory and practice, between the composition and pedagogic methods of teaching partimenti and solfeggi, existed side by side at least from the late seventeenth until the early nineteenth century. All these aspects stimulated and inspired one another.

Bibliography

BARAGWANATH 2014
BARAGWANATH, Nicholas. 'Giovanni Battista de Vecchis and the Theory of Melodic Accent from Zarlino to Zingarelli', in: *Music & Letters*, XCV/2 (2014), pp. 157-182.

BARAGWANATH forthcoming
ID. *The Solfeggio Tradition: A Forgotten Art Melody in the Long Eighteenth Century*, forthcoming.

BERNSTEIN – HATCH 1993
Music Theory and the Exploration of the Past, edited by David W. Bernstein and Christopher Hatch, Chicago, The University of Chicago Press, 1993.

---

[20]. See the suggestions from the Ms.1438 such as «La prattica in ciò fa divenir capace», f. 26^v; «[...] secondo l'idea del compositore che la pratica lo farà vedere», f. 33^r.

Two New Sources

Cafiero 1993
Cafiero, Rosa. 'La didattica del partimento a Napoli fra Settecento e Ottocento: note sulla fortuna delle Regole di Carlo Cotumacci', in: *Gli affetti convenienti all'idee: studi sulla musica vocale italiana*, edited by Maria Caraci Vela, Rosa Cafiero and Angela Romagnoli, Naples, Edizioni scientifiche italiane, 1993 (Archivio del teatro e dello spettacolo, 3), pp. 549-580.

Cafiero 2007
Ead. 'The Early Reception of Neapolitan Partimento Theory in France: A Survey', in: *Journal of Music Theory*, LI/1 (2007), pp. 137-159.

Cafiero 2009
Ead. 'La formazione del musicista nel XVIII secolo: il "modello" dei conservatori napoletani', in: *Composizione e improvvisazione nella scuola napoletana del Settecento*, edited by Gaetano Stella, Lucca, LIM, 2009 (= *Rivista di analisi e teoria musicale*, XV/1 [2009]), pp. 5-25.

Christensen 2017
Christensen, Thomas. 'The Improvisatory Moment', in: Guido 2017, pp. 9-24.

Cipriani forthcoming
Cipriani, Benedetto. 'La didattica musicale del partimento: la situazione del contesto romano tra figure chiave e nuove fonti', in: *Music, Individuals and Contexts: Dialectical Interactions*, edited by Nadia Amendola, Alessandro Cosentino and Giacomo Sciommeri, Rome, Societá Editrice di Musicologia-Universitalia, forthcoming.

Erhardt 2013
Erhardt, Martin. *Upon a Ground: Improvisation on Ostinato Basses from the Sixteenth to the Eighteenth Centuries*, translated by Milo Machover, Magdeburg, Edition Walhall-Verlag Franz Biersack, 2013.

Gjerdingen 2007
Gjerdingen, Robert O. *Music in the Galant Style*, Oxford-New York, Oxford University Press, 2007.

Gjerdingen 2009
Id. 'The Perfection of Craft Training in the Neapolitan Conservatories', in: *Composizione e improvvisazione nella scuola napoletana del Settecento*, op. cit., pp. 26-51.

Guido 2017
Studies in Historical Improvisation: From 'Cantare super Librum' to Partimenti, edited by Massimiliano Guido, Abington-New York, Routledge, 2017.

Holtemeier 2007
Holtemeier, Ludwig. 'Heinichen, Rameau and the Italian Thoroughbass Tradition: Concepts of Tonality and Chord in the Rule of the Octave', in *Journal of Music Theory*, LI/1 (2007), pp. 5-49.

Lester 1994
Lester, Joel. *Compositional Theory in the Eighteenth Century*, Cambridge (MA), Harvard University Press, 1994.

Lorenzini 1787
Lorenzini, Raimondo. *Grammatica per il bassetto composta dal Sig. Raimondo Lorenzini fatto Maestro di Cappella della Basilica di S. Maria Maggiore l'ann.87 copiata in quest'an. med da me e per uso di me Gio. Nicoletti*, [1787], I-Rc Ms 2546.

Mann 2013
Mann, Alfred. *Teoria e pratica della composizione: i grandi compositori come maestri e come allievi*, edited by Giorgio Sanguinetti, Rome, Astrolabio, 2013 (Adagio).

Sanguinetti 2012
Sanguinetti, Giorgio. *The Art of Partimento in Naples: History, Theory and Practice*, Oxford-New York, Oxford University Press, 2012.

Van Tour 2014a—
Van Tour, Peter. *UUPart: The Uppsala Partimento Database*, Uppsala, 2014—, <https://www2.musik.uu.se/UUPart/UUPart.php>, accessed November 2018.

Van Tour 2014b—
Id. *UUSolf: The Uppsala Solfeggio Database*, Uppsala, 2014—, <https://www2.musik.uu.se/UUSolf/UUSolf.php>, accessed November 2018.

Van Tour 2015
Id. *Counterpoint and Partimento: Methods of Teaching Composition in Late Eighteenth-Century Naples*, Uppsala, Acta Universitatis Upsaliensis, 2015 (Studia musicologica Upsaliensia, Nova Series, 25).

On the Origin of Partimento:
A Recently Discovered Manuscript of
Toccate (1695) by Francesco Mancini

Giorgio Sanguinetti
(Università di Roma 'Tor Vergata')

In my book, *The Art of Partimento*, which was published in 2012, I attempted to build a narrative on the origin of partimento based on the evidence available at that time[1]. My narrative is mainly based (but not exclusively) on the fact that the earliest known collection of partimenti with an author's name was found in the manuscript by Bernardo Pasquini in the British Library, presumably compiled between 1703 and 1708, for the education of Pasquini's nephew, Bernardo Felice Ricordati[2]. Pasquini, together with Alessandro Scarlatti and Arcangelo Corelli, formed a circle of elite musicians who gathered in Rome around Queen Christina of Sweden in the earliest years of the eighteenth century. This, and other evidence — such as an anonymous manuscript, which dates back to 1696 in the Berlin library[3], but clearly originated in Rome as evident from the watermarks on the paper — led me to speculate about the Roman origin of the partimento tradition and its subsequent move to Naples, following Alessandro Scarlatti's appointment as maestro di cappella at the royal court.

Only three years later, Peter van Tour, in his 2015 doctoral dissertation, made the existence of the manuscript dated 1695 and containing a large partimenti collection by Francesco Mancini public; this manuscript represents the earliest known document attesting the usage of partimenti as teaching material[4]. The Mancini manuscript — currently preserved in the National Library of Paris (F-Pn Rés. 2315), bearing the title *Regole o vero Toccate di studio del Sig. Abb[at]e Fran[cesc]o Mancini 1695* — is a large collection of (mainly) keyboard music: it probably arrived in Paris with the 'Selvaggi collection' and

---

[1]. Sanguinetti 2012.
[2]. London (GB-Lbl) MS Add. 31501, Facsimile edition: Pasquini 1988. Modern editions: Pasquini 1968; Pasquini 2006a; Pasquini 2006b.
[3]. *Regole per accompagnare nel Cimbalo ò vero Organo*, Berlin (D-Bsb) Mus.ms.theor. 1483.
[4]. Van Tour 2015.

was bought by the conservatoire in 1812[5]. The manuscript — whose existence Florimo suspected, which can be inferred from an oblique allusion in volume two of his history of the Naples conservatories — adds substantially to the meagre catalogue of the hitherto known keyboard music of Mancini[6]. The keyboard music in this manuscript includes titled works (a series of 21 *Toccate di studio*, 8 *Sonate*, 12 *Lettioni di sonare* and three isolated pieces) and untitled works, almost all notated as partimenti (the complete list is given in TABLE 1). Noteworthy is the fact that the toccate and the sonate are multi-movement pieces — a very unusual circumstance in later partimenti — and that they offer a remarkable amount of performance directions: hence, this manuscript can shed light both on the origin of partimento and on its early performance practice.

As it often happens with partimenti codices, the title and the author's name do not necessarily correspond to the actual content, which might not be entirely the work of Francesco Mancini. Rés. 2315 is in fact a *zibaldone* — a haphazard collection of material coming from different sources and authors. We cannot even be sure that all the material contained in the codex was composed in the year 1695. In fact, the dates on *zibaldoni* often indicate the year in which the manuscript was copied, or when it came into possession of the owner. Therefore, the content may have been composed earlier.

Before examining the content of the manuscript, I would like to spend a few words on Francesco Mancini. He was born in 1672 in Naples and entered the Pietà dei Turchini conservatory in 1688. In 1695, (the date on our manuscript) Francesco Mancini was 23 years old. He had been a student of the conservatory for seven years, having teachers such as Francesco Provenzale and Gennaro Ursino (more about Ursino later)[7]. In 1694, he began his six-year tenure as an organist at La Pietà dei Turchini conservatory; therefore, when the date 1695 was written on the manuscript, he had just started his duty as an organist. As one of the most outstanding composers of his generation, and one who worked as an organist for most of his life, very little is known of his keyboard works. As Angela Romagnoli had put it, «only a few traces are left of his keyboard toccate, written for pedagogical purposes, which must have been part of a larger corpus, given Mancini's long teaching career»[8]. This passage echoes Florimo's complaint, «Of all his other musical compositions that he, as a teacher of the conservatory, no doubt made in great quantity, nothing is known […] perhaps they were lost»[9]. Florimo's source is probably Giuseppe Sigismondo's *Apotheosis of the Music in the Kingdom of Naples* (now available in a modern bilingual Italian-English

---

[5]. On the Selvaggi collection: see CAFIERO 2007 and FABRIS 2015.

[6]. See footnote 8.

[7]. The most complete biographical account on Francesco Mancini is ROMAGNOLI 2018.

[8]. «È rimasta solo qualche traccia delle toccate per tastiera (scritte a scopo didattico), che dovevano far parte di un *corpus* più ampio dato il lungo impegno del M. nell'insegnamento». *Ibidem*.

[9]. «Di tutte le altre sue composizioni musicali, che, come maestro del Conservatorio, molte ne dovette fare, nulla si sa, salvoché di quelle esistenti nel Real Collegio di Napoli. Forse andarono disperse per trascurataggine di chi dovea aver cura di conservarle». FLORIMO 1882, p. 308.

edition)[10]. The discovery of this manuscript solves the mystery of the disappearance of Mancini's didactical toccate.

The manuscript has an oblong format and consists of eighty folios, or 161 pages. It contains 109 pieces (the content of the manuscript is shown in TABLE 1). As we can see, the content of this manuscript is composite in many ways. First, there is more than one hand involved in the physical making of the manuscript. The alternation in three different hands creates five groups, arranged in a rondo-like form.

TABLE 1: CONTENT OF MANUSCRIPT F-PN RÉS. 2315

GROUP	FOLIO	COPYIST
21 *Toccate*	1^r-21^v	copyist A
Una sincopa	21^v	
8 *Sonate*	22^r-31^v	
15 partimenti [no title]	32^r-35^v	copyist B
26 partimenti [no title]	36^r-48^v	copyist A
1 cantata «del Sig. Bononcini 1695»	49^r-49^v	
12 *Lettioni di sonare del sig. Francesco Mancini*	50^r-77^v	copyist C
1 intavolatura [no title]	78^r-80^r	
6 partimenti [no title]	80^v-84^v	
3 examples of diminutions [no title]	84^v	
1 partimento [no title]	85^r-85^v	copyist A
16 lessons [no title]	85^r-97^v	
Fantasia di capriccio	97^v-99^r	
Capriccio	99^r-99^v	
Cantata «Del Sig. Bononcini 1695»	100^r	
Cantata «Del Sig. Gio. Nardelli»	100^v	

Most of the content is keyboard music, with the addition of three short cantatas[11]. There are also differences in the notation of the keyboard pieces: most are notated as partimenti — on a single staff with continuo figures — and some are written as *intavolature* (the standard two staves notation). Yet, the two-staves notation is far from being thoroughly written out. In fact, the notation of the left hand often consists of a sketch of the bass, which needs to be further elaborated and composed. In this aspect,

---

[10]. SIGISMONDO 2016.
[11]. The textual incipits of the cantatas are: 'Ritorno Aquila amante' (Bononcini, cc. 49^r-49^v); 'Non sa che sia costanza' (Bononcini, c. 100^r); 'Se i tuoi sguardi furon dardi' (Nardelli, c. 100^v).

355

Neapolitan intavolature have much in common with partimenti, since they share a different kind of incomplete notation[12].

Multiple authorship is another problem with partimenti. Sometimes, the same piece is found in several different manuscripts with the attribution to different authors. So, how can we be sure that Francesco Mancini was the author of the entire manuscript? I immediately nurtured doubts on the authenticity of the *Sonate*, since several movements in this series open with long rests. This makes no sense in a partimento. In fact, the eight sonates are actually the continuo part of Corelli's Church Trio Sonatas Op. III[13]. Interestingly, the continuo part of Op. III appears in a manuscript in the Doria Pamphilj archive in Rome with the title «Bassetti», a synonym for partimenti used in Rome (in general, the term 'partimento' was hardly used outside the kingdom of Naples)[14]. This confirms that bass parts extracted from Corelli's works were used for teaching purpose, such as *bassetti*, or partimenti (a use also attested in Emanuele Muzio's studies in composition with Giuseppe Verdi in the third decade of the nineteenth century)[15].

Mancini's authorship is openly stated for two series only: the 21 *Toccate* and the 12 *Lezioni di Sonare*. But what about the rest? Today, we have tools at our disposal that were not available only a decade ago. I refer in particular at the UUPart — the Uppsala partimento database, freely available on the web — founded by Peter van Tour[16]. UUPart allows a string search of a single partimento, building instantly a table of concordance for each string. This feature is crucial, because it helps in analysing one of the biggest questions in partimento research: multiple attribution, namely the attribution of the same partimento to several authors. Thanks to the UUPart database, I found some concordances: nos. 63, 68 and 71 (all fugues) appear in other manuscripts with attribution to Durante and Leo (no. 71 appears in *seventeen* manuscripts)[17]. No. 79 (f. 80^v) is a special case: it is incomplete in the Mancini manuscript, but complete in only one other source. This other manuscript is I-Nc 33.2.3, a collection of partimenti, intavolature and more with a clear attribution to Rocco Greco (ca. 1650-before 1718), who taught violin at the Poveri di Gesù Cristo

---

[12]. On this subject: see SANGUINETTI 2017.

[13]. I owe this information to Peter van Tour. Corelli's Op. III was first published in Rome by Gio. Girolamo Komarek in 1689 (six years earlier than 1695) and in separate parts.

[14]. *Bassetti del Sig. Arcangelo Corelli*, Rome (I-Rdp) 276/B.

[15]. Emanuele Muzio described in great detail his studies with Verdi in his letters to Giuseppe Barezzi: see GARIBALDI 1931 and MARVIN 2010.

[16]. <http://www2.musik.uu.se/UUPart/UUPart.php>, accessed October 2018.

[17]. The numbering I am using is provisional, as Mancini's partimenti still does not have GJ numbers. When I am referring to a single partimento, I always give the folio indication as well. No. 63 (f. 47^v): D-MÜs SANT HS 1430, GB-Cfm MU.MS 709, I-Nc Roche A.5.6; no. 68 (f. 50^v) D-MÜs SANT HS 1430, GB-Cfm MU.MS 709, I-Nc Roche A.5.6, I-Mc Noseda Th.c.107, I-Nc 22.2.6/5, I-PESc Rari Ms.c.12: no. 71 (f. 52^v) D-MÜs SANT HS 1430, GB-Cfm MU.MS.709, I-Bc EE.171, I-MC 7-A-28, I-Mc Noseda Th.c.107, I-Mc Noseda Th.c.123, I-Mc Noseda Th.c.133, I-Nc 22.1.14, I-Nc 34.2.3, I-Nc 34.2.4, I-Nc Oc 3.40, I-Nc Roche A.5.6, I-PESc Rari Ms.c.13/1 and 13/2, I-Ria Misc.Mss.Vess. 283.

conservatory between 1678 and 1695 (the date on the Mancini manuscript). Rocco was the elder brother of Gaetano Greco, the teacher of Domenico Scarlatti and Nicola Porpora, who taught Haydn. Another significant concordance is with a manuscript counterpoint treatise whose author is probably (but not certainly) Gennaro Ursino, one of the teachers of Mancini (I will discuss this point later).

The 21 *Toccate di Studio*

The most distinctive series in the Mancini manuscript are the 21 Toccate, which also give their name to the manuscript. The title, translated, is: 'Rules, or Instructional Toccatas'. Two things are immediately evident in this title: first, if we mean by 'Rule' a written (verbal) instruction about some aspect of the theory, then in the whole manuscript there are no rules, not even the concise instructions offered by Furno, Durante, or Cotumacci. Second, the title suggests that partimenti, even at this very early stage, were already being used for teaching purposes.

The *Toccate di studio*, in comparison with the partimenti written by the later generations of maestri, are quite unique. They are generally longer that the standard Neapolitan partimento: the first toccata is 111-bar long, that is, from two to three times the average length of a Durante's *Numerato*. More importantly, they are multi-movement pieces whose style is close to the organ toccata, which was practiced in Naples during the first half of the seventeenth century, with authors such as Giovanni Maria Trabaci and Ascanio Mayone. Finally, these toccate are among the few partimenti having performance directions (other than tempo indications). Table 2 shows a list of these directions:

TABLE 2: Performance Directions in the *Toccate di studio*

Toccata 1:	«dolce; camina; pia[no]»
Toccata 2:	«piano, tasto solo»
Toccata 5:	«tirata di tasti»
Toccata 6:	«camina»
Toccata 7:	«staccato»
Toccata 8:	«tirata di tasti»
Toccata 9:	«tirata di tasti»
Toccata 21:	«tirata di tasti»

While most of the terms are self-explanatory, the term 'tirata di tasti' needs perhaps some clarification. According to Sébastien de Brossard, this term was used by the Italians to designate «all stepwise succession of several notes of the same value, ascending or descending. The *Tirata Aucta* or *Excedens* is the musical note achieved when it exceeds the borders of the octave, going one third, or one fourth, or even one fifth above or below the octave»[18].

As one can see in Ex. 1, the notated music already shows two *Tirate Auctae*: but why did the author (or the scribe) pen down what is already evident on the score? Is this a performance direction like *camina*, or *staccato*? Or has the sign a didactic intent, as to tell the student, «You see? This is a tirata»? Or perhaps, its purpose is to suggest the performer a specific accompaniment, such as a parallel run in the right hand by thirds or tenths?

Ex. 1: directions «tirata di tasti» in *Toccata nona* (f. 11ʳ).

The length and the variety of the 21 Toccate in this manuscript do not allow to focus on a single technical problem, as is the case with most mid-to-late eighteenth century partimenti, such as those by Durante or, even more, by Fenaroli. However, some of them do seem to focus on some specific issues.

The first toccata stands out for its bold modulations. The complete transcription of this piece in its original partimento notation is given in Ex. 2.

Ex. 3 reproduces the first 25 bars of the *Toccata prima* with analytical annotations. The home key is clearly E major, but with a key signature of two sharps only. The Toccata opens with a syncopated octave descent accompanied with alternating 4/2 and 6 chords and closed by a cadence — a standard partimento technique. An ascending fourth by stepwise motion, accompanied with the *Regola dell'ottava*, leads to A (in bar 5). This note sets in motion a descending progression by minor thirds, confirmed by a strong *cadenza doppia* on F sharp in bars 6-7 (indicated with the sign CD in Ex. 3) This progression

---

[18]. 'Tirata', in: BROSSARD 1703, pages not numbered.

Ex. 2: *Toccata prima*, transcription in the original partimento notation.

Giorgio Sanguinetti

repeats one minor third lower (on D sharp) and again one minor third below, on B sharp, thus delineating an overall motion by diminished seventh. The B sharp is then brought an octave higher (bar 10) and then sets in motion a passage with four notes a whole tone apart (bar 13), leading to a cadenza doppia in the key of A-sharp minor; the modulation is further confirmed by two progressions, the latter ending with a cadenza composta (CC) in the same key. The A sharp is again brought an octave higher (bar 19), and then a new pattern begins: a bass motion by 'third down, second up' six steps long. The pattern in itself is not unusual at all, but the scale in use actually is: the first five steps delineate again a whole tone scale A sharp - G sharp – F sharp – E natural – D natural, and finally C sharp as dominant of the new key, F-sharp minor (bar 25): this arrival point is emphasized by an expanded cadenza doppia.

Ex. 3: first 25 bars of *Toccata prima* with analytical annotation added.

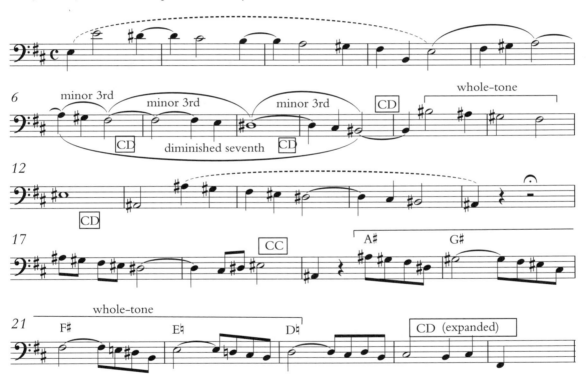

In the remainder of the *Toccata*, the bass line briefly touches F major and C major before returning to the sharp side passing through G minor, E minor and B minor (in this notation the flat has a double meaning: as a real flat and as a natural, depending on the context). Ex. 4a and 4b show two sections of the *Toccata prima*, bars 1-15 and 57-79, respectively in my essential realisation of these bars. By 'essential realisation' I mean a realisation that gives the essential harmonic and contrapuntal contour, leaving aside idiomatic passages and embellishments.

Ex. 4: essential realisation of bars 1-25 and 57-79 of *Toccata prima*.

On the Origin of Partimento

The Toccata features repeated modulatory patterns, which seem to indicate that it was intended as an exemplar, that is, a work written as a model for imitation and speculation: in other words, a theoretical work, but one that ought to be played too. But how could a single piece written in the second half of the seventeenth century modulate so many and such distant keys? My conjecture is that this toccata in particular (more than the other twenty, which do not modulate so boldly) was written with an enharmonic instrument in mind, such as the sambuca lincea, or the tricembalo. The sambuca lincea was invented and described by the Neapolitan musician, naturalist and botanic, Fabio Colonna (ca. 1567-1640), a scientist much admired by Linnaeus. Tricembalo was created by the priest and organist, Scipione Stella (ca. 1558-1622), who in his youth was at the service of Gesualdo da Venosa. In the seventeenth century Naples, together with Ferrara, was apparently affected by an enharmonic madness, at the point that even the famous Bolognese painter Domenico Zampieri, called the Domenichino, built his own archicembalo during his Neapolitan period[19].

According to Patrizio Barbieri, the sambuca lincea could modulate to 31 keys, and the tricembalo to 21, allowing the performance of music to 'circulate' through all the keys before returning home[20]. The daring modulations of the *Toccata prima* — something that disappeared with the onset of galant style during the eighteenth century — may be reminiscent of the fashion of harmonically 'circulating' music that permeated Naples during the early seventeenth century. Further, my evidence showed that the collection was actually composed in the seventeenth century, and perhaps much earlier than the date written on the manuscript.

Earlier, I briefly mentioned Gennaro Ursino with reference to another seventeenth century manuscript. A manuscript in the Naples conservatory library entitled *Lezzioni di contropunto*, dated 1677, contains a complete course in counterpoint, (from species to invertible to imitative) which apparently took many years to complete[21]. On the first page of the manuscript, the sign «Di Gennaro» indicated the owner/scribe of the manuscript, perhaps Gennaro Ursino (ca. 1650-1715). The first date in the frontispiece is 1677, but the owner marked the completion of the different sections with the respective dates: June 1679 is the date of a study of imitation, and August 1681 refers to the first, second and fourth species of (Fuxian) counterpoint. July 1688 marks a study on fugue. Then, a single partimento appears (f. 58ᵛ), followed by other fugues (this partimento is shown in Ex. 5). On the last pages of the manuscript, there are examples of cadences, including the 'cadenza lunga' progression.

---

[19]. BARBIERI 1987.
[20]. A transcription of an anonymous 'circulating' toccata is given by *ibidem* pp. 194-196.
[21]. Gennaro Ursino, *Lezzioni di Contropunto*, 1677, Naples (I-Nc 34.2.7).

Ex. 5: *Lezzioni di contropunto*, f. 58ᵛ.

The only partimento in the Ursino manuscript appears also in the Mancini manuscript at c. 32ʳ, as no. 1 of the 15 partimenti written by copyist B (section 4 in TABLE 1). Since the Ursino is a very clean manuscript, with almost no erasures and corrections, it was probably conceived as an exemplar: a collection of examples written by a maestro as guide to the student's work. This hypothesis agrees with the dates and the presumed author, who in 1677, was already an assistant professor of Francesco Provenzale at the conservatory of La Pietà dei Turchini. If this assumption is correct, the Ursino partimento could be the oldest partimento known, and also in the Ursino manuscript there is evidence of the use of partimenti at La Pietà as soon as in 1688. Therefore, the date 1695 in the Mancini manuscript does not necessarily refer to the year of composition of the material therein contained.

Earlier, I mentioned the Rocco Greco manuscript (I-Nc 33.2.3). This manuscript's title (*Intavolature per cembalo e partimenti di Rocco Greco*) was probably added by a librarian and misrepresents the content. There are indeed partimenti and intavolature for keyboard, but there are also five very unusual pieces written on a two-staff system, both with a bass clef, such as the one shown in Ex. 6[22].

---

[22]. The manuscript is acephalous: the first of the five pieces appears on the second page (f. 1ᵛ), in what seems to be a very old handwriting, the number 12, but afterwards the page numbering becomes erratic. The series interrupts after nine folios.

Ex. 6: Excertps from *Intavolature per cembalo e partimenti di Rocco Greco*.

On the Origin of Partimento

It consists of two bass lines: the lowest is simple and schematic, the upper one is essentially the same, but more complex. What is interesting, in my opinion, is that the upper line is not only a diminution of the lower but is also a complete realisation of its harmonic implications. So, it was indeed possible for a bass instrument player (in this case, a cello) to realise a partimento with no keyboard, using a single, polyphonic melody[23]. This answers a common question among theory teachers who want to introduce partimenti in their syllabus: how can I teach this to non-keyboard students? One possibility is using an ensemble with different instruments playing different voices of the texture. The possibility shown by Rocco Greco is perhaps more challenging because one should not only master simultaneously continuo realisation and diminution; but also stimulating, because by using this technique, a non-keyboard player can create a solo realisation.

In conclusion, we can say that today we know much more about partimenti than we did ten of fifteen years ago. But, much more is still to be discovered. I am sure that many other exciting developments will take place in the future.

Bibliography

Barbieri 1987
Barbieri, Patrizio. 'La 'Sambuca Lincea' di Fabio Colonna e il 'Tricembalo' di Scipione Stella', in: *La musica a Napoli durante il Seicento. Atti del convegno internazionale di studi (Napoli, 11-14 aprile 1985)*, edited by Domenico Antonio D'Alessandro and Agostino Ziino, Rome, Torre d'Orfeo, 1987, pp. 167-236.

---

[23]. On cello teaching methods in Naples: see Olivieri 2009.

BROSSARD 1703
BROSSARD Sébastien de. 'Tirata', in: *Dictionnaire de Musique*, Paris, Ballard, 1703.

CAFIERO 2007
CAFIERO, Rosa. 'The Early Reception of Neapolitan Partimento Theory in France: A Survey', in: *Journal of Music Theory*, LI/1 (2007), pp. 137-159.

FABRIS 2015
FABRIS, Dinko. 'L'art de disperser da collection: Le cas du napolitain Gaspare Selvaggi' (1763-1856), in: *Collectionner la musique: Erudits collectionneurs*, edited by Denis Herlin, Catherine Massip and Valérie De Wispelaere, Turnhout, Brepols, 2015 (Collectionner la musique, 3), pp. 359-394.

FLORIMO 1882
FLORIMO, Francesco. *La scuola musicale di Napoli e i suoi conservatorii: con uno sguardo sulla storia della musica italiana. 2: La scuola musicale di Napoli e i suoi conservatorii, con le Biografie dei maestri usciti dai medesimi*, Naples, Morano, 1882.

GARIBALDI 1931
GARIBALDI, Luigi Agostino. *Giuseppe Verdi nelle lettere di Emanuele Muzio ad Antonio Barezzi*, Milan, Treves, 1931 (Grandi musicisti italiani e stranieri).

MARVIN 2010
MARVIN, Roberta Montemorra. *Verdi the Student – Verdi the Teacher*, Parma, Istituto Nazionale di Studi Verdiani, 2010 (Premio internazionale Rotary Club di Parma 'Giuseppe Verdi', 5).

OLIVIERI 2009
OLIVIERI, Guido. 'Cello Teaching and Playing in Naples in the Early Eighteenth Century: Francesco Paolo Supriani's *Principij da imparare a suonare il violoncello*', in: *Performance Practice: Issues and Approaches*, edited by Timothy D. Watkins, Ann Arbor (MI), Steglein, 2009, pp. 109-136.

PASQUINI 1968
PASQUINI, Bernardo. *Collected Works for Keyboard*, edited by Maurice Brooks Haynes, American Institute for Musicology, 1968.

PASQUINI 1988
ID. *London, British Library, MS Add. 31501*, Facsimile edition edited by Alexander Silbiger, New York-London, Garland, 1988 (17th Century Keyboard Music, 8).

PASQUINI 2006A
ID. *Opere per tastiera: vol. VI*, edited by Edoardo Bellotti, Latina, Il Levante 2006.

PASQUINI 2006B
ID. *Opere per tastiera: vol. VII*, edited by Armando Carideo, Latina, Il Levante 2006.

ROMAGNOLI 2018
ROMAGNOLI, Angela. 'Mancini, Francesco', in: *Dizionario Biografico degli Italiani*, <http://www.treccani.it/enciclopedia/francesco-mancini_%28Dizionario-Biografico%29/>, accessed October 2018

SANGUINETTI 2012
SANGUINETTI, Giorgio. *The Art of Partimento: History, Theory and Practice*, Oxford-New York, Oxford University Press, 2012.

SANGUINETTI 2017
ID. 'Partimento and Incomplete Notation in Eighteenth-Century Keyboard Music', in: *Studies in Historical Improvisation: From 'Cantare super Librum' to Partimenti*, edited by Massimiliano Guido, Abington-New York, Routledge, 2017, pp. 149-171.

SIGISMONDO 2016
Apoteosi della musica del Regno di Napoli: Giuseppe Sigismondo, edited by Claudio Bacciagaluppi, Giulia Giovani and Raffaele Mellace, with an introduction by Rosa Cafiero, Rome, Società Editrice di Musicologia, 2016 (Saggi, 2).

VAN TOUR 2015
VAN TOUR, Peter. *Counterpoint and Partimento: Methods of Teaching Composition in Late Eighteenth-Century Naples*, Uppsala, Acta Universitatis Upsaliensis, 2015 (Studia musicologica Upsaliensia. Nova Series, 25).

«Taking a Walk at the Molo»:
Partimento and the Improvised Fugue

Peter van Tour
(Norwegian Academy of Music)

During the last few decades, the partimento repertoire and its pedagogical functions have been discussed in an increasing number of books, articles, and dissertations[1]. Although there is general agreement among scholars that partimenti were used in the Neapolitan conservatories for developing improvisational fluency at the keyboard, it has not been entirely clear exactly *when* students carried out their studies in partimento in relation to their studies in counterpoint. Were partimenti studied prior to the study of written counterpoint, or was it rather a certain part of this repertoire that had that function?

In recent years it has become increasingly clear that partimento, solfeggio, and counterpoint were applied as integral parts of the curriculum in the Neapolitan conservatories to teach composition through vocal improvisation, composition at the keyboard[2], and through written counterpoint and composition. It was necessary to have some basic skills in partimento playing before one could advance to the counterpoint class. The educational context has helped us to further define the term 'partimento', showing its double pedagogical function: on the one hand partimenti were used for developing musical imagination through the realization of figured or unfigured basses at the keyboard, on the other hand partimenti were used for developing fluency in written composition. In other words, the term 'partimento' can be understood as «a notational device, commonly written on a single staff in the F clef, either figured or unfigured, applied both in playing and in writing activities, and used for developing skills in the art of accompaniment, improvisation, diminution, and counterpoint»[3]. Partimento and

---

[1]. Borgir 1987; Christensen 1992; Renwick 1995; Renwick 2001; Gjerdingen 2007; Gingras 2008; Callahan 2010; Sanguinetti 2012; Van Tour 2015; Bellotti 2017, among others.
[2]. For a brief reflection on this term, see Bellotti 2017, p. 115.
[3]. See also Van Tour 2015, p. 19.

composition were fully complementary, in similar ways as was the case with thoroughbass and composition in German compositional theory[4].

A first account regarding the relationship between partimento and counterpoint is found in one of the counterpoint notebooks that describe Fedele Fenaroli's (1713-1818) teaching in counterpoint, entitled *Studio di Contrapunto del Sig.ʳ D. Fedele Fenaroli* (I-Nc 22-2-6/2), in which Fenaroli leaves no doubt about the propedeutical function of his first three books of partimenti:

> For those who want to learn counterpoint, it is necessary first to thoroughly study the first and second books of partimenti, and then the moti del basso of the third book[5].

At the Conservatorio di Santa Maria della Pietà de' Turchini, hereafter called the Pietà, counterpoint was taught according to a more conservative method of teaching counterpoint, in which partimenti were used to prepare students for their lessons in written counterpoint and fugue[6]. In the two other Neapolitan conservatories, the Onofrio and the Loreto, the writing of fugues had already declined, probably as a result of an increased interest for melodic writing, which evidently was esteemed to be greater important for writing of dramatic music.

In his *Biographie* of 1848, the Bohemian composer Adalbert Gyrowetz (1763-1850) gives some interesting anecdotal evidence of how students were mentally prepared for their future work as a composer. In this autobiography (because that is what it is)[7], Gyrowetz describes the path taken in counterpoint lessons with his teacher Nicola Sala (1713-1801) at the Pietà:

> *Maestro* Sala was in this subject [counterpoint] the most famous teacher and likewise, he was *maestro* in counterpoint at *La Pietà*, the most distinguished of the musical conservatories, of which there were three in Naples. Maestro Sala had already reached an advanced age and was happy to take care of a young German student who already had a good reputation in the field of instrumental music. The study of counterpoint started with exercises on the scale, and since Gyrowetz already had considerable experience combining chords, he proceeded with dispositions for two, three and four parts, then moving on with canons and fugues, etc. etc., in which art maestro Sala was an excellent teacher[8].

---

[4]. For the relationship between thoroughbass and composition in German eighteenth-century compositional theory, see: LESTER 1992, pp. 65-68.

[5]. I-Nc 22-2-6/2, fol. 1ᵛ: «Quelli che desiderano apprendere il Contropunto è necessario che prima studiassero bene il primo e secondo libro numerico, ed ancora li movimenti del Basso del terzo libro […]». .

[6]. For a description of the contrapuntal training at the Pietà, see VAN TOUR 2015, pp. 169-207.

[7]. RENWICK 1995, p. 10.

[8]. GYROWETZ 1848, p. 26: «Kapellmeister Sala war in diesem Fach in Neapel der berühmteste und auch zugleich Meister des Contrapunctes im Conservatorium della Pietà, welches unter den andern Conservatorien,

«Taking a Walk at the Molo»: Partimento and the Improvised Fugue

Adalbert Gyrowetz' lessons with Nicola Sala must have taken place at the Pietà within the time span between 1787 and 1789 (most probably in 1788 and 1789) and contain several interesting details. The lessons started with contrapuntal exercises written over and under the scale. This method of working is also known from Sala's printed counterpoint treatise the *Regole del contrappunto pratico* (Naples, 1794), where such exercises dominate the greater part of the first volume, and appears likewise in Benedetto Neri's counterpoint notebook written in 1796 (see Ex. 1)[9]:

Ex. 1: Benedetto Neri, 'Quarta specie a due' (1796) (I-NOd, Fondo cappella musicale 3387, fols. 7ʳ).

After these exercises, Gyrowetz's biography tells us that the counterpoint student advanced to what he terms «zwei, drei, und vierstimmigen Satz», that is dispositions (*disposizioni*) for two, three, and four voices. A great number of such dispositions are found in Sala's *Regole del contrappunto pratico*[10].

Finally, Gyrowetz's biography reports that the counterpoint studies led to the training of canon and fugue, «in which art Maestro Sala was an excellent teacher» (see the quotation above). After having expressed his admiration for his former counterpoint teacher, Gyrowetz gives us a few details about Sala's pedagogy:

> He had the habit of taking a walk at the Molo or near Mount Vesuvius together with Gyrowetz, after finishing the class in counterpoint and during the walk Gyrowetz was obliged to repeat orally what he had learnt; since the

---

deren es in Neapel drei gab, das vorzüglichste war. Meister Sala war bereits in einem hohen Alter, und freute sich, einen deutschen jungen Schüler zu übernehmen, welcher sich bereits in der Instrumental-Musik einen erfreulichen Namen erworben hatte. Der Anfang des Unterrichtes im Contrapunct wurde dann mit Ausübung einer regelmäßigen echten Tonleiter gemacht, und weil Gyrowetz in den Accorden-Fügung ohnedies bereits erfahren war, so wurde sogleich zum zwei, drei und vierstimmigen Satz und sodann zu Verfertigung von Fugen und Canons etc. etc. geschritten, in welcher Musikgattung Meister Sala ein ausgezeichneter, vorzüglicher Lehrer war. Er hatte die Gewohnheit, nach beendigter Lehrstunde immer mit Gyrowetz einen Spaziergang am Molo, oder in die Nähe vom Vesuv zu machen, und im Gehen mußte Gyrowetz das Erlernte ihm mündlich wiederholen; als der Unterricht bereits schon zu den Fugen gekommen war, mußte Gyrowetz ihm sämmtliche Bestandtheile einer Fuge, nämlich Thema, Umkehrung, Modulation, Imitationen, Verdopplung, Verengung etc. etc. bis zur Coda auswendig lernen, und mündlich vorrecitiren; das war eine sehr gute Methode, welche einem jeden Schüler in der Composition besonders anzuempfehlen ist».

[9]. Benedetto Neri (1771-1841), «Studio di contrappunto incominciato da me Benedetto Neri nell'anno 1796 alli 12. di Decembre 1796» (I-NOd, Fondo cappella musicale 3387).

[10]. See also BRANDENBURG 2003.

teaching already had come to the fugues, Gyrowetz had to memorize all the different components of a fugue, such as the theme, its inversion, modulation, imitation, augmentation, stretti, etc. etc. up to the coda and to recite these loudly; this was a very good method, which particularly may be recommended to any student in composition[11].

This quotation suggests that the extensive series of fugues that Gyrowetz wrote during his lessons with Sala had a pedagogical function reaching beyond the mere skills of putting a fugue together. As becomes clear, Sala demanded quite a remarkable level of mental skills in his contrapuntal teaching, urging Gyrowetz to vocally reproduce all components of the fugue, while taking a walk after their lesson in counterpoint.

In addition to this, an anonymous counterpoint notebook (F-Pn Ms. 8223) from about the same year (1789), which I recently identified as deriving from Sala's contrapuntal instruction, may here serve as an example of how the various components of the fugue were labeled.

I presume that the scribe of this counterpoint notebook may have been a certain Louis Julien Castels de Labarre (1771-?) who studied with Sala between 1788 and 1789[12]. The following two-part fugue from Louis Julien Castels de Labarre's notebook of fugues shows an example of how Sala introduced his students in the various components of the two-part fugue. Similar to what can be seen in a great number of counterpoint notebooks, de Labarre marked the start of these lessons on the first page of his notebook: «Du Dimanche 11 Janvier 1789, 1ᵉ Leçon de fugue a 2» (see Ex. 2):

---

[11]. GYROWETZ 1848, p. 26: «Er hatte die Gewohnheit, nach beendigter Lehrstunde immer mit Gyrowetz einen Spaziergang am Molo, oder in die Nähe vom Vesuv zu machen, und im Gehen mußte Gyrowetz das Erlernte ihm mündlich wiederholen; als der Unterricht bereits schon zu den Fugen gekommen war, mußte Gyrowetz ihm sämmtliche Bestandtheile einer Fuge, nämlich Thema, Umkehrung, Modulation, Imitationen, Verdopplung, Verengung etc. etc. bis zur Coda auswendig lernen, und mündlich vorrecitiren; das war eine sehr gute Methode, welche einem jeden Schüler in der Composition besonders anzuempfehlen ist».

[12]. Since the author of F-Pn Ms. 8223 also left two partimento collections with partimenti by Nicola Sala and Leonardo Leo, it seems likely that this author must have been known to Alexandre-Étienne Choron, and that he thus should appear in Choron's *Dictionnaire historique des musiciens*, published in 1810. At that time Choron had done extensive research in Sala's pedagogical writings, published and translated Sala's entire *Regole del contrapuntto pratico*. We know also, that Choron was aware of at least one other French student who studied at the same conservatory with Nicola Sala, in 1776: Étienne-Joseph Floquet (1748-1785). Floquet owned an autograph collection of Sala's partimenti which were reprinted in Choron's *Principes de Composition des Écoles d'Italie*. Given these circumstantial facts, it seems reasonable to assume that the author of F-Pn Ms. 8223 should appear in Choron's *Dictionnaire*. Investigation of this matter shows indeed that Sala did have a French student around 1790 by the name of Louis-Julien Castels de Labarre, who studied at the same conservatory with exactly the same teacher. However, Choron gives a slightly later date for de Labarre's studies: 1791 until 1793, instead of 1788 and 1789. Although we cannot be entirely sure about this, I assume that Choron did give incorrect dates for de Labarre's time of study. See CHORON 1810, p. 383.

Ex. 2: Louis Julien Castels de Labarre (?), Fuga No. 1, bars 1-20 (F-Pn Ms. 8223, fols. 1ʳ).

Even though it may seem clear that students wrote extensive series of fugues, the question remains how all this is related to the practice of partimento? Were the partimenti generally studied before these two-part written exercises and were partimenti intended to prepare the student for his studies in written counterpoint? And how could we possibly know this, when the partimenti in most cases survive in notebooks different from the counterpoint notebooks?

Luckily, in the case of Louis Julien Castels de Labarre's materials, there is a clear answer to this question: both his partimento notebooks and his counterpoint notebook were dated by de Labarre on the front covers: his first partimento collection is entitled «1.ᵉʳ Cayé de Partimenti de Basses d'accompagnement Del Signor D. Nicola Sala, Premier Maitre de composition du conservatoire de la Pieta a Naples a 15 Juillet 1788» (F-Pn 4° c² 343/1), while his counterpoint notebook is dated «Du dimanche 11 Janvier 1789» (F-Pn Ms. 8223), about six months later. The fact that both the partimento collections and the counterpoint notebook are written by the same scribal hand, suggests that this French student, who almost certainly belonged to the group of the paying boarder students, the *pensionaristi*, engaged himself for at least half a year of intensive partimento studies before advancing to the class of counterpoint.

In addition to this, it is revealing to take a closer look at the partimenti in the two partimento notebooks of De Labarre. The first 'cahier' of partimenti contains thirty-

Ex. 3: The front covers of two notebooks, the first containing partimenti, the second containing counterpoint exercises, both dated and written in the same hand (F-Pn 4° c² 343/1 and F-Pn Ms. 8223).

two partimenti by Nicola Sala and twenty partimenti by Leonardo Leo (1694-1744)[13]. All thirty-two partimenti by Sala in the first collection F-Pn 4° c² 343/1 are pieces of low to moderate level, all in F-clef and without any use of clef changes. This section is followed by twenty partimenti by Leonardo Leo that are slightly more difficult, containing clef changes and more elaborate imitative counterpoint[14]. The start of Leonardo Leo's partimento may here serve to exemplify how the course in counterpoint and fugue was prepared through the practicing of imitative partimenti (see Ex. 4):

---

[13]. The partimenti by Sala are those that are numbered nos. 143-176, and 178. I here use the numbering system used in VAN TOUR 2017B. The collection F-Pn 4° c² 343/2 ends with Nicola Sala's partimento no. 178. For the identification of the partimenti by Leonardo Leo in F-Pn 4° c² 343/1 and F-Pn 4° c² 343/2, see: VAN TOUR 2014—.

[14]. The attribution to Leonardo Leo of these pieces merit particular credibility, since the attribution to Leo is written under the authority of Nicola Sala, who was Leonardo Leo's successor as a teacher of counterpoint at the Pietà between the 1740s and 1799.

Ex. 4: Leonardo Leo, Fuga No. 1, bars 1-14, (F-Pn 4° c² 343/1, p. 39).

Louis Julien Castels de Labarre's two partimento collections F-Pn 4° c² 343/1 and F-Pn 4° c² 343/2 merit attention also for a second reason: they give no less than twelve *bassi seguenti*, which I have been able to identify in sacred vocal works by Leonardo Leo[15]. Eleven of these have been listed previously in my doctoral dissertation. In addition to these, only recently I was able to identify yet another partimento in F-Pn 4° c² 343/2 (no. 62 in this collection) as being a *basso seguente*[16]. The corresponding mass movement is the final *Cum Sancto Spiritu* at the end of the *Gloria* of Nicola Sala's Mass *Kyrie e Gloria intero* (I-BGc Mayr Fald. 53/4)[17]. Let us take a closer look at this basso seguente and its vocal counterpart (see Exs. 5 and 6):

Ex. 5: Leonardo Leo, *basso seguente* to the *Cum Sancte Spiritu* in G major, bars 1-24, (F-Pn 4° c² 343/1, p. 39).

---

[15]. See VAN TOUR 2015, pp. 279-289.

[16]. For the argumentation why these pieces should be called *bassi seguenti*, see *ibidem*, pp. 208-226.

[17]. It should be mentioned, at this point, that Nicola Sala's Mass *Kyrie e Gloria intero* (I-BGc Mayr Fald. 53/4), in which I identified this partimento (or *basso seguente*, to be precise) contains two fugal mass sections for which Nicola Sala used fugues by his teacher Leonardo Leo. These both fugues appear originally in Leonardo Leo's Mass in G major. For a list of concordant sources of this mass by Leo, see: KRAUSE 1987, p. 30. As can be noticed from the concordance list in this book, Krause does not mention this particular source for Leo's G major Mass, I-BGc Mayr Fald. 53/4.

Ex. 6: Leonardo Leo, *Cum Sancte Spiritu* from the Mass in G major, bars 1–24, (I-BGc Mayr Fald. 53/4, fol. 61ʳ).

«Taking a Walk at the Molo»: Partimento and the Improvised Fugue

The content of the two partimento collections F-Pn 4° c² 343/1 and F-Pn 4° c² 343/2 also raise a few other questions: 1) Why did Sala not use any of his partimenti that we know from two autographs I-Nc 46-1-34 and F-Pn 4° c² 344? 2) Why are Sala's partimenti followed by those of Leo? 3. And why did Sala include no less than twelve *bassi seguenti* by Leonardo Leo in these two collections?

It should be noted that these two partimento collections were written relatively late, in 1788. At that time, Sala appears to have abandoned the 131 partimenti that he had written in the 1750s and 1760s[18]. I suspect that the series of 131 partimenti had become too complicated for most of the students in the 1780s and 1790s, a time when there were many complaints about the decreasing standard of teaching at the Neapolitan conservatories[19].

It may seem somewhat surprizing that Sala in his partimento instruction used partimenti by his teacher Leonardo Leo from the 1730s and 1740, that is some 40 or 50 years later. It is not impossible that the reintroduction of Leo's partimenti represented a kind of 'nostalgia' for the 1740s and 1750s, the time when the Neapolitan conservatories had been in full bloom. Also in the case of Durante's partimenti it is possible to see such changes of stylistic orientation. As I have shown elsewhere, the twenty old-style fugues that commonly appear at the end of Durante's partimenti in early nineteenth-century collection, were almost certainly added to Durante's partimenti somewhere around the 1790s, probably with the aim of restoring some of the skills and knowledge that had been lost[20]. These fugues are compositions by early eighteenth-century composers. The twelve *bassi seguenti* by Leonardo Leo were introduced in the late 1780s, possibly for similar reasons. Also here, Sala may have had the ambitions to restore some important skills that had been the very essence of the contrapuntal tradition of the *Pietà* in the early eighteenth century.

Additionally, the two partimento notebooks of Louis Julien Castels de Labarre F-Pn 4° c² 343/1, F-Pn 4° c² 343/2, and the counterpoint notebook F-Pn Ms. 8223 shed new light on the content of a student's studies in partimento and counterpoint at the Pietà in the years around the French Revolution. A note added to the two-part fugue no. 12

---

[18]. This set of 131 partimenti have appeared as part of my complete edition with critical commentary, Van Tour 2017a, nos. 1-131.

[19]. See Sigismondo 1820, vol. iv, p. 173: «Cafaro se ne morì e Sala rimpiazzò il suo luogo. Introdotti nel *Collegio* i partimenti e solfeggi di Leo, poscia di Cafaro, egli non volle far uso de' suoi» («Cafaro died and Sala replaced him in his role. As he had introduced the partimenti and solfeggi by Leo and later by Cafaro in the *collegio*, he would not make use of his own»). Translation according to Bacciagaluppi 2016, 269. These circumstances are confirmed through the solfeggio collection I-Nc Solfeggio 250, containing Leo's solfeggi, not in the hand of Pasquale Cafaro, as the title page suggests, but in fact in the hand of Nicola Sala. The collection 'I-Nc Solfeggio 250' was probably used as teaching material at the *Pietà*.

[20]. None of the partimenti in F-Pn 4° c² 343/1 and F-Pn 4° c² 343/2 appears in the earlier collections of Sala's partimenti, such as I-Nc 46-1-34 or F-Pn 4° c² 344. Sala's partimenti in F-Pn 4° c² 343/1, F-Pn 4° c² 343/2, and in I-Nc S-1-94 were written rather late in his career and may have served to replace the previous collection of the 131 partimenti. See also Van Tour 2017b, vol. i, introduction without pagination.

in Labarre's counterpoint notebook F-Pn Ms. 8223, reveals Nicola Sala's answer to De Labarre's supposed question:

> The way to become skilled in constructing operas: after the fugues a 4, one must write 8 to 10 arias, five or six duos, five or six trios, five or six quartets, after that recitatives, and then the opera[21].

These notebooks show only the very start of this process, displaying a strong focus on counterpoint and fugue. At some point, De Labarre must have wondered how many more such fugues he would need to write, before he finally would be allowed to write any dramatic music. Sala's curriculum started quite rigorously with this «hard nut of counterpoint», to paraphrase Heinrich Schütz' expression in the forward of the *Geistliche Chormusik 1648.* The abrupt ending in the middle of one of the three-part fugues raises the question, whether De Labarre perhaps did end his counterpoint studies prematurely: the fourth three-part fugue was left unfinished, and the rest of the notebook remained empty too. From similar counterpoint notebooks we know that more three-part fugues normally would have been added, and after that even a similar set of four-part fugues. Probably the «hard nut of counterpoint» was somewhat too hard for De Labarre.

The partimento notebooks of 1788 by De Labarre and his counterpoint notebook of 1789 remind us of the fact that partimenti were not only used to develop skills in thoroughbass realization, but also, and most specifically, to prepare the student for his forthcoming studies in counterpoint. As such they enrich our present understanding of the educational function of partimenti.

Bibliography

BACCIAGALUPPI 2016
Apotheosis of Music in the Kingdom of Naples: Giuseppe Sigismondo, edited by Claudio Bacciagaluppi, Giulia Giovani and Raffaele Mellace, Introduction by Rosa Cafiero, Rome, Società Editrice di Musicologia, 2016 (Saggi, 3).

BELLOTTI 2017
BELLOTTI, Edoardo. 'Composing at the Keyboard: Banchieri and Spiridion, Two Complementary Methods', in: *Studies in Historical Improvisation: From 'Cantare super Librum' to Partimenti*, edited by Massimiliano Guido, Abington-New York, Routledge, 2017.

BORGIR 1987
BORGIR, Tharald. *The Performance of the Basso Continuo in Italian Baroque Music*, Rochester (NY), University of Rochester Press, 1987 (Studies in Musicology, 90).

---

[21]. F-Pn Ms. 8223, fols. 16r: «Marche pour se mettre en état de faire des operas: Apres les fugues a 4. Il faut faire 8. ou 10 ariettas, cinq ou six duos, 5 ou six trios, 5 ou 6 quartetto, après les recitatifs, ensuitte l'opéra».

«Taking a Walk at the Molo»: Partimento and the Improvised Fugue

Brandenburg 2003
Brandenburg, Daniel. 'Reisende Musiker in Neapel im späten 18. Jahrhundert: Adalbert Gyrowetz, Michael Kelly, Giacomo Gottifredo Ferrari', in: *Le Musicien et ses voyages: pratiques, réseaux et représentations*, edited by Christian Meyer, Berlin, BWV Berliner Wissenschafts, 2003 (Musical Life in Europe 1600-1900. Circulation, Institution Representation), pp. 113-126.

Callahan 2010
Callahan, Michael. *Techniques of Keyboard Improvisation in the German Baroque and Their Implications for Today's Pedagogy*, Ph.D. Diss., Rochester (NY), University of Rochester, 2010.

Choron 1810
Choron, Alexandre-Étienne. *Dictionnaire historique des musiciens, artistes et amateurs, morts ou vivants* […], 2 vols., Paris, Valade et Lenormant, 1810-1811, vol. 1????OK????, 1810.

Christensen 1992
Christensen, Thomas. 'The 'Règle de l'Octave' in Thorough-Bass Theory and Practice', in: *Acta Musicologica*, LXIV/2 (1992), pp. 91-117.

Gingras 2008
Gingras, Bruno. 'Partimento Fugue in Eighteenth-Century Germany: A Bridge between Thoroughbass and Fugal Composition', in: *Eighteenth-Century Music*, v/1 (2008), pp. 51-74.

Gjerdingen 2007
Gjerdingen, Robert. *Music in the Galant Style*, Oxford-New York, Oxford University Press, 2007.

Gyrowetz 1848
Gyrowetz, Adalbert. *Biographie des Adalbert Gyrowetz*, Vienna, Mechitaristen-Buchdruckerei, 1848.

Krause 1987
Krause, Ralf. *Die Kirchenmusik von Leonardo Leo (1694-1744). Ein Beitrag zur Musikgeschichte Neapels im 18. Jahrhunderts*, Regensburg, Gustav Bosse Verlag, 1987 (Kölner Beiträge zur Musikforschung, 151).

Lester 1992
Lester, Joel. *Compositional Theory in the Eighteenth Century*, Cambridge (MA), Harvard University Press, 1992, pp. 65-68.

Renwick 1995
Renwick, William. *Analyzing Fugue: A Schenkerian Approach*, Stuyvesant (NY), Pendragon Press, 1995 (Harmonologia, 8).

Renwick 2001
The Langloz Manuscript: Fugal Improvisation Through Figured Bass, edited by William Renwick, Oxford, Oxford University Press, 2001 (Early Music Series).

Sanguinetti 2012
Sanguinetti, Giorgio. *The Art of Partimento: History, Theory and Practice*, Oxford-New York, Oxford University Press, 2012.

SIGISMONDO 1820
SIGISMONDO, Giuseppe. *Apoteosi della Musica del Regno di Napoli in tre ultimi transundati secoli*, 4 vols. D-B Mus. ms. autogr. theor. Sigismondo, G.I., 1820.

VAN TOUR 2014—
VAN TOUR, Peter. *UUPart: The Uppsala Partimento Database*, Uppsala, 2014—, <http://www2.musik.uu.se/UUPart/UUPart.php>, accessed November 2018.

VAN TOUR 2015
ID. *Counterpoint and Partimento: Methods of Teaching Composition in Late Eighteenth-Century Naples*, Uppsala, Acta Universitatis Upsaliensis, 2015 (Studia musicological Upsaliansia. Nova Series, 25).

VAN TOUR 2017A
ID. 'Partimento Teaching according to Durante, Investigated through the Earliest Manuscript Sources', in: *Studies in Historical Improvisation: From Cantare super Librum to Partimenti, op. cit.*, pp. 131-148.

VAN TOUR 2017B
The 189 Partimenti of Nicola Sala: Complete Edition with Critical Commentary, 3 vols., edited by Peter van Tour, Uppsala, Acta Universitatis Upsaliensis, 2017 (Studia musicologica Upsaliensia. Nova Series, 27).

Abstracts

David Chung, *French Harpsichord «doubles» and the Creative Art of the 17th-Century «Clavecinistes»*

The seventeenth-century French harpsichord repertory developed from a largely improvised art in which notation served as an *aide-mémoire* to a form in which details carefully marked by the composer were expected to be observed meticulously by the performer. Through an in-depth study of the repertory of pieces with *doubles*, this paper delves into performance practice issues and explores the creative processes of how seventeenth-century French musicians in the quasi-improvisatory tradition played and taught. This paper considers three key issues in detail: (1) the possible variants (melodic, rhythmic, textural) between performances; (2) the role of improvisation; and (3) the ways how seventeenth-century musicians cultivated their individual artistic voices. A dozen concordant manuscript versions of Hardel's Gavotte, which inspired Louis Couperin's famous *double*, provide valuable materials for exploring the close relationship between imitation and creativity, as espoused by Jean Le Gallois (1680) and other seventeenth-century writers. The *double* by Louis Couperin has survived in multiple versions in a variety of manuscript sources, and virtually no two versions are cut from the same cloth. Although some of the differences among the manuscript sources could be explained as the inevitable result of aural transmission, it is clear that seventeenth-century scribes did not restrict their role to that of a faithful or mechanical copyist. Instead, they felt quite ready to impose their copying habits, musical tastes and their personalities during the process of writing out ornaments, rhythms, cadences, and other effects. In this context, the notation serves sometimes as an example of what could be done and sometimes as what had been done – a case in which many elements of the notation are not at all binding on the part of the performer. By identifying elements of the music that are decorative and those that are structural and integral to the musical fabric, this paper aims to encourage modern performers to nurture ways to be spontaneous yet stay faithful to the original spirit of the music through an increased awareness of the creativity embedded in the performance.

Massimiliano Guido, *Sounding Theory and Theoretical Notes Bernardo Pasquini's Pedagogy at the Keyboard: A Case of Composition in Performance?*

In a recent essay, Thomas Christensen calls for an 'improvisatory moment' and proposes the coexistence of two heretofore competing facets of music theory. Almost the entirety of our discipline is rooted in 'hard theory' and consists of prolix prose and myriad rules and corollaries. Music examples within this tradition only serve the words and do not reach a status of independence. On the other hand, we are slowly rediscovering a semi-forgotten tradition of 'soft theory': 'fragile texts' arising out of the aural-mnemonic praxis of Antiquity, exemplified in the 'artisanal' apprenticeship of music in which students had to 'analyze' didactic examples. The latter approach has been rejected for some time as 'real theory' because of the lack of surrounding discourse. In many cases music stands alone, and readers might not grasp its 'sounding theoretical' value. The concept of 'soft theory' is intimately connected to the Italian tradition of *suonar di fantasia* at the keyboard; this has been discussed by several scholars in recent years. Here I consider the didactic works of one of the most influential musicians in seventeenth-century Rome: Bernardo Pasquini. His *Saggi di Contrappunto* (1695), the *Sonate per uno o due cembali* (1703-1704), and the *Versetti con il solo basso cifrato* (1708) constitute a homogenous collection in which the learner is exposed to the complexity of composing at the keyboard. Pasquini's oeuvre stands in between the Renaissance tradition of improvised

Abstracts

counterpoint and Neapolitan partimenti. Its pedagogical value derives from the pleasantness of making music combined with the authority of theory. Why was Pasquini so famous as a pedagogue? What was so unique about his teaching method? I demonstrate how he connected keyboard technique with the art of composing in a coherent unity, providing the student with all the elements necessary to extemporize music at the harpsichord in the modern style.

JAVIER LUPIÁÑEZ – FABRIZIO AMMETTO, *Las anotaciones de Pisendel en el Concierto para dos violines RV 507 de Vivaldi: una ventana abierta a la improvisación en la obra del 'Cura rojo'*

The famous 'Schrank II' collection of the Sächsische Landesbibliothek – Staats- und Universitätsbibliothek (SLUB) in Dresden contains about two thousand music manuscripts, most of which were collected by the violinist and composer Johann Georg Pisendel (1687-1755), concertmaster of the Dresden court orchestra in the first half of the eighteenth century; he was also a personal pupil of Antonio Vivaldi. A careful analysis of these manuscripts reveals the presence of a large number of annotations by Pisendel that, for the most part, provide guidance for ornamentation and/or improvisation. Within this large corpus of manuscripts, Vivaldi's works are the most copiously annotated. Pisendel's copy of Vivaldi's Concerto in C major for two violins and orchestra (RV 507; D-Dl, Mus.2389-O-98) is particularly interesting by virtue of the fact that it contains annotations and ornamentation for both soloists. An analysis of these markings reveals a style that moves away from the one presented in contemporary treatises on ornamentation that generally adhere to the Corellian language predominant at the time. The style of ornamentation found in RV 507 shows significant similarities both with other Vivaldi works annotated by Pisendel (RV 202 and RV 340) and with certain slow movements in his concertos that adopt a particularly improvisatory language (*Adagio* in RV 195, *Grave Recitativo* in RV 208, *Grave* in RV 212a, *Largo* in RV 279, *Adagio* in RV 285, *Largo* in RV 318, *Grave* in RV 562). Additionally, there are similarities in the diminutions for the Concerto for violin and double orchestra, RV 581 (I-Vc, busta 55), written for another of Vivaldi's pupils, the famous violinist Anna Maria (1696-1782), a «figlia di coro» at the Ospedale della Pietà in Venice. These particularities of the ornamentation notated in the Dresden version of RV 507 appear to show that these annotations belong to a performative context in which the performer improvised and modified the musical text *ex tempore*. Moreover, they reflect the hypothesis advanced by numerous scholars that the works, given the similarities, may be Vivaldi's own.

JOSUÉ MELÉNDEZ PELÁEZ, *«Cadenze per nali»: Exuberant and Extended Cadences in the 16th and 17th Centuries*

The influence of humanism led composers of the sixteenth and seventeenth centuries to structure their works after the rhetorical processes of the ancient Greeks. *Conclusio*, also known as *finis*, is the part (or 'period') of a speech that defines its end. Joachim Burmeister subdivides a piece into nine rhetorical periods: «The Final, namely, the ninth, period is like the epilogue of a speech. This harmony displays a principal ending, otherwise called a *supplementum* of the final cadence [...]» (*Musica poetica*, 1606). The technique of extending a final cadence by prolonging its original time values can be found in compositions of the sixteenth and seventeen centuries. Extending the final note seems to have been common in polyphony of the early sixteenth century but as the century progressed and the thirst for rhetorical expressiveness grew, this musical epilogue was extended further by adding extra measures onto the penultimate – or, in some cases, also the antepenultimate – note. Late sixteenth- and seventeenth-century sources, such as those by L. Zacconi, G. B. Bovicelli, B. Barbarino, F. Severi F. Rognoni, H. A. Herbst, the Anonymous manuscript G239 (Estense Codex), the manuscript 'Carlo G', and the treatises of Spiridionis a Monte Carmelo show that this practice was originally improvised by performers. Other sources, such as notated diminutions, monodies and

Abstracts

instrumental music by composers such as Caccini, Mayone, Frescobaldi, Monteverdi, Castello, Marini and many others, appear to begin notating florid ornamentation on prolonged basslines at final (and sometimes intermediate) cadences. The vast documentation of this practice, both in notated musical examples and theoretical treatises of the time, gives us a glimpse of the interpretive skills that performers were expected to possess in the Renaissance and Baroque periods and encourages modern performers to study them and to include them in historical performances.

MARINA TOFFETTI, *Written Outlines of Improvisation Procedures in Music Publications of the Early 17th Century: The Second (1611-1623) and Third (1615-1623) Book of «Concerti» By G. Ghizzolo and the Motet «Iesu Rex Admirabilis» (1625-1627) by G. Frescobaldi*

Procedures such as diminution, the realization (and 'articulation') of the basso continuo, and modal transposition have been entrusted to the practice of improvisation for centuries. The information provided on the written page did not resolve all the problems that could arise in performance; such solutions could only be achieved by calling on the skills and experience of the performers. Therefore, musical sources that allow us to shed light on these procedures assume a great value and need to be examined with care. The cases examined here – the *concerti* from Giovanni Ghizzolo's second (1611-1623) and third book (1615-1623) and Girolamo Frescobaldi's motet *Iesu Rex admirabilis* (1625-1627) – reveal that the publication of a new edition could present an opportunity to review one or more previous published compositions, allowing us to focus on such issues as the articulation of the basso continuo line and its fixing on the written page, the modal transposition of compositions notated in *chiavette* and the possible presence of written indications referring to this practice, and the presence of diminutions written out in full in one or more voices. Each of these three aspects has been dealt with from two different angles, which consider both the consequences of these written outlines of improvisation procedures on performance practice and the implications they have on the practice of publishing. Taking for granted that the strategies to adopt in an edition should consider the specific history of each work's transmission, certain indispensable criteria should nevertheless be taken into account when preparing a critical edition. In particular, editors should avoid contaminating two or more distinct versions of the same composition, mixing parts or portions of one version with those of a later version. In the same way, editors should avoid fixing elements that were not fixed in the 17th-century edition. Moreover, all the indications contained in the ancient edition should be reported in the modern edition, so as to allow the player to glean all possible information from the different aspects of performance practice.

GIOVANNA BARBATI, *«Il n'exécute jamais la Basse telle qu'elle est écrite»: The Use of Improvisation in Teaching Low Strings*

The opportunity to imagine a method of teaching for cello or viola da gamba based on improvisation is offered to us from the rediscovery of the didactical and pedagogical practice of *partimento*. This method was based on learning directly at the keyboard and on the progressive memorization of patterns; from there, it rapidly led to composing or improvising on a given bass line. Given that low strings perform the double function of providing the continuo and the *cantus*, I investigated the possibility that a similar historical method that was suited to the cello and viola da gamba might exist; evidence found in the sources may confirm this hypothesis. I believe that historical improvisation was based on elaborations of pre-existing elements and patterns within a shared language that allowed for the development of individual formulae within the historical language. Here I suggest that, during the Baroque era, teaching methods were organised such that pupils could improvise based on patterns which could later be reused in different contexts. It was therefore a matter of teaching and learning patterns that the best students would later reuse with complete

Abstracts

autonomy. First we consider the improvisational demands of the repertoire, depending on different the bass instrument's different performative contexts: as a 'solo', as the principal voice, or as accompaniment. I then examine historical documentary evidence; I conclude by describing my pedagogical proposal, which suggests that the didactical method should be supplemented with schemes on which to elaborate from the beginning, while still leaving room for the student's creativity. Indeed, I believe that one can find a valid way to enrich one's skills on low string instruments while learning how to interpret and perform Baroque music more accurately with this approach.

Anthony Pryer, *The Borderlines of Improvisation: Caccini, Monteverdi, and the Freedoms of the Performer*

Improvisation during the Baroque period stands more or less at the mid-point in the documented history of the practice. This study draws on those traditions to illuminate the contexts in which improvisation might take place, and what its attributes and procedures might be. The argument proceeds in four stages. First, it suggests that the traditional division between oral and written cultures is rather unhelpful because a) most Western musical communities consist of a mixture of both, and b) the more important distinction seems to be found between 'prepared' and 'unprepared' musical activity. A 'Notation-Culture' grid is constructed onto which repertories combining improvisational and written features can be mapped. I then examine the role of 'common practice' styles. Since the Baroque period spent more time than most on defining its styles, that seems to have provided a particularly fertile framework for improvisational practices. Third, I look at Caccini's *Le nuove musiche* (1602) in detail as an attempt to 'write the un-writable' and to examine how it uses various types of notational function (archival, strategic, prescriptive, and descriptive) to capture the confluence between improvisatory performance practices and written compositional structures. Finally, I examine Caccini's 'Amarilli mia bella' and Monteverdi's 'Possente spirto' to show how they emerged via the essentially improvisational techniques of adaptation, re-combination and variation. Just where 'creative freedom' should be located in that process is a complex question. It is why and how people improvise that points to its social and artistic significance.

Laura Toffetti, «*Sostener si può la battuta, etiandio in aria*». *Testi e contesti per comprendere l'invenzione e la disposizione del discorso musicale nel repertorio strumentale italiano fra Seicento e Settecento*

The perception of the score as an unfinished work is the centre of this research. Since Baroque notation does not provide details for exact execution through interpretive signs commonly found in most modern musical writings, the examination of contemporary theoretical sources is necessary in order to understand and perform the musical text. The works of composers such as Girolamo Frescobaldi, of theorists such as Vincenzo Galilei, or of intellectuals such as Vincenzo Giustiniani clarify that Baroque composition is based on precise idiomatic formulations, arranged and adjusted according to rules inherited from classical rhetoric. These items or figures are comparable to semantic structures, which, linked together, build the musical statements. Identifying these gestures in the score and performing them, through the consideration of some important didactic works, introductory notes of music editions, and analyses of their cultural contexts, is the first objective of this research. I then focus on the evolution of musical terms such as 'tempo', 'figure' or 'numerus' as evidence of the analogy between musical language, rules of rhetoric and prosody, and the considerations of the communicative function of musical practice. Improvisation, a necessary step to realizing the unfinished score, thus acquires a new meaning. Broadened by different elements such as agogics, text organisation, or eloquence, this technique becomes a vehicle for expressive and semantic gestures: simultaneously *ex tempore* and rooted in an extremely precise cultural and aesthetic system.

Abstracts

Rudolf Rasch, *Improvised Cadenzas in the Cello Sonatas Op. 5 by Francesco Geminiani*

During the eighteenth century, composers developed the habit of creating room in their compositions for freely improvised passages; this practice was extensively described by Johann Joachim Quantz in his *Versuch einer Anweisung* (1752). These passages were called cadenzas because they were often connected with the final cadence of a movement within a larger work. Examples of notated cadenzas can be found in Corelli's Sonatas Op. 5 (1700) and Geminiani's Sonatas Op. 1 (1716, 1739) and Op. 4 (1739); they provide examples for performing such cadenzas where others are only suggested by a fermata. This article investigates how present-day performers perform the cadenzas that are indicated in eight places in the Cello Sonatas Op. 5 by Geminiani (1747). The cadenzas were transcribed from nine complete recordings of these sonatas, released from 1976 to 2015, and were then compared with the 'rules' given in Quantz's *Versuch*. Not surprisingly, the cadenzas as performed by these nine cellists vary greatly in length and style. Nevertheless, Quantz's suggestions are clearly recognizable.

Valentina Anzani, *Il mito della competizione tra virtuosi: quando Farinelli sfidò Bernacchi (Bologna 1727)*

In the summer of 1727, Farinelli, a rising star, and Antonio Maria Bernacchi, an older virtuoso and famous teacher, shared the same stage in Bologna. According to numerous versions of the event, Farinelli apparently challenged the older colleague in a contest of variations. The two engaged in improvisations and reciprocal imitations: Bernacchi got the better of Farinelli, and Farinelli was led to ask his competitor for voice lessons. This story has been important in establishing the relevance of Bernacchi's school and its notability in being a place for virtuosos' improvement in our collective imaginations. In reality, accounts of the meeting multiplied until the early nineteenth century, and the degrees of truth contained within them should be considered on a case-by-case basis. However, they share one aspect in common: they each describe the two virtuosos rising to *exempla*, one, the embodiment of the musical and human characteristics that being a virtuoso required and the other, the ideal representative of the good singing teacher. This essay aims to reconstruct (with archival foundation) what really happened between the two singers. It clarifies the ways in which the event has been changed in subsequent literature and also reveals how the event can be read as a representation of a diametrically opposite *topos* – and a positive one at that: that of two colleagues who imitate themselves in a virtuous relationship rather than as another negative commentary on the deistic attitudes of castrati.

John Lutterman, *Re-Creating Historical Improvisatory Solo Practices on the Cello: C. Simpson, F. Niedt, and J. S. Bach on the Pedagogy of «Contrapunctis Extemporalis»*

Clues to the technical means of re-creating the improvisatory practices of Bach's world can be found in a great number of sources, including Christopher Simpson's *The Divison Viol*, Friedrich Niedt's *Musicalische Handleitung*, and the rich trove of Italian *partimento* exercises. Viewed through an analytic lens, free from the blinders of a modern work concept, the written compositions of Bach and his contemporaries may be understood as inventories of formal models and as idiomatic vocabularies of motivic, harmonic, and contrapuntal ideas ripe for improvisatory appropriation and elaboration. *The Division Viol* is one of the most comprehensive treatises on improvisation, offering valuable clues to the nature of a number of historical improvisatory practices, including instruction in the art of extemporaneous implied polyphony, which Simpsons calls the 'mixt' style of divisions. The importance of Simpson's treatises for understanding the practices of seventeenth-century British musicians is well known, and copies of *The Division Viol* can be found in important musical archives throughout Europe. Indeed, the treatise remained popular enough to justify the printing of a third edition in 1712. Simpson's approach is more harmonically conceived than has been generally recognized, and the organization of *The*

Abstracts

Division Viol shows interesting parallels to Niedt's treatise, which Bach is known to have used in his own teaching, and which in turn appears to be indebted to Italian partimento practices. Although Simpson's treatise does not offer written-out examples of longer pieces, following his advice to use a bass from a pre-existent composition as a formal schema would result in a structured approach to improvisation similar to that which German and Italian *partimento* practices were designed to cultivate.

Francesca Mignogna, *Accompagnamento e basso continuo alla chitarra spagnola. Una cartogra a della diffusione dei sistemi di notogra ci in Italia, Spagna e Francia tra XVI e XVII secolo e loro implicazioni teoriche*

Interest in thoroughbass has long been nearly exclusively confined to its practice on keyboard instruments. Nevertheless, a considerable number of studies, all published during the 20th century, brought attention to thoroughbass as it would be performed on instruments with plucked strings. These studies, among them Thomas Christensen's excellent article that identifies Baroque thoroughbass practice as one of the most important applications of *rasgueado*, a Spanish guitar technique, have dated the appearance of stenographic systems of notation for plucked-string instruments to the turn of the 17th century. These systems consisted of a synthetic representation of the accompaniment that was notated by letters of the alphabet on a melody, bass, or text. They were derived from Spanish *rasgueado* handbooks and were subsequently used in the practice of thoroughbass, especially in Italy. The *alfabeto* Italian system, along with the French and Spanish systems, displays techniques of chordal variation that include, in some cases, dissonant sounds. These stenographic systems – looking to the past in the practice of reduction and toward the future theorization of Campion's *règle de l'octave* (1716) – allow for a realization of thoroughbass on the Spanish Baroque guitar that is strongly idiomatic yet free from predetermined schemes at the same time. Such systems aim to simplify concepts (such as transposition) that were considered abstract and complex at that time by using the gestures and the physical characteristics of the guitar itself to their advantage. These systems were not only a means of synthetic notation. They also functioned as non-intellectual didactical works that were aimed toward an amateur public who wanted to learn quickly. Their significance lies in their role in the evolution of music theory toward functional harmony (other than in the concept of fundamental bass). The goal of this essay is to offer an extensive list of the handbooks and songbooks containing instructions for *alfabeto* systems that appeared during the 16th and 17th centuries in Italy, France and Spain so as to undertake an analysis of their role in the evolution of the thoroughbass practice and the transition between counterpoint and the tonal system.

Guido Olivieri, *Naturalezza o artificio: riflessioni su improvvisazione e virtuosismo italiani in Francia nel Settecento*

Improvisation was perceived as a trait typical of the Italian tradition in 18th-century France. Connected to poetic and literary practices, improvisation became a distinctive characteristic of the style of the Italian virtuosi who moved to Paris at the beginning of the century and influenced the development of French music. This style rose from a performance practice that was transmitted from teachers to students, cultivated in particular by the teaching methods used in the Neapolitan conservatories. It is not surprising, therefore, to find that the virtuosi who introduced the Italian virtuosic approach to France came mostly from Neapolitan training. With their brilliant performance practice and flair for improvisation they helped establish the new image and career path of the international virtuoso.

Neal Zaslaw, «*Adagio de Mr. Tartini. Varié de plusieurs façons différentes, très utiles aux personnes qui veulent apprendre à faire des traits sous chaque notte de l'Harmonie...*»

A Parisian publication, the *Adagio de Mr. Tartini. Varié de plusieurs façons différentes*, widely known from its inclusion in J. B. Cartier's *L'Art du violon* (Paris, 1798), has been readily available since its re-publication

Abstracts

in facsimile by Alberto Bachmann in 1913 and by Hans-Peter Schmitz in 1955. (Subsequently, at least three more facsimile editions have appeared.) Because of its late date, apparent absence of an established pedigree, and dense notation, the *Adagio varié* has been received almost universally negatively by violinists and scholars. How could something this dense have come from Tartini, who was understood to have radically simplified his musical style in the context of the evolving aesthetics of the mid-eighteenth century? Uninvestigated in the negative critiques of the *Adagio varié* is an indication that its 1798 version was a «Seconde Édition». By investigating other known and putative editions, the earliest publication of the *Adagio varié* can be dated to no later than the 1770s, the decade during which his students published posthumously two other of his pedagogical works. Returning Tartini's *Adagio varié* to his canon re-opens questions about how he performed slow movements and how he trained his students to do likewise.

SIMONE CIOLFI, *Cantata da camera e arte del partimento in Alessandro Scarlatti.* «*An Historical Link between Baroque Recitatives and Development Section of the Sonata-Form Movements?*»

The partimento as pedagogical project begins with Alessandro Scarlatti's surviving partimenti. This article aims to examine basic elements of partimento theory, including the introduction of scale mutations as standard bass formulas (called here 'clausolas' because they are heritage of previous pre-harmonic clausolas), portions of the Rule of the Octave, and basses falling by thirds. These elements are found in Scarlatti's recitatives, arias and partimento exercises. Michael Talbot has written of a possible «historical link between Baroque recitatives and development sections of the sonata-form». Here I suggest that elements of the partimento technique, in combination with components of different musical genres, form the probable link between Baroque recitatives and sonata-form development sections. In fact, the composition of recitatives likely formed part of every Classical composer's training.

MARCO POLLACI, *Two New Sources for the Study of Early Eighteenth-Century Composition and Improvisation*

The study of partimento traditions has revealed a strong connection between the compositional practice of the eighteenth century and improvisational techniques. Pedagogical exercises, musical treatises, and other primary sources clearly indicate that improvising and learning the rules of partimento were essential aspects of musicians' training and study. Unsurprisingly, many European libraries contain a large number of manuscript sources related to partimento pedagogical traditions – a testament to the importance of improvisation and the knowledge of the pillars of Neapolitan counterpoint in musical practice at the end of the seventeenth century. To understand these methods of teaching counterpoint, studying musical sources such as the *regole*, *lezioni*, partimenti, and many other notebooks that demonstrate the relevant principles connected to the art of improvisation help us realize the importance of being skilled in the peculiar nature of these rules to every musician during that period. The Staatsbibliothek zu Berlin holds volumes of anonymously-written counterpoint exercises (D-B Mus. Ms theor.1483 and 1417) that have not yet been analysed. This study investigates the importance of these manuscript sources in connection with the compositional practices outlined in the texts *Principi di Cembalo* and *Regole per accompagnare nel Cimbalo ò vero Organo*.

GIORGIO SANGUINETTI, *On the Origin of Partimento: A Recently Discovered Manuscript of Toccate (1695) by Francesco Mancini*

When dealing with the difficult issue of determining when and where partimenti came into use, one can speculate about a Roman origin. Indeed, during the early years of the eighteenth century, Rome was considered to be the most advanced musical center in Europe; the earliest partimenti manuscript collection, signed by Bernardo Pasquini, originated here in approximately 1707. Later, following Alessandro Scarlatti's

Abstracts

move from Rome to Naples, a migration occurred. After my book *The Art of Partimento* was published, things became complicated. Newly discovered sources, such as the *Regole o vero Toccate di studio del Sig. Abb[at]e Fran[cesc]o Mancini 1695* (F-Pn Rés. 2315) prove that partimenti were in use in Naples already at the end of the seventeenth century – and possibly earlier. In fact, the Mancini manuscript, and in particular the *21 Toccate* for harpsichord, display an impressive level of sophistication and virtuosity. Other manuscripts, such as the coeval Rocco Greco manuscript (I-Nc 33.2.3) show that bass string players studied partimenti at the keyboard, but also learned how to improvise diminutions on standard bass patterns *harmonically* on their instruments. Musicological research thus gives us a better understanding of the origins of the practice and also helps us find a solution for the problem we face today when teaching partimenti to non-keyboard majors.

Peter van Tour, «*Taking a Walk at the Molo*»: *Partimento and the Improvised Fugue*

In this article I focus on the relationship between partimento studies and studies of counterpoint and composition. Were partimenti studied before students advanced to writing counterpoint and composition, and if so, it is possible to reveal more about how partimento prepared the student for studies in written counterpoint and composition? A biographical anecdote by Adalbert Gyrowetz (1763-1850) suggests that Nicola Sala demanded quite a remarkable level of aural skills from his students. Gyrowetz, who studied in Naples between 1787 and 1789, was invited to talk after his lessons in counterpoint, during which he was supposed to recapitulate the lesson by singing the theme, the countersubject, and the other components of the fugue. This article focusses further on how such aural skills were prepared through practical exercises, such as solfeggi and partimenti. In addition, I introduce a newly identified counterpoint notebook that is written in exactly the same handwriting as previously known partimento collections (F-Pn 4° c² 343/1 and F-Pn 4° c² 343/2); it is preserved in the Bibliothèque nationale de France (F-Pn Ms. 8223), The partimento collections are dated «15 July 1788», while the counterpoint notebook bears the date «Sunday 11 January 1789». These materials give a unique insight into how partimenti were used in preparation for counterpoint studies. The second partimento collection merits special attention as it contains no less than twelve *bassi seguenti* that I have identified in sacred vocal works by Leonardo Leo (1684-1744).

Biographies

Fabrizio Ammetto is a Full Professor in the Music Department of the University of Guanajuato, Mexico. He is a member of the 'Mexican Academy of Science' and the 'Mexican National Researchers System'. He holds degrees in violin, viola, and electronic music, and he received his Ph.D. in musicology from the University of Bologna. As a violinist, violist, and conductor, he has performed over 700 concerts in Europe and America, and has produced numerous critical editions and recordings of eighteenth- and nineteenth-century instrumental music. He has published several books, chapters and articles. He is a member of the international Editorial Committee of the Istituto Italiano Antonio Vivaldi (Fondazione Giorgio Cini), Venice.

Valentina Anzani is completing her Ph.D. at Bologna University with a dissertation on the castrato Antonio Bernacchi (1685-1756) and his pupils. Her research concerns castrati and the production of opera theatre. Her first publications are about castrati: 'Un soggetto equivoco al crepuscolo degli dèi castrati' (with Marco Beghelli, in *L'equivoco stravagante*, Fondazione Rossini, 2014), 'Castrato per amore: Casanova, Salimbeni, Farinelli e il misterioso Bellino' (in *Il Farinelli ritrovato*, LIM, 2015), 'Pseudonimi all'opera: un soprannome per la celebrità' (in *Il nome nel testo*, EdT, 2015). She was awarded the 'Handel Award' by the Handel Institute (UK) in 2017.

Giovanna Barbati (cellist and viola da gamba player) is a performer of early, contemporary, and improvised music. Her work as a researcher focuses on improvisation in early music and on historical didactics. She prepared a critical edition of Riccardo Broschi's opera *La Merope* for the Innsbrucker Festwochen der alten Musik in 2018. She was a pupil of Siegfried Palm (cello) and she studied the early practice with Christophe Coin and Jesper Christensen at the Schola Cantorum Basiliensis. She has been the principal cellist and viola da gambist of the baroque orchestra *Academia Montis Regalis* under Alessandro De Marchi for many years. She performed in the same role with many well-known European Baroque orchestras and groups in prestigious theatres and halls in Europe. She has recorded dozens of CDs, many of which are winners of awards and she has personally received rapturous praise from critics.

David Chung completed his musicological studies at Cambridge University and has published articles and reviews in *Early Music*, *Early Keyboard Journal*, *Journal of Eighteenth-Century Music*, *Journal of Seventeenth-Century Music*, *Music and Letters*, and *Revue de musicologie*. His edition of nearly 250 keyboard arrangements of Jean-Baptiste Lully's music has recently been published by the *Web Library of Seventeenth-Century Music* (<www.sscm-wlscm.org>). Chung maintains an active schedule as harpsichordist and has performed in cities across Europe, North America and Asia. Chung is currently Professor of Music at Hong Kong Baptist University.

Simone Ciolfi obtained his Master's degree (*laurea*) at the University 'La Sapienza' and his Ph.D. at the University of Rome 'Tor Vergata'. He has written articles on early nineteenth-century music, on Dallapiccola, on the programming of nineteenth-century Italian musical organizations, and on contemporary music. His areas of interest include the evolution of the concept of tradition in the music of the eighteenth and nineteenth centuries and the relationships between music theory and composition around 1700. He has worked on the artistic management of the Accademia Filarmonica Romana and has collaborated

Biographies

with *Concerto Italiano*, under the direction of Rinaldo Alessandrini for many years. He teaches Music History at Saint Mary's College (Notre Dame - Indiana, Rome program) and at the Conservatorio statale 'Arcangelo Corelli' di Messina.

Massimiliano Guido is a Senior Researcher in the Department of Musicology and Cultural Heritage of Pavia University, where he teaches courses in the history of music theory and history of musical instruments. He previously served as a Banting Post-Doctoral Fellow at the Schulich School of Music, McGill University, where he worked with Peter Schubert on a project about the art of memory at the keyboard as a tool for teaching counterpoint (2012-2014). He was the principal investigator of the research project *Improvisation in Classical Music Education: Rethinking our Future by Learning our Past*, funded by the Social Sciences and Humanities Research Council of Canada (2013-2014). He holds degrees in musicology (Pavia University, doctorate and *laurea*, Göteborg University, Master of Music Research), organ (Parma Conservatory, Italy), and harpsichord (Como Conservatory, Italy). He combines musicological research with organ teaching and performance.

Javier Lupiáñez holds, among other diplomas, a Master's (with distinction) from The Royal Conservatory of The Hague in Baroque violin, and a Master's in musicology from Salamanca University. As a performer, he has won six international awards and has recorded for Harmonia Mundi, Ayros, France Musique, Musiqu3, Concertzender, and Radio Klara. His work as a researcher led to the identification of new works by Antonio Vivaldi. He is currently a Ph.D. student at the University of Guanajuato, Mexico, where he is working on a dissertation entitled *Las anotaciones de Johann Georg Pisendel (1687-1755) en los manuscritos vivaldianos de Dresde*.

John Lutterman is currently an Associate Professor at the University of Alaska, having previously served on the faculty of Whitman College, the University of California, Davis, the University of the Pacific, Lawrence University, and the San Francisco Conservatory He holds a Ph.D. in musicology from the University of California, Davis, and a DMA in cello performance from Stony Brook University. He has given solo performances throughout Europe and America, and has performed with a number of prominent early-music ensembles. His research focuses on the relationship between notation, compositional theory, and historical improvisatory practices.

Josué Meléndez Peláez (cornetto and recorder player) studied music in Costa Rica, Guatemala, Mexico, Holland and Switzerland. He founded the first early music festival of Mexico, *Festival Santo Domingo de Música Antigua*. He is the founder and director of the ensemble *I Fedeli*, and has performed and recorded CDs with some of the most recognized European ensembles. He is a specialist in Renaissance and Baroque musical improvisation. He teaches Diminution/Improvisation at the University of Music, Trossingen, Germany and in various summer courses.

Francesca Mignogna is an Italian musician and musicologist who is currently a doctoral candidate at Sorbonne University in Paris. She studied saxophone and music composition at the State Conservatory of Campobasso (Italy). She obtained a Bachelor's degree and a Master of Music and Musicology at Sorbonne University of Paris. Her academic activities and research focuses on Renaissance and Baroque music theory and counterpoint. She collaborates with the IReMus (Institut de Recherche en Musicologie) on the publication of a critical edition of the works of Pierre-Louis Pollio (1724-1796).

Guido Olivieri is an Associate Professor of Musicology at the University of Texas at Austin, where he also directs the early music ensemble *Austinato*. He edited the collective volume *Arcomelo 2013. Studi in*

Biographies

occasione del terzo centenario della nascita di Arcangelo Corelli (Lucca, LIM, 2015), and the edition of A. Corelli, *Sonate da camera di Assisi* (Lucca, LIM, 2015). He has authored entries in *The New Grove Dictionary of Music*, *MGG*, and *Dizionario Biografico degli Italiani* and has published articles in journals and collected volumes on the developments of the string sonata in Naples and also on violin and cello repertories and performance practices in the 17th and 18th centuries. He is currently preparing the critical edition of D. Cimarosa *Il matrimonio segreto* for Bärenreiter.

Following his studies as a pianist, MARCO POLLACI graduated from the University of Tor Vergata in Rome. In 2018, he obtained a Ph.D. from Nottingham University. He specialises in diverse topics including music theory and music history – especially Italian – spanning the sixteenth to nineteenth centuries. He is also interested in music analysis and nineteenth-century opera.

ANTHONY PRYER is a Reader in Historical Musicology and Aesthetics at Goldsmiths College, University of London. He has edited Monteverdi's three earliest publications (*Sacrae cantiunclae*, *Madrigali spirituali*, and *Canzonette a tre voci*) for the new Collected Works published in Cremona, and has written widely on other aspects of his output. Recent publications on aesthetics include articles on Hanslick's *Vom musikalisch-Schönen*, Japanese concepts of Nature, and the challenge of performance to the ontology of music. For many years he served on the executive committee of the British Society of Aesthetics. He currently holds a Research Fellowship at Seian University in Japan.

RUDOLF RASCH studied musicology at the University of Amsterdam and was affiliated with the Institute of Musicology, later the Department of Media and Culture Studies, of Utrecht University from 1977 to 2010. His research focuses on temperament and the works of composers including Corelli, Vivaldi, Geminiani and Boccherini. He has published a number of articles, books and editions in these areas, including *Music Publishing in Europe 1600-1900* (an edited collection of essays, 2005), *Driehonderd brieven over muziek* (letters about music written by and to Constantijn Huygens, 2007), *Understanding Boccherini's Manuscripts* (an edited collection of essays, 2014), *Music and Power in the Baroque Era* (an edited collection of essays, 2014) and *Muziek in de Republiek* (about musical life in the Dutch Republic, 2018). He has also contributed to several volumes in the critical editions of the works of Luigi Boccherini and Francesco Geminiani. He has been the general editor of the Opera Omnia Francesco Geminiani since 2015.

GIORGIO SANGUINETTI is Associate Professor of Music Theory at the University of Rome 'Tor Vergata'. He has published extensively on the history of Italian music theory, Schenkerian analysis, form, and opera analysis. In 2011 he organized the seventh Euromac conference in Rome. He is a member of the scientific committee of the Istituto Nazionale di Studi Verdiani. His book *The Art of Partimento: History, Theory and Practice* (Oxford University Press, 2012) received the Wallace Berry Award of the Society for Music Theory in 2013.

LAURA TOFFETTI is a Professor of Baroque Violin at the Conservatories of Belfort and Mulhouse. After she graduated from the Conservatory of Milan with a degree in Modern Violin, she obtained a Master of Music in Performance Practice (Baroque Violin) from the Royal College of Music (London) and the «Certificat d'Aptitude en Musique Ancienne» from the Ministère de la Culture Française. As a member of several Baroque orchestras in Europe, she founded the *Antichi Strumenti* Ensemble (Music Award of Académie Rhénane 2011), and she has directed «Un Vendredi au Musée» at the Musées Historique des Beaux-Arts in Mulhouse. Her discography includes several cd and musical prizes, and she has published for Ortus Verlag (Germany).

Biographies

Marina Toffetti is an Assistant Professor of Music Theory at the University of Padua. She has won musicological competitions and scholarships, has given lectures, masterclasses, and seminars at different institutions, and has read papers at international conferences in Italy and abroad (including England, Germany, France, Poland, Slovenia, Slovakia, Czech Republic, Croatia, Sweden, and USA). She coordinates international research projects on the dissemination of Italian music in central-eastern Europe in the Baroque period. In 2013 she was awarded the 'Italian Heritage Award' international prize for 'Research, education and innovation in the protection of cultural heritage' for the restoration of the incomplete score of G. C. Ardemanio's *Musica a più voci*. Her main research interests concern the history of music and musical institutions (16th-18th century), music reception, assimilation and adaptation, musical philology, and musical analysis.

Peter van Tour is a Lecturer in Music Theory and Aural Training at the Norwegian Academy of Music in Oslo. As a scholar of musicology he has specialized in counterpoint pedagogy and historic composition. He studied Music Pedagogy at Brabant Conservatory in Tilburg (MA), Musicology at the University of Utrecht (MA), and obtained a Master in Music Theory at the Royal College of Music in Stockholm (MA). His Ph.D. dissertation *Counterpoint and Partimento* (Uppsala 2015) highlights the practical teaching strategies at the Neapolitan Conservatories during the late eighteenth century. In 1995, Peter co-founded the Gotland School of Music Composition, where he taught music theory from 1995 to 2014.

Neal Zaslaw is the Herbert Gussman Professor of Music at Cornell University, where he has taught since 1970. He is the author or editor of nine books and more than 75 articles on early music, historical performance practice, and the history of the orchestra. Zaslaw's revision of Köchel's venerable catalogue of Mozart's works will be published in 2019, as a book in German and online in English. His current research involves Italian music of the Baroque period.

A

Abel, Carl Friedrich 122
Acciai, Giovanni 79, 111
Agazzari, Agostino 82, 109, 123, 142
Alberti, Leon Battista 180, 191
Albicastro, Giovanni Henrico 45
Algarotti, Francesco 232, 236, 238
Amadori [Giovanni Tedeschi] 232-233
Amadori, Giuseppe 233
Amat, Joan Carles 262, 269-272, 274-279, 283-285
Amendola, Nadia 351
Ammetto, Fabrizio 43, 49, 61
Anglesi, Domenico 32
Anzani, Valentina 223
Antonio da Padova, Saint 90
Apel, William 263-264, 279
Appel, Andrew 210
Appiani, Giuseppe 233, 237
Arezzo, Guido d' 263
Arnold, Franck Thomas 104, 109, 335, 338
Arteaga, Stefano 231, 238
Artusi, Giovanni Maria 183
Aspden, Suzanne 232, 238

B

Babel, Charles 4
Babell [Babel], William 16-20, 47
Bacciagaluppi, Claudio 125, 145, 369, 379-380
Bach, Carl Philipp Emanuel 48, 82, 109, 155, 164-165, 170
Bach, Johann Sebastian 133, 155-156, 165, 199, 241-243, 250, 252, 254
Bachmann, Alberto 307, 309, 317
Bagnati, Tiziano 78
Banchieri, Adriano 37
Banti, Anna 192
Baragwanath, Nicholas 344, 350
Barbarino, Bartolomeo 68, 122, 142
Barbati, Giovanna 117, 138, 145
Barbella, Emanuele 296
Barbella, Francesco 296
Barberini, Francesco 183
Barbieri, Patrizio 364, 367
Barchi, Michele 210
Bardi, Giovanni 158-159
Bares, Alessandro 79, 145
Barezzi, Giuseppe 356
Barilli, Antonio 224, 229
Barker, Andrew 154, 170
Barnett, Gregory 62
Barney, Stephen 172
Baroni, Leonora 121
Bartók, Béla 155

Index of Names

Bassani, Oratio 68
Bassano, Giovanni 68
Basso, Alberto 323, 338
Baumgartner, Johann Baptist [Jean Baptiste] 133, 142, 243, 245, 257
Beach, Jennifer 172
Becker, Judith-Maria 210
Beethoven, Ludwig van 84, 156, 241, 337
Belli, Giulio 90, 91
Bellotti, Edoardo 31-34, 39, 41-42, 76, 78, 113, 368, 371, 380
Benda, Franz 44
Bent, Ian D. 279
Bentivoglio, Enzo 154
Berardi, Angelo 31
Berdes, Jane L. 302, 317
Bergé, Pieter 330, 339
Berghof, Oliver 172
Berkowitz, Aaron 169-170
Berlin, Isaiah 169-170
Bermudo, Fray Jua 269, 279
Bernacchi, Antonio Maria 223, 225-237
Bernstein, David W. 343, 350
Bertinetto, Alessandro 149
Bettinelli, Saverio 291, 297
Bianciardi, Francesco 82, 109
Bianconi, Lorenzo 326, 338
Biba, Otto 308, 317, 319
Bismantova, Bartolomeo 123, 142
Blackburn, Bonnie J. 122, 145, 282
Boccaccio, Giovanni 169
Boccage, Anne-Marie Fiquet du 290
Boccherini, Luigi 128
Boetticher, Wolfgang 267, 279
Boismortier, Joseph Bodin de 245, 247, 257
Bol, Hans 142, 145
Bombi, Andrea 317
Bonizzi, Vincenzo 68
Bonnet, Jacques 123, 143
Bononcini, Giovanni 232, 355
Bononcini, Giovanni Maria 180, 192
Bonz, Tobias 210
Bordas Ibañez, Cristina 282
Bordoni, Faustina 232

Borgir, Tharald 104, 109, 371, 380
Borio, Gianmario 41
Borman, Renate 61
Born, Georgina 171
Bovicelli, Giovanni Battista 65, 68, 78
Boyd, Malcolm 323
Boyle, Matthew 332, 340
Brainard, Paul 302, 310, 317
Brandenburg, Danie 373, 381
Breval, Jean-Baptiste-Sébastien 131, 143
Briçeño, Luis de 273, 279
Bronzi, Enrico 204, 210, 218
Brossard, Sébastien de 292-293, 297, 357-358, 368
Brosses, Charles de 314, 317
Broude, Ronald 28
Brown, Howard Mayer 77-78, 265-266, 268-269
Brumel, Antoine 275
Buelow, George J. 335, 338
Burden, Michael 298
Burmeister, Joachim 71, 78, 188, 192
Burney, Charles 236, 238, 301, 338
Butt, John 21, 28, 70, 78
Byros, Vasili 119, 145

C

Caccini, Giulio 67, 151, 154-155, 157-161, 163-168, 170, 172, 186, 189, 192
Caffarelli [Gaetano Majorano] 228
Cafiero, Rosa 117, 145, 343, 351, 354, 368-369, 380
Calcinotto, Carlo 315
Caldara, Antonio 133-138, 142-143
Callahan, Michael 120, 140, 146, 371, 381
Campeggi, Francesco 234
Campion, Thomas 274
Canale, Margherita 310, 317
Canguilhem, Philippe 118, 120, 146
Caplin, William E. 332, 338
Cappi, Giovanni 308-309
Caraci Vela, Maria 145, 194, 326, 338, 351
Caravaggio, Michelangelo Merisi da 184-185
Carchiolo, Salvatore 104, 109
Carideo, Armando 33-34, 41-42, 368
Carlani, Carlo 232

Index of Names

Charles Edward, Stuart, Prince 224
Carnoli, Pietro Paolo 233
Carter, Tim 158, 160, 165, 171, 340
Cartier, Jean-Baptiste 302-303, 306-310, 317
Caselli, Vincenzo 233
Castello, Dario 68, 78
Castiglione, Baldassarre [Baldassar o Baldesar] 264-265, 279, 291, 297
Cattaneo, Giacomo 45
Cavalieri, Emilio de' 158, 347
Cazeau, Isabelle 60, 62
Ceccato, Marco 145
Cerha, Friedrich 110
Cervetto, Giacobbe Basevi 129
Cervetto, James 129-130
Cesarini, Carlo Francesco 135
Chambonnières, Jacques Champion de 4-7, 12, 16, 20-21, 29
Chateaubriand, François-Auguste René, vicomte de 170-171
Chaucer, Geoffrey 169
Chilesotti, Oscar 266, 268, 280
Choron, Alexandre-Étienne 374, 381
Christensen, Jesper Bøje 104, 109, 210
Christensen, Thomas 41, 147, 262, 272, 279-280, 327, 338, 343, 351, 371, 381
Christina [Kristina], Queen of Sweden 353
Chung, David 3, 5, 28
Cicero 187, 192
Cimarosa, Domenico 126
Ciolfi, Simone xv, 323-325, 328, 331-332, 338-339
Cipriani, Benedetto 344, 351
Clayton, Alfred 146, 171
Cocset, Bruno 204, 206, 210, 217
Coelho, Victor 281
Coin, Christophe 130
Collins, Timothy A. 121-122, 146
Colomb, Romain 317
Colombi, Giuseppe 188-189
Colonna, Fabio 364
Columbro, Marta 139, 146
Colzani, Alberto 112, 114
Constantino, Fabio 95
Conti, Gioacchino 233

Cook, Nicholas 156, 171
Corbetta, Francesco 273, 280, 285
Corelli, Arcangelo 31, 47-49, 59-60, 135, 179, 198-199, 292, 310, 314, 353, 356
Corp, Edward 223-224, 238
Corrette, Michel 82, 109
Corri, Domenico 82, 109
Cosentino, Alessandro 351
Cotumacci, Carlo 357
Couperin, François 48, 128, 141, 143
Couperin, Louis 4, 10-13, 21-22, 29
Couperin, Marc Roger Normand 4
Coussemaker, Charles Edmond Henri de 263, 280
Cowling, Elisabeth 135
Crecquillon, Thomas 71
Crescimbeni, Giovan Mario 289-290, 297
Crivellati, Cesare 180, 192
Crocker, Richard L. 275, 280
Crouch, Joseph 210
Cuiller, Bertrand 210
Cumer, Nicola 113
Curry, Robert 172
Cuzzoni, Francesca 232
Czerniawski, Adam 258

D

Dahlhaus, Carl 120, 146, 156, 171, 241, 257, 275-276, 280
D'Alessandro, Domenico Antonio 339, 367
Dalla Casa, Girolamo 68
Damuth, Laura 325, 334, 339
Dandrieu, Jean-François 82, 109
D'Anglebert, Jean Henry 3-5, 7-12, 15, 20, 22, 28-29
Danner, Peter 269, 280
Darbellay, Étienne 96, 110
Dart, Thurston 265, 280
David, Hans T. 110, 257, 258
Davis, Miles 155
De Champs, Ettore 129
Decombe, Jacques-François 302, 307
Del Buono, Gioanpietro 71, 78
Dell'Abaco, Evaristo Felice 130

Index of Names

Della Libera, Luca 339
Della Sciucca, Marco 94, 111
Della Valle, Pietro 120-121, 143
Del Sordo, Federico 104, 109
De Marchi, Alessandro 135
Denis, Pietro 302, 309
Dent, Edward Joseph 324, 339
De Pascale, Enrico 185, 193
Derosiers, Nicolas 273, 280
Desler, Anne 234, 238
Devriès, Anik 309, 318
De Wispelaere, Valérie 368
Di Giacomo, Salvatore 139, 146
Diletskii, Nikolai 276-278, 280
Diruta, Girolamo 34, 37, 40, 42
Doizi de Velasco, Nicolás 277, 280
Donati, Ignazio 68
Dongois, William 140, 146
Doni, Giovanni Battista 183-184, 190, 192
Donington, Robert 165, 171
Dounias, Minos 313, 318
D'Ovidio, Antonella 62
Dubreuil, Pascal 192
Duckles, Vincent 310, 318
Duport, Jean-Louis 131, 133, 143, 243-244, 258
Durante, Francesco 77, 344, 346, 356-358, 379
Durante, Sergio 112, 313-314, 318

E

Eco, Umberto 182, 194
Eisenhardt, Lex 269, 278, 280
Eitner, Robert 307, 318
Elmer, Minnie 310, 318
Erhardt, Martin 343, 351
Erig, Richard 71, 78
Esses, Maurice 121, 146, 269, 281
Euripides 154

F

Fabbri, Moreno 297
Fabris, Dinko 112, 354, 368
Farinelli [Carlo Broschi] 223, 225, 227-231, 233-237
Fasch, Johann Friedrich 44
Fechner, Manfred 44, 61
Fei, Andrea 94
Fenaroli, Fedele 346, 358, 372
Fenlon, Iain 340
Ferand, Ernst T. 117, 146
Ferrandini, Giovanni Battista 233
Fesch, Willem de 199
Fétis, François-Joseph 225-226, 228-229, 236, 238
Findlen, Paula 298
Finotti, Fabio 290-291, 297
Fleischhauer, Günter 61
Florimo, Francesco 368
Florio, John 168, 171
Fontana, Giovanni Battista 68, 70-71, 78
Forkel, Johann Nikolaus 251, 258
Formisano, Marco 192
Forqueray, Antoine 142
Fortune, Nigel 158, 171
Forzoni Accolti 32
Foscarini, Giovanni Paolo 274, 281
Foscolo, Ugo 291, 297
Framery, Nicolas Étienne 122, 143
Franchi, Saverio 95, 109
Francone, Gaetano 296
Frescobaldi, Girolamo 68, 81, 84, 86, 94-99, 102-105, 107-108, 110-112, 156, 190, 193
Fuchs, Ingrid 308, 317, 319
Fuller, David 28
Furno, Giovanni 357
Fux, Johann Joseph 34

G

Gable, David 172
Gaffi, Bernardo 127
Gaffi, Tommaso 125-127, 143
Galassi, Mara 113
Galilei, Vincenzo xiii, 175-177, 192, 266
Galizia, Fede 185-186
Galli, Amintore 125, 146
Galliard, John Ernest 80
Gambia, Ezio 149
Garcia, Manuel 67-68
Garibaldi, Luigi Agostino 356, 368

Index of Names

Gasparini, Francesco 31, 33, 41, 82, 111, 125, 127, 143, 323, 335, 339
Gatti, Enrico 59, 61, 68, 79, 81, 111, 182, 194
Gavito, Cory Michael 262, 281
Geminiani, Francesco 44, 48, 195, 199-208, 210-219
Gentili, Mario 41
Gerber, Ernst Ludwig 122
Gerhard, Singer 65, 79
Gesualdo, Carlo, Prince of Venosa 364
Geyer, Helen 147
Ghielmi, Lorenzo 94, 110
Ghiselli, Francesco 224, 229
Ghizzolo, Giovanni 81, 85-86, 88-92, 98, 108, 111
Giacomelli, Geminiano 229
Gialdroni, Teresa Maria 127, 147, 326, 339
Giardelli, Claire 210
Gigli, Beniamino 159
Gingras, Bruno 371, 381
Giovani, Giulia 369, 380
Giuli, Paola 290, 297
Giustiniani, Vincenzo 184, 186, 192
Gizzi, Domenico 233
Gjerdingen, Robert O. 38, 41, 117-119, 126, 147, 326, 328, 339, 343, 351, 371, 381
Goede, Thérèse de 113
Goehr, Lydia 241, 258
Gordon-Seifert, Catherine 4, 28
Graun, Carl Heinrich 44
Greco, Gaetano 357
Greco, Rocco 296, 356-357, 365, 367
Grimaldi, Nicola 223
Guarducci, Tommaso 232
Guida, Antonio 139, 142-143
Guido, Giovanni Antonio 295
Guido, Massimiliano 31-32, 40-42, 343, 351, 369, 380
Gunn, John 131, 134, 144, 245-246, 258
Gustafson, Bruce 3-4, 16-17, 28-29
Gyrowetz, Adalbert 372-374, 381

H

Hall, Monica 269, 281
Halton, Rosalind 128, 147
Hamelin, Jean-Yves 120
Handel, George Frideric 44, 135
Hanning, Robert 173
Hardel, Jacques 4, 16-17, 19, 21, 29
Hardy, Henry 170
Harper, John Martin 96, 111
Harris, C. David 3, 29
Harris, Helen T. 323, 339
Hasse, Johann Adolf 228-229
Hatch, Christopher 343, 350
Hawkins, John 49, 61
Haymoz, Jean Yves 118, 147
Heble, Ajay 42
Heilmann, Luigi 194
Heinichen, Johann David 334
Heller, Karl 44, 46, 61
Herbst, Johannes Andreas 63, 65, 67-68, 79
Herlin, Denis 16, 21, 29, 368
Hill, John Walter 154, 172, 261-262, 272, 281
Hiller, Johann Adam 237-238, 301
Hitchcock, H. Wiley 155, 158-160, 163, 166, 168, 172
Hjelmborg, Bjørn 114
Hoffmann, Bettina 128, 131, 142, 147
Hogwood, Christopher 204, 210, 310, 318
Holtemeier, Ludwig 346, 351
Homer 169
Honea, Sion M. 66, 77, 79
Hotteterre, Jacques 121, 144
Hudson, Richard 276, 281
Humeau, Philippe 16-18
Hummel, Johann Julius 309

I

Illiano, Roberto xv-xvi
Ingarden, Roman 241, 258
Invernizzi, Roberta 160
Isabella d'Este, Marchioness of Mantua 264
Isidore of Seville 152, 172
Ivanoff, Vladimir 269, 281

J

Jacchini, Giuseppe Maria 125, 128
Jackson, Barbara Garvey 298
Jakobson, Roman 191, 194

Index of Names

James, Ivor 207
James II [and VII], King of England, Ireland and Scotland 223
James Francis Edward, [James III] Stuart, Prince of Wales 223
Jaquot, Jean 279
Jeffery, Peter 157, 172
Jensen, Claudia R. 276, 278, 281
Jensen, Niels Martin 96-97, 112
Johansson, Cari 309, 318

K

Kerman, Joseph 84, 112
Kinderman, William 156, 172
Kinkeldey, Otto 263
Kircher, Athanasius 188
Kirkby, Emma 160
Kirkendale, Ursula 147
Kirkendale, Warren 135, 147
Kirnberger, Johann Philip 248, 258
Knox, Hank 28
Kolenda, Konstantin 174
Kolneder, Walter 46, 60-61, 207
Komarek, Giovanni Girolamo 356
Köpp, Kai 62
Krall, Hannah 316
Krause, Ralf 377, 381
Kuhnau, Johann 335
Kurtzman, Jeffrey 90, 112

L

Labarre, Louis Julien Castels de 374-375, 377, 379-380
La Borde, Jean-Benjamin de 129-130, 143
Laghi, Simone 296, 298, 311, 318
La Gorce, Jérôme de 28
La Guerre, Jacquet de 4-5, 14-15
La Houssaye [Housset], Pierre(-Nicolas) 309
Lambert, Michael de Saint 82
Landini, Orazio Arrighi 290
Landmann, Ortrun 44, 61-62
Landshoff, Ludwig 44, 62
Lanzetti, Salvatore 122, 128, 133-136, 138-139, 141-142, 144

Lasso [Lassus], Orlando di [Roland, Orlande de] 71, 267
Laver, Mark 42
La Via, Stefano 62, 128, 148
Lavigna, Albert 280
Lavoix, Henri, fils 237, 239
Lawton, Philip 113
Lax, Éva 168-169, 172
Le Cerf de la Viéville, Jean-Laurent 293-295, 298
Ledbetter, David 5, 10, 20, 29
Leech, Peter 4, 29
Le Gallois de Grimarest, Jean-Léonor 7, 21, 29
Lemaire, Théophile 237, 239
Leo, Leonardo 344, 356, 376-379
Leonardo da Vinci, 175-176, 178, 192
Leonhardt, Gustav 110
Lester, Joel 343, 351, 372, 381
Lesure, François 113, 309, 318
Lewis, Eric 171
Lewis, W. 172
Li Causi, Pietro 192
Liepmannssohn, Leo 307, 318
Linden, Jaap ter 204, 210, 216
Lindley, Mark 266, 281
Lindley, Robert 129
Linnaeus, Pietro 364
Lionnet, Jean 193
Lippius, Johannes 275
Lisack, Lucille 146
Lister, Warwick xvi
Llewellyn, Timothy D. 234, 239
Locatelli, Pietro Antonio xiii, 199
Lockey, Nicholas Scott 44, 51, 60, 62
Lomazzo, Filippo 85, 88
Lomazzo, Francesco 70-71
Lorenzini, Raimondo 349, 352
Loulié, Étienne 180, 193
Lowinsky, Edward E. 122, 145, 263-264, 275, 281
Lucchese, Enrico 231, 239
Luisi, Francesco 95, 112
Lully [Lulli], Jean-Baptiste [Giovanni Battista] 4-5
Lupiáñez, Javier 43, 48
Luppi, Andrea 112, 114
Lustig, Monika 147

Index of Names

Lutterman, John Kenneth 241-243, 258
Lutz, Rudolf 147
Lymenstull, Eva 125, 128, 148

M

Machover, Milo 351
Macioce, Stefania 185, 193
Maione, Paologiovanni 139, 146, 339
Mancini, Francesco 353-356, 365
Mancini, Giovanni Battista 233-235, 239
Manfredi, Filippo 128
Manguel, Alberto 157, 169, 172
Mann, Alfred 343, 352
Marais, Marin 4, 122, 144
Marcello, Benedetto 128, 144
Marcocchi, Stefano 296
Marescalchi, Paolo 302
Maria Beatrice, d'Este [Mary of Modena], Queen of England, Ireland and Scotland 223
Maria Klementyna, Sobieska, Princess 223
Marini, Biagio 68, 183, 193, 232
Marino, Rosanna 192
Mark, Ryan 310, 318
Marotta, Cesare 154
Marshall, Robert Lewis 84-85, 112, 172
Martin, Margot 5, 29
Martinelli, Vincenzo 231-232, 239
Martini, Giovanni Battista, Padre 125, 144, 225, 235
Marvin, Roberta Montemorra 356, 368
Marx, Hans Joachim 326, 339
Mascardi, Agostino 127
Maschio, Francesco 135, 138, 145
Mascitti, Michele 295
Massaro, Maria Nevilla 317
Massip, Catherine 368
Mathurin Matharel 210
Mattei, Stanislao 82, 112
Mattheson, Johann 243, 248, 258
Maugars, André 121, 144, 179, 190, 193
Mayer Brown, Howard 279
Mayone, Ascanio 68, 357
McClintock, Carol 172
McGeary, Thomas 239
McGillivray, Alison 204, 210, 215
McGuinness, David 210
McSwiny, Owen 234
Meier, Bernard 326, 330, 339
Melani, Atto 325
Méléndez Peláez, Josué 63, 65
Mellace, Raffaele 369, 380
Melli, Domenico 158
Memel, Lorenzo 233
Mendel, Arthur 241, 257-258
Merighi, Antonia 223
Merrick, Frank 207
Mersenne, Marin 4, 273, 282
Merula, Tarquinio 68
Metastasio, Pietro 289
Meyer, Christian 381
Mignogna, Francesca 261
Milanuzzi, Carl 274, 282
Miles, Natasha Frances 273, 282
Minelli, Giovanni Battista 229
Mioli, Piero 240
Moelants, Dirk 149
Moersch, Charlotte Mattax 156, 172
Monteclair, Michel-Pignolet de 48, 288, 298
Montesardo, Girolamo 272, 282
Monteverdi, Claudio 123-124, 144, 151, 167-169, 182, 193
Monti, Vincenzo 289
Moore, Robin 117, 148
Morabito, Fulvia xv-xvi
Morehen, John 280
Morelli, Arnaldo 31-34, 36, 38, 40, 42
Moroney, Davitt 4, 12, 29
Mortensen, Lars Ulrik 210
Moser, Andreas 295, 298
Motuz, Catherine 63
Mozart, Leopold 48, 301
Mozart, Wolfgang Amadeus 156, 165
Muffat, Georg 31
Müller, Ruth E. 257
Murata, Margaret 326, 339
Musenga, Gabriele 230
Muzio, Emanuele 356
Myron, Richard 210

Index of Names

N

Nardi, Antonio 158
Nardini, Pietro 310-311
Nasillo, Gaetano 204-205, 210, 214
Navarre, Jean-Philippe 279
Neri, Benedetto 373
Nestola, Barbara 295, 298
Nettl, Bruno 152, 172, 173
Neumann, Frederick 165, 173
Neumann, Werner 259
Neuwirth, Markus 330, 339
Niedt, Friedrich Erhard 243, 248-249, 251-252, 258, 335
Nuti, Giulia 128, 148

O

O'Donnell, Aidan 272-273, 277, 282
Oliva, Patrick 316, 318
Olivieri, Guido xv, 133-134, 139, 148, 287, 295-296, 298, 367-368
Omosky, Ute 147
Ortiz, Diego 140, 144
Ortkemper, Hubert 226
O'Sullivan, Loretta 204-205, 210, 219
Ottenberg, Hans-Günter 61
Otter, Joseph 310, 311
Ottoboni, Pietro, Cardinal 135, 289
Owens, Jessie Ann 85, 112

P

Padoan, Maurizio 112, 114
Pagin, André Noël 309
Palestrina, Giovanni Pierluigi da 69
Palisca, Claude 158-159, 173
Pamphilj, Benedetto 135
Pandolfi Mealli, Giovanni Antonio 68, 189-190
Panzacchi, Enrico 227-228, 231-232, 239
Parisotti, Alessandro 159, 173
Pasquali, Nicolò 82, 112
Pasquini, Bernardo 31-42, 125, 135, 353, 368
Pauley, Scott 210
Pedio, Renato 194
Penna, Lorenzo 82, 112, 326, 340
Penson, Guy 210

Peri, Jacopo 158
Petrobelli, Pierluigi 301, 318
Pez, Johann Christoph 47
Philipsen, Christian 147
Pianca, Luca 210
Piani, Giovanni Antonio 295, 298
Pincherle, Marc 60, 62
Pinelli, Petronio 301, 319
Pirrotta, Nino 148, 155, 173
Pisendel, Johann Georg 43-52, 54-57, 59-60
Pistocchi, Francesco Antonio Mamiliano 227, 232, 236
Pitoni, Giuseppe Ottavio 31, 33, 41
Pitschel, Theodor Leberecht 242, 258
Plato 158, 314
Pleeth, Anthony 204, 206, 210-211
Pohlmann, Egert 154, 173
Pollaci, Marco 343
Porpora, Nicola 227, 233, 235, 344, 357
Porter, William E. 31-33, 39, 41, 326, 340
Praetorius, Michael 68
Pratt, Carroll C. 258
Preitano, Massimo 261, 274, 276, 278, 282
Prosser, Pietro 113
Protopopov, Vladimir 280
Provenzale, Francesco 354, 365
Pryer, Anthony 151, 167, 173
Puffett, Derrick 146, 171
Pujol, Emilio 269, 282

Q

Quantz, Johann Joachim 44, 48, 113, 152, 173, 195, 197-198, 206-207
Quinteiro, Eligio 210
Quintilianus, Marcus Fabius 187-190, 192

R

Raaff, Anton 232-233
Radicchi, Patrizia 298
Raguenet, François 292, 293, 298
Rameau, Jean-Philippe 248, 261, 282
Rasch, Rudolf xi, svi, 195, 242, 259, 338
Rasi, Francesco 163, 167
Rastall, Richard 265, 280

Index of Names

Ratti, Antonio 233
Raupach, Christoph 243, 258
Redi, Giovanni 234
Renwick, William 371-372, 381
Ricordati, Bernardo Felice 33, 353
Ridgewell, Rupert 308, 319
Riemann, Hugo 274
Rifkin, Joshua 71
Riley, Edward R. 173
Roberts, Helen 63
Robletti, Giovanni Battista 95
Rocchetti, Ventura 232
Roche, Jerome 95, 113
Rodari, Gianni 140, 148
Roger, Estienne 179, 325
Rogniono, Ricardo 68
Rognoni, Francesco 63-65, 67-70, 79, 193
Rognoni, Riccardo 79
Rohrmann, Leopold 302
Rolli, Paolo 289
Romagnoli, Angela 104, 113, 145, 351, 354, 368
Romanou, Katy 125, 148
Rosand, David 173
Rosand, Ellen 326, 340
Rose, Glori 120, 148
Rotem, Elam 74, 79
Rothstein, William 335, 340
Rousseau, Jean 298
Rousseau, Jean-Jacques 121-122, 144, 170, 287-289, 298
Roworth, Wendy Wassyng 298
Ruspoli, Bartolomeo 135
Ryhiner-Delon, Achilles 311, 313

S

Sabbatini, Pietro Paolo 82, 113
Sacaluga, Servando 289-299
Sacchi, Giovenale 225, 236, 239
Saccone, Eduardo 155, 173
Sachs, Curt 258
Sadie, Stanley 341
Sainte-Maure, Benoit de 169
Saint Lambert, Michael de 113
Sala, Massimiliano xv, xvi
Sala, Nicola 373-377, 379-380
Salimbeni, Felice 237
Sallis, Friedemann 85, 113
Salomon, Jean Baptiste Dehaye 302
Sama, Catherine M. 298
Sammaruco, Francesco 94
Sánchez de Lima, Miguel 278
Sandrin, Pier 71
Sanguinazzo, Nicolò 132, 144-145
Sanguinetti, Giorgio xv, 38, 42, 77, 79, 117-118, 125, 129, 134, 138, 147-148, 295, 299, 324-325, 327, 329-331, 335, 340, 343-346, 348, 352-353, 356, 369, 371, 381
Scarlatti, Alessandro 135, 290, 323-328, 330, 332-333, 336-337, 346-348, 353
Scarlatti, Domenico 135, 357
Scheibe, Johann Adolph 48
Schenker, Heinrich 165, 173
Schering, Arnold 44, 55, 62
Schmitt, Thomas 268, 278, 282
Schneider, Herbert 28
Schopenhauer, Arthur 151, 174
Schreyfogel, Johan Friedrich 44
Schubert, Peter 32, 42, 118, 149
Schulenberg, David 242, 259
Schultz, Walter 207
Schulze, Hans-Joachim 258-259
Schütz, Heinrich 380
Schwenkreis, Markus 63, 77, 79
Scimone, Claudio 317
Sciommeri, Giacomo 351
Scudo, Paul 227-228, 231-232, 239
Seeger, Charles 163, 174
Seletzky, Robert Eric 301, 319
Selma y Salaverde, Bartolomé de 68-69, 71, 78
Seneca, Lucius Annaeus 133
Severi, Francesco 68, 79
Sharrill, Paul 332, 340
Siéfert, Marion 146
Sigismondo, Giuseppe 354-355, 379, 382
Silbiger, Alexander 28, 111, 368
Simmel, Georg 81, 113
Simpson, Christopher 121, 132, 145, 243, 248-251, 253-257, 259

Index of Names

Simpson, David 204-205, 210, 212
Sirena, Galeazzo 169
Sisto, Davide 149
Smith, Anne 70-71, 79
Soldi, Luca Antonio 94
Solis, Gabriel 172
Somis, Giovanni Battista 45
Sørensen, Søren 114
Sorosina, Pietro 191
Spieth, Noëlle 210
Spiridionis a Monte Carmelo, father 63, 76-78, 80
Spitzer, John 62
Staehelin, Martin 311, 319
Staffieri, Gloria 326, 340
Steffani, Agostino 237
Stein, Daniel 129, 149
Stella, Gaetano 351
Stembridge, Christopher 95, 110, 114
Stewart-Macdonald, Rohan H. xv
Stiastny, Bernhard 125, 145
Stigand, Isobella S. E. 149
Stinson, Russell 259
Straw, Will 171
Strobbe, Lieven 118, 149
Strohm, Reinhard 340
Strunk, Oliver 158, 174
Suess, John G. 188, 194
Sueur, Agathe 187, 192, 194
Supriani, Francesco Paolo 296
Supriano, Francesco P. 133-135, 138, 142, 145
Suzuki, Hidemi 204, 210, 213
Szweykowski, Zygmunt 158, 171

T

Talbot, Michael 56, 58, 62, 336-337, 341
Tartini, Giuseppe xiii, 44, 128, 301-303, 306-314, 316-317, 319
Taschetti, Gabriele 91, 114
Tavella, Konrad 79, 111
Taylor, Rachelle 28
Telemann, Georg Philipp 44, 47, 57
Teni, Maria Rosaria 319
Terzi, Antonio 68

Tesi, Vittoria 229
Thom, Eitelfriedrich 61
Thomas, Antoine-Léonard 301
Thomas, Bernard 110
Tini, Simon 85
Todea, Flavia C. 117, 149
Toffetti, Laura xii-xiii, 175
Toffetti, Marina 81, 85, 94, 108, 111, 114, 194
Tomlinson, Gary 326, 341
Torchi, Luigi 120, 149
Torelli, Giuseppe 45
Tosi, Piefrancesco 226, 231, 234-235, 240
Tosi, Pierfrancesco 70, 80
Tosi, Pier Francesco 48
Trabaci, Giovanni Maria 357
Treitler, Leo 174, 287, 299
Tritto, Giacomo 346
Tyler James 269, 281

U

Ursino, Gennaro 354, 357, 364

V

Vaccaro, Jean-Michel 134, 149, 263, 266-267, 282
Valsecchi, Mario 110
Van Regenmortel, Hans 118, 149
Vanscheeuwijck, Marc 125, 149
Van Orden, Kate 171
Van Tour, Peter xiv, xvi, 343, 352-353, 356, 369, 371-372, 376-377, 379, 382
Veracini, Francesco Maria 128
Verdi, Giuseppe 356
Verdi, Luigi 230, 235, 240
Viadana [Grossi da Viadana], Lodovico 268
Vicente, Alfonso de 282
Vicentino, Nicola xiii, 183, 193
Vincenti, Alessandro 85
Vincenti, Giacomo 273-274
Vincioli, Teodora 189
Visée, Robert de 128, 143
Vitali, Carlo 223, 240
Vivaldi, Antonio 43-46, 48-49, 51-53, 55-60, 245

Index of Names

W

Walker, Jennifer xvi
Walls, Peter 319
Walther, Johann Gottfried 248, 259
Wasielewski, Wilhelm J. 121-122, 125, 130, 149
Watkins, David 133, 149
Watkins, Timothy D. 148, 298, 368
Webb, Richard 204, 210
Weinmann, Alexander 308, 319
Wertenson, Birgit Johanna 147
West, Martin L. 154, 173
Westrup, Jack 104, 114, 323, 341
Whenham, John 173
Whitmore, Philip 156, 174
Whittaker, Nathan H. 128, 149
Willaert, Adrian 71
Williams, Peter 327, 341
Wilson, Glen 4, 29
Wistreich, Richard 173
Wittkower, Rudolf 180, 194
Wolf, Christoph 257
Wolf, Peter 29

Y

Yacus, David 66
Young, James O. 119, 149
Young, La Monte Thornton 155

Z

Zacconi, Ludovico 65-67, 70-71, 77, 80
Zamboni, Giovanni Giacomo 32
Zampieri, Domenico 364
Zanetti, Antonio 231
Zanetti, Anton Maria 231
Zannetti, Bartolomeo 95
Zappi, Giovan Battista Felice 289-290
Zarlino, Gioseffo xiii, xvi, 181-183, 193, 261, 282, 314
Zaslaw, Neal xiii, xv, 62, 301, 310, 319
Zhu, Beilang 210
Ziino, Agostino 148, 339, 367
Zipperling, Rainer 210
Zuccari, Carlo 310, 319